A STRANGER
IN THEIR MIDST

THE SINS OF THE
MOTHERS

FRANK DELANEY

THE SINS OF
THE MOTHERS

A STRANGER
IN THEIR MIDST

HarperCollins*Publishers*

This omnibus edition published in 1999 by HarperCollins*Publishers*

HarperCollins*Publishers*
77-85 Fulham Palace Road,
Hammersmith, London W6 8JB

A catalogue record for this book
is available from the British Library

ISBN 0 261 67224 X

Set in Linotron Caledonia by
Rowland Phototypesetting Ltd
Bury St Edmunds, Suffolk

Printed and bound in Great Britain by
Caledonian International Book Manufacturing Ltd, Glasgow

For Susan

SPRING 1925

1

A mile from the village, the bus entered a tunnel of trees and dense hedges. The young woman turned her head to search for her reflection in the darkened window beside her. Peering, she opened her mouth a little, and ridged the back of her teeth with her tongue. The image of her face in the glass faded as the bus crested a small hill into a whiter daylight. She turned back again, and shifting on the hard wooden seat, craned her neck, fidgeting to see the road ahead past the driver: the fog still divulged only dripping trees looming over the high formal stone walls on either side. As *The Princess* crested the second hump by the New Quarry, the conductor, who had been leaning against the door, straightened up, readying for duty. The young woman withdrew her right hand from her pocket where her fingers had been secretly praying on a rosary; she touched an eyebrow, nudged her brown cloche hat in an unnoticeable adjustment.

Minutes earlier, as it did four days a week, the bus had driven past the verge of a damp forest where this morning, alarmed at the noise of the engine across the silent lands, a deer slipped on soft earth – the edge of a shallow grave. As the animal staggered and then recovered, drawing its fastidious hoof out of the stumble, another tiny shred of flesh slid from the decomposing corpse wrapped in the remains of a greatcoat beneath the ground.

The village materialized, a single one-sided street of low houses. Chimney smoke plumed upwards. Within, the villagers moved quietly, and the older people, their bodies slower to grow warm, still wore their night attire under such heavy coats as they owned. The bus engine vrammed and rattled; a black and white mongrel cat loped back from some small chill expedition in the hedges and squeezed under the planks of a warm barn in one of the yards. The curtains of the village twitched, yet doors remained closed.

The young woman on the bus massaged her forearms in the damp cold, then gathered her hand-knitted gloves and a small leather attaché case. At the helmeted pump, the dingy *Princess* halted with a gulp, and a bicycle on the roof spun one of its wheels; it looked a little like an insect's wings whirring slowly.

Her name was Ellen Morris. As the bus door slapped open, she stepped down briskly and innocently, and then jinked from the grass verge to the hard pavement beyond.

The driver took his time, did not immediately engage his gears. 'She could be foreign though, couldn't she heh?' said the conductor, the door still open. 'If it wasn't for the accent?'

Both men leaned over to watch where she went; they gazed at her shoes, her coat, her legs, and the driver puffed, 'Phwhoo-hoo then?' when Ellen headed for the only non-domestic building in the place: single-storey, uninspired, grey, municipal; two chimneys, and a small slate plaque on the porch wall: *Deanstown National School*. The bus driver returned to his steering-wheel, the conductor forced the stiff door shut, and *The Princess* cranked itself together and pushed away.

Ellen Morris pressed the small gate into the tiny yard and knocked on the door. A child opened, and Ellen asked, 'Is Mr Kane here?' by which time Mr Kane was already striding down the classroom from the fireplace. Before he could say a word, she spoke again, not quite blurting.

'I'm a day early, I'm Ellen Morris, you wrote to me, after I applied to the advertisement.' Ungloving her hands, she began to arrange the attaché case on her hiked knee. 'I couldn't come tomorrow but I didn't know that until yesterday, there's no bus I think on Tuesdays.' She thumbed the metal catches. 'Or if there is, we thought it might be too foggy to travel. But if I'm too early, or if it isn't all right . . .' From the attaché case she handed him a letter addressed, 'To Whom It Might Concern'.

The child who had opened the door returned to her desk shrugging her shoulders in curiosity and mouthing the whisper, 'A Mistress?'

The Princess, out of sight by now, stopped at the statue down in the hollow where the fog thickened; the conductor picked up the loose bale of empty jute sacks left there, inspected the string-tied label and then the bus clattered onwards to the east end of the parish.

Mr Kane said, 'Come in, so. Are you frozen with the cold? You're Miss Morris, so?'

To which she replied with the words, 'Both. Yes,' and he smiled.

She walked so directly through the door that he had to lean aside, and with none of the tentativeness of a stranger she stepped right in, as far as the classroom's edge between the squat, flaking pilasters of the school porch.

'Well. Now. Right,' he said, turning the letter back and forth in his hand, but not opening it.

He said, 'You're very welcome.' Stowing her gloves under her arm, she placed her attaché case flat on the windowsill, and said, 'How do you do. Mr Kane, is it, I suppose?' shaking his hand.

He stooped his head a little to walk through the inner door, waited, and when she had picked up her attaché case, he steered her into the body of the school and up to the fireplace.

'I can't give you a cup of tea or anything until later on. I didn't know about the buses. On Tuesdays, that is. Is today, what, Monday, yes, it must only be in the winter they do that, although I thought they go past here, but of course, yes, they only go as far as, yes.' He looked doubtful but polite.

He stopped and looked down again at the letter in his hand, then at her face. 'The Canon is expecting to. To interview you. But that's tomorrow. But sure what harm? Can't we go and see him today, he's there, I know.'

Ellen Morris had begun to organize herself: attaché case on the nearby table near the Globe of the World.

'Were there many on the bus?'

'Only myself.'

She swivelled her head confidently, looking around at the schoolroom: maps on the walls, *Mercator's Projection of Europe* and, shiny, new, *The Counties of Ireland in 1924*; the clock over the fireplace, *Made by Kneeshaw 1894* inscribed across its open, friendly face with the black Roman numerals; Breughel peasant paintings in profuse blues and yellows; *Curwen's Modulator* singing-lesson chart; on the easeled blackboard, chalked in careful, tall, joined lettering, 'Neither a Borrower nor a Lender be'; spreading stains of old damp by each of the three windows. Across the light blue, thick, flaking walls of both rooms spread the turquoise roundels of the twelve months, with their rhymes – 'January brings the snow; Makes my feet and fingers glow; February brings the rain; Thaws the frozen lakes again.' Turning to the attaché case in afterthought, she clicked it open again, and carefully handed forth

11

a large envelope to which had been pinned an advertisement clipping. *Qualified Assistant Required for Two-Teacher National School: to take charge of Low Infants, High Infants, First Class and Second Class. Higher Diploma not Essential but Desirable.* She held it forth before her, as if displaying a firm certificate to him. Mr Kane looked at it, then at her, then down again.

'My references. There.' She stabbed a finger at the letter in his hand. Then she presented the advertisement to him: her duties discharged, she held her hands out sideways to the fire behind her and flexed her fingers like a pianist warming up.

Mr Kane placed the letter carefully behind a tall box of loose chalks on the mantelpiece, then read the advertisement, and lifted it to see whether she had pinned anything beneath.

'Yes. Ye-ess. A copy of your letter. Ye-ss. H'm-h'm' – on a rising inflection. He opened and closed the fingers of his free hand to the general heat of the fire.

'I believe you speak French,' she said to him in her sudden way. 'Isn't that very unusual?'

He stared in the bright coals a moment, and then with his free right hand began to stroke his chin, leaving a fleck of chalk on it. The children in the desks looked on, a miniature audience, one or two whispering with giggles to those behind them. He rubbed the tips of his fingers back and forth together to loosen the ingrained chalk dust.

Mr Kane said slowly, 'The job here is for. A teacher. So you might. Well, I suppose, teach – for a bit.' Then he queried, 'H'm?'

She replied, 'You mean what an Inspector would want me to do?'

Winter sunshine began to illuminate the interior of the fog, and by the school window a woman walked into view. She wore a man's coat and a headscarf, and carried a bucket to the pump for water, her breath adding little punches of further mist.

'My references.' Ellen again indicated the letter on the mantel. She began to open the buttons of her coat, and loosened a little the cream silk scarf at her neck, tucked into her blouse like a cravat. The moment her eyes left his face as she attended to these easing tasks, he looked her up and down.

'Now,' Mr Kane said, in an air of turning to something new.

He faced the class. In one corner of the room hung an askew door, the entrance to the Juniors' room. Mr Kane had a tiny piece of food caught between two of his longer teeth. He rapped the front desk with a knuckle.

'Attention. Quietness please. Sit straight up and fold your arms.' The children's whispers, which had risen almost to speech, faded at the severeness, and the desks clattered metallically as they all turned.

'Continue with this headline. Do it three times. I'm taking our visitor into the other room. D'you want to bring your –?' He indicated the case and gloves on the table and led the way down the open aisle, stooping slightly to say softly, formally, 'At the most we have about sixty-six. That's with a full attendance, and it usually works out. About fifty-eight or -nine, and nearly half of them in this room. This is the Low Infants, the High Infants, the First Class and the Second Class.'

'As advertised,' she confirmed.

The door rattled lightly when opened, to a room where a fourteen-year-old girl stood in front of another fire.

'We never call it the Babies' Class. Miss Harrington, who retired, that's why the vacancy. She thought it offended them to be called "babies". Especially when they're big enough to go to school.'

Rows of little children at tiny desks were counting out small polished sea-shells.

'That's all right. Angela, you can go back to your desk,' he said to the girl who had been caretaking. 'Now –' he addressed the small ones, 'Quietness, please – this is Miss –' he paused, 'Morris, and she's to be with you until lunch-time.' To Ellen he murmured, 'I've been sending them home at half-past twelve every day. Until a new appointment is made. When the weather is *in*-clement. [He pronounced 'inclement' as two words.] I think I might send them all home early today. The fog and that.'

She said again how sorry she was, but felt it better to arrive a day early than not turn up tomorrow and have everybody waiting.

'No matter, no matter. All yours, so.'

Mr Kane gave her the classroom with a stern wave of his hand, and left, scraping the rickety glass-panelled door across the floor to close it behind him. She placed her attaché case and gloves on an empty, much wider table covered with a soft green baize loose cloth, took off her coat, but retained her scarf and hat, and said to the children, 'Hands up who can guess who I am?'

13

A hand or two crept up, then one or two more, then slowly the rest followed, until soon all the hands except one or two stood straight up in the air like a sweet little forest. Ellen looked all around, and then picked out a boy who had not raised his hand, and who sat looking down at his desk. She pointed to him and said, 'Now, what is your name?'

All the other children laughed, and Ellen said, 'Quietness, please.' The boy looked at her and his face reddened, and he looked down, and said nothing.

'You can put your hands down,' she told all the children. 'Are you going to tell me your name at all?' The little boy blushed deeper, and Ellen said with a smile to him, 'All right. All right. We can get your name from you later.' She stood with her back to the fire, and clapped her hands, 'All right. Since you all had your hands up you can tell me at the same time. Who am I?'

The children sang, 'A new Mistress, Ma'am.'

Ellen smiled and asked all to say together, 'The name of the Mistress you used to have?'

'Miss. Harr. Ing. Ton, Ma'am.'

Then she asked them where Miss Harrington was? This question produced no unison. One girl put a hand up and said, 'Re, re, re, re-something, Ma'am.'

Ellen nodded and, inviting them to 'repeat it after me', mouthed the word 'retired' several times. Next, with their sing-song help, she counted the children, twenty-one of them. When they had finished, she said, 'Now. What's the nicest prayer you know?' at which they fell over themselves to answer, 'Ma'am, Ma'am, Ma'am, Ma'am, me, Ma'am, me, Ma'am, me, me,' all except the same boy again, who, in the corner of her eye, said nothing.

'All right so,' said Ellen. 'We'll say the *Hail Holy Queen*. "Hail Holy Queen, Mother of Mercy. Hail, our Life, our Sweetness. And our Hope."'

They sang along willingly after her. 'To thee do we cry. Poor banished children of Eve. To thee do we send up our sighs. Mourning and weeping. In this Valley of Tears.'

Ellen tented her hands together like the roof of a toy church, and bowed her head up and down with the rhythm of the prayer.

'Turn then. Most gracious Advocate. Thine eyes of mercy towards us. And after this our exile. Show unto us. The pleasant fruits of thy womb, Jesus.'

14

Ellen looked down, then thumb-wiped a small fleck of wet dust from the toe of her brown court shoe.

'O Clement! O Loving! O sweet Virgin Mary. Pray for us O Holy Mother of God. That we may be made worthy of the promises of Christ.'

The children, with no vocabularial difficulty whatsoever, romped through the prayer, but although the little boy's lips moved, no actual sound appeared to emerge. Without looking at him directly, Ellen, during the praying aloud, next began to walk back and forward across the floor, and up and down between the rows of desks, bending to hear the words coming from sundry mouths, stopping subtly a little longer each time near him, sometimes behind him, sometimes a little in front with her back to him. His hair and ears had some congealed grease; he wore a hard, cheap jumper – as did most of the others – and although he held his hands obediently on top of his desk, he had scrunched them tight together. He had not been washed that morning, nor perhaps for a number of mornings.

Fourteen miles away, in the next town, *The Princess* bus had reached its morning destination, and to warm themselves, the driver and conductor addressed mugs of tea and slices of currant bread in *The Criterion*, where they told Miss Cronin about Ellen.

'She have a kind of a flat nose. Like she looks foreign.'

Miss Cronin when being shrewd dropped her voice to a stage whisper. 'That Harrington woman retired; she was left a farm in Waterford; that might be a new one, so, that must be it, isn't it, lads?'

'She's well shod, whoever she is,' said the driver. 'Well shod, yeh.'

'She looks like a Protestant,' said the conductor.

When the *Hail Holy Queen* ended, Ellen said, 'Now another prayer. Remember. All prayers go up to God.'

Again hands shot up. '"The Our Father", Ma'am.' And, equally breathlessly, 'Ma'am. Ma'am, the "I Confess".' Ellen again called them 'Very good'. She clasped her hands.

'The proper name for the "I Confess" is "*The Confiteor*". The what?' They struggled, and eventually managed with pride, 'The Con. Feet. Ee. Yor.'

She started them, as if pushing a cart until it picked up speed. '"I confess to Almighty God. To the Blessed Mary ever Virgin. To Blessed Michael the Archangel."'

Continuing her journey through the desks, she again chose at random to bend down beside a reciting child, chanting with it, nodding her head in good approval. 'To Blessed John the Baptist. To the Holy Apostles, Peter and Paul.' By each desk she inclined in order to listen, sometimes down on one knee, accompanying the child's chant with a mouthing of the prayer through an encouraging smile. 'And to all the Saints.' Her intention materialized: she wished to approach unalarmingly, and from the front, the silent boy, who mouthed a little, but definitely made no sound.

'That I have sinned exceedingly. In Thought, Word and Deed.'

The little boy, who until closer examination had a merry face, avoided her eyes, and then looked down. Ellen stooped low, continuing the prayer.

'Through my Fault.' She knelt. 'Through my Own Fault.' She placed her hand on the cheek farthest from her, and turned his face gently so that he faced in her direction. He screwed his eyes shut, and began to cry, the tears falling from one eye. 'Through my Own Most Grievous Fault.'

On his desk lay a matchbox. Ellen opened it, saw a moth inside give a tiny flutter, and she closed it gently. She gave the boy a secret, exclusive smile, and placed her hand on his hair.

Nodding to the rest of the class, and making her face into an encouraging expression, she stood straight again, and began to mouth the prayer exaggeratedly as she spoke.

'Therefore I beseech. The Blessed Mary ever Virgin. Blessed Michael the Archangel.' The boy's second eye oozed a tear, and she patted his face: he was no more than five years old, with, beneath the grease, fair-to-blond hair.

'Blessed John the Baptist. The Holy Apostles, Peter and Paul.'

The little boy did not open his eyes; nor did he move his lips.

'And all the saints. To pray for me. To the Lord Our God.'

The classroom yelled a great 'Amen', and Ellen walked to the head of the room again, having given the boy a final gentle tug on the hair.

Mr Kane opened the door of the classroom and announced that

16

a break might be taken, but if they wished to go into the yard to play, they had A, to put on their coats and B, keep running all the time.

'Who is that child?' Ellen asked, watching the released boy grab his matchbox, scamper into the porch and out through the door. Mr Kane beckoned her in the direction of the fireplace in the Senior room, and removing the tall brass mesh fireguard, stood nearer the coal glow.

'I should tell you a bit about the history of this place,' he said, 'before you meet the Canon, and before you make up your mind that it's a place like this you might want to work in. That is, if he offers you the job. Although with those references. Well, anyway.' He stopped short of the imminent compliment.

He said, 'You're probably used to swankier. There isn't anybody here worth a lot, they're a far-back crowd, the ones here. Some of them aren't, the big farmers' children, they're all right. But most of them are cottiers' children; we even get one or two of "no fixed abode". That young fellow, the one who won't talk, that you were trying to get to join in' – he ignored her eyebrows' acknowledgment that he had been watching and listening – 'they're as poor a family as you'd get anywhere in the world. There's fourteen of them in the house, and the father a bit of a – well,' and he never finished the sentence.

Ellen went to the window and looked out, where the children's breath condensed on the air, and Mr Kane said nothing for a moment or two.

'He doesn't seem to have any coat,' she said. 'That boy.'

Mr Kane looked down and ascertained the white handkerchief folded in the breast pocket of his tweed jacket. He patted it, then asked, 'The Canon? How would you like to make up your mind – if, I mean, the job is offered to you?'

She walked back to the fire, and said she didn't know. 'But I suppose I wouldn't have applied for it if I didn't want to take it. They're scarce enough, jobs like this.'

To which he replied, 'So are the right candidates.'

Mr Kane went to his tall, sloping desk, took out a speckled fountain pen, wrote a note on careful blue paper, folded and enveloped it, called in the girl Angela, the one who had been keeping the Junior classroom quiet, and sent her down the road to the Canon's house.

'How far away is the church?' asked Ellen. 'I mean, do they say Mass every morning here? Is it near enough to go?'

'Look. Look,' interrupted Thomas Kane, his head lunging forward gently towards the window-pane. 'That's the father. The boy you were asking about.'

Wearing a cap and a navy-blue, shabby overcoat, a heavy man pushed a bicycle ahead of him across the green, then clambered up and cycled away. Although she would recall that moment with great clarity, and prove capable nearly two years later of describing every facet of the man's appearance, and even the manner in which she herself stood when she first saw him — one hand on her hip, other hand still fiddling with her scarf — she now registered only cursory interest. Returning to the fireside, Ellen Morris at last removed her hat.

'That's nice,' she said. 'Who did that? Yourself?' With a knuckle she touched the drawing of a black and silver eel pinned to the wall.

'No. There's an itinerant artist. He comes around every few years. Some of those eels live to twenty years old.'

Ellen straightened the corner of the drawing.

'His full name is Jeremiah Anthony Williams. He's a bit, well, you know, a bit . . .'

As they walked down the hill under the dripping trees, Mr Kane did not finish the sentence, and Ellen did not press. He returned to it.

'Don't mind if he's a bit on the — rough side. What I mean is — coarse. He may be a Canon, but he hasn't ever been outside the county hardly. Except maybe to Dublin, once or so. He's capable of asking questions that he shouldn't. I mean, the sort of things he might ask in Confession.'

Ellen laughed, trying to keep up with Mr Kane's tall stride. Her coat brushed on a shrub along the Canon's avenue, wetting the upper sleeve extensively, although the light water merely sat glistening on the fabric. Inside, she sat alone in the tiled and musty hall, waiting to be called; and among the stale geraniums in brass pots she shivered in the cold. The housekeeper had ushered Mr Kane in to meet the Canon somewhere in another cave of the house. Soon, Mr Kane reappeared and, still wearing his coat, beckoned with one finger. Ellen rose, put her attaché case in her left hand and drew the glove from her right, prepared for handshakes.

'Oh,' said Canon Jeremiah Williams, when he saw Ellen. 'The last one was like a hairpin,' he said to Mr Kane.

They shook hands. The Canon, even lankier than Mr Kane, and with a ridge where his hat had been sitting on his hair, said, 'What's a good cure for the scour?' Ellen, with the air of someone who had not fully heard, begged his pardon; he did not acknowledge, and continued, 'Two of them calves have that hell's curse white scour and I can't pluck one single thing from a hedge anywhere in Christendom that'll stop the flow. They have the fields scuttered.'

Looking at Ellen's bosom – she had opened her coat: an oil heater formed the apex of their three chairs in the large, heavy room – he continued, 'There's some women say they can't eat turnips if they're feeding a child, and God almighty, we gave the cows turnips last week for the first time in years, and their milk is as hard and as yellow as dung.'

Mr Kane did not look at Ellen; she, seeking stability, began to assess the room. *Robert Emmet's Speech from the Dock*, a stained coloured print, hung above the mantelpiece, the young rebel, his hair black and plastered like a Napoleonic *beau*, standing defiant and poignant before a hostile courtroom a century earlier.

The Canon followed her gaze and misquoted Emmet's famous epitaph, 'Until Ireland takes her place among the countries of the world. Ah, yes.'

The housekeeper came to the door and said, 'Well, Canon?' He nodded his purplish face, and continued, 'Then and not 'til then let my epitaph be written.' To Mr Kane he said, 'Did you close the school early, that fog? Will you drink a glass of sherry wine, any of you?'

Ellen sat there and rubbed her hands to warm them, looking politely from one man to the other, then looking ahead when they seemed to ignore her.

'Do you know that Canavan man at all, Mr Kane?' the Canon asked, with no sign of interest in an answer. 'Do you know what he's after doing? He's after burying another wife. And the Curate has bronchitis again; I had to say the two Masses yesterday again.'

In the next hour, the housekeeper, who murmured unceasingly to herself, laid cloth, cutlery and surprisingly elegant napery on the bare table at which they had been invited to sit; she set forth thin soup dredged with rice; mutton slices on which white grease had been allowed to form like wedges of slush; turnip and mashed potato; and the Canon drank at least six minuscule glasses of sherry, while Ellen, feeling a little dizzy, resisted after two. Twice she had to ask the housekeeper for cutlery; the men had started eating before Ellen received, first her soup spoon, then a fork.

In a while, she asked venturesomely, 'Has the Curate been seeing a doctor for his bronchitis?'

'Mr Kane, I suppose the car is going great?' said Canon Williams. He wiped his mouth on his sleeve, kept up a stream of comment, observation, enquiry, never once referring to Ellen or acknowledging her.

'I found grand wild thyme the other day,' he said, 'down the Fourpenny road. That Curate of mine hasn't a penny to his name, the collections aren't enough at all. Do you know mountains called the Paps of Anu, down in the west, they're named after some pagan woman.'

Mr Kane ate in silence, his back straight; his food had a tall distance to travel from plate to mouth: he administered every spoonful and forkful with poised carefulness.

'I had a letter from the Bishop,' said the Canon. 'The Confirmation is going to be a month earlier next year, at the end of April; the Bishop has to go to Rome.'

Mr Kane said, 'We had better start the paperwork, soon, so.'

The old russet dog snuffled occasionally in front of the heater. 'That Coughlan woman,' said the Canon. 'I declare to God she's after having another child.'

Ellen, during a silence, asked, 'Do you have a big orchard here, Canon?'

The Canon threw back his head and laughed. After a moment or two, opening yet another new subject, he said, 'That young McCarthy lad is coming on well, isn't he, Mr Kane? He'll be on the senior team in a few years.'

The housekeeper returned. Ellen whispered to her, 'Where is the necessary?'

The housekeeper, very much more loudly than Ellen had spoken, said, 'You'll have to use a chamber-pot upstairs.'

Ellen half-folded her napkin and, ignoring Canon Williams's intense stare, left the table. The housekeeper showed her into a bare upstairs room where one shutter remained closed. In the gloom Ellen saw that at least eight chamber-pots stood around the floor, some of china, some the standard white enamel with blue rim. She had cause to wrinkle her nose.

The housekeeper said sourly, 'I'll empty it after you. That's what I do.'

She stood there. Ellen looked at her.

The housekeeper said, 'I'll wait outside the door.' She halted briefly then spoke back into the room. 'There isn't any paper, so you'll have to go easy.'

A smile on her face, Ellen chose a pot with a bright bunch of flowers on its floor.

When Ellen returned, the Canon stopped mid-sentence and looked at her, following her with his eyes from the door to her chair. He said to Thomas Kane, 'Did you ever hear of a song called "Barbara Allen"? D'you know that song was composed near here, up in Ballintemple. This is the centenary of it, 'twas written a hundred years ago next month. A famine emigrant took it to America. 'Twas John Quirke told me that last week.'

Abruptly, after a last, smacking spoon of lukewarm semolina and milk, the Canon said, 'The bus will be soon,' and rising from the table, left the room.

Mr Kane held Ellen's coat towards her shoulders and arms, and she whispered, 'Isn't he going to interview . . . ?' His headshake prevented her speaking further.

At the gate, as they began to walk back up the hill to the village, she said, 'Was that an interview?' Mr Kane laughed and told her that it was as much an interview as she would ever get.

'What was that he was saying about a song?' Ellen asked.

Thomas Kane said, 'A complete invention. He makes things up to please himself. They sound nice to him.'

'The Robert Emmet. Shouldn't it be "the nations of the world"?'

'Of course it should, wasn't that the whole point, Ireland a "nation", it is already a "country"; that's Jeremiah for you, always gets the most important bit wrong.' Mr Kane shook his head regretfully.

Neither said another word, and, audible for a long way through the leafless trees, the dank *Princess* arrived.

As she climbed aboard, he said, 'Goodbye now, Miss Morris.

21

Can you start next Monday, please? We're very shorthanded, as you can see. I'll fix up lodgings for you.' She looked at him and nodded.

'Thanks very much,' she said.

The conductor sloped down, edging with his hip between the empty seats.

'You have a ticket, Miss, haven't you, since this morning?' He punched it.

Ellen Morris looked back at the receding village and saw Mr Kane standing by the little gate of the drab school. She settled down, bulking the tails of her coat beneath her to comfort the wooden seat.

Opening her attaché case, she took out a notebook and fountain pen, and trying to wedge her writing elbow to her hip to prevent the bus shaking her hand, she began to write. 'Monday, 2nd February 1925. Deanstown. I could not see the place for fog.'

New mists for the coming night began to form in the fields behind the walls.

2

Her father said, 'They had a lot of trouble out around there, that place was very active y'know. The Irregulars were out in force there.'

Her mother said, 'How far away did you say the church was?'

'And that whole place out there,' said Bob. 'They all went against the Treaty, every single one of them.'

'Is the Curate young, even?' said her mother. 'Two old men, dth, imagine. A young priest is often better I always think.'

'I believe 'twas vicious out around there,' said Bob Morris. 'Vicious, by all accounts.'

In a week of buying and labelling, Ellen put together two suitcases, one large, one small, and a trunk. Her mother wondered about it all, and Ellen said, 'Mama, it is only thirty-six miles away. It isn't the far end of the world.'

On the Thursday evening, three days after her first visit to Deanstown, and three days before she was to take up residence out there, her father said to Ellen, 'Ellen girl, will you walk me down to Ginger Hill, I have to drop a letter into Tim Taylor's office?'

He paused from time to time to rest. 'This old damp. This time of the year.'

Bob always waited to speak until late in an opportunity. Climbing back up Ginger Hill, past the railings on Sarsfield Buildings, he said, 'I'm going to miss you, Ell.'

'Ach, Dada, it mightn't be such a gaudy place, but it isn't the North Pole I'm going to.'

'I was asking around about him,' said her father, 'your Mr Kane. And the great thing about him, they say. D'you know that he quit the Troubles? He did indeed. Gave it up. Left it all. The great thing was. Mind you, he was a hard man, as hard as Collins himself, Kane was. But they say the great thing about him was. That not as much as a pellet did he fire once he quit the Troubles. At the

Irregulars nor the Free Staters. Neither side, not a pellet. Not one.'

He lifted Ellen's hand, tucked it under his arm, and they returned to Brunswick Square.

The Canon, as School Manager, wrote to Ellen with her Letter of Appointment. It came enclosed in a note from Thomas Kane who arranged to meet her on the Sunday afternoon in Mooreville, not in Deanstown.

Bob Morris said, 'No, no, 'tis the least we might do and you going off like this,' as Ellen thanked him again for the car he had hired.

'Here, dab of Holy Water,' said May Morris, flicking her wetted fingers in the vague direction of her daughter's forehead, and both women's hands fluttered into the Sign of the Cross automatically.

'Now d'you know who's out there?' said the driver, who talked all the time. 'That Kane man, maybe you don't remember about him, he's the one did the big ambush at Tankardstown in 1919, d'you remember, a bunch of them, they took a man off the train and he heavily guarded? Oh, aye, he's the one, he's your man.' The driver wore a cap which he kept lifting and replacing on his bald spot. 'Aye, that's him. The train had a stop for only one minute. And yer man – he was on there as quick as wink, and a pair of guns on him. And came off it without a scratch. There was a Sergeant Enright killed in it, a distant cousin of my own sister's husband. Oh, aye.'

When Thomas Kane walked across the street to meet Ellen, as arranged, under the Maid of Erin statue, the talkative driver fell quiet and touched his cap. While Ellen shook hands and opened the conversation, the driver hauled out the cases alone, and then, a silent transaction, the two men together stowed Ellen's trunk in Mr Kane's car.

She sat bolt upright in the front seat, up and down the hills on the narrow roads, in air brilliantly clear with frost.

'It seemed best,' he said, 'to meet you in here. So that you can get an idea of the general area.'

As they drove, he pointed out sights: significant trees, one struck by lightning; he skirted the triangular beginnings of the forest: 'It is claimed that owls nest in there. Although I have to say I haven't ever heard any'; he showed her a house in which a man hanged himself; he drew attention to the blueness of the mountains: 'They say it is a sign of rain when the mountains seem near.' The ivy gleamed on Deanstown Castle, a spreadeagled, ruined *château* on old southern terraced slopes far from the road, and he told Ellen she should 'make sure to see the place when the weather gets fine'. Whatever the crispness of the air, he did not himself wear gloves, and she looked at the backs of his hands on the steering wheel: each hand had a thickset blue vein meandering upwards to the middle knuckle.

'He's very precise,' she said to her closest friend the following week-end. 'You notice it about him every day. He's not like my father, Leah, he's not a man I imagine everybody likes. He has a sharp cut about him, do you know what I mean?'

Leah, the wife of Herbert Winer: Jeweller and Watchmaker, said aloud on that Sunday night, 'What time is it, Herbert? I suppose Ellen is installed in her lodgings by now.'

Leah drew a picture of a dress she thought of trying to make for herself; she copied a drawing from a Butterick's pattern book. The caption beneath began, '*When fashion suddenly goes topsy-turvy, and ordains such things as waistlines and busts that have long been hidden*'. She wrote 'topsy-turvy' twice, and then beside it began to sketch a profile of her own bosom, looking in her bedroom mirror to do so. Sideways in the small cramped room, briefly dropping the wool wrapper from her shoulders to her waist, raising her arms above her head to improve the profile, shivering, her nipples cold and edgy in the air of the wintry room, Leah Winer dressed again, and called out to her husband in his home workroom down the passageway, 'D'you think she'll be all right out there, Herbert? A girl who was never away from home in her life?'

'Now that'll all help you to get your bearings,' said Thomas Kane. 'And here we are.'

He chugged into the yard of a good farm. 'We're about a mile from school. This woman is very clean.'

She appeared in the low doorway, shading her eyes against the descending winter sun.

'Hallo, Mrs Greege.'

'Hallo, Master. Is this her?'

Two awkward young men appeared behind their mother and came to the car to help with the suitcases and trunk. Mrs Greege surveyed the luggage as it passed by.

Ellen's room – not quite as large as the one in Brunswick Square, but what was? – roamed pleasantly beneath the roof, a long room, whose three windows, on account of the house's design, were at ankle level, and they looked out on the farmyard and the road gate. The room formed a square shape, with a little long neck right in the centre of one side; when writing home, she made a drawing of the room; 'it looks like an over-balanced, fat "T", a bit like a square tennis bat with a stubby handle,' she wrote. She loved the tobacco-brown rafters; the old chest on which she could stand a bowl of flowers; and above all the writing-table and chair: 'I find the room has a serene atmosphere.'

Ellen sucked a tooth as she gazed at the huge old newspaper engraving celebrating *Lord Roberts at the Relief of Kandahar in 1880*: 'But I suppose I will have to put up with it,' she wrote. 'I have plenty of storage, anyway.'

Just inside the door at the foot of her little corridor, a splendid wide space opened where her trunk and cases would dwell unencroachingly.

Ellen stooped to a window, watched for a moment the last flicker of gold in the evening sky: it caught the green paint of Mr Kane's car as he nudged out of the yard and turned left down the narrow hill. She stood and began to unpack. One by one, she opened the drawers in the heavy tallboy: the top one, which was above her eye level, stuck.

'I see,' she murmured aloud, and reaching into her lemon-coloured washbag, took a piece of soap and rubbed it along each upper edge of the drawer until it opened and closed with a smooth action. As she knelt to lay cardigans and skirts on the floor of the big bottom drawer, she glanced through the window again and understood that the distant house she could see must be that of Mr Kane, because as she watched, he opened his gate, climbed back into his car and drove through, lost to sight behind some tall evergreens.

Downstairs at supper, the two sons sat shyly, and ate very carefully. Ellen rounded the corner of the wooden stairs into the kitchen: Mrs Greege made a comment upon the knitwork in Ellen's cardigan.

'Did you buy that? Really? In a shop? Do you knit at all yourself? There's a very good woman over in Camas, cable stitching and that.' Mrs Greege spoke quickly, yet the words filled her mouth in clods.

Ellen said, 'No, but I do needlework.'

Thomas Kane padlocked the wooden door of the lean-to garage he had built with his own hands when he bought his car the previous year. He raised his head to admire the evening star in the bright sky, and walked across the gravel to his front door.

'This is lovely,' said Ellen Morris, referring to the cold bacon. 'Now, what are your names?' she said to the two young men, neither of whom answered.

'That's Liam, my eldest, and that's Shamie,' represented their mother, 'and did you meet Lily when you came in? She's my sister's daughter; she came over here to keep me company when my husband died, she's from the next county.' The aproned girl at the end of the table smiled at the two youths, but did not look at Ellen.

Ellen asked the sons, 'Did you go to school to Deanstown?'

Liam blushed, as he always would whenever Ellen addressed him, and as would his brother, and stumbled, 'Oh, aye. To Master Kane.'

'Wasn't he the man that was hard on them too, the same Master Kane?' said Mrs Greege. 'Wasn't he though? He put the fear of God in them all. Did you know him before?'

Ellen answered that she had not, and Mrs Greege said, 'Well, I'm the one to be telling you all about him.' She added, 'I suppose you'll be doing your own washing?' and moved on into another topic.

Ellen Morris, tolerant towards the newness of her situation, bit her independent tongue recurrently throughout this first conversation. Crockery clinked with cutlery: wood on the fire spat. Lily at the end of the table choked on a crumb and coughed herself vigorously to tears, releasing the boys' grins. After supper, the boys lifted the table and set it back against the wall; Lily cleared the utensils into a white enamel basin with a blue rim and took the unsteady pile – 'Lazy man's load,' called Mrs Greege – into a rear scullery, from which then came the sounds of washing-up.

'No wife, yet, the Master,' said Mrs Greege, 'and he what? Forty, I suppose, forty-one?'

Chairs scraped across the floor to the fire; wordlessly, the younger brother, Shamie, created a place with cushions for Ellen on the settle. All present in the semi-circle looked into the little flames, and little was said. Ellen's tentative questions, regarding farming, or the sports played locally, or the priests, met with either embarrassed monosyllables from the brothers, or increasingly intrusive observations from their mother.

Finally, Mrs Greege asked, 'Does the Canon know you brought all that style with you to wear?'

Ellen frowned and said, 'Style?'

Mrs Greege said, 'He's against style, the Canon. I don't think the man was ever in a city in his life.'

Soon after this, Ellen said, 'I think I'll start to get ready for bed,' and stood.

'Good God Almighty, but you're the early bird entirely,' said Mrs Greege. 'At eight o'clock in the evening only?'

'I have all sorts of things to do,' said Ellen, climbing the stairs. 'Good-night to you all.' Murmurs answered.

In her room she took out paper and pen and began her letter.

c/o Mrs J. Greege,
Mantlehill,
Deanstown.
8th February 1925,
Sunday night.

Dear Dada, Mama and all,

Well, here I am, hardly able to believe I am here. This is my address, and it is a farm, with hens in the yard and the cowshed within earshot and nostril distance! I am about a twenty-minute walk from the school, and I am quite excited about it all! Mr Kane met me off the bus with his car, 'the ninth car in the county' he informed me (a Singer, Dada and Jim). They all seem nice out here, very quiet, but I think some of them are going to be very inquisitive. The country is lovely, big fields and a lot of woods, and a wide, quiet river, and an old castle.

Ellen stopped, sat back and looked all around the room. She reached for a corner of the quilt and inspected it, front and back, stroking a piece of velvet she found among the patchwork. Rising from her chair, she then inspected the embroidery on the pillow-cases and the edges of the sheets, and the satin bindings on the heavy wool blankets. She caught sight of her face in the mirror-stand on the tallboy, and turned her hair a little in her hand. The oil-lamp's glow embellished the brass minarets on the bedposts. Returning to her table, she took an envelope from her leather writing-case and scribbled on it – 'Questions to ask Mrs Greege: 1. Ironing? 2. A larger heater?' then returned to her letter, and her little diagram of her room.

An hour later, she began to unpack the heavy trunk, typically methodically – if much more slowly than she might have done at home. Fumbling in the pocket of her coat hanging on its hook behind the door, she found the burgundy-coloured leather purse of her rosary beads and knelt in prayer, her hands across her eyes, forehead bowed; 'The Five Joyful Mysteries of the Rosary,' she began, 'the First Mystery, The Annunciation.'

Fifteen minutes later, she concluded. 'Dearest Lord, gaze down upon me, Thy servant, and teach me the strength to change the things I can, the fortitude to accept the things I cannot change, and the wisdom to discern the difference.' Finalizing with the Sign of the Cross, she rose stiffly and stretched. Partially undressing, shivering in the cold, she washed sparingly in cold water from the tall china ewer, put on a nightdress, drew her underwear out from underneath it, and climbed into the stiff bed.

Down the hill a mile away, Thomas Kane sat reading *The Idylls of the King* by the fire in his underfurnished and sere house.

'This is the only chair I could find in the county,' he told his sister some years earlier, 'that is tall enough to lean my head back against. Look?' He demonstrated. 'It comes right up. Whereas most of them only come up as far as under my shoulder-blades.'

Once, he rose, and poured the ageing tea into his mug from the pot sitting inside the fender. He looked at, but did not wipe clean, the ring of tea-stain the pot had made on the white fireplace tiles. When the clock on the mantelpiece reached exactly eight o'clock, he put the book down, rose and went to the table, where some papers lay near the lamp. Taking his speckled fountain pen from an inside pocket of his jacket, he unscrewed the cap and began to write in large, perfectly-spaced handwriting:

'Motion: That – if a National Teachers' Organization is to be formed, it should be for the entire country, and with a full-time Representative and Staff.' He underlined *the entire country*, and then wrote, *ISSUES: 1. Pay and Conditions; 2. Accommodation including the Right to Buy (Residences); 3. Pensions. 4. Compassionate Bursaries.*

In a writing-box on the table, two buttons from a military greatcoat jingled when he reached for a new sheet of paper. He wrote at a steady medium pace, as if he had long ago measured the use of his time and knew how to fill stretches of hours. Twice, he took from under the sloping lid of the mahogany writing-box a list of names, and ticked off one or two. After two hours, during which he rose once to fix the fire, he replaced the cap on his pen at exactly ten o'clock. He tidied everything away and turned the small key in the lock of the writing-box. Stretching his back and sighing through his nose, he rose and left the room, taking the lamp with him to the hallstand: to his annoyance, the wick's quick flare blackened the clear glass globe. From his front door, he walked the twenty yards to the green iron gate at the road, and checked its clasp firmly. He stepped back from the shade of the *macrocarpa* trees and looked at the sky. Weak light from the hallway fell on the gravel. In the summer, dogs barked at night, cows lowed, and bicycle tyres swished by as people cycled home from dances or public houses, sometimes talking quite loudly; last autumn nearby, a family of foxes sometimes barked. In the winter and the early spring, however, not a sound was to be heard from inside the house, only the scratching of a pen on paper, or the startle of coals resettling themselves on the fire. In the silence, he listened for the noise of the weir four miles away. Back in the house, he took the clock from the kitchen shelf, wound it, checked the bolt on the back door, turned the thick key in the front door and climbed the stairs to bed, holding the lamp ahead of him carefully.

By the mirror, he took off his collar, wetted his finger on his tongue and rubbed at a small dark mark where the stud had pressed. Hauling off his shirt, he examined the cuffs, and then laid shirt and collar aside to wear in the morning. He wore only a long vest underneath, and having removed his black shoes and socks, climbed into bed and blew out the flame of the lamp.

As Miss Morris arrived next morning, Mr Kane met her at the school door and asked, 'How did you get on at Mrs Greege's?'

She replied with a smile, 'I think I'm going to be talking to myself a lot there.'

He nodded pleasantly, and took out his watch.

'Well. Half-past nine,' he said, as he did every morning.

Thus, they began to work side by side five days a week in the small, insalubrious two-room school, with no other adults present, and most of every day a shared experience.

'Now – who gives out the plasticine?' Ellen asked, and all hands shot up.

'All right, all right. This is how we'll do it. This week the front two desks here, then next week the front two desks here. And then every week a different two desks. But. Before that. I want the names of every one of you. Who's first?'

They looked at each other and hunched their little shoulders. Nobody raised a hand. They giggled.

'Oh!' She swooped on them with a big mock of a smile. 'So you have no names?' They grinned wider.

'Oh, you're like sucky-calves, are you? They have no names either?' – which freed them to laugh openly.

'So,' she pressed on, 'I want to hear each of your names. Out loud. And I'm going to write each name on the board. And the names are going to stay on the board all this week. So you can look at yourselves. Like a mirror. I'll start with my name,' and she wrote 'Miss Morris' in firm letters in bright green chalk.

Their words tumbled out. Kitty. Joanie. Angela. Mattie. Mickey. Eddie. Mary. Paddy. Nellie. Dan. Mary. Jimmy. Gussie. Mary. Danny. Tim. Patie. Mary.

'The alphabet goes largely untroubled around here, I see,' she observed to Thomas later, as he looked at the board. 'Not to mention the Litany of the Saints.'

When she came to the small fair-haired boy, he of the great reticence during her first visit last week, again he said nothing. Two children in front turned and giggled, and she rebuked them with her first curtness. She walked across to the head of the row

31

in which the boy sat – dressed exactly as he had been a week earlier – and said, 'I don't know your name at all, so how can we talk to each other?' He put his head down on his arms.

'All right,' mollified Ellen. 'All right.'

To the boy sitting beside him she said, 'Now what is his name, because I am certainly not going to leave him off the board?'

A number of voices answered, 'Timmy Quinn, Ma'am,' and another piped from somewhere, 'Ma'am, he don't talk at all.'

In the same green chalk and in equally large letters Ellen wrote 'Timmy' on the blackboard. All the names completed, she then occupied the rest of the morning having them make small baskets from plasticine, and adding to their vocabulary the words 'fruit', and 'wicker', and 'weaving'.

Shortly after their break began it rained, and all rushed back in. They sat in throughout lunchtime, and Thomas Kane murmuringly guided Ellen around the school cupboards: the ink supply, in large black carboy bottles; the pencils, bought by the gross every August; the Progress Record. He instructed her in the school's meagre architecture. A waist-high wooden partition, surmounted with bright glass panes to the ceiling, separated their classrooms. The polished wood, a glossy light-brown oak, had married beneath itself, or else represented some kind of official apology, compensation for the general shabbiness of the building. In a corner of the partition, on the Senior classroom side, a knot-hole had dropped open in the wood many years ago; the children and the teachers traditionally used it as a mailbox, or last resting-place, for broken pens. 'The nib graveyard,' he now remarked to Ellen – and made her smile by wondering whether the cache accumulating daily on the floor within the partition would prove of great eventual interest to archaeologists.

When classes resumed, she had all her charges walk slowly around the boundaries of the room, hands behind their backs, saying 'One and One are Two. One and Two are Three. One and Three are Four', until they reached Twenty; then she marched them all back again in the opposite direction and took them to Forty. As they scrambled to get back in their desks, the little silent boy stood beside the board, and looking askance up to Ellen, drew a finger under his own name.

A moment or two after that, she started at a 'whh-ikk' sound from the outer room. As she looked through the glass of the partition, Thomas Kane, wielding a long-ish ash stick, gave a lanky boy four hard strokes across his palms outstretched. Each time the boy stuck his hand impersonally out from his body, the teacher steadied the uncouth young hand, lined it up for aim, and whipped the stick down: the arm bounced with the force. The boy stepped back to his desk, hands squeezed tight in his armpits, avoiding the eyes of his classmates, and Thomas Kane mundanely returned the stick to the grooved slot that ran beneath the blackboard and was designed to hold sticks of chalk. Ellen turned back to her task: for a moment she lost her place in the counting game.

Ellen's classes finished at half-past two and in the abandoned echoing classroom she began to rearrange the little drawings of farmyard animals, the large old paintings of flowers, and to make notes of what needed renewing. The Senior room evacuated at three o'clock, two senior boys and two senior girls remaining behind on a weekly rota to sweep the wooden floors. The Roll Book finalized, her basket rearranged for the walk home, the fires made safe – it all would take until twenty-five- or half-past three each day.

With the rain clearing, and the sky now a blue miracle, that Monday, her first day, brought again one of February's glorious, sunny promises of spring. Thomas Kane closed the cupboards, turned the key in his desk, checked the window latches, replaced the fireguard, then reached for his coat.

'I have to make a list,' she said, checking her sleeve for her handkerchief, and taking her gloves from her basket, 'there's an awful lot to be done.'

'Gorgeous sunshine.' He drew the wicket gate behind them. 'I'll walk on a bit the road with you.'

As they turned to cross the green towards the pump, curtains in two cottages flickered in little tics.

'That must be her,' the hidden voices of the village houses told each other. 'Look,' they called to those by the fireside, 'there's the Master and the new Mistress.' The village's eyes saw a pair of formal walkers: Thomas Kane and this very small woman with the new Red-Riding-Hood basket over her arm, and her gloves and her hat.

'Ha, boys-oh-dear, well, well?' said Mr Hand to nobody in particular in the kitchen of his pub. His wife said that night, 'D'you know what it is? She looks like a Protestant. A'course, she's a townie, isn't she?'

—

33

On the left ran the limestone wall of the Castle demesne, a circuit of three miles in all.

'Look at that?' Thomas Kane indicated the letter-box, now painted green since the Treaty, set in the wall outside Hand's public house.

'Do you know what they say? They say that was installed by Anthony Trollope himself. He worked for the Post Office all around here.'

Beyond the wall, wide fields stretched, tufted in the sporadic growths of winter.

'Even this time of the year,' said Mr Kane, 'the fields never lose their colour, the green is nearly blue, like they say about Kentucky.'

The mountains were pocked with little snows. On the right, they passed one last village house, painted ochre, and with leaded dormer windows; when their gardens flowered, he said, 'the cleanest of these houses could be on the lid of a chocolate box. They built the village like a toy, or an ornament – to make the estate look good. The Prince of Wales rode through here, did you know that? Everyone came out and lined the road and shouted their wishes to him that he get a good wife in Ireland, and he's supposed to have said to Dublin Castle later: "Rather a long way from getting shot by the Irish, don't you think?" That's what he's supposed to have said.'

He slowed his pace down to allow for Ellen's shorter steps; he then contrived to walk a foot behind her, looked at her face to view her in his surroundings. They walked past the Teacher's Residence, which he indicated.

Ellen said, 'Yes, I noticed it this morning. I can see it from my window. It looks quite new.'

'It is. The old one was burnt down.'

'Oh?' she said. Had he known her better, he would have recognized her inflection as a request for amplification.

A glossy crow flew off a wall; a flight of rooks swept out across the sky.

'Do you like the countryside?' he asked her. 'Do you know land at all, or fields. Hedges, and the like?'

She replied that she knew rural life mostly from books: when they went on holidays it was always to the sea, but that this place was lovely, really lovely. Without any context he said, 'It gets a lot of flies sometimes here in the summer. There are forty million species of fly in the world.'

'Well, so,' he said, his last remark as he turned from Mrs Greege's gate, and, with a serious nod, walked his fixed measured pace back down the road to his own house, remaining within sight. She glanced after him, and then, preparing her demeanour for Mrs Greege, went indoors.

'I am, thank you, yes, settling in fine. Yes, he seems very nice, a very nice man, and a good teacher, yes, very good.' Ellen answered the questions on the move, climbing the stairs.

Her skin glowed in the dimness of her room: too early to light a lamp. Since her first teaching job, a few streets away from Brunswick Square, she habitually changed after school; now she put on a white wool blouse, a heavy woollen red jumper which always went well with the dense blackness of her hair, a heavy tweed skirt and thick stockings: the larger oil heater she requested had not yet arrived, although she noticed that she had acquired a hot-water bottle. She sat on the bed to rest.

The room fell silent inexorably. She stared through the window to the quiet farmyard below. In a while, she looked around the room, seeking work, but she had now unpacked everything, had even rearranged her writing-case and her sewing threads. She sighed.

'Miss,' said Mrs Greege at supper two hours later, 'if you lock your door while you're out Lily can't clean your room.'

'Yes, I suppose so.'

Thomas Kane sat at his kitchen table. A red-faced man seated opposite him had brought with him a form for the Master to fill in, declaring an interest by kinship in a Will advertised in the papers last week.

'He was the wife's cousin, first cousin, Master, their fathers were brothers. The wife could tell you herself. That man's father married secondly, and this man who died went to Delaware when he was a young fellow, and he made money out of making iron.'

The Master wrote carefully on the solicitor's form, 'Mrs John Guiney, of Cappadun, Deanstown: first cousin on Paternal side.'

He said to Mr John Guiney, 'Has your wife any proof of the

family connection?' and Mr John Guiney brought from his pocket a very old and large envelope.

'She had letters from him, Sir, and a photograph and two Christmas cards.'

The Master said, 'Oh, that's excellent, John, excellent.'

John Guiney left, and Thomas Kane boiled two eggs and made tea and cut three slices of bread, heaping butter on them.

By the end of the week, Ellen had reorganized many of the boxes of chalks, counters and reading primers in the Junior room. She opened a 'Food Notebook'.

'Will they mind,' she wondered, 'if I ask them what they eat?'

He sawed at his chin with his fingertips. 'It might be a bit . . .'

'Suppose I make it a game?' she asked. 'Suppose I say we will do it so that we get to know all the kinds of food in the world? I have pictures of Africa somewhere.'

On each of the first four afternoons he walked with her to Mrs Greege's. On the fifth, the Friday, she caught the bus at a quarter past three from outside the school, her smaller suitcase in her hand.

'They'll think you're gone for good,' he smiled, and furtively indicated the village windows, 'when they see the suitcase,' and indeed the bus conductor asked the predictable question.

'No. Only for the week-end,' she smiled back.

'I'd say all the same 'tis a bit lonesome out around here for a city girl like yourself?'

'Everybody's very nice,' she riposted.

At half-past six, she walked from the corner by the railway station, down the sloped pavement past the railings of the park in Brunswick Square: shopkeepers in the by-streets had begun to plank up their shutters for the night. Sailors came to this park sometimes and smoked pipes, talking loudly in foreign languages. Many of the railings, particularly around the bandstand, had been manufactured, everyone said, from the cannon captured at Waterloo. The oaks on the western side were planted by a gentleman in honour of each of his early *amours*; later, the sole elm tree for his wife. Children tried in vain to measure with string the annual subsidence of 'the Sinking Church' at the lower end.

'Who's that, it can't be Ellen?' Her father slanted the newspaper outward. 'And how are you, girl?' standing over her in big affection. 'They're all out. Your mother is gone over to the Jesuits to say a prayer. Rina is down at Maud Joyce's house, and Jim is out, maybe with Mary Rose.' One of his large eyebrows rose to conspire with Ellen's amused nod. 'We got your grand long letter.'

Ellen colonized the hall table, chair and floor with gloves, hat, bag, suitcase, notebook, umbrella.

No matter what the time of day, Bob Morris always wore a suit and a stiff collar and a tie. His wife said he would have 'to undergo a surgical operation to remove them'.

'Your mother should be soon.'

He waited on her, as he had done since her birth. They sat at the kitchen table. A step fell in the hall.

'What's this? What's this?'

Coming through the door with some arms-raised business towards a hatpin, May Morris kissed Ellen who murmured 'hallo'.

May laid her hat on the kitchen's side-table.

'Have you no food in front of you? Bob, did you ask the girl has she a mouth on her, and she travelling?

'I'm just after talking to Father Watson,' her mother said, heading for the meatsafe. 'He was asking will you call and see him?'

Ellen said she would, but she wanted 'a quiet time', that settling in at Deanstown had been 'very tiring'. She stood and fetched a towel from the hot cupboard in the scullery.

Her father followed her to the hallway and whispered to her, 'D'you know what? You're getting to be a real handsome woman, a – a – smasher. That's it. A smasher.' She grinned at him over the baluster, hand on the rail, as she ran upstairs.

May called up the stairwell, 'If you're going out, 'tis going to rain. I'll have your tea here in a minute.'

Opening a door at the top of the stairs, Ellen, with the pleasure of renewed acquaintance, ran her hand along the side of the bath.

'Now, tell us all your news,' said Bob, elbows leaning in eagerness on the table.

'Bob, you're unseemly, wasn't her long letter enough for you?' said May. 'Did you find out about Masses?'

'Not every morning, except in Lent,' replied Ellen.

'What's the lodgings like?'

'Oh, Dada!' Ellen laughed. 'If you met Mrs Greege! She's like a bony wasp, she creeps around and stings.'

'Who is she herself?' asked May. 'Who are her people?'

'Farmers, there's pucks of money there, I mean all her clothes are good, and she keeps a very clean house, but she's always criticizing me.'

Ellen did an imitation of Mrs Greege's accent.

'Huh, Miss, where'd you get that shtyle from, you're like a doll that walks and talks and shtands, aren't you, huh?' – and they all laughed.

'She has her hair tied around her head as if it was a wreath stuck on, but I saw it one night when she was getting ready for bed and it was down to her waist and black and grey. She's the boniest woman I ever saw; she makes Mrs Halpin look fat.'

'Imagine!' said May. 'Mrs Halpin look fat.'

'And him?' asked Bob. 'The Kane man, what's he like? I was asking about him the other day; d'you know that Newman man from Newcastle West, he knew him slightly in the old days, don't you know? And he said, I'll tell you what he said, he said, "Thomas Kane is his own man to the power of three, Bob." That's what he said.'

'He's that all right,' replied Ellen, 'and – I don't know. He's – he's what I'd call "formal". They're all afraid of him.'

'But you're not?' asked Bob.

'Pwit,' said Ellen, 'no fear.'

'D'you know the story about him, do you?' asked Bob. 'He was Collins's man out there, he was the driving force, they said, and then, all of a sudden, he upped and left. Oh, in 1920, or so, as early as that. But I mean, he was the genuine job, so he was, there was a reward out on him, d'you know?'

They talked until half-past ten.

'Are you getting Mass in the morning?' asked May. 'Father Watson is saying a half-past ten, because he's going away tomorrow night so he won't be saying a Sunday Mass.'

'Oh, that's a good idea, are you going, Dada?'

'No, I'll be sane and wait for Sunday like the rest of the country,' said Bob, and Ellen punched his arm with her fist.

Thomas Kane spent Saturday cleaning his house from top to toe; he even cleaned the windows, and washed old dishes. A parcel containing two books arrived in the post from the mail-order book-sellers in London. Slowly he opened the knots, rolled the string into a tiny hank secured in the middle by a bow-knot, and then placed it in a corner of the kitchen table drawer. Turning the parcel from side to side, he eased off the brown paper, and folded it into a neat rectangle which he placed on top of the glass-fronted book-case in the corner of the kitchen. He clicked his tongue on his teeth as he saw in the bookcase, and took down, a book whose coloured jacket had been torn on the spine: two young men smiled at each other in a sylvan setting: *Under the Greenwood Tree*. Thomas tore a scrap of paper from an envelope in his pocket, wrote on it, 'Get some stamp paper and fix this,' and slipped the note inside the frontispiece of the novel.

He returned to the parcel on the table, still wrapped in heavy tissue paper from which he finally undressed the new books: *Moths of the World, A New and Important Compilation*. Taking it into the bay window, he made it fall open at 'L'. 'The Luna Moth (*luna*: the moon) is pale green in colour. *Actias luna*; it is predominantly found in North America where it has the reputation of great beauty. Very soon after the females emerge from their cocoons they begin to emit a radiant which attracts mates from up to four miles away.'

Thomas turned the book over and over in his hand and opened several other pages, still standing at the window. Then he returned to the table and exchanged it for the other book: *In Brightest Africa* by Carl Akeley. At random he read, 'The phenomenon of elephants helping each other when wounded is not general by any means. Only a few days after shooting the big bull, I had an instance of elephants abandoning one of their number that was wounded and not very badly wounded either. I had gone into the forest again, and had come upon another bunch in very thick country. I could only get little glimpses of a patch of hide or ivory once in a while.'

Beside the armchair in the bay window sat a small item of furni-ture, about two feet high, funnelling gradually outward from bottom to top, and covered in turquoise, yellow-flowered fabric, a gift from his aunt. She regularly obtained butter-boxes from her local creamery and covered them with furnishing materials – but she lined the inside in white cloth too thin to conceal the original black stencil: '56 lbs (Avoirdupois)' of the waxy yellow, soft, strong butter from the creamery. On the padded lid Thomas now set down his two new books, within hand's reach of his armchair.

John Watson, S.J., came swishing up the side aisle in his black soutane. One or two people still knelt in prayer: the sacristan, everybody said he had gone bald too young, doused the tall candles with his hooded stick. John Watson took Ellen's hands in his and whispered, 'Your mother said to expect you.'

'Do you know what?' Ellen once said to her father. 'He's the only man small enough for me to look in the eye,' and they laughed, but not unkindly.

In the porch, the noise of the outdoors allowed them to raise their voices a little.

'Oh, Father John, I have so much to tell you.'

He beamed. 'When I saw you at the Communion rails, I thought, dear Ellen, what a shame I have to go to Cork tonight, otherwise we could have had one of our walks tomorrow.'

'One walk wouldn't be enough, Father John. All I have to tell you.'

'Are you liking it out there? Is it exciting? You're not going to be buried out there are you, Ellen?'

'Oh, Father, there is so much to do. With those children.'

'I'll be listening out to hear will your accent change?'

Ellen laughed in a whisper. 'It will do no such thing!'

'Oh, I don't know, do I detect a slight broadening of the vowel sounds, do I?'

'Mind you, Father John, I have this landlady, Mrs Greege, and if you heard her? She might infect me all right. Especially as the place is so quiet out there.'

'Oh, but you'll be able to keep up with your reading?' They moved into the yard and raised their voices further, to normal. 'I thought of you the other day, and that grand essay you wrote, I was teaching Wordsworth. "I travelled among unknown men" . . .'

Ellen interrupted him and quoted, '"In lands beyond the sea" –' She laughed again. 'Father John, go away out of that, I'm only thirty-six miles away.'

'I thought that'd rise you. So now, you see, I told you. Janesborough is the hub of the globe after all!'

They laughed.

'Come in for a quick cup of tea,' he said. 'I suppose you'll be going round to Mrs Winer, will you, I met her the other day, we said hallo.'

'Tell me, Father John,' asked Ellen as they walked round the high brick building. 'Have you by any chance a copy of that other essay you asked me to write, d'you remember in the holidays years and years ago?'

'"The City of Janesborough"? I have indeed, do you want it?'

'I want to read it to the children. Because I wasn't much older than them at the time.'

'Oh, yes, oh, yes, I can see that,' he said. 'Now.' They sat down. 'Let me have a look at you.'

In the austere drawing-room, under the dark oil painting of Saint Ignatius Loyola, he spilled tea again on his chin, and apologized. 'I'm getting old, my hands have the shakes.' They laughed. 'Do you know, Ellen, I'm eighteen years a priest next week?'

'Hah!' she teased. 'I can guess your age now!' She mock-counted on her fingers. 'You don't look a day over a hundred to me,' she grinned.

'Close,' he said, 'close.'

'I'll tell you one thing, though, Father John, if ever I'm to be holy, I'll be holy out there; I think I'm saying two rosaries a night there, there isn't anything else to do. Although they only have Mass on Sundays.'

He left the room to fetch the essay for her, and returned reading it aloud.

'Here it is. "The City of Janesborough, where I was born and where I live with my parents and my brother and sister, has a population of forty thousand people. Most of its trade comes from the fact that it has a wide river port, and boats sail up and down. They come from Amsterdam and Genoa and Bordeaux and they carry jute and flour and wine. My father is a printer. He prints boxes and calendars and notices and advertisements." Now, wasn't that very good for, what age were you, eleven?'

'Stoppit, you'll make me blush, Father! Oh, and I have worked out your age.'

'You haven't.'

'Yes, I have. Eighteen years a priest, you said, and fourteen years before that in the seminary, from the age of what, eighteen?'

'Smarty!'

John Watson laid the school jotter on the table between them

41

and, switching to seriousness, said, 'I hope we're not going to lose you to them out there, Ellen, are we? I hope some strong countryman . . .' He leaned back, as a painter does to get a perspective on his canvas. 'Oh, now! Are you blushing, what?'

When Ellen left the Jesuit residence, Father John Watson climbed two flights of stairs to his room. For several minutes he stood at the window watching her walk the length of long Catherine Street; he stroked his face, drawing both hands from under his blond sideburns down to the point of his chin, where his fingers met each time in a brief praying tent before resuming their stroking. Turning away, he sat on his bed, took off his shoes and began to polish them.

Along with the parcelled books, the postman, always late on Saturday morning, brought Thomas Kane another of the letters he had been receiving for over two years. He opened it with a 'Dth' of mild annoyance. He had kept them all, when other recipients might have destroyed such correspondence.

'Never forget. I liked you the minute I saw you, and I will always feel like this. Signed. A Secret Admirer.'

He swept the backs of his fingernails in a tapping motion across the notepaper.

'I know who you are, Missy,' he said aloud, and half-grinned.

The writer, a handsome, often distressed woman, never dated her letters and often carried them around, sealed, in her handbag for days, even weeks.

Thomas Kane spoke to the letter in his hand; 'I danced with you a few years ago, so I did, Missy.'

Leah's bangles jangled against the table.

'Is that fresh air I see on your cheeks?' she asked. 'Come in, come in. Your letter, all that news. Let me look at you.'

Ellen sat on the little window seat, completely relaxed, content to let Leah's warm breezes blow.

'How do you like my blouse? I copied the embroidery. From my sister. Oh. But what can be done. She owns the blouse I copied from. But will she lend it to me? No. No, no, no. I have to go there, and sit there. I saw your mother, did she tell you?'

Leah put the teapot on the table and made a sucking-inwards

noise, a reverse whistle, as the over-hot handle caught her hand.

These women made friends fifteen years earlier, and would remain steadfast until death. Ellen had called at the Winer house when, aged ten, she was collecting for the Cathedral Building Fund, and Leah, a young wife of twenty, curly-bobbed and lively, laughed at the bright girl and said, 'Didn't anybody tell you that you shouldn't collect from us? But come in anyway.'

With a sweet homemade drink she told the fascinated child about Judaism, and then on the way out gave her a shilling for the collection. When Ellen tried to protest, Leah said, 'It all goes to God, doesn't it? You see to that, you see to it that God gets it, that the priest doesn't put it on an old race horse.' Her laughter, and her colours, and her curls, stayed in the little girl's ears and eyes, and one day the following week, as if in secret and a little timidly, Ellen called again.

Ellen's mother disliked Leah intensely, 'for reasons'.

'I know your reasons, Mama,' said Ellen. 'Your reasons are the same as everyone else's. This city hates the Jews.'

Ellen's father liked Leah, and said so in glances.

'Leah,' Ellen said once. 'You have what I call "a bonanza personality".'

'Bonanza. Bonanza!' Leah sang the words.

'The Jews always look after their own,' sniffed May.

'Sure why shouldn't they?' asked Bob. 'That's fair enough.'

Herbert Winer, as withdrawn as Leah was vivacious, also came of a Russian pogrom family, and now made a living as a jeweller, with a speciality in engraving silver pocketwatch-cases.

Ellen often said to Leah, 'Whatever Herbert says, he makes it tell. I always remember the things Herbert says.'

Herbert had given Ellen one or two of her favourite watchwords, such as, 'Always wait until a man has stopped smiling before you do business with him.' And – 'Never live in a house from which you cannot see the weather changing.' 'I love his advice, Leah,' Ellen said.

He had many more: he imparted them as sparingly and thought-fully as a chess-player's moves, in his thin, very slightly accented voice. 'What is bad is not people being bad. It is people being bad and pretending to be good.'

'Where do you get these sayings from, Herbert?' Leah would ask again, and then, turning to Ellen, answer her own question.

'He is his grandfather, they say, his very grandfather, down to the laces of his shoes.'

In private, Herbert found the anti-Semitism of the city unendurable.

'If they came and spat, I could understand,' he whispered to Leah, his voice sad on the pillow. Unlike her neighbours, who received deliveries, Leah always had to go out to shop.

'I don't mind, I like the walk, I meet people,' she protested. Yet she received cheerful shouts from breadmen, milkmen, the lot: 'Ah, how'ya, Mrs Winer, how's the children?'

'Explain to me,' said Herbert, 'if they are so friendly, why are we the only ones they won't deliver to? If only they remained silent,' said Herbert. 'It would be honest.'

The doctors alone did not treat them with that cutting edge of slight difference.

'You know why that is, don't you?' murmured Herbert. 'Look at what the Jews started in this country by way of maternity medicine?'

'So?' Leah settled now with the teacups. 'What. Is. He. Like?'

'Who?' asked Ellen.

'Ah!' Leah burst out. 'Who? This man, this what is his name?'

'His name, I told you, in my letter –' Ellen wore her patient teaching tone '– is Thomas Kane, Leah, and he is very. Very.'

'Very what?' asked Leah.

'Well – very. Very strong. In himself, I mean.'

'Is he now?' sipped Leah.

Thomas would grin to Leah months later, shortly before all their frightful days set in, that Ellen gave the impression of not observing him much on that first afternoon drive.

'No,' Ellen would butt in, 'I wanted to see the town, and all the places on the way out to the village. And you can't say I didn't notice anything, what about that lovely, fine-wool plaid rug you gave me for my knees? Herbert, he even has a spare pair of gloves for passengers.'

'It's beautiful countryside out around there, Leah,' she said.

'Oh, is it now?' mocked Leah, 'beautiful countryside, indeed, well, I didn't ask you about the beautiful countryside, I can see beautiful countryside anywhere, Miss Ellen Morris,' and she arched her eyebrows.

44

'All right,' Ellen caved in. 'I'll tell you four things about him.' She splayed her fingers. 'One, he doesn't look his age at all, more like a man in his early thirties.'

Secondly, she said, he has a voice and accent the likes of which she had 'never before heard. Kind of soft and hard and deep. And quite countrified, but he makes you listen to him. Thirdly, he is in a way quite frightening. He has, what is it? I don't know. He often seems so cross, nearly angry, impatient, and at the same time, he's slow and actually patient.'

And fourthly, Ellen warmed to her subject, 'How did such a man come to be in such a small country place? Leah, I'm not joking you, he was dressed like a tailor's dummy, like he came out of a bandbox. He had a blue striped shirt. And a lovely grey overcoat, grand.'

Ellen concluded, 'And another thing. He seems like he doesn't talk much, Leah, but he's talking all the time. But not inquisitive. He didn't even ask me as much as one question. Stop looking at me like that, Leah.' Ellen swiped a glove at her friend.

Coming back across Brunswick Square from half-past nine Mass next morning, Bob said, 'The thing is, Ellie, the thing to remember is – the thing people say about him is, he never fired a shot in the Civil War, that's the thing.'

'Dada. Stoppit. The man is my Principal, not anything else. And stop saying things out of the blue.'

'You're just like your mother. Ooh, well,' breathed her father. 'What age is he?'

'I don't know, now I'll get cross with you. Mrs Greege says forty or so.'

Bob rested on the doorstep.

At breakfast Ellen said, 'The night is very quiet out there. He –' she called Thomas 'he' in all reports to her family that first weekend – 'he says that in the hills above Deanstown there are people who only come out once a month, to shop down in Mooreville, and they never travel farther.'

'What do they do for a doctor?' asked May in wonder.

'Only if they're dying, I suppose.'

Her father said, 'Don't be too surprised if the people are suspicious. Strangers, you know. They mightn't warm to you straight off.'

'Dada, sure I won't be threatening them?'

He said, 'Ah, no, Ellie, but you have to think what they've been through, five years of gunfire, and then the whole Anti-Treaty business?' He pursed his lips and blew his breath out, a wry, summarizing noise. 'Sure, look. Brother killed brother. There was father against son. That's only two years ago.' He nudged the cat out of his way with his stick.

'Isn't it funny now that a man his age . . .' Bob did not finish the sentence, a habit that infuriated his family, and he moved on to another musing. 'I'd love to know some time why he gave up Collins and all that . . .'

'Dada!' said Ellen crossly. 'Stop grunting to yourself. And for once in your life, stop repeating yourself.'

3

In the beginning, they stood off from her. 'Sleek,' they said; and the clothes: 'all that style. Dth, dth. And poor people going hungry.'

Other things, too: 'the walk of her'; Mrs Leamy said to Mrs Hanafin, 'Isn't she very sure of herself altogether?'

They said, 'Them city ones.'

After some weeks, one ameliorating observation passed around: 'At the same time, she was very devout at Mass, did you notice that?'

Naturally, Ellen never guessed what they said: had she known she would have relished the content, if not the tone; to her Training College classmates she had insisted, 'Why shouldn't we have minds of our own?' To John Watson she had said, 'Oh, Father, I'm perfectly aware that I confuse the nuns, perfectly aware of it. If I was only independent by itself, they'd understand me, but the fact that I . . . that I –'

He interrupted to say it for her: 'That you are obviously devout? Yes, Ellen, it confuses them, what a revolutionary you are!' and they laughed.

The village roughed her up a little. On a morning when Thomas Kane had gone to a Diocesan Teachers' meeting, Mrs Leamy called to the school and rapped hard on the window.

Barging through Ellen's pleasant enquiry, 'And who are you now?' Mrs Leamy said, 'Joanie, my Joanie, Joanie Leamy, doesn't want to sit beside Danny Heaphy.'

Ellen said tartly, 'If you're so concerned about the way Joanie spends her days, why don't you wash her a bit more thoroughly in the mornings?' – not a retort Mrs Leamy could easily report to a neighbour.

Mrs Hand, from the public house, called to complain that the children were learning too many prayers.

Of her, Ellen enquired with some aggression, 'Who is responsible for the welts on the back of your child's legs? Because whoever it is should be reported.'

The children in her classroom raised no such boundaries. By the middle of Ellen's second week, their traditional morning reluctance had disappeared and they set off for school cheerful, returning in a mood of happy ease. To her Principal, Thomas Kane, Ellen said, 'Is it all right if I make some adjustments in the classes? Some of those children are not the same age as their class and they should be.'

And soon, while still keeping their distance, the parents began to speculate on the effect 'the New One' would have upon their aloof Thomas Kane. Late February sun warmed the village, bringing lemon light to the skeletal beeches.

The *Distinguished Monologuist*, Mr Val Vousden, sat in a room of Mrs Heffernan's, the house in which he was lodging overnight, and began writing down the words of a new recitation. He said aloud rhymingly, 'My many days,' and then, 'my worn-out gaze.' Licking his pencil, thereby leaving a thick dart of its blue lead on the front furrow of his tongue, he began to write on the rough thin paper of a school jotter, 'My son has brought me over to end my many days.' He sat back and said slightly aloud, 'Dah-da-da-Dah. Dah-da-da-Dah. Dah-da- my worn-out gaze.' Mr Val Vousden stood up, went to the door of his room and opened it, and putting his head into the next room, a kitchen, asked was there any way at all the woman of the house could dry a pair of socks for him for the morning?

'D'you remember that big puddle I walked into, Mrs Heffernan?'

'Of course I'll dry them, Mr Vousden. Give them out here to me.'

'O, thanks very much Mrs Heffernan.' Val held the socks out, lanky arm like a pallid semaphore, towards Mrs Heffernan's comfortable apron.

No man can go on onstage with a cold like this, Val Vousden whispered to his mirror, and sniffed and wiped his nose on a corner of the sheet. He moved to the door again and called, 'Mrs Heffernan, would you by any chance have another blanket?'

Back came the promise that she would bring it to the room in a minute, and he climbed into bed to anticipate her care.

Mrs Heffernan, when he first knocked on her door, did not fully disguise the thrill of meeting him, and with relish advised him not to venture out until he was better. Nonetheless, he began to place her in a considerable dilemma. His shirts proved no problem, she knew she was a good washer and a great ironer, and not just in her own estimation; and a little drop of paraffin would take the heaviest stains out of his swallowtail coat – but should she iron them narrow trousers? He said they had no crease in them, they weren't meant to have, but, in the name of God, who ever heard of trousers without a crease? Her Billy wouldn't go to Mass on a Sunday, God be good to his soul, without a crease in his trousers.

Within a quarter of an hour of his arrival, she had him comprehensively under her care. Now she brought the blanket, and then another, and tucked them in heavily from halfway down – nothing too encroaching – to the foot of the bed, where she heaved the mattress and folded them underneath.

'They're good Foxford blankets, the nuns make them up in Foxford.'

'You can't beat beef tea, Mrs Heffernan,' said Val Vousden from his bed, strewn papers around him, looking over his spectacles at her.

'I s'pose you're only passing through? Imagine anyone lining the pockets of a pair of britches with purple?' Mrs Heffernan held up the trousers and said, 'Isn't that very grand?'

'Well, the truth is, I'm here on a bit of, well, research I call it, Ma'am.'

'And if you don't want a crease in them, Mr Vousden, well, well? D'you go to Mass yourself, Mr Vousden, Vousden is an unusual name?'

'I have God in my imagination, Mrs Heffernan.'

'D'you know what, Mr Vousden, I never dream of God at all, I'd think it wrong of me.'

Val Vousden said, 'Did you ever hear, Mrs, of a famous brass band called *The Deanstown Brass and Reed Band*?'

'Ah, I did indeed, Sir. My father walked behind it. I'll tell you now,' she said, and was glad to rest on a chair for a moment, a good woman at sensing a conversation approaching. 'The man who knows about the Deanstown Band, now, is a schoolmaster out there. You'll know the name the minute I tell you.'

=

When Ellen stepped through the puddles to school on Monday morning, some agitation seemed to be taking place just inside the circle of the schoolyard wall. Thomas Kane, still wearing his coat which he never removed until both fires had begun to blaze truly, stood at the door, his hands raised in front of his chest, in a gesture of warding off, or pacifying, or dismissing – or, it turned out, all three. A girl of about twelve leaned back against the school wall, clean and neat, but confused: a woman in a hat implored.

'No, I can't, Mrs. I have a day's school to teach. Look. There are some children here already.' He began to step back into the porch.

Ellen, steering herself to the door, gave a glance of enquiry, and the woman turned to her.

'Will you ask him, Ma'am. You're the new Mistress, aren't you? He'll do it maybe if you ask him.'

Master Kane clapped his hands twice, and the crack resounded fiercely enough to make Ellen jump.

'Miss Morris.' He looked straight ahead and spoke sharply, 'improving' his accent. 'I would go straight into school if I were you.' Thomas moved aside to let Ellen pass.

'Ma'am. Ma'am.' The woman put out a hand that pawed the air, like an infirm dog. 'You ask him, Ma'am.'

Ellen stood, looking keenly at the young girl, who wore a fair-isle jumper and green skirt under her best coat. She addressed the woman.

'Ask what?'

The woman pressed forward as if to reach the Master physically. He stood there, rigid and unpleased, frozen into grey steel. Even Ellen recoiled; then she stepped out into the morning again, and interposed between Thomas Kane and the strange woman. In a voice of quick decision, she flattened the air with her hand: 'I don't know what this is about, but whatever it is, it seems to be too important to talk about in a hurry. Why don't you come back after school today when the Master has more time?'

Again she looked enquiringly at him; he raised his hands in a gesture of hopelessness.

'And bring the girl with you. What's your name?' Ellen turned to her.

The girl dragged the flat sole of her foot along the wall behind her, but said nothing. A little mollified, the woman asked, 'What time would that be? Three o'clock or so?' and upon receiving Ellen's affirmation walked away, the girl following.

Ellen asked, without bothering to smile, 'What's . . .? Who's that?'

Thomas Kane, jerking his head upwards, and already turning away, said, 'Ask me afterwards.'

Ellen watched the woman and the girl as they walked towards the gloom at the edge of the village. A dark cyclist overtaking them swished a little puddlewater towards their legs. Closing the school's outer door, Ellen did not pursue the matter: this was the day on which she had decided to show the very small children how water worked, and she needed all her energies and concentration to stop them from soaking themselves, while teaching at the same time.

At two o'clock, too early, the woman and girl returned, and hung like ghostly birds around the school walls; they peered in occasionally to see whether Ellen had finished with her classes. The last words of Ellen's last lesson consisted in the children chanting 'These are. The Four Cardinal Virtues. Prudence. Justice. Fortitude. And Temperance.'

'Now, what are the Seven Deadly Sins?' She intoned with them through the short aggressive litany. 'The Seven Deadly Sins. Are. Pride. Covetousness. Lust. Anger. Gluttony. Envy. Sloth.'

When they tumbled out and homewards, she settled her hair quickly, a pin or two in her teeth, her little mirror propped on the narrow metal mantelshelf, and went to the door to encounter mother and daughter. Mr Kane came down the Senior room quickly and tried to intercept her.

She shook her head. 'No. Not yet.'

Having failed, he stopped abruptly, with a brief glare.

'Now what's your name?' Ellen asked the woman. 'And what's your story? Step into the porch.' The girl followed, still silent, and to her Ellen said, 'I'm going to talk to you later.'

In the porch, the woman rested against the high sloped lid of the wooden box which housed the turf and coal for the fires, beside the chipped enamel handbasin on the wire trivet.

'Ma'am, we're McAuliffes, from over outside Millerstown. I want the Master to do a job for us, he's the only one in the world can do it, and we were sent here to ask him by Father Shine, the

Curate in Urlingford. He knows the Master well, and he says the Master is the man.'

As she began to speak, Ellen heard the heavy footsteps start again on the planked floor, and quickly she closed him off by shutting the door leading from the porch into the Senior classroom; the footsteps stopped, then receded: his baritone drone resumed as he returned to his class.

'The man for what? How do you mean? What is the Master the man for?' Now the girl edged forward, looking only at her mother.

'Ma'am, my husband. Things out around here. The Irregulars and the Free Staters. He was caught up in all that thing.'

Ellen asked, 'How do you mean?'

The woman said, 'I mean, Ma'am, what General Collins called the Civil War. And, Ma'am, my man hadn't a thing to do with it. The Master would know that.'

Ellen said, 'But Master Kane. He had nothing either – to do with "it"?'

To which the woman replied, 'Sure I know, Ma'am, sure I know, isn't that the very thing Father Shine was saying, Father Shine over in Urlingford. That the Master's the very man. That he hadn't a thing to do with it and that's why. But didn't he know General Collins well?'

Ellen said, 'But General Collins is dead this past three years nearly?'

The woman unhooked her spectacles and rubbed them on her coat. Her naked face stared like a moon at Ellen.

When she wished to become more authoritative, Ellen stiffened her back and chin, a trick they had been taught in *Teaching Discipline* class.

'Now, Mrs McAuliffe. You will have to make yourself plain. Come on now.'

'Sure, I'm trying to, Ma'am, and I will with the help of God. My husband, they said he was a Free Stater, sure he was nothing. He had no politics, and they said he was a Free Stater spy and he wasn't. Ma'am, sure he couldn't spy on himself. He was a bit of a talker, maybe, when he had drink on him, you know what that's like.'

Ellen drew her prim line across her mouth. 'No I don't actually, but go on.'

'Ma'am, you remember them "Orders of Frightfulness", don't

you? D'you remember, Ma'am? 'Twas when De Valera's side, the Irregulars, said that nearly anyone on the other side, that anyone who agreed with the Treaty, that was General Collins's side, should be shot. Well, anyway, my fellow, Sean, was taken from the house about six months after them Orders of Frightfulness was given, and we never seen him since. He was a distant cousin of Sean Hales.' Ellen nodded, recognizing the name of a government briga-dier assassinated in Dublin. The girl fidgeted more and more.

'But' said Ellen to the mother, 'that was nearly three years ago, those Orders? How does this affect the Master?'

The woman reached out, and Ellen now permitted her touch.

'Ma'am, they said my husband came into them Orders, because it was applied to a whole lot of people, and that's why he's gone. Nobody ever told us, 'tis only hearsay, like, but we never seen him since. He was working in the court office over in Johnstown. And this poor child, she can't sleep since, nor can I, there's only the two of us, and we haven't a pinch of money, and if we knew where he was . . .'

Ellen patted the woman's arm, releasing her tears. Mrs McAuliffe took a clean handkerchief from inside her cardigan and coat sleeves, and began, not to blow her nose, but to wipe her cheeks. Her hat had come slightly askew.

'So. You want the Master to find out. Where he. Where he, where your husband. Is?' Ellen looked from mother to daughter, and pursed her lips with approval at the cleanliness of the child's hair. The child nodded, her first animation.

Outside, on the road, *The Princess* bus snored metallically by, at least twenty minutes early.

'Ma'am. They came in the evening,' said Mrs McAuliffe, 'and he walked with them, they didn't drag him nor nothing, and the worst sign of all, they came the next day and took his coat off the nail on the back of the door. That's the worst thing.'

Ellen opened her mouth to ask, almost formed the words, 'Why is that the worst thing?' – but held back.

Mrs McAuliffe continued, 'Father Shine keeps telling me not to fear the worst, but sure, Ma'am, he was never married himself, how would a priest know? Don't you know that yourself?' Dropping her voice to a whisper, Mrs McAuliffe said, 'Ma'am, we can't hold a wake nor nothing. There'd be a widow's pension, if . . . if . . . if . . .'

The girl tugged at her mother's sleeve, in a half-tearing, half-striking motion, and made a worried noise.

'Now,' said Ellen, turning fully away from the woman to the girl, 'what's your name?'

The mother said, 'She's called Hannie, Ma'am, Hanora. After my own mother.'

Ellen patted the air between herself and the woman and said, 'No, Mrs McAuliffe, let her tell me herself.' She turned more fully to the child. 'Now, Hannie, what is your name?'

No reply. The porch door burst open: three o'clock, and the children from the Senior room began to tear out.

'Quietly. Quietly. You're not elephants,' called Ellen. Turning to Mrs McAuliffe in a way that the girl could not see, she mouthed the question to the mother, 'Stutter?'

The woman, looking at the child, nodded.

When the stampede of children had passed, Ellen led mother and daughter into the lower half of the vacated classroom. The Master sat at his high desk, writing up the Progress Record, a task he and Ellen had agreed they hated.

Mrs McAuliffe called out, 'Sir.'

Ellen shushed her swiftly, placed a finger over her own lips and whispered, 'No, Mrs McAuliffe. Leave this to me. I'll talk to him. You sit there,' directing the woman to one of the long benches by the wall. She placed the girl in a desk and sat facing her from the desk immediately in front. At the top of the room, Mr Kane continued to write, a hand now held laterally to his forehead like an eyeshade. Aware of his earshot, Ellen began.

'Hannie. Put your hands flat on the desk in front of you.'

The girl complied.

'Good girl. Now lift your chin. High. High. Higher. Good.' Ellen counted the motions, one, two, three.

'Good. Very good. Now, turn your head around like this. To the left. To the right. Good. Good.'

The girl looked terrified.

Ellen said to her, 'Hannie, you have a very nice face. Now. Put your hands on your jaws, each side. Like this. So that you can feel this. And this.'

To demonstrate, Ellen felt each of her own jawbones.

'Good girl. Now. Open your mouth and close it again. So that you can hear the click of your jaws. And feel it. Yes. Yes. That's

54

it. Good girl. Now put your hands flat on the desk again. That's it.'

Ellen put her own hands over the girl's, and said, 'Now, Hannie. I want you to say, with me, these words. "Miss. Morris." And "Hannie. Mac. Auliffe."'

The girl shook her head.

'Yes, of course you are able to say it. Try saying just "Miss Morris" first. That's me by the way.' She stabbed her own chest with her finger.

Ellen laughed, and thereby stirred half a smile in the girl, whose mother sat mute.

'Now, come on.' Ellen grew brisk again. 'Mmiss. Mmorris.' The girl began with tremendous hesitancy. 'Mm.'

Her nostrils dilated and she blushed with embarrassment.

'Mmm.' Ellen said. 'Now that is very good. Very good. Just say. Miss. Mm. Issss.' She tightened her mouth, then widened it open in accordance with the syllabic exaggeration.

The girl said, 'Mm. M. Mmm. Mm.' Then, with what seemed like a surprised expression, she said, 'Isssssss.'

Ellen nodded in affirmation. 'Yes. Yea-ssss. Good. Good. Now. Quickly. Try Morris.'

The girl tried immediately. 'Mmmaurr.'

Ellen said, 'the "-isss" is easy. You already said it.'

The girl went, 'Isss.'

'Quick, quick, while you have it,' said Ellen, 'Morr. Iss.' The girl repeated, 'Morr. Iss.' Ellen applauded. 'Now. The whole lot together,' she said. 'Miss Morris. You know. Just normally. Like me. Come on. We'll say it together.'

With some repeats and efforts the girl said it. 'Mmm-iss. Morr. Isss. Mmmiss. Mmmmmorrr. Isss. Mmiss. Mmorrriss.'

Ellen nodded approvingly each time, more and more enthusiastically. The girl said finally, 'Mmiss Mmmorris.'

'Oh, what a good girl you are, Hannie,' said Ellen. 'Now I'm going to give you something for that,' and she reached up and took the lavender ribbon from her hair and gave it to the girl.

'Wash it before you wear it,' Ellen laughed, and received a thin smile.

'Now, soon you won't be at all afraid of talk,' said Ellen.

She rose and crossed to the mother, who anticipated the question.

'Ma'am, she's like that ever since the night her father went. She was normal before that, fine, you couldn't shut her up. But she was her father's dote. Never left his knee when he sat in the chair. She's an only child. And she's stuttering that bad ever since.'

Ellen said, 'Do we know your address?'

'The Master has it, Ma'am,' she said pointing: he clearly heard, but ignored. Shadows drifted across the school.

When the McAuliffes left, Ellen put on her coat and hat and assembled the contents of her basket.

'We have to talk,' she said over her shoulder to the austere, sitting figure. Then she turned to face him fully, and said, 'I have to say. You should have talked to that woman more kindly.'

She blushed as she said it, and Thomas Kane, after a moment's hard survey of her face and eyes, smiled and smiled. 'Yes,' he said, thoughtfully. 'Yes.' From next morning he called her 'Ellen', although never, of course, in front of the pupils.

One evening later in the week, standing by the mirror in her room, Ellen counted off the days she had been in Deanstown.

'The first Monday doesn't count. From the day I came, Sunday night, Monday night, Tuesday, Wednesday, Thursday, that's five, home on Friday, back on Sunday night, that's six, then Monday, Tuesday, Wednesday and tonight, ten nights.'

On her bed sat a small pile of clean clothing; in the scullery an hour earlier she had completed her ironing, with Lily watching her silently – and blushing whenever Ellen said a word to her.

Outside, darkness had begun to fall. She reached for the matches, shook the lamp slightly to make sure the oil reached the wick, took off the clear glass funnel and struck a match, then sat down to write.

'Insect' book for school.

Ask Thomas K. about shopping in Mooreville.

Get my own hot-water bottle.

Ask Leah about 'Voller Corsets' advertisement in last week's Daily Mail.

'Small' towels.

Ask Thomas K. about cobbler: mend brown shoes.

Piano anywhere?
Ask Miss Humphrys about teaching children with stutters.
Ask Father John for loan of 'Imitation of Christ'.
Bring Janesborough essay to school.
Ask Thomas K. about houses to rent.
Get new vests from Cannocks.
Ask Thomas K. about McAuliffes.
Get dance book for the children?

Lily called up the stairs to say tea was ready. Ellen checked her hair and face and went downstairs. Mrs Greege, in one of her silent moods, dominated the morose table. Ellen made three bright efforts, and each one foundered: none of the others, the sons or Lily, had the capacity to break Mrs Greege's mood, which was expressed in gazing sourly down at her plate, and sighing at length from time to time. Ellen fell silent, too.

In school next morning, after the eleven o'clock break, Ellen inadvertently left the stiff door of her classroom slightly ajar. After some minutes, she realized that Thomas had been standing outside it, pretending to 'post' an old nib in the knot-hole, but actually listening to her. In the midst of telling the children about the suffragette movement, she stopped abruptly.

'No, Miss Morris.' He opened the door. 'Carry on, I didn't mean to interrupt you,' and he withdrew.

At lunchtime he said to her, 'That was very interesting.'

'Did you think so? You didn't think it was too much, or over their heads?'

He said, 'I found out in Belgium that no age is too young for education. Children can take in more than we think. And especially the way you told it. You shared it with them. As a great story, as a play, nearly.'

He stood by the window watching the children cavort outside.

'Of course.' He stopped.

'What were you going to say?'

He resumed slowly, 'If they were your own children instead of somebody else's.' He stopped again, and she waited.

'My brothers and sisters always say I never stop trying to teach them.'

She asked, 'How many have you?'

'I'm the oldest of nine.' Then he murmured, 'And one in Heaven.'

'Aah,' she said, 'that's a pity.'

He did not turn to look at her.

'Yes, it is a pity. That's what it is. A pity.'

After a pause she asked, 'What were you doing in Belgium?' He said, 'I was looking for a man whose picture had been painted by somebody famous, a Scotchman. But that's another story' – and accomplishedly left no room for further enquiry.

As school concluded, she enquired, 'What is Mooreville like for shopping?' and he offered to give her a lift there the following day, then reminded her, 'Now remember the Burkes on Sunday,' an invitation for both of them to visit one of the well-to-do farmers.

'I have to find out from you some time,' she said, as he rattled the school door to check that the lock had taken, 'about the Orders of Frightfulness.'

'Ah, yes,' but he closed down the mood, so that asking further questions would have felt uncomfortable.

That evening, Mrs Greege said directly after eating, 'I wonder, Miss Morris, that floor in the passage out there is very dirty.'

'I beg your pardon?' Ellen froze at the table.

Mrs Greege raised her head and said, 'Every woman around here does housework.'

Lily, on a nod from Mrs Greege, fetched from the rear kitchen an empty bucket, a scrubbing brush and some cloths. She filled the bucket from the huge black pointed kettle on the range, and, head held to one side, deposited bucket and steam, cloths and brush, on the floor beside Ellen's chair, but would not meet Ellen's eye. Ellen put a hand to her mouth; everybody except Mrs Greege left the kitchen. Without turning around, Mrs Greege pointed: 'Start from inside that door.'

An hour and a half later, Ellen sat on her bed, looking at her crinkled hands. She began to grieve. The small bowl of greenery she had assembled earlier in the week, culled from hedgerows and evergreens on the way home from school, lent the room a tiny glow. Ellen sat on the bed in a position where she could observe herself in the lamplit wardrobe mirror. She blew her nose and straightened up, rose, washed her face in cold water and sat down again.

27th February 1925,
Friday night.

Dear Father John,

It was very nice to have that cup of tea on Saturday. I forgot to ask you if by any chance you have a spare copy of the *The Imitation of Christ* you could post out to me?

I'm not going home this week-end so that I can get to know this place a bit better. As I was saying to you, the children are very backward and I feel I should stay here for a year anyway to get them started. The Principal did his MA in Dublin and says he knew some Jesuits in the University. I wonder if you knew any of them? Remind me to ask you the next time we meet.

If you get a chance, call around and see Dada some time as I feel he may need the company, too. If you get another letter from me in a day or so, then you'll know things are truly lonesome out here! Keep remembering me in your prayers, as I will you.

God bless.
Your affectionate friend,
Ellen

She sealed and addressed the envelope and began her next letter.

My dearest Leah,

I wish we had had more time last week-end, but I'll be in again soon to see you all. Things here are desperately quiet. At the moment if I stop writing and listen, I can't hear a single sound, except the odd creak from the house, or the rafters above my head. I have a Valor oil heater at last, and it is throwing diamonds of light on the wall, like a little picture-house.

Mrs G. here is terrible, and I don't know what to do about her. She made me wash the floor this evening, and I didn't know how to say 'No'. Thomas Kane, the

Principal I was telling you about, found these lodgings for me, saying it was the cleanest house in the parish. Now I know why it is! Maybe I'll ask him what I should do about her. He is the oldest of nine children, and he is proving very easy to work with, and very nice. He's actually quite gentle behind that terribly stern face he has, and he's giving me a lift to the town tomorrow to show me where the shops are. I haven't eaten an apple since I came here, and I need some things of my own. He's also taking me out to an invitation for our tea on Sunday, local farmers who want to meet the new Mistress!

I have to go to Mass here for the first time on Sunday morning and I'm dreading it a bit, going on display with a capital 'D'.

Leah, I miss you and Herbert and the girls, how are they all? Something very unpleasant happened at school the other day. A woman visited, whose husband has disappeared since the middle of the Civil War, and she asked Thomas K. to find him, but he won't agree. I'll tell you this and other news when I see you.

My best to you all.
Your affectionate friend,
Ellen

Finishing the letter, she began to weep a little again, then straightened up, put on her coat and went out for a brisk walk, startling the sitters around the Greege fireside as she slammed the front door shut. A half-moon sailed quietly and slowly behind orderly clouds. Ellen, familiar with the road, walked down the hill towards the village. Thomas Kane's house had no lights shining as she walked past. A cyclist without a light grunted behind her, and made her heart jump, as did the little dog trotting behind the bicycle. One or two small yellow glimmers lit curtained windows in the cottages. Defeated by the night she turned home quickly.

In the room, she took off her scarf, opened her coat, sat on the bed for a moment. Then, kneeling, she murmured, 'Friday, yes,' then began, 'The Five *Sorrowful* Mysteries. The First Mystery.

The Agony in the Garden. Thou, O Lord, shall open my lips, and my tongue shall announce Thy praise.'

Thomas called at noon, the car's roof glistening with the recent shower. Black spots of rain dotted the brim of his hat.

Above the noise of the engine, she called out to him as they drove, 'Could I rent a house locally?' He shouted yes, if she could find one.

'Should I buy a bicycle? Although I have an old one at home, I could bring it out on the bus.'

In Mooreville, he introduced her to *Careys, Tea, Wine and Spirits Merchants*, where the manager, Mr Gilsenan, in his brown apron breathed on her: 'This is the busiest day, the world and his mother come in of a Saturday'; she saw the Post Office and the banks, the bullet marks on the walls of the church, and *Wilkinson's*, the bicycle shop. She wrote everything down in her notebook. Thomas showed her the New Town, with the wooden slatted houses, built in the Land War: 'The tenants refused to pay rents any more to absentee landlords.' Sheltering in a doorway, he looked over her shoulder and corrected her on features of local spelling.

When a second shower began, Thomas steered Ellen into the *Mooreville Tearooms*; one other person sat there, a young woman wearing a scarf tied around her hat as if she too had been motoring. Thomas nodded 'Hallo' to her. The young woman had just finished and stood to leave: she looked at Ellen inquisitively.

'Ernestina Stephenson,' said Thomas, when the door's bell clanged closed, 'you know – the stud farm, that high slope up behind the school?'

'Oh, with the red roof?' asked Ellen.

'Protestants, naturally,' he said.

Nobody else came in while they sat there. Unawkward, comfortable from the experience of sharing breaks and lunchtimes at school, they drank tea and ate buns, two for him, one with jam for her.

She broached the subject. 'That McAuliffe woman?'

'Yes,' he said.

'Is there anything to be done for her?'

'I don't know –' he seemed to go no farther. Then, considering, he back-handed the crumbs from the corner of his mouth. 'The

61

whole thing is . . . peculiar. Look.' In an outburst he continued, 'What is most known around here is the least talked-of. The more a thing is common knowledge the more secret it is. And the other way around. Do you know what I mean?' Not giving her a chance to answer, he forced a change of subject. 'I have to go to Outrath, would you ever mind coming with me, it's only a few miles out the road?'

He explained when they got there, 'This is a co-operative cream-ery, and I'm on the Committee; we're applying to the Government for a grant. We have to get some of these new separators, I have to drop in a form there.'

She sat in the car, watching the rain pour down. After ten minutes or so, he came striding back, seven-league-booting over the puddles in the cart-ruts.

'Ah, no, don't apologize,' she said. 'I enjoyed waiting. I like looking at the rain. You never see the weather in a city.'

Just before he got out again to start the car, he peered through the windscreen to assess the wide circle he would have to turn in the creamery yard.

She said suddenly, 'There's something you might know what to do about. I don't know what to do about something' – and in full detail told him about Mrs Greege and the scrubbing of the floor.

He clipped his words, 'We can't. Have that. You're the Teacher. They try to do this to authority around here.'

'What could I do about it? I feel that if I go to live somewhere else, she will talk about me all over the place. And I don't have enough. Enough . . .' She hesitated.

'Enough what? You have plenty of energy, anyway.'

'No, not that.'

'Enough experience, maybe?'

'Maybe.' Ellen took the rope he threw her. 'Yes, enough experi-ence. To stop her.'

'Well.' He spoke in a straight line. 'I could interfere. But I don't want to. The best thing is to show her you'll not put up with it.'

'And how do I do that?'

'By saying to yourself, "I won't put up with it." You might have to say it over and over again. I had to take a decision once that was very difficult, and I decided to do what I did on the basis that what was going on – was doing me harm. Inside myself.'

=

62

Another quiet and tense night for Ellen. She sat in her room all evening, asking Lily to bring her meal up on a tray.

'Ma'am,' said Lily, desperate with embarrassment, and manoeuvring the tray clumsily, 'my Aunt says are you sick or something, because there's not trays in this house, she says, no one waitin' on anyone?'

'Never mind, Lily,' said Ellen. 'Thank you, anyway, I'll talk to your Aunt. Don't you mind. And thank you for the tray.'

Next morning, among candles and silence and the smell of mustiness, and maps in damp on the walls of the church, Ellen Morris and Thomas Kane had their first opportunity to observe each other in public.

She walked to Mass: camel coat, brown hat, black shoes – brown shoes still not mended. Outside the church, a long line of men formed in chatter against the wall; inside the yard, women conversed animatedly. Ellen walked through, returning a 'Hallo' here and there. One woman came forward and said, 'You're very welcome. I hope you'll like us,' to which Ellen said with her lovely smile, 'I do already.' The men all looked at her legs.

She dipped her finger in the marble font, made the Sign of the Cross patiently, chose an empty pew about a third of the way back from the altar, genuflected and knelt. A quarter of an hour early, she prayed on her knees for five minutes, then rose and sat back.

Mantlehill's sacristan always tolled rapidly: he blamed a heavy rope on a light bell. The church began to fill: folk joined Ellen's high-backed pew on each side, nodding to her in seeming recognition. A few minutes before the due arrival of the priest, she saw Thomas: he walked up the aisle to her left and took a seat a little ahead, licensing Ellen to scrutinize him. Then she concentrated on her prayers once more.

At Communion, Ellen went to the altar-rails first. She passed abreast of him on the way up the aisle; he viewed her hips and legs, then folded his hands. On her way back, since she had her head down in an attitude of devoutness, he could gaze at her from the front without being observed in return.

Thomas went last to the altar-rails, almost in a shepherding and summarizing role, and as he walked back, his eye caught her looking at him: he did not smile, that would have been unseemly.

=

63

Outside Mrs Greege's at five o'clock that afternoon, he said to Ellen, 'There's a great stretch in the evenings now,' and held open the car door for her: he wore the clothes she had seen on him at Mass.

The thatched farmhouse, long and powerful and low and pink, lay at the end of a mile-long avenue with pot-holes and occasional gravel.

Ellen offered to open the many gates, but Thomas refused and stepped down each time, bending his head to avoid the canvas roof of the car. One of his fingernails had a little residual stain underneath, as if he had failed to remove oil. Fixing the stiff catch on the windscreen, his hands tensed.

Mrs Burke, Thomas said, 'had ideas about herself.' She also had silver hair and a lazy eye, and a bone-breaking handshake, and pictures in the hallway; 'That's my son the engineer, the Master here taught him; he has a great job now over in Wolverhampton, but he'll be back one day, please God. Now, what'll I call you, Miss Morris? Your mother, now, is a friend of Mrs Joyce, who's married to a cousin of my late brother-in-law, they're Burkes over in Croom.'

They stood on the smooth flags of the big glistening kitchen and Mrs Burke said, 'Oh, we're not sitting here, you have to come into the parlour, the parlour,' and led them along a dark and tidy passage-way to a room of lace, and peacock feathers in tall green vases, and small brown cameo photographs in huge black frames; men with starched moustaches, and women with blouses made of chilled linen, standing formal and stiff, or sitting on large chairs, the couples never looking at each other. A fire roared before a table set with china, and a tier of three plates stacked up on a silver rack: sand-wiches, scones and small plump buns in filled, fluted-paper cases.

'Now, my husband.' Mrs Burke began every sentence with a firm statement of the subject matter. 'My husband Martin is a distant cousin of W. T. Cosgrave's wife. In fact, he'll be in in a minute, he's dying to meet you, but I won't ever let Martin into the parlour in workboots, you know what the men are like.'

Thomas told Ellen afterwards that in Mrs Burke's boasting of her husband's family relationships, she conveniently left out the fact that the Burkes 'were on the Irregular side, they were very bitter too; they'd never vote for Cosgrave now, no matter what she says about him.'

Martin Burke, quieter and graver than his wife, came silently in, still buttoning a clean waistcoat, a small man, with his highly polished brogue boots.

Mrs Burke said, very kindly and approvingly, 'They tell me you have great style, Miss Morris, that you've a different outfit for every day of the year. I suppose a single girl can afford clothes these days, 'twasn't like that in my day, although not that my father stinted us for a thing, not at all. You see this?' She fingered her own cream silk sleeve. 'That was my grandmother's.'

'Very nice,' said Ellen, who watched carefully Martin Burke's thoughtful respect as he shook Thomas's hand, and then accepted the introduction to Ellen.

The talking began. Would Mr Burke be 'taking any con-acre this year?' (The more prosperous farmers, and Thomas 'definitely' included the Burkes, rented extra land most summers.) He might, but last year he got 'a bit of a sickener. I took eighteen acres from the Horans and the river flooded up into it, d'you remember that heavy rain we had in May, and I never got it dry 'til 'twas too late.'

So there was not to be a new Sergeant after all, which was just as well, as 'the man in the Barracks, didn't he know everyone and wasn't that the main thing?' said Mr Burke.

Peggy, in a black flowered print crossover apron, brought in plates of bacon, black pudding, egg, glistening glands of sausage and kidneys; later, to much acclaim, a wide apple pie arrived, in a deep dish, not a round plate.

Ellen tasted and asked.

'That, now,' said Mrs Burke, 'is my grandmother's own invention, extra cloves and, mind you, brown sugar; she was an O'Connor herself, her nephew, Surgeon O'Connor, is very well-known, very well-known.'

Peggy left with the hot-water jug, and Mrs Burke said to Ellen, 'Did you know that Parnell stayed in this house?' Ellen discussed, very interesting, Mrs Burke's pronunciation of the name, her mother's aunts argued about it, but her father always said that the man himself liked it pronounced 'Parn-l' and not 'Par-knell'.

Mr Burke nodded, 'Your father is exactly right. Exactly right.'

Mrs Burke said, 'That woman. Dth. Such an awful thing to happen to a fine man that he falls in with a bad woman.' She fussed on. 'Of course, she didn't stay with him in this house, not at all, he was on his way to a meeting in Cork and he stopped here. I can show you the very bed he slept in, but he sat in that chair the Master is sitting in now. He made a joke to me, that at least he wouldn't trouble me for hot water to shave in, you know, on account of the beard. "I won't be any trouble to you, Mrs Burke, for hot water in the morning anyway," he said.'

As they stood on the Burke doorstep, clouds flying unthreateningly across the waxing moon, Mrs Burke said to Ellen, 'Now you're as grand a girl as I met in a long time. If I can ever do anything for you, you just get the Master to drive you up here and we'll have a good chat. Martin, isn't she an awful nice girl?'

Mr Burke shook her hand diligently, and Ellen, half-buttoning her coat, blushed a deep red.

Thomas hummed a ditty in the car. 'Oh, Kitty O'Shea. Oh, Kitty O'Shea. You're as black as the night and as bold as the day.' Cattle snorted unseen in the fields as he opened and closed gates. Ellen drew the rug around her knees. At half-past nine, they reached Mrs Greege's gate and Thomas turned off the engine.

She asked, 'Did Parnell really sleep there?'

'He did. But what was unusual was that for all his politics, Parnell usually only stayed in Protestant houses, and that's another reason why the night in the Burkes' house was such a noted episode. And Mrs Burke nearly had a heart attack of delight. She walked like a woman on stilts up the church the next Sunday.'

Ellen told Thomas that she liked Mrs Burke. 'I didn't mind the snobbery too much. I mean, if you knew my own mother?' She added, 'You have a great appetite.' Thomas had eaten the apple pie almost singlehanded.

'What did you think of him?' asked Thomas.

'A nice man. Genuine.'

Ellen said, 'You know – for years I never knew what the Parnell scandal was, because nobody would say he was brought down by a woman. All my father would say was, "and just as he was going to govern Ireland and get us Home Rule". That's all.'

The lamp steady in the quiet bedroom, Ellen wrote in her notebook, 'Mr and Mrs Martin Burke, The Red Farm. The walls of the kitchen are about three feet thick, and the windows have deep shelves wide enough to hold the sewing machine. The poker in

66

the fireplace in their parlour is the biggest I have ever seen, with an eagle's head.' Then she wrote underneath, 'Thomas Kane'; and again, 'Thomas Kane'.

She stood up, moved the lamp to gain a better light from the mirror of the wardrobe door, angled her body sideways and smoothed her figure, from her shoulders down her breasts, finishing with a flourish, her hands flying off her hips. Capping her pen, she put the notebook away, and stood directly in front of the mirror, this time mouthing words, like an actress rehearsing lines. Then, walking downstairs very slowly, she rounded the corner into the kitchen and drew a deep breath. Mrs Greege, alone in the kitchen, was sewing under the lamp.

'Mrs Greege. I want to say something to you, please. I am the new Mistress in this parish. As such I must, and will, have the respect of the people. I am not your maid, and I never will be. As long as you know me, never think to ask me to do a menial chore again.'

Ellen gripped the end of the balustrade. The woman in the black clothes half-leaped from her chair beneath the oil-lamp. The wick flared and Ellen walked back upstairs; shaking and with eyes closing and opening repeatedly, she reached her room.

Next morning, Monday, Thomas handed Ellen two brown paper bags: one contained ginger snap biscuits. 'You might like them for your lunch. I have a bag too many of them.'

In the other brown paper bag he had placed a small silvery stone, with a tiny white fossil embedded in it.

At lunch he said to her, 'Here, this is what they were talking about' – and handed her some verses of a monologue written out in his own hand. Martin and Bella Burke had recalled a gathering at which Thomas memorably gave them a recitation; 'D'you remember, Master, what was it, Percy French, wasn't it, "The Four Farrellys".' All had smiled; Mrs Burke conspiratorially assuring 'Lovely, lovely' to Ellen, who, later, had asked Thomas for the words.

In a small hotel in London I was sitting down to dine,
When the waiter brought the register and asked me if I'd sign.
And as I signed I saw a name that set my heart astir
A certain 'Francis Farrelly' had signed the register.

=

At three o'clock, as the last children left the school, it began to rain, and at the window she said, 'That's bad, now. I have no umbrella.' They sat by the fire in his classroom for almost two hours, and he showed her the Roll Book which went back to the school's foundation in 1847.

'In all that time,' Thomas often pursed his lips between one sentence and another, and Ellen, when he talked, rarely took her eyes off his mouth, 'in all that time, hardly one family in this half of the parish has ever gone on to Secondary Education.'

The rain still fell; it fell and fell, on the fields, the trees, and on the ochre, leaded-windowed, gabled houses of the village.

'One or two boys or girls from farmers' houses,' said Thomas, 'like young Burke, went on to the convent or the secondary school, and I had one lad who was as brainy as you could ask for, and we even got him a scholarship, but the parents took him out of secondary school after a year or two, and sent him working, to England or Dublin, or somewhere. He's a barman now, over in Kent, when he should be a barrister or a surgeon. Oh, and we had one priest. But the rest of them are in shops, or working for farmers. Or doing nothing.'

The rain slackened a little, and they quenched the lamp and locked up. When they had left the village, the rain intensified again, and Thomas said, 'Here. Put your head under my coat,' and held it out high to her for shelter, which drew her in close to him. Within sight of Mrs Greege's, although by now it had grown fully dark, he took the coat's wing back gently, saying, 'You know what they're like if they see us.' Yet they stood in the shade of over-hanging ivy on the demesne wall, talking for another hour. Nobody passed by, not a bicycle, nor a cart, and still the rain quietly fell.

'It rained like this the night my father died,' Thomas said, 'my brother nearly got pneumonia on his way to get the priest.' Ellen's shoulder touched Thomas's arm as they stood in the growing cold. Abruptly he stopped speaking – then after a moment's silence, said, 'If you don't go home next week-end, we might go out for a drive.' They parted.

Two days later, on Wednesday, when the children went out to play at noon, Thomas walked into Ellen's classroom; he held something behind his back, and was smiling. He handed it to her: an egret's feather.

68

Ellen rhymed in delight, 'Oh. Oh. How did you know?' and told him that her mother's two aunts had always admired one lady 'of their acquaintance but not of their knowledge': they said of her that 'she was never without an egret-feather hat'.

Next morning, he handed to her a book: new, carefully covered in brown paper, and with Ellen's name in his handwriting on the cover: *In Brightest Africa*, by Carl Akeley. On the way home, walking with her as far as Mrs Greege's, he said, 'March is coming in like a lion.' On Friday afternoon outside his house he said, 'Wait a minute,' and he reappeared with a cushion cover of black satin embroidered with tea-roses; it had never been taken out its original tissue-paper. 'My aunt sent it from San Francisco.'

That evening she jotted down a snatch of poetry in her notebook:

When the winds are breathing low
And the stars are shining bright.

Browsing through her possessions, she sought her old notebook from Teacher Training College, the one with the Morocco thonging along the binding, and smiled at notes she had taken from Miss Humphrys: *The Modesty of the Person*:

All daytime clothing must hang loose, no belt, nothing tight: nowhere on the body must the wearer be alerted to the flesh. Undergarments must also flow, never knowing constriction or pressure, only the loosest of cords. Even in the gymnasium, nothing of the body may perform in public; the legs must not be divided by pantaloons or bloomers. When taking a bath or a shower, always wear swimming costume in order not to give offence to yourself.

Throughout the week-end it rained and blew, too wet almost to go to Mass: Ellen got soaked: nowhere did she see Thomas in or near the church. For the rest of the day, although not quite sitting at the window waiting and watching for him, Ellen realized that Thomas had not appeared for the drive he had suggested. On Monday morning he told her the car had broken down again.

4

A bugle blast rings out. Then another blast, then another, too
musical and varied for an ordinary hunting horn, and besides,
no hunt is meeting anywhere nearby. The children in the Senior
room jump; the Juniors have left already. Thomas cranes his body
aside to see through the open door. When the bugle rings again,
followed by cheers and 'Halloos', Ellen moves to her window, then
looks back through the glass-paned partition at Thomas, who by
now has begun to move quickly.

He shoos the Seniors out: they raise a little cheer in the porch:
he shouts at them in an angry voice Ellen has not previously heard.

Wheeling in sharply by the pump and the handball-alley, into
the space between the green and the school, swings a *caravanserai*
of one rickety motor-vehicle, neither a coach nor a truck, and two
gaudy carts drawn by flighty piebald ponies, behind which trot a
further two such animals tethered on halters. These carts bear high
piles of mysterious boxes, crates and flat folded objects, all painted
in blue and red and yellow. At the head of the procession rides a
man on a motorcycle wearing a leather helmet and goggles pushed
up on his forehead. He is the bugle-blower, and he also leads the
'Halloos', and waves his bugle arm aloft vigorously while shouting.

Across the handlebars of his motorcycle he has fixed a placard
reading *'Joe-for-Yells'*. The last high horsedrawn cart has a message
across the front, *'Emily-for-Laughs'*, and the motor-waggon's side
bears the curly legend, *'Mrs MacReady's Famous Travelling Herbal Show – If You Suffer from Coughs or Threatening Notions.
We'll Kill You with Laughs or We'll Cure You with Potions. Two
Shows Nightly – Sunday Matinee – Many Cures Worldwide – Only
Natural Herbs Used from the Fields of Our Own Fair Land.'*

'Oh, my God,' says Thomas. 'Oh, Jesus Christ!'

Ellen joins him at the door, stepping on tiptoe in a hopeless
attempt to peer over his shoulder. The parade halts.

'Good day to you, Sir,' shouts Joe-for-Yells, and blows on his
bugle again. The motor-waggon's horn toots a vulgar, louder toot,

and someone on one of the carts screams a loud whistle. A boy jumps down and bangs cymbals.

'What in the name of God is this?' asks Ellen, finally getting past Thomas's hips.

'What is it, Thomas?' repeats Ellen, but observing Thomas's agitation. He does not answer, makes an 'I'll tell you later' sign, and, racing back up his classroom, begins to put away into the tall glass-fronted cupboard some objects he normally leaves out all the time: his gleaming ebony ruler; his own private brass-capped inkpot; his pens; his box of good writing paper; the ivory set square and protractor on the windowsill; the Roll Book and the Progress Record.

His hands tremble as he locks away his compass; and an old silver watch he uses to demonstrate the mechanics of clockwork in one of his beloved *General Knowledge* classes; and the music-box he bought in Bruges and is always promising himself he'll try to mend some day. As he locks the drawers beneath the glass cupboard doors, he looks over his shoulder and sees the children outside, talking and laughing with the people from the travelling show.

He rushes past Ellen and reaching the door again shouts, 'Home with you! Stop hanging around here! You're slow enough to get here in the mornings! Home now!' He turns back into the classroom and looks at Ellen, and he is trying in vain to slow down his responses.

'Isn't that a bit harsh?' she says. 'Children always love a circus.'

He takes the clock down from the wall and puts it into another cupboard, the key of which has always lived in the lock, but now he pockets the key.

'Good day, Sir.' The laughing voice outside again, followed by another blast on the bugle. The man comes to the door, a seedy fop with missing teeth and a drowned, lank-haired complexion, then calls a third time. 'Good day to you, Sir.'

Thomas stands with his face to the wall beneath the blank patch where the clock has been. All of this has happened within the space of two or three minutes, all of it frantic, and to Ellen, still unexplained, and she now grasps Thomas's arm, and repeats her enquiry urgently.

'Ellen, this is trouble. This is trouble.' He will not turn around. 'This is bloody trouble. These fellows are scavengers and hooligans.

71

Put away everything you have.' She looks mystified, and begins to make some resistance.

'Look.' He holds up a hand, and his authority has returned. 'This is what has happened. Who is the School Manager? Who is the Manager of this school? Not me. Not you. The Canon, isn't it?'

Ellen makes no objection, simply listens.

'What does the Canon do in his spare time? What is he famous for? What? What do you see him doing on Sunday afternoons and on other occasions, you even asked me about it just after you came here?' Still he does not let Ellen speak.

'He gathers herbs, doesn't he, the Canon? And he "cures" people with them, doesn't he? His famous "cures". That bunch out there – they belong to that same fraternity and they have him hoodwinked. They persuade the Canon every few years to let them use this school every night for a while, for their herbal cures and their vulgar shows. They put on sketches that are blue.'

Mrs MacReady, hair white and powdered and pomaded like a third-rate Regency portrait, rouge on her cheeks, with the nose of a crone and the step of a dancer and filth beneath her finger-nails, comes out from behind the motor-waggon. She raises a hand dramatically in the air.

'We took Wicklow without firing a shot. Our *Colleen Bawn* was the best show they had ever seen. Emily is a *tragédienne* as well as a *comédienne*. But Carlow gave us our best cures. We cured half Carlow and all Tullow in one evening.'

Ellen wrinkles her nose as Mrs MacReady jinks forward.

'Where is that fine man?' she cries. 'Let me see that fine Mister Kane. The Man all the women want. The Man with the Motorcar.'

Thomas turns from the porch in disgust, but Ellen catches his jacket and he turns back.

'How long will you be here for this time?' Thomas calls out, with all the charm of a writ-server. One of the horses on the halters rears and whinnies. Joe-for-Yells blows his shattering bugle again.

'Who knows? Who knows? The Gaiety of Nations. Until cock-shut time. I am Napper Tandy's fancy. Oh, I met with Napper Tandy and he shook me by the hand.' Mrs MacReady raises her skirt like a little girl and does a small waltz to accompany her snatch of song. 'We have wintered in Wicklow, my dears, but here we may spring. The Cat, the Rat and Lovell the Dog.' Children appear behind her, followed by a girl of about Ellen's age, mid-twenties in a black jumper and stained jodhpurs.

Ellen turns to Thomas and begins to joke. 'Soap and water in short supply.'

He shakes his head angrily, and comes forward from the door to halt Mrs MacReady's progress.

'You will have to give us a few minutes to get the school to rights,' he says. Ushering Ellen ahead of him, he shuts and locks the door, stranding the noise outside. She asks for explanations.

'The Canon gives them the right to camp out there and use the school outside of teaching hours to put on their shows. They make a holy mess of the place. This is the fourth time. Oh, this is desperate, this is desperate. They leave it filthy. You can see what they're like.' He hits his desk with his fist making the lid jump. 'They stole two of my best fountain pens, they tore pictures out of my books to decorate the walls during their sketches. The smell of that stuff they call medicines. Uegch!'

Ellen draws up a chair, and sits him down.

'Have you complained to the Canon?' she asks calmly. 'Have you ever done anything about the missing things?'

Thomas tells her the Canon would never hear a word said against Mrs MacReady, he believes her to be 'saintly', and 'a near-genius'. When Ellen asks what they should do now, Thomas replies, 'There's not a thing we can do. Not a thing. We have to give them the key and go.' He tightens his mouth to a line like the edge of a slate.

Ellen says, 'That's not good enough for me. I'm going to come and see their show.' He argues that if she does that, it will be seen as supporting them.

'Not if their show is as bad as you say it is. That will give me something to say against them.'

Through the school window Ellen sees a pony-and-trap draw up on the road near the pump. A young woman sits watching the circus. It is Ernestina Stephenson, and Ellen says irrelevantly and involuntarily to Thomas, 'Lovely pale complexion that Stephenson girl has.'

At seven o'clock that evening, in drizzle, Ellen returns from Mrs Greege's to the school, and in her handbag she brings notebook and pencil. A crowd has gathered, already over a hundred people.

Mrs MacReady sees her, and says, 'There's no room,' but Ellen has bought a ticket from one of the children in the yard, and she pays a further five shillings to book a medicine 'exclusively' later: this fact unmans Mrs MacReady's initial opposition to Ellen's attendance.

All the desks have been removed, and piled high in Ellen's room; in the process her blackboard with tomorrow's letters on it – the junior infants have reached 'J', 'K', 'L' and 'M' – has been knocked half off the wall, and the surround has been cracked. One or two people smile at her and say 'Hallo, Miss', or 'Hallo, Mistress': many others nod, point, whisper.

A wide canvas sheet, with mountains, snow-covered Alps, and waterfalls daubed on it, some of the paint now crazed and chipped, hangs across the front of the room, from Thomas's dais to the maps above the library boxes and science cupboard. It has been fixed to the ceiling with nails, around which spread huge jagged coins where the plaster has been broken. On Thomas's blackboard easel perches a large placard. *To-night. Joe-for-Yells and Emily-for-Laughs in The Rose of Killarney. Star Attraction. From the Stage of London and Vienna. Madame Rose MacReady in a Selection of Dramatic Roles.*

Ellen takes out her notebook and squeezes along the second row of benches. The globes of the oil-lamps, kept pristine by Thomas who polishes them every day with a special duster, have already begun to blacken with uncontrolled smoke. A smell of sulphur fills the room.

'Jayzes,' she hears a flat anonymous voice behind her say, 'Kane'll go mad in the mornin' when he sees the cut of the place.'

Somewhere a pair of hands claps twice, a whistle blows, then cymbals bang, then a bugle calls. From behind the Alps, quick as a foxtrot, springs Joe-for-Yells carrying an enormous accordion on which he begins to play a jig. He dances across the open space of floor in front of the first bench, swaying the huge gleaming box, pressing its buttons, punching its keys, and dancing, dancing. From behind a waterfall comes the girl, in a green and white peasant blouse with shamrocks all over it, and as the oooh-ing room says 'Aaaah!', Emily-for-Laughs sings,

'There is not in this wide world a valley so sweet,
As that vale in whose bosom the clear waters meet.'

Ellen makes a note: 'Words of song wrong. "Bright" waters, not "clear".'

'Oh, the last rays of feelings and lives shall depart.'

Ellen writes: 'Wrong, too: "of feeling and *life* must depart". She sings "of feelings and *lives shall*".'

'Ere the bloom of that valley will fade from my heart
Ere the bloom of that valley will fade from my heart.'

'Not "*will* fade", it should be "*shall* fade"': Ellen notes down eleven further errors in the remaining three verses, including 'Sweet Vale of Have Woke You' for 'Sweet Vale of Avoca'. The attendance, still piling in, claps, cheers and joins in the singing. A child blows out one of the lamps. In the dramatic shadows Mrs MacReady materializes, her head hooded in a wide Kinsale shawl, black, lined with red, 'heavily patched' Ellen observes, 'hence the dimming of the lamps'.

Mrs MacReady comes forward.

'A dramatic recital. "The Traveller", by Walter de la Mara.

'"Is there anybody there," said the Traveller,
Knocking at the moonlit door,
As his horse in silence chewed the grasses
Of the forest's leafy floor.'

Ellen's pen races. 'Not called "The Traveller": the poem's *correct* title is "The Listeners". Not "de la Mara", but "de la Mare". "Chewed" should be "Champed". "*Ferny* floor" not "leafy".'

'And the bird flew up out of the tower,
Above the traveller's head;
And he smote on the door a second and a third time,
"Is there anybody here?" he said.'

In the spellbound room, the racing ferocity of Ellen's pencil almost becomes audible. '"Turret" not "tower". Where did she get "a third time"? It doesn't even scan.'

To cheers and applause, and heads turning wonderingly to their neighbours to share the enjoyment, Mrs MacReady takes her bow.

'Here's a riddle,' shouts Joe-for-Yells as he bounds into view. 'Riddle me this. Johnny had a long thing. Mary had a hairy thing. Johnny stuck his long thing into Mary's hairy thing.'

'Wee-heeeeee,' the hard men at the back shout. 'Waaayy-haayy,' and others laugh nervously. 'Yeh dirty things,' shouts Joe-for-Yells. 'Answer – a man putting a handle in a brush.'

Ellen leaves, and the room falls silent as she walks out. By doing so, she misses *The Rose of Killarney*. In the darkness she hears footsteps coming towards her along the road, and she recognizes them.

'Is that you, Thomas?' He says he has been coming to ascertain that she is all right, and he walks her to her lodgings, asking anxious questions about the condition of the classrooms, the blackboards, the desks. She gives all details.

'What is the point,' he asks – of himself, not of Ellen – 'in fighting, in struggling all the time, to banish ignorance and vulgarity?'

She removes a glove and gives him a warm handshake.

'You'll get it all right again,' she says.

In her room, Ellen began a long letter to Leah, but she never finished it, nor did she ever post it. In the letter she asked questions such as, 'What was it like when you met Herbert? How did you feel?' and – 'When are feelings morally wrong, Leah?' and – 'Before you married, Leah, did you ever feel very excited just in thinking about someone?' She did not sleep, her mind racing between the problems of the MacReadys and the excitement of Thomas Kane.

Next morning Ellen finds both classrooms clean and tidy.

'Did they clean up after them?' she asks Thomas, and receives an askance glare.

She returns that night. Mrs MacReady greets her. 'You missed *The Rose of Killarney*, so we're putting it on first, and you never collected your medicine. Isn't Joe-for-Yells a scream? Sometimes he goes a little too far; I have to say to him, "Joe-for-Yells, tone it down, tone it down, there are ladies present," but he gets so excited he doesn't hear me.'

She preens in front of Ellen, pink lipstick and a high-necked frilled blouse with stains all around the collar. 'Do you know who's coming tonight? Mr Val Vousden himself, he's in the area and he sent word to Emily-for-Laughs, aren't we honoured? Oooooh, did you hear about last night, two of the boys outside got very excitable, oooh, excitable, and they did not like each other. A bit too much of the other medicine, maybe?' and she winks.

Ellen makes a note when she sits down, 'Ask about two "excitable" boys? Drink taken?'

A squeezing strain on the accordion comes from behind the Alps; then a tune, soon recognizable as 'Believe Me if All Those Endearing Young Charms', then the voice of Joe-for-Yells:

> 'O, believe me, if all those endearing young charms,
> Which I gaze on so proudly today.'

Ellen's pen flicks into action. 'The correct word is "fondly", not "proudly".'

Mrs MacReady's voice announces, 'Ladies and gentlemen. Mac-Ready productions, in memory of the late Mr MacReady, have pleasure in presenting the romantic drama, *The Rose of Killarney*, by the late Mr John MacReady.'

A child appears, a little fair-haired girl, in what had long ago been a sweet black velvet dress. Wringing her hands she says, 'Oh, if my Daddy would only find a pretty wife, because my Mammy has gone to Heaven.' The packed room moans a soft, 'Aaaahh!' From behind the waterfall on the other side of the room, Joe-for-Yells appears, singing again the first two lines of 'Believe Me if All'. Ellen notes, 'Are they the only two lines he knows?' He takes the little girl by the hand and says, 'Never mind, my darling, we will find a lovely new Mammy for you. Look, who is that over there?' By the window, Emily-for-Laughs stands on a bench, and rubs her head as if washing her hair. 'Oh,' says the child, 'it is a beautiful lady.'

Ellen said to Thomas next morning, 'And it went on like that for about twenty minutes, it was awful. But everybody clapped like mad when it was over and I looked around and there inside the door clapping hardest of all was the Canon. Then she took out this medicine, and she called it "sycamore oil", from the leaves, she said, "of the biggest sycamore in the country", and she claimed it cured boils, and coughs and baldness. How could any one thing do all that?'

Thomas said, 'Look.' He pointed to the door of his cupboard; someone had tried – and failed – to force the lock. 'I'm going to come down here tonight,' he said. 'They've been using the side wall outside as a lavatory.'

At darkness, he walks to meet Ellen; about halfway between her lodgings and his Residence, he hears her footfall, stops, turns about, then falls in step with her.

'The Canon won't be there anyway,' he says. 'He's gone to a meeting over in Rosegreen, I met the housekeeper on the road. Of course, she's going to the show as well. Wouldn't miss it, she said.'

By the time they reach the village they have to push through the crowd, and by then all seats have been taken. Thomas stands there, all the authority of his school stripped from him. He and Ellen move to a standing position by the wall; Mrs MacReady avoids them, hugely busy with bottles for people around the room.

'Did you keep that stuff you bought?' whispers Thomas. 'I'm going to take it to a chemist.'

Emily-for-Laughs appears, and announces in her glum way, 'This evening we're going to begin with a medley of songs and jokes from –' she gestures dramatically towards the canvas backdrop – 'Joe. For. Yells.' So far, whispers Ellen to Thomas, Emily-for-Laughs has not smiled once.

Joe appears; tonight, ribbons flutter from the huge accordion, his flattened hair glistens; a red spotted cravat at his thin neck, he sings, switching lithely from verse to verse, pieces from many songs, all of which either Ellen or Thomas, comparing notes long afterwards, recognize, and thereby know that in most he has the words wrong. Then, after the applause, he begins to tell jokes.

'There was this woman. And she wasn't backward in coming forward.' He makes an explicit gesture with his hands to shape a large and pointed bosom. He makes the gesture again, and amid the sporadic laughter he sees Ellen turn her head away. Joe-for-Yells prances over to her and, addressing the audience, his finger aimed almost in Ellen's face, chants loudly,

78

'My dearest dear and dearest monkey,
Your face is like the Divil's donkey.
With your awful hands and your cloven feet,
You stole out of Hell while the Divil was asleep.'

He raises his hand with a flourish and says, 'Yerra, give us a kiss, Missus.' Ellen pushes his hand away, and Joe-for-Yells, backing a step into the centre of the 'stage', makes the bosom-outlining gesture again and winks sideways at the audience.

The quick hush in the room suggests that Joe-for-Yells has gone too far. Something whisks past Ellen's shoulder and hits Joe, just on the ear beside a sideburn, and he staggers back against the canvas Alps, an urgent wheezing groan coming from the accordion; something hits him again, and splits his nose as he straightens up. He does not fall, but holds the accordion out in front of him. The flying right fist of Thomas flashes out a third time, but connects with the accordion. Women in the front benches squeal and lean away, and a man whom Ellen has seen with Mrs MacReady's group, attending to the horses but never appearing in the performances, comes out from behind the canvas, an unwieldy length of planking in his hand. He tries to reach beyond Joe-for-Yells to hit Thomas, but does not get quite that far. Thomas, gleaming in the lamplight, his face as grim and hard as a miner's at the coal-seam, tears forward now, picks up Joe-for-Yells who has fallen to his knees, pushes him to one side, drives towards the man with the plank and kicks him viciously on the knee. The people at the front of the room begin to back away: the men at the rear try to see what is happening; Mrs MacReady stands on Thomas's dais by the far window, shouting. Thomas hits the man with the plank twice, hard, in the face, and when the man falls to his knees, Thomas kicks him in the face, knocking him backwards. He then reaches down to Joe-for-Yells and, grabbing him by the hair, begins with great speed to drag him to the door. People scatter, clearing a pathway, and some run out under the night sky, as Thomas drags Joe-for-Yells across the little yard, out through the small gate, to the motor-waggon, hits him in the eye, very hard. A bystander says, 'Jayzes. Them travellers eats nearly nothin'. You'll kill him.'

Thomas turns to him, 'Are you looking for something, too?' The man backs off, 'No, Master, Jayzes. No, no.'

People pouring out of the school run back in again to get out of

79

Thomas's way as he returns. The second man, much shorter than Joe-for-Yells, has risen to his feet, and Mrs MacReady is standing by him. Thomas picks the man almost right off the ground by the hair. The man screams, and Thomas runs him to the door and flings him into the yard. When he returns, Emily-for-Laughs comes at him, shouting, 'What are you after doing to my husband?' Thomas hits her with the flat of his hand across the cheek, and she staggers sideways. He grabs both Emily-for-Laughs and Mrs MacReady by the upper arms, and hauls them to the door. Two of the children run after them, weeping. It all takes place within two minutes.

Ellen comes forward as Thomas returns. He motions her with his hand and hisses, 'Don't. Move.' As he rips the canvas curtain from its moorings, little showers of plaster fall from the ceiling. Wrestling the painted canvas into a large, cracking ball, and gathering some other bits and pieces – a 'magic wand', with a star on top; the top hat of Joe-for-Yells; the black, patched Kinsale shawl – he goes to the door again and throws them out over the wall of the yard in the direction of the parked *caravanserai*. Nobody has left the vicinity: all stand around with no wish to interfere. On his last ferocious errand Thomas picks up the accordion and, almost running, launches it hard against the motor-waggon where it crashes near the head of Joe-for-Yells.

'Master. Ah, Master for Jayzes' sake . . .' Another bystander appeals. Thomas walks to the man and raises his fist. This man also backs off.

Thomas stands on the doorstep of the school. 'All of you,' he shouts. 'Go. Home! Now! You. Mrs MacReady! I'll give you five minutes. If you're not out of here in five minutes, I'll set fire to the lot of you!' He goes inside the school.

The people begin to slope away. Some move a short distance from the school and stop to confer. Those still inside drift out: one or two say, 'Good-night now, Master, good-night, Miss,' to Ellen, who stands by the door. In the distance, the door of Hand's public-house opens with a yellow glow.

'Those children are frightened,' Ellen remarks, and moves towards the MacReady *entourage*.

Thomas holds up a hand. 'Don't go. Near them.' She stops instantly.

Returning to the schoolroom, she picks up her basket diffidently, and, as Thomas, breathing hard, begins to tidy up, she moves over near him, strokes his arm briefly, slips out and walks quietly home through the darkness, avoiding the two or three little knots of people who stand around the village in dumbfounded conversation.

As she draws near Mrs Greege's house, she looks back and sees approaching from behind her the unsteady lights of a procession. Under the dark trees Ellen cannot be discerned, and the motor-waggon and the carts rumble slowly by her in the night. She watches them until they vanish into the dip at Hogan's Bend.

5

All next day, Thomas said not a friendly word, not to Ellen, not to any of the pupils, not even the ones he liked particularly. Systematically, he recovered the objects he had locked away. Standing on a chair, he measured with a ruler the plaster damage in the walls and ceiling; he tried to remove a 'medicine' stain from the white windowsill; he had not polished his shoes, nor had he shaved well.

He taught at his most impersonal. Taking a piece of light wire he said, 'Look at this. If you have a perfect geometric shape, then you can bend it into any other perfect geometric shape. In other words, a perfect square will also make a perfect rectangle, a rhomboid, or a perfect circle.'

After school, Ellen said, lingering at the doorway, 'I'm off, so. Are you finished yet?' and he shook his head, bending to the dais.

Next morning at ten o'clock, she heard raised voices, and rushed to the door. The Canon, standing in the porch, pecked his walking-cane hard on the floor; 'Mr Kane. That woman is a saint. I know it. She's . . . she's a . . . a scientist. A pure scientist. And a pure saint. She was here at my invitation. This is a very serious matter. I'll have you know.'

Thomas said, his voice louder too, 'I told you before, Canon Williams, that those people are dirty and dangerous and I will not have them corrupting my school.'

The Canon replied, 'Your school? I think you're forgetting yourself, Mr Kane. Your school?'

Ellen, walking into view, said, 'Canon, I was there. I saw everything.'

'Oh, good morning, Miss. Good morning.' He raised his tall-crowned hat.

Ellen said, 'And it was very serious. I was here three nights of that show, and those people should not be touring the country.'

The men backed off in different directions. Ellen continued.

'Canon, I made notes of what was going on, and it was nothing short of disgraceful. They had every song wrong. Every song. Completely wrong. I was going to visit your house after school tomorrow. With my notes of what went on.'

Thomas folded his hands behind his back, but fidgeted with his fingers. The Canon half turned away, then came back at Ellen.

'What kind of a Miss . . . a Miss – a "Miss Prim" objects to people getting the words of songs wrong?' The Canon stalked off.

On the road home, Ellen, her hand pumping up and down, spoke insistently to Thomas.

'I am going to tell him that teaching here is also about setting some standards, that we try to teach the children how to learn to live decent lives, and to say their prayers and to speak cleanly.' Her head bounced in emphasis. Thomas made no comment.

The Canon himself opened the door. As she sat down, he said, addressing a point above her head, 'I have a touch of lumbago. They tell me elderberry wine is very good for it? Do you know anything about it?'

'I'm afraid I don't, Canon.'

Hands trembling, Ellen took out her notebook, and stiffened her neck, held her head up high.

'Right. Now, Canon. Mrs MacReady.'

'Of course, my mother had it, like a martyr. To see that poor woman getting up out of a chair.'

'Canon, I made a note of what they were doing. In a school. Where people are supposed to be taught things the right way around.'

The Canon coughed. Then he coughed again, and made the bout of coughing last, until it rang as hollow as a false laugh.

He poked the dog with the toe of his boot, 'Out, Rusty, out, out. He's fourteen this year. Or is it fifteen, that'd make him, what, a hundred and five? One of the dog's years is seven of ours. Did you know that?'

Ellen said, 'Do you know that they damaged the school building and tried to break into cupboards?'

Canon Williams folded his arms tight across his chest and looked out of the window. Ellen pressed on.

'Did you know that one of them began to molest me in front of

83

the whole parish?' Canon Jeremiah Williams stood up and turned away, his lips wet.

'Canon, you called me "Miss Prim" for worrying about the words of songs. What words would you like me to teach wrongly in *The Apostles' Creed*? Would you like me to teach, "I believe in God the Father Almighty", and leave out, for instance, "I believe in Jesus Christ His only Son our Lord"? Is that what you'd like?'

'You don't understand the country people. The past goes away here slowly. The people here need the bit of entertainment. Look at what they're used to. 'Tisn't that long ago since the Famine. And the Troubles. And the Irregulars. You're trying to say they have no past. They're entitled to their ballads. You should have joined in with the songs instead of correcting them. Miss Prim.'

'Canon Williams, I'm a teacher.'

'What songs anyway?' asked the Canon surlily.

'*The Wearing of the Green.*'

He turned round to face her, full of interest; 'How in the name of God did they get that wrong?' he asked. He pursed his lips. 'Could you teach them the right words? If they came back?'

Ellen shook her head. 'I want your assurance as our School Manager that they will never be allowed back. The Department of Education wouldn't like it, would they? Grants and that, for school repairs.'

After a long silence, Ellen eventually rose, gathered her coat and her basket, and moved to the door. The Canon followed, and in the stained-glass porch, pointing to some withered plants in brass pots, said, 'Did you ever grow geraniums?' Then, he said, 'You're a lot older than your age. And you're not married at all, they tell me.' He had closed the door behind her before Ellen could blush.

Ellen stopped at Thomas Kane's gate, but found it closed; the house looked empty.

'Herbert,' said Leah. 'Do you know who I met on the street?' She often leaned against the jamb of his workroom door when the girls had gone to bed. 'Rina Morris. She was in her school uniform, she's a good deal taller than Ellen already. She has a year to go at Privet Hill, and then she says she doesn't know what she wants to do, but she doesn't want to teach.'

Herbert nodded. Leah went back to the kitchen and began to clear the table, and sing. Thinking of something else, she returned to Herbert's door and said, 'She's very observant, Ellen's sister. Do you know what she said to me? I asked her had they heard from Ellen, and she said the letters were getting full of the man Ellen is teaching with, that Kane man.'

'Ah, yes, yes,' said Herbert, in that facilitating tone of voice which always left Leah guessing whether he intended a comment, or was merely acknowledging her remarks.

Lent began, with Evening Devotions at the church on Wednesday and Sunday evenings, and Ellen declared to Thomas her intention of attending every one. 'It will get me out of Mrs Greege's. A bit of a nice sound in the evening, at least.'

In the silver glitter of the altar, and yellow light of the candles, and the high, raised gold of the starry monstrance, the *Tantum Ergo* echoed. On the frosty Sunday night, he waited outside the church, and said, 'I didn't bring the car, 'tis such a fine night. My God, the Canon can't sing.' She laughed.

He walked her to the top of the Norman motte-and-bailey near the church, and said, 'From here you can see the moon at its best,' which proved true; solemn and bright, it lit the surrounding countryside so clearly that houses and woods quite far away could be picked out.

'Who was that woman in the camel coat?' asked Ellen, as they walked down the slope.

'With the headscarf? Thin?'

'About four seats back from the altar-rails?' asked Ellen.

'I think,' said Thomas, 'she must be the new Doctor's wife.'

'She reminded me,' said Ellen, 'of my grandmother, she had the same cut about her. The famous Helena.'

Thomas said, 'What was she famous for?'

'She was a character,' replied Ellen. ''Twas from her I got the clothes, I mean the interest in them. She had a bombazine mourning skirt for my grandfather's funeral. A woman used to come to the house with a basket and a brown paper bag. Patterns. They had to open out the dining-table, all the leaves extended. Then the famous Helena climbed up on the table.'

Ellen did a mimicry.

'I will wear my black silk blouse. Will my emerald brooch be too much? Too frivolous for the dead? I can never bear to have no colour anywhere.' Thomas laughed.

Ellen continued, 'So the dressmaker – and her mouth spiky with pins – said the custom in some places was for women in mourning to have a scarlet, or a cream silk waistband on the skirt, "on the inside, of course, Madam". And I wasn't let go to the funeral but I wore a nearly-best dress. I still have it, green organdie, with red flights of ribbons on the edges of the sleeves, made by that same Mrs Moody and her pins. And then when they all came home from the funeral, my grandmother, when no one could see, winked at me, and turned her back to the crowded room, and twisted her waistband inside out quickly, to show me the red lining. She had lovely long legs.'

Thomas laughed again. 'She sounds a character. Did you hear what they're saying about Mrs Doctor Hogan? That she has no luck because she wears green, very unlucky, and that that's why she and her husband are always arguing.'

Matters had altered in Thomas Kane's life. The silent watchers of the village behind their curtains saw and understood. His homeward stride had changed: now he paused to talk further to his new teacher, and if he did not always walk as far as her lodgings with her, he detained her outside his own gate with one more comment, or walked a few steps after her to call her back and say one last word. Mrs Greege observed Ellen Morris at close quarters, saw her switch between excitability and introspection, watched her walk out from the house most fine evenings and return flushed not long later. Did she meet someone? Mrs Greege, an accustomed and experienced watcher, did not need to ask, knowing that time would reveal everything, and in any case, she had a clear understanding of the nature of the inevitable. However, she did make one comment to test the waters of Ellen's affections.

'Didn't I tell you he was a hard man, the Master? They're all talking about him and the way he gave them MacReady men a hammering?'

She watched Ellen's colouring face carefully; 'Any man would do what the Master did. They were wrecking the school. The filth of them. They didn't respect anything and when that man offered me offence – well, what would any gentleman do except what the Master did?' But by now Mrs Greege knew her young lodger well

86

enough to recognize the furrow of anxiety when it cut into Ellen's forehead.

On Friday, Thomas waved a letter excitedly after the postman had gone: he came to her classroom door laughing with pleasure.

c/o Mrs Nancy Heffernan,
Ballinagown.
Wednesday,
1st April 1925.

Dear Master Kane,

I am trying to find out about the famous Deanstown Brass and Reed Band that won the All-Ireland Championships in 1897 at the Royal Dublin Society Showgrounds in Balls Bridge.

How many men were in the band, and is it true that they played for King Edward the Seventh when he was over here as the Prince of Wales? And for the Count de Jarnac the day he left to become the French Ambassador over in London? The reason I am asking is that I am arranging a new series of monologues for my Summer Tour, and I want one to be about famous musicians who are now forgotten, on account of nostalgia, etc., etc., always such a potency, as I'm sure you know.

I am staying here at kind Mrs Heffernan's, having been infirm etc., for some weeks now, but recovering very well, thank you. Then I have to go off for about a month, to Dublin and that, but I'll be back in these parts in the first week in May. If you would do me the esteemed favour of writing to me, my address is usually, 2 Pavilion Terrace, Patrick's Hill, Cork City, County Cork. I would be ever so grateful for the courtesy of an answer. Thanking you in advance,

I remain, Sir,
Yours truly,
Val Vousden (Mr)

Thomas said, 'Well, well, well.'

=

Ellen had a letter too, from Father John Watson; no more than a note, on the white paper with the jet-black address;

Dearest Ellen,
   I have only one copy of Thomas à Kempis, but when next I'm in Dublin, I'll get a copy especially for you. So sorry to have missed you. Your Mama tells me you are settling in well. When are we going to see you again?
Yours in Christ,
Father John

Thomas took the calendar from the wall under the clock and held it out at arm's length; he had left his spectacles in his coat pocket. She walked the length of his classroom.

'That new chalk. It is easy to break, if you lean on it the slightest bit.'

He said, 'Use shorter lengths. Break the stick in half.'

'Oh,' she said.

He asked, 'Are you going home the week-end?'

'I don't know yet.'

Ellen began to give Timmy Quinn little tasks to do. He handed out pencils; and knobs of plasticine – she encouraged each child to recognize the piece they had been using yesterday – and the small pictures that formed numbers. When she needed to demonstrate something such as height, and tell them feet and inches, she stood Timmy beside her. His hesitation at singing stopped; he yelled with the rest, and Ellen said to Thomas, 'I feel I'm making some progress. I wish I could say the same with the young McAuliffe girl.'

They had returned to the school twice, Mrs McAuliffe and her daughter. The child's demeanour had deteriorated; the mother's anguish increased. Ellen managed to pin Thomas down, and extracted from him at least a clear picture of the difficulty.

'The talk is,' Thomas said, in unease, 'that Sean McAuliffe got in with the wrong crowd. He had a job in the courthouse and of course it gave him plenty of information. And it was a bad time to have information. He wasn't the only one who disappeared.'

Ellen asked, 'Why won't anybody talk about it?'

He said, 'Your father would probably tell you why. People don't.

I told you. They never talk about the truest things. Too dangerous.'

Then, dismissing it, he said, 'Look. This all came up two years ago. The same thing. Her brother asked me. The Sergeant said not to do a thing about it. And he said the Superintendent said the same.'

'And who will?'

Thomas said, 'Nobody.'

'But the poor misfortunate woman?'

Thomas shrugged his shoulders.

'Can't somebody? She can't get a widow's pension or anything?'

Repeatedly, Thomas pinched his lips with his hand. 'The people responsible are still around. I mean – very around. Local. If a body is found – well.' In finality he said, 'The gun isn't gone away in this country yet.'

Thomas scrubbed and scrubbed: the blacking had lined the pores and wrinkles of his hands, even if the range did glow. Next he explored each paper-wrapped item in the large cardboard box he took from the cupboard in the corner of the kitchen. In a clean basin of water, he washed each new cup and saucer and plate, polishing their thin gold edges. From a flat, rectangular parcel which had lain in a drawer for two years, he shook a clean white damask tablecloth: the creases had become so folded they seemed almost grubby. Spreading this cloth on the parlour table, having moved all his books and his writing-box to the sideboard, he set the table for two people. He checked a circular cake-tin; in it lay, like a trove, a dark, glistening thick fruitcake with almonds and currants on top, set like nuggets.

Ellen leafed through *The Leader*, to a large drawing of the plans for the new boat club at Athlunkard which would have 'a sanitary annexe and chamber'. *The Coliseum*: Wednesday, Thursday, Friday and Saturday, twice nightly at seven and nine o'clock: *Moon of Israel* by H. Rider Haggard. 'Greatest Drama Ever Screened. A critic reports: *The production has been made on such a truly stupendous scale as to leave us gasping with wonder and admiration. A Picture of Artistic Splendour, Magnificent and Enthralling. The Crossing of the Red Sea and the Drowning of Pharaoh and his hosts is but one of the thrills, Matinee Thursday and Saturday at 3.30 p.m.'

A horse whinnied in the yard and a woman's voice called Mrs Greege. If people stood beneath the eaves talking, Ellen could hear every word.

'Ah, hallo,' said Mrs Greege. 'How's Ernestina today? Won't you come in out of the rain itself?'

Ellen stooped to the window. The girl in the pony trap wore a man's hat and coat.

'No, I have to hurry. Can Shamie come up to help? We've two pigs to kill. Would you like the puddings?'

'Of course he can, sure that'd be grand. Are you sure? Sure, a cup of tea out of your hand is no harm, on a day like this?'

'I can't, I can't.' The girl spoke briskly and in a loud voice.

'Aw,' said Mrs Greege, 'sure that's a shame, sure the man who made time made plenty of it.'

'Not for me. Is Wednesday all right?' asked Ernestina.

'Grand, grand. Tell me is it true you're getting an engine up there?'

Ernestina barked. 'Oh, my blessed brother. Whick! Whick!' she said to the pony, and hauled the reins around. 'Stay, boy! Stay, boy! And he says he's going to plough with it, did you ever hear the likes of that?'

At supper, Mrs Greege volunteered, 'There's a great row in that Stephenson house, she's entitled to half the place but if he marries she mightn't get it, and he's after one of them Merrigan girls. From a cottage.'

Hearing a loud noise passing by on the road outside, Ellen perked up. Mrs Greege noticed and said, 'There's more than the Master with a car, the new doctor has one.'

Ellen changed the subject. 'Do you know a Mrs McAuliffe at all?'

Mrs Greege replied, 'Everybody knows that old story, that woman has people tormented looking for pity.'

It was Thomas's car. After school he had driven to Kilgobnet to see Stewart the tailor, to collect the new suit. Stewart, a Scot, had been in the Army.

'I was lucky,' he said to Thomas. 'Most of the officers were tall men like yourself. Very hard to make clothes for a small man.'

=

Eight weeks had passed since the dank fog of the February morning through which Ellen first peered at Deanstown. Two days later, her life changed forever. On a Thursday afternoon, just after her pupils had left, Thomas gave her a packet tied with a ribbon. It contained papers bequeathed him, he said, by an aunt: an account written both in letters, and in some unpublished articles, of the life of one of his ancestors, a man called Timothy Nash.

'He was a great-grand-uncle of my mother, he was a hedge-schoolmaster,' Thomas explained.

'But this is an heirloom?' said Ellen.

He smiled. Ellen could not forbear, and dipped into the pile there and then. The first document she opened, a brief 'history' of Nash attempted by Thomas's aunt (also a teacher), outlined the relevant history in general.

In the days of the Penal Laws, Catholicism was banned. Only a few priests were allowed to continue in their parishes: other priests went on the run, saying Mass across the country at Mass Rocks, convenient tables of natural stone set in remote places from which any arriving soldiers could be seen a long way off. No ordinations were permitted, therefore the Church secretly arranged for boys wishing to become priests to flee the country and be ordained in Irish Colleges abroad, such as Salamanca, or Louvain, or Paris, or the Irish College in Rome. Most of these men never returned, choosing instead, for safety's sake, to work in the country of their adoption; many thereafter annealed their angry souls by writing virulent and seditious tracts. A few, not as many as a hundred or so, came back in disguise to Ireland and went into hiding. They roamed the country, saying their secret Masses, and also, since all education was equally forbidden, teaching the Catholic people and their children. Under the trees and the hedgerows, in isolated smallholdings and broken farms, on the sides of the hills, they held lessons in religious instruction, and in Virgil and Plato and Horace.

Timothy Nash was one of those hedge-schoolmasters, and he taught for several years before going to England. For a detailed account of his early life, please refer to the other papers in this box which I have collected from my own father and my aunt, especially the words of Mr Nash himself. I will just give a short account here for the moment.

He was born in a house on the edge of the woods near Bruree, not far from the route of Sarsfield's Ride. His grandfather had been a well-off farmer whose family lost the farm under the Penal Laws to Timothy's uncle, who became a Protestant and added an "e" to his name to indicate that he had changed his religion. The original family kept the dwelling house, however, where Timothy grew up, and it can be seen to this very day, a pleasing enough house.

The letter went on for several pages: Ellen folded it and put it away to await reawakening.

'Can I take this home?'

'Oh yes, 'tis yours,' Thomas said.

The packet's bulk filled her basket. A slightly closer scrutiny told her that one piece in particular seemed to have sources of all kinds in it, notes on books, translations and brown newspaper cuttings and official-looking documents. Ellen asked Thomas how much he knew about Timothy Nash: he could only offer that people said he 'carried the Nash looks'. They had, in any case, been a colourful family, the Nashes: one of them had been with Sarsfield at the Siege of Limerick, and may even have been on Sarsfield's Ride, or Hogan's Ride, some people called it, the famous midnight break led by the Rapparee, Galloping Hogan, to blow up the Williamite siege train at Ballyneety.

That night Ellen discovered among the papers, as she spread them out on her writing-table, a tiny folded lace handkerchief which smelt of ancient flowers: she read on:

Timothy was admired as a child for his intelligence and as a result the parish priest, a Father Tobin, took a special interest in the boy, and gave him lessons on the quiet. Timothy proved a very good student, and showed what Father Tobin called 'a true thirst for knowledge'. Father Tobin therefore approached another family in the next county who still had money and who were well-disposed towards educating Irish boys, and told them that he had in his parish a boy of unusual cleverness who would make a very good priest. This family put up the money and Timothy, aged fourteen, was smuggled out of Janesborough port on a boat going to Spain, to join the Irish university in Salamanca.

Two nights after he left, obviously acting on the tip of some informer, soldiers called to his house and took away Timothy's father to the barracks in Kilmallock. He told them the boy had run away, and they tortured him but could not get any more information out of him. They hung him upside down and kept dipping his head in a bucket of water, holding him down long enough to make him think he was drowning. Still, he gave them no information. They let him go, and he returned home, walking, even though they had taken away his boots and never gave them back to him. Mr Nash (Senior) never recovered from this and his health grew worse. Timothy was never to see his father again. A year and two months later Mr Nash died, and when the word was brought to Timothy in Spain he did not react in the way the priests who had charge of him expected. He did not weep. Instead he flew into a terrible rage and had to be held down. It took, they said, two full-grown men to restrain him. He was a very tall young man.

Next day, Thomas said to her, 'I have to slip home early,' and he muttered words which sounded like, 'something to do. So would you ever lock the door and drop in the key to me?'

He greeted her at his house in a new suit and dazzling white shirt.

'Come in, come in.' She had only stood in the hallway once before; now he ushered her into the right, through a doorway to a room where a fire blazed, and a table, with white linen and cups and saucers, sparkled.

'Oh,' she said. 'Are you expecting somebody, I shouldn't be here?'

He smiled. 'I am, I am expecting somebody. Take off your coat.'

She blushed deeply, and with never a question, and with a meek air, sat in the chair he pulled out. He poured tea for her, and sliced cake, then sat opposite.

Desperately she blurted, 'Those papers you gave me, they're very interesting, but, they're your family, I can't keep them. I mean I'd love to read them and that, but they're your family belongings . . .'

He looked across the table. Her eyes diverted – to the ring of white stain made by a glass or a cup on the dark piano, which had one candlestick missing.

'I hope you'll be able to keep those papers,' he said. Pausing, he then continued, 'The reason I asked you here, was is there any chance you'd marry me?'

She put down the piece of cake she had picked up and looking at her plate said, in perhaps the quietest tone he or anyone had ever heard her use, 'There's every chance.'

'Does that mean you will?'

'It does.'

They said nothing more about it, or about anything else, for several moments.

Eventually, he said, 'Good,' then he said again, 'good.' He exhaled, and would not stop looking at her, no matter how she looked away.

'You'll have to understand,' she said, as if in sudden, new thought, 'this is whirlwind. I mean, I don't mean, I didn't expect and I didn't, I'm not surprised. But I know nothing at all about being a wife, and they'll all say you're an awful lot older than me.'

'They can say what they like,' he said. 'And anyway, what does anybody know before they get married? Sure everybody has to learn.'

'But. I've never even walked out with anybody much, I was always at home,' she said.

'Same here, I mean I wasn't always at home, but.'

'You've travelled, though,' she said. 'And you were out a lot in the world . . .'

'Is it too sudden for you?' Thomas asked.

'Oh, no, no, no.' Then she stopped. 'No.'

'I was at the hare coursing the other day,' he said, 'and when I saw them let the dogs off, I thought. That's what I felt when I saw you first. I was like a dog racing out of a box to get to you before anyone else did.'

Ellen's eyes filled with tears.

They probably exchanged no more than a hundred words in the next half-hour or so. She finally said, 'I'll have to go. If anybody saw me come in, then I'd better go before dark.'

He said, 'I know.' Then, 'Hold on a minute.' He left the room: she heard him climb the wooden stairs, and return, something hidden in his large hand – a small, square, high-domed red box, of fading leather: he stood above her as she opened it, and she found inside a ring: small diamonds clustered inside a circlet of tiny pearls.

'It used to be my mother's and her mother's,' he said.

She put her hand to her mouth. 'I suppose – I shouldn't wear it yet. Until everybody has been told.'

'I suppose that's right.'

She sat in the chair, looking at the ring in the box, inspecting even the jeweller's name in gold lettering on the white satin. 'Kneeshaw's,' she said. 'The same as the clock in school.'

He said, 'Here,' and she looked up. He bent down and kissed her, and the force, not just the physical pressure of his face, left her gasping. When the kiss ended, he clasped her hand. She stood and put her head on his shoulder and said, 'I want to walk back, please, Thomas, I want to sit quietly by myself, and think quietly.'

'You're sure,' he asked, 'you won't change your mind?'

'Oh, no. Oh, no!'

Inside the door, as she put on her coat, he said, 'I have enough money for us to live very comfortably. I have, in the bank and the post office together, about . . .'

She shook her head. 'My mother will ask you anyway. I won't.' Then she said, 'When – did you have in mind?'

He said, 'June. Just at the school holidays.'

'That's an ideal time. You mean this June?'

'Yes, this June.'

'What will they say?'

'No matter.'

She talked to herself the whole way home up the hill, in breathless gabble, with an occasional laugh.

'Oh, God, Lily,' she said merrily to Mrs Greege's niece in the kitchen, 'do you think your aunt would ever install a bathroom in this house?'

'She won't, Ma'am, nor hear of it, she thinks 'tis bad for one.'

The dying sun caught the tips of the trees in a distant hillside wood where a deer nuzzled a young green shoot at the base of a tree. The deer shook its head to free its teeth from a piece of heavy cloth inching a fraction above the surface.

SUMMER 1925

6

Mrs Greege herself called up the stairs to announce breakfast. Ellen clunked firmly down.

'So 'tis a big day for you, today?'

Thomas was calling for Ellen at twelve, then driving to Janesborough to meet the Morris family.

'And I have those black puddings you like.' Mrs Greege bent to the long scrubbed deal table. Ellen cocked a suspicious head at the good china: she did not have long to wait, not even until the second cup of tea.

'Will there be many coming to the wedding?'

Perhaps the white teapot picked up light and threw it on Mrs Greege's face, or perhaps she just sat in a shaft of morning sun; in any case the grey tufts of hair in her nostrils appeared as never so clearly before. Thomas said Mrs Greege planted them there deliberately, to give her face drama, or for the greater glory and honour of God. Today she wore a heavy skirt of grey twill: the geese hissed in the yard at some sudden agitation.

Ellen deflected: 'We haven't finished the lists yet; there's a lot of family.'

Mrs Greege served fat speckled quoits of black pudding – and angled again for an invitation.

'I suppose linen is always an acceptable wedding present?'

Thomas had said that he would with his own two hands throw Mrs Greege out of the church if she turned up.

'Or a bit of silver, it always brings good luck, Miss Kneeshaw was saying the other day? Kneeshaw's sell a lot of it for wedding presents, or a clock? But I suppose ye'll get plenty of clocks, the Master being such a man for keeping good time?'

A breeze stirred, then suddenly billowed the lace curtains; a shiny red-brown hen raced briefly across the yard to flee a hostile scurry, and wound to a halt clucking in dust and indignation; the yellow morning began to warm up – by noon it would be hot again today, beaten gold.

Ellen decided to collude with the conversational mood; 'Mrs Greege, who do you think will end up marrying us, the Canon or the Curate, they're fussing over which of them should do it?'

'What about that friend of yours, the priest?' Mrs Greege sawed at the soda bread. 'Lovely clothes.'

Ellen looked down, smoothed her blouse into her light skirt, with an expression on her face of not-quite-grasping Mrs Greege's compliment.

'D'you mean Father Watson? Sure, this is an old skirt, I have it five or six years; I always think the summertime is the only time you can wear yellow.'

Mrs Greege's skirt creased as she hoisted one long knee across the other. 'I had a cousin whose sister ran off with the man she was going to marry. Is that his name? Watson? What is he, is he an Englishman or something? No, I meant the underclothes.'

'He is not an Englishman, he's a Dublinman. What?' Ellen's tone sharpened as it dawned. 'The underclothes? What underclothes?'

It burst like a shell.

'But they were in a parcel,' she snapped. 'Addressed to me!'

Mrs Greege spoke in a flat tone. 'I opened it by mistake.'

Ellen picked up her knife and put it down again. 'And it was you who re-tied it? Is that what accounts for it?'

Not even Mrs Greege with her great gifts of obtuseness could mistake the chill in Ellen's face and voice.

'I suppose you could never let yourself be married by an Englishman, could you?'

'He's not an Englishman, he's a Dublinman, I said. And besides Father Watson is a Jesuit priest. If you don't mind?! Irregardless of that – what business had you opening that parcel? What else have you opened? That is an offence under the law.'

'If a parcel comes to my house, I am entitled to open it. That's the fact,' said Mrs Greege, tough of face and voice.

'It was addressed to me!'

'Care of me.'

'I'll report you.'

Mrs Greege handed Ellen the breadboard, with the fresh soda bread on it.

'What have you to be ashamed of? Sure you'll never wear them again anyway. 'Tis an overall you'll need to run a house.'

Ellen fell into the trap. 'But I'll still be teaching.'

Mrs Greege, having won the information she sought, snapped the trap shut. 'Hach! Isn't the Master the crafty man? Two salaries coming in, his and your own.'

Ellen, defeated, rebelled into monosyllabic answers, finished her breakfast, returned to her cool, dim room and washed her face again with the corner of a damp towel. She locked the door, and lay on the bed for five minutes: still an hour and a half before Thomas would call.

Had she looked out the window in the direction of the Castle, to the south-east, Ellen might even have seen the black figure speeding through the fields towards Thomas's house.

'Completely charmed, completely charmed.'

His hand worked like that of a man at a stiff water-pump. Thomas, stripped to the waist as he shaved in his bare bedroom, had first caught sight of him in the mirror, then for about fifteen or twenty minutes watched him from the upstairs window, this extraordinary creature beetling down the morning fields from the Castle, the tails of his coat flying out behind him, a hat in one hand and, over the opposite shoulder, a kind of large leather satchel, which bounced off his hip as he hurried. Thomas sometimes counted half-aloud the strokes of the razor on his face: he paused in mid-count. As the man drew closer to the house and Thomas stepped back to one side of the window, lest he be seen watching, it became apparent that the man talked to himself all the time, and gestured, sometimes half-stopping to make a wider gesture. Where his white hair receded on the dome of his forehead, sweat shone in the light; the perspiration also made little rat's-tail curls at the other end of his hair, which had been allowed to grow into flowing locks. Patches of damp appeared at the neckband of his shirt which he wore without a collar and he had opened the buttons of his waistcoat: the thin legs of his stovepipe trousers clung and wrinkled.

'How on earth did you happen to come from across the fields?' Thomas asked with a smile.

Mr Val Vousden apologized with a little rueful face for the wind he had just broken in Thomas's hallway, and said, 'I am not accustomed to such exertion, and I ate rather well last night. That lovely black pudding. Somebody killed a pig.'

His voice see-sawed in a warm tune.

'I stayed with the O'Donnells and you know them, I'm sure, they certainly know you, so you know full well what their hospitality is like, and it was their suggestion to come across the fields, and it was grand with me, the morning is when I compose.'

During the night, a full bladder had awakened Thomas and he decided to go downstairs and outside. True darkness had never fallen; the wall of the house still had some heat to his touch. The leaves of the sycamore rustled above his head.

'Would you like a cup of tea or something, you're an early bird?'

Val Vousden stepped out of the hallway again, into the sunlight, and with another tiny, quick slap-wheeze of escaping wind, 'Oh, pardon me again,' sat on the green iron-and-wood garden seat under the bay window, easing his hands with downward strokes along the shins of his trousers, while through the window came the noise of cups and cupboards and the clank of a kettle's lid. Val Vousden raised his nose and sniffed, and said in a loud voice, 'Honeysuckle,' and to this remark, Thomas's voice called, 'What was that you said?'

He repeated, 'Honeysuckle. Or is it eglantine?' and from within, in polite momentum, 'Oh, yes.'

Thomas emerged through the hall-door, a cup and saucer steadied gingerly in one hand, in the other a plate with a small stack of thick-sliced bread and butter and jam.

'Oh, gracious,' said Val Vousden. Thomas went back to get his own breakfast, and Val Vousden shuffled along the seat to make room. The two men sat in the sunlight eating, and then leaning forward and down almost simultaneously, to pick up the heavy blue-banded cups resting in their saucers on the gravel at their feet.

'I. Fmlst.' Val Vousden swallowed a bite suckingly, and began again. 'I fmlsts say. I.' He sprayed some crumbs. 'Must say.' More crumbs and a swallow. 'How much I enjoyed. Our correspondence. You write a great letter, Master.'

Thomas coughed. 'I don't think I'm a hundred per cent clear. On what you want.' He blew out his cheeks, puffing after a mouthful of tea. 'Is it that you want to start the band up again? They didn't play for the Prince of Wales, by the way. And that story of them –' coughs '– playing for the Comte de Jarnac?'

Val Vousden pointed wordlessly with a finger at the privet bush in front of them where a dewed cobweb glistened like a crystal snood.

Thomas paused and took it in, nodding and continuing.

'What they did was. They played at the Union Farming Society Show, and it so happened it was the last one where the Comte de Jarnac was the President, because he left not long after that.' Thomas flicked crumbs and jam from his fingers fussily. 'A thrush nested in that bush last year, and she used to dive at me every morning I came out. I had to start using the back door.'

'No, I didn't think at all about restarting the band,' said Val Vousden, 'but what a lovely idea. I only wanted to write a recitation about an old musician who retires, and who comes out of retirement for one last glorious marching day.'

Thomas said, 'I have a few bits and pieces for you. An old programme, and a thing from the newspapers, and there's something one of the bandsmen wrote. Now there is a fellow, he's down there in Boss Glen. Called Egan. He played in the old band. He was in the Munster Fusiliers.'

Val Vousden traced his finger along the rim of his still-steaming cup and said vigorously, 'Oh, imperial echoes. Imperial echoes. I remember the military bands well when I was a child, I was always following them.' He started. 'Oh, I suppose, of course, maybe I shouldn't . . . Be talking about the military to yourself, Sir.'

Thomas smiled. 'Oh, nonsense, man, nonsense, there's nothing as good as a military band, not at all.' He smiled again. 'Not at all.'

Val Vousden said, 'This man, Egan?'

'Now he'd know a lot,' said Thomas, 'you see, several of them were killed, the Somme and Ypres and places. I had an uncle killed there myself. But I know for example that some of the Band's uniforms are still around, I don't know who has them, or even if they're still more or less intact.' He rose and went indoors. 'I'll get you those papers.'

Val Vousden stuffed them carefully in his satchel and shook hands as if with an emperor.

The postman came.

Dear Mr Kane,

Is it true? They are saying you are great with that new teacher. Say that it isn't true. I have been asking you to

103

leave a message for me on your pew in the church, and
then I'll have the courage to meet you. You know my
feelings. Have you any feelings for me? If you met me
you would have, but I can't make the arrangements, it
is the man has to do that. Please. Please.

Your Admirer

P.S. I feel like tearing her eyes out if it's at all true.

Ernestina and Cyril Stephenson agreed that the best day might be
Sunday, 26 July.

'Rory will be here, and will Constance be home? In which case,
we haven't much time, we'll have to start writing soon. Mama,'
continued Ernestina, 'always said politeness demanded eight
weeks before a summer party, twelve in the winter.'

Her brother said, 'Yes. Yes.'

'Cyril, you are certainly not going to invite that bloody little
domestic of yours, that shop-girl or whatever she is.'

'You shouldn't swear.' Cyril yawned.

'I'll do more than swear if you try that on. That little bitch,' she
said. 'If we hadn't Mrs Cullen coming in every day, she'd be washing your bloody shirts by now. That's how they connive, those dirty
little Roman Catholics. And don't you dare sell that bloody yearling
either without telling me.'

Cyril yawned again. 'We have too much meat,' he said. 'I knew
we should only have killed one beast. We'll soon have no more left
to kill.'

Ernestina snapped, 'Well, we have to kill our own, we owe the
butcher too big a bill. And when are you going to fix the green-
house, you'll have to do it before we have any party?'

Cyril whistled a tune.

'You said ages ago you'd fix it. If it rains what'll we do?'

'That sky. It won't rain for a month. Anyway, you can't fix that
glass until the laburnum is cut back.'

'I'm not touching that laburnum! You cut down the one in the
yard.'

'It was poisoning the horses.'

A brown terrier ran across the lawn and disappeared behind the
high brick wall, yapping. Ernestina leaned forward and opened the

window wide. Cyril toyed with a chess-piece from a board that had several of the pawns missing. A light breeze through the window stirred the yellowing newspapers on the chair.

Ellen jumped with relief when she heard the car, and stooping to the low window, saw the lovely brass lamps, like two wonderful ancient helmets. Thomas had taken the hood down. Ellen ran downstairs. She never replied when Mrs Greege called out, 'Aren't you going to ask the Master in?'

Ellen climbed into the car, even though he had begun to clamber out of the other door. Up the road, beyond Hogan's Bend, he stopped the car to listen to the underclothes story.

'From now on,' he summarized, 'and 'tis only for a few weeks, try and have every parcel sent to the school.'

Ellen put her arm in his, and placed her head upon her new favourite resting-place, the top of Thomas's arm, the broadest, hardest part, just beneath his shoulder.

'I get very confused.' She pressed her head tighter to him.

Children gathered around the car, haw-ing their breath to make condensation on the brass lamps; Ellen's father opened the door and came to the front of the top step, beaming. In the hallway deep behind him, a figure moved.

'This is him, Dada,' said Ellen, as she stood with Thomas on the street, looking up.

'Now, how are you?' said Bob Morris, as pleasant as ever. He held his hand out to Thomas, and turned to Ellen, saying, 'No wonder you were hiding him from us, an ugly man like that.' All laughed.

'Come in. Come in.' He called to his wife. 'Mama! Mama!'

Nobody moved. They stood in shadow, as the sun had not yet westered sufficiently to reach their side of the square.

'And you drove in?' he asked.

'No, we walked,' said Ellen, and they laughed again.

'Come in. Come in,' said her father again.

Ellen's mother came forward, making actions as if she had just taken off an apron, which she had not; and then other gestures to fix her perfectly all right hair.

'Mama, this is Thomas.'

May stepped forward, then back.

'Well, I declare to goodness. Let us have a look at you. You're very welcome to our house.' She spoke emphatically, and then began to blush – from the neck up, and it spread, and spread, and spread, until it reached her under-chin, then her veined cheeks, and then her forehead. She shook Thomas's hand; then stumbled backwards and led the way in. 'Jim and Rina are both out, they'll be in in a little while, are you famished with the hunger, isn't the weather lovely, if it keeps up like this for the wedding we'll all be blessed.'

'Father Watson left a note,' said May to Ellen. 'He's gone to Dublin for his annual Retreat, you know, Rathfarnham Castle.'

Thomas admired the stuffed fox in the glass case, and as he put his hat without forwardness on the pegs of the hallstand, inquired politely as to the identity of the powerful lady in the large studio photograph – Ellen's great-grandmother, Bob Morris's grandmother, an eagle of a woman, portrayed beside a pillar with ivy. May led the way to the drawing-room, where the piano gleamed and the smell of furniture polish rose warmly with the sun's heat. Tall cream plumes of pampas grass, and a large basin of pinecones, filled the fireplace, now empty for the summer.

'I hope you don't mind my asking,' said Bob Morris, 'but is that a Harris tweed by any chance?'

Thomas, looking down, plucked the cuff of his rust jacket.

'It is actually.'

'Did you offer the man a drink, Robert?' said May. 'You'll think we have no manners at all,' she said to Thomas.

'I'll get it, Mama,' said Ellen, and to Thomas, 'we have Locke's, or a Paddy.'

'Or some of that good Midleton whiskey, give him some of that, that's very good altogether,' said Bob. 'D'you know you can't get Harris tweed in this city. They used to bring it in, but you can't get it for love nor money. And 'tis a thing you have for the rest of your life.'

May had already left a glass jug of clear water on the tray, and Ellen brought it to Thomas's chair, along with the round heavy tumbler.

'Dada?' she asked.

'I will, girl, special occasion.'

'I got this in Glasgow,' said Thomas, again inspecting his sleeve.

'Glasgow?' said May. 'Imagine! Ellen said you're very travelled.'

Ellen perched on the wide arm of her father's chair. The four people sat disposed around the room, and the sunlight caught as yet just one corner, where a tall black lacquer screen, inlaid with mother-of-pearl birds, stood behind an empty chair. Thomas crossed his long legs.

'How old is this house, as a matter of interest?'

Ellen looked at her father, and Bob responded with practised knowledge.

'This house was built by the grandfather of that lady in the picture in the hall, he'd be my great-great-grandfather; he'd be what? Three greats to Ellie here. He was a Morris from over Carlow direction, they had mills and they came here when paper started to come into real demand. Now he was born in 1725, two hundred years ago this year, he put his date of birth on the deeds of this house, and he bought the site, this was green fields –'

'Imagine,' said May.

'– and he built the place in 1750; it took two and half years, and d'you know, the roof has never needed a bit of repair, and still doesn't; there was workmanship for you. And not a bit of rot, or a thing.'

'Well, well,' said Thomas in approval.

'But that's not the most surprising thing,' Bob continued. 'The most surprising thing of all is the age of the man when he built it, he was only twenty-five years old.'

'Imagine,' said May. 'Of course they were Protestants. The family converted afterwards.' She always affirmed religious good news with a little bob of her head.

'He did a lot for a man his age,' said Thomas.

'Who's that?' sang out May as the front door opened.

'Rina,' said Ellen.

'My younger daughter, Catherine. She arranged that,' said May, pointing to a bowl of roses.

'Very nice,' said Thomas, 'very nice. How old is – Catherine – Rina?'

'Seventeen,' said May.

Thomas got up and they shook hands, Rina's gloves half-on, half-off. She sat down, blushing.

'Did you see any sign at all of Jim?' asked her mother.

'He'll be here,' said Bob; 'he said it when he was going out.'

'But will Mary Rose be with him, that's what I want to know. I don't know how many we're to cater for?' said May.

'I always say 'tis easy to take a name out of the pot again once you have it in in the first place,' said Bob.

May opened tall double doors and they moved to the dining-room.

'I have to keep those blinds down all this summer, or that table would fade entirely,' said May as they sat.

A leg of cold ham had been carved into huge slices, which lay on a willow pattern dish in the centre of the long table.

'Now those napkins were Ellen's grandmother's; she bought them in Vienna. Imagine,' said May. 'Now, d'you like cold chicken or cold turkey or cold goose with your ham?'

Glass shell-shaped dishes of preserves paraded down the table-cloth. 'I pickle my own apricots,' said May. 'There's a man out there in Ballysimon, he bought a very old house, Bob knows him, and he has an apricot orchard, imagine, and we go out there every August and come back with baskets. The plums are our own, look you can see them there under the blind, on that far wall, reams of them.'

Thomas lowered his head and shoulders, and gazed politely, then turned back to the table and, with the tentative decisiveness of good manners, chose cold goose and cold turkey, and some of the apricot and plum preserve, then accepted the large bowl of soft green lettuce leaves with sliced tomatoes and sliced hardboiled eggs.

'Hallo, I'm sorry I'm late.' A red head poked around the door, followed by a cheerful face. Thomas rose and shook hands across the width of the table, amid smiles.

'Are you on your own?' said May.

Jim sat down, and said, 'She couldn't, she had to help her aunt or something, their stall.'

May said aside to Thomas, 'We have our Bazaar tomorrow, for the church: 'tis a pity you can't stay for it.'

'Ach,' said Bob, 'the man must have seen a hundred bazaars.'

Ellen said to Thomas in front of Jim, 'He won't tell us whether it's serious with Mary Rose, but he's been walking her out for the past four years.'

Jim laughed and said, 'The less you know.'

=

108

Cakes had been both baked and bought, and scones, and cream for the tea, and home-made jam and apple jelly. Thomas's performance at the table drew admiring comment from his prospective mother-in-law, 'There's nothing like a man who likes his food.'

He amused them with stories of the neighbours in Deanstown, and made Ellen's father laugh more than once with descriptions of the children's remarks in school – how, for instance, he could not get one little boy to come into school on time. Finally when he asked him why he was late, this child, the youngest of a large and very poor family, simply stammered, 'H-ha-h-had I a spoon, had I?' Another, when sent to the pump to wash his face, inevitably returned with what Thomas called 'a high-water mark on his forehead', and when asked why he didn't wash all his face, replied that his shirt-tail would 'only reach so far up'.

'D'you know what?' said Ellen to Thomas, as they walked slowly to Leah's house later. 'You subdued Mama. She was. No, not frightened exactly. In awe, I suppose. And as for Dada, well – I never saw him like that before. So excited.'

'You'll come back, won't you,' asked May, 'and have a cup of tea out of your hand before you go?'

Leah, when introduced to Thomas, held on to his hand after the handshake, and looked at Ellen, saying over and over, 'My, my. My, my.'

After that initial response, Leah's restraint took Ellen aback a little. The girls giggled and ran off; then the three of them sat and talked for a little less than an hour, then Leah had to shoo them out because it was the Sabbath and she had to prepare the house. In the hallway – Thomas had gone to the bathroom – Ellen whispered, 'But – do you like him?'

'Yes, yes, of course. Such a big man, so distinguished, and you are really going to marry him? This is dramatic news, dramatic. Your letter. I was amazed.'

Thomas returned at the moment observing that they must persuade the Canon to put running water and electricity into the house.

'Now, you have to come back soon and meet Herbert, my husband,' said Leah. 'He's out at his prayers.'

Ellen said, 'We'll have to be here several more times before the wedding, anyway, there's so much to do.'

Late on Saturday afternoon, Ellen travelled with Thomas in the car to the outskirts of the city, kissed him goodbye at a place where nobody could see them.

'I meant to tell you,' he said. 'I had a dream about you last night.'

'Aaah?' she said.

'I dreamt. Do you know that cat on the marmalade jar? The one that sits looking in at the fire in a lovely homely room? I dreamt that we were sitting together on the sofa behind the cat.'

In the evening sunshine Ellen walked the mile or so back to Brunswick Square.

'What are you doing?'

Rina lay on the drawing-room floor copying an address from an American magazine. 'Sending away for something.'

The *Ladies Home Journal* offered a Hickory Shadow Skirt. 'THOSE FRESH CRISP LITTLE VACATION FROCKS – keep them smooth and wrinkle-free! The Hickory Shadowskirt of cool lingerie fabric, and light, fine rubber. It prevents body warmth and perspiration from reaching your dress. Wrinkleproofs and shadowproofs perfectly. In flesh color. As low as $1.50.' (The item never arrived: her father said it fell over the side of the ship into the Atlantic and was floating away somewhere near the Azores.)

'You missed the Leonards,' said Rina. 'They brought that.' A brown paper parcel, large and flat and tied with strong white twine, lay on the table. 'Mama says 'tis sure to be linen.' At which Ellen moaned.

'Mama says you can never have enough linen,' said Rina.

Ellen sat at the piano and played a halting piece of minuet.

'Where's everyone?' She turned on the piano stool and twirled the full three hundred and sixty degrees.

That night, Leah said to Herbert, 'But it is all very fast. "Marry in haste, repent at leisure." I don't know, Herbert.'

'She's very intelligent, Ellen is.'

'Yes, but is her heart intelligent? I mean – too much determination can be a bad thing too, and she seems very determined, but she has no experience of the world at all, has she? What do you think, my dear?'

Herbert put down what he was doing. 'If Ellen wasn't a teacher. Say if she was something else. Say she – what? Say she painted pictures or something? What would she paint? I often ask myself that about other people. What would they paint?'

'Not big bright colours, like I would,' said Leah.

'No, no.' Herbert mused on.

'Very small and neat? Is that what you mean?'

Herbert said, 'I think they might surprise us. I think they'd be neat, yes, but I think they might be more baby-ish than we think.'

'Should I talk to her, Herbert? I'm uneasy.'

'No harm in writing to her. I mean. Behind that very – that very organized exterior of hers, I mean?'

Leah said, 'That's what worries me. I know she's very warm, but she's very cold as well, and I think she's doing this without taking everything into consideration. I mean, he's an awful lot older than her.'

When Thomas met the bus next evening, he suggested a drive and a walk. Where the river forks two miles from Deanstown, people gather and sit on the wooden seat on summer evenings, when the senior men of the farms and the cottages discuss the county's prospects in the championships, while watching the hardy boys from the farms cavort in the cool water after a day's dusty work. On occasions, one of the men brings a fiddle, someone else a deck of cards. Tonight, the old makeshift seat beneath the willows, completely obscured from view – except from the water or the woods on the far bank – was empty: a football match in the next village had attracted everyone. Thomas glissed a flat stone along the water, one-two-three-four, then it died.

Private in the remote open air, they held hands, they leaned shoulders. Ellen wore a cream dress and took off her short coat, too warm, turned it inside out and folded it to make a cushion on the wooden seat. Thomas kissed her at dusk and kissed her again, and then, with no objection from Ellen, he put a hand up under her loose clothes and quite easily felt her – all over, thighs, knees, hips. His hand came to rest for some time, flat like an offering, on the plain of her stomach just beneath her waist, and with tenderness covered the soft plateau completely. Ellen looked straight

111

ahead, at the dark sluggish water of the river, at the swirling reeds. Her face seemed grim; an expression she wore when concentrating, or requiring a moment of courage. She turned her face inwards to Thomas's lapels, and just once more, very slowly, those strong fingers, that hard palm, swept slowly over her again. Raising her head and looking out across the dark water and sedges, Ellen sat perfectly still, neither accommodating nor impeding, blinking very fast at first, and then closing her eyes, and swallowing like an excited child.

She added one prayer at bedtime, not habitual in her repertoire, except after her Confession on the first Saturday of every month. 'O, my God, I am heartily sorry for having offended Thee. And I detest my sins most sincerely, for I have sinned exceedingly. In Thought, Word and Deed. Through my fault. Through my own Fault. Through my own Most Grievous Fault. Therefore I beseech. The Blessed Mary Ever Virgin. Blessed Michael the Archangel. Blessed John the Baptist. The Holy Apostles Peter and Paul, and all the Saints. To pray for me to the Lord Our God. Amen.'

As the weeks passed by, they stayed behind in the school, eating sandwiches, drinking tea from a flask, or red lemonade from the village shop. Ellen made her final bridal lists, and Thomas enlightened her with snippets from the newspapers, local and national.

JUNE ROSES
June has come. The first day, at all events, brought us a little sunshine. Hope it will continue and that straw hats will be more in evidence than umbrellas. The latter, though not invented by an Irishman, suits our Irish climate. After the initial miraculous weather, cold bitter showers and lowering skies marked the end of May. Soft, fleecy, wool-hued clouds hovered to the north and north-west. The nip in the air reminded us that icebergs were breaking up, perhaps, in the Gulf Stream.

'Icebergs?' said Ellen. 'As my mother would say' – mimicking May Morris's accent perfectly, 'imagine.'

O, HOW THE WHEEL BECOMES IT
The Whitsuntide demand for Raleighs has exceeded all previous records. It is a modest estimate that the Whitsuntide holiday

saw not less than twenty thousand fresh Raleigh bicycles and their riders on the road.

When she first mentioned that her grandmother had a household ledger, Thomas told Ellen that he would buy her one too – when they went to London on their honeymoon. In anticipation she clipped various pieces – domestic use, recipes, gardening or cleaning tips, advertisements, or simply items of interest.

Fancy! A man still living who saw the great Napoleon. And a hardy old fellow for his 140 years. He is Haji Tahir, an Arab, born at Mecca, who went to Palestine in the year 1799, at the age of 14, when he saw 'Bony' who was then operating on the Syrian coast.

* * *

BUTTER! BUTTER! BUTTER!
We are open to purchase this Season as usual large quantities of Unsalted Butter at Highest Market prices. Butter will be bought on Thursdays, Fridays and Saturdays throughout the Season. Highest prices will also be paid for Fresh, Clean Eggs. Edward Ryan & Son, Ltd, Brewery Stores, Thurles.

Deanstown,
Friday

My dearest Leah,

Thank you for your long letter. The weather here is still lovely. Please God it will keep.

You will be pleased to know that your letter did make me 'think again' – although it would be a bit late in the day to change my mind! Not that I want to.

Yes, it is 'a plunge' – and 'a whirlwind romance', as you say. But without any doubt Thomas *seems* very good to me (as your letter generously said) and also *fond* of me, and I have to take things for how they affect me. What other, fuller knowledge do folk have? Although you didn't say it, you might have been wondering how much I knew about him before deciding to give him the rest of my life. The

113

only thing I can say is – what can anyone know about anyone else?

I think I must have exaggerated to you in my letter about that fight with those travelling show people. Yes, I did ask myself – Was this a very violent man I had agreed to marry? But as you know, Dada had told me that Thomas never got involved in anything bad after the Troubles, and even then he left the Flying Column in the height of things, which I think showed great courage. When he attacked those show people Thomas was provoked, and he was nearly even challenged to fight; those people would have stopped at nothing, and they had ruined the place, and I must say that I was very proud of the way he dealt with it. Even though I think any woman would be frightened of how strong he was with his fists, I don't think he'd ever be that angry with me, or use violence towards me.

I know you think I'm probably too young to be getting married, or that this is too short a courtship. But isn't that what married people always say to those who are getting married?

Dear Leah, I'm only teasing you. Naturally enough, though, I have worries, but I feel that I can get enough of my own way with Thomas. He makes me feel very good, it is not like marrying a man my own age who has still to grow up. He says that this is what he always wanted, a wife he can devote his full attention to, so that really I have to do very little, it will all just happen, which is lovely for me.

The thing I find, no matter what you say about my not having walked out with enough fellows so far, is that it seems very easy to get men to do what you want in any case, and Thomas is always around me, always near me. The other odd thing is that I don't find anything at all strange in the notion of sleeping in the same bed with a man, even though I hated it whenever we had visitors at home and Rina and I had to share. Maybe I'm not shy, or something.

Leah, soon I'll be 'Mrs Thomas Kane'. Imagine! I keep practising the name, and wondering what it will sound like

114

when people say it to me, although around here I suppose they'll only call me 'Mrs' or 'Ma'am', or 'The Mistress'. You must write to me immediately after I'm married, so that I can see what the name looks like on an envelope!

Will the girls be coming to the wedding after all? Your letter never said. Because I need to teach them how to stand a little back from me at the altar.

I have lots more things to tell you, only I haven't the time now, as Thomas says we have to go and look at some furniture. I won't let him buy a thing without my seeing it first.

Thank you again, dear Leah, for your dear sweet letter, and I didn't take offence. You have always meant well towards me.

Your affectionate friend,
Ellen

On her last visit to the city before the wedding, Ellen had a conversation with Father Watson.

'Have you prayed for guidance?'

'Oh, Father John, endlessly.'

'Well, if you have no doubts?'

'Father, when you meet him, you'll see.'

They sat in the grounds of the Jesuit Provincial House.

'Have you doubts, Father? About me, I mean? As a candidate for marriage?'

He thought.

'Have you, Father John?'

'There's one thing, my dear.' He hesitated then hastened. 'But I may be wrong!'

'Oh, Father?!'

'No, no, don't get alarmed, more alerted is what I mean you to be, dear Ellen.'

As she reported to Bob later, few people could be as thoughtful and kind as John Watson when he tried.

'What crossed my mind, Ellen, was this. You recall that you told me about this – travelling show, what was it?'

'Oh, I know what you're going to say, I know what you're going to say! Thomas's violence, isn't it?'

115

'No, no, my dear, not as simple as that. Just – well, we've had very odd, very hard times in this country. I get told strange things on the few occasions I hear Confession, morbid things. But if you're sure.'

'Father John!' Ellen turned to face him. 'You're not jealous or something?' For a second before he laughed, just for a second, no more than that, the priest looked away. When he turned back, he asked, 'And how's your Mama enjoying the preparations? She must be very excited?'

There seemed to be ribbons everywhere – the handlebars of the bicycles, the lamps on Thomas's car, on the hats of the girls. A young teacher, from Ellen's Training College class (she too was to marry a teacher) chased a red ribbon that had fallen and was being swept by the breeze across the yard of the church, and she tied it to the straps of her handbag and everybody laughed. Men jingled the coins in their trouser pockets; smiling, they held out closed fists to the children and made them pry open the big knuckles to find the sixpence inside. Little Rachel clung to Herbert's legs, and although she smiled up, and even chatted, would not come out. Mrs Martin Burke buttonholed May Morris in the porch, and the two women had a wonderful, competitive conversation about whom they knew and to whom they were related.

One of the Kane boys had brought a small handbell, and sitting on the saddle of his bicycle outside the church gate, under the trees, rang it like a giddy town crier to get the procession started. Ill Uncle Denis, not seen at a family function for something like seventeen years, had a complexion like prison pallor. The three priests gleamed together as they accepted the envelopes of the bride's family.

Pushed by a dozen playful hands, the car lurched forward: Thomas had had the foresight to reverse into the church gateway. Ellen clung to her hat and veil with one hand, her bouquet with the other, and everyone squealed as the cheering men finally slapped the back of the departing car.

Along the road, people stood waiting at the doors of their houses; they smiled and waved, and relished a full, uninhibited stare. Some had slipped into the back of the church to watch the ceremony, and they now stood on the hilltop gazing down. Even when the parade of two motor-cars, many, many bicycles and two pony-drawn traps went out of sight into the tunnel of thick hedges down at Hogan's Bend, those up at the church could still hear the cheering, and the halloo-ing, and the singing, and the merriment of the handbell. Then the sound freshened again as the road swung back into view, and the colours, not yet so far away, could be seen: the purple, the bright green, the blues and the reds, and white.

Four of Thomas's brothers rode their bicycles along beside the car like furiously happy outriders, on a day so hot and sunny that the road threw up dust which puffed every time a brother hit the shiny paintwork with his cap. In a pony and trap behind – the car only held two, Thomas and Ellen – came the bridesmaid and best man: Rina and Thomas's brother Arthur, back from America for the wedding, and his sister Margaret, who did not want to be called a Matron of Honour, so could hardly decide whether she was an attendant or not. The Morrises had hired the car of the talkative driver, and Father Watson travelled with them: Canon Williams and the Curate would cycle.

Thomas stopped at the crossroads to accept the greetings of a line of carts on the way home from the creamery; they had all been at the village pump filling their empty churns with water for the livestock: in the ferocious heatwave, many streams had gone dry: even a famous well was threatened. The men in their waistcoats and collarless shirts, some even wearing overcoats notwithstanding the sun, raised their caps to Ellen, and said, 'Well, now,' their indelicate teeth beaming and gapped.

In this vivacity, among the men who got down and crowded around the car, nobody took much notice of a walking vagrant, a strong, thickset and quick man. As ten farmers and their labouring-men shook hands with Thomas and Ellen – 'I hope you'll have all luck, Master. And yourself, Ma'am' – this hobo, unseen until too late, reached in towards Ellen's bosom and twisted and wrenched away without any difficulty the gold cross and chain she was wearing, and then he ran.

Too late she called out, or, rather, too late Thomas heard her in all the din: the man was gone.

'Thomas! Look!' she cried, pawing the top of her breastbone, and looking around her awry, but Thomas turned too slowly from his pleasant outreached handshaking, and Ellen, although half-rising from the car, did not know the man nearest her, and could not ask him by name to follow the tramp.

She pointed with her finger, and Thomas, not comprehending, asked, 'Who is it?' Everybody looked, but nobody moved.

'Thomas, Thomas! He has my cross! My good cross! He's after whipping it off me!'

'Who? Who?' asked somebody else, but another horse and cart drew up outside, further cutting off any quick pursuit.

'That man, the one running, he whipped off my cross, Aunt Bridge's cross!' cried Ellen, pointing. The cross and chain had been in the family for at least a century, perhaps two. Aunt Bridge, still hale, was coming along to the wedding later. 'She says she's seventy-five,' in Ellen's words: 'You could add five years to that and not be uncomfortable.'

Thomas had admired the crucifix: knew how old it must be: the cross had a Penal Laws motif, Christ on one side, Mary on the other, comprehensive worship in one image, to be treasured in the days when the next Mass might be six months away, and then only out on a secret hillside.

Thomas started the engine. The running tramp, hearing, looked back, and rushing to the demesne wall, climbed into the fields and disappeared. Ellen should have cried out more significantly. Thomas should have taken more notice of the short outcry she did make. Between them it fell: nobody, upon later enquiry, knew the tramp, or had ever seen him before.

Earlier at the altar of the church Canon Jeremiah Williams celebrated Nuptial Mass, assisted by the Curate and Father John Watson. Thomas wore a dark grey suit, his head held as correct as an officer, bowing only to put the ring on Ellen's finger: both looking straight ahead exemplarily.

Intoning the prayers with the Canon, John Watson's long hands fingered the Missal as if it were sheets of music.

'You know how much I like him,' said Ellen to Thomas, 'but he has little oddities about him. He never bought me a cup of tea in my life. I know priests have no money, but . . .'

She said nothing about a certain lack of personal fastidiousness, Father John's ears, and clothes, not always what they might be, the opposite of the things she liked so much in Thomas and unusual too in a countryman.

When Ellen fell in love with Thomas, she described the intensity to only one person – surprisingly not Leah. Obviously she did not go into detail; not even to her notebook could she express as she thought.

'Oh, Father John,' she said to him about Thomas, 'I laugh at myself when I think of it, but his voice is like fire in my ears. Wouldn't you think I was suffering from calf love?'

'Of course, the problem, Ellen my dear, if problem it be, is that you have the mind of an intelligent woman and the innocence of a girl.'

Since she first came to know Father John Watson, she found that he often made a remark which took her days to decipher. This, and a difficult balance between intimacy and reserve, led to her fashioning devices of conversation: for example, she used questions as a means of trying to tell him what she felt. Did he know or had he ever encountered sudden instant attraction between people? What were the moralities involved, by which, she hastened, was it all right to feel you wanted to give your life completely to one man, even at the expense of what you knew were certain gifts you had? What were the dangers involved in spending the rest of your life with a person, even one to whom you felt so committed? Should not a person experience several such relationships before committing herself finally to one partner for life – 'I mean, Father, of course, observing the norms of chastity and so on?' He never answered directly.

Thomas did not meet the Jesuit until yesterday, in the rush of last-minute preparations.

'Aha,' said Father Watson looking right up at Thomas, 'the man we've all been hearing about.'

'And which of us is that, now?' asked Thomas agreeably, but the pleasantry did not ignite. Nor did the priest take it wholly genially when Thomas completed a quotation for him: Father Watson, looking at his watch, said, 'Well, we'll have to hurry or we'll tire the sun with talking and send him down the sky,' and Thomas, again intending amiability, murmured, 'They told me Heraclitus, they told me you were dead.'

'Oh! The classics out in Deanstown,' recoiled Father Watson a little. 'Well, Ellen, you never told me.' Whatever Thomas noticed, she certainly caught the edge in the Jesuit.

In the preceding weeks and months, however, Father Watson had been assuring her that, yes, what she seemed to feel for Thomas could accurately be described as love as known to humans, and desired by God so that people could bring themselves to Him, and if it expressed itself, as he hesitantly put it, 'in a sacred way',

120

that was part of God's desire too, and that the love of man for woman was created by God, but that love of the mind must also be a part of Christian marriage, just like love of the flesh. Ellen said, 'It often makes me a bit uneasy' – but did not elaborate on the images and curiosities that flashed through her mind whenever she thought of Thomas, or the heat that made her mind's eye blink whenever he touched her: 'Father John, you always make me less confused.'

At the altar during her wedding, she looked at the little Jesuit again, his head bowed a little, the glistening chin: who would ever think he was nearly ten years older than Thomas?

'What I feel is not exactly . . . affection for him,' she struggled to explain to Thomas more than once; 'I mean not the way I am towards you; what I like is the respect he makes me feel for him.'

Father Watson, by arrangement with the Canon, gave the briefest of sermons, without a text.

'Dearly beloved brethren. Thomas Kane and Ellen Morris are two people we see this glorious summer morning at a moment of important ritual in their lives. Both have the intelligence, and the sensibility, not only to rise to the individual importance of the occasion – but to observe this ritual. And not just observe it for themselves, but on behalf of all of us. All of us who love them. All of us, their families. All of us, their dear friends. And perhaps even more importantly, all of us, all of you, the community they serve as teachers and leaders.

'As teachers and leaders, Thomas and Ellen, now Mr and Mrs Kane, they each know, both by instinct, and by education, they each know the importance of ritual in our small communities. They each know furthermore, and I know they have discussed this, that they both feel a part of our emerging nation. Our nation which so badly needs ritual and leadership.

'When God's own ritual, such as the Sacrament of Matrimony, is consummated as suitably as this at local level, ritual will pervade us, and our new nation, at national level. And thus we will heal all the wounds of a generation which has seen three wars – the War of Independence, the Great War and the sad Civil War.

'My dear brethren. It is our great pleasure to meet here this morning as witnesses to this loving union. I happen to know that Ellen takes a particular spiritual pleasure in reading that wonderful work, *Of the Imitation of Christ*, and therefore, I salute her and her new husband, Thomas, by quoting another Thomas – Thomas à Kempis himself, who said: "Would that we had spent one whole day well in this world."

'"Well", my dear brethren, "one whole day *well*": I feel we will all look back on this day, and see how we have indeed spent this "one whole day well". Spent it *well* observing this inspired wedlock between two remarkable people.'

When the couple and their best man and bridesmaid went around the back of the altar to the sacristy to sign the register, the congregation barely managed to maintain the decorum of silence in church. Children swung from the high peaks of pews, or scampered along the aisles to inspect some curious, or winking, or playful, beckoning man or woman. May Morris, long embroiled in attention-seeking indecision, had chosen light grey: 'Dear God,' she whispered now to Bob, 'how could Auntie Neenie be serious about that lilac frock? On a woman her age?'

The glee was at last released in the church porch and soared outwards among relatives who had not met since the last family funeral or wedding. They used these occasions to record the passage of time on each other's faces and bodies, to run comparisons on ageing, to measure family competitiveness and progress. 'And I hear Ally is doing great? Isn't that great?' to which a gratified mother would say of Ally's new-ish husband, 'Of course, he's a very steady fellow, Sean is, he doesn't drink nor smoke, and he takes con-acre every year of his life.' No mention made of the age difference between Sean and Ally, nor Sean's resident old mother who was still holding on to the rights of the farm, nor the baby every relentless year. They all greeted each other in the friendly impersonal mode, as when Auntie Neenie hove in view: 'And how's Rina at all? Are we getting a bit stout, are we? Sure we all had puppy fat' – this to a seventeen-year-old girl enduring remorseless shyness.

All on Ellen's side, first intrigued by the resonance of his difficult fame, had been more or less captivated by Thomas; 'Even "herself",' said Ellen: – 'And God knows, to be perfectly straight about it, she's a "b" with an "itch", that's what she is.' The said Auntie Neenie clamoured that she had at long last met a man who could make her change her mind 'about the married state', the reason she herself never married being, of course, that she never found a man who 'would come up to my expectations'. (Causing Ellen's father's famed observation: 'Nothing to do with the port-wine stain on her face.')

The families differed widely. All the clothes on Ellen's side matched; Thomas's people had broader, open-air complexions. Ellen's people talked a lot; Thomas's, fewer, smiled more than they spoke, hung back farther than Ellen's relatives, waited until approached. The women, formidable and with great jutting round-nesses, dominated Ellen's family: the men seemed more prominent in Thomas's. To his brothers, with both parents long dead, Thomas was their father, their hero, their point of reference, their good security. The four boys looked up to Thomas, crowded around him, laughed at his jokes, teased him about his suit as they had long begun to tease Ellen, revelling in her friendly gullibility. 'Now – you have to polish his shoes every morning. He likes his egg boiled soft. And whatever you do, don't ever bake him a caraway seed cake, it goes straight to his head and he falls down in fits.' In the future, whenever any one of them appeared at the house, they consistently brought some present for Ellen: a salmon, or a pheasant, or eggs, or some plant or shrub.

To the Kane brothers, Leah's presence at the wedding was as exotic as a little carnival, or a dancing clown. When Ellen introduced them just outside the doors of the porch, they loved her, and her good humour, and her fun. Leah, delighted to be sur-rounded by so many men and all so much taller than her, and taller than her husband Herbert, laughed and joked with them, and got Herbert to explain his skull-cap to them, and asked them their names, and whether they could dance, and whether they had girls? None of them had, and she chided them, saying she knew girls who would come and chase them if they did not make a move to marry soon. They loved it all, and later that day they each danced with her. With two out of the four, Leah had to do the asking – but then each one of them swung her around the room, laughing out loud at her stumbling, breathless dizziness.

Given that the marriage took place 'on Thomas's territory', as Ellen's mother put it, they came to an arrangement. Contrary to custom, Thomas would attend to all the day's costs: Ellen's parents would spend their daughter's wedding money on furniture for the happy couple. Thomas conferred for weeks – mysterious meetings with farm women in faraway corners of the parish.

An army of wives provided hot and cold food. Most guests, given the weather, opted for the salads, white-and-gold hardboiled eggs, harems of gleaming beetroot everywhere; the huge baked hams like sweet babies, the long pink salmon, the cold turkeys and chickens. He even had cold pheasant, taken as a great favour from the old ice-house at Moore Abbey – but nobody ate it: 'Hot pheasant is bad enough,' one man murmured to another. Drinks of all kinds stood on every table, bottles of whiskey and brandy, and forests of black stout bottles: Arthur devoted himself to pulling corks. Ladies drank wine and sherry, huge jugs of orange squash with the slices of orange floating in them (prepared by the Misses Harpers' niece who had spent some time in London). A long continuous table reached from the back wall of the parlour, making a causeway out through the bow windows (frames removed for the day) as far as the privet hedge, so that half of the people at the feast sat indoors in the shade, and the other half, although at the same table, sat outside in the bright light. A pigeon swooped into the high *macrocarpa*, and out again quickly. The men hooked their caps on the sides of the chairs; the women placed nests of handbags beneath the table. An accordionist and a fiddler played on and on and on, their notes squeezing and scraping across the wall of fifty conversations.

Thomas and Ellen sat on slightly raised chairs, backs to the piano which was covered with cloths, and dishes of cakes, opposite the mantelpiece, across from the picture of *Vesuvius Erupting*.

'How are you?' whispered Ellen. 'I've hardly had a minute to say hallo to you?'

He whispered back, 'Do you think everything is going all right?'

'Oh, grand, grand! Look at them, look at the way they're enjoying themselves?' Then she whispered with a chuckle, 'What about Auntie Neenie?'

'She gave me a big kiss,' said Thomas.

'Oh, God! How did you avoid the birthmark?'

They dissolved into laughter.

Ellen said, 'I don't think I'll be able to eat a thing,' and devoured a plate of cold meat and salad.

=

Five speeches: the Canon; Ellen's father; Arthur Kane, the best man; Thomas; and Father Watson. The Canon blessed the wedding.

'I'm the lucky man today,' he said, and everybody laughed.

'I'm the Manager of the school and now the school has a great wife. And the Pope can't say a word agin it.' More laughter. 'And what's more,' he said. 'As any man should be with a wife – I'm afraid of my life of her.' They roared.

Outside, by the road, three of the older boys had captured a six-year-old cousin: they threatened to take his trousers off and send him in to all the girls. The boy wriggled away and ran off, and from a safe distance began to call them names again, hoping for another chase.

Ellen's father reminisced: Ellen in her mother's shoes and hat; Ellen on a rug in front of the fire; Ellen learning to read; Ellen growing up; Ellen on long walks: 'I can tell Thomas one thing. He'll never find a better listener than Ellie.'

Arthur, like a showman, made everybody laugh with stories of sharing a bed with Thomas when they were little and how Thomas would never cut his toenails, but said he was leaving them grow long to torture Arthur, 'and he used to rake his nails up and down my legs. I hope he's changed. People buying a horse look at the animal's teeth. Ellen, you should have looked at Thomas's toenails; you've probably discovered an addition to the Impediments to Matrimony.' Much laughter and cheering.

Thomas stood. He made a speech full of kindness and tenderness, towards his brothers, towards his dead parents, towards all their past, hard life together.

'I think of my father often, I think of where he came from, and sometimes I see him in my mind's eye. On fine Sundays he used to ride out across the country on a horse he borrowed from our neighbours. Just for pleasure, the way other men go for a walk. And my mother would see him coming back, and go out to meet him, and so would we, and he looked great.

'And I think of my father's life, and how he was as a young man with his own brothers, some of whom are here today, Uncle Matt, Uncle John, the two of you are so welcome. And I think of how he was as a young man, how he was lively and good, and all his folks up there in the north of the county, a big, bright crowd of people. He liked my mother very much altogether, and I thought of them many times in the last few months when I was walking out with Ellen. And how they would have liked her.'

Stillness and affection had fallen on the room, as Thomas continued, unaware how he moved them, these his guests and friends and kin. Any spoor or chill which his person may have carried from his own history had evaporated; he stood as a man who had put awfulness behind him, and who now looked to his future with warmth, and confidence, and a friendly sense of safety. When those who had proved ambivalent about the role and purpose of the Flying Columns overcame their diffidence, even hostility, towards the more prominent individuals, they lionized them, especially in the glow of hindsight: from this latecoming adulation Thomas now benefited, and their faces turned up to him ready to like and admire.

'My father and mother gave me a valuable gift, and it was this. They told me many times that I never had to set out to do anything to please them deliberately, that I did not have to think of pleasing them, that my being there and just trying to be good and decent, that was enough pleasure for them. Now I have married Ellen, they, to my sadness, are not here to see her, or to dance with us all, and even though I would not have been marrying Ellen to please them – well – I know they would have been delighted.' Around the room, Thomas's family could not look at each other; the girls sniffled and blew their noses; the boys looked downward.

Thanking everyone, Thomas began praising Ellen.

'I told her myself, and she knows what I'm going to say. When she came out here last February, I know what the fellows around here are like. And I was like a greyhound out of the traps.' They roared.

'And I know I speak for her when I say, that anyone of you here is going to be welcome under our roof at any time of the day or night. Only, try that you don't all arrive at the same time.' He sat down to cheers, laughter and applause.

Father Watson, the last speaker, then rose. He said, 'I had a speech prepared, and I wanted to give it. I wanted to talk about the sanctity of marriage, and what a man must be for his wife, and what a woman must be for her husband. I've known Ellen Morris for ten years and I met her through circumstances where she behaved with great compassion to a child who was dying. Ellen befriended her –' May Morris could be seen nodding, and mouthing to her neighbour, 'That's true, that's true' – 'and Ellen made that little girl's last days bearable and cheerful. I know therefore that she is utterly capable' – his Dublin accent, and mannerisms, and phrases sounded foreign in the long room, and his trained speaking voice rang out into the air – 'utterly capable of being all the things a man could wish for in a wife. I hope for a lasting and vivid friendship with Thomas, and now that I have heard him speak here today, anything I have to say about the prospects for a marriage between these two exceptional people would be superfluous.'

Many of the people in the room did not quite fully comprehend the meaning of the word 'superfluous', and would never have used the word 'utterly' – but they knew that this 'odd little man' was paying their Thomas and their Ellen a huge compliment, and they applauded him sincerely.

'Quick,' whispered Thomas, 'that photographer is going to be drunk if we don't get him working now.' They stood in front of the door, in a rotation of groups and poses. 'The nick of time,' murmured Thomas, 'he's well on already,' as the man had difficulty unfolding his 'sticks'.

Tables were pushed back. A piper arrived, and the other two musicians cleared a space in front of them. Arthur rushed over and grabbed Ellen. Everybody shouted, 'Yeee-ow, go on there, Arthur!' Dancing furiously, Ellen pawed up to feel the cross and chain flying at her neck, and missed it. She danced on. Uncle Michael, her mother's uncle, looking on and, tapping his old feet, said to his wife, 'You used to have a bosom like that.'

Men and women and boys and girls drifted here and there. Aunts admired the peony roses on the tables. Cousins talked about jobs in Dublin. Lavatory arrangements became informal; the small shed at the side of the garage (Thomas had whitewashed it the previous Saturday) had people standing beside it, therefore men walked into the acres near the house: others walked deeper into the fields. Girls on tiptoes, and with fat bottoms and ribbons, giggled and skipped a little up the road, in the opposite direction from the village, then slipped in past the hedgerows in twos and threes. Ellen was called by a cousin to attend to a tearful Rina: she had torn the hem of her dress when she caught her heel in it, and feared her mother's wrath: a needle was found, and Leah helped.

Aggie O'Carroll, the girl from the Training College, gave Ellen an illuminated scroll the nuns had given her: *The Housewife's Prayer*: Ellen read the first lines:

> *'Lady who with tender ward*
> *Didst keep the house of Christ the Lord,*
> *Who didst set forth the bread and wine*
> *Before the Living Wheat and Vine;'*

'Oh, this is lovely, lovely,' Ellen squealed. 'Thomas, stop them playing for a minute. Aggie – read out the rest of it.'

Aggie, not at all shy, stepped over near the lulled musicians and read on,

> *'Be beside me while I go*
> *About my labours to and fro,*
> *Speed the wheel and speed the loom,*
> *Guide the needle and the broom,*
> *Make my bread rise sweet and light,*
> *Make my cheese come foamy white;*
> *Yellow may my butter be*
> *As cowslips blowing on the lea . . .'*

– and when she came to the end,

> *'To me Thy gracious help afford*
> *Who art the handmaid of the Lord'*

– and after the word-swooning and clapping had died down, Ellen exclaimed, 'Oh, I'm going to have that framed the minute we get back from our honeymoon.'

Thomas and Herbert met for the first time at any length; previous encounters had been fleeting (all on Saturdays), and now they could not be prised apart. In the corner of the sitting-room they sat, Herbert, with his quiet courtesy, questioning Thomas intently late in the afternoon.

'I've always wanted to find out about Collins.'

Had Ellen heard, she would have caught her breath, knowing Thomas's astringent reticence on the subject of his own past.

'And tell me, was he a big man?'

Ellen had tried over and again, in an effort to break through the mist of dropped hints from the people of Deanstown. All she had really gleaned, apart from the fact of their connection, was that Thomas and Collins had quarrelled violently. When the news came through of Collins's assassination – Mrs Burke had passed on this nugget – Thomas, shopping in Mooreville, knelt in the street, as people did all over the country, and wept. He let it be known that he would lead a candlelit vigil to the church the night of Collins's funeral, and the whole parish turned out, irrespective of political affiliations.

'Not as big as people think,' he told Herbert. 'About five foot ten or so, or eleven. And he had a curious way with him. Whenever he met somebody, say you were in one of his Command Units, and you came to see him, and he was fond of you, and he hadn't seen you for a while, the first thing he'd do was wrestle with you until he overpowered you down on to the ground.'

Herbert then pushed back the lock of fair hair dipping down into his spectacles, and delivered the next slow but passionate question; and from their first moment, the two men discovered their mutual, if passive, commitment to politics.

'Oh, undoubtedly, undoubtedly,' said Thomas when Herbert asked him if Collins would have gone into politics had he lived. 'God, to think of it. What? Thirty-one? And all he had done? Where were you when you heard of his death?' It was to Herbert, and to Herbert alone, that Thomas revealed the extent of his involvement with Collins, and only in that roundabout way did Ellen ever come to hear of it, and only then in the most appalling of her days a year and more later.

When Herbert first asked, Thomas brushed down each arm of his new suit thoroughly, five brisk strokes, then fixed the cuff of each sleeve. He patted the front of his jacket, and straightened the pens in his inside breast pocket. He transferred an envelope from one side pocket to another. After these comforting preliminaries he began.

'Well, we had three ferocious years, him and me, I sort of worked alongside him. My house, the Teacher's Residence, was burnt down by the Black and Tans while I was away doing the Master's degree. Although I was never suspected of any involvement. It was burnt in reprisals for an ambush I set up, and they'd have burnt down the whole village if it wasn't for Captain Johnson. He was a retired army man, India, that type of thing, and he stopped them. The Sunday week after they burnt the house, Collins involved me in a series of things in Dublin which I'm sure you remember, a lot of shots and that.'

Herbert asked, 'Bloody Sunday?'

Thomas said, 'Yes. Anyway, to cut a long story short, I began not to be able to sleep, and a few weeks later I got notification that I couldn't go back to the school here, because the Inspectors had decided to close the school until the Teacher's Residence had been rebuilt.'

Thomas concluded his tale. 'I was finished the thesis, and I wasn't going to be examined on it until about August, so I saw my chance and I went to see Collins. I told him I was out of it, that I was out of it altogether, that I couldn't do any more the things he wanted. We met in a room in Aungier Street.'

Thomas sat up straight: Herbert leaned forward.

'Why? Why were you out of it?'

'I can't do that sort of thing. I never wanted to. I mean – I agreed with the principle, the Cause itself, and in the beginning I agreed with the actions we had to take. But it got too much for me.'

Herbert nodded. Rachel came over, shaking both her legs. 'Dadda, wee-wee, wee-wee?'

Herbert said, 'Look, my love,' and pointed, 'there's Mamma.'

'No, Dadda, you. You!'

Leah rescued.

Thomas smiled after them, and after a moment resumed. 'Anyway, I said more or less the same to him as I'm after telling you. And do you know what he did? He hit me. Across the face. He had these brown leather gloves he used to wear, winter and summer, cycling, and he hit me with them. This was the middle of June. I said if he hit me again I would . . .'

Thomas stopped, then continued, 'Anyway. The upshot was he threw his arms around me, and said I was to go with his blessing. The following night I left on the Mail Boat with my bicycle. I was in bits. I went off to Antwerp and places.'

Both men sat and reflected.

'But will we all fit?' asked Leah.

'Of course we will,' said Bob, 'won't we?' he asked the driver.

'Bit of a shqueeze, Sir, but you will, I'd say.' Bob smiled at his own mischief, knowing May's opinion of Leah. Herbert sat in first and the girls, asleep, were handed in to his arms.

The end of the day had come slowly and good-humouredly. At ten o'clock or so, as twilight gathered, people began to leave. It had become known that the couple were to spend their wedding night in their own house – but Thomas had successfully sealed the stairs.

'They'll make us a French bed if we don't watch out,' he laughed to Ellen.

Together, the Morrises took their leave of their daughter. Bob shoved a roll of notes into Ellen's hand; 'For something nice in London.' Father Watson, formal once more, made promises to visit the pair when they returned.

Thomas's brothers stayed until last. They hung around until all other farewells and laughter and goodbyes had floated away on the dusk and then, one by one, they came and shook hands with both Ellen and Thomas. When the youngest brother, Des, aged twenty, tall and lanky, with fair curly hair, came forward, he burst into tears. 'Ah, Thomas,' was all he could manage to say, and Thomas caught his arm with one hand, and with the other pulled his hair gently, and then they all slipped away into the darkness, crackling their shoes on the gravel, their low conversation fading down the roadway amid the clanks of bicycles.

Thomas turned to Ellen, and said, exhaling, 'Des. I often think of him. He's the one I reared, really.'

They went in and sat down among the happy debris of their own wedding.

'A pity to have to close the doors such a fine night,' said Thomas, 'but the cats will get at the turkey. Or the ham.'

'Or the salmon,' said Ellen. 'We'd better put the milk in the pantry. What time are the women coming in to clear up?'

'Twelve. What in the name of God is that?' asked Thomas, pointing to an ungainly brown paper parcel with angles sticking out of it.

'Auntie Neenie's present,' said Ellen. 'Diamonds the way she was going on. Open it' – a set of five washboards, from tiny to large – 'for everything,' said Ellen, 'collars up to sheets. You can hang them up for me when we come back.'

'Look at this.' He held out to her a stiff brown envelope: she opened it and took out an old newspaper. 'Your mother gave it to me,' he said.

'Heavens above!' said Ellen. 'Well. You are privileged.'

It contained a newspaper advertisement from 1811 – the Notice of Sale of the farm by whose purchase the O'Kellys, May Morris's people, became rich.

They stood. Thomas said, 'You looked grand. All day.'

'The funny thing is,' Ellen said, as if thinking aloud, 'I'm not a bit tired. And I thought I'd be exhausted.'

8

Ellen inched her head towards him, to lay it beside Thomas's shoulder, gently touching, yet not waking him up. Sunlight slanting down at a tangent through the cream net curtains made patterns on the wall; dust danced in the beams of honey light above the dressing-table. Ellen stretched carefully, easing each leg. On the back of her neck she fingered a small line of soreness where the chain of the cross had cut into her skin when the beggar whipped it away outside the church; it had broken easily, and at the wedding the incident was a nine-hour wonder.

She touched the back of her teeth with her tongue. Her ears began to focus; Thomas's breathing; the birdsong, every trilling a separate and energetic sound; a calf 'mwaaah'-ing for, or at, its mother. She eased up on her elbows and began to look at Thomas. 'He has hairs on his chest!': his new pyjamas, blue stripes, a stubble, mouth slightly open, a hint of saliva, like a tiny tide-mark of foam; face peaceful, the black brows a fraction away from meeting; one tooth at the side slightly broken.

Ellen scanned the brightening room. On the mantelpiece stood a small photograph of a man in uniform. Uncle Eddie, he told her last night, died on the Somme, 'for the defence of small nations,' said Thomas with sarcasm. Two brass candlesticks held the white coiled remains of last year's candlegrease.

Ellen lay back again, slowly raised her arms in straight parallel lines above her head, studied the satin ribbon on the little puffed sleeve of her nightgown, looked at her hands side by side: a thin, thin gold ring.

'Marriage,' she whispered. Then, 'Married?'

Quiet as a mouse she sat up. In the side mirror of the dressing-table whose angled glass held the window in its reflection, she could see the branches of the sycamore, and in the distance the forecourt and gate of the Castle, lit brightly aslant by the morning sun.

'Married. Ellen married?' she said in the smallest of whispers.

She put a hand beneath her hair and lifted it out from the back of her neck and let it fall twice, three times, held her hands out again for inspection, turning her head to one side as if preparing to paint or draw. She dropped her chin, stiffened the back of her neck, raised her head and yawned with her mouth as closed as she could keep it; she leaned forward and stretched her hands down along her sheet-covered legs towards her ankles. On the marble-topped washstand not far from her face, inside a wide matching basin, stood a large white jug with blue flowers. The soap dish of the set nestled beneath the shoulder of the basin. Several towels hung from the mahogany rail beneath; she had folded them herself last night, in heavy layers, blue, and striped blue-and-red, and plain white: wedding gifts, all. Ellen stretched her legs and thighs, moving her stiff hips with pleased caution. Leaning forward she could see the small clock with the bright open face on Thomas's little bedside table, half-past five. She lay down again softly, but still woke Thomas, who half-smiled.

'Ahunhh.'

Ellen placed her face fully into the folded joint of his shoulder and arm.

'Good morning, Mrs,' said Thomas, sleepy and good-natured. 'And how are you this morning?'

In a series of large wiggles of her body, she moved closer, pushing her face up to the hollow of his neck and jaw.

'I was just wondering.' Thomas stopped and yawned. 'Heeaannh, I was just wondering. Who was this stranger in my bed?' He brought his right hand over and began to stroke her head and hair.

'Listen to the birds,' said Ellen. They lay for a moment, Thomas slowly waking up.

'God in Heaven, this room needs a coat of paint,' she remarked.

Thomas yawned, 'Aisle. Altar. Hymn.'

'You and your old jokes,' said Ellen. She rubbed her itchy nose on his arm with a 'nnnnn-hing' sound.

'Different altogether,' said Ellen, her finger twisting a vacant buttonhole on Thomas's pyjama-jacket.

'What's different?' he asked.

'Different skin, different muscle, different shape.'

Thomas yawned again, blinked his eyes as slowly as a frog several times, then did reverse blinks, opening the eyelids as far as he could. He eased his jaw away from Ellen's head, brought his other hand up behind her and began to stroke her shoulder.

'The pigeons,' said Ellen, 'listen to them. Listen.'

They lay in the bright room. The curtains began to blow a little as a morning breeze dropped by from somewhere, then subsided ever so quietly.

'Different what did you say?' asked Thomas through a yawn, pushing air from the sides of his lips. Ellen rolled the back of her head on to his hard forearm.

'You aren't awake yet, are you? I think – the shoulders. Different from women, from girls. Men's shapes. I taper. You're more. Rectangular.' She sat up, hanging her face down so that her hair fell forward. The hand with which she propped herself touched his and he closed his fingers over her.

'The raven's wing,' he said. 'Black is blue, isn't it? Your hair.' She lifted a hand high above her head, then placed it on the pillow.

'I'm always telling you. I have a flat nose. Like a boxer,' she said. 'And freckles.'

He lifted her hand and kissed it, throwing her slightly off balance. She looked down at him without turning her face fully.

'My legs are stiff,' she said. She began to whistle a little. 'Wasn't the dancing great?' She put her hands behind her and bounced her ankles on the bed beneath the single sheet.

'Is it the dancing made your legs stiff?' Thomas asked in a whisper, and with an expression of tender roguery. She looked at him quickly through the side of her hair, then looked away, then turned around sharply and pressed her head down on his chest, her arms reaching up to his shoulders.

'Thomas.' She moved her face from side to side, as if feeling his chest with each eyebrow. 'Thomas. I wish.' She raised her head, looked at him very seriously and put her head down again. 'I wish the word "tender" were longer and had more letters in it. And had more "n's" and more "r's" in it, and a few "l's". Soft letters. For a soft word.' She began to spell it. 'T.E.N.D.E.R.'

A small bird, robin or sparrow or something, landed briefly on the windowsill and fluttered away again quickly. Ellen's face lifted and dipped on the swell of Thomas's breathing.

'Ellie?' She grunted in response.

'Nothing,' said Thomas.

After a few more moments Ellen bounced out of the bed. She

went to the window, parted the net curtains and raised the lower sash to its fullest height. Leaning far out, she gazed all around her, at the sycamore, at the currant and gooseberry bushes in the garden, and the tall green-white pampas grass on the lawn, and the red-hot poker flowers, and the two apple trees. 'One sweet, one sour,' Thomas had said, 'like myself.' They had closed the gate last night, and a white glistening cobweb of dew had formed on the latch.

'Somebody left a bicycle.' The saddle had large shiny spots of bright black, from the dropping condensation on the leaves of the sycamore. 'There's Blackie.' The cat crossed lazily from one privet hedge to a corner growing sunnier as the light moved around. Ellen half-turned to Thomas, rubbing her arms.

'Are you getting up, or what?' He canted himself over to one side, and stretched, then put his feet on the rug.

'Come over here. You look like an Algerian girl in a painting,' he said. 'Come over here and sit down,' patting the bed. Without looking at him she backed across the room from the window.

'Yes, sir?' she said, in mocking obedience. He ran the back of a hand down the side of her face, caressing, then back up again, then traced the shape of her head.

'Yes,' he murmured. 'That's right. An Algerian girl.' She flounced off the bed and went to the door, saying back over her shoulder, 'If you knew I took size seven shoes would you have married me?' and continued to the room that Thomas said they should make into a bathroom if they ever got running water, a bare-floored room, where he had kept the chamber-pots and some spare kitchen chairs.

'I'm only putting on second-best clothes yet,' Thomas called after her. 'We're going for a walk.'

She answered, asking what time the train was?

'Not 'til twelve. We've nearly six hours. Are you hungry?'

She closed the spare room door behind her.

They agreed to just a slice of bread each, with butter, and honey from a new comb, and have full breakfast later. Standing in the kitchen, plates and bottles and glasses everywhere, she walked over to Thomas and put her head on his chest, then stepped back again. Then she dusted the white soda-bread crumbs and flour from her fingers and walked out into the small cobbled yard.

'I'm wearing no shoes,' Thomas said, following, 'it'll be a bit cold at first, but not for long.' Stepping gingerly on the gravel, he held the gate open for her. Ellen took her shoes off and left them on the wall.

'The Mathews had these stones mortared in here,' said Thomas, as she climbed, and rested on the wall, 'like the steps of a stile – so that they could get onto the road easily when they came down from the Castle for a walk.' Cautiously, she got down the other, steeper side, and stood on a little grassy mound waiting.

'When my father first visited this parish,' said Thomas, 'all these fields were filled with trees; there was a whole forest here, sloped down to that long hollow, see that –' he waved a hand – 'that was the Castle's ornamental lake.'

Ellen shaded her eyes with a hand and looked. They set off together, walking a little apart.

'I didn't sleep very well,' she said, 'but I'm not tired.' She took his hand briefly then let it go. 'Though I suppose with the journey ahead of us I should have stayed in bed a bit longer.'

Under the beech tree Thomas broke off a small branch and handed it to her, the leaves gleaming in the light.

'Here.' Ellen snatched it and deliberately bumped him with her shoulder, then swished the leaves like a fan. She looked up at the sky, and turned all around in a circle like a child playing dizzy.

'Look. Look! The moon.'

A faint, fading disc hung high to the west, soft, benign. Thomas began to sing in a low voice. 'Then awake 'til rise of sun, my dear. The sage's watch we shall shun, my dear. For in watching the flight. Of bodies of light. He might happen to take thee for one, my dear.'

Reaching the ditch that led into the big broad expanse of fields sloping up to the Castle, Thomas led Ellen to a sturdy hazel, showed her where a gap opened if she pushed the lower branches, and she scrambled through.

'Now that bush, d'you see it, up there?' – he pointed to a stunted dwarf tree standing all alone in the middle of the fields ahead of them. 'That's standing on what used to be the bank of the ornamental lake, and that bush never grew. Because the nurserymaid from the Castle let the only son and heir drown at that spot. The child was only two. She was out walking with him. And she let him wander away. They jailed her. And she put a curse on the place.

137

That it would only become a nesting-place for rooks and jackdaws. And that is exactly what it is.'

From the edge of the sunken fence, and then farther up, by the ramparts, they could see for miles in a circle, and he talked in his quiet deliberate voice, breaking up his sentences for emphasis, as he did habitually.

'That house off there. No – there.' He redirected her pointing arm. 'The man in that house. He was in the Crimea. A groom. Best man with a horse for miles. And the worst temper.'

Ellen's eyes picked up the flight of a small dipping bird from the point where it took off on a turreted gateway, and traced it down, down the fields, until it became lost against the foliage. Behind them, far away, the mountains in this light seemed as compact and precisely located as if placed there in a great toy – tidy foothills, orderly peaks. In the near distance, the light caught two farm-houses and a hilltop copse; much nearer, beside the Norman motte, stood the church in which they married yesterday, and far, far beyond that, Ellen could see, as Thomas promised she would, the spire of the cathedral in which she had been baptized, a full thirty-six miles away. Down on the big Castle pond, waterfowl screeched and flustered; Thomas said swans lived there, on a large high knot of earth with rushes in the middle; and migrant geese came.

'Oh, by the way,' he said suddenly. 'Val Vousden. He wrote. Do you know what he told me? And I forgot to tell you in all the excitement? He has traced most of the instruments of the old band. Their banner, everything. The uniforms, some of them are still all right, lovely, blue and gold jackets, the county colours. The blue of the sky, the gold of the corn.'

Ellen looked at Thomas as he talked quietly on. She had developed a way of standing dutifully while listening, hands held simply behind her back. If sitting down, she nested her hands in her lap, or rested them folded on the table or desk in front of her. In this pose, she had the capacity to listen for a long, concentrated period, and she tried diligently not to interrupt, even when questions coursed through her mind. She told Thomas frequently how much she liked hearing his stories. Now, when he finished telling about the band, and the number of members it once had, and a meeting he might hold to try and have it revived, she moved away a little and looked at him.

'Thomas Kane, I am going to do something especially nice for you one day soon. No. Don't ask me what it is. I'll think.' She looked away. 'Perhaps . . . perhaps I will plant a greengage bush for you and make you some greengage jam? But you mightn't like greengage jam, of course.' She looked at the Castle walls. 'Ooh, Thomas, look, that face, what is it?'

She pointed to a scowling, bearded head carved in white limestone above where the door had been.

'That, Mrs Kane – how d'you like being called Mrs Kane? – is a riverine god. It is the head that represents the spirit who lives in the river Nore. There's one for every river, but the stonemason who did that one, it was supposed to be a different river, he only knew the Nore.' He strode on. 'If it's greengages you're after, here, come on.'

She followed, watching her feet make footprints in the dew. 'It looks Greek, that head,' she said. 'Like Zeus or one of those, Poseidon, or the one always changing, that one. Proteus.' Then, 'Good God above! I never said my prayers, last night or this morning. I'll have to say them later. Isn't God very good to us, this weather?' She chattered on like this from time to time, a detail in her that Thomas loved: soon, he would particularly come to enjoy standing quietly outside the door in their house before he entered a room, eavesdropping on his young wife talking to herself.

They emerged under the arch of the tower gateway, the east entrance to the Castle, and turned down the Bell Walk towards the wood. Nobody in the world had yet awakened; they might have seen foxes or badgers, so early had they risen. Not even the cattleboy from the farm, nor one of the farmer's many daughters, had yet come to call the animals in for milking, and the cows grazed in the fields away down near the main road, placid brown-and-white miniatures. Ellen ran in across the old terraced, formal Viennese gardens with their repeating circles of tall, pointed box trees set on gravel beds. She skipped from tree to tree, disappearing from Thomas's view, reappearing, smiling, waving, squinting one eye closed against the sunlight as in her later photographs. He leaned against the crumbling parapet, arms folded, watching, pleased with her. She slowed her cavorting, then walked in procession along an aisle of the trees, bowing to him as she approached, and they grinned at each other, then covertly eyed. So began their marriage, governed by reticence in the face of intimacy, obligation at the head of their community, filled from the beginning with the decorum of their religion: the transactions of the night would never be talked about, never discussed, and if hinted at by either, would be greeted with oblique humour, or embarrassment, by the other.

Distance had softened the village's dinginess, and restored some of its old calendar prettiness in the early light. The yellow ochre, the leaded panes, the pointed gables gleamed.

'They diverted this stream, you know,' Thomas said, as Ellen splashed her feet, stretching her toes in the thin friendly mud and the watercress. 'It used to come in over there, just under that bank, but they changed the direction of it so that it could flow over a course of stones in here, behind that wall. And the Castle kitchen servants used the stones' – he cupped a hollow with his hands – 'as a little flat, square box in which they kept the milk fresh in the summer. Now. There you are. There's all the greengages you could want, Ellie. They're wild, now, of course, but they were properly cultivated. I suppose those are over a hundred years old.'

Ellen went forward, with Thomas watching her. He looked at her legs, and her shoulders, and her behind; he stood with his legs apart.

'*Espalier* plums, Thomas, look. Pears. A red-currant bush. This place is a bower.'

Thomas sat down on a broken stretch of the brick wall, and Ellen picked her barefoot way over grass-covered stones and masonry. She peered at each new discovery, making pleased sounds, ran her hands around the shape of a small and pretty window. 'This must have been a pantry or something,' she called out. Then, head down, concentrating on placing her feet carefully in the brick-strewn long grass, she made her way back to him, looking up with a dazzling smile just as she reached him. He held out both hands for her to grip and hauled her up near him, kissing her hair as she drew level.

'Do you know what I have at home?' he said. 'I have the original planting-map, and the drawings, of this kitchen garden. I'll show it to you.'

'At home,' she said, immensely happy. She let him kiss her on the mouth. Climbing down from the bricks, she stumbled on ahead. Back in the fields, and heading diagonally towards their house which had never been out of their sight, she said, 'Thomas?' paused, resumed, 'Are we blessed or something?'

He said nothing, walked beside her as she swung her arms, and they reached the two white, overgrown posts that marked the entrance to the old avenue. When he helped her over the wall and then down onto the road, her skirt caught on the wall and revealed a thigh, and he looked away.

'Yes, you're right,' he said, 'blessed.'

Inside the door he caught her arm, and began to say, 'I think . . .'

She hunched her shoulders and leaned towards him, making shushing sounds, and then followed him as he walked ahead of her, through the kitchen.

9

Ellen looked out of the window towards the distant Castle, on whose terraced slopes the white paths of the gardens intersected in broad-ribboned cross-hatchings; black specks, crows, sat on the tattered dovecote. Her breast touched the windowpane. She wore a skirt, and had draped a towel around her shoulders.

Thomas sat up and said, 'I'd better shave,' then stood. 'Look – new razor, in honour of you,' and held the blade up, swishing it, a small rectangular scimitar shining in the light. 'I'll go and get fresh water,' and as he went she shivered in the sudden cold air coming through the door, and quickly, before Thomas returned, put on a bodice. She continued to hang clothing in the wardrobe, fetching things from suitcases they had left in one of the empty rooms.

When she had fully dressed, he, wiping his razor, observed that she looked different in the mirror, that he had never noticed it before. He stood behind her as she straightened her waistband before the long glass in the wardrobe door. The back of her head came up to the middle of his chest. He kissed the crown of her hair, and placed his fingers where he had kissed her. Then, with her wide eyes watching their reflections in the mirror, from behind her he ran his hands slowly all over her, touching first her hair, neck, ears, eyebrows, and mouth; his fingers stroked her throat, shoulders, armpits, lifting her arms a little to do so; the large hands roamed slowly over her breasts, down lazily to the rib-cage, hips, then stomach, down through the valley of her pelvis into her thighs; and kneeling, he touched her shins, her ankles, caressed her feet over and over. She turned around to face him as he stood, and kissed his chest.

'Thomas, I want to talk about this.'

'Yes?'

'To make sure. Of . . . That there isn't anything wrong in any of it.'

'We're married.'

'Yes. That is true. That is true.'

He stroked her hair, then ran his thumb along the side of her breast by her upper arm, then with his fingernails softly raked her side from armpit to hip.

She said, 'But we could. We could be more, more – enlightened, about it, and all of it, and that. Know more.'

She had once asked the question in the Training College in biology classes, why women were not given more information about their bodies?

'Because there is none,' the embarrassed doctor had said.

'None?' asked Ellen. 'None at all. You mean, none in England, or in France, or America?'

'We're not in England or in France or in America,' she was told. 'We are in Ireland. This is a Catholic country, and these things are not discussed.'

'But why not? They're our bodies,' she persisted.

'You had better take that up with Mother Agatha,' the doctor said, a decent enough man, middle-aged and with a large family of his own.

She did take it up with Mother Agatha, or rather Mother Agatha took it up with her. The conversation only led into the usual *cul-de-sac* of authority, which always happened when Ellen tried to create some innovations, such as dramatizing history, or discussing feelings.

'That is not the way this College is run,' she was firmly told.

Thomas asked her hesitantly, 'Have you ever talked to anybody about it?' He took the towel from over his shoulder and rubbed his face and neck.

'No.'

'Not even Leah?'

'Not yet.'

'And how did you know . . .' He tailed off.

'There was a book they gave us in Teacher Training, written by a priest. It had diagrams.' Then, taking his hand, she asked, 'Have you ever talked to anybody about it?'

He answered evasively. 'Men talk. A coarse sort of way.' He did not elaborate – on the fact that men in the country, on the farms, workmen and the like, discussed women in crude terms as 'mares', good for 'a ride'; or in terms of dogs and bitches; or bragged of what they wanted to do to local flighty girls in terms of 'bulling' them.

He said, 'We should get going. Arthur will be here soon.'

He hummed a tune, then looked out of the window.

'I have all kinds of good ideas in my head,' Thomas said half to himself, and pulled on his new waistcoat.

Arthur came cycling in through the front gate.

'Hallo, Mr and Mrs Kane!' he called upwards. Thomas and Ellen both put their heads out of the window.

'Where's the car? 'Tis going to be a very hot day again.'

'In the garage,' said Thomas, 'but we'll have to push it out, there's no room to turn the starting-handle, I left it too close to the wall. Hold on, I'm on my way down.'

'The two of you look like a framed picture up there,' called out Arthur. They laughed and withdrew.

The train, almost empty, passed through the woods where Thomas's grandfather had lived, and he pointed out to Ellen the thatched roof of the family house, barely visible through a swoop in the trees. Somebody walked past the First Class compartment, stopped in the corridor beyond their door, walked back again, stopped on the other side, and passed the door a third time. Gazing out of the opposite window at the sunny morning, neither of the newly-weds paid attention. A sharp rap on the glass made them jump, and the compartment door opened. A woman stood there, in a white dress that had gathered smuts from the engine and the flying steam. She held a straw hat in her hand.

'Oh,' said Ellen recognizing her.

'I just came in to wish you all the best,' said the woman. 'You were married yesterday, weren't you?'

'Oh, hallo,' said Thomas.

'And you had a great wedding, we could hear the music, we nearly joined in.'

'You'd have been very welcome,' said Ellen in stout hospitality.

'But we'd have had to bring you a present,' said the woman. 'How and ever, here I am now, and I suppose you're off on the honeymoon.'

'You're Mrs Doctor Hogan, aren't you?' asked Thomas.

'Miriam's the name. After Moses's sister. Watch me,' said the woman, who spoke in little tunes. She put her hat on the empty seat, opened the compartment door wider so that they could see her and, singing loudly, waltzed up and down the corridor, her arms held out in a meeting curve as if dancing with a partner.

'Oh, the days of the Kerry dances,
Oh, the ring of the piper's tunes.
Oh, for one of those hours of gladness,
Gone, alas, like our youth – too soon.
When the boys began to gather
In the glen of a Summer's night.'

She stopped and bowed. Picking up her hat she lilted airily, 'People should dance for other people's weddings. I'm off now.' She closed the door and they heard her lurching back along the corridor.

Thomas and Ellen looked at each other and laughed.

'Was she drunk or what?' asked Ellen.

Thomas said, 'Did you know whether she had the words right?' – and Ellen thumped him, and they laughed again.

'Well. We heard she was a bit odd,' said Thomas.

They saw Miriam Hogan again at Kingsbridge, hauling a suitcase to a porter and asking him to lift it, then arguing with him when he refused, fanning him threateningly with her hat.

At the Mail Boat quayside, a difficulty arose. Although Thomas had booked and paid for a full cabin, the boat in service had no berths. Thomas could not improve the situation, and he began to rage. Ellen took his arm.

'Thomas. This is a lovely night. We can wrap ourselves up warm and sit out on the deck.'

'That's not the point, Ellen.' He jerked his arm away. 'That's not the point. We booked and paid for . . .'

'But they're giving you a refund.'

'I don't want a fucking refund.' He stopped suddenly. 'I apologize, I swore to myself I'd never swear in front of you.'

'It's all right. It's all right. Come on, it's all a strain, a wedding is.'

She calmed him, led him aboard: Thomas fidgeted in guilt. When the boat had cleared the intricate harbour, a sailor brought them tea and biscuits on a tray, and offered them a drink which they both declined. They went out on deck, and still holding the teacups, stood at the rail. The night beamed on them, a starry sky with a white moon rising.

'We're like the pictures of romance in the magazines and on the book covers,' she said.

They walked a little, then leaned over the rail watching the rush of the water by the dark keel. Sitting in the stern's lee, they looked backwards at the receding lights, and then up at the sky.

'God!' muttered Thomas. 'Look.' At the far end of the deck, Miriam Hogan walked up and down with a sense of drama, a cardigan thrown across her shoulders. Upon disembarkation, she also boarded the smoky, jerky London train.

In the hotel, Thomas looked at everything; inspected the light switch, the brass taps on the bath, the ceramic waste-pipe hood; the curtain-pulls; the lights. To Ellen's confusion of embarrassment and delight – although she made no remark – he wandered in and out of the bathroom while she bathed, and talked to her easily, even though he seemed to avoid looking at her.

In the tall bedroom, she said to him, and in a moment regretted it, 'You scratch yourself a lot?'

'Yes-I-do' – in a short tone.

In the next ten days, he seemed to Ellen to have brought a lot of money; he kept it in an inside pocket the flap of which he secured with a safety pin. She said, 'Thomas, aren't you spending a lot of money on me?'

'No matter. I'm a very prudent man.'

Sitting in the hotel dining-room, he turned back the tablecloth and looked at the wood beneath.

'Mahogany, I'd say. Not white deal, anyway.'

'Prudent? Lovely word. Yes, you are, Thomas, you are prudent.'

'We ate no meat in our house for several years, except at Christmas; my mother's widow's pension was one shilling and sixpence a week, and a houseful of us.'

Ellen said, 'When you tell me something like that, it dawns on me that I don't know you at all yet.'

He grinned. 'Plenty of time now. Look.' He pointed out to her a man sitting alone reading a newspaper. 'The thing he's picking his teeth with. I'd swear it is made of silver.'

=

146

In Selfridge's he bought her a 'gown', as the saleswoman said, a good grey dress; and another for wearing at school, so that as he looked at her through the glass partition he would be reminded of their honeymoon. Back at the hotel, she asked, 'Thomas, do you feel very proud of doing all of this?'

'Proud?'

'Well, you know, coming from where we do, and here we are like big people.'

He said in a quiet voice, 'We are big people. We are ordinary human beings like everybody else. That's big people.'

Unhooking garments, she asked, 'Will you ever tell me? I mean one day, about – the things you were involved in?'

He generated silence in the room by standing still.

Ellen said, 'Nothing. Sorry.'

The days followed in heat and movement. A train to Bath, to see the Roman Springs. To St Paul's Cathedral. To the British Museum. To Kensington Gardens.

'Did you know,' said Ellen, 'that Queen Victoria had a plaster cast made of Prince Albert's hand? At her dying request it was placed in her coffin.'

In Oxford Street, she bought a straw hat with a maroon ribbon: 'The money Dada gave me,' she said.

One afternoon, after they had lain in bed late, he said, 'We are going for a long walk and a surprise.'

She saw him ask directions from the hotel porter, note them down carefully on an envelope, and they set off. They crossed a bridge going south, and entered a neighbourhood of small streets and burly warehouses. The children looked at them and shouted things, and Thomas and Ellen smiled, agreeing that in their hats and finery they must have looked unusual. Soon they came to a row dominated by huge tanks, and Thomas, checking his notebook, said, 'Down here.' As they stopped outside a funny little, long, two-storey building, he said, 'This is where we get your housekeeping ledger,' and grinned at her.

At the sliding glass panel he asked the girl, 'Mr Alton, please?'

'Who wants him?'

'I do.'

'No, I mean the name' – she pronounced it 'nime'.

'Mr Thomas Kane. I wrote to him.'

'Aren't you the dark horse?' whispered Ellen.

He replied, 'You said you wanted one.'

'But I thought you forgot.'

At the end of a room with long, long tables, where men measured card, and glued book bindings together, Mr Alton, ageing and ingratiating, showed them a variety of ledgers: the very large, with many columns for cash entries; or the more compact, cash-book type. Ellen looked and looked, at over twenty in all.

'What kind of business are you in?' Mr Alton asked.

'Teaching,' said Thomas.

Finally she chose a large book, measuring twenty inches by twelve – 'like the school Roll Book' – with a mauve cover staked out by red, deep corners, like large photograph angles. Inside, past the lavishly marbled endpapers, the pages, though ruled in part into little boxes and squares, also had enough lines to write upon. She needed a book she could organize in a way that permitted her to paste in recipes, cuttings and any other items on the box-ruled sections, while leaving room to write the captions, such as the date of the newspaper from which it came, or any other observations. She hefted the book in her hand, measured it side to side, end to end, spread the covers out as if writing in the early pages, then the middle pages, then the end pages. Mr Alton admired her rigorousness, and proudly pointed out to her how the spine, their own development, their own invention, had been deliberately made flexible so that a user would not have to wrestle with the pages; with most such ledgers, he informed them, comfort in writing only came as one drew close to the centre of the book, but in this case comfort was 'assured the whole way through'.

Next, Ellen sat with the ledger, as she might if writing in it, to ascertain that the top of each page came within her easy reach, that she would not have to stand up, for example, when writing at the beginning of every page, and then she judged the distance between the bottom of the page and the bottom of the book itself, so that her hand would not have an awkward struggle when writing on the very bottom line. Then she gauged how it would be writing overleaf, assessing that the paper proved thick enough not to allow even a heavy hand's ink to show through.

'Almost vellum, almost vellum,' Mr Alton kept repeating. 'Three hundred and sixty pages.'

She decided to take it but worried immediately about the weight of it, but, Mr Alton said, 'for another shilling' it could be sent by Royal Mail. Then Thomas and Ellen had a discussion as to who should pay for it; Ellen felt strongly that she should, and Thomas, although he had established that he had wanted to make her a gift of it, gave way. She paid Mr Alton in cash, waited for a receipt and, thanking him, they left.

They crossed the river again, and by now the afternoon had grown very hot. Thomas asked Ellen to wait for him outside a public lavatory on a busy street. She took off her hat and began to fan her face with it. A small-ish man unstretched himself from railings where he had been leaning and, unnoticed by Ellen, walked towards her. She only saw him when he first stood in front of her, and she strained politely to hear what he was saying, could not quite catch the words.

'Are you on, love?' he repeated.

'On?' she asked.

'Come on, love,' and he reached out and touched her arm and then squeezed. Ellen, baffled, looked down at the hand, then drew back a little. He reached out again, and only then did she say, 'Stop, stop,' and somewhat comically began to swat at his hand.

'Come on, love, stop pretending,' the man protested.

'Pretending what?'

'Come on, come on.' He cajoled, but in a tone which grew more determined. Stepping beside her he attempted to put an arm around her shoulders, while grabbing her left hand.

Bewildered, Ellen said, 'What do you want?'

'Well, what do you think?'

A heavy woman approached, a puffy face rouged.

'Hoy,' she called. 'Who's she?' The man tightened his arm on Ellen's shoulders, and began to try and walk her forward. Ellen resisted.

Thomas appeared at the top of the steps under the blue 'Gentlemen' sign, looking around pleasantly for Ellen. He stopped, puzzled, then pressed forward and grabbed the man by the shoulder. The man shouted, released Ellen and struck out at Thomas, partially connecting. Thomas tried to lift the man off the ground, and the shouting intensified, with Ellen joining in and Thomas shouting abuse. Thomas tried to slam the man's face into the high railings around the lavatory stairwell. People walking by stopped, and stood back. The man wriggled out of Thomas's grasp and began to run. Thomas ran after him but stopped when he heard Ellen calling. The puffy woman drifted away.

Another woman, seeing Ellen's shock, had stopped to sympathize. Thomas came back. 'Are you all right?'

'Yes, yes.'

'She shouldn't have been standing here,' a man said to Thomas. 'This is a beat.'

'Why not? What's a beat?' Ellen and Thomas asked in bewilderment.

'Where are you from?' asked the sympathetic woman.

'Ireland, we're on our honeymoon,' said Ellen.

The man said quietly to Thomas, 'This is a beat. You know, tarts.'

'Prostitutes?'

'You got it.'

'Oh, God,' said Thomas, looking shocked. He stopped a cab. At the hotel, Ellen sat on the bed, clinging to the brass rail, her face buried in her forearms, beneath her drifts of hair. She rose and filled the bath. He sat alone in the bedroom, and she emerged silently. After some slow pottering, she asked, 'But I don't look like one of – "them", do I?'

'How do you know what "they" look like?' his voice grey.

'We used to see them on Dickson's quay when a new ship came in. Tight skirts and bosoms.'

'This place,' he said, not unbitterly. 'How can people live here?'

'I thought you were going to kill him,' she said.

'I would have done.'

'I was frightened –' she began, but whether at being accosted, or at Thomas's response she did not specify.

Ellen stretched cautiously on the bed, wrapped in towels and a dressing-gown, and Thomas, still fully dressed, lay beside her; they confessed to feeling shocked, and drifted off into a sleep, a knight and his lady lying side by side on their naïve slab.

At dinner in the hotel dining-room that evening, Ellen, more forthright by then, told Thomas that she was 'really frightened' when she saw him picking up the man who had accosted her, and he said it was no more than his husbandly duty.

'Do you remember before we were married –?' They had returned for a last walk to Kensington Gardens.

'Those are nice words,' he interrupted.

'Aren't they? Do you remember before we were married –' with a wide smile '– we said. You said, I could ask you any question.'

'Yes?'

She had begun to emphasize, an indication that she found a subject uncomfortable. 'We said that we could talk about – being married.'

'Yes.' This time he did not look away.

'Did you ever hear of a woman called Marie Stopes?'

'No.'

'She's a woman in her mid-forties, she's a sort of doctor, interested in women and marriage.'

'And?'

'Well, she has a place here in London where people can get advice about marriage.'

'Advice?'

'Advice about, you know, what we've been doing.'

'Advice?' Again, Thomas shifted.

'No. I mean deeper information, knowledge, babies, so on. I know nothing about all that.'

'How do other women manage?'

'I suppose they talk to their friends and sisters or whatever. But I want to find out more. About myself. About you.'

'But what more is there to find out? Don't we know enough? Do you want to go and see this woman?' he asked apprehensively.

'No. Not really. But I thought we might get one or two of her books. She wrote a book called *Married Love*, we could get that. There's another thing.' Ellen blushed and brought it out in a rush. 'My father and Jim, they wear cotton pants beneath their trousers.'

Thomas also blushed.

They bought postcards in the bookshop too, and to Leah Ellen wrote, 'Weather and hotel and everything lovely. Hope you enjoyed the wedding. See you soon.'

Thomas remarked that the postcards would probably travel on the same mail train and boat they were taking home. In the street they opened *Married Love*, glanced at one or two of the pages, and then put it in Ellen's handbag. As they began to walk, a photographer persuaded them to stop, and Thomas paid him to send on the photograph.

10

'I'll tell you one thing,' Ellen said.
   'What's that?'
   'I don't feel the need to go to Confession at all. Even though I know we're all supposed to. But I've nothing to tell.'
   'Same here.'

From the date of the end of their honeymoon, they had seven weeks of settling down before school reopened in September.
   In tiny Deanstown, with its farmhouses, cottages, the school, a public house, a pump and a village green, the grass still grows voluptuously in the summer, and still, as Thomas once upon a time repeated so fondly, in a shade closer to blue than green.
   When Thomas Kane and his wife Ellen, née Morris, settled down there in the first weeks of July 1925, the population was larger than today. Most of the gabled, yellow-ochre cottages have long fallen into disrepair; Hand's pub closed a long time ago; the long demesne wall has been breached many times by the fences of new farm owners; several ornamental gateways here and there throughout the locality, those beautiful, hand-cut limestone pillars, have simply keeled over into the grass.
   The drays of the farmers no longer rumble through Deanstown every morning with aluminium churns bound for the creamery two miles away in Silverbridge on the river: lorries, from farther away, collect the bright sweet milk. Six miles to the west, the town of Mooreville then provided all of the Kanes' immediate needs: groceries, stationery, some books, a selection of clothing: it still could. That summer, the helmeted pump plunged out cool, lead-dark water which Thomas fetched at least twice daily, a bucket lugged gently spilling at the end of each arm. The distant mountains, as ever did, gave them their weather forecast.

For a while nothing touched their charmed lives. Their bodies moved in the warm space around their house and garden, in their busy marrying of each other, in their sweating, thoughtful beginnings of mutual understanding. Their fingers and thumbs and lips found new muscles, a new language; in each of the partners, new people came to dwell, unquestioning, and free. That summer the weather proved extraordinary, as if it intended to heat up the air in anticipation, or warning, or premonition. Not more than five years ago, Thomas had hidden in these fields, lain in these hedgerows, his peaked cap turned backwards, a gun in each hand, waiting to kill. Now, in the tremendous silence of a different urgency, his hips and his back ached similarly – as did those of his new wife. With a not dissimilar savagery, he surged towards her bringing her life, as he had lunged towards others bearing them death.

Yesterday (reported *The Leader*) was so far the hottest day in the county since the heat wave began. The mean temperature was 106 degrees, but at 2.55 it reached 112 degrees in a confined area. The temperature at 1.15 today was 102 degrees in the sun. Barometric and other indications, we are informed by an authority on the subject, point to a continuance of the present fine weather.

Ellen cut out the report, and pasted it into her ledger, the first record of their married life. Thomas, tapping the glass at midnight, marvelled at the temperatures. Ellen, wearing a light nightdress of lawn cotton, bought in London, could not sleep. Over and over again, they drenched themselves in perspiration wordlessly, and then achieved brief, deep sleep before the morning light and the birds awakened them. Each came to know something of the rhythms of the other's body, whether the other lay awake or had fallen asleep. If Ellen awoke first, she lay perfectly still, or tried to look down at his face. If Thomas had been awake, he turned to her as she stirred; after his own sleep, he reached for her the moment he opened his eyes. The summer had rendered the nights bright, and some light always hung in the room. Profound stillness could be heard through the wide open windows; inside, the walls and timbers ticked, contracting after the expansion of the day.

When they met around the house or the garden, they always touched. She wore the minimum of clothing beneath the lightest of dresses; he stripped to the waist and wore cotton trousers and plimsolls, and they kept the gate closed to discourage visitors.

Sometimes through the day, she went upstairs, undressed and sponged her legs and torso with a cold flannel. One afternoon, when she sat with her ledger beginning to shape its future, Thomas came and sat opposite her. She smiled up at him and pasted in the cutting from *The Irish Independent* very carefully, using a paste of flour and water mixed in a large egg-cup.

HINTS THAT HELP

Rub new boots with a slice of new potato, and they will then polish as easily as old ones.

When stewing meat be careful not to put in too much liquid.

Tablecloths and shirts should be taken off the line before they are quite dry, folded smoothly, and laid on one side to be ironed the next day.

An excellent aluminium polish is a mixture of borax, ammonia and water. Apply with a soft brush.

If, instead of a hard carpet-brush, a damp cloth is used to clean the stair carpet, the nap will not come off and it will wear twice as long.

Do not put away for any length of time linen that has been starched. It is apt to crack. Rinse the articles free from starch, dry, and fold in blue paper. The latter keeps them from turning yellow.

Every time she could, Ellen went and stood near Thomas. Through the window she often watched his bare back bent working in the garden.

Thomas smiled at her all the time. He looked down on her face, called her 'wife' in a teasing way, stroked her hair, held her hand if they sat out in the evening, on the bench in front of the bow window. He looked like a man who had just encountered great fortune; he indulged her, and when she did ask the occasional awkward question, like querying his violence towards the porter on the mailboat when they had no cabin reservation, or raised again the immense force he had threatened towards the man who had accosted Ellen on the street in London, Thomas smiled and said, 'Another time,' or 'Eh-yeh,' and went on stroking the back of

154

her hand, or twisting her wedding ring softly round and round: she never returned to the MacReady affair, and he ever evaded her inquiries regarding the missing McAuliffe man.

Their intimacy, now flying high in all its sensations and urgency, became to both a business of assumption, rather than spoken agreement, and developed into a matter of great, silent importance. Only once did Ellen ask anxiously, 'Thomas, is this all right, is it all right for us to be like this?'

He replied with a smiling question, 'Married love?'

The process of Ellen's joining the local community now began in earnest. Numerous invitations came: tea on Sunday afternoons; to join in farmers' wives' guilds; the Canon asked her would she play the harmonium in the church? Where previously she had respected Thomas's exalted place in the community, now she relished it as part of her own life; she took pleasure in the parish deference now embracing her.

The Stephensons held their garden party – a hundred people on the lawn in front of the paddock. Thomas and Ellen walked there, up the long shaded avenue, past the woods Captain Johnson had planted years ago. Ellen wore a notable red dress.

'I'd love to see the inside of the house,' she murmured as they drew near. A table held bottles and jugs and tea-cups and saucers. Old wicker chairs reposed under trees, and a croquet mallet. The tablecloth flapped a little in the breeze. Nobody came to host them, or take them around. They greeted a farmer they knew, who stood on the edge of the crowd awkwardly, and with him, holding cups of tea Ellen had fetched, they drew back a little.

'That's the brother.' Thomas pointed out a large, heavy slow man, in his late twenties, wearing a thick tweed check jacket.

'He'll roast in that coat today,' observed Ellen.

'You'd need a magnifying glass to see the sandwiches,' said the farmer standing with them, and abruptly left.

Thomas and Ellen stood under a wide spreading tree.

'Who is that in the warlike yellow?' asked Ellen. 'Oh, that's, that's . . .' She struggled to recall the name.

'The daughter,' said Thomas, 'Ernestina.'

'How in the name of immortal God,' said Ellen, 'could she let herself go out of the house in that dangerous colour of a frock?'

'And,' said Thomas, 'she's no oil painting at the best of times.'

They gazed, absorbed. Most people there had passed the age of fifty, and had dressed as if for winter; a few women wore light skirts and blouses or thin coats, but many wore tweed skirts and tried not to perspire. Their heads bobbed as they listened closely to each other and they never stared at anyone else; they wore old brooches.

A tall, thin man, with a stoop, came to where they were standing.

'Now who's this pretty girl, I thought to myself?'

Ellen shook hands.

'I'm Henry Wallace, I'm the uncle you will have heard about. The Indian one.'

'You're not an Indian, are you?' Ellen asked, much less shy than Thomas.

'No, no.' The man laughed. 'I lived there. Bombay. My sister married in here. Dead now, I'm afraid. What are your names?'

Ellen replied, 'Mr and Mrs Kane.'

Thomas added, 'Only just.'

'I'm Ellen. He's Thomas.'

Henry Wallace said, 'Thomas Kane. Kane. Oh, I say. I know who you are. You're quite famous. Although I s'pose I shouldn't be saying that here.' He giggled, and indicated the party over his shoulder.

Ellen saw Ernestina advance to a few yards behind Henry Wallace, look very hard, intercept a passing woman by the arm, indicate Henry Wallace, and say something. The woman stopped to look, shading her eyes against the sun, then murmured to Ernestina, who waved a hand strongly, as if shooing her forward.

Henry Wallace said friendlily, 'I always wanted to meet you, Kane. You were a great gunman, weren't you?'

Ellen winced. 'Oh, Mr Willis, I don't think . . .'

Thomas looked down at the cup and saucer in his hand, and shook his head a little.

'Wallace, it is. I think I've said the wrong thing,' said Henry Wallace. 'Haven't I? And I think I've got it wrong right through, haven't I? Oh, dear. Look. I mean it. I am genuinely interested in what you fellows did. I always felt we got it wrong our end. I used to be a soldier, just like you.'

This seemed to surprise, and even mollify, Thomas.

'I say. Would you like to talk about it some time? I'd love to hear how it was all planned.' Henry Wallace leaned forward in a kind and eager way.

The woman to whom Ernestina had spoken materialized in their group. Smiling tightly at Thomas and Ellen, she said, 'Henry, Ernestina needs your help.' She obliged him to wade off.

'Well, that was a bit of a surprise,' said Ellen.

'I normally hate those fellows,' said Thomas.

They drifted a little, had a conversation or two with people of similar unease. One man, a veterinary surgeon with a moustache, said, 'Of course we're a Republic now, we have the Catholics here as guests. And the Sinn Feiners. You can't beat that for fairness, can you?'

Ellen tugged Thomas's arm. 'He said it to rise you. Take no notice.'

Thomas leaned towards the man. 'It seems we had too few bullets,' he said with a smile.

'Oh, now!' said another man in outrage. 'Oh, now! Really!'

An anxious man chimed in, 'We all have to get on now, don't we?'

They saw the Canon, and, under the mulberry tree, Miriam Hogan: she waved a hand at them and munched on a pie or something. When they made a move towards her she turned her back.

'God, she's odd,' said Thomas, 'look, she's talking to no one. And eating everything she can get her hands on.'

Ellen said, 'She's very handsome, though.'

The Canon came over to them and said in a loud voice, 'Haven't the Protestants very dry old faces? And 'tis no wonder they're thin, did you see the size of the sandwiches at all? And the tea. Holy Mother of God! Like water. You could baptize a child in it.'

Thomas and Ellen left, walking down the drive under the trees.

'That crowd,' said Thomas. 'Whatever they have they took from us.'

'But that was all long ago,' appeased Ellen, 'and we have most of it back now. And at least they're educated.'

'But we're not, I mean, the people around here.'

'They will be,' soothed Ellen.

'I doubt it,' said Thomas.

They turned back for a last look: Henry Wallace waved a farewell.

=

Ellen and Thomas went to Mass every Sunday morning in the car, the hood down in this glorious weather. Their arrival always seemed an important moment, and for the first few weeks people came across to introduce themselves, and congratulate the Master on his good fortune, and then add a word to Ellen about how it was 'high time a good man like that got himself a decent wife'.

By tacit understanding their pew, halfway down the aisle, was reserved for them alone. The Master and his wife led the movement to the altar for Communion, and their joint demeanour, dictated by Thomas, set the standard for outward expressions of devoutness among the rest of the congregation.

They dressed for Mass with great care, Thomas in a dark or a grey suit, Ellen in grey or navy, always with hats: he removed his in the porch, she affirmed hers in place with a long and powerful hatpin. They sat erect during the sermon; the Curate short and sweet, or the Canon, rambling and interminable.

Mass-going brought Ellen information and advice. She wanted hens, chickens, pecking beneath the apple trees. Wives outside the church door on Sunday gave her cuttings from the papers, the long weekly lists of providers, some of which Ellen had already clipped. In Herbertstown, Grouselodge and Ballingarry she could buy Rhode Island Reds, White Leghorns or White Wyandottes, as well as Indian Runner ducks; in Killeglass and Broadford and Doon she learned she would find Brown Leghorns, some geese and what seemed like a larger, more vigorous strain of Rhode Island Reds; she pasted these and related matters in her ledger.

CHICKENS! FOWL! YOUNG TURKEYS!
Thousands cured of Gape or Pip by the famous 'Pipuline' Dusting Powder 1/3d, postage 9d extra. H. Bell, Ltd, 62, Quay, Waterford. For discoloured heads, drooping, etc., use Bell's Liver Tonic Powder; a great cure, 2/6d; smaller size, 1/6d. Postage 9d.

'I have to have a messenger,' said Ellen to Thomas. 'I'm going to catch the first schoolboy I see at Mass.'

Outside the church porch she asked Michael Quinn, 'Will you come and do some jobs for me?'

'I'm left school, Ma'am.'

'I know that, but the Master says you can run quickly.'

'All right, Ma'am.'

'Drop down today after dinner.'

'All right, Ma'am.' She neglected to tell Thomas.

The Misses Harper befriended Ellen, sent her little notes from the large grey Georgian house, The Rectory; their late father while still the Protestant minister had bought it outright from the Church of Ireland. The spire of his church stood down by the river in Silverbridge, among trees populated with rooks. They called their boxer dog Marcus, and they spoke with pronounced English accents. Called Georgina and Judith, they cooed over Ellen.

'You look as if you just arrived off the boat from Dresden.'

'You are a china doll, dear Mrs Kane, of great value, great value.'

Recipes, preserves, flower arranging tips, crochet patterns – they offered all of these with enthusiasm and courtesy, with flourishing delicacy and charm. On various Saturdays, Ellen learned how to transplant the corms of flowers; how 'difficult' dahlias could be; how to prune a rose bush; how to make damson jelly; why to split the end of a beech twig before putting it into water: 'The leaves stay fresh longer.'

When she walked to their house, they strolled, sometimes arm-in-arm, to meet her – letters had, of course, been exchanged – and the meeting on the tree-hung road was a model of good manners and some incongruity, the little bright-eyed, refined, fulfilled, pretty teacher, and the two tweed-skirted spinsters, one with tinted spectacles and the other with a permanent straw hat. Georgina told harmless jokes, such as the one about the man who remarried somewhat hastily after his wife died, and justified it by saying, 'The light of my life has gone out – but I have struck another match.' The Harpers had a brother who never appeared in public, said to be 'a little delicate', and whom neighbours had come across on many mornings early, sitting stark naked in the reeds by the river, playing a violin.

The sisters relished Ellen's company; she had come from a city, and therefore must know about fashion and society. Ellen loved their naïve good manners – and their polished accents suggested that the wider world might after all be introduced safely into this worryingly closed, however idyllic, community.

=

On several afternoons of this unprecedented hot spell Thomas and Ellen cycled, or sometimes drove, to the river, to the place where they had first walked, where Ellen had worn her cream lace dress, where Thomas had first 'laid hands' on her (as she once called it). Down in the dark water they delved, gasping cold at first, then delightful. Ellen learned to swim properly under Thomas's guidance, and in a blue swimsuit and little white rubber cap she waved her hands slowly like fronds, up and down, up and down, to the fork where the tributary joined the big swifter river, and back again.

Nobody else ever came there by day, only the waterbirds, some coots, and a crane. In the near fields they heard corncrakes: in the distance, always in the distance, a cuckoo. Nearby, Chadwick's Well, a round, deep, bright structure of white cement, sparkled full of turquoise waters.

In the early cool of the evening, before they ate, they often walked the fields – sometimes to the Castle again, of which Thomas never tired, sometimes to the old kitchen garden where the ancient *espalier* pears and plums, and the greengages, were ripening, much to Ellen's anticipation.

The food she prepared surprised not only Thomas but herself. She had natural taste and a flair for cooking, even though she stuck to what she had learned in Domestic Economy, and what she had scantily gleaned from her mother or now picked up from local women. She made him 'Fancy Lady', an Irish stew, but using brown gravy and a tablespoon of sherry; all over and around the chunks of meat hewn from chops, she packed potatoes from Thomas's garden, and his hard, fat onions from the hanks inside the back-kitchen door. Once they even had wine, a bottle Thomas had been given at a Teachers' Conference the previous year. They drank some of it on a Sunday at lunch, and put away the rest in a cupboard where it lived for five years – and when Ellen eventually found it by accident she burst into screaming tears.

On the last Sunday in August, with a week to go before the opening of the school, Ellen, having arranged herself carefully, sat down to begin reading the heirloom Thomas had given her, his aunt's inherited papers and letters about Timothy Nash, the hedge-schoolmaster. The handwriting was steady and elegant.

I began assembling this in 1882, and hoped to expand it wider and wider, but as I found out more and more about my subject I felt that I should stop.

Ellen fingered the pile and methodically began to rearrange the package. Under the heading 'The Life of Timothy Nash' she made five notes on her writing-pad, '1. Rearrange all the papers in chronological order. 2. Buy folders at Hickey's, and labels to keep the parts separate. 3. Ask Thomas for the name of a good Irish translator. 4. Call to library in J'borough.'

She looked at the clock on the mantelpiece, counted out forty pages, enough, she reckoned, to occupy two hours, and began to read, skipping the illegible bits until later.

The original writer, from whom Thomas's successive aunts had inherited, first described Timothy Nash's classes:

. . . lying in a sunny meadow surrounded by impoverished children and their bedraggled parents. Most of them had once been wealthy, before being displaced by Yorkshire or Somerset yeomen families planted into their lands. In his hedge lessons Nash took these dispossessed Catholics into other worlds, the realms of gold. These poor, miserable people, deprived of learning, and of land, and of living, encountered the ancient writers, Horace and Livy and Virgil . . .

Some of these hedge-schoolmasters died in the open air in the wintertime because they were always on the run . . .

We used to see Mr Nash coming across the fields to us, always down the same pathway by the headland of the Hill Field, a long black coat down to his ankles, and a fading black hat like an Italian priest. He came to our house about four times a year and we took turns to watch for the soldiers who hunted him if they thought he was in the area. He would either have been dragged out of our house and shot on the spot, or hanged after a quick trial. By that time, there was nearly as big a price on the head of a hedge-schoolmaster as there was on a priest, and we were always afraid of informers . . .

Sometimes, if it was raining, he taught inside, and he made us chant *Amo, Amas, Amat, Amamus, Amatis, Amant*. He told

us about Euclid and Pythagoras. In the open air he was at his
best, and out there in the haggard field, most especially when
the grass was long and there were buttercups, he taught Latin
poems.

Ellen made notes. 'Go and see the Nash house over near Bruree.
Look up the Penal Laws and see the details regarding education.
Find out what the population of the Irish Colleges abroad was.
When was Salamanca founded? What regiment would have been
stationed nearby in 1770?' She read on through the details of
Timothy Nash's scholastic career, which, it appeared, had dazzled
the whole College.

At the back of an account of his brilliant capacity to translate
sight unseen from the Greek, she found another page, folded in
four and pinned tight; the pin had long rusted. Fearing blood-
poisoning from the rust, she did not handle the pin directly: she
forced it from the pages with the corner of her writing-case, opened
the paper and read in the same hand.

He was disciplined several times for [two words that looked
like 'moral insubordination'], and on four occasions for [was it
'excessive' or 'extreme'?] and unnecessary violence, resulting in
one student [the ink had splodged: perhaps 'needing the care'
or 'cure'] of the College's physician. He struck a tutor with an
[Ellen could not make it out: it might have been 'oar', but boats
had not been mentioned] and rendered the man ill. A following
line had been heavily scored out, and the passage concluded
with the words, 'concern but not astonishment'.

Ellen sat back, thinking deeply, then shivered. She stood up,
walked to the bay window, fiddled a moment with the long lace
curtains, touched the fronds of the palm, and turned back again to
the table. Delving further into the package of papers, she took out
the ones in Timothy Nash's handwriting and held them up to the
light as if examining banknotes; she turned them over, moistened
a finger and touched the black, insect-like ink until one word
ran a little, then laid the papers back on the table with a little
shudder.

=

At supper – cold beef and tomatoes, with Thomas drinking a glass of stout – she said, 'Thomas, what kind of a man was Timothy Nash? I mean was he a violent man?'

'I have no notion,' said Thomas.

Michael Quinn came almost every day to the house.

'Michael, you're going to be invaluable to me.' She addressed him more as adult than boy, and invited him to bring his little brother, the unspeaking Timmy – who, on his first appearance, hung around the gate, peeping in like an elf, with a big beaming smile. Ellen lured him forward with a slice of apple pie. Timmy's nose ran permanently.

Michael cleaned Ellen's bicycle; he helped her wash potatoes; Timmy followed her around the house, always a few steps behind. Once, she grabbed him unexpectedly and washed his face in warm water and soap. After a first quick struggle, he stood, caught between embarrassment and pleasure; she held her own good handmirror to him, then let him take it in his hand; he stroked the back, trying to touch the lace inside the glass.

Michael worked beside her at the scullery table, topping and tailing the gooseberries, taken too late from the garden and quite squashy, and he willingly entered into her games to help Timmy speak.

'Goose. Gog,' Ellen said. Michael repeated it equally slowly.

Ellen procured from her mother discarded shirts which had once fitted her brother Jim, and gave them to Michael. She showed him how to clean windows, she inside, he outside, and made him go over smears again and again. When Timmy climbed on the chair behind Michael, Ellen teased him through the glass by pretending to speak, but uttering no sound. This brought forth a number of words from Timmy.

She praised Michael, gave him apples, and paid him in half-crowns.

'That's too much, Ma'am.'

'No, Michael, the labourer is worthy of his hire.'

She said to Thomas, 'That Michael – there's something very endearing about him. He's invaluable to me.'

'His father's a bad egg,' Thomas grunted.

'But you should see how nice he is to the little fellow. He plays with him, and talks to him.'

'Eh-yeh.'

=

Thomas and Ellen went back to school on the first Monday of September.

'I have a sudden craving for an orange,' said Ellen, then continued, as they stood watching the children play, 'Isn't it extraordinary? How much has happened? Since last February.'

Arms folded, he merely smiled.

'I love all the new books,' she said, 'and the chalk from last year's boxes and the smell of the ink – I know it isn't last year, but you know what I mean.'

Leah arrived the next Friday to stay for just one night, a rare treat, Herbert had given her 'a Sabbath off', even though she had, dutiful wife, as she said, prepared everything before she left: the food; the children's clothes; the prayer books; Herbert's suit and shawl. She stepped off the bus in the middle of the village, a wonderful, coloured creature, with a suitcase that would have sufficed for a four-week stay. She wore a bright pink coat, and a hat of curved feathers, and high heels.

Thomas and Ellen both met her, Thomas carrying her almost empty case the few hundred yards to the house, Leah's heels sinking in the soft tar of the road. Eventually, seeing how her shoes might be ruined, she took them off and walked along the grass borders of the road. Thomas, looking at the shoes, said, 'You can take that tar off with butter.'

Ellen said, 'Can you? Leah, Thomas knows everything: I'm going to put that in my ledger' – and proceeded to tell Leah about the recipes, the household hints, the short poems.

'She even cuts out the advertisements,' said Thomas. They all laughed.

After school, Thomas had to go and help a farmer fill forms for a drainage grant. Ellen and Leah took their cups of tea out to the garden bench which, during the summer, Thomas had moved under the sycamore tree at the side of the house. The women began to talk.

'You look very well,' said Leah. 'And happy. It is possible to be happy living with a man, although with Herbert I often think I have to make the happiness, he worries so much.'

'Leah, tell me something,' said Ellen. Leah sat up, sure in her wisdom and experience that something 'interesting' was about to be addressed.

'You know, when you and Herbert got married first.'

'Ye-es?' asked Leah.

'Ah-m.' Ellen halted. A breeze stirred. Ellen put a hand to her mouth.

'I read. I read in this book we bought in London. Well, no, in a magazine Rina got from America. That married women should always consult a doctor.'

They murmured for half an hour, obliquely, thoughtfully.

Leah, earnest and quiet, summarized, 'They don't talk about things like this in our religion, either. Although we seem to understand more – more about, I suppose, about – joy.'

The leaves in the tree rustled. Leah shivered, pointed to the sky, to a cloud moving slowly over. 'I told Herbert the weather would break. He said it would probably never rain again, there would be no crops this autumn, and did we have enough packages of food laid in?'

Ellen smiled, and Leah continued.

'I can't afford any of those things in packages. Do you know, Ellen, I can get skim milk for a third of the price of real milk, and the children don't notice it in their tea, and if Herbert does, he doesn't say anything.'

'The next time we're going to see Mama and Dada, I'll make sure Thomas throws a bag of potatoes in the back of the car for you,' said Ellen.

They took the cups in and the rain came. It poured all night; Thomas came home soaked to the skin but very pleased that the ground would have water. He and Ellen lay in bed listening to a sound they had never heard before together, the rain on the slates of the roof.

Next morning, being Saturday, they slept a little late, and then downstairs could hear Leah moving about and singing in a sweet voice. Thomas lifted the window high and put his head out, breathing the air.

'Oh, the coolness.' He turned to call Ellen and found her leaning against the dressing-table. She had grown very pale and looked disturbed, shaken.

'What's wrong?'

'I don't know, I'm feeling terrible, I can't swallow, I'm all dizzy.'

'I'll call Leah.'

'No, she'll see the bed, how tossed it is.'

'She's a married woman.'

He went to the door.

'Leah. Leah!' and she answered from the hall.

'Ellen's feeling off.'

'Off?' Leah climbed the stairs. 'Not off, surely? How can she be off?' and quite unabashedly sailed into the room. Leah felt Ellen's forehead, sat her on the bed, then made her lie down. Turning to Thomas, she said, 'A glass of water, or a cup of tea and a rest, I think.'

Thomas hurried downstairs and Leah said, 'Dear Ellen. You are going to have a new little person in this house, I think,' and counting on her fingers, starting, 'August, September, October, November . . .' she said, 'And in May, I think.' Outside it began to rustle with rain again.

'Don't say anything to Thomas,' asked Ellen.

'If you're all right,' said Thomas later, 'we could go to the pictures when we take Leah back. There's one on at the *Grand Central* called *Sinners in Silk*. I'll read it out to you. "Featuring Eleanor Boardman, Conrad Nagel and Adolphe Menjou. A highly dramatic and unusual story of Life. And then – Realization – comedy and interest. The Rejected Woman. In seven parts. Featuring Alma Rubens." Would you like to do that?'

Leah said, 'Ooh, I like Adolphe Menjou.'

Ellen still lying down, said, 'Thomas, I don't think I want to go into Janesborough today.'

'No,' said Leah, leaning against the jamb of the bedroom door, 'I will get the bus.'

'No, Thomas will drive you, won't you, Thomas?'

'Certainly.'

'No.' Leah put up a hand with the air of somebody who would not lose this argument. 'I will go by bus.'

Thomas stood at the door, looking out at the rain. He whistled a little.

Ellen said, 'Leah thinks I might be going to have a baby.'

His hands hung by his sides. Then he rubbed his mouth.

'Well, well, well. That's great news.' He said no more, and did not look at Ellen, who fiddled with her hair. 'Great news,' he repeated.

In a moment, he strolled downstairs. First he stood by the book-shelves, then went into the parlour and rearranged the small clock on the mantelpiece, then back to the kitchen. He opened the drawer, took out some stamp-paper he had been saving, fetched down the copy of *Under the Greenwood Tree*, and began to repair the torn jacket. When he returned, undressed and climbed into bed, Ellen had begun to drop off to sleep. His hand found her forearm, which he clasped.

AUTUMN 1925

11

Ellen suggested they take 'nature walks', so that she could learn about the countryside.

'With a heart and a half,' Thomas said, and, not un-wryly, continued, 'I know every stick and stone of these fields.'

Laying it out like a campaign, he planned that they walk every second day or so, with varied moments for the different sights: pastureland in the morning, marshland at evening, woodland by day during the week-ends, and he taught Ellen the values and liabilities of each field. He showed contempt for farmers who allowed moss to grow; plucked blades of silverweed for her; identified the different fescues and clovers in the opulent aftergrass of the summer's meadows. She learned boys' lore: how to stand motionless if glimpsing the rarity of a fox; where to sense a nest in the grass: 'Go to where the bird has flown from, not to where she seems to be leading you'; how to find downwind on a seemingly calm day: 'Put your finger in your mouth, until it is wet and warm, hold it to the air: the side that gets cold first – that's where the wind is coming from.'

'I wish we had owls around here,' said Thomas, 'an owl can eat nearly twice its own weight in mice of an evening.'

'Aach!' said Ellen.

'Or wouldn't it be lovely if we had nightingales? "Thou wast not born for death, immortal bird,"' quoted Thomas.

'But wasn't Keats an immoral sort of fellow?' asked Ellen.

Together they admired the slender form of the lark, and its flirrup-flirrup of flight away from them; analysed the difference between an occupied badger sett and a disused one, according to the freshness of the earth at the entrance; what will put off a thrush's attacking dive as it protects its nest?: 'Wear tall-ish headgear, like a hat, not anything flat, wear something with a crown to it'; that she should never, ever approach a nesting swan – 'A swan can break your arm with the beat of a wing'; where to find the variety of wild briar that smells like roasted apples: 'At a stone wall, and facing south or south-west'; the impression of a shod hoof, complete with nails, the twig formation from which the horse chestnut got its name; how a trapped bee or wasp sent down a rabbit burrow will have the same effect as a ferret. Thomas captured a dozen or so wasps in an unwashed empty jamjar, and sealed it with a punctured lid: 'They can't get out but they still get air.' They walked to a warren near the Castle ice-pit, and arranged themselves on either side of the entrance. Waiting several minutes – 'Give the burrow a chance to calm down' – Thomas threw some jam down the earthen hole as far as it would go, then opened the jar and shook the wasps out. He smiled across the grassy bank at Ellen, as her eyes widened when she heard the thumping. Next, a posse of rabbits galloped out of the burrow, raced to a few feet away, their noses twitching unstoppably, then seeing Thomas and Ellen raced farther and urgently. They were followed by a slower thumping and tiny, hairless, sightless bodies rolled out, down the earthen hillock, as two large females heaved out baby rabbits hardly two days old. The adults climbed over them, began to haul at them, then they too raced away in several directions, abandoning their young to the humans. Having inspected the babies to their satisfaction, Thomas ostentatiously led Ellen away, far down the field until they had moved out of the territory of the burrow. There they hid behind hazel trees, and could see that the adults had returned and engaged in some transaction, presumably returning the babies to safety, or, as Thomas believed, 'either sniffing them to decide whether to abandon them, or moving them to a safer place.'

'Isn't that cruel of us,' she asked, 'disturbing them like that?'

'No, it's only animals,' he said. 'Wait 'til the spring, 'til you see the hares kicking.'

They returned from these walks exhilarated and breathless, and Ellen found that Thomas, no matter what chore was about to pre-occupy him, seemed never far away from the bedroom as she went upstairs to change. He sat on the bed, talking, or listening: one afternoon she asked sharply, 'As a matter of interest – do you mind me looking at you while you're dressing?'

He fidgeted. 'I don't know. I mean . . .'

For some days he avoided the bedroom when she went there,

until, on two successive occasions, she called to him, and when he arrived, engaged him in conversation, and the issue was soon smoothed over.

Mrs McAuliffe and Hannie came again to the school.

'I can tell, Miss, that you're not someone who has much time for people with a sad story.'

Only for the sake of the child did Ellen hold back a sting of her tongue.

Mrs McAuliffe now said to Ellen, in Thomas's presence, 'You know, Miss, they all told me the Master here wouldn't help, but Father Shine said that wasn't the case at all, no matter what people said about Master Kane.'

Ellen said, 'Now, Mrs McAuliffe, you shouldn't be talking about the Master like that. We're here to help. You know that.'

'He did a very good turn, the Master, a couple of years ago, didn't you, Master? For a man whose hay burnt down. The Master got every farmer for miles to give a small bit of hay of their own, until the burnt barn was all filled up again. Didn't you, Master? Ma'am, the pension and all that, I have to clean houses for people; the eggs I sells only brings in a few shillings.'

'I'll tell you what,' said Ellen. 'The Master and myself will be making enquiries about . . . about your problem. Will that do for the moment?'

'Ah, Ma'am, it won't do, no,' said the woman. 'Sure, how am I to know anything, we've no funeral, nor wake, nor nothing.' She looked again at Thomas and said in an accusing tone, 'Master Kane, you should be doing something.'

Thomas reddened, not in embarrassment; in anger.

'Now that's enough,' he snapped, 'that is. Enough.' He walked back into his own classroom. Ellen shepherded the woman out, running back to get a book, *Stories of the Saints*.

'Here, Hannie, there's a present for you.'

'Ma'am, I'd rather give her her father back.'

Ellen returned to Thomas, and asked with vehemence, 'Does that woman think you're supposed to know about something?'

Thomas said, 'Look, I spoke to the Sergeant. That is a bad case. That man is dead. The people who killed him and buried him are still around. And nearer here than you'd think. I told you that before. If they find out that anybody is looking into that case –

well, there's danger in it. Now leave it alone like a good woman.'

Ellen said, 'But – that's terribly unjust. That child is missing her father. I'd take it as a great favour if you did something.'

'No, I won't.'

'I think you should, Thomas.' She bobbed her head. 'It would be a kindness, and a good act, and a fine example. Why should such bad things be buried? Besides, isn't it very clear that she thinks – and so must other people – that you were involved in things like that, and you should show them you weren't.'

Thomas closed the lid of his desk.

Ellen pressed. 'I'd think a lot of you if you did.'

He looked at her with a statue's sightless glare.

Ellen asked, 'Did you know her husband?'

Thomas said, 'A little useless scut of a fellow, but he had one good point, he was very reliable. If you asked him to be somewhere to do something, he'd turn up as promised, not like most people, but he was useless when he got there, as lazy as sin.'

They walked to October Devotions, and prayed and sang before the white-and-gold altar of the church. On crisp evenings of moonlight and frost, Thomas pointed out the stars to her on the way back. They could hear their footsteps echo, and now she also longed for an owl, never having heard one. Sometimes he stopped and hushed her, and they listened to a scurry in the roadside, or a cough not far away – a badger. One Wednesday evening she stopped.

'Euch!' she said, 'what's that smell?'

He sniffed the air. 'A dead animal probably. There's a dead beast inside the ditch somewhere.'

Ellen turned to the list of contents in the handwriting of Thomas's aunt, and found the Flora Callaghan letters, four in all. The first one, addressed, 'Dear Miss Kane' had been written in 1850, and said,

> As you suggest, I am writing herein my memory of the first time I saw Timothy Nash. I have taken the liberty, and I am sure you will not take offence at it, of consulting my brothers and sisters so that a full picture of the unfortunate man may emerge.

174

Unfortunate? Ellen sat up. She flicked through the other letters and then stopped herself, thinking that the story must unfold in its own natural way, that she must not jump from source to source. Her bladder was full: would the Canon ever be persuaded to install running water and electricity?

'"Unfortunate"? Timothy Nash "unfortunate"?' she queried half-aloud, and read some more of Miss Flora Callaghan's first, very long letter.

> My father had arranged for a hayloft above the cows to be set aside as a place where Mr Nash could sleep and teach. Mr Nash had no slates like the modern schools do, all he had was a curious, very large leather bag out of which he took many books, small volumes that must have travelled a long way. At the beginning of every class he would arrange these in a neat pile and throughout the lesson he would read from them in turn, telling us about the people who wrote them.
>
> We never thought of laughing or giggling in his class because he had a severe nature which rendered children quiet in his presence.
>
> He wore linen that required much attention, and a blue bandanna at his neck which also deserved washing. He had a waistcoat the colour of burgundy wine and he frequently smelt of a smell I knew later to be strong drink. In appearance he was a tall man with dark brown, nearly black curly hair, which had a little grey in it. He had a flared nose and eyebrows which met in the middle, and gave the appearance of a handsome, erect man who could be most distinguished if he chose.
>
> When he read to us he would rise from the palliasse on which he had been sitting, the same upon which he had slept, and stand as if acting the words, the book held out at arm's length, reading in a strong voice.

Ellen exclaimed half-aloud, 'But that's just like Thomas!'

> My father once asked him whether he thought it could prove more prudent to hold classes in softer tones, lest passing soldiery or an indiscreet servant be attracted to

175

this unusual sound, and Mr Nash's reply left no room
for further discussion. He was a strong man, of large
physical capacity and fiercely-held opinion. He had
difficulty once or twice with some people of my father's
acquaintance to whom he showed extreme violence . . .

Ellen exclaimed to herself, 'Oh, my God!'

and I feel certain that his very forthright demeanour
played no small part in the unfortunate continuation and
outcome of his life, but his love for learning could never
have been gainsaid.

I cannot think what assistance my poor recollections
may be to you, dear Miss Kane, but I will write again
and see if I can offer something more illuminating than
this humble meal from my memory.

In the meantime I would be grateful if you would
convey my simple affections and notice of regard to your
brother and his wife, and to your respected self

I remain,
Yours Most Truly,
Flora Callaghan

'Thomas, this sick feeling won't go away.'

He looked over the top of his spectacles. 'I told you. You should
go and see the doctor.'

'Leah says there's no need. Mama says there's no need, they
all say 'tis perfectly natural in the first six weeks, even three
months.'

Upstairs, she took off all her clothes and stood in front of the
mirror peering intently at her stomach. She rubbed a hand over it
and turned this way and that watching the candlelight reflect from
mirror to mirror, and did not hear Thomas step softly into the room
behind her. He put his hands gently on her bare shoulders from
behind, kissing her neck.

'You look like a painting,' he said. 'You look like a picture in a
gallery.' For the first time ever Ellen did not attempt to cover
herself in his presence.

=

After school in the evenings, Michael Quinn came to do his chores. Ellen asked Thomas to show the boy how onions should be plaited into a hank: Thomas did so with scant grace.

'Don't be so gruff with him,' Ellen hissed when Michael had gone to the pump to fill the bucket.

The boy showed Ellen how to wash a bottle clean: put a handful of little gravel pebbles in the bottom, some water, then shake it hard, and all the scum of the old cream will disappear. One afternoon, Thomas walked into the kitchen while the boy was sitting there at the table, having tea and a piece of apple tart, with Ellen reading to him from *Treasure Island*. Thomas walked out again.

At supper he said, 'I'm telling you, Ellie, there is bad blood in that house.'

'Well, Michael's all right, you have to admit that. And he's very useful to me.'

Thomas said, 'I have taken to putting certain things out of sight.'

Ellen flared. 'Now, isn't that very pompous of you? Look at the way that boy protects Timmy from that father of theirs? Look at the nice way he talks about that hopeless mother of theirs?'

Thomas retorted, 'You see? You're saying it yourself. They're a useless tribe.'

'Thomas, I'm surprised at you. That poor boy – he walks as if expecting a blow on the back of his head all the time. Where is your compassion? I'm very fond of him, and the more I see of him, the fonder I get of him. He's completely trustworthy, and he's very willing to learn.'

The following Saturday, Ellen and Thomas drove to Janesborough. They called to Brunswick Square first, just before noon. Ellen's father had decided not to go into the printing works that day, and they found him in the little front garden behind the railings, lifting bulbs. He had in mind, he said, to clear that ground for some standard roses from now on, only he did not know how far back from the railings he should put them, and did he have enough room?

'Did you go to the doctor yet?' whispered May in the kitchen.

'I'm just going to go, Mama.'

Thomas said to Ellen's father, 'The thing I'm thinking is, it solves one problem, at least I'll have something comfortable to call you now. I can call you Granda or Granddad, or whatever the child says.'

Mr Morris said, 'Right enough, I never knew what to call my own father-in-law.'

'Yes, you did,' cut in his wife. 'You used to call him "the oul' shite".'

'But not to his face,' her husband replied, and everybody laughed except Ellen who protested, 'Mama! Really!'

Father Watson greeted Ellen in the dark-brown camphor-smelling drawing-room.

'And how is the wonder-man?'

'You mean Thomas? Fine, Father John, he's grand,' she replied, too preoccupied to catch – or perhaps ignoring – the edge in his voice.

They decided to go for a walk, with Ellen realizing that somewhere on the way she would be buying him a cup of tea, and probably something to eat.

When they had swung onto the parkway path towards the river, she told him the news about the baby. He took her arm briefly, squeezed it gently and said how pleased he was.

'Birth is a miracle,' he said, 'though I have always thought that death is a miracle too in its own way.'

'Does that baby know anything now?' she asked, stopping to take a piece of the cinder from the path out of her shoe.

'Not knowingly, not until it begins to experience life. But of course it is life, it is part of you and Thomas, part of your joint being.'

'I don't remember anything before I was born.'

'It is not given to us to know anything before birth.'

'How do I know I shall know anything after death?'

'Because the Lord has said so, we have the evidence of Christ himself and the Gospels and the whole Testament. But I take your point. If you didn't know anything before you were born, it may not be given to you to know anything after your death. Therefore – what has the whole experience been for? That is what you are saying, is it not?'

'More or less.'

'That, Ellen,' and he laughed, 'is what centuries of theologians have discussed. I have a simple view. This child of yours and Thomas's, he or she will grow a little like you, a little like Thomas, with your eyes, perhaps, or Thomas's curly hair; he or she will copy a gesture of yours, or walk like its father. That is the root, is it not, of Christian belief, that God made us in his own likeness? Is it not also a kind of immortality, a kind of eternal life, that one day, if we had family portraits, your descendants would see that one of them would look exactly like you? That's why rich people have portraits painted, especially non-Catholics, because they have no safe after-life.'

He asked Ellen how she felt about the baby, about how she felt spiritually.

She said, 'I feel in two minds about it. I have a kind of natural joy, but I also have a kind of fear.'

'Apprehension?' he queried.

'Is that the word?'

'Yes, it's a natural enough feeling. It probably comes from wishing to protect the new life, Ellen dear. How is Thomas feeling about it all?'

'Well, naturally he's hoping for a son.'

'Naturally.'

'And he says he's very pleased, quite excited, but of course he has reared children before, he had to be the father to his brothers and sisters when his own father and mother died. And I think he feels the responsibility.'

'And —' Father Watson cleared his throat as if embarrassed, then looked off to the distance, as far as he could see, before planting his spike: '— And, Ellen, he is not too worried, I take it, about the marital quietude?'

'How do you mean, Father John? What's "marital quietude"?'

'I mean, he is not upset at the loss of marital rights?'

'What loss?' Ellen blushed, and stopped to face the priest. Behind them a pilot boat set out down the choppy river to guide a cargo ship in from the sea.

'Well, my dear Ellen —' the priest put on his most serious tone and raised himself to such height as he possessed. 'When a woman is bearing fruit, it is of course the Natural Law, and therefore the law of God, that congress must cease.'

'Father John,' said Ellen, consternation growing, 'you are not serious? You are not serious? You mean we could be committing sin?'

'Yes, I'm afraid I do. I admit the Church, the teaching is a little hazy, but it has been a generally-held belief that this is a sacred time for a woman, for you, in this case, and must not be profaned.'

They had reached a café on the edge of the park, where a busy street ran down to the water. Two drays and their horses and carters stood by the kerb, thudding barrels into a public house cellar, the street grille of which had just been raised. The priest and the pretty young woman skirted them and entered the café: he ordered tea for them both, and bread and marmalade for himself, and then a jam roll.

Ellen could not look at him for a moment or two, then raising her eyes and staring him in the face, said, 'Father John, can you make sure about that. Please?'

The priest's face darkened and then grew embarrassed.

'Ellen, I said it was a confused issue. But it is there, in Canon Law.'

'Father John, you know I like everything very clearcut, no shadows, no doubts, I want no possibilities of being anything other than on the right side. If there is any doubt I find it, even if I have to dig it out, and then it worries me even more.'

'Yes, Ellen, yes. But you do not need to have scruples to get by in life and to stay in the sight of God. God doesn't want you to be perfect.'

'I do!'

'But that's impossible.'

'Father, would it be a Mortal Sin or a Venial Sin?'

'My dear, I don't know.'

'Yes, you do, I know by your face. It is grave, isn't it?'

'Well, anything like that is grave. Yes, I have to tell the truth, it was supposed to be a Mortal Sin, but I don't know if it still is.'

'Things can't shift their ground like that, Father.'

'Ellen, I spend my life dealing not with moral certainty, but with moral uncertainty. I'll do all I can to establish the certainty in this. The point is. Congress between man and wife has as its intent the procreation of children. Once conception has been achieved, anything thereafter according to Canon Law is no better than bestial.'

'Bestial? For something God Himself has blessed? Bestial?'

'Well, that's what they say. A bit strong, I grant.'

'And in the meantime?' Ellen leaned forward, clearly in anguish: the serene and passionate bedroom she shared and so adored with Thomas had just been invaded uglily, confusingly.

'Ellen, if you don't know something is a sin, then you can't be committing one. And you don't know this is a sin.'

'You've just told me it is!'

'I've just told you that it was once regarded as one. I don't know what the most recent thinking is, that is what I'm going to find out. In any case,' he continued, 'think of the good fortune you have now created for this child by choosing such a fine man as Thomas to breed with.'

'He isn't a racehorse, Father John.' The priest laughed.

'He may not be, but there is some very interesting thinking going on over in Europe right now – about people choosing ideal partners, for the purposes of producing even higher strains in their children, ever finer types of child. All lawful and above board. Though I can see where some doubtful morals might creep in.'

'Does it follow that they will also inherit . . . ?' Ellen did not finish her sentence, said instead, 'You've confused me terribly, Father John.'

She reported to Thomas immediately they got in the car. He looked at her aghast. 'You talk to him too much. Why the blazes did you say anything at all to him?'

'I didn't mean to,' Ellen said apologetically. 'He actually said it to me. We were just talking about birth, and then he asked me how you felt about this.'

'What do you think yourself? Do you think it'd be sinful?'

'I don't know,' said Ellen, angry and wan at once. 'I'm up and down and in and out about it. I don't know what to think.'

'Feeling is sometimes better than thinking,' said Thomas. 'What do you feel? Do you feel it would be a sin?'

'I won't know until –'

'Until we do it again?' He grinned, seeking to ease matters. 'So I get one more go, do I?'

'Oh, Thomas.'

That night, she saw him go to the bookcase and take down *Married Love* by Marie Stopes. When he saw her glance of enquiry he laughed and remarked, 'Just fighting fire with fire.'

'There's nothing in it about all this,' Ellen said.

'How do you know?' Thomas asked suspiciously. 'Were you looking for it?'

'No, but I've read it from cover to cover.'

181

A page fell open. 'What's this?' asked Thomas, and began to read. '"This little crest, which lies anteriorly between the inner lips round the vagina, enlarges when a woman –"'

Ellen snatched the book out of his hand: he chased her and they wrestled but she would not give it up, and they concluded in laughter.

When, hours later, they climbed into bed, Thomas said, 'It is not a sin, it can't be a sin,' he said quietly, and with all his authority, 'for a man and his wife to be married. Remember what the Canon read out at the altar. "With my body I thee worship." Ask the Doctor when you go to see him.'

'But will we be punished?' she asked.

'Punished? For what? That's a strange God that would do that,' Thomas said. 'How would he punish us?'

'Perhaps the old stories, you know, the birthmarks, maybe that's what it all means?'

He grimaced in the dark: nevertheless he bundled her up in his arms and rocked her, holding her head on his chest.

In the church the following morning only Thomas noticed the hesitancy in Ellen as she rose to go to the altar-rails for Communion.

12

Dr Morgan said, 'You left it long enough. What are you, three months gone?'

'About that.'

'When did you get married? Late June? Ah-ha. Honeymoon job. Well, well. And no complications of any kind?'

'None.'

'Good man, good man. At the same time, why didn't you come earlier?'

'Well, isn't it very selfish to pay myself such attention?'

He said tartly, 'Well, you went to school to the nuns, that's for sure.'

Examining Ellen very carefully, he checked her eyes, her ears, her pulses, made her undress completely and drew a blanket over her; piecemeal, he unveiled her as he continued his examination. He became brusquer still when she did not raise her legs to the required height and angle. She lay as still as a peaceful animal, her face peering up at him from the rim of the white blanket, hands held above her head, never taking her eyes off his, a direct response to her own embarrassment, while inspecting his matter-of-factness as if to learn how he achieved such a manner. When the examination had been completed he invited her to dress and sit at his desk, and he began to ask her questions.

'Now do you know what happens to a woman when she is having a baby? The reason I ask is that if you sat here at my desk day in and day out, you'd be amazed that anybody ever got born.'

Ellen, typically, summarized, as if in a classroom, what she had learned, what she knew, about conception, pregnancy and child-birth. Though amused, he was pleased that she had taken the trouble to learn so much, and then burst out laughing when she mentioned Marie Stopes.

'Where did you hear about her? You'll get yourself excommunicated from the Church if you mention her name.'

183

'But there's a letter from a Jesuit printed in the preface of her book?'

'Yes, but that's only window-dressing. D'you remember what the letter said?' Dr Morgan reached for the shelf behind him and took down his own copy of *Married Love*, grinning at Ellen's surprise. His hands shook a little.

'Listen to this. This is the Jesuit, what's his name, Father Stanislaus St John, though I suppose he pronounces it "Sinjen", this is what he has to say: ". . . the case you give of the worn-out mother of twelve. The Catholic belief is that the loss of health on her part for a few years of life and the diminished vitality on the part of her later children would be a very small price indeed to pay for an endless happiness on the part of all." Blah. Pure blah.' Dr John Morgan grinned.

Ellen smiled. Then leaning forward, suddenly urgent as if her life depended on it, and as earnest as a child, she said, 'Doctor, I have a problem – raised by a priest too.'

The benign man blew through his yellowing moustache. 'You're not the first and you won't be the last.'

'No, seriously, and by a Jesuit as well.'

'They're the boys for the problems. Don't I know it, wasn't I at school to them?'

'A friend, a Jesuit, an old friend, told me that it is a mortal sin for my husband and myself to go on –' she stopped.

'Having "connection"?' asked the doctor.

'Yes.'

'Did he now? Envious old buggers, the priests.'

'Is it?'

'Is it what? A sin? I don't know. There's all kinds of superstitions about it. Did he tell you the baby will have a birthmark?'

'He didn't, but I heard it.'

'That's the sort of thing,' said Dr Morgan, 'there's a basis in superstition, and sin has a lot to do with superstition.'

'He says,' Ellen pressed on, 'that the purpose of the relationship between man and woman is to have children, and once that has been achieved, then anything else is sinful until it is necessary to try again.'

'Yes, I know. And that's all designed to keep the Catholic Church growing in numbers.'

'He says people will grow in strength towards each other through their self-denial.'

'You mean,' said the doctor with a snort, 'if I deny myself my little night-cap every night by the fire, I will come to like whiskey even more? More old blah!'

'He says' – when Ellen got the bit between her teeth she was difficult to shake off – 'that Thomas and I must stop immediately, that we are committing sin every day and every night.'

'What does your husband, Mr Kane, what does he think?'

'He hasn't said much, so far, but I know he's upset.'

'This is awkward. And 'tis awkward for me, as well. I'm supposed to be a Catholic doctor. If I tell you anything, or say to you anything that contradicts Catholic teaching, and if it gets back to a priest or a bishop or any of those boys, they can – and will – make a complaint about me. But I'm also a man who has travelled a lot, I have seen a lot of the world. My wife is German, I have a daughter nearly your age, I was in the British Army in the Far East – this bloody malaria –' he held out his shaking hands – 'and I have my own views on this and other matters. But I can't tell them to you, but neither can I condemn you or anybody like you for disagreeing with the official line. A nod is as good as a wink to a blind horse. The reason there are superstitions, and the reason why people made it into a sin to have marital relations while a woman is expecting, is probably a social matter too.'

'How do you mean?' asked Ellen, who sat on the edge of her chair all through this conversation.

'I mean a matter of protecting the woman and the child in her womb.'

'How so?'

'Pweh!' said Dr Morgan. 'Listen to me. I have women coming in here from all over the county and the city. I had a woman here the other day who couldn't, she thought, have children. But, she thought, it might be her husband was at fault, but of course she'd never be allowed to say that, the man's pride must be kept intact. And not only that, but every effort to have children nearly "tore her apart", she said. I asked her a few blunt questions.'

'I bet you did,' interposed Ellen.

'I certainly did. I asked her was her husband's member big? And she said, "What'll I compare it to, Doctor?" What could I say? A bull? A stallion? A sheepdog? A ferret? Anyway, we worked out some rule of thumb – literally' (he glanced across to see whether Ellen smiled: she did) '– and then I said to her that maybe her own private parts were too tight. She lay down there where you were lying a few minutes ago, on that couch, the poor innocent woman took all her clothes off without a blush, that's how desperate she was, and I examined her. D'you know what was wrong? I'll tell you what was wrong. No matter what feelings she had for her husband, or where she had them, the man ignored her, and insisted – these two were married eight years, remember? – he insisted on going in the wrong entry. Up her backside, if you don't mind me being blunt.'

He leaned back. 'Yes, of course, you may look shocked, but he had never seen it done any other way, or so he thought, from bringing the cow to the bull. Or watching the dogs in the yard. Going to a stud farm, I suppose, was his education.'

'The misfortunate woman,' said Ellen.

'Haven't you married women friends you can ask?' said Dr Morgan, bringing the consultation to an end.

'There's one, but it's different,' said Ellen.

'Different how?'

'She's a Jew, different faith.'

'Isn't she alive?' asked the doctor sardonically.

Thomas asked her, 'How was Dr Morgan?'

'Mind your own business,' she snapped. He looked at her and flared.

'I am minding my own business. You're my business. Or aren't you?'

He got out, slammed the door of the car and walked down the street out of sight. Returning five minutes later, he swung the starting handle viciously, climbed back into the car and said nothing.

She said, 'I didn't mean to say that.'

'You did!'

Then they both spoke together: she said, 'What I meant was, he was talking about . . .'

He said, 'Ever since that blasted priest got his hooks into you . . .'

She said, 'He hasn't got his hooks . . .'

Thomas shouted, 'What the hell right has he –?' then clammed his mouth shut, fixed his hat, chugged the car out in the middle of the street and set off for home. By the time they reached Deanstown, both had calmed down at least into silence, although he spent at least half an hour in the garage, doing some chore or other with the light of a lamp. Indoors, Ellen had fried liver and onions, one of his favourite meals, and when he came in to wash his hands, the table looked calm and likeable: she had taken down the milk jug he liked, with the broad blue band around its belly.

That night she pleaded a headache and invented some nausea, and allowed Thomas to walk alone to the church. The moon shone clearly as she stood at the door to see him off, and he took his walking stick and hat and gloves. She could see his tall back in the long shaft of light thrown from the door as he walked down the gravel to the gate, disappearing into the night, and she stayed there for several moments until his metallic footsteps on the hard road faded completely.

AD MAIOREM DEI GLORIAM

The Provincial House,
The Terrace College,
Janesborough.
Sunday, 15th November 1925

My dear Ellen,

Perhaps I should also address this letter to Thomas, as it vitally and intimately concerns both of you, and I hope you will share its contents with him; in fact you must. I know you have been waiting to hear from me, and I apologize for the delay, but the matter seemed so vital I thought it best to obtain the fullest possible spiritual advice.

You will recall that while we walked and talked, the question arose over the sacredness of birth and its preludes. We considered whether in the sight of God it would be morally unlawful for man and wife to continue to engage in congress once a wife had conceived.

Although Canon Law is unclear as to the actual or precise dimensions of sin on this specific point, we may

187

infer the moral stance from clearer points on related issues. The Church says quite clearly, and this is dogma, therefore handed down by God and preached infallibly by the Pontiff as Christ's Vicar of Rome and Visible Head on Earth, that the purpose of congress must be directed exclusively for the procreation of new souls. Once this objective has been achieved, any other form of such intimacy is obviously licentious.

Therefore we may assume that any other form of intimacy includes congress after the event of proven conception – which is your question, dear Ellen, is it not?

Therefore we have to assume that, once conception has taken place, congress between married couples is grievously sinful. Obviously before conception has occurred it may be of an unlimited, though always of course respectful, nature, as this is the Lord's way of ensuring our continuity in His image and likeness.

If such a ruling may initially seem to cause distress, then I can assure you that in the eyes of the Church the spiritual reward accruing to both parties on account of their willing and loving abstinence, is far greater; and it is of course of a temporary nature, as relations may resume once the child has been given the gift of birth.

I am sure that this restraint will only strengthen the love between you, dear Ellen and Thomas, and I send you all my best wishes and blessings.

Yours sincerely in Christ,
John Watson, S.J.

Thomas took the letter from Ellen. He looked confused, blinking as he read it.

'What does that phrase mean?' he asked, pointing to 'we may infer the moral stance from clearer points on related issues'. 'Oh, yes, I see,' and he read on.

'Ellen, do you believe him?' he asked. She nodded.

Thomas stood back. 'But that means we can't hardly touch each other any more, or until the baby is born, I mean. And that's not 'til next May?'

Neither seemed to know what to say.

Thomas looked into the distance, the letter floating in his hand. The school break for play had already run on too long. Thomas blew on his whistle.

In the afternoon he found her in tears.

'I'll make a bargain with you, Thomas,' she said, barely able to speak. 'I'll let you touch me with your hands, but that's all.'

He said, 'No, that's no sort of a bargain.'

They spent the evening avoiding each other at home, ate an almost soundless meal, and that night in bed, as they lay side by side, he asked in the dark, 'Is it even wrong to hug you? Can't we find out more about this? There's another six or seven months before the baby is born.'

An invisible wedge parted their bodies in the bed, from shoulder to ankle, a high, thick, hard, cold wedge, reaching from the soft warm mattress up to the ceiling as surely as if it had been a gigantic version of the steel-blue wedges Thomas used to prise a cord of timber apart before he split it finally with the axe. Within days, another wedge, even thicker, and colder than ice itself, and flecked with blood, would prise them farther apart.

WINTER 1925

13

Whenever the District Court sat in session, Thomas, on account of his standing in the community, frequently appeared as a character witness. The visiting judges also called for his impartial opinion, providing 'extra knowledge of the circumstances', and he rendered other services, such as the explanation of implications in various cases. Although serious violence had generally dwindled, the Land Division still rankled: when some estates were distributed among local people after the 1922 Treaty, a few inevitably claimed unfair treatment. Civil War revenge occasionally played a part in an assault, or a shooting at a house: Thomas usually knew both parties, or their kinfolk. The visiting judges liked him because he gave his opinion very forthrightly, without fear.

He owned a special, dark, double-breasted suit which he kept almost exclusively for court: many of the officials, both the locals and those who travelled with the judges, told him repeatedly that he should have been a lawyer, not a teacher. He enjoyed the compliment, and if time permitted he stayed in court listening to the cases, even when his duty had been discharged. Some of the judges sought his company afterwards for conversation and local history, and he was one of the chosen few nominated to accept guns, handed in by those availing of the gun amnesty. When no criminal cases came before a Sessions, it sometimes fell to Thomas to buy the traditional white gloves presented by counsel to the bench.

His status, his forthrightness, and his reputation for strong discipline brought with them a task that Thomas never relished: he was asked to birch offenders. On the two required occasions he carried it out with punctiliousness: both of those assignments had been requested of him by Mr Justice Hipwell (whose wife had a club foot: they were known as 'Hipwell and Hopwell'). Justice Hipwell sat again in the first week of December.

Thomas received a notice of the charge-list the previous evening, handed in to the house by the Sergeant. The letter lay unopened until he had finished his chores and washed his hands.

'You like the court business, don't you?' asked Ellen with pleasant interest.

Thomas said, 'Look at this.'

She leaned over his shoulder.

'Oh, my God! Oh, Thomas, no. Why didn't he tell me, he was here on Saturday? Awww!' Ellen squealed. Michael Quinn had been charged with theft.

'Thomas, you'll have to get him off, you'll have to vouch for him.'

Thomas said nothing, other than, 'We'll have to see how it is.'

'Thomas,' she charged, 'you knew about this, didn't you? You must have known?'

Leaving Ellen – by agreement with the Canon – in charge of the whole school, Thomas hoped to return to the classroom by lunchtime. Tuesday morning, however, vanished in licensing renewal applications, at which Thomas gave some testimonials as to the good character of two pub owners. After the brief lunch adjournment, awaiting the Quinn appearance, he listened to two further hearings.

One concerned a man from Rosegreen who was apprehended, according to the charge, 'while drunk and shouting at the sky'. The man was bound over to keep the peace and fined three shillings and sixpence. The second hearing concerned the larceny of a tree from the yard of the Church of Ireland. The man who took it offered no explanation: he was fined two shillings and sixpence and ordered to retrieve the tree from his own garden and replant it in the church grounds at Silverbridge.

The third hearing began. Michael Quinn had allegedly stolen two watches from farmers' jackets at a sports day the previous summer. Late delivery of the charge sheet had given Ellen no time to see the boy. She had handed to Thomas a letter of good character, and in it she offered the court her services in the boy's hoped-for probation.

'Thomas, I implore you. That boy tries to look after his brothers and sisters, and he has nobody to look after him. Now you know I'm especially fond of him. Please, Thomas.'

=

When Thomas re-entered the courtroom he saw the Quinns, father and son, sitting at the back, in the narrow public benches waiting to be called forward. He went across to them, to say an encouraging word, that he would volunteer to appear as a witness on the boy's behalf, that he had been talking to the court solicitor. The boy's father – the man whom Thomas had pointed out to Ellen the very first morning she came to Deanstown – turned on Thomas abusively.

'You're all part of this crowd, you're all the same sort of Free Stater crowd, your justice was never any good for anyone.'

The boy, white-faced and edgy, looked away in distressed non-chalance. Thomas rested his hat on the seat and indicated his desire to help; the man knocked the hat to the ground.

'I know you of old, Kane. You were a Collins man. Keep your help. We don't want your help.' The boy's father spoke savagely, yet in the kind of hushed whisper he might have used in a church.

Michael continued to try and look uninterested.

The hearing began: the boy, his arm taken firmly by the Sergeant, stepped forward into the dock, and stood there white-faced against the wooden grained panelling.

'Are you Michael Quinn?'

The Sergeant nudged the boy, who answered. Mr Justice Hipwell asked the clerk where exactly did this alleged crime take place.

'I know it was at the Sports Day in New Inn, but where, which field? Was it during the running? Or the three-legged race? Or what?'

Nobody knew. Two farmers gave evidence and said that they found their watches missing out of their pockets; they had laid their jackets on the ground during the tug-of-war. When they went to the pub later they heard that a boy had been down at the stalls outside the church gate trying to sell a watch to a tinker.

The boy said only 'Yessir' and 'Nosir' to the judge's questions: 'Did you know this was wrong? Did you mean to steal these watches? Isn't it wrong to go around the place like a little thief taking things from people's pockets?'

Thomas gave evidence.

'My wife in particular knows this boy and feels that he is a good boy, that he is not a criminal. The boy left school a year ago at fourteen, he is not really strong enough to work for the farmers.'

He handed in Ellen's letter: Mr Justice Hipwell read it and only commented, 'Oh, Mr Kane, I forgot. Congratulations on your marriage, I wish you all the best.'

Thomas told Ellen later that he tried to build a picture of 'difficulty requiring leniency', in sentiments that, as he pointed out, he did not fully feel. He appealed further on the boy's behalf – that he diligently brought the younger children to school; that he looked after a mother who had much illness, she had lost several babies. He, Thomas, had taught the boy, had never known him to give trouble, could even give a guarantee about the boy's future behaviour.

'I take your point, I take your point.' Justice Hipwell always nodded in agreement with Thomas, and then asked whether the boy's parents had come to court. With Thomas still at the wooden rail of the witness box, the father rose from the rear. He shouted at the bench that no justice would be forthcoming in this court, that all this country had done was exchange one system of discrimination against Irish people for another, and that the court had no power anyway in his eyes, it was 'Free State fraud'.

Mr Hipwell gave the man a choice – he could leave the court, or be arrested and bailed to the next session on a charge of contempt: he chose to leave – noisily: Justice Hipwell sentenced the boy to twelve strokes of the birch.

The Court Clerk asked – whom would the judge nominate to administer the punishment? Normally a parent was commanded by the court to do so: here the court found that the relevant parent had shown himself to be unsuitable: what was to be done?

The judge deliberated, whispering it further with the Clerk. Thomas saw them looking at him and, by now back in the well of the court, he began to slip away towards the exit. The judge called him back.

'Mr Kane, you've helped in a similar matter in the past. You'll oblige again? The court would be in your debt.'

As Thomas opened his mouth to protest, the judge continued, 'And as you know the court can actually command you to do so, though I am sure that will not be necessary in your case. If you have a word with the Clerk he will inform you of the necessary forms that have to be filled in, specifying time, date, witnesses, etc.'

The court rose; Thomas had no more influence in the matter. He went forward to the Clerk's desk, and gathered the forms. The

Clerk said, 'I know 'tis a bit hard to have to do it, but the Justice is very grateful, and I suppose your wife might want to be the official witness.'

They parted, and when Thomas turned to go, Michael, still standing in the dock, stared at him across the empty room. He rushed out of the dock and half-ran across the courtroom to Thomas and stood there, not saying anything. Thomas quite simply did not know what to do and turned on his heel and left. The boy, quite a tall boy for his age, but, as Ellen was fond of saying, 'woefully thin', followed to the car and stood again.

Thomas had to attend a committee meeting at Outrath creamery at half-past four, and by the time he got home at seven o'clock, Ellen already knew the verdict of the court, and that Thomas had to carry out the punishment. She had intercepted Michael on his way home, had taken him in, given him tea, consoled him.

'Why, Thomas, why?' Ellen stood shaking in front of him, shaking as if cold, and rubbing her hands, screwing her eyes in pain. 'Why did you agree to it?' She tugged each cuff of her cardigan. 'You won't do it, will you? You'll pretend, won't you?' She came around and stood before him each time he turned away.

No matter how patiently he tried to explain – 'Will you listen to me, Ellie?' – she interrupted.

'But if you do commit contempt of court, if you don't whip him, that's only a fine, that's all, isn't it? Even if your standing in the court is affected, what matter? And anyway what's your standing, compared to that poor boy's wellbeing? You have standing. You'll always have standing. He'll probably never have standing. Or wellbeing. Thomas, he hasn't a pick of flesh on him, you'll cut him if you whip him.'

Patiently, Thomas said, 'It isn't "whip", it is "birch", I can't avoid doing this task.'

'But it could be. This is like you being a hangman.'

'Now, you're going to get yourself upset, Ellie.'

'Thomas, please don't do it. Go back and tell the court . . .'

'The court is gone now, for another two months.'

'Tell the Sergeant, Thomas.'

'No, Ellie, there's a duty.'

'You never liked Michael, you never liked him.' She turned away and said, 'This is terrible, this is terrible.'

197

He said, again patient, 'This is not terrible, this is the way it is, this is the law.'

Ellen burst into tears and hugged her arms tight across her bosom. 'You can stop it. You can! You don't have to do it. You don't have to be so high and mighty to that child.' She waxed. 'You're going to like hitting him, aren't you, like you like hitting everybody, like you like slapping the boys in school? What's this you call them, "paw-warmers", isn't that what you give them on their hands? I see you at it every day.' She backed away and crashed into the kitchen table behind her.

He said, in a very cold voice, 'You have a child inside you. You should be calmer than this,' then walked out of the room, left the house and went firmly to the school, where, with candlelight, he sat at the high desk and read for two hours.

When he returned, all the lights downstairs had been extinguished except in their bedroom. From the hallway he heard Ellen climb into bed. He undressed on the landing, hung his clothes over the banisters, put on pyjamas, climbed into bed beside her and lay in the rigid, cold silence.

Thomas had agreed with the Sergeant to have the boy fetched to the school on Saturday morning. At eight o'clock on the night before, Ellen, sitting alone in the kitchen waiting for Thomas to come back from a nearby farmer's house, heard somebody shuffling across the gravel to the front door. She scarcely waited for the knocker to be lifted; three figures stood outside, like waifs and strays from a sentimental painting – Mrs Quinn, and Timmy, and one of his sisters.

'Won't you come in?'

They refused and asked for Thomas.

'He's not here,' said Ellen; 'he won't be home for a while.'

It transpired that they knew this; the Quinn children had been watching the house.

'You are very thin,' said Ellen to Mrs Quinn, who wore a coat that had once been fawn, and the children had no coats on this freezing evening. 'You'll have to have a cup of tea.'

Mrs Quinn refused and made her request straight out.

'I can't,' said Ellen. 'I can't. I don't like it either, but I can't stop it; the law's the law, the Master says.'

The woman stood looking at Ellen, then looking away, then

looking back. To her next remark Ellen replied, 'No, he's not a hard man. The Master is a fair man. Very fair. Everybody around here knows that. He's only doing what the Judge asked him to do. The Master is a Justice of the Peace, and Justices of the Peace often have to do things like this.'

Mrs Quinn ignored her, talked through her, and Ellen stepped back. 'If you want to come in and sit down and talk about it, do. I don't know when the Master will be home.'

Mrs Quinn muttered something and turned away.

Ellen stepped after her. 'Don't curse me. Do you hear? Don't you put your curses on me. I've looked after your young fellows and I will continue to do so. So don't you curse me.'

The little girl looked up and said, 'Sorry, Ma'am.'

Timmy waved a little hand as he walked away.

Thomas came home, having seen the departing trio. 'Oh, God Almighty.'

Ellen did not reply directly; she arranged the table for supper. After a few minutes she said, 'What do you expect? And now I find myself having to defend my husband. She said you were a hard man. What could I say?'

In the discomfort and hurt of unaccustomed silence, they began to eat. Rescue came in the form of Miss Harris, the poultry instructress, to whom Ellen had written. Miss Harris was one of the great talkers of the world, untroubled by the necessity of context.

'There's a girl from Broadford, that I was with last week, who was in the same class as you, Mrs Kane, she's marrying a vet from outside Croom, he's a fellow with a hare lip, you might know him, every old stocking meets an old shoe, his mother is a big stout woman, he has a whole lot of sisters, a Maguire man, the vet, his mother is Mrs Maguire, there's a great row, he's not getting the farm on account of him having a job already as a vet, they're dividing it up between the five sisters, achh, the commotion that's going on, 'tis a fine place, there's nearly three hundred acres, though some of it is boggy, what harm sure even a tin knocker will shine on an empty door.'

Miss Harris's volubility enabled Thomas to slip away to bed early. Next morning, Ellen had risen long before him and he found a note at nine o'clock: 'Gone to the school to light a fire. Somebody has to do something *kind*.'

Thomas dressed in the court dark suit, and his best coat and hat. From the front door he turned back to get gloves.

Smoke rose in a blue unwavering plume from the school chimney; the Sergeant's bicycle stood against the wall, and he, in a heavy coat, the silver buttons shining against the dark blue fabric, stood flapping his hands at the fire.

'Hallo, Master.'

Ellen was bending near the grate, in coat and woollen hat, foraging in her large canvas shopping bag.

'I s'pose I'd better get him, so, Master.' Thomas nodded. The Sergeant walked across the planked floor, his boots making a pleasing ring. He turned.

'Master, what'll you use?'

Thomas looked up, looked out the window, looked carefully at Ellen, rubbed his chin.

'I'll get the lad himself to cut a stick.'

Ellen drew a breath, was about to say something, stopped, blushed, turned away, bobbed her head hard, and frowned. The Sergeant spoke again.

'Two lads of mine, Sir. Out of the barracks. They're gone to the house to stop the father coming here. D'you know, like?' Thomas nodded.

When the Sergeant had gone, Ellen looked at Thomas and half-smiled.

'I think,' she said, 'I have a solution. I brought this bag. Now any noise made hitting that with a stick will sound like a beating. And I brought this too.' She took from the bag a long, quite thin alder cane. 'I broke it last night off the tree near the back door.'

Thomas shook his head.

'Thomas, if he cuts it himself –' Ellen now spoke in the voice of someone trying a different tack '– will you mind if he only cuts a light stick. Otherwise isn't that very cruel? I mean, proverbially cruel, "cut a stick to beat yourself"?'

Thomas told her that was precisely his point, that the punishment was likely to have greater, more lasting effect.

'Thomas, is there anything I can do, that will . . .'

He told her kindly and carefully that he felt obliged, felt it important. 'I need your support in this, Ellen; we have a joint place here. They look up to us.'

She opened the door, from which one could see down through

the village, down to the end of the long sloping hill past the Canon's house. Soon the frost would begin to drip from the gaunt trees. Figures appeared, materializing as two adults and two children: the Sergeant wheeling his bicycle, Mrs Quinn, the little daughter and the boy Michael. Thomas and Ellen, disregarding the cold from the open door, watched them. They stopped; the Sergeant said something to the boy and they started forward again, much more slowly. Down to a snail's pace they reached the school wall and stopped again. As the Sergeant began to make some arrangements with them, Ellen stepped outside, her breath billowing white. She heard the Sergeant explain to Mrs Quinn that nobody would be allowed in; Ellen reinforced this, and told the woman she would take care of the boy, warm him, make things as easy as possible.

Michael refused to come in; the Sergeant began to drag him. Ellen took over, and led him gently in through the door, and walked behind him up to where Thomas stood.

'You know why you are here?' Thomas asked. The boy nodded.

'You have to answer me,' said Thomas, 'that's part of it.'

The boy, on Ellen's prompting, answered a 'yes'.

'You have a choice,' said Thomas, not looking at Ellen, 'I can either use this,' indicating the ash stick with which he kept discipline in the class, 'or I can send you out to cut a stick.' The boy pointed to the stick lying in the chalk-groove beneath the blackboard.

Michael had no coat, and still wore short trousers. He had socks and boots, not in good condition, and the suit, bought very cheaply for his Confirmation four years before, had been much worn since, winter and summer. He wore a shirt with a collar, very unclean, and nothing else, no underwear.

Thomas, having asked Ellen to close the door, said to Michael, 'You have to turn around and bend over that front desk.'

Ellen went to the door as if she had become a wind-up toy, little bobbing mechanical movements, and almost ran back.

'I am supposed,' said Thomas, 'according to the law, to birch your bare flesh; you are supposed to lower your trousers.'

Ellen made a tiny, whingeing noise, and clenched and un-clenched her hands with great rapidity, and hammered them in the empty air by her hips.

'But,' continued Thomas, 'on account of the *in*clement weather,

201

I will let that pass. Now you know that you are to receive twelve strokes for stealing other people's property.'

The aspect of a beating which most surprises, and which people often most remember long afterwards, is the noise of the first stroke. Ellen rushed her hands to her ears, then spun her head around. Last night's frost had the whiteness of light snow; the breath from the cattle rose like a nativity in the fields across the road; a bird nipped past the window.

Thomas struck again, the firelight catching his face as he lifted his arm. The boy shook each time. The third blow seemed especially severe and the desk clanked.

Ellen had by now begun to tremble in her entire body: her shudders punctuated each blow. Thomas never moved quickly, but had he ever moved so slowly? At the fourth blow a new noise started, a pushing of air from the stifled calls of Michael who seemed to wish to get up from his doubled position, but did not dare. Thomas struck again, changing direction this time, and by laying the stick flat across the thin body, he caught new angles. Michael screamed. Ellen began to breathe like someone in heavy exertion, and now was almost spinning on her feet. As a small child when severely agitated she seemed determined to change the orbit of the world by spinning against it: she repeated this movement now, drumming her shoes on the boards of the floor, turning a full circle, her hand to her mouth.

The door burst open; the little girl had escaped from the Sergeant. 'Mikey! Mikey!'

The Sergeant's huge hand reached in and grasped her, 'Sorry Sir, Ma'am. Carry on,' and he closed the door.

As the sixth stroke descended, Michael twisted and Thomas missed, catching the boy's thigh. He yelped appallingly. Thomas paused, which seemed almost crueller to Ellen than anything else he had done. At the seventh stroke, Ellen saw a trickle of blood on the boy's thigh and said, 'Thomas, Thomas,' and pointed to it. Thomas made a helpless gesture and laid on three more strokes. By now the boy squirmed so much Thomas had to hold him down tight with his left hand, and he became so angered by this, that when he might have eased off, he intensified his efforts. The last three blows, Ellen afterwards said bitterly, were harder than the first four. Outside a scream had begun and they could hear the

Sergeant saying, 'Now shut up will you, shut up now, you're disturbing the peace.'

Michael's thigh blood became a wider trickle. Thomas stopped, out of breath. He laid the stick along its groove, took his coat from the hook, and his hat, and walked from the room, hands deep in his pockets. Outside he nodded to the Sergeant and walked in the direction opposite to home.

Ellen eased the boy up from the desk: he could scarcely move.

'He didn't hurt me that bad, Ma'am, the Master.' He had to stop, lacking breath. Tears leaked into runny lemon mucus from his nose. Ellen stood him carefully at the tall mesh fire-guard and fetched three hot-water bottles from her large bag. She emptied one of them into a basin and from a towel unwrapped soap, a face-flannel, a jar of ointment.

'You'll have to help me,' she said, trying not to be embarrassed, 'you'll have to turn around and let down your trousers.'

When he did so, she cried for the first time, wept hot tears. It seemed as if she could count ten different stripes, red, and red-blue, mottled at the edges, and not a few of them had opened and begun to bleed. Nor was the boy accustomed to any basic hygiene. Ellen dipped the face-flannel in the warm water and as gently as cotton wool patted the angry stripes. The boy all but fainted; his mother came in, the Sergeant held on to the sister outside. Mrs Quinn stood helplessly by.

It took almost an hour and the other two hot-water bottles before the boy could actually think of walking. Ellen emptied the basins out of the back windows so that the little girl would not see the bloodstained water. Ellen talked to herself all the time, heaped coal on the fire, gave the boy sweets, soothed him, 'It will never happen again, don't you know that?' held his hands and rubbed them, and finally wrapped him in her own coat and saw them off. She then mopped the few small bloodstains from the floor beneath the desk and stood by the fire, and wept like a child. After some minutes she dried her tears, then remained for a long time looking into the flames.

'What is this all about?' she asked herself, over and over again, aloud. 'What is this? What is this all about? What kind of man am I married to? What is this business, this business of marriage, supposed to be? Is this what marriage is like?'

She blew out the lamp, doused the fire as much as possible, locked the door and walked very fast down the three hundred yards to the house, coatless and carrying her shopping bag. She flapped her free hand repeatedly. As she reached the gate, she heard the swish of a bicycle behind her and turned as the sound came to a halt right by her heels. The Quinn boy's father, to whom she had never spoken before, loomed over her. Ellen, a hand on the gate, said to him, 'He'll be all right, Mr Quinn, Michael will be all right.'

'Ma'am,' said the man bitter as acid, 'anyone who'd do that to a child should get a taste of the same himself.'

'I understand you, Mr Quinn,' said Ellen, piously and impetuously. '"He who takes the sword shall perish by the sword." Isn't that what the Bible says?'

'That's right, Ma'am,' said the man. 'That's right.' He shook his fist in the air, turned his bicycle around, and Ellen opened her front door. She knelt at a chair in the kitchen, as close to the black, shiny range as she could get without burning herself, and, of a sudden more uneasy than she had ever felt, began to pray.

When Thomas walked from the school he intended to stay out all day. His pace increased as he left the village and turned along a deserted by-road; he walked maniacally fast, sometimes clamping his hat tight to his head. Once or twice a cyclist or a horse and cart passed by; he did not return their greetings. Reaching the abandoned bridge at Griffinstown, a full six miles from home, he ducked under the parapet and crouched in the flood arch, under limestone which kept out the cold. The water flowed by, black and sluggish, and he hunched there, staring at the river. When he came home, walking much more slowly, in the dusk of the late afternoon, he called in a quiet voice, 'Ellen? Ellen?' as he took his coat and hat off in the hall. She did not answer, and when he opened the kitchen door, it took him a moment or two to pick her out in the gloom, by the glow of the range.

14

Thomas provided the means of recovery from their dreadful *impasse*. He did not relent upon what he had seen as his duty; nor did he apologize for having done it. Ellen did not address him nor provide food for him for eight days, during which he behaved as he had always done: lighting the fires; closing the shutters at night; bringing in potatoes from the pit; cleaning the globes of the lamps and nipping the wicks of the candlesticks. He helped himself to bread and butter and tea and eggs; he fried bacon.

On the Sunday, a week and a day after the birching, Thomas walked into the kitchen after Mass, his coat still on. Ellen stood by the tall cupboard, folding her scarf, and putting it away.

Thomas said, 'Ellen. Enough is enough. Do you understand me?' He said it slowly and clearly, and only once, then turned to the hall, closing the door behind him. She stuck her tongue out at the closed door, and when Thomas returned to the kitchen some time later, she said brightly, 'Wasn't that a useless sermon the Canon gave this morning?'

Thomas said, 'What would you expect from a pig but a grunt? He hasn't what you'd call a silver tongue.'

Ellen laughed. 'Made of lead, more like.'

From this time, questions of Thomas's violence became part of the daily swirl in Ellen's mind, causing her affection towards her husband to undulate erratically. Always a great enumerator, she was sometimes observed by Thomas as she stood gazing without looking, and silently counting on her fingers. If he offered a penny for her thoughts she said 'Nothing': but what means could she have found of telling him that in the silent counting on the fingers of one hand she was listing the violent incidents she had witnessed of him: the MacReadys; the bad language to the boat steward; the man in the street in London; the birching of Michael; the casual use of the cane in school? All Thomas knew was that after such a bout of introspection he could never expect closeness or friendly warmth from her for several hours.

205

At other times, she overwhelmed him with tenderness. That Sunday afternoon, for example, standing behind his chair she began to stroke his hair, then leaned forward and wrapped her arms around his chest, making a complete mess of his newspaper.

He had grown reconciled, though with difficulty, to the Church's 'intervention', making only one bitter remark, a cutting reference to the fact that she had taken to keeping her underwear on beneath her nightgown: 'Most people take clothes *off* when they go to bed.'

Otherwise, he remained constant, saying, typically, in the bedroom that evening, 'You've no idea what I think of you,' and he held her hand and pinched her cheek with gentleness: she butted his chest tenderly with her head. Looking down, she saw a bruise on his thigh, and learned that he had bumped off the edge of the gate.

'It looks just like the bruises on poor Mi –' she began, and stopped, and her mood went cold.

When the next huge tweak of her worries came by, she displayed a little more calm, and in the face of what seemed to her further evidence of the cruel strain in Thomas, she did not panic – but afterwards, she flinched for days if he touched even her hair.

An old chest of drawers had been one of the few articles salvaged from the night the soldiers set fire to the previous Residence. Never usable again as domestic furniture – blackened, and with the splats of huge heat blisters – it had been kept, almost for old times' sake, by Thomas, in the farthest of the three sheds leaning against each other to the new house. There, Ellen found Blackie, in a drawer, while actually giving birth, the round, wet spheres plopping to the old blanket scraps on which she had nested, and the cat licked the wet gossamer filament off the five kittens, one after another.

Thomas went along with Ellen's excitement, and discussed progress every day for over a week, until the kittens' eyes had opened and their crawling changed to endearing fluffy-scrawny lurches.

'But we have, how many? Ellie, we have one, two, three cats already, and Blackie four, we can't have another five cats. Give them away if you can, but I'm telling you, this parish has more cats than people, and you'll not get takers.'

She did not enquire into an alternative solution, and subsequently reported with glee that several children next day shot their hands up when she asked, 'Who here would like a kitten?'

Thomas advised that she should wait until they returned with permission from their parents. Next day, all fell by the wayside: not one parent had agreed: all had too many cats or other domestic animals already. Ellen did not report this to Thomas until asked.

'What did I say to you?' He reached for the butter. 'Some of them can't feed themselves, let alone pets.'

Animals strolled all over Deanstown. A loose cow, a mad jennet, two bad-tempered geese, several ducks, mangy dogs, innumerable cats; all were dirty, mucky from the passageways between the houses, or the dungheaps of the yards. Only Mrs Greege's hens had any scrap of decency about them, but she might well have polished them, for all anybody knew.

Two days later, Thomas raised the subject of the kittens again. Ellen ducked it, saying she would discuss it later, and in school tried the children once more, with no success whatsoever.

On Saturday morning he said, 'Ellie, those kittens.'

'I know, I know.' She looked flustered.

He asked, 'What are we going to do about them?'

She replied, 'Would you run me to Camas, to the vet, and see if he'll take them?'

'Ah, woman,' he said, half-amused, and a little irritably. 'The vet has more to be doing than dealing with a few kittens. He'd put the run on you if you walked in there like that.'

'But the kittens are animals, too?'

'If you walked into a vet's yard,' said Thomas, 'with a litter of kittens under your arm, he'd give you a strange look.'

Ellen asked, fearfully, 'What do people do with kittens they don't want?'

'What do you think they do?'

That afternoon, averting more than fending off Blackie's half-hearted, mewling defences, Thomas picked up the five kittens one by one and plopped them into a potato sack. Ellen did not appear: Thomas had told her very clearly that he intended to remove them 'before they get any bigger'.

'New life,' she said. 'It's not fair,' but she put up little fight, other than a last suggestion of giving them away as 'Christmas presents. Or couldn't we keep one for our own baby?' He merely looked at her over his reading spectacles.

=

Thomas left the house and walked diagonally across the Castle fields; in one hand a shovel sloped gun-like over his shoulder, the other hand held the squirming sack stiff-armed out from his side to avoid little soft poking claws: the piled-up kittens mewed, tossed in the brisk walking motion. He followed the muddy cow-path by the Castle stableyard walls, until he came out into the open ground under the plane trees, and soon reached the sluice at the old pond.

In summer, the pond, replenished from a small underground source, fed the stream from which farmers watered their cattle along the way for eight straight miles until, a minuscule canal, never widening nor deepening, like the lives of its neighbours, it reached the river. The sluice-gate, therefore, though by now the colour of rust, always worked: its hinges were kept well oiled. At the point in the pond where the sluice wall dammed the water at the stream's beginning, gathered a small black pool, a yard square, but as deep and threatening as a filled canal lock.

The winter sun came out, low in the sky, and weak, and Thomas raised his face to it. He laid the sack on the pond shore, crushing small sedges, and walked around the field, intently examining the ground, bending almost double here and there, prodding the earth with the point of the shovel's blade. This narrow section, generally infertile, and too neglected even for the farmer to slash the 'Thistle, Ragwort and Dock' in response to every year's notice in the police stations, had turned into a cemetery for unwanted, small domestic animals drowned by their owners at the sluice. Thomas found the site of a recent burial, and tracing its lines, eased the turf sward off the old grave. The traces of a rotting sack appeared. He then worked the shovel into a space beside the bits of jute, availing of the softer weakened ground to dig a new, equally shallow hole.

Returning to the sack he picked it up and measured the new trench with it, then dug some more and continued to measure it with his sack's volume, until the little pit would completely accept the entire bundle. Then satisfied he stuck the shovel in the ground, leaving it to stand erect, stepping on the blade's shoulder to make it fast. He picked up the sack again, at which the kittens mewed afresh. Thomas strode over to the sluice-gate and, squatting on the wall, lowered the sack into the water, dousing the mewing. He angled the sodden bag in such a way that it caught under a jutting ledge just beneath the surface. The sun continued to shine, warm on his neck, and a bird fluted, unseasonably pert. From the sack in the water came a brief, puny thrashing, then a series of small bubbles rose to the surface.

Thomas secured the neck of the sack to the sluice wall under one booted heel, fumbled inside his heavy coat and drew out a watch. He gazed at the mountains, so near and welcoming and mysterious in the winter light, and referred to his watch once or twice. After five minutes or so, he returned the watch to its pocket, lifted the inert load from the sluice, and evading its plashings and cascades, stepped nimbly from the wall to the shallow grave, and buried the drowned kittens.

Had he raised his head from his labours and looked back in the direction he had come, he might have seen his wife. Standing by a haw bush on the height of the sunken fence, a distance of about two hundred yards away, she had a clear view of all Thomas had been doing. By now, she knew him well enough to feel safe following him across the fields: an intent man, he rarely looked back while walking, and in any case she had travelled by a different field. She stuck her gloved hands deep in her pockets joining them across her stomach; afflicted, she went home along another diagonal path on which the woods would shield her. Not a word did she say when he returned: she accepted casually the cup of tea he made. Later, sitting reading in the kitchen, he remarked, 'I notice you didn't ask me anything about the kittens?'

She said, quite slowly, 'No. I didn't.'

'Don't you want to know what happened to them?'

No reply.

He lowered the newspaper further, and looked kindly. 'What I want you to know is – two or three of those kittens would have litters of their own in a few years' time, and then two or three of them; all the females would have litters and so on, and we wouldn't be able to feed them all, nobody would. Much kinder to get rid of them. So I drowned them. Up at the Castle sluice, and then I buried them. These are small laws. It's not like humans.'

She said, 'I know, I know,' thoughtful and pacifying in her tone. 'I suppose these are things I'll have to learn. I was wondering – if I lived alone out here, would I be able to do it myself?'

He replied, 'My mother never managed it, one of us, or my

father before that, we always had to do it. How will you go about killing the turkey?' They laughed. Next day, however, Ellen relapsed into one of her worried silences. He joshed her once or twice, but getting no response, occupied himself elsewhere.

It poured with rain the week before Christmas, and Ellen – who had used her own money, as she pointed out to Thomas – had to dash from the car each time, to the doors she visited with the parcels of sugar and tea she had been buying, thick string-tied paper bags, blue and large for the sugar, brown and smaller with the bags of tea. Briefly bewildered children, or their mothers, opened their latched doors and saw their schoolmistress standing there, her hat heavy with raindrops, and bowing her head as if sheltering under their eaves, and thrusting forward these parcels, saying, 'Just something for the Christmas.' All accepted, except at Quinns where the father opened the door.

'No, I don't want them.'

'But they're only for the Christmas. And the children.'

'I don't want them. I've enough for my own family.'

'No, but really,' Ellen pressed again.

He said, 'I have enough for my own family. I'm in work the whole year.'

Ellen pushed a little past him and placed them on the windowsill inside the porch.

'It's Christmas,' she said. As she left, he tossed the parcels in a small arc after her: they burst open either side of her feet, spilling the white sugar and the black-brown tea in the puddles. Not knowing what to do, she bent for a moment, then realized nothing could be picked up, and she reached the safety of the car.

'Did you see that?' she asked Thomas breathlessly. 'Did you see that? He threw them at me.'

'Did he hit you with them?' She shook her head. Thomas drove away, saying, 'I told you not to go in there. He's unreliable, that's saying the best about him.'

'But the example for the children?' protested Ellen.

'Ah, God help your head, Ellie,' said Thomas. 'People think you're giving them charity, and they mightn't like that.'

She said, 'I haven't seen him around for ages, not since . . . Oh, God . . .' As if about to confess something, she bit her lip. Thomas did not press; in any case, she would not have told him what she had just remembered: the pious 'Perish by the sword' remark she had made in the heated aftermath of the birching.

All week, especially when the weather improved, people visited with gifts. Mrs Mahony brought a pair of geese; 'The Master loves a goose, Ma'am, doesn't he?'

Ellen replied, 'Is that why he married me, d'you think?' but the joke may have been too sophisticated. Denis MacLoughlin's wife brought a large ham. 'We cures this ourselves, Ma'am, and we smokes it.'

'We cure. And we smoke,' said Ellen, unable not to correct.

'Do you, Ma'am, isn't the Master blessed so. I thought, saving your presence, a city girl wouldn't know anything about that class of a thing at all.'

'No, no, it isn't that,' said Ellen and, recognizing that she was about to get hopelessly lost in the intricacies of colloquialism, gave up, rescuing herself by getting from Mrs MacLoughlin details of how they cured and smoked the ham.

'The bad thing is, Ma'am, wet turf is good for it, but it'd kill ourselves with coughing, and Denny's always saying we have to kill ourselves to cure the ham, like. But the good turf, it ed not make enough smoke, like.'

Ellen said to Thomas as they ate, 'Mrs MacLoughlin, where's her accent from?'

'The planet Mars,' said Thomas. 'I never know a blind word she's saying. Ask her some time about the flowers in her garden? She'll tell you she grows "chrystantrums", and "germaniums" and that when she got married, her aunt gave her a present of crockery, "the finesht set of bowels in the county". When I met her first, I needed an interpreter.'

'But very good-natured, though?' said Ellen. Thomas nodded.

Mrs Quinlivan brought two porter cakes still in their tins. 'Don't eat them now, Ma'am, keep them for the Confirmation, or something, they keep grand.'

Thomas said, when Ellen reported this, 'What a shrewd piece of advice, in case you were going to dig them out of the tins there and then, with a trowel, and tear into them. What else did Mrs Quinlivan say? Any funeral news?'

Ellen turned from the washing-up: 'Now why do you ask that?'

Thomas laughed. 'Go on, tell me. Did she say anything about a funeral?'

'Well, she did, as a matter of fact.'

Thomas asked, 'Was she just back from one?'

'She was. How did you know?'

Thomas asked, 'And did she tell you how old the unfortunate man was, how many children he left, what he died of, and who he left the place to in his will? And how in the name of the good God above in Heaven will the widow manage at all, at all?'

Ellen replied, 'Yes, more or less, that's nearly exactly what she said. How do you know? Did you meet her on the road? Because if you did, why didn't she give you the cakes?'

'I didn't meet her at all. But going to funerals is her hobby. That woman has been known to travel fifty miles to a funeral. Her husband the same. D'you remember that train crash? The one at Tarr's Bridge? Her husband went to the scene of the accident, and he got around one of the ambulance men to get him the dead train-driver's bootlaces and he brought them home as a souvenir. Mind your feet, Ellie.'

The rain of the past week had raised the water-table all around the house, and Thomas was laying armfuls of straw on the weeping stone floor.

On the eve of Christmas Eve, the weather changed for the better. Ellen finished the last Christmas pudding and vowed to Thomas that henceforth she would have them all made by October. He laughed and told her his mother always said that too, but 'was always up to her elbows in candied peel the Sunday before Christmas.' As Ellen took off her apron, she smoothed her stomach, and said, 'Have I begun to look anything yet?'

He turned her in an angle to the light. 'Oh, you certainly have,' he said. 'Although in clothes it's hard to tell.'

With the burst of speech that always signified intense anxiety in her, she blurted, 'There's something worrying me. That I want to say to you,' and sat on a kitchen chair: he leaned against the table.

'D'you know the way the Stephensons breed their horses, you know, the thoroughbreds, a good hurdler, or a good filly for the Guineas, or whatever the race is? Well, I was wondering – Can the same be done with human beings, the same breeding?'

'You mean are we going to enter that child –' he pointed at her stomach '– for the Derby?'

212

Ellen did not laugh. 'No. What I mean is – will it, can it, will it bring forward, in it, as part of it, exactly what we, you and me, are like?'

Thomas said, 'I don't know. I suppose, not all of it, and not exactly any of it, maybe. It will have to be – itself. Why, what are you driving at?'

'Well, you won't talk about it, but if it is a son we have, and if he turns out to have your temper . . .'

'You mean – my violence? Don't you? Now who were you talking to this time? Not your "dear Father John" again?'

He spread his arms impatiently. 'The night after next is Christmas night, tomorrow night is Christmas Eve night, and I'm not allowed to have connection with my own wife in my own bed; she even wears her knickers when she goes to sleep, and we're not allowed even to question it. How, so, do you expect me to talk about something that's only an indefinite, when there's an urgent definite that we're not allowed to discuss at all?' His voice rose.

'But there isn't anything to discuss, we know it's a sin while a woman is expecting.'

Thomas barked. 'On one man's say-so. We don't know for certain. What I do know is a sin is – denying kind friendliness, that's a sin. It goes on all around us, has for years, and we're adding to it here, privately, between us. No wonder it spreads.'

'Oh, Thomas, I don't deny you anything, look around you, look at the house, look at the baking I've been doing, look at the shine of the place, and the way I pray for you. Come on, Thomas, be fair.'

Since he had begun the long and difficult attempts to control his anger and his physical violence, Thomas avoided provocative situations, and now he walked out of the house, into the yard, and then through the leafless hedge into the empty, quiet garden and its ridges of last year's drills.

On Christmas Eve, the houses of the countryside drew into themselves. Men finished last tasks at noon and changed into Sunday clothes, in order to do some last-minute shopping, or drink in crowded public houses. Wives tried where possible to accompany them, in order to prevent excess. Shopkeepers gave extra measure, or a cake, or a bottle of something in gratitude for the year's custom (and carefully drew attention to the gift). Spouses did not exchange

213

presents: Santa Claus came to see many of the children; some, from the poorest cottages, avoided meeting playmates for several days, or pretended Santa Claus had indeed come and brought them sweets which by then they had eaten. By seven o'clock on Christmas Eve, apart from stragglers – swaying on carts, or walking unsteadily along the dark roads wheeling bicycles – all had come to rest indoors, and in each home the youngest lit the Christmas candle in the window to guide the family wandering towards Bethlehem to a friendly light.

Ernestina Stephenson envied the Catholics that tradition. Certain that nobody would enter her room – the house had fallen silent: her brother must have gone 'carousing' – she put her bedroom lamp in one of the windows for a short time. She scraped her hands violently through her hair – 'He's a fool! He's a fool!' Dr Hogan was a fool: telling her that the way she felt now might not necessarily be the whole truth: the last few days she had been feeling much better: she might even go for a drink on New Year's Eve to the Harpers. And the nightgown and bedjacket, ordered from a magazine – why not? Why not a Christmas gift from herself to herself?

'You will never get me inside a hospital door,' she told Dr Hogan. 'Never.'

'All serene, so?' he asked. 'All serene?'

He said the same words to his wife.

'No, Jack,' she snapped. 'No. Not all serene. You can cook it.'

She stood in the kitchen, arms folded tight, her coat still on, face red after her long walk.

'And by the way, when are we going to change the name on this house, why does it have to be "The Dispensary"? Why does it have to have a name at all?'

'It was called that when it was built, Miriam. You know that.' He rubbed his hands. 'The car was freezing. Would you like a cup of tea?'

'You're always making tea. No wonder you get on so well with my mother, Jack.'

He put the kettle on, still rubbing his hands, and poking the stove.

'Where did you put the turkey anyway, Miriam? Even if you're not going to cook it?'

'Down a manhole, Jack, where do you think?'

He took it as a joke.

At the crossroads, as the bus approached, casting a rectangle of shaky yellow light, Val Vousden raised his hand, and manoeuvring his precious Gladstone bag, accepted the respectful greetings, and acknowledged the smiles of the Christmas homegoers. Through the dark bus windows, he could see tiny lights here and there in the hills, each one signifying a window and a home. The bus dropped him at Patrick's Bridge; Val walked briskly to Shandon, and began the slow climb up the hill to his sister's house. He never understood their family's tradition of having Christmas dinner on Christmas Eve: it was an odd, old custom: they should have dropped it years ago: 'The bells of Shandon. That sound so grand on. The pleasant waters of the river Lee,' he hummed to himself, out of breath by the time he reached the door.

'There's a parcel here for you,' said his sister.

'Oow, ow, ow,' yelped Val, 'is it Mrs Heffernan? It is! It is!' shouted Val, feeling the crinkle of careful paper inside. He opened it and spread it out on the table for all to see, and held it up against himself.

'Isn't it splendid?' he said. 'Isn't it splendid?'

In the gaslight the blue of the blue uniform, and the gold of the gold, seemed to him made of precious metal.

'Ow, Ow!' he yelped again, sheer delight.

The father of the Quinn children drank all day, and then he attempted to drink all of the evening, going from the earliest closing bar to a later, then a later, then a later. He greeted all and sundry, and only those who did not know him – and there were many – returned his greetings. However – nobody refused him a drink: not on Christmas Eve, and in any case he had long since learned only to drink in bars who did not care what colour his money was. He did not grow violent under the influence of drink: he grew mellow, and with his huge frame he could drink an enormous amount. On the carrier of the bicycle he had tied a large paper bag; it contained sweets and biscuits, and small dolls and toys. To a little girl sitting in the corner of one pub, waiting silently for her father, he handed a packet of biscuits and a sixpence.

=

'Happy Christmas,' said Leah Winer to her neighbours, for which she encountered Herbert's mild protest.

'It doesn't matter. It is their festival. Yes, Herbert, I know they don't greet us on ours, but if they knew when our festivals were, they might.'

'We have a festival every week,' he said.

'Herbert, do you want everybody going around saying "Happy Saturday", do you?'

'Didn't the church seem extra golden?' said Ellen as they took their coats and gloves off after Mass next morning. 'People don't shake hands here at Christmas, do they? They don't even say "A happy Christmas", do they?'

Thomas closed and locked the gate, as if to give the impression they had gone away for the day. An overcast sky darkened the house, so they secured the shutters at noon, lit all the fires and lamps, and spent the day in peaceful, fond quietness with each other. Thomas gave Ellen a piece of especially beautiful cut stone he had found in the Castle ruins and had polished by the monumental mason in Mooreville; Ellen gave Thomas a wide, warm scarf, with tassels at the end.

'I was going to give you gloves but that's unlucky,' she said.

He read to her as she prepared their dinner; *The Gifts of the Magi* by O. Henry, a story of lovers making sacrifices to give each other Christmas presents; the story made Ellen sad. As he finished eating he said, 'You should be praised to the skies for that food. To the skies.'

She had put hot-water bottles in the bed. As she finished her prayers and climbed in, Thomas raised himself on one elbow and reached out his arms. She drew back. 'No, Thomas, no. I promised God and his Blessed Mother at the altar this morning, and at the very moment the Canon put the Host in my mouth, that I wouldn't give in to temptation.'

'Oh, Jesus, Ellie, I'm not temptation, I'm your husband.'

Ellen shrieked from the kitchen next morning.

'You thief, you thief!'

One of the cats had hidden overnight, and made inroads into the remains of the goose. Thomas laughed as Ellen wailed. 'Now I can't even use the carcass for stock. I've a good mind not to give the rest of it to them.'

'Come on,' argued Thomas, 'they've earned it.'

At noon they decided to walk to the ploughing championships at Ross: the frost had hardened the fields sufficiently and, as Ellen said when she closed the door, who could resist the brilliant sunshine? Thomas did not act as a judge, but should a dispute arise, especially in the measuring of a plough's deviation within a drill's length, they turned to him for an adjudication and his word was final.

'It's not that I'm a ploughing judge, or that,' he explained, 'it's more mathematics really, measurement, and it's not even that, it's really a sort of court of appeal and to stop them fighting. Anyway, it's a good thing, because they'll stop betting if I'm here.'

The first competitor was calming his horses as they arrived, and ploughing began within minutes, watched by a scattered crowd of absorbed, talking spectators.

'Each man has to open two headlands,' one of the organizers explained to Ellen, 'and do seven drills each turn, and each turn is measured. And the marks are given for the cleanness of the headland and the evenness of the drills and the evenness of the turns between the drills.'

'And does the whole field get ploughed?' she asked.

'It does, Ma'am.'

'Very handy for the farmer.'

Another man who was listening laughed. 'Ah, now, Ma'am, sure he'd pay a man to plough it ten times for what he'll spend on the drink today above at the house afterwards, but don't tell the Master that.'

Thomas, overhearing, said, 'What was that, Paddy, I didn't hear a word you said,' and they all laughed. He wore his new scarf. They kept moving, slapping their hands together, and Thomas showed Ellen what to watch for as the brown earth heaved behind the blade in thick slices.

'The real experts never look behind them to see what they have done, they concentrate on what they have to do, on what's before them. Look at that drill. He couldn't do that cleaner with a razor.'

Ellen dropped on her hunkers beside Thomas, and wonderingly traced the clay where it met the old unploughed land, a hard and straight edge. Gazing up the length of the rising field behind the man with the two horses, watching the satin back of his waistcoat shine in the sunlight, and seeing the powerful steel silver of the

217

ploughshare make slabbed earth waves through the loam, she asked Thomas, 'Why does the plougher walk to one side instead of directly behind the horses?'

'That's another sign,' he said. 'A good ploughman never ruins his own work by treading on it. I remember an old fellow from Callan, over near the Kilkenny borders, telling me once that a good furrow should look as if God himself reached a knife down and whipped it along the field.'

In the event, Thomas was not called on for what he called 'any Solomon business'; they declined the offer of a drink up at the house and walked home, their noses and cheeks glowing in the twilit frost.

On Tuesday, school reopened, and the postman brought a rough and mysterious parcel, crude handwriting, yellow binder twine, higgledy-piggledy postage stamps. Thomas winked at Ellen and said, 'I can guess what it is, and don't ask me 'til we get it home.'

As he unwrapped it that afternoon, his meticulousness – balling the string, folding away the paper – made her jig with agitation from foot to foot, and she even tried to snatch the parcel away, but he laughed and fended her off easily. When he removed the thick inner layers of newspaper, a salmon lay disclosed, raw and pink like some newborn, mythic thing. No note, no letter.

'I know fine well who this is from,' Thomas said, 'and I know how he came by it too. That's my Uncle John, so it is. And his good strong net. Now that's a great compliment to you. He was always promising me one, but it never arrived 'til this year.'

For an hour or so that night, in the yellow light of the lamp, Ellen settled down to *The Story of Timothy Nash*. She had chosen a separate notebook: selected carefully with stiff covers and one hundred and twenty-four pages. Having discussed it with Thomas, she intended to write it like a dissertation. The story began to emerge quickly and clearly in her large careful writing.

After a long period of education in Salamanca (see note) *(here Ellen turned to the back of the notebook and made a detailed note about the Irish Colleges in Europe and the Penal Laws which provoked their existence)* Timothy disappeared from the

College, seemingly inexplicably, shortly before he was due to be ordained as a priest. It is believed that he spent some time working for farmers in Spain (by then he had a fluent grasp of the language), and then made his way into France and down into Italy. From his own papers it is clear that he spent some time in Rome, though his existence there may not have been an edifying one.

We encounter him most interestingly when he appears in three southern counties, Limerick, Cork and Waterford, in the year 1786. He found a patron, a wealthy farmer named Callaghan near Mallow who, the father of a large family, changed his religion from Catholic to Protestant in order not to lose his farm and livelihood. But James Callaghan secretly continued to worship as a Catholic, and therefore engaged Timothy Nash to educate his children. The first document from outside the circle of Nash's relatives is a letter from the late Miss Flora Callaghan (deceased 1860 approx.) describing the encounters her brothers and sisters had with Timothy Nash. I shall quote.

Ellen fingered through the papers, copied several passages of Flora Callaghan's letters, and opened out a large family tree, showing where Nash entered the family. The dates of each member had been entered beside their names, as had the places of birth and death. Beside Nash's entry stood an asterisk, referring to a footnote.

As you will note, Timothy Nash is the only member of the family so far to die outside his own parish.

Ellen checked the place-name beside Nash's entry: 'Beaumaris'.
'Thomas! Where are you?'
'Yes,' he called.
'Where's Beaumaris?'
'Never heard of it. Is it in Italy?'
He came through the door. 'Check the atlas.' They searched futilely.

In the weeks after Christmas, Ellen ate more and more: ever larger plates of porridge and cream for breakfast; six, eight, nine potatoes, at a time: 'Ah, Ma'am,' the solicitous women at Mass said when she told them, 'sure why wouldn't you, sure you're eating for two.'

'Thomas, I'll be fat,' she said.

'When the baby is born, all the fat will go,' he said.

'And I hardly feel the cold,' she said.

'But you must be careful if the roads are slippery,' Thomas warned; 'sometimes you can't see that ice.'

This time, Ellen opened the letter.

February 28th, 1926.

Dear Mr and Mrs Kane,

Isn't it a good job this isn't a Leap Year, or that last year wasn't either, otherwise I'd be claiming my silk gown, and I'd be using it now as a shroud, not for myself, though, but for someone else, and her little head of black hair would ornament it fine. Too sweet to be wholesome, that's what they're saying about you, Mrs Kane, although everybody should be calling you Miss Morris still, because you came in here and took what wasn't rightfully yours, namely one of our men, and our best at that. But I have my eye on you, Miss Morris, and I watch you wherever you go, at the ploughing, or coming out of Carey's with your boxes of messages, and the boy from the shop running behind you like you want all the men to be. The law may say you're married to him, but I don't.

Yours watchfully,

Through the glass of the partition, Thomas saw Ellen reading the letter, and raced towards her.

'Give it to me.' She followed him to the school porch where he stood reading it.

'Ah, dth.' He seemed more exasperated than angry.

'What's that about a silk gown?' Ellen asked.

'Oh, just an old joke around here. If a woman proposes to a man during a Leap Year, and if he refuses her, he must buy her a silk gown. This woman – if it is a woman – is sick in the head.'

'I'm frightened,' said Ellen, arms clinched shivering to her bosom. 'I never saw an anonymous letter before.'

Thomas dismissed it. 'They're always going on around here.'

'Did you get some before?' asked Ellen.

'Several.'

'Oh, Thomas, if you showed them to me I wouldn't be as frightened, maybe.'

Thomas said, 'Let me think about it.'

Ernestina Stephenson sat on the long window-seat, her breath frosting the glass, watching two of the men fork hay across the fields for the cattle.

'You, dear brother, have no intention of marrying your little Roman Catholic. Isn't that right?'

Cyril gulped from a mug of tea.

'You shouldn't be saying things like that,' he said, in an unconcerned tone. Ernestina did not look any less anxious.

'But she has every intention of marrying you, and that's what's worrying me, you know what a fool you are.'

Ernestina had a gruff, abrupt way, mannish, and her thick spectacles repelled people even further.

'I could confront her,' said Ernestina.

'What?' said Cyril.

'If you were a man, you'd tell me what your intentions were.'

'I'm going to the hunt tomorrow,' said Cyril.

'Yes.' Ernestina looked at him. 'Yes, I bet you are. Listen, can you give me money? I have none.' Cyril reached into his pocket and took out two notes.

'Ten pounds?' said Ernestina, 'that'll only do until Friday. Is that all you have?'

Cyril reached again.

'Twenty. A bit of an improvement. Another fiver, please? I hate these Irish notes.'

'If you had enough of them you wouldn't,' said Cyril.

'Would you ever think of saying something new or original?' asked Ernestina, as he drank some more tea.

Ernestina said, 'If you're not going to tell me what your intentions are towards little Miss Merrigan and her dirty little family – her dirty big family – I'll ask her myself.'

'Off you go, so,' said Cyril.

221

15

The frost lasted for six weeks, right through to Saint Patrick's Day. Ellen, though large, had expected of herself a greater ungainliness, but instead spoke of being limber, of wishing to walk.

'Although I think I'll draw the line at climbing walls,' she said to Thomas, 'and can't we go by the gate anyway?' The schoolchildren had told him the Castle pond had frozen solid, fit for skating, and Thomas decided, 'I'd better check it for safety.'

'Oh,' said Ellen blushing as they walked through the fields, 'I forgot one little detail.'

Thomas laughed and said, 'I'll wait for you. And I'll watch out to see there's nobody coming.'

She disappeared behind some bushes, and when she caught up with Thomas who had strolled on, he said, 'I never saw such steam.'

The tease took a moment to register, and then she punched him.

Two boys careened, yelling, on the slide the locals had made down the length of the pond: when they saw the Master and the Mistress, they drew themselves to a halt by drifting off to one side where the rime of the frost sat like light snow.

'I'd love to but I'd better not,' said Ellen, 'you have a go.'

Thomas said, 'I'd better test it first,' and stood with all his weight on the closest edge. He had brought a chisel, and began to lever the ice away from the sedges.

'Look,' he said, 'frozen solid, right enough. Did you hear about the Stephensons' engine. Stuck. On the field. They can't budge it. Everyone's laughing.' He stepped on the lake, bouncing, bending and flexing his knees. 'Look. Not a give. Not a trace of a give.' He walked gingerly outward. 'It's six feet deep here.' He bounced harder. 'Ellie, this is extraordinary. Look.' He drummed his heels on the ice. 'I can't even make a crack.' Taking the chisel from his pocket he attacked the frozen surface. 'Not a mark.' He strolled-skated over to the little island at the very centre, while Ellen watched clapping her hands in the cold.

'Aah,' he called out sympathetically. 'There's a water-hen.' He bent down, struggled with something in the reeds and stood back having failed, then began to return to Ellen. 'A water-hen, dead,' he called out, 'it got caught or something, frozen to the ice. Stiff as a board.'

The whiteness of the landscape lit his face reddening from exertion.

'Thomas, you're a disgrace,' she said. 'Anyone would think to look at you now that you were no more than twenty-five years of age.'

He took her arm. 'Come on. I'm going for a skate,' he said, and they walked around the shore.

The two schoolboys stood back in sheepish respect, as Thomas had a run at the slide. He took off by locking his feet and whizzed by Ellen, waving to keep balance. Then his arms began to windmill and he fell crazily, crashing on to the ice and spinning a little on his hip. The boys laughed, and Ellen had difficulty in not joining in. When Thomas picked himself up, he held his elbow gingerly and made his way slippily to the bank.

'What are you looking at?' he asked the boys. 'Go on. Skedaddle.' They looked at each other, then slunk away.

'I've hurt my blasted arm,' he gritted. She inspected, turning the arm a little this way and that, making him squeak with pain.

'Come on,' she said, 'we'll go and call in to Dr Hogan. It'll be an excuse to meet him.' Thomas had previously remarked that the same new doctor had not had 'the manners to come and introduce himself in the last six months', but Ellen pleaded the stranger's case, saying the man was still settling in.

He himself answered the door of the Dispensary, younger than they expected, but still almost Thomas's age, and wearing something Thomas hated, a bow tie. Nevertheless, Dr Hogan immediately disarmed Thomas, when he exclaimed, 'But you're the man with the Singer car. I have an Austin Seven myself.'

Thomas asked, 'The green one?'

'Green is right.' He ushered them in. 'Green for glory. With a nice little yellow stripe. Here. Sit down there. Don't mind the mess. It'll be better than this, I have to do a lot myself, the wife is very busy. You know the Tierneys, I believe?'

'Which Tierneys?'

'From Glaslyre.'

'Oh, I do well,' said Thomas.

'We met your wife on the train,' said Ellen. 'And she was on the boat.'

'She has cousins in England,' said Dr Hogan. 'And the Tierneys are cousins of mine, that's how I heard of this job. What happened to us?'

Thomas said, in quite a short tone, 'I fell; I slipped on ice.'

Ellen laughed. 'Tell the man the truth. He was playing on the slide up at the Castle.'

'Slide?'

'The schoolchildren made a slide on the pond,' said Ellen, 'and Thomas was playing on it.'

Thomas said, irritably, 'I had to make sure it was safe.'

'Are we able to take off our coat?' asked Dr Hogan, and helped Thomas out of it. 'Funny, I was going to call to the school and say hallo on Monday, but sure you brought yourselves to me here.'

'What is your wife busy at?' asked Ellen.

'Ah, she's always doing some old thing.' He stood examining Thomas's coat before laying it on a chair. 'And our jacket. Oh, we drew blood a bit, that's hopeful. I'll tell you one thing. You have a lively bit of life around here. Did you hear about your rabbit-catcher?'

'What's up?' asked Thomas.

'The Sergeant called this morning, see if we can lift our elbow a bit higher. They can't get into the house. They're gone away to get a crowbar. Higher.'

'Ow!' Thomas winced and jerked. 'Crowbar? I'll get in there. What do they want to get in there for?'

'Now the other way. When are you due, Mrs Kane?'

'Early May.'

'A good time, child'll grow up in the warmth of the summer. The fresh air. Watch out for the wasps, though. Now back this way. I see. Does this hurt? Whose patient are you?'

'Dr Morgan's,' said Ellen.

'Hah! I did a locum for him about six years ago. Ex-army, yellow moustache.'

'The very man,' said Ellen.

'"Malaria Morgan" we used to call him. Now does that hurt us? H'mmmmm. D'you know what it is? I think we have a chipped elbow. Was it our elbow we fell on?' He turned about and speculated towards some half-prepared shelves.

'We'll have to fix that up for us, that's no good.' He began to hum.

'Are you musical?' asked Ellen.

'Love it,' said Dr Hogan. 'Balfe is my man.'

'Because I'm getting a choir going,' said Ellen.

'I'm the wrong man for that, I'd never turn up,' said Dr Hogan. 'And anyway, d'you see, I'm no good in a chorus, I'm a great man for the *tour de force*, that's what I am. Here we are.'

He unwrapped an awkward package and took a yellow slab of hard cloth from it. 'This is what they call a plaster, it has plaster of Paris in it, I don't know how they do it, and it's supposed to be very good. Now we have to hold our elbow like this' – he bent his own elbow three-quarters of the way closed, then stood over Thomas's elbow and eased the plaster on, while Thomas winced again.

'And we'll have to wear a bit of a sling. The scarf'll do lovely. Well, well, a Singer Roadster. About ten days, I'd say, and we should be all right, 'tisn't a bad chip.' He hummed again, and, the sling finalized, washed his hands in a basin. 'What about the rabbit man, d'you see? I s'pose we should go and see him?'

He invited them to squeeze into his Austin Seven, and then had to go back to the house for the starting-handle.

Thomas, staring straight ahead, murmured to Ellen, 'Look at the top window.' A face pushed aside a net curtain and Miriam Hogan stared down, dark-eyed. She withdrew when Ellen saw her, and the net curtain flickered back into place.

On the edge of Deanstown, where the trees ended, the Sergeant flagged down the overloaded green Austin Seven. Johnny Halloran's house was known locally as 'The Hotel', a building of acute dishevelment, noisome and broken-paned.

'Oh, the very man yourself, Sir,' said the Sergeant, when he saw Thomas. 'Hallo, Doctor, there's a great stretch in the evenings, isn't there? Hallo, Ma'am.'

Thomas squeezed out of the car, wincing, and the Sergeant began to explain. Nobody had seen the old man of the house for two to three weeks: the son had been evasive. The son's wife had seemed more than usually 'off the main road', as the Sergeant put it, and had barred entry to the nurse who wanted to 'put ointment on the baby'. Now the Hallorans had refused to open the door at all.

'Could you give them a shout, Master?' asked the Sergeant.

Thomas walked to the door, knocked, then tried it: the latch shifted but not the door. He knocked again.

'There's someone in there,' said Ellen, who saw movement in a curtain of newspaper at a top window.

Thomas retreated several paces and tilted his head back to address his voice upwards.

'John Halloran, come out of there! At once. Do you hear me?'

Dr Hogan looked aside at Ellen, raised an eyebrow and bulged his cheeks at the force of Thomas's authority. The door shook under Thomas's fist. 'Did. You. Hear. Me?' He stepped back again.

The door opened abruptly and the infant scrambled out, followed by the distraught man.

'I didn't do nothing, Sir. Sir, he was that way for days before we copped on.'

The wife followed, barely dressed, talking to herself.

Thomas beckoned the Sergeant who went in, and after a moment came out holding his nose.

'Jesus. Begging your pardon, Ma'am. No, Sir, don't go in,' he said to Thomas, who pushed past – and who returned just as quickly holding his nose with his un-slinged arm.

'Phewack,' he said. 'You're needed, Doctor.' Jack Hogan shrugged and entered.

Returning, a white handkerchief pressed to his face, he asked, 'Sergeant, what do we do for an ambulance around here?'

'We haven't one, Doctor, usually the Master's car, and that's no ambulance, that's a job for a hearse.'

'No, we have to determine cause of death, Sergeant.'

The Hallorans stood by the wall, where Ellen had gone to hold the small child's hand: a little boy, he was naked from the waist down, and wore only a flimsy vest. Dusk gathered, and a flicker of snowflakes.

'We have to do something before this child gets his death of cold,' she said briskly.

'I'll take the woman and the child into the hospital,' said the Doctor.

'Master, don't be hard on me, I didn't do it, I didn't do it,' said the husband.

226

'Johnny, in the name of God how many rabbits have you in there?' asked Thomas.

'I don't know, Sir.'

'Didn't I teach you to count?'

'You did, Sir, but I forgot again.'

'How long is your father dead in there?'

'I don't know, Sir.'

'Well, when was he last alive?'

'I don't know that ayther, Sir.'

Thomas drew him away from the knot of people and began to talk to him quietly. Ellen helped the wife and child into Dr Hogan's car, and smiled at the way he looked forlornly at the hitherto clean seats.

'Ma'am, no, Ma'am, I can't let you in there.' The Sergeant moved too late: Ellen had already reached the edge of the kitchen, and just as quickly she slapped a hand to her nose and mouth. She could make out the many shapes of rabbits hanging all around the dim room lit by a small oil-lamp, and a flameless fire smoking heavily up the chimney. On a low mattress lay a figure, but her eyes did not wish to register the condition of the skin on the face beneath the matted grey hair, and she fled.

The old man had died over a week previously. Lacking the intelligence or the will to move him, the family sat there looking at him; the child even rambled across the corpse, playing 'horse-y'. In milder weather, rapid decomposition would have set in earlier: it had just begun.

'What happened,' said Thomas back at home, as they dried their hands, and stood in front of their kitchen range, 'was that the father died, and Johnny had no money to pay for the funeral, and he didn't want the indignity of a pauper's grave for him, so he thought he'd wait, and with luck the frost would break and the ground would ease, and he'd sneak him up to the graveyard one night, across the bar of the bike or something, and bury him himself.'

Thomas laughed. When he went to throw the water out into the yard he held the back door open and called Ellen. Together they stood and looked at the snow falling.

'Well, that's the end of the frost,' said Thomas, 'rain next.' The snowflakes, like millions of soft tumbling insects, fell into Ellen's eyes and pleased her, as she looked up into the night sky. They bolted the back door.

After supper she asked, 'How bad is the elbow?'

'Ah, the blasted thing is a nuisance,' said Thomas. 'Good job it isn't my right arm. At least I can still use the chalk.'

She went to the parlour, and returned with a bottle.

'You deserve this,' she said, getting a glass.

'I always thought port was red,' he said; 'this is black.' He sipped. 'Sweet. Well, goodness, I never knew. D'you want a taste? I'll get a glass for you.'

'Oh, Thomas, in my condition.'

'Arrah, woman, half the infants in the country were carried floating on a pond of Arthur Guinness.'

She drank equally wonderingly.

'Isn't this nice?' he said. 'I wonder how it'd go with onions?' and she giggled, the port, and the fire, and the pregnancy, flushing her face. Thomas had another glass, but Ellen declined. He sang her a little song:

'If I were a blackbird I'd whistle and sing
And I'd follow the ship that my true love sailed in.
And on the top rigging I'd there build my nest,
And I'd pillow my head on her lily-white breast.'

'You changed the words,' she accused happily.

As eventually they stood for bed, he gave her a large gentle hug with his good arm, curving his hips out backwards to accommodate her pregnant stomach.

'You made all the difference to me when I met you,' he said. 'All the difference in the world.'

As Ellen undressed, Thomas held the candle to the mirror, casting light farther into the bedroom. At a chosen moment he turned around from the reflection to the reality. As she stood by the basin undressed to the waist, he walked towards her, skirting the end of the bed, his scarf-sling incongruous against his pyjamas.

'I want a kiss. That's all,' he said.

'And you can have one and welcome to it.' He drank from her mouth. She moved back and said, 'You are lovely. You are great.' Reaching out, his right hand traced across the blue veins on top of her breast, as a child follows a map with its finger.

—

In school next day, Thomas called out a boy and made him stand at the top of the class. Drawing the ash stick from the groove beneath the blackboard, Thomas told the lad to hold his hand out straight. Out of the corner of his eye, he saw Ellen appear right up close at the partition, watching closely. Thomas gave the boy one reasonably mild slap across the palm and put the stick away, telling the amazed boy to return to his desk. Nevertheless, Ellen frowned.

The snow had begun to melt under soft rain. Leah came to spend the night, complete with her big suitcase. The schoolchildren looked at Leah with wonder and she smiled at them all, shaking the drops from her umbrella like a swimming dog. Thomas sent the Senior room home early, and he and Ellen walked home, with Leah between them trying to shelter all three with the umbrella, and getting all three of them wet.

'Now, we're going to have a real good chat,' said Ellen, as they drew their chairs to the fire Thomas had lit in the parlour. 'I'm going to make a cup of tea, and Thomas is going out, he has a meeting.'

'Are you off, so, be careful,' she called to Thomas from the hall, 'what time will you be back? He won't be back until late,' she tossed to Leah, and closed the hall door.

'Did you see this?' asked Leah, and handed Ellen a cutting, who read it, and said, 'Great! But, Leah.' She halted. 'Sure how will I know what size I'll be?'

Leah said, 'A first baby? You won't change too much.'

Mrs Gleeson, who is retiring from the Drapery business, having disposed of her Winter Goods, is offering her last Summer's Stock at exceptionally low prices. Wonderful Value in Ladies' frocks from 75/6d, Latest Style in Ladies' Costumes and Coats from 20/-. Children's Frocks from 2/6d. White Voile and Silk Frocks in great variety for 4/6d. Wreaths and veils from 2/-. Ladies' and Children's Hats from 7/6d. Children's White Shoes from 7/6d. Blouses and Jumpers from 2/-. Cardigans, 6/-. Underclothing of all descriptions marked less than cost. Boys' suits from 8/6d. Odd knickers from 2/6d.

A TRIAL WILL CONVINCE.

'Now how are you?' said Leah. 'Is everything all right?'

'I'm fine,' said Ellen, 'just fine.'

'And Thomas?'

'He's fine too. Oh, Leah, I have so many things to tell you I don't know where to begin.' She leaned forward and touched her dear friend's arm, and they smiled broadly at each other for no reason other than pleasure at the prospect of several uninterrupted hours together.

Their history of friendship permitted them a shorthand language, the mutually understood references of common ground: children, neighbours, fashions, households.

Leah asked again, 'And how are you, I mean – how are you? Herbert said to ask.'

Ellen said, 'Well, grand, really. Everything fine. A cake collapsed yesterday, you should see it, Leah, I had to throw it out. The waste, I think I put in too much fruit, and there was an awkward breeze down the chimney, the fire in the range was irregular.'

Leah looked at her and said, 'Your complexion is lovely – but are you a bit peaky?'

Ellen said, 'Well, I had a bit of a blow this morning, in the post –' and when Leah looked startled, Ellen said, 'No, I mean, no bad news, but not good either.'

She began to tell Leah the story of Timothy Nash: that Thomas had never really looked in the heirloom papers: that it had proven fascinating: but that beneath it ran a great undertow of anxiety.

'He so reminded me of Thomas, Leah, and it worried me.'

'But the letter this morning?' asked Leah.

Ellen said, 'Well, I'll tell you. Thomas's aunt had written out a whole family tree, and in it, it said that Timothy Nash died in Wales, in a town called Beaumaris on the island of Anglesey. We thought it was in Italy. So, to cut a long story short, I wrote to the local authorities there, to see if I could get some information.'

Leah said, 'Ah, why didn't you leave it alone?'

'You know me, Leah, I can't drop a thing once I start it. Anyway, I had this very peculiar letter back this morning, which said should I "wish to pursue any further details of Timothy Nash, who died in Beaumaris in 1806", I should "write to the Courthouse". I haven't told Thomas yet.'

'Hold on. Hold on. What is worrying you about the Courthouse?'

'I don't know, but I have a very bad feeling.'

Leah asked, 'Why, Ellen, are you so interested in this hundred-years-ago man?'

Ellen took another deep breath, and said, 'The thing that worries me is that I never expected Thomas to be so, so rough. I don't mean rough, and not to me, he's not, I mean –'

'You mean violent?'

'– Well, yes, I suppose so. And I'm frightened of it.'

Ellen's dam of tears burst. 'I've never said it to anyone.'

'But he has never hit you? Or has he?'

'Oh, God, no, nothing like that. But it is there in him, and children might have it in them, and what will I do if I breed a murderer? I'm serious, Leah, I'm serious. You haven't seen him when he's like that, I have.'

Ellen recounted again in greater detail than ever before, the MacReady incident. 'Leah, we could have lost our jobs over that.'

She told Leah of the birching of the Quinn boy. 'The unfortunate lad's bottom was cut and bleeding.'

Leah opted for a cool position.

'Do you seriously feel threatened by the way you have seen Thomas behave?'

'Not for myself, no,' Ellen said. 'But this worry won't go away.' She told Leah about the honeymoon incident, and the intensity of Thomas's behaviour on the street in London seemed to have the same resonance as Nash's violence to a policeman who almost arrested him.

'It is all there, in the papers about Nash, Leah. And of course, the whole "Canon Law" thing doesn't help,' said Ellen as an afterthought.

'The what?'

'Oh, nothing. I mean, I never told you. I thought it was too – too private.' Ellen unfolded the story.

Leah sighed. 'I wondered, I must say. I mean – it isn't the first time I heard a story like that with the Catholic Church. But if you want my opinion –'

Ellen cut in, 'Oh, Leah, don't confuse me any more than I am already.'

Leah halted, changed her direction. 'You've been worrying too much,' she said. 'You married a good man, then you stopped being a wife to him, all for the sake of your religion. Do you know – Herbert hinted to me that something like that might have cropped up, and he wanted me to ask you.' Leah sighed. 'I should listen to him more often. He's always right.' She continued, 'And then you saw Thomas being very angry and brutal, and you thought you'd made a big mistake, and now you find you think he has bad blood in him, and that your children will carry that bad blood.'

Ellen asked, 'Wasn't that what your letter was about, do you remember – before the wedding?'

Leah reached forward and took Ellen's hand: 'No, that was about things you should really understand, every girl should understand, before marrying.'

Ellen said, in a bitter little tone, 'I know, I know, "Marry in haste. Repent at leisure." I know.'

Leah gripped her friend's hand. 'Oh, Ellen, no, I feel for you, I feel so sorry, what you've been worrying about. And telling nobody about it. You'll worry the baby too, you must stop. Thomas is a good man. Herbert says so, too.'

'But, Leah, you know that Thomas did a lot of. Things. You know, Collins and that. The Troubles, I mean – for God's sake, Leah. He was a gunman!'

'I know. Herbert told me. He told Herbert.'

Ellen said, 'He never told me.'

Leah said, 'He told Herbert in detail. And if you're this frightened, aren't you glad he didn't tell you? Look – why don't you let the baby's placidness just – just take you over?' They sat in thought for a moment.

Leah asked, 'How much of all this has there been lately?'

'Almost none. And in fact, I wonder if he isn't trying to get "it" under control.'

'There you are. People can change, Ellen, and we must not so much help them to, as allow them to. If Thomas changes, don't say anything to him about it, just find other ways of rewarding him. But the point is – he is violent, he probably is truly a violent man. That doesn't mean that your life will be the worse off for it. I mean – there are things about me that Herbert hates. I flirt, he says, and he hates me flirting, says I shouldn't be "cocking my backside" he calls it, at men. And there are things about him that I think are wrong in any human being, I mean Herbert is quite mean with money, Ellen, and keeping small things to himself around the house; he buys himself little treats that he doesn't share – but that doesn't mean that I can't live on and on with him.'

'But, the fear. Won't go away.' Ellen provoked another fit of weeping in herself. 'And I have no choice in the matter, that's the real difficulty.'

Leah reached a handkerchief across, clean from beneath her cuff.

'I knew I was right to come out and see you. I said it to Herbert. Now you've cried enough. You don't want the baby crying too. Has all this been bottled up in there for months?'

Ellen snuffled. 'It's not so much bottled up, as much as it feels as if it is all in another room, and when I open the door it all comes tumbling out.'

Leah read silently the letter again from Beaumaris. 'Do you really want to follow this up? You'll only be a month or so off the baby?'

'It'll ease my mind, Leah.'

Leah poured more tea. 'But Thomas seems thrilled with the thought of the baby, doesn't he?'

Ellen leaned back and closed her eyes.

'And you love each other, and he's very tender to you? Despite everything? I see it in his face. And is that all that's worrying you? I mean, you're not worried about Thomas being a father? Forty-one or forty-two isn't young for a man to learn these things?' Leah wore her 'fishing' expression, but she caught nothing.

'No,' Ellen lied, 'that's the thing I'm really worried about,' and touching upon a greater concern, said, 'I mean, Leah, if you'd seen that poor Michael Quinn's bottom after Thomas birched him. I can't get it out of my head.' She did not mention the 'Perish by the sword' remark, by which she frequently felt haunted.

Ellen subsided, her eyes closed. Leah said, 'Take a little sleep there, I'll wash up these cups. I always felt weepy at this stage before the girls were born. By the way, what happened to that poor woman whose husband disappeared?'

'Oh, nothing.'

An hour later, they said good-night on the landing. A few moments afterwards, Ellen nipped back downstairs, took down a fresh pot of the Miss Harpers' prize gooseberry jam, that she knew Thomas loved, and set it on the table for his breakfast: she was fast asleep by the time the car's lamps floodlit the front of the house.

=

Val Vousden came offstage at the Opera House, thrilled with the reception: they wanted him back for another curtain call, and then another, oh, my! And another!

'Home was never like this,' he quipped to Willie Crosbie in the wings.

'Go back again, boy,' said Willie Crosbie; 'they can't get enough of you.'

Val bowed low, reversing his twirling legs sideways. Val pranced forward again, obeying to the letter the trouper's rule of curtain calls – on quickly, off slowly.

'He wouldn't milk a herd of cows better,' said Willie Crosbie to Geraldine, his favourite usherette.

Val darted out one more time, bowing lower than a weeping willow and twice as flourishingly, then straightening high, the high dome gleaming, and kissing his hands, and mouthing 'thank-you-thank-you- thank-you- thank-you- thank-you- thank-you- thank-you-thank-you-thank-you-thank-you-thank-you-thank-you-thank-you' he bravely stepped up and quick-marched off, his back view releasing the audience from their rapture.

Val had a wonderful gesture of imploring, both hands held out palms upwards, like a prince pretending to be a beggar.

'Aren't they great, Willie? And they loved "The Deanstown Band".'

'You see,' Willie said. 'There you have it, boy. Brand-new material. They love a new recitation.'

'Ah,' said Val, 'I thought as much.'

'A great piece, Val. The best piece you've done with a long while.'

In the blue of sky and gold of corn,
They marched their glittering uniforms,
With fife and drum and bright trombone,
They played the tunes their folks could hum.
This little band of village men,
Of humble birth and lowly breed,
Made music fit for Count or King,
To gladden hearts of every creed.

'Great stuff,' said Willie, leaning against the wall, reading it.

Val snatched it back, signed it and gave it to Willie, 'personally autographed'.

Val entered his dressing-room and shook hands with the tall young man there, who brown-haired and shining-eyed, congratulated him.

'Bernard, I have great plans. That band, you know –' and Val closed the door.

In the corridor, Willie read on for a moment or two, then, with Geraldine, vanished through an emergency exit like a rabbit.

SPRING 1926

16

Hushed, the church heard the lists.

'Monday, the 12th of April – John Ryle, Lackendarra: Tuesday, the 13th – John Tobin, Piercestown: Wednesday the 14th, Spy Wednesday – Michael Connors, Newtownbeg; Thursday, the 15th, Holy Thursday – John Relihan, Kiltynan. This parish is very honoured [the Canon pronounced it 'onnurd'] to have Easter Stations this year, it being a Confirmation year. And it being Holy Week, I needn't say –' The Canon paused for emphasis – 'there will be none of the usual practices, that is to say, there will be no drink. And no card-playing, but there will be a dispensation in each house for the day, and the usual Lenten fasting of only one meal and two collations will be lifted.'

On the way home, Thomas explained. 'The Stations are regarded as a great honour because the Blessed Sacrament comes to the house, 'tis like the church coming to the home, but most people find them very difficult. Because the Canon won't announce them in time, that misfortunate Mrs John Ryle won't have a minute to get her house clean, or food in, before the Canon and a whole crowd of people descend on her tomorrow morning. Everywhere else in the country, they get several months' notice, but he thinks here it will stop them having the time to buy in drink. The opposite is the case, they need the drink after all the fluster.'

'Are we going?' Ellen asked.

'We're expected to go to at least one. Our Station is on Thursday, at Relihans.'

John Relihan's house in Kiltynan lay within a long walk's distance, but Thomas decided to drive, on account of overcast skies and Ellen's largeness and occasional breathlessness. Wednesday, closure day for Easter, was her last day at school: an untrained deputy would take over until September.

'It is a bullock you have in there?' the Canon asked Ellen after Mass, looking at her stomach.

'Subtlety and delicacy,' sighed Thomas afterwards, 'Canon Jeremiah Williams's hallmarks. Known for them from here to Timbuctoo.'

Ellen was greeted with warmth, and chose a chair at the back to kneel against: that way, she could view the whole proceedings.

'Ah, Ma'am, sure you mustn't kneel, never mind the knees, sit up, sit up, sure if God'll not forgive you now, He never will.'

The women pressed around her, in her small celebrity.

'God bless you, look at the complexion of you, nature's boon.'

They intended to make her as welcome as they knew how.

'Ah, Ma'am, you have a sheen on you, that'll be the healthy child. And the lucky one. And the Master looking great? I never seen a man look so well. Sure every man needs a wife, don't they?'

The Station, essentially a Mass celebrated at the farmhouse kitchen table (which had been elevated on four butter-boxes), brought the ceremony closer to her than Ellen had ever felt, and, almost excited, she said to Thomas later, 'I never enjoyed anything as much. I never felt so devout.'

The Station Mass ended; the Canon intoned, 'God bless all here. And the crops for the market and the house. And the beasts for the fair and the table. And the women for their children now and the future. And the men that they will have strength and health and purpose. Now and in all the times to come, Amen.'

The fifty or so people there shuffled to their feet. John Relihan, as head of the household, moved forward to the Canon and put an envelope into his hand, the cue for neighbours to do the same. Connie, the sacristan, took the vital packets one by one as the Canon handed them to him, and when this ritual ended, the Canon moved off up the house to the parlour to disrobe, followed by Connie who would count the cash. The men lifted the table from the butter-boxes, and redistributed the chairs; the women began to assemble the tablecloths.

Neither Thomas nor Ellen took any part in this. Fittingly, as host, the head of the house, John Relihan, a stocky man with short black wiry hair, whose face shone, engaged Thomas, next most important guest after the Canon, in conversation: Thomas stooped as he listened, his hands behind his back, his head inclined away.

=

A stout woman approached Ellen, and introduced herself, John Relihan's sister-in-law, married to his brother.

'Tell me now, is your time good?'

Ellen did not fully comprehend.

'I mean, were you sick at all in the morning, or did you have wind in the stomach? I have a great cure for wind in the stomach.'

Ellen said, 'Oh, hold on, hold on, I'll write it down,' and from her handbag came the ever-present notebook.

'This is it. Now. You take a cupful of milk, that's about half a pint, and you boil it well [she pronounced it 'bile'] and you let it cool down to drinking heat.' Ellen wrote quickly, the pad on her knee. 'Then. You take four teaspoons of soot.'

'Of what?' Ellen looked at her.

'Four teaspoons of soot. Soot from the chimney.'

'You do not!?'

'You do, Ma'am. Four teaspoons of soot.' Ellen wrote it down, but slid in a question mark.

'And you mix the soot well into the cooling milk and you drink it.'

'But doesn't that taste terrible?' asked Ellen.

'It do, Ma'am, but sure anything is better than the wind.'

Ellen looked up speculatively, and from the far end of the kitchen saw a thin, handsome, young-ish woman staring at her, who quickly looked away. Thomas beckoned Ellen over.

'Do you know John Relihan at all?' The man shook her hand heartily. 'I'm sorry I missed you when you came in. You're very welcome. How are you settlin' in here with us all, at all?'

Ellen replied, 'Oh, sure I'm nearly a native, I'm here now, what? Over a year.'

'Oh, sure, one of our own. One of our own. And you have good news on the way.' He also indicated Ellen's stomach.

'Well, I hope so, I hope so.' Ellen noticed both the man's shyness and the determination of his courtesy in acknowledging her condition.

'I have five myself, Ma'am, and one in Heaven, and sure we liked every one of them.'

'And one in Heaven? Aah,' Ellen said sympathetically.

'Ah yes, Ma'am, sure the little thing was dead before 'twas alive, sure that's the way.'

Conversation continued: neighbours, the Land Commission

rulings, boundary fencing, arguments over inheritance in families: Ellen loved these conversations and listened avidly, barely tearing herself away when 'breakfast' was called.

She gasped when she saw the table. One of the reasons why people such as Thomas condemned the Stations had to do with social rivalry: householders, even those who could scarcely afford it, outdid each other with food. The Canon returned to the big kitchen, and said, 'Glory be to God' when he saw the feast, raising his right hand and making the Sign of the Cross over it all.

Along the centre of the main table ranged seven large, long dishes in a row, three by three, a leg of pork, a leg of mutton, a leg of beef, each huge: Thomas and Ellen would get a fortnight's eating out of any one of them. On the next three dishes, a turkey, a goose, and a pair of chickens. All the meat was cold, mostly cooked the night before: in the middle of the seven sat the largest dish of all, a huge pink ham: 'There's a quarter of a pig there,' Thomas whispered to Ellen. All around these sat little satellite plates: sliced hardboiled eggs; sliced onions; bowls of cold potatoes; dishes of glistening chutney. The two adjoining tables had been packed even more tightly: two large glass bowls of cream; Ellen counted nine varieties of cake – Madeira, chocolate, sponge sandwich, two seedcakes, a fruit cake, Swiss roll, lemon layer cake and a wide flan covered in cream, with slices of orange layered across it. No fewer than five apple tarts, circular and golden brown, had been baked, in dishes more than a foot in diameter: a further eight plates contained small buns in cases; cream horns filled with home-made raspberry jam added to the cream; small apple tartlets with pastry striped across them in an 'X'; large, hot plump currant scones, that had been opened, buttered and closed again gently and the butter oozed out; another plate of soda scones, no currants, had been opened and spread with butter and homemade gooseberry jam; on the sixth plate a little arrangement of jam tartlets, with gooseberry, raspberry, blackcurrant and loganberry jams, all home-made; the seventh plate bore slabs of dark cakes, long and with smooth chocolate spread along the top; and on the eighth sat lordly, high buns, the tips of which had been slit and filled with blobs of cream. Around these, several small dishes had been laid out, with all the available homemade preserves Mrs Relihan commanded, from herself and her relatives and neighbours who, in the previous rushed days, had arrived bearing gifts.

The Canon sat at the head of the table, John Relihan on his right and Thomas on his left. No woman joined this sitting, with the sole exception of Ellen, given a place of honour at John Relihan's right hand. Fifteen people ate at this first serving: two more sessions would follow, and at the end of it all, the servant-girl of the Relihan house, and the others lent for the morning, all of whom had tea and sandwiches standing up in the rear kitchen, would clear everything.

Amid exclamations, the men were given heaped plates, the Canon's, Thomas's and Ellen's the most heaped of all. Other than the declared hierarchy of Parish Priest, his Principal Teacher and the head of the house, no social lines were drawn: men from cottages sat alongside the men on whose farms they worked; any guesswork regarding the strata in which people belonged would depend entirely upon the quality of their clothing and the grades of sheepish shyness on their faces.

For once Ellen listened rather than talked, and briefly, out of the corner of her eye, she saw again the long, handsome woman, this time having put on her coat, and making her excuses to Mrs Relihan, preparatory to leaving. Ellen tried to catch Thomas's eye and indicate the woman, who inexplicably made her feel uncomfortable, but the opportunity passed, and through the window she saw the woman mount a high bicycle and ride away. She reconnected with the table's conversation in time to hear the Canon say, 'The Mistress, there, is a fearless woman, I'd say.'

'What was that?' Ellen smiled.

Thomas told her, 'We were talking about which is braver, a man or a woman?'

'A woman has more to lose,' said Ellen. 'That is, if she has children, she has to look after them.'

'Fair point, fair point,' said the Canon. 'But would a woman use a gun?'

'What about the Countess Markievicz?' asked Ellen.

'Ah, sure what was she?' said the Canon. 'A Protestant woman from the west of Ireland caught up with ould romance, and parading the streets of Dublin in 1916 with a gun in her hand; sure she never fired a dangerous shot. They tell me her gun was never fired at all.'

All eyes except the Canon's turned on Thomas. He said nothing,

243

and chose to concentrate on a wedge of pork. Mrs Relihan poured tea in his cup.

'Not the case,' Thomas told Ellen on the way home. 'Her gun was fired. Several times.'

'Their teeth are generally very bad,' said Ellen, 'aren't they?'

They had developed a habit of sitting in the car when they reached home, talking there for several minutes. Ellen now said, 'Who was that tall, good-looking woman?'

Thomas asked which one, and Ellen continued, 'She had her hair drawn back from her forehead; I was expecting it in a bun, but it wasn't, it was cropped at the back. She had a black cardigan.' They climbed out of the car. Thomas had taken to coming around to Ellen's assistance. 'I saw her looking at me very hard.'

Thomas replied, 'You're still something of a curiosity, they haven't all seen you yet.'

'No,' said Ellen, 'no,' but she was not replying to his observation. 'Who was she, Thomas?'

'Her name is Edel Crowe.'

'I told you I would,' said Ernestina to her young brother, 'but you never take a blind bit of notice of anything I say. So I'm going up there now. This minute.'

'To the house?' asked Cyril? 'You're not going to the house, are you?'

Ernestina said, 'I certainly am.'

'In your best bonnet?'

'I don't wear a blasted bonnet. Who do you think I am? Little Bo-Peep?'

'No time like the present,' Cyril said, although he looked less than contented.

'I wish you would stop trotting out those proverbs of yours.'

Ernestina went to the hall. Cyril called, 'She won't be at home, she'll be at work.'

'No she won't. Thursday is her half-day.'

'You know everything.'

'I do and I know something else, brother dear, I know that the gig is tackled.'

A pony and trap awaited in the yard.

'Are you too lazy to walk?' called Cyril.

'I'll leave that to you for the night-time, you'd know your way there blindfold by now,' said Ernestina, who knew perfectly well she might want to leave quickly. In the yard she halted, her breath catching – again: she winced in pain.

Ernestina drove fast, the Stephensons were known always to have a good pony. One skilful hand slapping the long leather reins just on the stinging point of the pony's shoulders, she rested an arm along the mudguard of the trap, whose yellow wheels flashed in the sunlight. Thomas Kane stood at his gate as she drove by, and he saluted her: she raised a hand.

Her destination – a high-peaked cottage, a woodsman's in the days when the Castle precincts had been extensively forested. As the Land Commission divided the estate after the 1921 Treaty, the Merrigans were given permanent title to the cottage on a peppercorn annual ground rent, plus five acres of land on which they grazed one cow, and some goats. Nothing distinguished the cottage, no flowerpots, nor bright colours, nor pretty curtains. Ernestina drew the pony to a halt, and took off her thick spectacles to polish them. She shouted.

'Hallo! Hall-ooo!'

The ajar door opened back fully, and a girl stood there.

'Hallo,' Ernestina called, 'Joan, is it?'

Joan Merrigan stepped a little farther forward, and said a tentative 'Hallo'.

'I wanted to have a word or two,' said Ernestina, in what Cyril always called her 'as nice-as-pie' voice.

Joan Merrigan answered, 'Yes,' and walked towards the trap, taller than Ernestina, and quite heavily built. 'What do you want?'

'Just a few words,' said Ernestina, in whose hands the initiative trembled.

'I want to know what . . .'

Ernestina stopped as the girl laid a hand on the back door of the pony-trap.

'I was wondering,' said Ernestina, still sweetly, and now in a lower tone, 'about you and . . .'

'About me and what?' Joan Merrigan spoke neither enthusiastically nor surlily, but with no overwhelming respectfulness, either.

'About you and my brother. That's what,' snapped Ernestina.

'What about it?' asked Joan Merrigan, who wore a pink butterfly slide in her hair.

'Well. What is it you're doing with him?'

'When?'

No give whatsoever from Miss Merrigan. Ernestina blinked vigorously; those bloody glasses again, how often she cursed them.

'When what?' she asked.

'When what what?' came the Merrigan reply. 'What are you going on about?'

'I'm talking about you and my brother,' said Ernestina, 'and I want to know what you're doing with him?'

'And I'm asking you when?'

'How do you mean "when"? What I mean,' said Ernestina, reverting to her 'reasonable' tone, 'is what your intentions are to my brother, who after all is a considerable citizen. I'm Miss Stephenson, by the way.'

Joan Merrigan looked at Ernestina.

'Ah, would you come down and look at yourself above. "Miss Stephenson".' She withered further. '"Miss Stephenson". Your brother may be a "considerable citizen" but he's not above shifting around here. "Miss Stephenson". We're not anybody's tenants any more, are we? Why don't you ask your brother?'

Ernestina said, 'I thought that, well – as women . . .'

Joan Merrigan looked at her once more, walked away from the gig, and went into the cottage, not even bothering to close the front door.

When Thomas saw Ernestina pass by in her trap, he was preparing to walk down the road to the school: Ellen had taken to bed for a rest. The postman had forgotten the dates of the school closure for the holidays, and had lazily pushed some letters under the door. One marked URGENT, came from the Department, a most unusual occurrence, and Thomas opened it immediately: it contained not a letter but a promulgation.

> A virulent, and often fatal disease, thought to be but not
> yet confirmed as, a strain of contagious poliomyelitis, has
> been reported in Thurles; a second suspected case has
> been reported in Ballingarry. Experience in other
> countries has shown that this disease spreads like wildfire
> if contracted in a small community: children of
> schoolgoing age are particularly exposed, especially if

undernourished. Accordingly, the Medical Officer of
Health has ordered that the schools in your area must not
reopen after Easter until further advised. Your School
Manager has been informed, and it will be announced at
all Masses on Sundays and Holydays in the interim.

Thomas spread the notice out and read it again. He folded it carefully and put it in his inside pocket for Ellen to read at home.
The second envelope had that deadly, familiar handwriting, and,
although addressed to Ellen, he slit it.

I have now seen the whites of your eyes, Ellen Morris,
you who call yourself Mrs Kane. Your child, whatever you
say, will be born a bastard, because you came in here and
stole that man.

Thomas read no more. Snapping the letter shut, he said, 'That's
enough! That's enough,' and sat down. After a moment or two, he
unlocked his desk and took out a black metal oblong box with
Japanese designs on it: long ago it had held fancy biscuits. In it he
had put all the other anonymous letters and now he spread them
out, one by one, on the floor, too numerous for the desk, and he
forced himself to re-read them, from the very earliest, passionate
declarations of love, to this, the most recent and most poisonous.
  'Always look for a pattern,' was Collins's phrase when analysing
military operations against him: Thomas now took out a sheet of
paper, and, kneeling, began to make notes. He noted down phrases
in common, or repeated word usage, from letter after letter – there
had been eighteen in all over three years – and he noted the dates,
if dated, and the frequency, and then made a note to try and trace
where he, and then he and Ellen, had been immediately before a
letter arrived. He looked for any pattern of mood in the writer,
which would authenticate them as genuine, and not some hoaxer;
he compared the lengths of the letters, counting the paragraphs in
the longer ones, the words in the very short ones, and he wrote
every finding in his tiny, immaculate handwriting. He even marked
the two letters he knew Ellen had seen.
  A rap on the windowpane alarmed him. The face peering in
shading its enquiry with a hand in order to see better: Dr Hogan,
in a different bow-tie. Thomas, not thinking quickly enough in the

small sudden fright, went straight to the door and admitted him, then realized he could not cover up the letters spread out on the floor.

'I saw you through the window, did I give you a fright? Did you get the Department notice?'

Dr Hogan spoke rapidly, and sent a hand over his thinning sandy hair.

'How serious is it?' asked Thomas.

'Ah, it is bad. I'm after coming from a meeting of Dispensary men, and apparently there's a case nearer home, a Carroll girl from over Scullystown.'

'God, that's a bit close. I know that family, they're originally from here.' Thomas whistled. 'How old is she? And how is she?'

'Nine. Hard to say. She has two of the symptoms, and vomiting a lot. The mother is nearly out of her mind, and I told them nothing about the others, and when you see a mother worried like that, you always know. The thing is, if she hasn't been that well-fed, she'll go like a light'; he snapped his fingers. 'By the way, there's another Department promulgation on the way, and I think you might be best to keep it to yourself. I advised they shouldn't put it out at all, except to the afflicted relatives, because it's going to cause havoc.'

'What is it?'

The doctor sighed. 'It's about burial. D'you see, it has to happen immediately a doctor certifies, within twelve hours if possible and with no attendance other than the family at the funeral. People are going to find that very hard.'

'And very alarming. Like the Black Death or something,' said Thomas. 'What eejit thought that promulgation up?'

A sharp clip-clop rang on the road, and the men turned to look through the open school door.

'The Stephenson girl from the stud,' Thomas answered the doctor's enquiry.

Dr Hogan turned around; 'Ernestina?! What's she doing out? She should be at home. Bit of bother there.' He looked down at the floor. 'Were you working?' he enquired, indicating the letters. Thomas took a deep breath, looked at Hogan, took a decision.

'Will you keep a secret?'

The doctor said, 'Isn't that what I'm paid to do?'

Thomas, by example, invited him to get down on his hunkers,

and began slowly to tell him the story of the letters. The two men stayed there for over an hour, Thomas soon lighting a lamp. After thoughtful conversation filled with pauses, the doctor finally took away several of the letters in his pocket, wrapping them carefully in unused notepaper Thomas had given him.

'The weather seems very settled,' Ellen said, sitting up in the half-darkness. 'Would you do me a favour,' she asked, 'and hand me over that,' indicating a white squat jar with blue lettering on the cover. She sat up and began to rub the hand-cream into her palms in a slow circular motion. 'Do you know, I know I look heavy, but I don't feel heavy yet. Leah was saying it won't really bother me until the last week or so. That's dreadful about that Carroll girl. Do you know them?'

Thomas said he did, and after some other desultory conversation, Ellen rose, and Thomas lit a second candle to give her light by which to dress.

'I hate tomorrow,' he said. 'I've always hated it. I hate that whole idea, fields of skulls, that, Haceldama, all of that, field of blood.'

'Oh, I love Good Friday,' said Ellen. 'It's the only day of the year I wear lipstick, because it reminds me of the blood and passion of Christ. Why don't you do what I do on a day I hate. Do something nice, something that you enjoy.'

'Well, I can't do that, can I? You and Mother Church and Canon Law won't let me,' replied Thomas, with spirit. Ellen, despite herself, laughed.

'No, no, that's not what I mean, do something else that you enjoy. I'll tell you what you'll do. You know how you like honey? Why don't you walk over to Connells and see if they have any combs of honey left? It'd be good for me too, with the baby.'

Thomas sat beside Ellen on the bed as she brushed her hair and began, pins in her mouth, to make a small rampart of it high on her crown.

'Whatever I say,' he began, 'I can't wait for that little thing to come into the world. Did you notice John Relihan's remarks at the Station? No matter how rough a man is, a baby will move him.'

He held Ellen's hand for a moment, and she allowed her hair-piling to be interrupted, sitting quietly, looking straight ahead where the mirror caught the dim reflection of them in their moment of quiet, she in her large white nightgown, he visible by the face only, his dark clothes augmenting the shadows.

'There is such a thing as religious mania,' said Thomas. 'I've heard it.'

'You're mocking me again, Thomas,' sang out Ellen.

'No, I'm not.'

'Yes, you are!'

'No, I'm not. People get it, and they foam at the mouth.'

'They do not. I've never heard of it.'

'I saw you at the altar, Ellie, and you were nearly in a trance.'

'How can I help it if I love God, too?'

Thomas was opening a sack of seed potatoes. 'I think I'll start putting these in. Seriously, Ellie, do you really feel as strongly as that religiously?'

'But isn't it a lovely feeling?'

'I always feel anxious when I pray too much. It opens up things I know I can never reach.'

'But isn't that the point?' Ellen put two cups, saucers and plates on the table. 'Do you want milk in your tea?'

'Don't I always have milk in my tea?'

'But today . . . ? I'm not having any.'

Thomas straightened up. 'Penance or no penance. Mortification or no mortification. Good Friday or no Good Friday, you are to have your nourishment.'

'But.'

'But rubbish, Ellie. How d'you think God will thank you for not looking after your health right now.'

'My health is fine.'

'Good. Make it finer.'

She laughed to take the small head of steam out of things. 'Thomas Kane, for a sensible man you're ridiculous. Come on, sit down. You have to go and get that honey.'

Thomas had always wanted to write, and had achieved a small distinction with anonymous book reviews, some local history journalism, and for a national newspaper, an account of Dean Swift's visit to Deanstown: Thomas wrote it in 1917, to coincide with the 250th anniversary of the Dean's birth, submitted it to the editor and received a cheque for three guineas. This encouraged him, and at the time he further reasoned that any such literary or journalistic activity would offer perfect cover if questioned by the military; nevertheless, not one other piece was accepted, and he gave up, through a combination of disappointment and the pressure of his 'extracurricular activities', as he privately called them.

When he returned from Belgium and France, in the autumn of 1920, and settled into the newly-built, empty house at Deanstown, he tried again. This time the failure had nothing to do with editorial rejection: as if a huge boulder had been put in his pathway he found any free direction forward blocked, and no matter how he pushed and heaved with his mind, he could not run ahead as he wished. After a few paragraphs the light darkened, and he could not make it bright again. Everything he wrote seemed to him slight and thin, hollow: he tried writing doggerel, to see if that would loosen things: he even copied out paragraphs from *Under the Greenwood Tree*, a book he particularly liked. He made lists of the matters which interested him, and even wrote nature notes for himself, recording the bird life in the garden during that winter. Once, recalling assiduously all the things that had made him laugh, he attempted to write humour, but found that the most difficult of all and gave up.

His habitual control of the details in his life meant that all these attempted pieces had now been assembled in two large notebooks, so cohesively gathered, and in such uniform writing, that a stranger might at first assume his eye had fallen on a journal of sorts. Thomas had never shown them to Ellen; in some sort of hope, he looked at the notebooks from time to time, and when he did, he inevitably turned to one page, the only piece in the entire collection which half-pleased him. One wet Sunday afternoon he had made a dart for freedom around that boulder blocking the cave of his imagination – he wrote, quite quickly, and without labour, an imagined description of the Castle as it must have been had he visited it in the mid-eighteenth century, when it had the reputation of being the finest demesne in the land.

Seen from the road to the village, a belt of ornamental woods in a circle formed a fringe very like a ruff, above which rose the Castle in all its spires and grandeur. Through these woods several paths have been cut radially, each path opening onto the shore of the ornamental lake, from the far bank of which terraced fields

251

rise in a parterre to the sloping lawns immediately before the Castle door. On the left, as I walked up the fields, my hat in my hand, a long line of exquisite trees and bushes culminated at each end in a gate: this was the Bell Walk, so called because Grand George Mathew, the owner of the Castle, had hung it, his main avenue, with bells which tinkled to warn the Castle of approaching guests, so that he might welcome them as warmly as he hoped to do.

Where the Bell Walk ended stood a sunlit wall, decorated with ivy and flowers, and along this wall in alcoves stood a number of brilliant white statues and busts of famous figures and gods. In the distance, I saw a maze, reached by a gravel path along each side of which grew tall sunflowers like columns, each taller than a six-foot man. As I approached, a servant in a blue apron and a large white wig called out, 'Hallooa' and walked down the sloping green lawn to greet me, offering me wine and biscuits from the silver tray he carried.

Although he liked to reread this passage, it also made Thomas a little uncomfortable, principally because he had never developed it, and also because he knew that he had not entirely originated it all, that some of the description had come from local word-of-mouth, and from the written descriptions in the library at Thurles, recorded by an English visiting clergyman called Campell, who had called to Deanstown in 1775. Nevertheless, Thomas found some pleasure in the thought that one day he might find the freedom to pursue this strange man with the hat walking up the fields to the Castle, a figure that he, and only he, had invented. He played with the notion now and again, and especially every time he walked to the house of the Connells which lay a good two miles on the far side of the Castle.

On Good Friday afternoon he drank tea there. Brother and sister, both unmarried, the Connells complained strenuously of the Canon's appeals for money, and told Thomas something he had heard rumoured but never confirmed. One of their workmen had caused trouble with a gun: 'that Quinn man. I never felt safe with him around the place,' Nora Connell said, and her brother chimed in, 'That fellow's – well, he's not good, not good.'

Nora Connell said, as Thomas stood up, 'Now that honey'll do the Mistress grand, now, and her time so near.'

'Sure how would you know?' asked her brother humorously.

'Don't I talk to people, don't I?' she riposted.

Thomas took a different route home, heading for a high brake of trees from which the widest and highest view of the surrounding countryside could be had, a full three hundred and sixty degrees of the landscape he loved. No cowpath wound this way, and he walked over the new grass, tussocking already in the mild spring weather. The last climb to the coppice was always the steepest and, holding out the string shopping bag gently so as not to break the eggs he had bought, nor damage the honeycomb, he scrambled up the bank and leaned his back against the outermost tree in the group.

Facing first to the west, he saw the spire of Ellen's cathedral, in the shadow of which Leah and Herbert lived; in shorter focus, on the nearest, next highest hill, beside the motte-and-bailey, stood the church in which they had married. To the south, the mountains had changed to velvet. Suddenly, Thomas heard behind him in the distance the rattle and chink of a cart. He turned to face east, and down below, caught in a late shaft of sunlight, sat the small cemetery of all the scions of the Castle families, their private burial ground.

As tiny and whitened as a graveyard in a Mexican story, it had fallen more or less into disuse, and although some local families had claimed rights to be buried there, no funeral had been taken to it for at least two to three years. Beyond it now, and approaching the gate, on the wide, almost overgrown gravelway, a cart approached, drawn by a large pony, rearing its head. Thomas stood, transfixed, recognizing the family: on the cart sat a man holding the reins, and across from him a woman wearing a black headscarf. Dangling his legs at the back, but with bowed head, sat a schoolboy of about twelve years of age. In the centre of the cart lay a medium-sized coffin with a white cloth partially draped over it.

The cart reached the gate of the cemetery, and the man jumped down, followed by the boy. Thomas could hear the sound of conversation, but could not discern its content. With some difficulty – a stiff lock, and overgrown grass – the man and boy forced the little gate open, and spent some minutes as if looking for something in the near corner of the graveyard. The boy returned to the cart, and while the father began to uproot great bunches of grass with his hands, the boy fetched two shovels and a pickaxe.

While Thomas watched, the men dug, toiling and grunting, their heads bent. After a time they removed their jackets and piled them on the coats they had already spread along the little white wall. The sun had begun to set and a small mist could be seen, vaporous and white-grey, a foot or so above the ground: tiny steams rose from the bent working backs. The boy rested for a moment.

Without warning his mother jumped from the cart, ran to the cemetery, wrenched the shovel from the boy's hand and began to dig furiously. The man restrained her, argued with her, and eventually she handed the shovel back to the boy and retreated to the rear of the cart, where she put her head down on her hands and began to sob: the sound carried, it seemed to Thomas, for miles.

Soon the grave was complete: the man and boy approached the cart, and took the coffin, half-sliding, half-lifting it, on to their shoulders. The woman led the way, praying. In a slow, crouching, and obviously taxing movement, the man and his son lowered the coffin into the ground and stood for some minutes in prayer. The boy began to weep, and then the man: the woman walked over to both and comforted them, an arm held out to each. They filled in the grave much more slowly than they had dug it, and replacing some green sward, and then some fistfuls of grass, they closed the gate of the graveyard; the man and boy took their coats and jackets from the wall, donned them, and joined the woman on the cart.

The pony wheeled around and they left. Thomas made the Sign of the Cross, spoke a small prayer almost aloud and stood there, growing cold, for several more minutes, until he could no longer see the departing family in the gloom, and then until he could no longer hear the strong creak of the cart.

Ellen met him at the door, had heard his footsteps.

'Dr Hogan called,' she said. 'That poor Carroll girl, Thomas, she died.'

He replied, 'I know.'

17

'If I don't get these potatoes in,' Thomas said next morning, Holy Saturday, 'we'll have nothing to eat for the winter.'

He moved into the farthest corner of the garden, over beyond the blackcurrant bushes, where, at the cherry tree, the hedge began separating the Teacher's garden from the Quarterground, the village allotments. Ever methodical, he had two buckets which he carried from the sheds to the drills. One contained the seed potatoes, innocent tubers, sitting there like little babies: the other bucket bore Thomas's measuring stick, exactly a foot long, cut from a straight piece of ash; another longer measuring stick, flat, the handle of an old hurling-stick, two and a half feet long; his 'line', made of two pointed pegs wrapped together in a ball of binder twine; a sharp penknife with a pearl handle, and a two-pound bag of lime. He returned for the spade and the fork.

Ellen appeared, pulling on her coat.

'Thomas, there are Confessions in the church from eleven o'clock, aren't there?'

He stuck the spade in the ground. 'Do you want me to drive you?'

'No, the walk will do me good.' He did not comment on her red, swollen eyes.

In a corner of the prepared ground, where flat, well-dug loam glistened brown, Thomas stuck down one of the pegs with the binder twine. Unrolling the other from it, he walked backwards until he reached the other corner. Measuring with his eye, and using the hedge as a general marker, he stuck the other peg in the ground. Using the line of cord as his guide, he then took the old hurling-stick and laid it flat on the ground, one end just touching the 'line'; and at intervals up along the cord, measuring all the time, he made marks in the earth. Looking back, he had now delineated the first drill – the cord 'line' would form the right-hand side, and the marks, two and a half feet from the cord, the left-hand side. Between those two parameters, he dug with the spade a narrow trench. He then took the fork, and from the heap of farmyard manure in another corner (acquired with compliments from Michael Connors's cowsheds and delivered by cart) filled a wheelbarrow and returned to his drill, which he filled with manure to a point level with the general earth of the patch, so that he had a long narrow trench comfortably plump with straw-flecked cowdung. Taking one of the buckets, he next flung with his hand, all along the drill, little fistfuls of the lime from the paper bag; the lime made puffs of white in the air, and coloured the shins of Thomas's blue dungarees.

'Bless me, Father, for I have sinned, I am three weeks since Confession.'

'Yes, my child?'

'Father, it isn't that I have any great sins to tell, but I need help and advice.'

'Yes, my child.'

'Father, do you believe in Original Sin coming down through a family?'

'How do you mean, my child?'

'Father, do you believe that a grave flaw in a parent may be passed on to a child?'

'Do you mean like – madness?'

'Not so much that, I mean – more a characteristic?'

'Do you mean – contrariness or meanness? Like a nose, or the colour of a pair of eyes?'

'Ye-ess, Father.'

'I've never heard of it, my child, do you want to tell me any more?'

The old head in the dimness behind the wire mesh grille shook itself awake: the Canon sat up. He astonished Ellen with his kind, almost mellifluous manner.

The postman, skidding his bike to a halt outside the tall hedge, brought four letters.

Dear Master,

Regarding that matter we were talking about, I have some information that might help. When it suits, will you walk up to see me? I hope the Mistress is fit-and-well.

Yours faithfully,

Jack Hogan (Dr)

=

256

'Father, I married a man who for part of his life, before he met me, was involved in the – in the . . .'

The priest waited. Ellen tried again, hesitating, like a child pre-emptively telling of an undiscovered misdemeanour.

'Father, I am very worried. My husband . . .'

'Yes, my child.' No voice could have sounded more sympathetic. Ellen began once more.

'Father, I am married to a fine man.' The Canon inclined his head, only in encouragement, not to give any sign that he already knew: the Seal of the Confessional extended to preservation of identity.

Ellen said, 'But he was once involved in the Troubles, and I know that he had to do things then. And now I've discovered that there is violence in his breeding, and once or twice since I came to know him, I've seen him behave very violently, and I don't know what to do, and I'm expecting a baby next month.'

'And you're afraid this will carry down to the child?'

'Yes, Father' – careful not to call him Canon, to use the universal address instead.

'Dear Madam,' the letter from the registrar at Beaumaris had said, 'Further to your enquiry of the 9th inst., the person regarding whom you write, one Timothy Nash or Nashe, was tried on counts various (see below), and sentenced at Beaumaris Court on 28th March 1806, sentence being carried out seven weeks later, on 17th May.'

'You say you believe he's a fine man?' asked the voice of the confessional.

'Oh, yes, Father, and everyone looks up to him, respects him. People consult him.'

'And he goes to Confession and Holy Communion?' – again, the fine line between knowing and asking.

'Oh, yes, Father.'

At the bottom of the standard form, Ellen had read the words: 'Nash or Nashe, T.; (Irish): Charged with: (1) murder of a police-man, one R. A. Edwards at Chester on January 29, 1806; (2) bodily harm to a warder, one T. Bowen, Beaumaris, on February 2, 1806:

(3) serious bodily harm to a policeman, one R. Hampson, Beaumaris, on February 2, 1806: (4) actual damage to Crown property, Beaumaris, on February 2, 1806: Sentence: hanging: executed Beaumaris Gaol, 17th May 1806; confirmation H.M. CORONER, E. A. Bolton, cert. 17th May 1806.'

The Canon asked, 'Has he ever been violent to you?'
  'Oh, no, Father, never.'
  'Nor ever shown signs of it?'
  'No, Father. Quite the opposite.'

The Registrar at Beaumaris had attached a note, in wide, looped handwriting.

> Dear Madam,
>   Like you I have an interest in local history, and was pleased to receive your inquiry. This sketch of Nash or Nashe, made by a Beaumaris artist in the courtroom during the trial, became very popular in this town, as Nash's name became a byword for villainy. The local newspaper printed it and postcards were made of it. I hope it assists you.
>
>   Yours truly,
>   N. S. R. Hughes

Ellen gasped: the face in the picture might have been Thomas's, only less composed. Just as cruel, though. It had the wide cheekbones, and the strong black hair, and the looming black eyebrows meeting in the middle, the straight line of mouth, the unpleasant dimple in the chin.

  'Thomas, if he walked in here now, people would say he was your older brother.'

'Do you fear him, my child?'
  'It's not that, Father. What I'm afraid of is – with the help of God we're going to have several more children.'
  'Please God,' murmured the priest.
  'And I would be terrified if one or more of them turned out to be. Murderers.' Ellen gasped the word out.

=

Thomas, his thumbnail black with clay, recognized the writing.

> My heart is broken. You knew how I felt for you. Does
> your 'wife' know about your past? If you do not meet me
> I will start to inform her, and perhaps she won't any longer
> look at you with the sheep's eyes she has been making at
> you. This is your last chance.

'How long have you been worried about this, my child?'

'Just a year or so, Father, since the first time I saw my husband being angry, although he wasn't my husband then. It was very frightening.'

'But you married him?' the priest said.

'I did, Father.'

'And since then?'

'Well, there were other things. On our honeymoon, he beat somebody who insulted me.'

Setting out for the church, Ellen had said to Thomas, 'It'll be very odd going to Confession to a priest I know.'

On her return she reported, 'It wasn't odd at all, it wasn't like talking to a person.'

As if to a stranger, Ellen said, 'Father, it feels as if I'm confessing what I think are his sins.'

She told about the birching of Michael Quinn.

The old voice countered, 'But he did that in the line of duty?'

'Yes, Father?'

'And when he was involved in the Troubles? Duty again?'

'I suppose so, Father.'

'Was he excommunicated during that time, my child?'

'I don't know, Father.'

'And he attacked somebody who offended you? In public I take it?'

'Yes, Father.' She stopped. 'But there's something else, Father' – and plunged into the story of Timothy Nash.

When she had digested the letter and the etching, Ellen asked, 'Thomas, did you know any of this?'

'Now that you mention it, there was a bit of a cloud,' he said.

'That's a bit airy of you.'

'Ach, Ellie, if we were to dig up and drag out everything in our past, we'd spend our time killing each other,' he dismissed.

Ellen tried to peer harder through the wire grille of the confessional. The voice said, 'And no man is responsible for what his ancestors did, if that was the case we'd all be in queer street, wouldn't we?'

Ellen's lips pressed on each other as if putting on lipstick.

'My child, your story, although you may not think so, is not unusual. A number of women worry greatly about what their husbands and sons did in the last ten years or so. But they were hard times. God forgives men for hard times.' He straightened.

Thomas opened the other two letters: a formal note from the Canon confirming the date for Confirmation, unless 'the current poliomyelitis outbreak affects it.' However, the fourth letter contained a new promulgation from the Department, saying that if to all intents and purposes, the outbreak seemed to have passed locally, the countrywide experience suggested it might be safe to reopen the schools in ten days, making a closure of four weeks in all. Coal Money should be adjusted in the annual budget, etc., the Progress Record should be marked thusly, etc. 'Eth! Don't they know anything?' cursed Thomas, then put the four letters in the inside pocket of his good coat hanging on the hallstand and returned to the garden.

'Is there anything else, my child?'

'There is, Father, there's this other thing I want to ask you.'

She outlined Father Watson's advice, and the outcome of it, the abstinence. The voice sighed. Ellen could smell him, a combination of tobacco and what might have been slightly sour milk. He sighed again.

'My child, aah. This is a matter of. Well. This is not something.' He stopped. 'My child, I'm an old man, and I don't keep up with things. But I'm no heretic. I believe in the love of God. That is why he gave us all the wonderful herbs that grow in the fields and bushes.'

Ellen smiled in her mind.

The Canon went on, 'And your friend the priest, who advised

you regarding Canon Law, is correct, within the laws of our Holy Mother Church. He's right. So, how can I advise you in a way that is contrary to Canon Law?'

Ellen bent her head, fumbling in the darkness, looking for a handkerchief, quiet as dust. The old priest shook himself, as if at a sudden chill.

'My child, this is my opinion. There are Laws of God, and there are Laws of Man made in honour of God. The Laws of God move within us with a natural force. The Laws of Man made in honour of God have to be learned specifically and applied. That may only be a simple man's view, but I, for one, would never do anything to interfere with the flow of goodness from one human being to another, especially when blessed within the sanctity of marriage.' He slumped back, and Ellen thought he had finished speaking. Then he began again.

'I would say this to you. If you and your husband, when you discovered you were expecting marriage's greatest blessing, that of a lovely little babby, if you and your husband . . . If you and your husband while you were expecting – provided there was no danger.' The Canon had slowed down to less than half his usual snail's pace. 'If. You. And. Your. Husband. Well, do you think God would cast you out if you stood before him at the gates of Heaven? Ah, no. Ah, no. Not at all. Canon Law is a thing for priests to debate. What would your husband think?'

Ellen said, 'He would agree with you, Father.'

'Then, my child, go in peace and above all, in love.'

The priest raised his hand, and began, '*Te absolvo. In nomine Patris, et Filii, et Spiritui sancti.*'

Ellen interrupted, 'Father, you haven't given me any Penance?'

The priest replied, 'Aren't you after doing Penance enough, if all this was bothering you? You're about to bring a young life into the world. I see no need for Penance. Go in the love of God.'

Turning to the bag of seed potatoes, Thomas crouched, opened his pearl-handled Sheffield steel penknife, and began to cut them in half. In this small but complex manoeuvre, he could not slice at random across the tuber: he had to ensure that each half bore a quota of 'eyes', the black points in the tuber through which the potato propagated itself. This completed, he took his bucket and, walking in a crouched position, his buttocks almost tipping the clay beneath, he planted the potatoes in the ground, on the limed manure, precisely a foot from each other: he measured the separation by the short ash marker which he pressed down forward from each tuber. When a full row had been completed, he stood and eased the ache in his back, and checked with his eye whether any of the little white-faced half-tubers had tilted over in his wake. With his hurling-stick he measured two feet from the outer edge of the drill and then re-set his 'line' and from it, with the fork, dug the earth and smoothed it over the newly-made drill – and then began the whole procedure all over again.

Ellen reached the house. She said to Thomas in breathless half-amusement, 'You know, when I start out walking, I'm fine, and then I start to waddle like a duck. Oh, I'm so fat, Thomas.'

He looked closely at her face, and, heeling off his boots, walked upstairs in socks and silence behind her.

In the room, she took off her hat, looked with a sigh at her puffy face in the mirror, frizzed out her flattened hair with a hand, and turned to Thomas. She walked over to him, took his two hands and wrapped them around her shoulders like a cape, so that she could lay her head on his chest. For several minutes, she stood there, saying nothing. She began to weep, and, still holding carefully his hands clay-ey from the garden, he sat her down on the bed and knelt beside her.

She said, 'Thomas, it is all all right, it is all all right.' She repeated it over and over, and then recounted everything she had said in Confession.

Thomas sat on the floor, like a boy, looking up at her. For that brief period the relationship had changed, and Ellen became the leader. Thomas accepted every detail of her great affliction, even when she implied that she had been believing he would breed a race of murderers.

'Thomas, I have something else to tell you.' At that moment his eyes filled with tears.

'I asked him about Canon Law.' Ellen hung her head and looked up from beneath her black brows.

Thomas laughed. 'Jeremiah makes his own Canon Law. I bet he gave you short shrift?'

'No, he's a different man in Confession altogether. He's not nearly as crude.'

'That's what I said to you beforehand.'

'He said the Law of God was what mattered.'

They both laughed and cried at the same time.

Thomas laid his head on Ellen's knee, and she stroked his hair.

She said, 'Here, do you want to feel my stomach, it's moving a lot.'

He said, 'I wouldn't. No. I wouldn't think it right.' She bent down awkwardly and laid her cheek along his face raised towards her. He took her hand and twisted her wedding ring around and around.

'When my sister died,' he said, 'and when I had to put her body in the coffin. Ellie, she only weighed a stone or so, she was so wasted, and a child of seven weighs about three stone. They brought the wrong size coffin, they brought a grown-up coffin, we had to pack it with blankets. I took the best blankets and sheets in the house, so that she didn't shift around inside the coffin. And I remember saying to myself, and I said it over and over during tough times later, I said, "I'll never be happy in my lifetime, I know it, never." And I was wrong.'

'Oh, you were. My dear man.' In half an hour or so, after whisperings and silences, Thomas went downstairs and laid the table, and fried eggs and black puddings for lunch, and then boiled potatoes.

Thomas had to flee the April showers, and indoors he stood at the window, near Ellen, his dirty hands dangling by his sides, and in peaceful silence looked out at the rain, and the clouds sweeping over from the west. When the sun came out again, he returned to his task.

At nine o'clock, unusually early, they prepared for bed. When he climbed in beside her, Thomas discovered that Ellen wore no nightgown, her stomach large and almost blue in its whiteness. Thomas, in pyjamas, lay beside her.

'Thomas,' she said, 'if it were medically safe, and I feel it isn't . . .'

'Shh,' he said, and laid a hand on her breast, stroking it, and repeatedly sending his palm smoothly across her rubbery nipple.

'There were times, in the early days,' he said, 'when I thought that – if we hadn't stopped – I would somehow pump strength into the baby.'

'I often thought that, too,' said Ellen. 'But I even thought that was a wrong thought.'

'Will you say anything to Father Watson?' asked Thomas.

'I don't know. I don't know. I suppose he acted in good faith.'

'I'm not so sure,' said Thomas, 'I'm not so sure. But we won't talk about that.'

He arranged his shoulder so that Ellen's head could rest on it, and there she fell asleep, and slept without moving, while Thomas stayed awake for hours, looking into the darkness. Eventually, he could bear no longer the numbness in his arm and shoulder, and he moved Ellen with infinite gentleness, and settled his own head to sleep.

18

'A bit erratic, d'you see. Is that what you mean, Mrs?'
'Well, yes, what I mean is – don't pay any attention if Miriam
is a bit of an oddity from time to time.' Mrs Gardner's other daughter, Alice, had married a vet from Reynoldstown. Miriam, at home
with her mother, did little except play the piano and go for long
walks; the worse the weather the longer the walk.

'She was immensely attached to her father, God rest him,
immensely, and I always say that a good daughter makes a good
wife,' says Mrs Gardner. 'And her father doted on her; I never told
Alice, because she'd rightly think it unfair, but their father left
bigger provision in his will for Miriam than he did for Alice. I
suppose that was because Alice was married, and well married too,
before her father died, God rest him. So don't ever breathe a word
to Alice will you, we never thought . . .'

She stopped just short of saying, 'We never thought anyone
would want to marry Miriam.'

In the drawing-room of the house near Mountshannon, on the
heights above the river, watching the dark stream reflect the clouds
overhead, Jack Hogan grew besotted with Miriam Gardner. He
watched every movement. At a meal he observed her every bite.
Across the room he never took an eye off her.

Earlier in the afternoon, unobserved, Miriam looked in through
the side window at the pair drinking wine.

'She's very pale. Is she a bit on the anaemic side?' Jack asked.

'No, Miriam was born pale, I think,' said Mrs Gardner.

'Will she marry me, do you think?'

Mrs Gardner smiled, and tried again to settle a wisp of grey
hair.

'I like a man who worries about winning a woman's hand in
marriage,' she said. 'Miriam's father was afraid of his life that I
wouldn't marry him, and in the event we had twenty-eight good
years together.'

'When will I ask her?'

Mrs Gardner gazed down at the Shannon, and at the gigantic rhododendrons, and at her adored cypresses, and the row of willows by the steps far below.

'I'm playing whist tonight, here at home. We have a card drive for Father Cooney. We play in the large dining-room, the one we only use at Christmas. If you and Miriam sit in here, by the fire, you'll not be disturbed, and she'll feel safe with all those people around. I'll make sure Madge makes us all a good supper first.' Mrs Gardner looked at her garnet ring, and breathed on it, then polished it on the cuff of her grey cardigan.

'D'you drink much?' Miriam stretched her long legs by the fire.

'I learned it in the Army,' said Jack Hogan. 'It was almost *de rigueur* in France.'

'*De rigueur*. That's nice. *De rigueur*. As a matter of rigour': a lazy way of speaking, sometimes halting completely in the middle of a sentence: she fascinated Jack.

'As a matter of necessity,' said Jack. He consumed the long hair, the small but obviously hard breasts, the green stockings, the plaid skirt.

'I've never had. A drink.' Miriam moved her head from side to side as if exercising a muscle in her neck. 'Were there nice girls in France?' All those rising inflections.

'Would you like a sip of my wine, Miriam?' he asked. 'No. And certainly, Miriam, none as nice as you.'

'Tell me about babies. Mama said we all took the pledge and we're not allowed to drink.'

'Oh, I see,' said Jack. Then, nonplussed, he asked, 'About babies?'

'Yes. You're a doctor.'

'What do you want to know?'

'How to get one. Mama won't tell me. And Alice won't tell me.'

'Well.' Jack took another drink from his glass.

'Mama said, if I got married I'd find out.'

'If you married me,' said Jack, speaking more carefully than he had known he could, 'I would tell you.'

'I will marry you,' said Miriam. 'Mama said you were going to ask.'

'May I kiss you, then?' asked Jack.

Miriam held up her face. Jack rose from his sofa, almost missed his footing, put down his glass, crossed the fireplace to her sofa, and bending over double, kissed her cheek for a long time. She never moved. He moved his face around and kissed her mouth, and she never responded. He returned to his sofa.

'Is that settled then?' he asked.

'Yes,' said Miriam. 'Will you look after me well?'

'Oh, very well,' said Jack. 'Oh, very well, indeed.' Then he grinned, and said, 'You're a terrible chancer, you know all about babies, don't you?'

Miriam rose and pirouetted in waltz-time, singing, 'I'll be your sweetheart. If you will be mine.'

On their wedding night in the Shelbourne Hotel, she thumped him on the shoulder as she climbed into bed, and said, 'Shove over, don't lie so close to me. And go to sleep now. Go on. Move over. Turn your back to me.' In Geneva, she made him book two rooms, one each, before she would agree to check in. He called to collect her for dinner downstairs; she had locked her door, and he had to stand in the corridor waiting.

At dinner, he said, 'Married people are supposed to . . . to have a relationship that is . . .'

'Shhhhhh,' she interrupted. 'I know. I heard. I read about it.'

Later that night, he entered her room after knocking. She sat at her dressing-table, still apparently fully dressed, the buttons of her blouse open down half-way. A pool of cream satin lay on the floor. She pointed to it and warbled, 'I always simply step out of my underclothes.'

As she scratched vigorously at her shoulders and upper arms, she continued, 'I have a rash.'

'Let me see it, Miriam. Maybe it needs a bit of ointment.'

'No fear. You're not my doctor.' She laughed. 'Isn't that a scream? You're not my doctor. You are, but you're my doctor husband.' She stood. 'Stay where you are, Jacko.' In front of him she undressed completely. 'Have you red hair down there, Jack, or are you going thin on top there too?' she chortled, and climbed into bed so quickly he had to shift from where he sat.

'Miriam, you should be putting ointment on that rash, your arms are bleeding.'

'Good-night, Jack. Switch out the light when you're going.'

She tore at her shoulders with both hands. He closed her door and slipped back to his own room. Miriam's dowry, handed to Jack in a bank draft by Mrs Gardner, was much, much larger than he had ever considered, and there were stocks and shares to follow.

Ernestina Stephenson, although very different from Miriam Hogan, née Gardner, had some characteristics in common. The tendency to 'fly off the handle' without warning; the abrupt change of direction in conversation; the unexpected little shows of force; and Jack recognized them from his own wife, and also from the conversations he had been having with medical colleagues in Cork. One significant difference appeared clear, however – Miriam had been like that almost as of nature: Ernestina had become that way through fear. Only thinly could she answer Jack's questions on that very first evening she allowed him to examine her.

'You'll have to tell me everything as clearly as possible, Errr-nestina,' he said. 'D'you see?'

She sat there, like a frozen person.

'I need,' said Jack in a tone gentle enough not to frighten Ernestina, 'to see what these bumps, you call them, are like.'

'Why?' asked Ernestina. 'Don't you believe me?'

'Now,' said Jack Hogan. 'I'll make a note or two. Date of birth?' Ernestina said, dully: 'Thirteenth of November, Eighteen ninety-four.'

'So that'd make you, what? Just gone thirty-one? Parents alive?'

'Both dead.'

'Ah, that's tough.'

'No it isn't. I hated the two of them.'

'I have to ask, you know, family history, what did they die of?'

'Father a bullet. The war. Mother cancer.'

'Were y'ever ill before?'

'For a while.'

'Since when?'

'My father had a jacket like that.' Ernestina touched Jack's check cuff. A tear rolled out of one eye. 'I started bleeding all the time three months ago. Non-stop. I started getting very much thinner, and I'm eating nothing. And then the other day, I found.' She stopped abruptly.

'Found what, Errr-nestina? The bumps, is it?'

She sat looking straight ahead, her eyes closed behind the thick spectacles, the same lone tear rolling, rolling downward. As if choosing a place on a map, Ernestina pointed one stiff finger to her right breast; then, to Jack's horror, to her left. Her misery accentuated her plainness.

Jack said, 'I'll have to have a look. Why don't you sit here on this armchair, but you'll have to take off some of your clothes. You'll have to let down your straps.' Ernestina had been sitting on the bed, then she rose, and Jack turned away to his bag, taking some time to fetch his stethoscope. After some rustling, he heard her sitting in the chair, and she said, 'I'm ready.'

He turned around, and without yet looking at her, showed her with a smile how he warmed the gleaming disc of the stethoscope between his hands, 'So that it won't make you jump with the cold of it,' he said. He knelt on one knee beside her, and she sat with her arms draped on either side. Her body, Jack noted, had greater beauty than her poor face: ah, dear, the number of women who were like that, if the world could only see.

He listened at her breastbone, then made her lean far forward, and he listened at her back.

'Now,' he said, 'show me where you found the bumps.'

'They're like eggs,' she said, and again her mapping finger pointed out, on the right breast, one, two, three, four and on the left, one, two.

Jack Hogan said, 'I'm going to have to see what they're like for myself. Guide my hand.'

She took both his hands and, laying them flat on the surprisingly firm tissue, introduced the planes of his top three fingers to each lump in turn, one, two, three, four, five, six – and he found number seven. One was large, hard as eggs: others the size of a hazel-nut. Jack sat back on his hunkers, then stood up, uncoiling the stethoscope from around his neck.

'Now this bleeding, Errr-nestina? How heavy is it?'

'I've used up all the small linen towels we had in the house. I'm down to table napkins. I throw them away. Or I'm cutting up towels into squares. I have cardboard boxes of them hidden around the house.'

'Oh God, girl, you should be in the hospital.'

'I told you, I told you. I can't go to hospital.' This time a brace of tears squeezed out. 'If I go to hospital, that little Merrigan bitch'll be in here behind my back, washing his shirts, and I'll be ousted. She's after my brother.'

'Whooo-phooo!' Jack Hogan let out a long exhalation of breath.

'Well, you have to go to bed, Errr-nestina. And you have to go now. You're to take a good rest.'

'You're the only man who was ever nice to me,' said Ernestina, looking away from him in a panic. 'Your wife must be very lucky to have you.'

Jack Hogan said, ''Tis very easy to be nice to you. You're a very nice girl. But you're not well, and you have to rest. Now, are you in any pain?'

'Sometimes.'

He promised to call again in two days – 'to see how you are.'

Ernestina dressed again and lay on the bed. As Jack folded and clasped the lugs of his Gladstone bag, and prepared to leave, she held out a hand and shook it.

'Thanks very much,' she said. Jack went.

Cyril strolled in. 'What did he say?'

Ernestina said, 'That I have to rest a lot.'

'Well, I must say. The things some people will do to get attention.' About to leave the room, he turned and remarked, 'Imagine you having a Catholic quack? H'm?'

In the week before Confirmation Day Thomas came home in despair.

'Ellie, what in the name of all that's high and holy are we going to do? They know as much about Catechism as a pig knows about a holiday.'

Eleven children were going forward from the school to be confirmed, and Thomas had a high reputation for the preparedness of his pupils.

He said, 'I think I'm just going to have to say to the Archbishop that on account of the polio scare we couldn't get them ready properly. But you know perfectly well what they'll all say all over the place, "Hah, the new Master must be too busy with the new wife." That's what they'll say.' Thomas's rough mimicking of the local accent made Ellen laugh.

'How's Miss Kellett shaping up?' asked Ellen, regarding her temporary replacement.

'Useless. She doesn't know "B" from a bull's foot,' said Thomas.

Ellen said, 'Why don't you send the children down to me at lunchtime. I'm doing nothing here. We've ten days left.'

Every day the eleven candidates straggled to the house, and

270

Ellen arrayed them in the kitchen, taking them through the Bishop's likely questions.

'What is chrism?' Blank faces again.

She led them into the answer, beating her tuning fork on the air as if teaching music.

'Chrism is the anointing oil for Extreme Unction, the Last Rites of the Church.'

'Good,' Ellen nodded. 'Now, what is chrism made of?' and without waiting for them not to know the answer, she began another chant, beckoning them like a choir-mistress to recite with her: 'Oil of olive mixed with balm and blessed by the Bishop on Holy Thursday.'

'Where is chrism applied? Anyone? No? Very good. You'll know it yet. Don't worry. Come on now, after me. Chrism is applied to the Five Senses: Seeing, Hearing, Smell, Taste and Touch. First the priest puts chrism on the eyelids, then on the lobes of the ears, then on the edges of the nostrils, then on the lips and then on the palms of the hands and on the soles of the feet.'

The house rang with the young, thick voices, led by Ellen's spoken melodies of instruction, as she sat there, voluminous in a powder-blue smock and a pretty blouse: Blackie, sleepy, sat on the folded-down table-top of the sewing-machine in the bay window. Ellen told Thomas that for the last three days those children should spend all day with her, and she would continue the instruction, and slowly but surely she took them through the greater part of the curriculum.

'For a sin to be a Mortal Sin, what must it have?'

'It must have Grievous Matter, Perfect Knowledge and Full Consent.'

'Full Consent, what?' They stared at her and at each other.

'Full Consent, "Your Grace"; it's the Archbishop you're talking to, so you call him "Your Grace". You must end every answer with "Your Grace"; if it was a Bishop, what would it be? It would be "My Lord". Not what a boy I taught once called the Bishop, he called him "Our Lord"' – which made them laugh.

'Name the Nine Choirs of Angels?' By now she had them all chanting together in a kind of unison which at the end of the week would shine under her polishing.

'Cherubim, Seraphim, Thrones. Dominations, Principalities, Powers. Virtues, Archangels and Angels.'

=

271

To their great surprise one day, Father John Watson called, stepping out of a shiny car which someone else drove. He did not stay long. Ellen greeted him warmly, and Thomas distantly, but with perfect good manners and offers of hospitality, which Father Watson refused, saying he was *en route* to somewhere else, and when he realized how near he was he thought he had better call and say hallo. He knew Ellen's time was coming up soon, and standing on the gravel in front of the house, he twisted his hat in his hands, saying, 'Remember how splendid your wedding day was here? Your dear parents are well, Ellen, and very excited. I met Rina the other day, and she is thrilled at the prospect of being an auntie.'

'Now what was that in aid of?' asked Thomas, policing the car out of sight.

'I'm not criticizing you, Thomas,' said Ellen, 'but I'm sure he felt your coldness towards him. I certainly did.'

'I hope he did,' said Thomas. 'He can stew in his own juice for a little while.'

Ellen smiled. 'It doesn't trouble me too much,' she said; 'the two of you will become great friends one day. You're both too intelligent not to.'

> *Faith of our Fathers living still*
> *In spite of dungeon, fire and sword.*
> *How our hearts beat high with joy,*
> *When e'er we hear that glorious Word.'*

Ellen, her huge pregnancy obliging her to sit far back from the keyboard, pumped hard at the pedals of the harmonium. Each member of the congregation sang at their own individual tempo, in their own personal key.

'I could have been playing *The Mountains of Pomeroy* for all they cared about accompaniment,' she said to Thomas afterwards, 'or a polka.' The church was packed, and sixty priests – 'A record,' claimed the Canon – attended.

'Why was the Canon so nervous?' asked Ellen afterwards.

'Can't you guess?' said Thomas. She shook her head. What she called her 'boxer's nose' seemed flatter, and like a snub-nosed child's, and her complexion darkened with the restfulness of placid days.

'Jeremiah was afraid,' said Thomas. 'Didn't you threaten at the time of the MacReady business to report him to the Bishop?'

'Oh, I had forgotten all about that,' said Ellen.

'But he hadn't. These people forget nothing.'

The choir began the second verse, so slowly that Ellen doubted they would reach the end in decent order.

'Our fathers chained in prisons dark
Were still in heart and conscience free.
How sweet would be their children's fate,
If they like them could die for thee?
Faith of our fathers living still
We will be true to thee 'til death.
We will be true to thee 'til death.'

The Archbishop, beneath the yellow and white Papal banner of the Papal Tiara and Crossed Keys, raised a hand to the congregation.

'I'll say this for the Archbishop,' said Thomas on the way home. 'He's a great blesser. I haven't felt as blessed in years.'

'The grammar in those hymns.' Ellen shook her head. 'Awful.'

The other half of the parish, Silverbridge, hosting the Confirmation this time around, had priority, which meant that the Deanstown children were the last to be examined and confirmed. Ellen picked at her fingernails. In perfect acoustics she heard each question, and her tutored ones rattling off the answers. 'Oil of olives, mixed with balm, and blessed by the Bishop on Holy Thursday. Your Grace.' One by one they sparkled haltingly, the boys' hair slicked down with oil, the girls' hands twining behind backs, bunching their gloves into a ball. One by one, the Archbishop patted them on the face, and nodded.

The potentate of an alternative empire, this fat-faced man had a great, semi-secret power. Archbishop Edward Ahern governed the Archdiocese, and thereby controlled every moral detail of every Catholic existence within his territory. He had the right to pronounce on everything, and be sure of receiving at least profound respect, and usually unquestioning obedience. Above reproach, any man who became a Bishop, still more one of the country's four

273

Archbishops, lived a notable life: the Guest of Honour wherever he appeared; the focal point of all gatherings; never a second fiddle, except perhaps to the President himself, or the Cardinal.

Parallel to the civil authority, the Church worked as a political entity, unacknowledged as such, and with the ultimate freedom of having to declare responsibility to nobody other than its own God. Committed only to a Master whose existence was not even provable, obliged to nothing other than the great intangibles of faith and morals, it had abjured unto itself the cleverest kind of power – that created by impressive doctrine and decree, based on the abstract rather than the concrete. Using prayer, ritual and cloth-of-gold ceremony, it preyed upon the workings of the human imagination; it capitalized upon Man's oldest need, for some force which both acknowledged and warded off personal fear, while at the same time guaranteeing the eternal survival of the primal force, the force of life itself, and by corollary, the defeat of death. In return for no more than responding to the Church's guidelines, the Catholic human being was granted the opportunity never to die. By offering to every person in its fold, no matter how humble, the promise of such Eternal Life – and within the sight and favour of God Himself – the Church achieved its greatest power among such people as those in the parish where Thomas and Ellen attempted to educate: simple people who never challenged in spiritual matters, and who belonged as of breeding, in a continuity of superstition. And, lest learning interfere, the Church had seen to it that the clergy controlled the schools.

Most of all, in the same way as any elective civil power needed to garner votes, the Church needed births among its faithful, the numbers had to be kept up; and the greatest blessing a couple could bestow on their country, and the greatest benison they could bring unto themselves – and so they were told repeatedly – was the gift of a large family. Domestic economics did not enter Church doctrine.

Accordingly, there sat Edward Ahern in Mooreville's rural-baroque little church. A tall arched mitre of white silk, of gold thread and scarlet lining, was fastened to his plump head: a pair of wide grosgrain ribbons fluttered down to his shoulders: atilt in his left hand stood a tall crozier of gold and gilt: a giant episcopal ring squatted like a big, brilliant insect on his finger. He wore white-and-gold slippers made with the love of duty by the nuns, who also washed his white socks. His vestments gleamed with the power of tradition: were it not for the general knowledge that this was a man of the cloth, a man of God, and barring some dreadful personal secret, surely destined for the ranks of the august in the next world, he might have been taken for some kind of visiting Sultan, here to levy from his homageous people. No property, emotional or intellectual, of any other human being in the vicinity, assailed him.

Edward Ahern had risen – from a poor cottage in the north-west of the next county – through acquired skills: an ability to hide his shrewdness behind a mask of seeming *naïveté*; general good-natured *bonhomie*, tempered with the steel of authority which he had learned to flash at just the moment, and for just the appropriate length of time, in convocations such as a Diocesan Schools meeting, or some such other useful stage.

He built an impeccable career path: an exemplary seminarian; then a young and zealous pastor who did not cause his colleagues the discomfort of competitive piety – although he was very devout, of course, and with a particular devotion to the Blessed Virgin Mary. Next, he taught for some years in the seminary which bred him; whence he was appointed Secretary to his predecessor; then bishop in a smaller diocese, and now lord of his own land – a model Churchman.

His astuteness burgeoned with status. He led men well, capable of a not-too-familiar joke; astride the sporting references; author of competent Lenten pastorals; he could even take a glass of stout on occasion, and above all, when voices had been raised calling for the excommunication of Collins and the other guerrillas, Edward Ahern was remembered for nothing, for no kind of controversy whatsoever.

In his public appearances, in which a Parish Confirmation ranked high, he paid very considerable attention to his demeanour and had been thoroughly, if informally, instructed by English and French churchmen encountered in Rome. From them he learned the little tricks of good presence: grooming; an impressive watch; excellent shoes always and, extra touch, a discreet white scarf in winter with the very best clerical black overcoat. Nobody, not even those close to the personal side of his life, speculated at a secret vice. In any case, he had none.

=

This morning, His Grace pronounced himself well pleased with all the states of learning in every candidate for Confirmation. For his text, he chose one of the Beatitudes, his favourite one, 'Blessed are the meek for they shall inherit the Earth'. As a seminary teacher, he had been fond of telling his future pastors that in their preaching they could find the finest outlets for expressing themselves.

'When you find God in your own life – and he is there, he is there everywhere – tailor your sermon to the importance He has for you, and then you will speak with the courage of your own experience.' Edward Ahern understood that politics – called by whatever name – began in the personality.

He concluded. 'My dear people of the parish of Silverbridge and Deanstown. I promised not to keep you long on this sunny and blessed morning. This is your day, not mine. I am your servant here. I am God's servant here. I am your servant and God's servant here, in this parish, among these fields where you earn your bread.

'This morning, we have had the pleasing spectacle – and how it must gladden the heart of Christ and His Blessed Mother Mary; how it must cause delight in the alcoves of Heaven – this morning, we have had the pleasing, the holy, spectacle of young people being confirmed.

'Let us lastly examine the word. Confirmed. Confirmation. To make firm, to say something with determination. With authority. With pride. But, my dear brethren, I am not the one confirming. I know we use the phrase "the Archbishop is confirming". Or "The Archbishop is holding Confirmation".

'No, I am not. Just as we say, "the priest married a couple", the Canon "married John and Mary". But the priest, my dear brethren, does not marry a couple. You are surprised. But marriage is a holy sacrament, and yes, of course the priest is there. But – it is John and Mary who marry. The sacrament is entered into by you, the faithful.

'Today I have been privileged to officiate at Confirmation. By young people. By these young people – who confirm that they are willing to become strong and perfect Christians, and soldiers of Jesus Christ.'

As he began the telling phrase, Ellen's lips synchronized with him: 'Strong and perfect Christians and soldiers of Jesus Christ.' She moved her buttocks on the wooden pew and the baby kicked – awake again: the woman next to her tried not to yawn. Ellen could see Thomas in the church ahead, sitting at the outermost edge of the front left-hand pew, the place of honour for the teachers. His head – and she had never remarked upon this before – showed not the slightest trace of baldness.

Many people stood, leaning against the walls; the sweat on the Canon's forehead picked up the light from the candles and the sanctuary lamp; on the right-hand aisle, the rows and rows of priests in their white surplices and black soutanes sat still and comfortable in their accustomed professional environment; the altar boys, three on each side, squatted at the foot of the altar steps, and tried not to fidget.

Ellen looked at her watch – a quarter past twelve; at this rate they would be finished, what, about half-past one? A slow Communion – probably for every human being she could see, except the very young children, although several priests would minister, then the procession to the statue, all before they would be finished. Half-past one, at least. Craning slightly to see others, she recognized – with a lurch – a headscarf. Mrs McAuliffe. Ellen sat straight again, easing upwards and outwards to take the pressure off the small of her back, and giving a small 'Kehh' of release.

'Why aren't you blushing?' Ellen teased Thomas when she met him at the church door after the procession. The Archbishop had included some unexpected remarks.

'Lastly, my dear brethren, I want to bring to your attention something for which we should all be grateful. I am a child of this Archdiocese as are all of you. We have all lived through terrible turmoil. We are now building our own country after eight hundred years of oppression. In this pattern, one member of our society will be, and already is, of the utmost importance – our Teacher.

'The moulding of the young mind: the building of the young character: the making of the young Catholic. In this we are especially blessed to have the likes of Thomas Kane, who since I was last among you has married and, I am told, Mrs Kane is an equally splendid teacher; we have been able to judge the fruits of their work today. And they themselves are about to be blessed, with the help of God, with the beginnings of what I hope will be a large family, and I want you all to think of them in your prayers.'

Thomas said to Ellen, 'That's only his way of keeping us in line.'

=

In the crowd they were separated. Ellen went to congratulate her young stars, who stood more or less in a bunch, creaking in the stiffness of their clothes, gloves and hair-oil.

'You were great, the lot of you, you gave him the best answers he ever had.'

They, naturally enough, did not know where to look, and one or two shrug-hunched their shoulders and allowed themselves a grin. People greeted Ellen, and gathered around; the women wishing to know when? and how was she? and what she was hoping for?

'I don't care, so long as it has ten fingers and ten toes,' laughed Ellen.

'Errah, Ma'am, didn't I dream once I had a litter of pigs,' said a woman with very quick speech, and everyone cheered her.

As she left that group to find Thomas, someone plucked her sleeve. Ellen turned, and her smile died when she saw how haggard Mrs McAuliffe had grown, suddenly an old woman.

'Ma'am. You won't forget, will you, Ma'am?'

Ellen patted her stomach. 'Well, we're very busy at the minute.'

'Ma'am, has the Master any news for us at all?' Ellen could see Thomas, head bent, listening to a couple of elderly priests, but she couldn't catch his eye.

'Ma'am, I know we're awful trouble to you, but – we can't even mourn the man. And sure every Christian creature has the right to mourn.'

Ellen looked down at her shoes. 'That's true. That's true,' she murmured, and looked up again, blinking in the sunlight to try and catch Thomas's eye. She scraped her lower teeth on her upper lip again and again: Thomas emerged.

The woman clutched her.

'Ma'am. Aw, Ma'am.'

Thomas came over, and decided to pacify. He bent his head to speak to Mrs McAuliffe; to tell her that he had had a number of conversations with the Sergeant; that the police assured him they had made exhaustive enquiries; that he could see no sensible means by which he could assist. Ellen, too, murmured soothing words: together she and Thomas affirmed their own remarks; both nodded their heads repeatedly.

—

Sean McAuliffe had been shot with, unnecessarily, two bullets; the first had gone straight into the head from the back and it never emerged; the second, half a moment later through the side of the head, burst open at the other side. He never felt either shot, all happened too quickly: what he felt was a kind of fear he had never even heard about: he looked straight ahead, and saw one man standing on his left, in a heavy old navy-blue bodycoat, and felt the presence of another, his wife's brother, directly behind him.

'Lads, listen to me, listen to me.' He whimpered. 'Look, I said nothing to no one.' He begged. 'Lads, I'm neutral, I'm neutral, I'm neutral. I was only at the door of the dance, selling the tickets.' A clandestine member of the Anti-Treaty Forces had been at the dance when Free State soldiers called: they could not have known him: someone had to have identified him.

They had held McAuliffe the previous night in a cottage from which the occupants, relatives of one of the two men, had been asked to depart for forty-eight hours. McAuliffe's mood went through many changes – from innocence to defiance to truculence to despair and back to blandness again, then once more through the whole cycle.

'If it wasn't serious,' said one of the men, 'would you be here?'

'Or tied to the chair?' said the other.

When they left him alone for some hours, although absolutely secured in his bonds, he began to hope that they might have intended him to escape, and he rocked the chair back and forth, back and forth – but he only succeeded in falling over and bruising himself in the process. On their return, he pretended not to recognize that the coat they carried belonged to him: he put it on, thanking them for the warmth.

'Did you tell herself, or the child, did you tell the child I was safe?'

'We didn't. You're not.'

In the sequences of little actions that make up cold-blooded murder, where both parties have become incontrovertibly aware of what is about to happen, logic drifts away. Time, the most important factor in the all-round equation, loses its texture and its tempo, and becomes an elastic matter. Noise is altered: a cough sounds different, a whistle unreal; every infinitesimal movement, every sound, every sight, is promoted to a stature never normally attributed to it; men already hard, indurate themselves further in order to carry out their deeds. Those holding the weapons handle them with extraordinary casualness, even, for instance, scratching themselves with the gun, finger already inside the trigger-guard. Those about to be killed choose one of a number of courses of response. They soften uncontrollably and become jelly, helpless; they dignify themselves with a last raising of the head; or they weep quietly; or they struggle to the last; or they rail and curse their executioners; or they beg captors to forgive them; or they offer bribes, or try to strike deals, to divide and conquer with promises; they speak incessantly to themselves as if to rationalize the awfulness of what is happening; or they soberly ask to have a last message delivered to loved ones; or they give themselves up to the arms of sheer terror, every black thought and innate fear realized, every night-time spectre of fear from their tenderest childhood stored away to roar out of the cavern at this moment; or they join the ranks of the mobile animate insensate – rigid and uncomprehending.

When the trio had been walking for ten minutes or so, in the later stages pushing awkwardly under low branches – several scratched his cheeks, because with his hands tied behind his back he had no way of keeping them from slapping into his face – McAuliffe saw the freshly-dug pit, the brown earth and leaf-mould against the dank wood's floor, and began to scream.

'Shut up,' said one of his captors, 'or I'll shut you up,' and hit him on the back corner of the head with the heel of his hand.

'The priest! The priest!'

'Where was the priest for Tony Lawlor?' they asked, referring to the soldier for whose betrayal they had abducted McAuliffe.

In the lifetime of Thomas and Ellen Kane, and of McAuliffe's young daughter, Hannie, and for the rest of the life of Archbishop Edward Ahern, and ever thereafter, very few people in Ireland would ever, ever, even in private, discuss the events of the Civil War, the secret, livid dreadfulness of field and valley and night-time and river bank and woodland, as these beautiful places were defiled with revenge and death. The whole vast, mutual crime went unpurged.

'Aaah.' Half a scream, half a sigh. 'Oh, Jesus. Jesus. Jesus. Oh, my God, I am heartily sorry . . .'

They took McAuliffe's bonds off, then took off his coat, turned it inside out, put it back on him; he stood there unbound and made no attempt to escape. His eyes tried desperately to weep, and failed.

Up close, gunshots seem never as loud as reputed; the crack too thin, too narrow, a plank of sound rather than any fat explosion. When fired close to the skin, so swift is the sound, and so short-lived, unless the local acoustic breeds a long echo, that the rip of flesh and the crack of bone may even be heard, and if there is one, the burble of flesh. The birds whirred away, more of them than the winter's day seemed to have been hiding, and some deer stampeded. The men, one at the back, one at the side, one, two, used two handguns, a Colt and a German gun, the one they called 'Peter the Painter'. Only a little smoke hung in the air, grey-blue, mingling with the condensation from the breaths of three men, now two. Both men instinctively held their noses, though not through a distaste for the smell of cordite: McAuliffe's last bodily action had been involuntary. He did not fall quite accurately into his grave, they had to adjust him to it, before with grunts and pantings they shovelled with their feet all the loose soft earth piled around.

In the thronged church precinct, when seen from a distance without being heard, when observed by one other pair of eyes on the edge of that good-humoured Confirmation mêlée, the Kanes, especially Thomas, looked like people giving full help and information to someone in distress. Regrettably, Thomas pointed to the west – but a watcher out of earshot would not have known that he had only been telling Mrs McAuliffe that he himself, at the time, had helped the police search all those fields and woodlands for her missing husband. His bodycoat slung over the handlebars in a loose bale, and tied with the belt, the watcher in the crowd, the heavy man with the cap – who continually beat his small boy until the boy had difficulty in speaking, although Ellen's efforts in school had helped – cycled away.

At home, Ellen, by now climbing slowly and resting halfway, went upstairs. She opened the wardrobe door to put her hat on the top shelf, then unhooked the hooks and eyes at the back of her maternity dress. As it hung loosely about her, she reached to adjust some of the garments in the wardrobe. One skirt had not fitted for ages, and she took it out, saw that the buttons at the waistband had forced a little of the fabric apart: she must have worn it too long before switching to smocks, and she put the skirt on the chair to stitch later.

Turning to the mirror, she held a jacket up against her swollen bosom, and turned this way and that. She sat on the bed in fatigue, looking down with pleasant aimlessness at the garment in her hand. Bought in Todd's a month after she had met Thomas, with that nice braiding, not too much, on the reveres, a darker effect, same on the cuffs, with that little dart there at the bust. Should it have had buttons covered with its own cloth? Or, maybe, even shiny buttons, not full brass, no, too like a blazer. For several minutes she sat there examining the cream piece of clothing, running her hand along the shoulders, puffing the sleeve a little, tugging it, straightening the satin lining.

SUMMER 1926

19

'How is it spelt? C. A. U. L.? Or W?'

'"U",' said Ellen, looking again at the letter. Thomas had left his spectacles upstairs and held the dictionary at arm's length, the page slanted towards the light of the window. 'Cattle. Well, we know what they are, anyway. Caudex.'

'What's that? Caudex?'

'Shh. Stop interrupting me. It's the stem, it says, of a plant, a palm. Caudicle. Cauk. Caul. Here we are. "A kind of close-fitting cap worn by women, often richly ornamented; a net for the hair".'

'Isn't that ridiculous. How could a baby be born wearing one of those?' asked Ellen.

'Try this,' said Thomas. '"A membrane enclosing the foetus before birth; or a portion of it, sometimes enveloping the head of the child at birth, and adadadadadada . . ."' He broke off into a mumble.

'Read it all out, Thomas!'

'. . . "Superstitiously regarded as of good omen; sought by mariners as a safeguard against drowning" . . . There you are.'

'For goodness' sake,' said Ellen. 'Good Lord above!'

'Oh, I remember something.' Thomas reached up for another book. 'D'you remember *David Copperfield*? Here it is. "I was born with a caul, which was advertised for sale, in the newspapers for the low price of fifteen guineas." There you are, Ellie. So we're doing well.'

Bohercreen,
Mooreville.
27th April 1926

Dear Mrs Kane,
    You won't know who I am, but your husband knows my
husband's brother, Father Ryan. I heard from him that
you were expecting a baby and may God's blessing

descend on you. My own brother is a sea-captain in the Merchant Navy, sailing out of Liverpool, and he has only recently taken over a very big ship. He always has me on the lookout for a Caul, and if God blesses that your own Child is born with one, I am instructed to offer you fifty pounds for it, or we could discuss the price.

God be good to you and Master Kane and the New Infant.

Yours faithfully,
Julia Ryan (Mrs)

'I know them well,' said Thomas; 'her husband is a fussy sort of man. A great fisherman, great salmon man. They're not a family I like, they're a bit full of their own importance. He's a great friend of Uncle John's.'

'I never heard of that before,' said Ellen, 'a caul for good luck, wouldn't it be exciting? But I don't think I'd sell it.'

'You mean you'd keep it,' asked Thomas, 'in case you took up seafaring?'

Ellen swiped at him, laughing.

'No. I'd give it to them.'

'Oh, you can't do that. They have to buy it. You'd break the luck of it otherwise. You know if someone buys you a present of gloves or a knife, you have to give them a little money to preserve the friendship? This is the same principle, sort of having to purchase your luck.'

Ellen said she'd write that very moment to Mrs Ryan and say she was welcome to have the caul, if there was one, for the price offered.

First came *The Heather Clan*, dancing girls in kilts and bonnets and white blouses, doing sedate sword dances. Then Mrs Mac and her Mops.

Time for the main attraction. Val came out like a young thing, like a gambolling lamb, and took his bow. Dublin was never as thunderous as Cork, but they certainly knew who he was. The silver buckles on his shoes gleamed. He held up a hand and began to recite *The Roads around Rathoe*.

> *'My son has brought me over to end my many days,*
> *Amidst his wealth and comforting that meet my worn-out gaze,*
> *I'm sure the boy means well enough and the wife's a treasure*
> *too;*
> *She calls me 'Pops' and 'Popakins' and smiles with eyes of blue.'*

The applause fell a little short of wonderful, to Val's way of thinking, and would be described by next day's newspapers as 'appreciative'.

> *'Although they do their best to make me feel at home and safe,*
> *I'd rather tread this moment the brown of autumn leaf,*
> *That makes a thickened carpet along where streamlets flow,*
> *I'd rather be a-strollin' the roads around Rathoe.'*

How Val had also struggled for that third and fourth line rhyme.

In Furnace Wood, near the old lime-kiln, spring had truly become established. Under the beginnings of hard shiny little shoots, other buds were forming down near the floor of the wood; tiny wild strawberries would bloom here in August, bittersweet on the tongue. A wren had nested, its domed roundhouse in never-ending construction, with small twigs being ferried in to reinforce the moss, the wren's wings whirruping softly whenever the bird, its tiny tail indicating the sky, landed on the branch high above the protruding cloth in the earth. The woman and the girl walked through the wood slowly, looking here and there; like diviners, they prodded the ground with sticks.

Late Saturday evening: 'Am I ever allowed to write in your ledger?' asked Thomas. Ellen sat there, copying in a recipe.
   'No,' she said laughing. 'Go away. All your old seeds, and potato varieties and things.'
   'I have a formula for Macassar oil,' Thomas fought back.
   'You never use it. Just as well, think of the mess on the pillow.'
   'I know how to mix gentian violet,' said Thomas.
   'The next time I get a sting from a wasp I'll send for you,' countered Ellen. 'Thomas, go and do something, will you?'
   'I can't. I'm just waiting.'
   'I'm the one who's expecting,' said Ellen. 'You're like a child.'

She dropped a hand on his knee in affection. 'You could pick up that goosewing and dust the place.'

'Will I read to you, instead?' he said.

'All right, love,' she conceded. 'You're the dearest man.'

'What are you doing, anyway?'

LEMON CREAM TARTLETS

(from Mrs Annie Dalton, 28/4/1926)

Three eggs, I use between two and four depending on how many people I'm expecting. Separate the yolks from the whites and keep the whites to one side in a cup.

'A recipe Mrs Dalton gave me; d'you remember those lemon little tarts she had?'

'I thought you used Mrs Beeton for everything?'

'She hasn't these.' Ellen consulted the thick, black-covered volume. 'Mrs Beeton has, look – lemon-and-acid drops, lemon biscuits, lemon blancmange, lemon cheesecakes, lemon cream, lemon jelly, lemon pudding, baked *and* boiled, lemon sauce, lemon sorbet, lemon sponge, lemon water ice, but she has no lemon cream tartlets.'

Ellen, when concentrating, never lifted her head.

Beat the yolks of the eggs to a frothy consistency. While you're beating, keep adding nearly a cupful of sugar if it's two eggs, a full cupful if it's three eggs, and just over a cupful if it's four eggs. Grate the peel of a lemon, and add the juice of the grated lemon and the juice of another one to the mixture. Roll out enough pastry, the lighter the better, and with it line some cake-pat tins, that you have already greased every little compartment of with butterpaper.

Thomas returned with his book.

'Now,' he said, settling down beside Ellen.

'Not for just one minute, Thomas, I'm nearly finished.'

Add about a cup of cream to your mixture, folding it in thoroughly, and then fill each of the pats on the tray with the mixture. Do not fill too full. Bake medium to hot, until the pastry is as brown as you like and the custard setting on top good and firm. Take the tins from the oven, and keeping them level(!) put them in a cool corner. Take the whites of the eggs and with two to three tablespoonfuls of castor sugar whip them into meringues. When the tartlets are cool enough, dollop the meringue on top of them, and then put the trays back in the oven, in a slow heat so that the meringues set.

'You can if you like,' Mrs Dalton had added, 'pour cream on these as well, but I only do it for the men, as I think it is too much otherwise.'

Ellen sat back. 'Good! Lovely! I'll make those the minute I come out of the nursing home.'

Thomas began. 'Now. Are you ready?'

Ellen tidied her papers, slipping back in some loose cuttings and notes not yet fixed in the ledger.

'Guess who this is?' Thomas began to read. 'Here we go. "The cuckoo, as has been said elsewhere, makes no nest, but deposits its eggs in an alien nest, generally in the nest of the ring-dove, or in the nest of the ground-lark, or on a tree in the nest of the green linnet." Any ideas?'

Ellen shook her head: she loved these book games Thomas played with her: he had covered the spine and cover with one large hand.

'I'll read on. "It lays only one egg and does not hatch it itself, but the mother-bird in whose nest it has deposited it hatches and rears it." Well?'

'No clues?'

'No. "And, as they say, this mother-bird when the young cuckoo has grown big, thrusts her own brood out of the nest and lets them perish"? You'll never guess, Ellie, in a million years.'

'Who?'

'Aristotle, you eejit.'

'You eejit yourself. Oh, Thomas!'

'What?'

'My back!'

'Here. Come on, get ready for bed.'

Thomas had bolted the back door and was winding the alarm clock to take it upstairs when he heard her cry.

'Thomas! Thomas!'

He rushed up the stairs.

'Don't come in! Don't come in! Hand me in a towel from the landing cupboard.' He handed a towel in through the door.

'Get out the car, Thomas!' Ellen called, half-flustered, half-laughing.

'Where's your bag?'

'Talk about on time, I only got it ready this very day.'

By then he was halfway down the stairs.

'Oh, shite,' he said, remembering something, and turned back, almost falling. 'What about the doctor?'

'We'll call to Dr Hogan and take him with us.'

He pushed the car back far enough to get the starting-handle in, and twisted: it fired first go: he reversed carefully from the garage.

'Hold on, Thomas.' Ellen dived back to the door, opened it, dipped her finger in the little brown, bakelite holy water font on the wall, blessed herself and dabbed a little on Thomas's forehead, and he also made the Sign of the Cross.

Dr Hogan's lights were on: 'I'd better get the bag.'

'He sleeps in that bow tie,' observed Thomas.

'Any pains yet?' said the doctor cheerfully.

'Just a hint.'

'Good girl. Good girl.'

'Will your coat be warm enough on you in the dickey-seat?' said Thomas.

'Fire away,' shouted the Doctor, once he had crammed himself in: his bag was placed inside the car, on the floor at Ellen's feet: he fought to prop himself up: the dickey slanted outwards and upwards like the lid of the car boot.

'That reminds me – I never went to see that poor Stephenson girl,' Ellen remarked.

'You can when you get out,' said Thomas. 'We'll go up there then. Show her the baby.'

Within seconds of knocking on the door of the nursing home, Nurse Cooper herself appeared, a coat over her nightdress.

'Hallo. Oh, Dr Hogan?'

'Hallo, Nurse, you were expecting Mrs Kane, weren't you?'

'You're very punctual indeed,' said Sheila Cooper. 'And what about Dr Morgan?'

'I could go and get him,' said Thomas.

'But how long would that take at all?' asked Nurse Cooper.

Thomas pulled out his watch. 'There and back, what, two and a half, three hours?' he said hopefully.

'Great God in Heaven, sure the child'll be out and up and running about in short trousers by then,' said Nurse Cooper.

Jack Hogan said, 'John Morgan can't do it, anyway, he's after getting another case of malaria.'

'You'd think a bottle of it would be enough,' said Thomas.

Ellen leaned with one hand against a wall, laughing.

'Show me your hands,' said Nurse Cooper to Dr Hogan. He put down his bag and held out his hands.

'God.' She glared at him. 'Look at the cut of those hands. In there, like a good man, and wash yourself.'

'Only the hands?' he asked. 'Is that all you're going to look at? What about the lugs of the ears, or the navel?'

Thomas asked Ellen, 'Are you all right?'

'I am, but I won't be in a minute.'

'Come on, now,' Nurse Cooper said to Ellen, 'this is your first, isn't it? I have the nicest bed in the place kept for you. Would you like a cup of tea, maybe?' She took Ellen's bag and led her upstairs, and then looked back at Thomas.

'Well, go on, what are you looking at, go on.'

'Where will I go to?' asked Thomas, who still had his hat on, most unlike him.

'Mauritius. Where d'you think? Stop standing there looking out of your mouth, and go.'

Ellen had never heard anybody speak to Thomas like that before, and she would have intervened, had a pain not hit her, the first real one, knocking her breath out, making her gasp.

Thomas stiffened, and Nurse Cooper, observing, held up a hand, and spoke softly, 'Mr Kane, a bit of calm.' She nodded seriously. 'A bit of calm' – one moment, harpie: now, carer.

'But –'

'– A bit of calm!'

The women disappeared round the corner of the staircase and continued to the landing above.

And Thomas drove home in the darkness, the headlights shafting up to the night sky as he climbed the hill, and then the long white and amber beams flashing into the fields as he swung around Hogan's Bend, first lighting up little puzzled, glazed, opaque lamps in the eyes of the cattle as they chewed large and silent in the fields behind the low stone wall, and then the lights closing back in on his own eyes and straight features as he entered the tunnel of trees and high hedges.

At a quarter past six the knocking awakened him out of a deep and late-arriving sleep; then a pebble hit the window.

'Master,' the voice called. 'Are you there? Master.'

Thomas clambered over, raised the sash, and peered out into the half-light. 'It's me, Jack. Jack Hogan.' In such circumstances do people learn to drop formalities and begin thereafter to use the first names of others.

'Jack. Oh?'

'A girl. Lovely and healthy.'

'A girl?'

'Grand and strong.'

'A girl,' said Thomas, the word ending in a little gasp.

'Hold on.'

He ran down the stairs, feeling his way in the dark, not bothering with a candle, and opened the front door in his pyjamas.

'Come in, come in, hang on I'll get a lamp.'

'No, no. I only called to give you the news.'

Ellen's hats hung on the hallstand.

'And all well?'

'All serene,' said Dr Hogan. 'She's a great girl, great girl.'

'She's all right, so?'

'Ah, grand. I mean, for a first birth, d'you see, she's a miracle. She must have been practising for years.' He laughed and so did Thomas.

'You'll have a cup of tea, come in here 'til I find the matches.'

'No, no, no. I have to be going, the wife will have heard the car passing the house, and she always has the breakfast ready if I'm out on a night call.' He left.

Thomas lit the lamp, and then set up the small Primus stove on the scullery side-table, shaking it first to check that it had enough paraffin; he made a cup of tea for himself. Blackie had slipped in while the door stood open to Dr Hogan. Mewling, she painted Thomas's shins with her tail. Two of the other cats, Jen and Soot, clambered on the windowsill and prowled against the glass, ghostly in the opening glim of day. Thomas, cold, fetched a coat from the hallstand, wrapped it around him, refilled the large cup, smiled at how fiercely Ellen would have clucked at him for eschewing a saucer. He opened the door of the range: a few embers from last night glowed; Thomas poked at them, threw in three, four, small pieces of wood, dusted the disturbed ash off the rail with the goosewing. The little timbers flared and Thomas chose two small pieces of turf, then a third, made a tiny tent of them, watched for five minutes.

'My thanks – will be inadequate,' he had said to Dr Hogan at the front door, 'no matter what I say.'

'Ach, what thanks?' dismissed the doctor.

The fire built a little, and Thomas repeated the process, first a wigwam of small firewood, hemmed in by walls of turf pieces, and within twenty minutes the blaze began to speak for itself.

Not even Ellen knew that Thomas talked aloud when alone. Had the pattern been mapped by an invisible watcher, it would have become evident that he did so only on specific occasions – when recalling an acute embarrassment; when severely troubled by a bad memory; when inordinately excited; or, as now, when flummoxed.

'I don't even know what it means. A daughter.' He put his hands between his knees and rubbed the palms together, a gesture of bemusement as well as warming himself.

'I suppose it'll be Helena?'

They had talked out names, and came to the traditional agreement: if a boy he would be called after Thomas's grandfather; if a girl, after Ellen's grandmother; a second son after Thomas's father, a second daughter after Ellen's mother; a third son after Thomas himself; a third daughter after Ellen; then, they would switch the preferences; a fourth son after Ellen's father; a fourth daughter after Thomas's mother, and so on.

'We'll be in right trouble when number thirteen arrives,' Thomas had said; Ellen scolded him.

'Helena, that's it,' said Thomas aloud. He had left the clock upstairs and had to guess the time: about a quarter to eight, he reckoned, and the grey light had begun to take over from the lamp: the cats still paced, wraiths against the windowpane.

'Sunday. Nine o'clock Mass. No post. No bus. Should I drive in and tell all the relatives? The best thing to do. Now, if I go to Mass here. I'll have to tell everyone, and might it get to the folks before I have time to tell them?'

Thomas resolved, ticking it out on his splayed fingers, to (a) Call in to the nursing home, see Ellen and the baby if possible, but anyway verify everything, see did Ellen need anything, he'd surely only be let stay a short time? (b) Get Mass in town, there's an eleven o'clock Mass, he'd get that straight away after coming out of the nursing home; or maybe get Mass first, then call to the nursing home; (c) Head for Brunswick Square; they'd give him his dinner, he could drop a note into Dr Morgan, and tell Leah and anyone else Ellen wanted told; (d) Get back in time to visit Ellen and the baby again, and be back in Deanstown, what? some time around eight or so tonight? Good.

Nurse Cooper stuck her hand out in a formal congratulation. ''Tis never easy, but this was as easy as it could ever be. In grand fettle, the two of them.'

Long-hipped and starched, she led Thomas upstairs; he smoothed his hair and stood outside the door, as candidates hesitate before an interview.

Nurse Cooper first checked her patient, then held open the door: 'Here's God the father.'

She stepped back to admit Thomas, and then closed the door behind him and went away. He stood with his hat in his left hand, and said, 'I heard the good news.' Approaching the bed, he said, 'How are you, Ellie?' and stood for a moment, then asked, 'Where is she?' Ellen, sitting up, washed and combed, pointed to the crib on her side of the bed, and Thomas stood on tiptoe to lean over.

'You and your left-handedness?' he smiled. 'How are you feeling?'

'A bit sore,' she rued. 'Glad to have it all over.'

'They said you were great.' He walked to the end of the bed and came halfway up to where the baby lay on its side, soundless, wrinkled and asleep. Again he stood on tiptoe, although he didn't need to.

'The mop of hair,' he whispered, in a slow and foolish awe.

'And no caul,' joked Ellen. 'Poor us.'

'We have luck anyway?' Thomas consoled. 'How are you feeling?'

He came around to the side and sat on the chair beside the bed, as Ellen lifted a towel to make way: his overcoat seemed huge in the room.

'D'you want to take off your coat?'

'No, I'm grand.'

'Oh,' she said, catching sight of his tie and shirt, 'you're in your very best.'

He looked down. 'Why wouldn't I be?'

He asked for no details, no account of what birth entailed, no specifics regarding soreness and its location, nothing other than asking whether Ellen had much pain, and how long did a pain last, and what was it like, was it very hurtful? Ellen gave him the weight of the baby, people would ask.

'And when you saw her?'

'At that stage, I was exhausted, and I thought, "Oh, so that's what I looked like when I was born," and then they told me she was fine in every detail, and then I thought, "Oh, what am I supposed to think?" Do you know what I mean? The doctor and the nurse were like a circus together.'

In the inner corner of Thomas's eyes, tears almost appeared, and he blinked them away. He sat erect and said, 'You're a great girl.'

'Imagine,' said Ellen, mocking her mother's tone.

They organized. He would drive on to Janesborough, and take care of all that, and then through the week call in every day after school; he would also make arrangements for exactly which day the Brunswick Square contingent would visit. Ellen said perhaps she would take up Leah's offer to visit for a while, and would Thomas make sure the spare room was made up, and then Leah could come out the day before Ellen and the baby were due home? They agreed on the following Sunday – Nurse Cooper's advice: 'a first baby needs the full week for the both of them' – and Thomas left promising to see Ellen later.

In the belled and Sunday-empty city, Dr Morgan's wife brought him Thomas's note as it fell through the letter-box.

At Brunswick Square, Jim opened the door.

'Hallo, Uncle Jim,' said Thomas, and May, ever vigilant, over-heard. Eagerly they all found a place at the table for Thomas, who gave them all the details he knew, prefacing every stage of the proceedings with a timetable.

'At exactly twelve minutes past ten, she called me, I was

downstairs . . .' ending, many minutes later to their agog attention, 'and the baby was born at exactly twenty-six minutes past four.'

To Leah and Herbert, the word of the new baby, safely born, might have been a personal blessing: Rachel and Sarah wanted to know what colour hair, eyes; did she have fingernails; what would she be called? Herbert gave Thomas a crown piece to press in the baby's hand; 'More than he ever gave me,' ribbed Leah, who handed Thomas a mysterious small parcel for Ellen, revealed in time as a small jar of home-made hand-cream accompanied by a note. Thomas made arrangements to meet Leah off the Deanstown bus the following Saturday.

Back at the nursing home, Ellen was receiving instruction on how to hold and feed.

'Here – you take her,' said Sheila Cooper, thrusting the baby into Thomas's arms, and he, unprepared, dropped his hat on the floor. 'I'm always trying to get the fathers involved too,' she said, 'and most of them would be more at ease holding a calf.'

Thomas sat ramrod straight, inspecting every visible fibre of his daughter.

'Oh, she does have fingernails?'

'What are you talking about?' said the nurse. 'Is it that you have none?' He laughed, and told them of Leah's little girls; he marvelled on the smallness of the baby, and the frailness, and the tininess.

'Yes,' said Nurse Cooper, 'and you should see what some people do to them, frail and all as they are.'

Thomas asked to see Helena's feet: they unwrapped the swaddling clothes and he inspected her little toes, setting their minute wrinkled redness to rest in his huge palm.

Thomas's week passed in a blur of wellbeing. He walked to school smiling: he never told the schoolchildren, but they knew. Naturally enough, the postman, knowing everything, congratulated him, as did the bus conductor, dropping off a parcel of schoolbook samples for the changed curriculum next September.

Alone in the house in the evenings when he returned from the nursing home, his solitude had a completely different texture from the life he had lived before he met Ellen. It felt almost as if he now tenanted her house: vases, empty at the moment; the mystical arrangements of jars in the pantry; the washboards fixed in ascending sizes on the left-hand scullery wall; the peremptory notes in her handwriting pinned to sundry surfaces: 'Every vessel likely to hold milk must be scrubbed severely; every bottle cleansed out by a little gravel in the water and Shaken Vigorously, then Rinsed'; '*Do not Boil* the Master's Shirts'. He brought the newspaper to the nursing home every day, and, with the exception of Wednesday, when the Morris family visited, he read Ellen the day's news, and from time to time held the baby as gingerly as if he had just landed a sacred fish. People who encountered him found an unbent and warmer man.

Ellen, in her turn, regaled him with the many details of Nurse Cooper's humour, or the characters in the other rooms. She showed him the envelope with five hundred pounds in it that Bob Morris had given her.

'Better than a caul,' Thomas commented.

Ellen struggled on with the bottle-feeding, as she did with the bathing and changing.

On Thursday when he visited, having resisted again the temptation to close the school early, and not trusting the temporary teacher, he slipped in, as had become his wont, through the unlocked front door. Ellen was not in her room. He found a maid, who found Nurse Cooper, who had a story to tell him.

'That Mrs Stapleton isn't well at all, and her child just will not take the bottle. I asked your wife would she help, and she's down now in Mrs Stapleton's room feeding the child. Would you give her half an hour and call back?'

When Thomas did, he found Ellen a little out of phase, and when he pressed, she grew embarrassed. Briefly she told him.

'Nurse Cooper said the child was even more poorly than the mother and it didn't look at all good, and she asked me would I wet-nurse for it a few days?' Ellen paused, then truly blushed. 'Actually she didn't give me any choice, she said I had enough to feed triplets. So what could I do?'

Thomas said, 'But where's the harm in it? How is the child?'

'Apparently,' said Ellen, 'there's a great recovery.' Thomas did not ask why she blushed, nor did he understand.

—

The month of May grew warm quickly in 1926, as hot as high summer. Leah came on the Saturday bus, to stay and settle Ellen and little Helena Sorcha in easily. That night, Thomas wrote Ellen a note and placed it in her dressing-table drawer where she would be sure to find it, perhaps when he was at school on Monday.

8th May 1926.
Saturday night.

Dear Ellen,

Do you have any idea of how I feel now? After all the things that have happened to me, all the awful things, some which were not of my creating, and worse than that, many which were my own doing?

I suppose that very few men get a chance to make for themselves a good life. I have, and it is mainly thanks to you.

Now, I have a daughter of my own, God bless her, and you have therefore given me something I have always wanted, ever since my own little sister Sorcha died, R.I.P.

All I can say is, that I will do my level best to provide for you and the baby, and any others that come along.

Thank you very much.

Your sincere husband,
Thomas

On Sunday morning, Nurse Cooper and one of her other two nurses stood at the door to see them off. Thomas had been to nine o'clock Mass in Deanstown and the entire half-parish, it seemed, waited to congratulate him. Leah had made him a breakfast so large he could scarcely finish it, and she stood at the door waving him off, and saying the house would be aired and fresh and warm for the baby, and she expected them about twelve noon, or just before.

Unaccountably, Leah then stood at the gate and watched the car climb the hill and go out of sight, then she put out saucers of milk for the cats, and cleared the table.

Halfway through the washing-up, Leah dropped the cloth in the basin, and said aloud, 'Oh, my God!' She never told Ellen this, and when recounting it to Herbert late the next week, said, still on the verge of tears, 'I don't know why, Herbert, I don't know why. But at that moment, I felt something awful, something black and awful.'

The Canon's sermon droned on even longer than usual, and when Thomas went round to the sacristy with the Collection afterwards, he could not get away from the Canon who seemed excitable – but Jeremiah Williams never mentioned Helena's birth.

'Umpteen people, the Relihans, the Ryles, Mrs Dalton, they were all asking for you, and they all want to call and see you,' Thomas told Ellen.

'It'll be fine if they come during the day,' said Ellen.

'Now,' said Nurse Cooper, 'you've to look after yourself too, you know.'

'How will the Stapleton child be?' whispered Ellen, as Thomas prepared the car.

'He'll be fine now,' confided Nurse Cooper, 'you started him, and this morning's bottle was the best he had. Sure, the poor little fellow is getting a variety of food very young.' They laughed.

Ellen called from the doorway, 'The hood, Thomas. Put the hood down.'

He called back, 'But what about the baby, won't she get cold?'

'Oh, but such a gorgeous day,' said Ellen, and looked to Nurse Cooper for support.

'She's very well wrapped,' agreed Nurse Cooper, and Thomas lowered the hood of the car, although only to the three-quarter mark: the brass headlamps shone; he had wax-polished them early yesterday morning. The two nurses on the doorstep waved goodbye.

The Deanstown road declines as it leaves the town, and then climbs a steep hill past the cemetery, to one of the highest points for miles around: on a clear day, Thomas always pointed out the Castle, a comforting landmark. They passed a woman and her son walking on the left, going home from Mass: the couple stopped to look at the car going by, and stepped out in the road when it had passed, then toiled on up the hill; the fair-haired curly boy remarked to his pleasant and plump mother how handy it would be for them to have a car. Just before the brow of the hill, the car, as it always did, struggled a little, and, with Thomas humorously urging it on, the car made it.

The plateau of the hill runs on for forty yards or so, with a slight curve, then dips with corroborative steepness. The midday sun lit Ellen's face from the side: her hair streamed out from under her brown hat: she held the quiet baby firmly in her arms.

Ellen heard the fat and booming crack before she registered what it was: Thomas heard it too. With his experience, he must have known what the noise meant: they both saw the split second of milky-white little cracks, and then the shatter appearing on the erect windscreen. Ellen heard the second crack: she never found out if Thomas did. He swung violently towards her as if something had punched him terribly hard on the side of the head. Blood flecked her cream skirt: Thomas's left hand clawed towards her, his right hand seemed to get its elbow locked at the steering wheel. His head hit her shoulder, his hat half-squashed off. The car slewed onto the grass margin, and climbed the bank; the engine made several banging noises, and one of the white-walled spoked wheels flopped along; the car slewed on, drifted down the grassy bank, eventually being brought to a halt by the density of the earth, and by some low-growing haw bushes halfway down the hill. Green and shining in the sun, the car attempted to heel over and did so halfway and leftwards, pinning Ellen and the baby under the weight of Thomas's body. She called out to him, and received no reply; then something final hit her on the head, too.

At the top of the hill, the woman and her fifteen-year-old son walking home from Mass had heard wild sounds, and the boy ran on ahead to see around the bend. He called his mother, who broke into a scurry. Coming from the opposite direction, a man on a bicycle saw the smoking car lying almost on its side and recognized it. He reached it at the same time as the boy. The panting woman arrived: the trio heard the baby crying: the man despatched the boy to the nearest dwelling, a farmhouse two hundred and fifty yards from the road. From where they stood they could see the people, one, two, three, emerge from the house and, shading their hands against the sun, look from the hollow up in the direction of the boy's pointing finger, and still the baby cried.

The man with the bicycle told the woman, 'Master Kane out in Deanstown owns that car.'

'I know that. The wife had a baby last week in at Nurse Cooper's,' and they stood there, helplessly surmising that 'the Mistress would be in there so, too, and that must be the baby we're hearing.' They plucked uselessly at the green metal of the car.

From the farmhouse a horse and cart and two men, twin brothers, arrived. With great care they righted the car, found the baby safe and sound, and the woman took the child and cradled it. The men gently disentangled the two adults from the almost undamaged car. The woman was unconscious, but bore no trace of serious injury: the man bled profusely from the head, his white collar was soaked with red darkness, and nobody could think how to stop the bleeding. Both adults were laid side by side on the back of the cart.

'She don't look too bad,' said the farmer, preparing to turn the horse around in the direction back to town and hospital, 'but I'd say he's done for.'

20

Holding the baby in her arms, and sitting on the front of the cart, the woman suggested that instead of the hospital they should go to Nurse Cooper's on account of the child and its mother.

The farmer led the horse, walking beside it, trying to keep jolts to a minimum. His brother knelt on the cart facing backwards, attempting to hold steady the heads of the two unfortunate people. The journey, little more than a mile, and helped by the fall of ground back into the town, seemed to take for ever: the man with the bicycle had been detailed to cycle ahead and tell the Guards, and in the distance they saw him returning, accompanied by a cycling officer.

The policeman vacillated – between accompanying the stricken load, inspecting the car, finding a doctor or alerting Nurse Cooper: duty called for the first or second; humanity and practicality governed the third and fourth. Guard Burke resolved his dilemma by, first, sending the man on the bicycle to Nurse Cooper (who then sent him farther, to fetch a priest); second, calling to the barracks on the way (he had been intercepted on the Main Street) and requesting that one of the dayroom men be dispatched out to the car; third, by sending the boy – on the police bicycle – to find a doctor, while he walked along beside the swaying cart. He felt certain the Superintendent would endorse his decisions. (He did not: the man got a flea in his ear, and was told – albeit only when all the circumstances came to light a long time later – that he should have inspected the car, or searched the fields.)

The boy showed the greatest perspicacity: he rode the policeman's bicycle along the back road – to the golf club, where, in the bar, he found not one, but two doctors, one of whom was Jack Hogan.

Nurse Cooper drew on all her phlegmatism learned in time of military and civil unrest: as the cart arrived, she waited on the pavement outside her door with stretchers already prepared. The horse and cart turned the corner, and she saw to her vast relief Dr Hogan's Austin Seven sweep around the other end of the short street by the market gates. The assistant nurse took the baby, and with a silent thanking nod to the woman, hurried indoors: the policeman and the farming twin brothers, under the supervision of an untypically grave Dr Hogan lifted first, Ellen, onto a stretcher, and then Thomas. For a moment the bodies lay there on the side of the street, mute and slack, and the farmers edged their cart away a decent distance, and tied the horse to a lamp-post. The man with the bicycle returned, saying Father Herity was on his way: it felt to everyone as if those were the only words so far spoken in the activities at the nursing home door – not the case, merely a breaking of the spell.

'Which of them first?' asked Guard Burke.

Dr Hogan's friend, Dr Dillon, straightened up and said, 'He's bleeding very heavily,' so they took Thomas in first.

'Good job that baby is on the bottle,' said Nurse Cooper to nobody. A few people had gathered, interrupting their Sunday mealtime to inspect a commotion they had sensed rather than heard.

'The room inside the door,' said Nurse Cooper, 'the bed there is empty. And take her upstairs.'

She led the way up to the bed Ellen had vacated some hours earlier: it had been stripped of its sheets and not yet remade, a detail to which Nurse Cooper now attended as if by magic, and she had a sheet spread on it before the bearers, grunting to keep the stretcher level all the way upstairs, manoeuvred it through the doorway.

Dr Hogan and Dr Dillon divided their responsibilities; Dr Hogan attending his recent maternity patient, Dr Dillon, with much more surgical experience, washing his hands in the corner of the downstairs room where Thomas stretched on the only bed. The man on the bicycle was sent on one more errand – down the street to call in Nurse Cooper's other nurse, and if not her, the Jubilee Nurse: in fact he called both.

Another car drew up outside, another doctor, a MacDonnell man, the word had spread fast: then Father Herity arrived on foot, and was kept waiting, not hugely to his pleasure, until a preliminary examination had taken place. He was then only granted minutes with each patient while the doctors conferred. Dr Dillon whipped off Thomas's tie, unbuttoned his waistcoat, and cut away the shirt and vest. Blood ran everywhere and he tried to wipe it away with a towel he took from a pile on a chair. He worked with deft furiousness, called one of the waiting men to get off Thomas's jacket with him, and cut at the clothes until Thomas was naked to the waist. Removing the rest of the clothes proved no difficulty: they jack-knifed Thomas softly upwards at the hips, and, having taken off his shoes, slid off his trousers, under which he still wore nothing. The strenuous actions elicited no response from the tall wiry man lying supine. Dr Dillon prised open the eyelids and then let them slip shut again.

Upstairs, Nurse Cooper and Dr Hogan found heavy bruising on Ellen's right temple, found a cut over her right eye, and very severe bruising and contusion to the lower jaw.

'No scarring,' observed Nurse Cooper.

Ellen's right hand, badly cut, bled heavily: Nurse Cooper covered her with a sheet while Dr Hogan examined her.

Downstairs, Dr Dillon sponged and sponged and sponged with his towel. Another nurse arrived, and without taking off her coat began to help him, until all the early blood had been washed away, although it still continued to pour from somewhere in Thomas's hair on the right-hand side of his head. Dr Dillon found some bruising to the left-hand ribcage, surprisingly not excessive; he located an unserious injury to the left hand; the nurse pointed out some spots of deep purple, as if caused by heavy pinpricks, on the back of the right hand, on which Thomas appeared to have broken a finger. They returned to the catastrophic injury, the substantial wound on the right temple, high up, between the top of the ear and the forehead. From here, the blood flowed: in this position it filled Thomas's ear: Dr Dillon could not yet gauge the extent of the head wound. Dr MacDonnell fidgeted from foot to foot, felt all Thomas's extremities, noting changing temperatures.

The doctors went to the hall and called Dr Hogan: the priest approached Thomas's bed, muttering prayers: the baby, sensibly, had been removed from all the agitation. Dr MacDonnell, the newcomer, opened his mouth to speak when Nurse Cooper shouted. Dr Hogan raced up the stairs again: Ellen had begun to flicker. But she subsided: Nurse Cooper rubbed the back of Ellen's neck even more warmly, then held the cold, wet cloth to Ellen's forehead. Ellen flickered again, and turned her head.

'She's coming, she's coming,' said Dr Hogan, and bent his head: the other doctors stood, urgent-looking, at the door.

'Mrs Kane, can you hear me? Ellen. You're all right. You're safe. And the baby is fine. Can you hear me? Nod your head if you can.' Nurse Cooper brought her head forward: 'Ellen, it's all right, you're safe. Everything is all right. You're all right.' She stroked Ellen's face, and continued to speak in a mixture of insistence and kindliness. 'You're all right. The baby's safe, dear. The baby's safe. Can you hear me?'

Dr Hogan whipped open his bow tie, undid the shirt button at his throat, and began to massage Ellen's fingers, kneading them in his own: all almost fell over each other at the bed: Dr Dillon went back downstairs to Thomas who had continued to bleed in the two minutes they were away.

'That man is dead,' said the priest. 'He's gone to God.'

'Not if I can help it,' said Dillon; 'will you go out now, please.'

'The Last Rites,' protested Father Herity, who had a piece of food stuck in the corner of his lip.

'Out!' said Dr MacDonnell, and the priest reluctantly drifted away: the nurse continued to sponge Thomas's face.

Ellen woke up – and lived: severely shocked, terribly sore and bruised, hysterical. She calmed momentarily when Nurse Cooper shrewdly sent for Helena, then became agitated again and tried to get out of bed when she asked about Thomas. They told her, 'He's downstairs; Dr Dillon and Nurse Lynch, and another doctor are with him. Now lie back and rest, just put your head back gently, that's it. The baby's safe, she's fine. Fine.'

The doctors, in a second hurried conference, decided to move Thomas to the hospital, as they could not staunch the blood: the hospital was only half a mile away and had more equipment than a private maternity home. No ambulance: in Dr MacDonnell's car, larger than Dr Hogan's, they could slump him across the back seat. On the way to the hospital, Thomas's head lolled over and the bleeding appeared to have slowed. They rounded the corner by the Post Office, and in the lurching of the car, Thomas's dead weight fell on Dr Hogan – who could not reach Thomas's pulse to check whether Thomas had died at that precise moment.

Dr Hogan, wrinkling his nose searchingly, murmured to Dr MacDonnell when the car stopped, 'At least there's no evacuation of the bowels so far.'

Out in Deanstown, Leah had grown almost frantic. Too stable ever to give way utterly to unfounded alarm, she paced and paced, walked to the gate and back a dozen times. She folded her arms and rubbed them to remove the contradictory coldness she felt in the hot sunlight. Around her, not a sound could be heard; the countryside sat quietly in the orange warmth of a Sunday in May. She rearranged the flowers she had put out for Ellen's return; readjusted over and over the place settings for lunch on the kitchen table, fidgeted in a variety of disquiets, even took down the iron and began to heat it. Unlike the city, no people could be seen, and she did not wish to walk down to the village in case Thomas and Ellen arrived in her absence, or in case she gave cause for unnecessary anxiety which would be talked about: Ellen had told her how they gossiped.

Had Thomas by any chance said they would call somewhere on the way home? No: lunch had been agreed: chops rather than a roast on account of any delay in settling down the baby. At three o'clock, when they had not arrived, Leah put on her coat, locked the door, hid the key under the stone, went to the garage, took out Ellen's bicycle, walked it to the gate which she closed behind her, and mounted it awkwardly. Wobblily, she cycled the six miles to Mooreville, her red hair lifting in the breeze. First, on the hillside, she saw the car overturned and some people standing near: fearing their answers, she did not ask any questions. Next, she had to find Nurse Cooper's, and when she saw the cars and the bicycles and the people standing at the door, she knew something awful had happened. Dismounting, she walked into the sombre aftermath.

Thomas did not die. In what passed for an operation late that afternoon, they removed a small piece of metal from his head, and his pulse and breathing grew stronger, and in time normalized. Leah took some kind of charge, concentrating at first on Ellen and the baby. Nurse Cooper came into the room to call Leah out and say that a surgeon had been summoned from Janesborough, and another from Cork (who subsequently wrote a book-length account of the entire case). Ellen, in total shock, took no decisions, took no part in discussions.

The town rang agog: all three had been shot, one by one; the car had been riddled with bullets; the baby only had been shot; the baby only had survived. People cycled, or took out their pony-traps, to view the overturned Singer Roadster. The Master was dead; the Mistress was dead; the Mistress was fine and up and about; the Master and the baby were dead. Nobody knew the truth, nobody attempted to ascertain. The Guards said little; the Superintendent could not be found – he and his wife had gone to visit his wife's mother over by Pallas, a fifteen-mile cycle for the Guard who had to fetch him.

Next day, the surgeons discussed; they deliberated: no further operation – 'for the moment'. Jack Hogan hung like a schoolboy near their edges. With instructions for acute observation, they left Mooreville. One, an old colleague of hers, called to see Nurse Cooper before he departed the town; she told him Mrs Kane was sleeping and she even let him look in, and then let him see the sleeping baby who had a tiny scratch just between where her eyebrows would grow.

'There's a friend of Mrs Kane's here,' said Nurse Cooper. 'A very capable woman, a Mrs Winer,' and then whispered, 'she's a Jewess, but she seems very sensible.'

In the shadows of early Monday evening, the surgeon told Leah and Nurse Cooper in the small downstairs sitting-room, 'We have no idea how he will turn out. He's unconscious, probably not very deeply. He responds to some things, his lips withdraw from a pinch, that sort of thing. But 'tis in waves, at times he seems to lapse deeper, at other times he comes very close to the surface. What we're hoping for is some kind of steadiness.'

Leah asked, 'What is to be done?'

The surgeon replied, 'How is the wife? Will she be capable of looking after herself?'

Nurse Cooper said, 'The shock is the big thing, that's the big problem. She has only small injuries, I think she has a sprained wrist, but the shock . . .'

Leah asked, 'When you say you don't know, what do you know? Is the man going to live or die?'

'That,' said the surgeon, 'is what we don't know.'

Leah pressed, 'But how long could he live like he is now?'

'We don't know that, either.'

'What do you know?'

The man pulled at his ear and said, 'We know he has had a bad head wound, from a gun. He was shot at. We know he is not conscious. We know that he is as strong as a horse. He could recover. If he doesn't – he'll die. But we don't know when.'

Leah said, 'There is something you are not saying?'

With an embarrassed look, the surgeon asked, 'Are you next of kin?'

Nurse Cooper reassured him as to the proprieties.

Leah went on, 'What you're not saying is – he could live like this for a while?'

'Yes,' said the surgeon, 'that's the worst possibility.'

'But how could he live?' asked Leah. 'How could he eat?'

'It happens.' Surgeon and nurse spoke together. 'He will be able to swallow soft food if it's placed deep in his mouth.'

'But otherwise he will just lie there?' asked Leah. 'Like a living corpse?' The man nodded his head, twice.

Thomas did not recover consciousness: the same surgeon, who called several times in the next weeks, had predicted accurately. Most of Thomas's body returned to a normal physiological state, and he existed somewhere between coma and general lack of consciousness. His eyes opened from time to time but they were as blank as blindness, and flapped closed slowly again, like a dying fish. He had, they surmised, suffered irreparable brain damage, and longevity did not seem a prospect. Nevertheless, as Leah had been told, and it was not an unknown curiosity, he could swallow liquid and semi-solid food. The doctors had encountered a similar case only by repute: the patient – a Collins man, too, as it happened, and with worse injuries than Thomas – had lived for eight months, and then died of pneumonia.

In Thomas's case, who could say? He had immense vitality and physical strength. Wasn't it ironic, said the doctors, that such properties could prove a disadvantage, as now they did? All his bodily functions had to be attended to by others: he had almost no physical response of any kind other than breathing, sometimes even snoring; he took the soft runny food, provided his mouth was held a little closed after each mouthful, obliging him to swallow involuntarily. The doctors had no medical literature to which they could have had recourse: the one and only case of which they knew had not been written up, on account of the Collins connection and the attendant secrecy in the mood of those times. Dr MacDonnell said to the others one Sunday, as they stood by the prostrate bedside, that perhaps a radiograph would help, but he doubted it, and besides they did not have one; the nearest was in Dublin, he thought. Nobody mentioned radiographs to Leah, or even to Ellen when she resumed her capacities. The men conferred one last time in the room where Thomas lay.

'It's a terrible bind,' said Dr MacDonnell, an unsentimental Northerner, 'that man is too strong to die.'

Thomas's room in the hospital took on the atmosphere of an oratory: people tiptoed in to see him, as to a figure lying in state, and the less charitable folk, who had disliked him, or feared him, or, since the old days, hated him, muttered things about the 'living dead': in truth, commented Jack Hogan, it described him well.

Leah stayed overnight on the Sunday at Nurse Cooper's, making sure to be in the room on Monday morning when the sedated Ellen awoke to find Leah simply holding her hand and smiling carefully.

'Helena's yelling for her bottle,' said Leah.

'You've cut your hair,' said Ellen. 'Why am I so weak?'

'You had a very bad accident,' said Leah. 'No wonder you're weak.'

Leah cycled out to Deanstown, and arranged changes of clothing for herself, then cycled back to the nursing home. Each time, she averted her eyes as she passed the askew car gleaming and brutally sad on the roadside. She walked around Ellen's room, cradling Helena, whose eyes remained mostly shut, and whose lips made endless little pink sucking motions. Leah kissed the child softly over and over.

'And Thomas?' Ellen asked again and again. 'How is he? I know something dreadful happened to us. Tell me.'

Leah said, 'Yes, but you are all alive. Thomas is in the hospital. He is unconscious; he had an operation and the surgeon was telling us yesterday about his extraordinary strength.'

On Thursday, Ellen rose, helped by Nurse Cooper and Leah, and she stood and then walked, then sat in a chair by the window. For hours on end she scarcely spoke. The Guards removed the car: someone had stolen the rug: the car now sat in the yard of the barracks in Silverbridge, and parish ghouls came to view it.

One afternoon, Nurse Cooper, Leah and Ellen, a day before her homegoing, left the nursing home and walked to see Thomas, taking a route that avoided Mooreville's main street. At the door of the hospital, Nurse Cooper said, 'I'll wait out here.'

Leah said, 'What?' and Sheila waved a hand: 'I'm not allowed in; I'll explain to you later.'

In the hallway, people looked curiously but knowingly at Leah and Ellen: nobody came forward. The girl at the desk said, 'Wait here a minute,' and returned with the Matron who shook hands, a woman of forceful earnestness.

'He is down here,' she said, 'although how long we can reserve this room for him I don't know. The surgeon is coming in in the morning.'

'Mrs Kane is going home tomorrow,' said Leah.

Pale, diminished, Ellen walked along the corridor as if encased in glass. The Matron opened the door and ushered them in, then stood back, unveiling her exhibit. Leah knew what to expect, Ellen did not. At the end of Thomas's bed she looked at Leah, then at the ceiling, then forced a glance again.

Leah snapped at the Matron, 'Why isn't that bandage clean? When was it changed?'

Matron defended. 'There's still the occasional oozing. We can't stop it, 'tis only very slight.'

Leah threw her hands apart. 'Get a nurse to change it. Now!'

Matron assessed her and left the room.

Leah said to Ellen, 'Come and hold his hand.'

'I can't.'

'Come on!' She took Ellen's arm and drew her to the head of the bed. 'Stroke his face.'

When Leah began to rub Thomas's jaw gently, Ellen did the same.

'He's so white,' she said. 'He's so white. And that's a huge bandage. Leah, what happened to him? Poor Thomas.'

Matron returned with a nurse who began to rearrange the bed, so that Thomas's bandage could be removed from his head. Matron said to Leah, 'At least they were able to get out all the lead.'

'Lead?' said Ellen, from the edge of a trance; Leah had been unable to shush the Matron.

'All the shot. It was a shotgun,' the woman blundered on: they had not yet told Ellen.

'Come on,' said Leah, 'that is enough for one day.' She did not let Ellen see the tears in her eyes as she walked from the room.

21

In Deanstown, Thomas's misfortune moved the parish as nothing had ever done before.

'They say he'll never stir again. Never stir. He'll live for a while. But sure . . .'

All became medical experts. 'A living death. That's it. A living death.'

Heads shook; tongues clicked. 'Well, sure. Dlokk. That's the way. You never know what's going to happen in this world. And no notion of the next world. Well, well.'

They stared into their fires, watched the pictures in the flames. 'Do you know what it is? She'll be a living widow, that's what? Did you ever hear of such a thing? Whoi-oi.' They blew soundless whistles through their lips.

One evening, as if by accident, five of the men drifted together in a farmhouse to consider whether they could make any contribution to Ellen's new circumstances, improve the Master's shattered life.

'Nineteen twelve. That's when he came here. God, wasn't he the hard man, though, when he came? All that skelping he did to us in the school, hauh?'

'All the same a fair man. And sure, who'd be able to read a line, sure we couldn't post a letter if he wasn't hard on us, so we couldn't.'

A third voice said, 'Jayzes, there's many the form he filled in for me. An' I don't want to take any of them forms to the Canon. Or the Sergeant. The one thing about the Master, you never knew him minding your business.'

'Oh yeh,' said a fourth, 'as silent as the grave' – at which irony the company fell quiet.

John Relihan offered one last thought: it entered forbidden territory. 'He was as good a man as any of them when the time came, wasn't he? He was as good a man as Ernie O'Malley, or Sean Treacy. Or Michael Collins himself come to that.' Someone coughed on the draw of a cigarette, and the conversation changed tack.

Exactly one week after the event, several of Thomas's family came by various means to the house in Brunswick Square, and mournfully discussed the matter with Ellen's parents. May arranged cold meats and tea and cakes, apologizing all the time for the fact that she had to buy everything: 'I hadn't the heart to bake.'

To the faces whitened with shock and hurt, Bob asked a general question, 'Do the Guards know anything yet?' and received no conclusive reply. The group fragmented into several smaller groups, having quiet conversations, anxious to get off the subject as soon as possible.

Bob asked another question. 'Is there anything anyone thinks we ought to be doing?' and was answered by a few mumbling, shaking heads, and a vague, 'Sure what can we do, what can anyone do, until the doctors know one way or the other?'

Jim Morris, unusually grave, answered the door knocker and ushered in Father John Watson, who accepted May's cup of tea promptly.

'What is the latest news?' he asked through crumbs, 'and is there such a thing as a visiting arrangement?'

They told him what they knew: Thomas showed no responses; Nurse Cooper had recommended as few visitors as possible for Ellen who remained 'extraordinarily shocked, but, thank God, no injuries at all, hardly'; the baby was fine. John Watson looked around the room with a most kind expression on his face and addressed them.

'May I say just one thing? This is a dreadful occurrence, and my heart and prayers are with you all. I have little to offer you by way of practical assistance, as you know. But I have two things I can give you. One, whenever you need anyone to talk to, about anything, however worried you are, write to me and I will write back. Or call and see me: if I am teaching at that moment just wait for me, and then my time will be your time. And two, remember this. You are all decent, good people, and it is that decency and goodness that will carry you, and dear Ellen, and the baby through this dreadful thing.' He did not mention Thomas: nobody noticed.

Father Watson put down his cup of tea and spent the next hour moving through the room, talking to each individual there: May and Bob Morris, and Rina and Jim; Thomas's two sisters in their identical navy hand-knitted cardigans; his brothers who did not know where to put themselves, and who stood awkwardly near windows and doors. When the little priest had spoken to them all, and then left with a general wave, and wish, and a wipe of his hand over his wavy fair hair, the mood in the room had almost lightened.

'Ah,' said Bob Morris, when the door closed, 'isn't that man a good man?' and the conversation took such a relaxed turn, that by the time they began to leave the house, all seemed somewhat cheerful.

Just before Ellen came home to Deanstown with the baby, John Relihan and Michael Connors met by arrangement, and collecting Tom Dalton, they drove in John Relihan's trap to Dr Hogan's, where 'that peculiar woman' let them in, and, sidelong, sparsely, told them the doctor was 'out'. They waited in the room with the palm in the pot, and just as they discussed leaving, heard his car.

Dr Hogan listened carefully. 'I perfectly agree with you. I perfectly agree with you' – and would willingly lead a delegation to the Canon on the following Sunday after Mass.

Jeremiah Williams listened to them in silence and said, 'I have to talk to the Curate.'

'Sure, what can we do?' asked the Curate.

'They want me to give her his job.'

'Ah, sure you can't do that, that has to be a man,' said the Curate. 'The Department'd be up in arms.'

'They would, they would.'

'Sure how could we do that?' asked the Curate. 'Don't Principals always have to be men?'

The Canon inspected another young apple, as the Curate followed him at a distance, avoiding the branches.

'Apparently there's a Mrs Sweeney over in Callan or somewhere,' said the Canon, 'and she got the job when her husband died, but she had only a year to go before retiring or something. And it gave her a better pension.'

'Sure this is a different case altogether,' said the Curate. 'That woman is only in her twenties.' He paused for reflection. 'And she's a fiery bit, into the bargain.'

'Hah, don't I know it?' said Jeremiah Williams.

'I know 'tis a sad case,' said the Curate, 'but sure God alone knows what trouble you'd have with her.'

'The men are saying I have to do something,' said the Canon.

'Did you try the Department?' asked the Curate.

'They say that technically she has to vacate before the school reopens, 'tis the Principal's Residence. But that, of course, I'm the Manager, and 'tis up to me.'

'Sure what can we do so?' asked the Curate. 'I mean, if she wasn't a woman . . . ?'

'D'you know what it is, Father?' said Canon Jeremiah Williams, peering at a green apple. 'These'll soon be ripe at this rate of going.'

Dr Hogan collected Ellen and six-weeks-old Helena.

'I hope you don't mind, Ma'am,' he said, as he settled them in the car, 'but I have to go a small bit out of my way. I have to go out by Carrig, I know 'tisn't the straight road, but 'twill only be a few minutes extra. Glorious day again, thanks be to God.' The baby blinked in the bright light.

In the event Jack forgot to make even a pretend call, and thereby exposed his good intention of not taking Ellen past the scene of the shooting.

Leah heard the car, stood at the open door, and reached out to take Helena. 'Hallo, hallo, hallo, you little pet, you little sweet one.' She fingered aside the shawl to see Helena's face better; Helena pursed her lips.

'Will you have a cup of tea, Doctor?'

'I won't thanks, Ma'am, I have all sorts of oul' things going on. I'll skedaddle.' He turned to Ellen. 'Good luck now, Ma'am, I'll drop in and see how you're getting on, and I'll keep an eye on the boss'; he glanced resignedly at Leah over Ellen's head.

Leah led the way; on the kitchen table sat a blue Moses basket, readied for Helena who began to whimper when Leah laid her down in it.

'Ah, little puss'ms, I'll warm a bottle for you.' Leah let Helena clutch a finger. 'Oooh, your grip, already, you dear little sweetheart.'

The light caught Leah's ring: Helena tried to focus on it, still grizzling a little. Two prepared bottles and teats stood on the shelf.

'Leah, you're here again, you're a champion. What can I say to you?'

'Now, now,' said Leah, 'none of that.'

315

Ellen had seated herself on a chair just inside the door. Still holding the handle of her suitcase she looked around the kitchen: Thomas's chair; the book he had been reading, and the careful bookmark torn from a newspaper; the case for his spare set of spectacles on the windowsill; the calendar on the wall directly opposite his head, with all the school holiday opening and closing dates ringed – at which Ellen closed her eyes tight, notwithstanding the tears squeezing out.

Leah watched while pretending not to. Leah said nothing. Leah warmed the bottle of milk. Leah lifted Helena and began to feed her.

Ellen released the suitcase handle, turned her head away from Leah as if to look through the window, and slipped a wiping hand up to her eyes. Leah made soothing, affirming sounds to Helena, who began to fall asleep halfway through. Eventually, Ellen rose, took off her coat and hung it on the hallstand.

'Will I unpack down here, d'you think, Leah? Or should I do it upstairs?'

'Down here I would say,' said Leah, 'all that washing, you might as well.'

Presently, with shrewd management of the moment, Leah contrived to get upstairs ahead of Ellen, and carried the fed, changed, dozing Helena in the Moses basket to the stand in the corner of the bedroom. Pondering for a second – should she hide Thomas's razor, and deciding not to – she called Ellen. She called her again. And again. Then went downstairs.

'Ellen, dear, we'd better decide which corner of the room for the baby. Are there draughts? – from the chimney or the window?'

Leah went back upstairs leaving Ellen no choice but to follow her.

'See what I mean?' she said when Ellen stood in the door. 'This corner looks like the best, although it's a tight squeeze past the end of the bed. Oh, Ellen, dear.' She came and stood in front of the younger woman and took her in her arms as she would a child, sat them both on the bed and rocked Ellen gently. 'Dear God,' said Leah, over and over. 'Dear Ellen.'

In the following two weeks or so, little happened. Ellen's mother, having been to the nursing home and the hospital twice already, came for a day, with a note from Bob enclosing some money. He had bronchitis again – 'In weather like this?' queried Ellen.

Letters poured in. Surprisingly few neighbours came; those who did brought baked cakes, or home-made puddings, or meat from freshly-killed animals, or their own butter. All avoided the subject of the man lying still, the warm statue, in the Mooreville Hospital bed six miles away. Michael Connors, with not a word to anyone, took to leaving a can of new milk inside the gate each morning. Mrs Ryle called with tea, sugar, butter.

Miriam Hogan stood on the road, but would not enter the house, perhaps picking up the hesitancy in Ellen's invitation. She said, 'Have you a good book to read? Distraction is very useful you know. I'll bring you something.'

The Sergeant called again, as he had to the nursing home.

'When'd be a good time to talk to you, Ma'am?'

'Now,' said Leah, 'get it over with.'

'No,' said Ellen. 'Nothing more. Only what I told you so far. All I remember was – it was very warm, and we had the roof of the car folded down, and there was a crack.'

'You mean, like a shot? You must have heard shots before, Ma'am? You know, in Janesborough, like, a few years ago and that?' The Sergeant's wife had a terrible turned eye, Ellen told Leah later, a squint that went out to the west.

'Yes, I suppose. A shot.'

'We found cartridges, Ma'am, well, a cartridge. There's a man down from Dublin, a detective. He found it inside the ditch. You see, if, if – God forbid, if the Master. If anything happened to the Master. I mean to say, something is after happening to him, but if anything more happened to him.'

'You mean if Mr Kane died?' asked Leah abruptly.

'Well, sort of, Ma'am, it ed be murder, so it would.'

'Who fired the gun?' asked Leah.

'We don't rightly know, Ma'am, I mean. Ma'am, we've to be very careful. I mean did you see anyone?' The Sergeant put away his notebook. Ellen shook her head.

'Are you suspecting anyone?' asked Leah, again abrasive.

'We can't suspect anyone unless somebody saw someone, that's the way of it. Unless the Mistress saw anyone, or if anyone threatened the Master. But if nobody saw nothing, I mean to say, if there was nothing seen by anyone . . .'

At the gate, the Sergeant said to Leah as he left, 'There's'n't a thing we can do, Ma'am, and that woman here with no man in the house. You'll have to move her. Out of here, Ma'am. And the baby. 'Tisn't safe, so 'tisn't.'

Leah did not report this to Ellen. She did make a tentative suggestion that Ellen should return to Janesborough, but Ellen told Leah that under 'no circumstances, point blank' would she leave Deanstown; nor would she stay in Brunswick Square, not even for a few weeks; nor would she think of getting a job elsewhere.

'I've made my bed, I have to lie on it,' she said over and over, and did not amplify, other than saying, 'And anyway we have to wait and see . . . what happens . . .'

Thereafter, Leah directed Ellen's attentions concentratedly towards Helena, and the housework, and towards picking up the generalities of a life. Leah said, 'No, Ellen, it is not a sin to miss Mass in these circumstances, you will go to Mass when you feel able. And you can't until you have somebody to help you look after the baby.'

'Leah, what in the name of God am I going to do when you go?'

'You'll manage. You'll be surprised. Wait and see. Sheila Cooper said she'll keep on calling' – as she had done twice in one week already, arriving like a descending fowl, red-faced, the bicycle almost running on out of her grasp.

On Sunday, Leah said to Ellen, 'Right. Washing tomorrow. Blankets. All your woollen things. And Thomas's. The whole house!'

Ellen came downstairs next morning with huge armfuls. Three times Leah had to ask her to fetch Thomas's two V-neck pullovers, and his three warm, long-sleeved undervests.

Leah said, 'He's going to need these.'

When Ellen set up a wail, Leah repeated, 'I said – he's going to need these.'

She held them up to the light, inspected them for any darning needs and handed them to Ellen. 'Here. You wash them.' Leah stood on a chair and took down three of the five washboards from the scullery wall.

That evening, Ellen said, 'Whew, my back.' She stretched her upper body forward and pressed her hips with her hands.

Baby feed and change four times a day; cooking – a new recipe even; cleaning – the range had to be blacked; the women worked all week side by side, talked quietly, and sometimes silences fell; in the evenings they sat at the kitchen table and went over and over again what had happened.

'There are no reasons, Ellen, there are no reasons. All you can do now is get yourself going again; there's the new life there, the baby.'

'Leah, what about Thomas? What about Thomas?'

If she asked the question once, as Leah reported to Herbert, Ellen asked it a hundred times.

'We can't push anything, Ellen. It has to wait. The old saying: doctors differ.'

'And patients die,' said Ellen, completing the proverb.

Standing on the road on Saturday morning, seeing the bus in the distance, Ellen said, 'Will I be all right, Leah?'

Leah said, 'You will. You will.'

Silence in Deanstown. Silence in the Teacher's Residence. Ellen Kane closed her gate, and closed her door, and at the hallstand pressed her face into the folds of her husband's good grey overcoat.

They came to see Ellen in two cars, one of them Dr Hogan's. The tall man whose name she did not quite catch, said, looking down at the Moses basket, 'Well, at least the baby is very healthy. How are you feeling, Mrs Kane?'

They sat in the parlour. By now Ellen had re-familiarized herself with all corners of the house, and had begun to address the stabs of pain at each encounter with Thomas's domestic life: his gardening cap; the old paint drum for holding the oil he drained from the car; his piles of newspapers that she had complained about – 'they're always in my way, Thomas'; the sharp brightness of the spade and shovel blades that he cleaned so assiduously with a flat mutton-bone after each use; the tray that had been his mother's, on which one of their wedding-gift tea services now sat.

'It's like this,' said the tall surgeon to Ellen. 'We don't know. He can eat soft food, mush, bread-and-milk –'

'What they call "goody", d'you see –' interrupted Hogan.

'I know what "goody" is,' said Ellen impatiently.

''Course you do. The baby'll be on it soon,' said Dr Hogan.

319

Ellen said, 'My father had it for his gums when he got his teeth out, that's all he could eat.'

'Your husband can swallow that, provided he's fed properly,' said the tall man.

'Nurse Cooper showed them down at the hospital, she went over the other day,' smiled Dr Hogan, 'and read the Riot Act over them.'

'I thought she wasn't allowed in,' said Ellen.

'She reported them once for hygiene,' said Dr Hogan, 'and they barred her, but this time she forced her way in.' He laughed.

'But something has affected the brain, and that's the case as I see it,' continued the tall surgeon, who had a white triangle of stiff good handkerchief in his breast pocket.

'Will that "something" ever stop affecting it?' asked Ellen.

'We don't know,' he said. 'We don't know.' The remainder of their visit grew sombre.

The other two doctors said little, until the end. One then remarked, 'Even if he is comatose, and even if it seems that he's going to remain comatose –'

Ellen interrupted. 'Comatose? I've never heard that word? Is it from "coma"?'

'– Yes, and if it appears that he'll be comatose, then he'll need constant attention.'

'The hospital can do that, can't they?'

The doctors looked at each other and the tall man said, 'We'll watch how it turns out.'

When they stood and began to take their leave, the fourth man had yet not said a word. At the very last moment, he turned to Ellen: 'I'm a great believer in human contact, Mrs Kane, a great believer. It is also part of the medical process.'

'Tell me one thing?' Ellen leaned forward. 'How much life is in him?'

'A lot,' said the man. 'A lot.' The others had climbed into the cars. 'He is near enough to consciousness to have muscles that work in order to take in food. He may even flicker into some kind of awareness, and then relapse again. We don't know – that's the truth. He's taking food, as we said, so long as it can slip down his throat. His breathing is very strong and normal. God knows what will happen. We have nothing to go on.'

=

320

'Oh, isn't she grand!' Nurse Cooper wagged her face up and down at Helena. 'Grand. Aren't you, you little thing? You have her grand and clean. If a fraction of the babies I saw were as grand as that, aren't you grand?' Helena and the lightly bearded nurse beamed at each other.

'Now, my lady, let me look at you.' She led Ellen to the window, turned her face this way and that. 'That eye, is that a stye starting, or is it a bit bloodshot? You may be a bit run down, my lady, we'll have to get you a tonic, or a few rose-hips or something. What about the tummy, are you eating all right? And what about down there?' She nodded her eyes towards Ellen's pelvis. 'Is the after-the-birth over? Well, your hair is grand anyway, your crowning glory, let me see.' She drew Ellen's head towards her and fingered through the abundant hair; she scrutinized Ellen's hands: 'You should use a bit more hand-cream, the water round here isn't all that soft.'

Sheila Cooper had twice been unlucky in her life. Her training in London from 1891 to 1894 had given her a penchant for men in uniform.

'Not good,' rebuked her aunt. 'Men in uniform die.'

As did her first love, Dick Speight, descended from a Janesborough family. When Sheila met him in London, they found much in common, knew many people from entwining strands of life. He died of blood poisoning in the Transvaal, was buried out there: Sheila lit a candle in some church she wandered into in London.

Ellen said, 'You were at the hospital?'

'I was, dear, I was. That crowd. I'd box their ears for them.'

Sheila's second love, a relationship more mature, firmer, than the first, was an officer too, posted to Ireland, and the staff car in which he was a passenger crashed not fifteen miles from the Cooper family home on its way to the aftermath of an ambush. In London at the time, she missed his funeral: he, a John Gibbs from Hertfordshire, a morose and slightly irascible man, was being taken to his grave in the opposite direction as she crossed from Holyhead on the Mail Boat. Regarding all of this, Nurse Cooper only ever made one remark. To a *confidante* she said that although everyone is supposed to have three great loves in life, she would 'never risk a third'.

'How is he?' asked Ellen.

'He's just the same. You weren't in yet?'

Ellen deflected the question, 'The doctors, they were all here.'

Ellen looked at her to gauge how the remark had been received. Nurse Cooper and she had discovered something steadfast in common: as in Ellen's family, a Protestant had married a Catholic a forebear or two ago, and although the ensuing generations were reared as Catholics, the Protestant veneer and its waxy odour had lingered refiningly.

'Well, I'll tell you now.' Nurse Cooper began to take off her coat. 'You know that young man, that young Condon man. Well. I asked him to call here today, now if you don't want him he'll go away again. He knows that. But he has the car nearly fixed, there wasn't a whole lot wrong with it. Anyway. I'll stay with the baby, to let you go in and see himself.' She paused. 'Probably you should tidy yourself up.'

When Ellen came downstairs, Sheila Cooper looked her up and down, then put aside the baby's bottle, lifted Helena to her shoulder, rose and said to Ellen, 'Come over here to the window so that I can see you' – then added, 'Haven't you something a bit brighter you can wear?'

At the hospital door, Ellen paused, looked back at the respectful Michael Condon; she had faced getting back into the car; they had driven past the scene of the incident. She hesitated again, then broached the hallway. The girl stopped her and said surlily, 'You can't go in anywhere. 'Tisn't visiting time.'

Ellen said, 'But – the Matron said – I could come any time, my husband is Master Kane.'

The girl said, 'Visiting time isn't 'til half-two. There's the notice about it there.'

A man put his head round the door: 'Eily, he's gone in, so don't let anyone –': he stopped abruptly when he saw Ellen and retreated: the girl's face reddened, and grew furtive. Suspicion flooded Ellen: she charged at the double doors and ran down the corridor after the man, all her fearful tentativeness dissolved. At the door of Thomas's room she caught up with the hurrying little porter – and found Jacks, the photographer, actually in Thomas's room setting up his 'sticks' to take a photograph of her prone husband: he had even dragged the bed into the window to get the light.

322

She kicked Jacks so hard that he later went and complained to the police, who did nothing. Ellen rushed back to the hallway and shrieked at Michael Condon. 'COME ON!' she screamed. 'Come on. HELP ME!'

He blinked his brown eyes and clambered from the car.

'COME ON!'

She beckoned and beckoned, leaving him no choice but to follow her down the corridor: the girl had vanished from the hall, and Thomas lay alone in the room.

'Under his shoulder.' She directed Michael to one side of the bed, as she whipped off the thin and grubby blanket. 'Under his shoulder,' she repeated, snapping. As Michael grasped Thomas's slack hand, Ellen took the other arm and lifted it: together they raised Thomas into an upright position.

'Jesus, Ma'am. This isn't the right thing at all.'

'Shut up, will you? Lift him. I can't do it by myself.' They hauled. Amiable Michael Condon abandoned his reluctance. Swivelling around slowly, they dragged Thomas's dead weight clear of the bed, and carefully, although they could not prevent some bumping, allowed his legs and feet to crash-flop to the floor.

'Get out of the way!' she shouted to a dumbfounded maid who had materialized from somewhere. 'Out! OUT!' The girl jumped back and then ran.

As they reached the main door, the Matron appeared.

'Where do you think you're taking my patient?'

Ellen spat at her, 'I'm taking MY husband home to clean him up.'

Two panting figures; and between them a sagging, nightgowned white spectre with the beginnings of his dirty beard, stale food traces messing his chin; and a hefty woman in white with her nurse's cap and its narrow blue band: 'Look at him?' Ellen roared at the Matron. 'Look at him.'

The woman tried reason. 'There isn't a lot we can do.'

'Look at the cut of him. Look!' Ellen simply could not stop shouting. 'He's FILTHY. That man was always SPOTLESS!'

'If you're discharging him you can't get him back in here.'

'I'll discharge you if I get my hands on you!' Ellen yelled. They manhandled Thomas into the passenger seat of the car.

'Take off your coat and put it round him. How do you open the dickey seat?' asked Ellen, frantically. Months later she discovered that the hospital porter had been permitting people to view Thomas like a freak at a carnival: many of the Deanstown neighbours had sneaked in.

At the house, Nurse Cooper displayed no astonishment. They propped Thomas in an armchair in the parlour. Michael Condon dismantled the single bed in the spare bedroom, and they staggered it down the stairs.

When Thomas had been stretched on it, Nurse Cooper said, 'You need an invalid bed-chair, I have a spare one, I'll get somebody to bring it out.'

Ellen asked Michael Condon to put the car in the garage.

'There's still work to be done on it, Ma'am, I'm waiting on the bit of paint . . .'

'It'll wait, and thank you,' said Ellen. 'How much do I owe you?'

'Oh, Ma'am, nothing, I mean, I don't know yet.'

He left. Ellen did not close the door; instead she turned to Nurse Cooper, who said, 'He has to walk seven miles home.'

Ellen ignored the remark and said, 'I have to be on my own now.'

'But listen . . .'

Ellen said, 'I have to be. I have to be. I have to be.'

'I see. I see. Well, look. I have to call and see the Harpers anyway, the mad brother again. I'll just take a spin over there and when you're settled in, I'll drop in on the way back. Make yourself a cup of tea now, there's a good girl, you're after a shock, aren't you?'

'I have to be on my own,' repeated Ellen. 'I have to be on my own.'

'All right so, all right.' Sheila Cooper soothed, put on her coat and wheeled her bicycle out on the road. Ellen closed the gate and padlocked it.

On her return Nurse Cooper could get no reply, not even when she shouted from the road, nor could anyone else for the next three days: the postman took the letters back to the Post Office in Silverbridge and said, 'The Mistress must be in a terrible way; we'll hang on to them here, I suppose.'

Ellen made 'goody'. She took two thick slices of white bread, boiled a large cup of milk and let it cool a little; she broke the bread into larger chunks than the ones she and Thomas fed to the birds last winter, added the warm milk and a little sugar, pounded it all into a mess as soft as porridge – and sat by Thomas, raising his head with a pillow.

Silently, in an attitude composed of morbid curiosity and numbness, she spooned the warm soft mixture into his half-open mouth. Each spoonful sat somewhere in there, and then, each time with a suddenness, his throat muscles contracted. Sometimes the food threatened to lurch back up out of his mouth; most went down his throat. She repeated the procedure again at six o'clock, and a smaller amount at nine, and even tried to pour a little warm tea into his mouth.

During Helena's chores in between, Ellen normalized somewhat. After one last look at Thomas she blew out the candle, returned to the kitchen, tidied it, folded the cloth she had been repairing, lowered the sewing machine into its recess, heaved the table-top back up into place, clicked the machine shut, and went to bed, checking Helena's sleeping face.

Next morning, when she awoke and lay still for a moment, a procession of implications began to march by, the first and most distasteful of which were later confirmed by the smell whose source she located and understood immediately she entered the parlour downstairs where Thomas lay.

22

My dear Leah,

This is going to be the worst letter I have ever written. I am beyond the Vale of Despair. I have no idea where to turn, what to do, what to say even when I talk to myself. At twenty-six years of age my life seems to be gone as bad as a life could be. Even, God forbid, if poor Thomas had died, I would have something definite. I can't sleep, I can't cope with the day, it gives me all I can do to feed Helena – who is a little dote it has to be said. And on top of all that I am frightened – until whoever did it is caught.

Leah, I don't know what to do, or where to turn. My prayers seem to have lost their power of consolation, although I'm sure that is only temporary, and that God will come back to me. But why has He sent me this awful Trial? And what am I to live on? The Canon is coming in the next few days, and I know he's going to either tell me I can't have the house, and if I don't agree, he'll give me the sack, because he has to find a new Principal. I can't teach children any more in this frame of mind. Then where will I live? This house is owned by the parish, and neither the Bank nor the Post Office will allow me to draw Thomas's money. I have some that Dada gave me when Helena was born, but although it was very generous it won't last for ever.

The house is grey with sadness through and through. The nurse managed to get me a kind of bed-chair for Thomas with castors on it; it came this morning, and the parlour has now become Thomas's bedroom (so that I don't even have a good room for visitors any more, which is just as well because I don't want to see anyone).

So here I am, Leah, with this man I depended my life on, stretched out like a grey ghost in a corner of the house, silent and damaged for ever. I get up at seven or so, change Helena and do something the same with Thomas, and feed them both before I have my breakfast, which I then can't eat because my stomach is still turning. I feel I've aged twenty years. And after breakfast there isn't anything to do, there isn't anybody to talk to.

Please think of me. Remember how we used to laugh – already I think of those days as if they were dreams I had a long time ago. And please don't tell the girls too much of this yet.

Your affectionate friend,
Ellen

Leah handed Herbert the letter when he came home at one o'clock. Before he touched his food, he read it, then put it to one side, and read it again.

'What's wrong, Mamma?' asked Rachel.

'Poor Uncle Thomas isn't very well,' said Leah.

'Is he going to die?'

'No, he's not.'

'Oh, good, then,' said Rachel, and looked puzzled at her mother's sad face.

Herbert paused while eating his food and re-read the letter. He took off his spectacles and polished them.

'I think I will go out there,' he said.

Ellen was trying to dig some of the potatoes Thomas had sown at Easter. Every such task anguished her. When she stuck the spade in the ground (not knowing she should have used a fork) she found that the potatoes got sliced across uglily. Nor did she know how to stake the pods of peas on their runners. She even had to learn how to wind Thomas's old alarm clock.

Fear intensified the hopeless learning of small essential tasks. The locking-bar of the shutters was too stiff for her to manage alone, and the shutters remained perilously unlocked at night.

Every noise outside the house made her jump: even when going as far as their little lavatory beside the garage she carried Thomas's heavy blackthorn stick, with its silver band.

Throughout the day, she made raids on the outside, the garden, the garage: otherwise, she kept the front and back doors bolted, and only opened the upstairs windows wide. If she heard footsteps she shouted, 'Who's there?' often waking Helena and making her cry – but never even causing a flutter in the comatose Thomas. His long body, wrapped to the throat in a white Foxford blanket, lay semi-reclined, with only the occasional rattle of a slightly caught breath – each of which in the first two days caused Ellen to run and stay there watching for any increased sign of consciousness.

As Herbert rattled the gate, he saw another figure approach from the opposite direction, a lanky, bustling man.

Ellen, hearing more clearly when the noise of the bus engine had abated, shouted, 'Who's that?' and froze among the drills of the garden.

'Ellen, me! Herbert.'

'Who?'

'Herbert. Leah's Herbert.'

She walked cautiously around the corner of the house, her hands covered with clay, the blackthorn stick in her hand.

'Leah, I wish you had seen her,' said Herbert that evening. 'No washing of the hair. Skirt was torn a little, here, just at the waist-band' – he indicated. 'The jumper she had, oh, all stains. The shoes . . . and neither stockings or socks . . .'

'And she who thought out every stitch,' said Leah.

The hedge obscured from Ellen's view the other arrival, and he reached them just as Ellen released the padlock on the gate.

'Mrs. Mrs!' he called.

'You can't see him, Mr Vousden,' said Ellen, retreating a little.

'I know that, Ma'am.'

'And did you ever see her being rude to anyone, ever?' Herbert asked Leah late that night, as they sat before bedtime.

'A bit brisk, maybe, rude not,' said Leah.

=

Ellen said to Val Vousden, 'Can you go away? Just clear off.'

Val said, 'I've come down from Dublin specially. How is he?'

'He won't see you or anyone else. He's –' Ellen hesitated. 'Now will you go?' She almost barked.

Val, taken aback, opened his mouth again, and Herbert said, 'Ah, hold on.'

He spoke softly to Ellen. 'Is it all right if I correspond with this gentleman, or speak to him later?' Ellen turned on her heel and walked towards the door.

'Mr Vousden, is it? My name is Herbert Winer and my wife is an old friend of Mrs Kane.' He lowered his voice. 'The thing is, there's been an accident.'

Val said, 'That was no accident. No accident. I just want to know how the man is.'

'I wonder – will you, would you, wait around the village or somewhere, and we'll meet at the evening's bus. The Castle up there is very interesting.'

Val said, 'No need, if there's anything I can do, tell her to tell Mr Kane, that I'm doing very well reviving the band.'

'Reviving the band?' repeated Herbert.

'He'll know,' said Val, then corrected; 'she'll know.'

Herbert, trying to pick his way in his light shoes to where Ellen had been digging, took the bucket and moved towards the house. Not since the pogrom in Janesborough had he seen a face so troubled: the memory convinced him of the rightness of the approach he had come to suggest. They reached the scullery together and Herbert put the bucket on the floor beside the table: dishes from several rounds of meals stood unwashed, but at least there was some evidence that a start had been made on them.

'I'll give you a hand with these,' said Herbert, and Ellen fetched a kettle of hot water from the range in the kitchen. Herbert took off his jacket and rolled up his sleeves. Neither said anything: she took each cup, saucer, plate, knife and spoon from him and dried it and stacked it for putting away. He wiped his hands, turned to her and said, 'Ellen, dear. Listen carefully to me. I came out specially to say something to you. Just one thing.'

Ellen stared at him; a fixed stare.

'Before I do that, I want to see Thomas, then I want to see Helena.'

'I can't let you see Thomas.' She bit the words off. Then she paused: 'Helena's due a bottle soon.'

Herbert said again, 'I want to see Thomas.' He said it very softly and Ellen began to tremble.

'You can't. I won't let you.'

Herbert stood, saying nothing, just looking steadily at Ellen, whose lip crumpled.

'Nonononono, don't touch me!' She stepped back as Herbert moved to take her hand. She began to cry like a child, standing there, one hand leaning on the table beside the basin of dirty soapy water. Herbert, not very much taller than Ellen, in his soft brown waistcoat, put his hand on her shoulder, and said nothing.

When she stepped back and could speak, she said, 'I'm so ashamed of how he looks. And you know how Thomas kept himself. I try to clean him, and there always seems to be a smell off him, and I can't comb his hair the way he used to, and now there's a smell in the room, so what will it be like when he's here another month – or a year.'

Herbert asked, 'Has anybody else seen him?'

'No,' said Ellen. 'They come and they try. They slow down on their way home from Mass, looking in as if we were animals or something.'

'Is that why the shutters are closed?'

'I'd never let them see him like that. And the feeding is so messy.'

'What about the nurse? Leah said she's very capable?'

'I'm not letting anyone in.'

Herbert said, 'Where is he, Ellen?'

Ellen took the key from the pocket of her skirt, and before turning it in the parlour door, listened at the foot of the stairs for Helena. Then, unlocking the door, she led Herbert into the dimness of the room.

Herbert said, 'Yes, I see what you mean about the smell,' a remark which seemed to give Ellen some relief.

'Can he hear us, do you know? Thomas, can you hear us?' Herbert asked.

Ellen said, 'Even if he can, there's nothing he can say or do.'

'What do you do when someone is like that?' asked Herbert,

thinking aloud. 'Do you have a conversation about them or with them, do you include them or what?'

'Doctors always talk as if you're not there,' said Ellen.

'Can I roll that blanket down a little?' Herbert asked, and Ellen helped him, until Thomas's neck came into view, his Adam's apple protruding through the growing beard.

Herbert stood away and looked at Thomas very carefully. A knife-edge of light came through the joint of the shutters. Herbert then moved himself into a position for an even better observation, and asked Ellen to wheel the bed-chair back a little. 'The room is very dark. How do you move him?'

'I don't. He's too heavy for me to shift him much. I can lift an arm or a leg, that kind of thing.'

Herbert approached the moribund, slanting figure and looked very closely at Thomas's right temple, remarking in little 'h'ms' as he did so.

'May I see his hands?'

'They've gone terribly white and useless,' said Ellen, and she drew them up, limp chalk-white stalks, from far below within the blanket. Herbert examined each of Thomas's hands in turn, and then caressed each hand and gave it back to Ellen to tuck away.

Overhead, Helena woke and began to whimper.

Ellen shrugged hopelessly. 'See what I mean?'

'Leah says she's lovely,' said Herbert. 'Can I just stay in here a minute?'

Ellen went out. Herbert opened the shutters wide, flooding Thomas with sunlight, then opened the window's lower sash; the breeze rushed in like a friend. He drew up a chair. A foul smell came from Thomas's breath, and his mouth fell a little open, as foolishly as that of somebody asleep on the bus: white slime coated his teeth. Could this be the sleek, authoritative man whom Ellen had married?

Herbert had said to Leah, when he first met Thomas, that it took a little time to adjust to someone as young and girlish as Ellen marrying such a distinguished-looking figure – but that it obviously suggested something about Ellen that they had not yet realized. Herbert now reached out and touched Thomas's forehead: it felt normally cool, if a little clammy, not in any way feverish. Not that Herbert knew anything about such things, he felt Thomas's pulse, and found it not at all unusual in any way – Herbert felt his own pulse several times a day as if to verify, as Leah used to tease, that he was 'still here with us'.

'Thomas, my friend,' he said. 'Thomas, my friend –' but he did not pursue.

He patted the blanket back around Thomas's throat and smoothed Thomas's hair as he heard Ellen coming downstairs muttering to the baby.

Herbert wheeled Thomas's bed-chair forward a little towards the open window, and left the room, closing the door behind him. He caught up with Ellen in the kitchen and spoke many delights over Helena, taking her in his arms while Ellen made a bottle.

As they sat there, with Ellen feeding Helena, Herbert said, 'It must be like having a living corpse in the house with you, and it must be most dreadful of all at night. I opened the shutters and the window.'

Ellen's only respite came when dealing with Helena's needs. Even if the despair had never shown a single sign of lifting, it became fractionally more tolerable when feeding Helena, and even daring to play with her a little while washing or changing her – procedures in which she still did not feel confident.

'That's what they were calling him in the hospital,' said Ellen. 'That's why I brought him home. "The living dead". They were treating him like something in a sideshow. The whole country knows about it.'

'It was all in the papers, of course. Hallo! Hall-low, sweetheart!' cooed Herbert to Helena, who puffed her cheeks placidly on the bottle. 'It remains a mystery.'

'Nobody around here ever talks,' said Ellen.

'And no idea who did it?' Herbert murmured.

Ellen glanced at him.

'I read your letter to Leah,' said Herbert; 'she showed it to me. I suppose this is about the worst thing that you could imagine happening to you.'

'Sometimes,' Leah complained, 'you have to strain forward to hear what Herbert says in that soft voice of his.'

'Unless to be tortured or something?' replied Ellen, 'but I can't think of anything ordinary that could be worse. I can't look at a calendar in case I have to think of what next month will be like, or next year, or ten years from now.' She spoke in a dullness of which she was once incapable.

'No,' said Herbert, 'no, I suppose not. I see you! I see you!' he cooed again to Helena, who frowned round the shoulder of the bottle.

Herbert said in a most even voice, 'The night before the pogrom in 1903, Leah's mother's brother was walking home along the banks of the Shannon and three fellows caught him and threw him in. Maybe they only meant to give him a ducking, but they didn't know there were only two feet of water there, and beneath that, several feet of soft mud. He fell on his face and never appeared again, until they dragged his body out.'

'This would be Leah's uncle?' exclaimed Ellen. 'I never heard that!'

'Too painful, even now. The following day, when those boys were arrested, because in their fright one of them talked, the pogrom began in earnest.'

Herbert spoke without bitterness of any kind.

Ellen interjected again, 'I wonder does my father know about that?'

Herbert continued, 'Leah's mother blamed herself for it, said she should never have allowed Simon out alone. I was sitting with her the day of the funeral and she kept on blaming herself, over and over.'

'Blame?'

'Well, what I really mean is that she felt responsible, or that she felt she ought to feel some responsibility in the matter.'

Ellen put the bottle down and tilted Helena over her knee: the little face grew red and bulging, then drooled a little as she belched.

'That's what kills me, Herbert. That Thomas can't see any of this, that he can't even help with the baby.'

'I said to her, "But why do you blame yourself, he went out all the time, he was a normal eighteen-year old?" And she said to me, "Unless I can give myself a part in it, I can never understand it." I'm still trying to work out what she meant.'

Ellen heard Herbert, looked away and did not look back at him for some time, busied herself with Helena, to whom Herbert also chatted.

'By the way,' said Herbert, 'a couple of things. I can show you how to shave Thomas; my uncle was an undertaker and I know how to shave an inert figure, I watched him. And Ellen – and Leah agrees with me – you'll have to make a list of your choices. That's what I really came to say to you.'

'I don't understand you fully,' said Ellen.

'We'll talk about it later.'

Val Vousden sat in Hand's public house and had a tall glass of red lemonade, and Mrs Hand made him a cheese sandwich and said, 'I declare to God,' when he asked her for mustard.

Dreadful it was, what happened to the Master, and what was the Mistress going to do at all, surely she was only a young one? At which Val remarked, 'She seems well able to look after herself.'

To which Mrs Hand replied, 'She'll have to be, for the Canon will have her out of that house like a shot.'

Val, fishing for information, asked, 'I suppose that's the very first motor-car "accident" around here?'

'It must be,' said Mrs Hand thoughtfully, re-tying the thin strings of her crossover apron. 'I never heard of another one anywhere in these parts. Although there was military lorries and cars, the Tans and that. That Nurse Cooper, her intended was killed in one,' she said.

As he saw the Curate off at the orchard's little door, the Canon said that he could not confirm whether he would call tomorrow to see the Mistress, or whether he would leave it until after he came back from his two weeks in Lahinch, and anyway there wasn't time to advertise before then for a new Teacher, and the sea air would clear his head, and besides, all the teachers would be on holidays themselves, and he wondered aloud whether he might meet somebody in Lahinch who might even know of a Principal looking for a job or who might move.

The Curate said, 'I'd love to do it for you, Canon, even while you're away, but 'tis a sensitive business, and it has to be done by yourself, you're the man with the authority to do it.'

The Canon knew he had a reputation in the Archdiocese for not getting on well with his curates, but God Almighty, how could you get on with a foxy man like that?

'Well, Father,' he said with some asperity to the departing man who bent to put on his bicycle clips, 'what'll we say to the Archbishop in four years' time when we have children who aren't nearly as good as this year's crowd were?'

The Curate straightened up. 'Sure, the point is, of course, Canon, we can't get a new Principal until we have a house for them to live in. I don't know when the Mistress can move out of there. I mean she can go on teaching, can't she, if she can manage, with a small child and that man the way he is, but she'd have to move into another house, wouldn't she?'

It suddenly occurred to the Canon to ask, 'Have you somebody in mind for the job, Father?'

'I haven't yet, Canon, but I'm sure if I thought hard . . .'

The Canon watched his Curate mount the bicycle.

'The thing is, Father, what sort of Christians are we that we're not out in force trying to find the man who did it?'

'Sure, how would we do that, Canon, sure, who has that kind of information? And anyway, sure who'd want any man hanged, I mean if the Master died?'

The Canon watched his Curate, whom he did not like at all, cycle away down the short winding avenue.

When Helena had been returned to her crib, Ellen and Herbert ate a light meal, and then, at Herbert's suggestion, sat outside on the seat in the sun. Initially, Ellen jibbed at this – the seat was right outside Thomas's window, but Herbert insisted. In an atmosphere between them of increasing intensity, and in hushed tones, even though there was nobody for at least a mile around to hear them, they talked for two hours, with Ellen arguing all the time, but eventually giving way on each of the points Herbert made in a series of upraised fingers.

At four o'clock, Herbert said, 'How long 'til the bus?'

She peered through the window at the clock. 'An hour and a quarter.'

He promptly rose from the seat, and went indoors, with Ellen following. At his request she filled a basin of water, the temperature of which Herbert tested with his elbow, and he asked her to fetch Thomas's favourite razor, the stick of shaving soap and the brush. 'And the scissors.'

By Thomas's side, Herbert drew up a chair, placed the basin and shaving things on it, and then with love and care tucked a towel under Thomas's chin. Outside, a horse and cart clipclopped past the gate.

'Now watch me very closely,' said Herbert. 'And let me just tell you one thing.' Herbert, according to Leah, believed very firmly in fixing matters to one point: if he could find one mooring, he believed, one means by which to guide or judge the matter in hand, then any man could cope with anything.

'And the one thing is this – don't be afraid of the razor. The way to defeat it is to go right against it, to oppose the thought completely. If you were shaving the baby,' he asked, 'would you cut her?'

'Oh?' said Ellen. 'I never thought of that.'

'Exactly,' said Herbert.

He clipped the heaviest hair from Thomas's face and neck. This took ten minutes or so, after which he ran his hand all around the cheeks and jaws to feel the consistency of the remaining stubble. Herbert wrinkled his nose to keep his spectacles from slipping. Next, with a vigour that surprised Ellen, he began to lather Thomas's face. He showed Ellen how to pull Thomas's cheeks this way and that, how to begin by declaring a line under the ears, depending upon the length Thomas liked to grow his sideburns, and then how to sweep down the face to the chin, holding the open razor, as it were, backwards in the hand.

'The point is,' he said, a phrase over which Leah sometimes threatened to slaughter him, he used it so often, 'the point is, that Thomas himself would never go through a day without shaving, or would he?'

Ellen said, 'Under no circumstances. He hated not being shaved. I used to joke him about it. I used to threaten to tie his hands behind his back, as a torture, to stop him shaving.'

Herbert pressed down on Thomas's lip to flatten it into a plateau.

'The thing,' he breathed, 'we are never taught is, that caring is about making the other person feel the way they want to be, not the way that will make us feel nice and good. In Thomas's case, the way he himself would want to be, the dear man.'

Ellen said, 'No wonder Leah married you.'

Herbert towelled the side of Thomas's face he had shaved, and the chin and upper lip, then said to Ellen, 'Now you do the other side.'

She flinched.

'Go on,' he said, 'I'll guide you.' He showed her how to make the lather begin to work by rubbing it very hard on the heel of her thumb.

'If it still doesn't work, pinch the brush when it's wet, pinch it right up all the way from there, where the bristles meet the handle right up to the top, and that will bring up all the existing soap.'

She began to lather the other side of Thomas's face. On the far side of the road Val Vousden sat on the wall opposite the gate, his legs dangling: Herbert could see him through the rustling net curtains.

'Harder, harder, don't be afraid,' Herbert said. 'Did you ever watch him lathering himself? I bet he didn't do it timidly.'

Ellen took the razor from the basin, and wiped the handle.

'Hold it out like that, in front of you,' Herbert said, 'let me see. Look, your hand is perfectly steady. Now, off you go.'

Ellen began, gingerly.

'The point is – not to scrape but to sweep, an even movement,' said Herbert. 'Let me see, oh, that's ideal. Yes, yes.' He praised her.

'My hand keeps wanting to shake,' she said.

'Remember. It's the baby's face you're shaving,' said Herbert, and watched how Ellen's concentration upon the task developed.

'It's a mixture of care,' said Herbert, 'care-ing and care-ful. Good, steady. That's it.'

Ellen's hand swept steadily down Thomas's jaw; she moved back and held her head at an angle to allow better light on his face, and soon she had shaved down to the neck. She towelled the remains of the soap away.

'Now, Thomas, let me tilt your head forward,' said Herbert. Suddenly, like a man with a brainwave, he said to Ellen, 'Have you a small looking-glass, you know, that you use yourself?'

'But he can't see, Herbert, and he can't hear you,' she said, her teeth gritting in frustration.

'No matter, no matter,' Herbert said, 'get it, will you? Please.' She went upstairs and fetched it.

'Now, I'll hold his head up straight and you hold the glass in front of him. Come round here to the side, so that you can see his face in the mirror. All right, Thomas? I'll just move your head a little.'

Thomas had given Ellen the hand-glass as one of many wedding gifts, along with a comb and a hairbrush of the same set: they were backed with green glass, inside of which had been fixed the piece of lace so fascinating to little Timmy Quinn. Ellen held

337

the glass in front of Thomas's face, and could see his lifeless reflection.

'Now,' said Herbert, 'doesn't he look better? That's how he would see himself if he had just been the one doing the shaving. What d'you think of that, Thomas?' he called, as if to an elderly, slightly deaf relative.

'No, he doesn't look better. And he can't see himself. Herbert, what are you doing, this is so stupid!'

Ellen burst into tears and flung the mirror on the floor where it shattered, the handle breaking away from the cracking rear, the glass of the mirror spreading in slivers on the floor. 'Now look what you've done; Thomas gave me that. Oh, Jesus. Now I'm going to have seven years' bad luck!'

Herbert laid Thomas's head back.

'Ellen, you'll see what I mean,' he said, 'you'll see what I mean.'

She spun on her heel and walked from the room: Herbert followed her, deliberately leaving the door wide open, with Thomas framed in it.

On board *The Princess* bus, Herbert told Val Vousden the story of Ellen Morris and Thomas Kane, ending with the afternoon's scenes. Owing to the softness of his voice, Val had to ask this odd little man several times 'What was that?' and 'I'm sorry?' and 'I beg your pardon?'

In his turn, Val told Herbert of his correspondence with Thomas Kane, and the background to it, and the dialogue they had been having, and how Thomas had embraced the idea of reviving the Deanstown Band: 'And I'm going to revive it myself, so I am.'

At home with Leah and the girls, Herbert took off his shoes immediately he sat down.

'It's my tongue that's tired out. I can't remember a day when I talked so much.'

Leah gave the girls their supper and plied Herbert with questions. Typically he frustrated her with superficial and cursory answers, and then disappeared to his home workroom with a tray, saying he would speak to her later. He always did, of course, it was just that Leah found the waiting so unendurable.

=

338

When Helena was settled to sleep, the dreadful silence fell again on Ellen and the house. Her mind failed to function at these moments. Every position in which she chose to sit or stand felt so listless. The only difference this evening was that she actually managed to wash the dishes in the scullery, and she even put most of them away: yet, she could not bring herself to face the bucket of napkins outside the back door. The cats had not been fed for days, and came hopefully to the window from time to time. A year ago, 'in Thomas's day', as she had unwittingly begun to describe it, Ellen often perched on the end of the kitchen table, her legs swinging, while he sat in his chair, his body turned towards her, and they chatted until the twilight obscured the expressions on their faces from each other.

Remembering, she said aloud, 'Tired the sun with talking. And sent him down the sky.'

And then, after a quick turn in the warm night air, to bed together, to fall asleep eventually, in silent exhaustion: 'the merry newlyweds' Thomas called themselves: next morning, as she washed at the basin and ewer, he would tangle her hair gently and say, 'And how are the merry newlyweds this morning?'

Now he lay, a grey, mansize slug, in there, across the hallway, and his pretty baby daughter, growing plump, asleep upstairs. The light had not yet gone, no need yet for the lamp: what in the name of God was she going to do in the winter? She slid the knives and spoons away in the ordinary cutlery drawer, and then searched in the other drawer for the carving-set box. As she drew it out, the box's catches caught in a ball of string which fell, unravelling, to the floor. Ellen bent to pick it up and she wound it back into its shape again. Thomas's meticulousnesses could still be seen all around the house – string, and paper, and small empty tins into which he put his nails in the garage, and the polishes for his shoes every night, and his regular oiling of the locks and window-catches.

She replaced the rewound string in the drawer, and went to the kitchen door to look across the hall. A breeze had blown the door slightly to, but she could see the blanket where it wrapped around Thomas's feet. On the wall, just at her shoulder, hung her favourite Thomas joke – his certificate from Primary School declaring him qualified at the age of seven in 'Reading, Writing and Ballframe': on the day Thomas showed it to her, she asked him for it, and then she had it framed, because she always wanted to imagine the little boy of seven, with curly hair, long before this dreadful life had come out of the fissures of the earth and foully breathed fire on him. Thomas gave her the certificate, but accused her of sentimentality. On the sewing-machine table-top stood the bag of fruit Herbert had brought, which she had not opened.

Ellen stood for a long time in thought, her eyes red and sore from crying. She could see her reflection in the window, in outline only, not in detail, but knew that her hair seemed stringy and greasy: in the clothes she wore she could not trace her figure with any clarity, no matter how she turned.

She spoke aloud.

'I promised Herbert.' She turned back and went to the far corner of the kitchen, poked about in the bureau, found her blue tortoiseshell fountain pen, took her ledger from the drawer beneath the bureau's flap, dragged herself to the sewing-machine table-top, moved the fruit to the seat of the chair Thomas used to sit in, and sat at the table-top to write. The ledger hadn't been opened for over two months: the first thing Ellen saw was Mrs Dalton's recipe for lemon tartlets, entered before she went into the nursing home to have Helena.

Ellen spoke aloud again, fiercely: 'No, I am not crying again, I am not, I am not, I am not.' She shook her pen on her blotting-paper, verified that it contained ink, and began to write.

More or less simultaneously, Leah finished reading to the children, and Herbert emerged to sit in the living-room. A pigeon landed in the tiny yard outside. Leah had a handful of socks and things, which she left on the living-room table.

'I don't even know where to begin,' said Herbert, 'my jaw is still tired.'

Ellen, thirty-six miles away, wrote on an unlined piece of paper, using the lines of the ledger as a guide, 'I promised Herbert that I would make a list of my choices.' She stopped, sucked the end of her pen, folded the sheet of paper, tore it in four, and in the ledger, on the fresh page opposite the lemon tartlets, wrote, 'My Choices'.

Outside, on the road, unseen by her, a heavy man stopped his bicycle, and holding it stationary by touching the road with the toe of his boot, looked in for a moment, then cranked up the bicycle again and rode off.

'So I said to her,' continued Herbert, 'was there one thing she did every day, rain or shine, when Thomas was, you know, in the whole of his health? When things were normal?'

Leah leaned forward, not missing a word, eyes as glittering as a bird's.

'Anything, no matter how trivial, but anything that was part of their life together, you know, like polishing shoes, or always putting a certain dish away in a certain way, or making a cup of tea at a certain time; this is something for herself, I meant, not something she used to do for the two of them, and that she should go back to doing that, to see if she could get herself started up in some sort of pattern. You see, this is the point. She has no pattern yet that has not been imposed on her by these terrible circumstances, and it's, what, getting on for between two and three months since the baby was born, do you know what I mean?'

'Yes, yes,' said Leah, 'go on, go on. What did she say?'

'Oh, yes, well,' said Herbert, 'actually it was very good, she said she had a housekeeping book that she put hints in, and recipes, and that, and I said, ideal. Ideal.'

'She has,' said Leah, 'her ledger. I know it.'

'And I made her promise me, because she has to promise somebody, that she'd do it, and if she promises I think she will.'

'Oh, yes, Ellen will,' said Leah. 'That's the religion in her.'

'And I put it to her that she now should use the book to write down, like she was making a plan or something, to write down what kind of life she could now make for herself, because she has to make some kind of life. She has to choose, to make some kind of choices. I mean, will she keep him there, will she stay out in that place, what? They're the choices she has to make, Leah.'

'She has,' said Leah. 'She has.'

'Well, the second thing we talked about was, that she must get Thomas turned every day, and that was very interesting,' said Herbert. 'You see the house is dirty already.'

'Oh, no?' Leah interrupted, consternation beginning.

'And untidy, and there is no nurse coming in because she had a row with her, and with the hospital, and she has also forbidden the doctor to call.'

'But that house was like a new pin?!'

'And if Thomas gets sores, and she has to call somebody in, she will be judged unfit to look after him, and maybe even unfit to care for the baby.'

'I hope you didn't say any of this, Herbert?'

'I did, I said it all.'

'You shouldn't have.'

'I should've, if we're her friends.'

'No!'

'Yes, Leah.'

'But what did she say?'

'She looked desperate, and then she told me about the house. It isn't theirs, it is the official house of the Principal Teacher, but only insofar as whosoever that may be.'

Leah put her hands over her face.

Herbert said, 'So I asked her to promise me, for Thomas's sake – that she would ask the one person she really trusted in the whole place, provided they lived any way near her, to come in and turn Thomas every day with her. She resisted that too, like she resisted everything, but eventually she said she doubted there was anybody, so I told her to find somebody. Anybody.'

While Herbert told Leah of his day, Ellen wrote under *My Choices*: 'I have the following choices as to what to do with my life and this predicament.' Then she stopped.

Herbert did not tell Leah the full story. He left out several of the details – such as the fact that he refused to help Ellen with what might be a course of action she could choose to make matters easier – to get Thomas into a home or a mental hospital; or that he did not minimize the greatness of the threat to her dwelling-place when the Canon eventually called. Nor did he tell Leah that against Ellen's will, he held Ellen's hand firmly in his, and told her that she had to begin pulling things together, not pulling away – as she tried to do now with her hand from his; that no matter how harsh that might be, she had to begin accepting help. Nor did he tell Leah that Ellen should find where she was to blame in the entire matter, and how he chose not to use the word 'responsibility', and even said to Ellen, 'You will understand the word "blame" from your religion. After all, you worship in a faith which is based on

blame. Jesus's fame came out of the dreadful punishment of cruci-
fixion. Therefore, you have to purge your "blame".'

He did say to Leah, 'She looked a little, what? – deranged from
time to time.'

'Patchwork,' said Leah suddenly, 'she has to make something,
something like patchwork, so that she can see it and others can see
it, and admire it.'

Herbert said, 'I tried to persuade her to ask her mother to come
and stay.'

'No,' said Leah, 'no, she won't do that, not at all.'

Lying in bed, with Leah's arms around him, her face between
his shoulder-blades, Herbert asked, 'Did I do all right, Leah? Did
I do the right things?'

'Oh God, I hope so, Herbert.'

Ellen wrote one letter, just a note; she had promised Herbert
and she could not renege. She did not write another word, and,
despite her best intentions, cried herself to sleep again. In the
morning she awoke to another day when even the summer sunlight
shone grey on her face.

23

Mrs Greege arrived two days after the postman handed her Ellen's note. Ellen, upstairs, putting Helena down after her morning bath, heard the catch of the gate clicking and looked out of the window. Then, consciously for the first time in weeks, she checked her appearance in the dressing-table mirrors. Dreadful – and too late. Panicky, Ellen stood back on the landing, hands in consternation to her jaws, then had to run downstairs in case Mrs Greege's calling disturbed the drowsing Helena.

She unlocked the gate. 'Come in,' she said, and held the door open, directing Mrs Greege to the kitchen.

'She is a bitch,' Thomas said, 'and she always will be a bitch,' as he reversed the paper on the parcel of wedding-gift linen Mrs Greege had sent them, and posted it back to her. When Ellen wondered if this might not be a little extreme, he reminded her of Mrs Greege's behaviour. Now, here, the woman stood in Ellen's own kitchen, waiting as Ellen closed the front door.

'Will you sit down?' Ellen asked. The woman looked, wiped a chair with her hand, sat down, put her tall, brown handbag on the table, clearing a space for it by pushing it forward, and stared all around.

'You were a deal cleaner and tidier when you were with me.' She looked at Ellen. 'No fine clothes today, huh? What happened to all the underwear?'

Ellen said slowly, 'No, that's true enough.'

'You look a hundred,' said Mrs Greege, wading straight in. 'I thought you had better stuff than that in you. Although I never liked you.'

Ellen sat down, tentative in her own kitchen. 'No,' she said again.

'Where is he?' said Mrs Greege. 'They're all saying the hospital wasn't good enough for him, that you were too posh, too big in yourself.'

Ellen moved a breakfast plate out of the way, spilling the crumbs from it.

'There's not a lot of people sorry for the two of you,' said Mrs Greege. 'Notions, the two of you had, going up the aisle there of a Sunday morning, Lord and Lady Muck.'

Ellen, white-faced and bleary, ran the back of a hand across her forehead. This morning, she had not had even enough energy to attend yet to Thomas.

'And the two of you thought you were so popular.' Mrs Greege stared at Ellen, and gave the impression of some relish. After a slab of silence she said, 'You wrote me a note?'

'It doesn't matter,' said Ellen.

'You mean I wasted my time coming down here.'

Ellen shook her head and lowered her gaze. 'No, it doesn't matter.'

Mrs Greege reached for her handbag. Instead of preparing to leave, she opened it and took Ellen's note from it.

'There it is,' she said, 'the note you wrote me. It says here, "Please will you call to see me? I need your help. Yours faithfully, Ellen Kane." And in your writing.'

'I know I wrote it, but it doesn't matter now.'

'And I have that sort of time to waste?' asked Mrs Greege, in what Ellen used to describe as 'her whipping rhetoric'.

'No.' Ellen shook her head. Mrs Greege studied her, looked around the kitchen again, then back at Ellen, who raised her eyes and said, 'I didn't mean to waste your time. I apologize. 'Tis just that –'

'Just that what? That Lady Muck can command the parish?'

Ellen shook her head.

Mrs Greege said, 'My wedding present wasn't good enough for you. That mouth of a postman told everybody it was thrown back in my face. How did he know that unless the Master or yourself told him?'

'Oh, no,' said Ellen, 'I would never do such a thing,' and realized that Thomas felt so strongly about Mrs Greege anything could have been said. 'Nor would I approve of it.'

'Well, it happened,' said the widow, thin ring solitary on her long hand. 'We're decent people, and you used the biggest mouth in the parish to make a laughing-stock of us.' Another silence fell. Neither woman looked at the other.

Ellen said, 'I'll pay you.'

Mrs Greege looked at her.

'I always knew there was malice in you,' she said.

'There isn't, there isn't.'

Mrs Greege broke the silence by asking, 'What help was it you wanted, anyway?'

Ellen said, 'No, it doesn't matter.'

'You owe me for my wasted time to tell me.'

Ellen, her head down, said slowly, and barely audibly, 'A friend told me that my husband would get very ill from bedsores if he wasn't turned every day. I can't do it myself, he's too heavy, and I'd hurt myself. If he goes wrong on me, and anyone gets to hear of it, the authorities might call, the Cruelty Man or someone, I might be judged unfit to look after my husband, or to look after the baby. I'm ashamed to let anyone see my husband in the state he's in now. This friend asked me was there anyone at all I trusted completely hereabouts. That's why I wrote to you. That's all there's to it.'

Had Ellen not forgotten – again – to bring the alarm clock downstairs to its habitual daytime place on the bookcase ledge, its ticking would have dominated the silence in the kitchen. Mrs Greege, resting her elbow on the table, arranged all the fingers of one hand vertically over her mouth: the fingernails touched the grey nostril hairs of which Thomas and Ellen once joked.

The woman stood up, straight as a rifle.

'I'll be back in an hour in my overalls,' she said, 'provided you wash yourself, and provided this place starts getting cleaned. I'm not having anything to do with a house this dirty. You shouldn't be bringing up a child like this. Lady Muck is right.' Pleased with her little joke she let herself out.

She returned in exactly an hour, dressed as she did when working in her own kitchen. Hanging her coat in the hallway – Ellen, for once, had not closed the front door – she confronted Ellen, who was still washing her hair in a basin on the scullery table.

'Where is he?' and then said, 'No, I'll go by myself.'

Minutes later, when Ellen, her hair piling in a towel, entered the room where Thomas lay, the curtains blew in the breeze from the open windows. Mrs Greege, having cleared away into a pile the towels and other clothing strewn on chairs in the room, was opening the blanket down to Thomas's waist, and preparing to prop him up.

'Are you all right now there, Master Kane?'

'He can't hear you,' said Ellen, who had a look of dismay on her face.

'How do you know?' The woman seemed a little less harsh than when she first sat in the kitchen.

'The doctors . . .' Ellen stopped.

'I've no time much for doctors. Is there water on the boil?'

'No.'

'Is the fire on?'

'No.'

'Have you anyone coming in to help you here?'

'No.'

'I hear you had a fight with Dr Hogan.'

'He came to the gate and complained to me for taking Thomas out of the hospital.'

'I hear you threw a stone at him.' Ellen didn't answer.

Mrs Greege looked down at Thomas, then sucked her lip and said, 'I'll be back in a minute, Master Kane,' in a normal tone, not shouting, not slow-speaking-to-the-hard-of-hearing.

'Have you clean towels?'

'I don't know.'

'Did you do a wash yesterday?'

'No.'

'Did your mother come out to give you a hand?'

'No. I wouldn't let her.' Then Ellen, looking at Thomas, and the dried, unpleasant saliva at the corners of his lips, said, 'That's what my friend did, my friend's husband, I should say. Herbert. He talked to my husband. To the Master.'

'My husband. The Master,' Mrs Greege mimicked. 'Call him his name, can't you? And why wouldn't anyone talk to him? Isn't he alive?' said Mrs Greege, crossing the hallway to the kitchen. 'Now. Where's your turf, and where is your kindling? Do you know how to light a fire?'

'I've only seen the Master do it.'

Mrs Greege showed her how: her method was identical to that of Thomas's, tepees of sticks and coal.

'What water do you use for washing?'

'From the tank in the yard.'

'Have you rain-barrels?'

'We have. Four': one at each corner of the house, only half-full in summer.

'They're enough,' insisted Mrs Greege, who made Ellen fill the two large black kettles out of the nearest barrel, and set them to boil on the range.

'What do you do your washing in?'

Ellen lugged out the large and the smaller zinc baths from under the scullery mangle-table. Both had been filled with soiled clothes, mostly Helena's.

'How long is it since you did a wash in the name of Jesus Himself?' asked Mrs Greege.

Ellen started to cry, and Mrs Greege said with hissing viciousness, 'If you start that, I'm walking out the door this minute. Do you hear me? Sort them clothes into four piles – your own, the baby's and the Master's and the linen for the house. I'll get the others from the room,' and she returned piled to her chin with all the clothes discarded near Thomas's bed-chair.

'It'll be an hour before them kettles are boiled. Go and put clean clothes on yourself, and open every window in the house except the baby's room. And bring down all the dirty bedclothes.'

When Ellen returned, Mrs Greege had folded all the towels and any sheets she found, and said, 'We'll send these into the nuns' laundry. Now, tidy the kitchen to the state it'd be in if the Master was coming in for his dinner.' For the next hour she bossed Ellen, made her dust with both duster and goosewing, saw to it that every piece of crockery and cutlery was washed again and returned to its normal habitat. Mrs Greege then filled a bucket from one of the kettles and set to scrubbing the floor: 'And I'll make a better job of it than you made of mine. Now, refill that kettle. No, don't take it off,' she barked. 'Use the can or the bucket,' as if to a slow-learning child.

The kitchen began to look clean and fresh: the bow window sashes were raised as high and open as they could be; the table was pushed back against the wall and the chairs tucked beneath it, and the top of the range gleamed; a through draught blew its pleasant breeze from the window to the open back door.

Mrs Greege fetched two basins which she made Ellen fill from one of the boiling kettles.

348

'When we've finished this job, you can go and get a few flowers from the garden and put them there on the sewing-machine,' said tall, bony, sour Mrs Greege over her shoulder as, followed by Ellen, she marched into Thomas's room, 'and then we'll start on this place.'

She put the basin on the floor. 'Now, Master Kane. We're going to give you a good wash, and we're going to turn you.' Her voice was more relaxed than the tones she used with Ellen, to whom she said, 'You take the far side.' Ellen went around the back of the bed-chair.

'Now, we're going to let the back down, Master Kane,' Mrs Greege said, and to Ellen, 'the least you might do is talk to your husband.'

'Hallo, Thomas,' said Ellen, uncertain and wan.

'Ask him how he is, can't you?'

'How are you, Thomas?' said Ellen feebly.

They lowered the bed-chair into the recumbent, flat position. Mrs Greege pulled down the rest of the blanket covering Thomas, exposing the large towel Ellen had clumsily fastened on him as a napkin.

'What's this?' asked Mrs Greege, who removed without fuss or comment the filthy, noisome towel from around Thomas's groin: his thighs were covered with urine stains.

'You poor man, Master Kane, they must be stinging you,' said Mrs Greege conversationally. 'Your backside must be in an awful mess.'

Ellen, although she winced, ventured a question at Mrs Greege's deftness: 'How do you know so much?'

'I had a bedridden father and I had a bedridden husband. Aren't you the lucky woman to have me.'

It took an hour and a half, and three changes of water, to wash Thomas. They washed his hair and his genitals and his back and buttocks and feet, and almost lovingly Mrs Greege dried him, and beginning-to-be-lovingly Ellen dried him too. She did score one victory: Mrs Greege acknowledged the skill with which Ellen shaved Thomas: 'I never learned how to do that properly,' she said.

When he lay there, naked and white, and no longer, it seemed to Ellen, as grey as he had been, and cleaner than at any time since his incapacitation, Mrs Greege said, 'What clothes will we put on him? We'll have to put on a good towel until we get something better, and you're going to have to watch what food you put in his mouth on account of the other end.'

Ellen, weary, said, 'Clothes?'

'Of course clothes. Wouldn't he wear clothes if he was all right?' Her waspishness to Ellen scarcely varied. 'Get him a shirt, a pair of trousers, socks and slippers and a pullover': and they dressed Thomas.

'He looks like he's only asleep,' said Ellen.

'Tell him that,' said Mrs Greege, and left the room with her redundant basin held at her hip.

Ellen stood in front of Thomas, gazing down at him where he lay, his eyes closed, his mouth open a fraction, his breathing sound and regular. She had chosen his favourite blue wool shirt, and a navy pullover and corduroy trousers.

'Thomas, love, you look like you're only asleep.' Ellen bent and kissed his forehead, something she had not done since he came home. Mrs Greege, about to return, saw her from across the hallway – but moved aside out of Ellen's line of sight.

Mrs Greege's only signs of a capacity to thaw came when Helena was brought downstairs. She held the child, and cuddled her, and told her what 'a grand little bantam she was', and even murmured a half-compliment to Ellen for the manner in which Helena seemed to thrive. Otherwise, for the rest of the day, washing and hanging out clothes, and scrubbing the kitchen table, and then, in a slow tortuous way, changing the manner in which Ellen fed Thomas, she behaved in her usual curt and acid fashion.

She left at six o'clock, promising to return next day at nine, leaving Ellen exhausted in her wake, but for the first time in weeks not tearful at the end of the day. With Mrs Greege, Ellen had changed Thomas again into pyjamas, and a fresh towel-napkin for the night, and fed him spoons of warm milk with rusks melted in them. She went to bed directly after she had settled Helena down at half-past eight, and slept until Helena woke her at six.

Next morning, as Mrs Greege fastened the buttons on Thomas's shirt, she exclaimed, 'Ah, good, she's here.'

Ellen working on the other side of Thomas looked out of the open window and saw, wheeling her bicycle through the gate, Nurse Cooper in full white uniform under a blue coat.

'What?' asked Ellen.

'I sent Liam in with a note. We need an expert.'

Nurse Cooper came in and shook Ellen's hand rather formally. When Mrs Greege left at one o'clock in the afternoon, again promising to return the following day, Nurse Cooper, standing in the kitchen, put her arms awkwardly around Ellen and gave her a hug.

Ellen said, 'I'm sorry I wouldn't let you in.' From behind the curtains of the top window she had watched Sheila Cooper on five occasions try to find some means of getting past the padlocked gate; had not even opened Sheila's letters.

Now Ellen began to talk: she did not weep, she did not become hysterical.

'I realize now what has happened, that my life has been destroyed. The thing I can't manage at all is not so much the physical caring, in fact that's probably good for me in some queer sort of way.' Nurse Cooper nodded.

'The thing I can't manage is – is –' Nurse Cooper waited.

'Is the fact that none of my feelings have changed for him, that when I look at him like that, I feel exactly the same as if he was, as if he was – sitting here talking, or, if he was getting up in the morning in the room, or winding the clock as he walked up the stairs last thing at night . . .' She paused. 'In fact, if anything, I have stronger feelings for him now. Fonder of him.'

For the rest of the day, on and off, Nurse Cooper listened as Ellen talked, and told the whole story of her marriage to Thomas. Of her fears, of her hopes. Of how she had never really liked, or met seriously, any other man. 'We were always quiet at home. Mama is so bossy, Dada is so quiet, we never met anyone except our cousins.'

Of how when she first knew she felt something for Thomas; 'I got very confused, it was all lovely and it was rosy and like the magazines and books say, and yet what I liked about him was not that. 'Twas that he made me think.'

Of how when they first got married, 'I didn't know that – I didn't know, I didn't know – what marriage was like, it wasn't at all like our religion says it is. That Thomas's respect for me didn't cut across his fondness for me, or the excitement we, the excitement, I, him and me, what we felt together, I mean we didn't talk about it, except a little but we both knew that this was lovely, and that we had such freedom, I mean, there was no having to go to Confession, or anything. I could go to Communion every Sunday, even in spite of all the – of all the, all the excitement. The being married.'

Of how Thomas's anger with others worried her. 'And I got this idea, and it grew all over me, like weeds growing inside in my head, that any children we had, especially if they were boys, that they would be violent too, and that the whole thing would never stop . . . And then a priest friend of mine, he told me that once I was expecting, that Thomas and I should, that we shouldn't, that we should have no more, that we –'

Sheila Cooper cut in: 'I have a friend, they've six children, and when they had their third – she always has them with me – her husband never again talked to her during the whole nine months she was expecting, and I said to her, why, and she said she didn't know, and I knew she wasn't telling me the truth, and then eventually it came out, that on account of her condition the priest told her in Confessions she had to have no more to do with him until the baby was born.'

Ellen agreed. 'That was the same as us. I don't mean the not talking, but the rule, although I heard the opposite in Confession, from the Canon, of all people.'

Sheila Cooper said, 'Jeremiah has a mind of his own. D'you know who his closest friend is? Father Ferris, d'you know who I mean, he's always giving out about the Church, they call his sermons "Feresies", he's about ninety.' They laughed.

Ellen continued. She traced the weeks before Helena was born, their lovely peace together, the way Thomas had been about the baby.

'I remember saying it would be grand if she was born on the first of May, and he had a bit of poetry, he always had a bit of poetry –'

'– Always *has* a bit of poetry,' corrected Sheila Cooper.

Ellen continued, 'And he recited it, "May Day, delightful day". And then when she was born, not on May Day itself, that few hours after, as you know, he said to me inside in your nursing home, "Sure aren't women always late for everything?" D'you know why she's called "Sorcha"? Because he had a little sister who died, she was called "Sorcha"; as you know, that's the Irish for "Sarah", and the first time he ever talked about it, he told me, talked about it to anyone, was just before the baby was born.'

Ellen's spate of talking ended when she told how she could face nobody, had not been to Mass since she finally came home from the nursing home with Helena, and had generally deteriorated into the condition in which Mrs Greege had found her.

At half-past five, Nurse Cooper said, 'We'll have one last cup of tea before you have to feed Helena, and then I have to go. Now, these things I brought with me –' she had a small parcel of nursing equipment, including incontinence materials – 'I'm sending another parcel out to you, you'll have to pay for them I'm afraid, but I'll get them for you at cost, at the wholesale price. Now Mrs Greege is coming in every day for the time being, and I'll call out every second day for a while, and I think you should mend your fences with Dr Hogan, don't you? Jesus, Mary and Joseph, that daft wife of his.' Sheila Cooper would always make Ellen smile. 'And if you want to write a quick note to your mother I'll post it for you at the Post Office, it will go more quickly.'

Shrugging on her coat, she said, almost slyly, 'You're a remarkable girl, you know. Don't ever let anyone gainsay you that.'

In those first two weeks of August, through a combination of hard practical assistance and new emotional support, the worst rampart of Ellen's crux was thereby broken through. By talking to Nurse Cooper, she managed to regain some purchase on her life.

'Look, you might as well know,' said Sheila, 'you have a very hard time ahead of you.'

By now, they had all helped to conquer Ellen's main fear – that through lack of care for Thomas she might be judged unfit even to look after him or Helena.

Her next great anxieties, the house and the school, showed no signs of being resolved. At Nurse Cooper's prompting, she wrote to the Canon, and received a reply from the housekeeper to the effect that the Canon was on his holidays in Lahinch for a fortnight.

'Then write to the Curate,' said Nurse Cooper impatiently.

The Curate wrote back saying it was the Canon's business, and could only be dealt with when the Canon returned.

'But the school is supposed to open in three and a half weeks,' wailed Ellen.

On one of the mornings, Nurse Cooper arrived, not red-faced and glistening on her bicycle, but unfurling from Dr Hogan's car. He followed her up the pathway to the front door, and came in, not unsheepishly, his stethoscope hanging from his pocket. Ellen greeted him.

'I owe you an apology,' she said.

'Ach, what apology. Not at all. Not at all. Sure you missed, your aim is bad. And 'twasn't a big stone anyway,' and Ellen smiled a little, not just at his warm response but at the fact that he was wearing the virulent bow tie Thomas especially despised.

'It would be no harm,' said Nurse Cooper, 'if he had a look at all three of you.'

'She's not the worst,' said Dr Hogan, grinning at Nurse Cooper.

'No, then, she's not,' agreed Ellen.

Helena lay in a crib on the table, kicking her heels in the morning air. Doctor and nurse together tapped the child, looked in her eyes, listened to her little chest, looked in her ears and at her fingernails and whispered to each other, while Ellen stood at a distance, watching them, but not hearing what they said to each other, which made her nervous.

'Right, so,' said Dr Hogan as Nurse Cooper replaced Helena. 'Well, you have her in grand fettle. She's like a thoroughbred, she's stall-fed. D'you see, if she was anyone else's child, I'd be remarking on how well they were looking after her, but in your case, all credit to you, under all the circumstances. She said –' he indicated Nurse Cooper – 'that you were a good bit of stuff.' He approached Ellen, and held out a chair. 'We'll have to look at yourself, now.'

She sat down, and took off her blouse, and he checked her breathing, her pulse, the eyes, the ears. He asked her questions about sleeping and eating, whether her body had returned to 'its monthly normal'?

She dressed again, and he sat in front of her, eyeing carefully, and said, 'I'd say you were on your way to a good recovery. You had bad shock. And shock is a fright altogether, a fright to recover from. That's an awful time you're after being through, I've nearly not seen as bad in the war. We'll be keeping an eye on you, though.'

Then he asked to 'have a look at the man himself'. They stood beside the reclining bed, and Nurse Cooper joined them.

'Haven't you him grand?' exclaimed the doctor. 'Good God above! And you say you're only after starting to do this properly. A hospital wouldn't do him better. A nursing home would, of course,' he said to Nurse Cooper with alacrity. 'Good morning, Master Kane,' he said. 'How are you this morning?'

Ellen made no remark, accustomed now to Mrs Greege and Nurse Cooper addressing Thomas all the time. Dr Hogan examined first the location of the crucial wound. He pushed the hair aside and looked very carefully at the temple, trying to get the maximum light to bear on it by turning Thomas's inert head a little.

'Dth. Is there ever any bleeding from this?'

Ellen acknowledged that once or twice a little blood had appeared on the towel, but she put it down to her own clumsiness in washing Thomas's hair too vigorously, and perhaps rubbing the healing wound.

'No. For some reason,' Doctor Hogan spoke musingly, 'that's taking a long time to heal fully, like there's something stopping it at the core.'

Nurse Cooper bent to look at it.

'If you have an antimacassar at all,' said Jack Hogan, 'put it there behind his head; it'll stop him from going bald where the head is rubbing on the pillow.'

He stood back. 'I want you to do something for me,' he said. 'I want you to start an observation pattern. Will you do that?'

Ellen asked what he meant.

'I want you to watch him, to sit here and watch his face, for long-ish stretches of time. Bring the baby in and let her kick there on the rug, or if you're having a cup of tea. Just sit here for not less than ten minutes at a time, to begin with, and then up to a quarter of an hour, then twenty minutes, and bring a notebook with you, and if you see any change of any kind at all, write it down.'

'What kind of change?'

'Anything. If he suddenly jerks his breathing, or if an eyelid even moves. I don't even know what I mean myself – yet. But write down the time it happens at.'

He began a long examination of Thomas, and said, unable to avoid a hint of despondency, 'He's as strong as an ox.'

As he took his leave, promising to call back and collect Nurse Cooper around five, he said to Ellen, 'I've another favour to ask you. A harder thing altogether. Do you think you could manage it?'

Ellen replied with the first ever hint – and it was only a small and distant vapour – of her former amused asperity: 'I can't know until I know, can I?'

'I'll tell you what it is. Poor Ernestina Stephenson up there is in a bad way. Lot of pain. But like yourself she's a great battler. Any

355

chance you'd call up and say hallo to her some day Nurse Cooper is here to let you free.'

'I'll see,' said Ellen.

'Did he not say anything else to you?' asked Nurse Cooper.

'No. What else?'

'Well, something good. A bunch of them is putting pressure on the Canon over your case. Time the men around here got off their backsides and stood up to the priests.'

She did not add that so far they had run into a stone wall, and that the Canon and Curate were both saying Ellen was going to have to vacate the house to make way for an incoming Principal.

Although Ellen strengthened every day, her mood still dipped terribly every evening when she found herself alone. On four separate occasions she returned to her ledger, faithfully attempting to carry out Herbert's request. Nothing flowed from her pen, no list of choices, no plans, no hopes.

Her father arrived unexpectedly on the bus, carrying a big cardboard box full of meat and fruit which the conductor unloaded for him. Ellen, overjoyed to see him, also found herself flipping back to the awful greyness of those early days, when she had Thomas at home to herself and she did not know the first thing as to how she should nurse him. Five minutes after her father arrived, she went upstairs saying she wanted to change into something cleaner, but in reality seeking a moment in which to recompose herself.

Bob, to her surprise, got on immediately well with Mrs Greege, and when Ellen came back down the two were deep in conversation. He turned to give Ellen his attention.

'Can I see – himself?' he asked.

'Yes,' said Ellen.

'Thomas, Dada is here to see you,' and she arranged a lapel of Thomas's collar. She had taken to folding his hands in his lap, and even though his head lolled sideways, Thomas still seemed like somebody sleeping.

'He looks – fine,' said Bob.

'No, he doesn't, he looks grey, and older than he is – but he doesn't look dead,' said Ellen emphatically. 'Now Thomas, we'll be back later. All right? We're just going to sit on the seat outside and have a chat,' and they left the room.

'Can he actually hear you?' asked Bob.

'No,' she replied curtly.

'Do you know,' asked Ellen one day, 'the history of my relationship with Mrs Greege?'

'I got a fair idea from her,' said Nurse Cooper. 'That's one of the reasons I told you you were a remarkable girl.'

At long last, a note came from the Canon, but not with the crucial news Ellen desired: instead, he enclosed a letter of permission from the Department to postpone the opening of the school for a minimum of two weeks.

Next day, Sheila Cooper said, 'Mrs Greege has a surprise for you tomorrow.'

In this, the third week of August, the temperature climbed.

Mrs Greege, when imparting something of importance, always spoke over her shoulder, as she did now: 'There's a girl in Kilkenny, a lay sister in the Mercy Convent. She's coming over to see you, she's leaving the Convent.'

Ellen said, 'For what?'

Mrs Greege said, 'She's a great worker.'

Essie Doherty had a slightly cleft palate and the energy of a steam engine: she had been as thoroughly trained in domestic work as a human being could be.

'Another debt clocked up to Mrs G.,' reflected Ellen to Nurse Cooper.

'Not debts, Ellen,' said Nurse Cooper, 'not at times like these.'

Essie's arrival lifted huge burdens. On her bicycle, this large mild woman with her elephantine suitcase tied with a pair of leather straps, sweated under a heavy winter coat. She lugged the case up the stairs behind Ellen, and when she came down shortly afterwards she had already put on her overall. No discussion of any kind took place; no length of stay was discussed. Like a ploughhorse Essie strode into the housework, and could 'bake, sew, iron and cook', she told Ellen, who, at first, had a little difficulty understanding Essie's rather difficult speech full of the letter 'n'. They agreed terms – a pound a week and every second Sunday afternoon and evening off. Ellen stood looking at Essie, and smiled at her.

In the late afternoon, hearing voices, Ellen turned from where she sat observing Thomas – in whom she had so far not noted down a single change for Dr Hogan – and saw, on the road outside, Canon Jeremiah Williams, brown from the sun. He stood pointing out the house with his walking-stick to a man and a woman dressed in good clothes.

'Oh, Jesus, no,' she said, and went to the door: when the Canon saw her standing there, he led the strangers away, back down towards the village.

It took Ellen several hours to overcome the feelings of panic: the need to answer Essie's questions as to where she kept things, and other domestic procedures, afforded some distraction. In bed that night she lay awake for hours.

In the morning she discovered another bonus in Essie: the convent where she worked was also a retirement home for senile priests, and she had had to look after old men as if they were babies. With Thomas, Essie proved expert, and swift, and respectful.

At one o'clock, with Helena and Thomas fed and settled, and changed until the late afternoon, Ellen said to Essie, 'If I go out for an hour, will you be all right?' Upstairs, Ellen went through her wardrobe. Any summer clothes belonged to last year, and everything she touched had some memory of Thomas. She chose her cream dress, her good brown court shoes and decided not to wear a hat. She also, for the first time since last May, chose the best underwear she had, and some scent.

The most difficult part would be the walk through the village. In the event she met nobody, and she swung to the shaded side of the road and quickly down the slope to the Canon's house. A passing cyclist, or horseman, or a rare motorist would have seen a woman who looked older than twenty-six years, but would have been drawn to her presence. The slightly frizzy hair, the quick, swinging walk, the good clothes and the brown bag over her arm; not a farmer's daughter or wife, and, though not a native, a woman who had some sort of belonging to the place; and an air of determination.

'He's in,' said the hostile housekeeper, 'but he's reading his Office.'

'I'll wait,' said Ellen.

Half an hour later, the housekeeper came back. 'The Canon says he has to have his dinner yet.'

'I'll wait,' said Ellen, in the tiled hall with the spiders and the dried-out potted plant.

Half an hour later, 'The Canon says he has a letter to write to catch the post.'

'I'll wait,' said Ellen, her heart growing heavier on the hard mahogany chair, behind the stained-glass front door.

He kept her waiting two and a quarter hours. When the housekeeper showed her in, Ellen opened fire, her patience gone.

'Canon, what kind of manners have you, keeping a woman in my circumstances away from her responsibilities for over two hours? You wouldn't do it to me if my husband was up and about.'

Having arranged himself behind his table, Jeremiah rose, and immediately knocked some things over, on the table's surface, not to the floor, but it was enough.

Ellen stormed on. 'And what do you mean by showing people the house where I and my stricken husband and our baby live, without ever coming and having the manners to talk to me about my future as your employed teacher?'

Jeremiah Williams fought back. 'I hear you have Jews as friends, and that you had a Jewman calling to visit you?'

Ellen almost ran across the room, then stopped.

'My God!' she said. 'My God! I'm going to tell the world on you.'

Eyes wide, she stared at him. For a moment she touched the edge of his table, then turned, left the room and the house and walked home, where she raced upstairs and collapsed on the bed in the heat of the afternoon.

Essie called up.

'Ma'am, there's someone at the door. A woman.'

Miriam Hogan's straw hat made Ellen smile.

'I love your flowers,' she said, 'will you come in?'

'No, no,' said Miriam. 'I brought you these.' She had an armful of magazines.

'My husband will be cross,' said Miriam, 'when he thinks I've finished with them he cuts out the corset advertisements,' and she tripped away.

=

Next morning at half-past ten, Essie, on her way to the clothes lines, turned back and said, 'Ma'am! Ma'am! There's a man in the garden.' She rushed in and closed the back door.

Ellen turned pale. 'What's he like?'

'A big fella. Awful big.'

Ellen ran upstairs and twitched the lace curtains in the left-hand bedroom. The Quinn man, a bucket near his feet, nonchalantly dug Thomas's potatoes, filled his bucket and strolled away the way he had come, through a gap in the Quarterground hedge. Ellen, paralysed with fear, sat on the bed.

When she returned to the kitchen, Essie said, 'Ma'am, I don't know anyone around here, but I don't like the look of that fella.'

Ellen said, 'Oh, Jesus, help me, Oh, Jesus, help me. I'll have to do something about it.' Later, after a preoccupied day, she sat at the table and wrote a letter.

'Essie, do you know the Parochial House?'

'No, Ma'am.'

'Go down the village and carry on down the hill, the big cream house on your left, there's an orchard beside it.'

'Oh, I seen it and I coming here, Ma'am, with an avenue?'

'That's it.'

> Dear Canon,
>   This morning at half-past ten, that man from the village came to my garden and dug a bucket of our potatoes and took them away. I don't know what to do.
>
>   Yours faithfully,
>   Ellen Kane (Mrs)

'Essie, just say to the housekeeper that it is urgent, but there isn't an answer required.'

When Essie returned, Ellen asked who took the letter?

'A woman who put on a holy face,' said Essie, making Ellen laugh.

Next morning, Essie said, 'Ma'am, look! Coming in the gate! With a fork and a bucket.'

Again Ellen watched from behind the curtains. It took Canon Williams half an hour to fill his bucket, then he walked to the front door and knocked.

Ellen said, 'Good morning, Canon.'

He said to her, 'This is my own bucket. If you empty the potatoes out I can take this away with me, have a clean bucket for me here tomorrow, would you?'

'Won't you come in, Canon?'

'You should be pitting them potatoes fairly soon, Mrs.'

Essie brought back his bucket and he strolled away.

He returned next morning, and dug some more, and the morning after that, and the morning after that. On each occasion he walked slowly through the village, the fork angled over his shoulder. Nobody else appeared again in Ellen's garden.

On the fifth morning, the Canon said to Ellen, 'Can you open the school for me on Monday the 13th of September. Officially.'

AUTUMN 1926

24

The weather continued bright and hot. The routine of the house promoted a semblance of normality, and by the end of August Ellen had analysed this mood as the shape into which things would settle, rather than any reminder of the way they once were. Essie burgeoned, a docile boon, country wife to Ellen's leadership of the home. Ellen's looks began to return when she permitted them, but despair still ambushed her – when she opened the post; or when feeding Thomas proved unusually difficult – sometimes he gagged; or in the stillness of an afternoon when a bird suddenly sang nearby; or feeling the dew on the bushes in the morning as she fetched some of 'his' vegetables or fruit, as she considered them. She had not even paused to consider how she might address the gardening problems in the coming year.

On the morning of the second Sunday in September, the day before school opened again, Ellen went back to Mass, for the first time, and most apprehensively. She expected to be stared at from the moment she stepped off her bicycle to walk the last hundred yards up the hill; she anticipated the feel of their eyes on her up along the aisle.

'I have to be as normal,' she told herself. 'As normal.'

At the point where the churchyard wall began, some twenty yards from the actual gate, a woman Ellen only knew by sight came forward. Of her, Thomas had said, 'Watch that one. She'll talk sweetly and with a big smile, and when she's gone you'll feel the sore spot where her jab landed.'

Not this morning.

'Ma'am,' she said, 'how're you off for eggs? And how are you yourself? And how's the baby? And how's the Master?' She fell into step beside Ellen, and said, 'Sure we're all praying for you.' A dozen women walked and drifted towards Ellen before she had even reached the church gate, all talking to her and nodding, mostly gravely, and wishing her well, and asking was it all right if

365

they called to see her, and was there anything she wanted?

'Ma'am,' said one of them, 'Mrs Greege was telling me herself, out of her own mouth, what a great woman you are; she said she never seen a woman bear a burden like yourself.'

Another said, 'Ma'am, that Essie, she's a horse of a woman,' to which Ellen replied, 'Oh, she certainly is.'

From a third, 'And you have your figure back an' all, after the baby, Ma'am, isn't that awful quick, that's great.'

In a sober and concerned sorority, they virtually blocked Ellen's path, and their soft rising-and-falling voices said, over and over, 'Don't forget now, if you ever need a day's work, or a woman to look after the baby and the Master, or the blankets washed . . .'

One shy young woman who had wed into a cottage the week before Thomas and Ellen themselves married, said, 'Ma'am, I had my baby last week, and inside in Nurse Cooper's you're the talk of the place. They say you're great altogether.'

Mrs Martin Burke walked across the road and said, 'You're not to think of stirring out of that house. My Martin knows people high up, and we're related to W. T. Cosgrave. Martin is after talking to the Canon. And my nephew knows someone well placed in the Department.'

Ellen replied, 'Thanks, thanks. You're very good.'

As she reached the corner of the church wall, and began to turn toward the gate, the men standing in their habitual confabulation, thirty or so of them, straightened up in their leaning line, and one by one touched their peaks, or raised, or even took off their caps. This proved too much: Ellen lowered her head, and failed to stop the tears. By the time she parked her bicycle and reached the church door, the bell began to ring. Never had Ellen paused to consider how she and Thomas had been a nightly discussion point in the quiet homes.

But as she left the church she saw the large figure of the Quinn man standing alone, a horse's bridle over his arm, just outside the gate on the right-hand side. She looked away.

On that afternoon, with Essie on her half-day, Ellen finally managed to put into practice the first of Herbert's suggestions: she wrote a timetable for herself, and pasted it in the inside front cover of her ledger.

6.00. Rise; say my Prayers; wash: dress in housework clothes.

6.30. Breakfast.

7.00. Begin Thomas: wash, change, dress, turn and feed.

8.00. Helena – feed, change, wash (every second day a bath) and settle: play with her for ten minutes.

9.00. Change: Leave for school.

12.30. Essie to give Thomas short feed: to feed and change Helena.

3.15. Home from school: dinner: me to change and feed Thomas.

5.00. Housework: own washing and darning: bills: any school work: Progress Record, etc. school forms to fill in, etc.

6.00. Helena: long play: observe Thomas.

7.00. Thomas's last feed: settle him for the night: then settle Helena.

8.30. Rest!

10.00. Bed!

Opening the school door wrenched her: the musty smell, the clock long stopped without winding for the summer; ink dried to the bottoms of inkwells – none of this would have happened if Thomas . . . She could have cracked apart when she saw a child posting a broken nib through the famous knot-hole in the corner of the wooden partition. The new temporary Assistant Teacher, a Miss McGoldrick, did not seem much good: Ellen took the Senior room, freezing all her emotions and concentrating on giving out new books, pencils, exercise copies, arranging chalk, ink, pens. Opening Thomas's main cupboard she saw all the supplies laid out in rows – the blotting papers, his rulers, spare inkwells.

In the afternoon, she departed the day's curriculum in order to relieve her tension and created the pleasure of a Singing lesson.

First she took them through *Curwen's Modulator* and variations:

'*Doh, Ray, Me, Fah, Soh, Lah, Ti, Doh.*
Doh, Ti, Lah, Soh, Fah, Me, Ray, Doh.'

She began a new song, teaching them the words of the opening verse:

'*O'er the ocean flies a merry fay,*
Soft her wings are as the clouds of day,
As she passes all the blue waves say,

Marionina, do not roam:
Whither, whither is your home?
Come and turn us into foam.
Marionina! Marionina!
Come, oh, come, and turn us into foam.'

By the end of school, the whole room, Third, Fourth, Fifth and
Sixth classes, boys and girls from eight years old to just short of
fourteen, had satisfactorily begun to speak the lines from memory:
then Ellen briefly hummed them through the notes.

As the four pupil 'sweepers' clunked about after three o'clock,
she sat at Thomas's desk to finalize the Roll for the day, but child-
like, could not reach up or forward sufficiently to the top of the
Roll Book: she made a note to bring some cushions. Timmy Quinn
was absent: he had been sent 'to live with an aunt'.

On that first Monday, Ellen came home from school exhausted, so
tired that she had to look in her ledger to check what the schedule
commanded next. Mrs Greege had looked in and had left word
with Essie that she was going to call tomorrow after school with
some stewed apple for Thomas. Helena had started taking
solids – 'Not before time,' said Nurse Cooper, 'don't mind these
old wives.'

'Blast,' said Ellen, more to herself than to Essie, 'that means I'll
get no chance to talk to Sheila Cooper' – who was also expected.

Ellen finished her dinner, a stew she had prepared with Essie
that morning, went upstairs, changed her clothes and came down
to begin on Thomas. Hitherto, she had only spoken to him a little
self-consciously, always stopping when Essie came near, although
Essie rambled on to him all the time, and even said to Ellen, ''Tis
the first time I ever talked so free to a man who never talked to
me,' and Ellen managed to see the humour.

Between them they had begun to deal very efficiently with
Thomas, apart from the feeding which would always be difficult.
Now Ellen provided the finishing touches – some milk from a large
spoon – while Essie cleared away the bits and pieces, and took the
big basin out to the scullery.

Without thinking – and perhaps even thinking aloud – Ellen
said, 'Thomas, dear, would you by any chance remember where
the Inspectors' Reports are kept?'

So preoccupied was she, that she did not realize for a hugely absent-minded moment why he didn't answer.

'Are they in your high desk – or did you bring them home?'

Abruptly she stood up. 'Oh, God, Thomas, I'm sorry, I really am. I forgot.'

Then, hand to lips, she addressed herself aloud, 'No I am not sorry. What are you doing, Ellen?'

A new sensation began to materialize in her – an entirely different kind of loneliness, not at all like the feeling she knew when she first came to Deanstown and spent those nights in Mrs Greege's; or in those awful first days alone in the house with Helena; or during the worst times of all so far, directly after she took Thomas home from the hospital: this anguish was sharp, and the more bitter for its unexpectedness. She paced a little beside his chair, both fists flailing up and down in her small agitated beatings of the air. 'Now I see why they wanted me to talk to him – to you. Now I see it.'

Crouching on one knee, she held Thomas's fish-like hand, and said fiercely, 'From now on, my dear Thomas, I am going to talk to you every day. And every night.'

That evening she relaxed more easily than she could remember having done for months. In her ledger, on the page after the (still blank) one headed, 'My Choices', Ellen copied in the address in London from which she could get, by subscription, the *Ladies Home Journal: The Rolls House Publishing Company, Ltd, 2, Breams Buildings, E.C.4.* She made a note to order pattern no. 5088, for *a tailored georgette dress: in navy, or any plain colour desired. Shirring at the shoulder seams in front, a slightly bloused bodice, and a gathered front section of the skirt soften the strictly tailored effect of the long tight sleeves with their flaring cuffs, and the wide flat belt that extends all around.*

Standing at the parlour door, she said, 'Thomas, I'm going to keep a record of things I know you'd like to know about eventually. Deaths, auctions, and that,' and returned to the ledger. She took a cutting from the *Irish Independent*.

FARMER COMMITS SUICIDE

Our Abbeyfoyle Correspondent writes:

A respectable well-to-do farmer named Cornelius MacCurtain of Kilbaha, committed suicide on Saturday by tying a large stone around his neck and throwing himself into a quarry pond

on his farm some ten feet deep. Deceased was about sixty years of age.

Under this she noted:

Perambulator for sale (almost new); very little used; cost £8.10s. For further particulars apply to Box 115 this office.

> Monday, 13th September 1926.
> 9.00 p.m. The house is silent. Helena is asleep. Is dear Thomas asleep or awake? How can I ever tell? How long will he live for like this? How can I ever tell that either? All I know at this moment is that this is the first time since Tuesday, 11th May, that I have not felt terrified.

At which point she closed the ledger, put it away, sat in thought for several minutes, then went to bed, checking Thomas and Helena *en route*.

The new routine strengthened Ellen: the joy she found in teaching renewed her: her anguish came within her control – she became somewhat capable of her own distress. Initial problems now containable, others grew approachable – and major pieces of outstanding business needed attention. The Canon had not said one word regarding her position, or the house, or her future. In the garage, that idle, bright car tantalized her; it could prove so useful. Tax and other forms had to be filled in. Thomas's money remained a problem, although she would now have her own salary back again (it had been paid to him by arrangement from the date of their marriage). Essie did the shopping; Ellen no longer had to rely upon Mrs Greege, her sons, or the convenient parcels of meat brought by Sheila Cooper.

Four months had passed since the shooting of Thomas. No culprit had been found. Fears of further violence against Thomas, or even against herself and Helena, had abated a little, in a natural way. Sometimes, despair made a raid: however, school and home together now so exhausted her that Ellen had less time to think.

Deeper questions remained: they concerned, among other things, her own guilt at how she had 'misjudged' – as she put it to Sheila Cooper – the conduct of her own marriage. When this thought surfaced, she reminded herself that she had not yet replied to Father John Watson's two letters.

Her appearance at Mass and in front of her pupils began to give the impression that she had returned to the community, and people felt licensed to call.

To the Sergeant she said, 'Any progress?'

'Ma'am,' he replied, 'Not hide nor hair.'

Softly she enquired, 'And nobody suspected?'

'Ma'am, sure how could we suspect any Christian creature when we haven't a thing to go on?'

'Sergeant, have you a conscience?'

'Ma'am, there isn't a thing in the world anybody can do about anything in all this. I mean to say, things are going very quiet around here, that's one good thing, there's a lot of guns handed in under the amnesty, and that.'

'Very well, Sergeant. I won't say another word.' He looked uncomfortable.

'Talking of conscience, Ma'am, the other thing, Ma'am, is – knowing yourself and the Master, and the way the two of you are regarded, the thing people are saying, Ma'am, and now that the two of you have a little babby, they're all saying that anyone who'd do such a terrible thing, sure such a person'd feel terrible regret altogether.'

'Regret?' echoed Ellen with a note of sharp doubt, and said no more.

She pounced on Dr Hogan. 'How many times do I have to ask you? I'll ask you again. I want you to get me all the medical information you can. I know I've been trying to keep myself together, but now I have time to pay attention to the real issue.'

'But you said yourself there was an improvement in him?'

'Mild, Dr Hogan, mild. That's all. I want him cured. C.U.R.E.D. I want him to be operated on. Or whatever. It might be in Cork, or in Dublin, or in London. Anywhere. But I want it done.'

'Ma'am, I'm asking everyone. You see yourself, he's as close to conscious as you could get.'

'Dr Hogan – my husband, Thomas Kane, cannot speak. I do not know whether he can hear. Or see. His eyes are half-open, but only now and again, and when they are half-open there is no expression in them. And what will the winter do to him? Yes, I agree, his response to food in his mouth has slowly improved. But he is still, to all intents and purposes, "living dead". Now, what can you find out? And don't show your face to me at this front door until you find out something? Do you hear me, Doctor?'

By creating new arrangements with Mrs Greege and Sheila Cooper during the first week back at school, Ellen guaranteed that some reassuring senior presence came to the house every day of the week. Not for almost a month had Mrs Greege made a snide or cutting remark. Ellen began to answer the correspondence which had mounted all summer. The weather continued unusually hot.

On Thursday night she stood at the door of the parlour, *The Leader* in her hand.

'Thomas, did you ever hear this Household Hint? "Paraffin will last longer and produce a better light if a piece of salt, the size of a marble, is placed in the reservoir of the lamp." I'll put it in, I think,' and she cut it, and pasted it in the ledger.

On Friday, an Inspector of Schools arrived, to her initial dismay, as she recalled how Thomas hated them.

'They don't know our jobs, and they don't know their own,' he always said, and indeed one of his planks in the policy-making discussions for a Teachers' Union had been the formulation of a national demand to have appointed as Inspectors only those who had originally been fully trained teachers.

This Inspector turned out an angel in disguise.

'I only called,' he said, 'because someone in Dublin, a friend of a neighbour of yours – do you know a Mrs Burke? – asked high up, in case you needed a hand, but I can enter it as an official visit, which means nobody will come near you for three or four years. I'm not going to do an Inspection, or anything.'

Ellen told him the Canon had not yet resolved the Principalship, and that she had formally asked to be appointed to the position, 'given the unusual circumstances'.

The Inspector, bald as an egg, rubbed his head and chuckled. 'I know Jeremiah of old,' he said, 'I knew him when he was a Curate, and damn troublesome he was then. But he's afraid of Bishops and

Government departments. I'll call down and put the heart cross-
wise in him.'

Sheila Cooper had told her in August about Power of Attorney –
how she might be able to have Thomas's money released. On
Saturday she received a letter from the Bank's Legal Agent in
Dublin, confirming the probability of her enquiry's success.

Val Vousden called to the school.
    'Ma'am, I've great news for you and the boss. I have nearly all
the instruments, bar one cornet and one trombone. I'm after tracing, you'll never believe me, eight of the original fourteen or fifteen
musicians, they're some of the rest of them dead, and there's some
emigrated, but out of sons and cousins and nephews, there's a
chance now that I could get well a dozen, maybe, together.'
    'You must have worked very hard, Mr Vousden.'
    'Everyone calls me Val. I did, and Mrs Heffernan is after making
a pile of uniforms for me. Blue and gold, Ma'am, they're gorgeous,
with a red stripe down the trousers. She made the first one last
Christmas. Now, the thing is, Ma'am, would the boss ever let us
use the school for practising in?'
    'He would, I'm sure, Mr Vousden. When d'you want it?'
    'If we could have it of a Saturday or a Sunday, Ma'am, we'd be
very careful, we're not them MacReadys.'

Four days later, the Post Office Legal Officer wrote to Ellen enclosing the Power of Attorney forms for Thomas's savings, and instructions on how to proceed. The essentials had begun to come right,
and yet, hour upon hour, Thomas, pitifully supine, lay a hundred
and fifty yards from the school in what had been their adventure-
some parlour, its new furniture now pushed to one side to make
way for the mahogany, slanting bed-chair.

Her success with the day-to-day practicalities had given Ellen's loneliness only light succour, and, as she said in an unguarded moment
to Mrs Greege, she dreaded a day when she would have mastered
her burdens so fully that time would hang from her hands. Her truest
relief – and she resisted admitting it to herself – began slowly to
materialize when she talked to Thomas nightly.

—

Herbert and Leah and the two girls arrived, tripping off the bus, the girls carrying posies and wearing shiny shoes and insisting they inspected everything at once, inevitably seeking the baby before anything else.

'But – on a Saturday?' asked Ellen in surprise. 'What happened to your Sabbath?'

'We are allowed to do the works of God, and that includes visiting the sick,' said Herbert, although Leah whispered to Ellen later that he had had an argument with their new Rabbi, a Cork man, who was not turning out to Herbert's liking, and that anyway, when they got home that evening, Herbert would spend an hour or two reading prayers.

'Some day,' said Ellen, 'I will ask Herbert to tell me the whole story of how he prays, and what he says to God, and where he's different from me.'

Leah asked, 'Your prayers must have stood to you in all your trouble?'

'Yes and no,' answered Ellen, surprisingly evasive, and then availed of a question from Rachel – 'Does Helena eat potatoes and meat?' – to quit the subject.

They all had a grand, busy lunch, with Leah giving Essie the benefit of all her warmth, and praising Ellen for finding her. Herbert sat at the head of the table and the children, summoned from the cats and the garden, had more lemonade than was good for them.

The adults unspokenly feared the moment when the children would tire of their distractions and forget their manners. Finally they asked. Leah and Herbert had already called in to the parlour to inspect Thomas, and say 'Hallo': the subject then slipped into abeyance during the pre-lunch bustle.

Ellen surprised them all by answering, 'Now, girls, do you know what to expect when you see Uncle Thomas?'

'Mamma says he isn't well,' said Rachel.

'Oh,' said Ellen, 'he's much more than just not well. Uncle Thomas had a very bad accident to the side of his head. Since then he hasn't spoken to us, or seen any of us, and we don't know if he can hear us. He just lies there and we care for him very much. We wash him and feed him, like a big, tall baby, and maybe you can even help.'

Hand in hand, she led the two from the kitchen to Thomas's

room, while Leah and Herbert looked at each other with raised eyebrows.

'Thomas, look who's here?' Ellen called. 'I talk to him all the time,' she explained in a lower voice. 'I tell him what the weather is like, and I tell him who has written us letters, and I tell him who was bold in school today, and I tell him what's in the newspapers, and sometimes I cut things out of the newspapers for him to read when he gets better again.'

'There's a funny smell?' wrinkled Rachel, who reached out a hand to touch Thomas's bed-chair.

'Rachel is wearing a lovely yellow ribbon, Thomas, and Sarah has new black patent shoes with buttons on them,' said Ellen.

The girls stood there, holding Ellen's hands tightly and looking transfixed.

'Aren't you going to say hallo to him?' asked Ellen. 'No? All right,' she pacified, 'maybe you can come in and say hallo later.'

She led the children back to the kitchen: with relief they escaped, to Essie in the scullery, and thence to the garden to find the cats again, leaving Ellen, Herbert and Leah alone at the table.

'We were just saying,' said Leah, 'what a change, how things have improved. You keep Thomas beautifully, and Helena looks grand.'

'You must have made a huge effort to get this far,' said Herbert. 'How are you yourself?'

'I am destroyed,' said Ellen, matter-of-factly, elbows on the table. 'I feel – I feel dismantled. I keep going because I must, because I have responsibilities, but I feel destroyed inside me. From time to time I break down, and then I seem to recover some ground, and get better for a few hours, even a day at a time, but then I think – "God this is the rest of my life I'm looking at, and no hope of it getting better." I mean the best thing that can happen to me, if you think about it, is that Thomas might die. What an awful choice?'

'What about prayer?' asked Herbert.

'I pray. But it's like it's coming out of a machine,' said Ellen.

'Any further medical ideas?' asked Leah.

'Not one. Not a single one. No hope. I keep thinking there must be someone somewhere who knows. Although I'm supposed to be talking to Dr Hogan tomorrow.'

Sarah came in claiming Leah's attention: Rachel had fallen in the clay of the garden.

Herbert said in Leah's absence, 'How did you get on with what I suggested to you?'

'Not very far. I tried. I'm going to try again.'

'If you're very angry,' said Herbert, 'that might . . . I don't know, it might open up something?'

'Angry?' said Ellen. 'I'm too busy to be angry. Angry?'

Ellen waved them off, standing in the middle of the road, watching in the white dust the small faces of the girls at the back window of the high bus. When she could see it no more, and could only hear a distant growl of the receding engine, she looked despondently at the house where in a few minutes she would begin another drudging, hauling round of feeding, cleaning and changing her two dependents. Turning her back to the house, she walked the three or four paces to the high stone stile in the wall, over which Thomas and she had climbed on the morning after their wedding night.

Only one September in living memory, in the 1880s, an Indian summer forty years earlier, compared, they said, for such golden beauty. Now, the fields of 1926 had wide patches of parched irregular patterns, as if the colour of beige straw had been dragged any which way across the grasses. Aftergrass shone brilliantly blue-green from a meadow harvested in July. Up beyond the Castle, stubble of a cornfield wore a kind of black gold. Across this glorious serenity the earliest short shadows began to fall: a dog barked somewhere very far off, rounding up, no doubt, the cows of the evening to take them home to the yard for milking. On the grass verge beneath Ellen's feet, white dust had coated the broad, bending grass and the purple shiny berry clusters fallen from an elder tree.

From upstairs, where she had gone to lift Helena, Essie drew down the sash of the window, now that the sun had moved around to the side of the house, and the room had cooled. She saw Ellen raise her arms until they rested on the top of the wall. Ellen placed her chin on her arms and stood there, motionless, in grey jumper and grey skirt. Essie chaired the baby up in her arms and, moving the net curtain back a little, pointed to Ellen and said through her half-cleft nasal palate, 'Nlook. Nlook, nthere's your'n Mamn.' The thrush that Thomas liked so much began to sing, 'Your-tea. Your-

376

tea'. Essie and Helena saw Ellen put her face down on her fore-arms, then raise, shake herself and turn towards the gate.

'Ma'am, who's this coming in, look at him, an apparition?'

Ellen twisted, peering round the high back of the chair, and looked out of the window. A dapper man with a white moustache, and carrying a suitcase, walked with a bounce up the path, on the gravel and to the front door. Ellen checked her face in the little hand-mirror on the shelf, and said, 'Essie, look at me, I'm a show.'

With the front door wide open towards the cooling evening, the man was in the hall.

'G'day. Have I the honour of addressing Mrs Thomas Kane?' He pronounced it 'Kine'.

'Yes, and who are you?'

The man put out his hand; he had a white handkerchief like a set of flat triangular sails in his top pocket: one of the triangles had the letter 'J' embroidered on it in red.

'I am a cousin of your husband's. My name is Joe Johnson. I am from Melbourne.'

'Essie, was it the Lord who sent us such entertainment?' Ellen asked hours later when Joe Johnson had left. 'Although my heart sank when I saw the suitcase. I thought he was coming to stay.'

The encounter began unpromisingly.

'Oh, Mr Johnson, I don't know, I didn't know . . .'

'Never mind that, Mrs Kane, I'm on a visit to this old country and I'm tracing every cousin I can think of or find out about. And your husband is the man to meet, they tell me.'

Ellen said coldly, 'Do they now?'

'My great-grandfather was the brother of your husband's great-great-grandfather.'

'I'm afraid, Mr Johnson, that at this moment . . .'

'And that makes me your husband's second cousin once removed –'

'I'm afraid,' protested Ellen once more –

'And you know what they say,' quipped Joe Johnson, 'a second cousin once removed is very difficult to replace.'

In spite of herself, Ellen burst out laughing. 'Come in,' she said, 'only for a minute, though. And anyway, that would be second cousins twice removed.'

'Twice removed? Worse again,' cracked Joe. 'And here I am.' He sat down at the kitchen table and accepted the offer of a cup of tea.

Ellen began to explain. 'You don't seem to have heard about my husband, Thomas.'

'Is he in clink?' said Joe. 'That is how his Australian cousins began. I hope he's not away leaving a little beauty like you on her ownio? The Kanes always liked handsome women.'

Ellen smiled and blushed.

'Or is he out on the rant, eh?'

'No. He is in the next room.'

'Oh, great, can I see him? Is he decent?'

Ellen asked, 'You don't know at all, do you?'

Joe Johnson replied, 'I know he was a handy man with a point three-oh-three rifle, I know that.'

Ellen shuddered. 'Mr Johnson, my husband, your cousin, is very ill.'

'Oh, my dear girl, I am very sorry.'

'He got – injured. And he has been – unconscious, I suppose you'd call it, since the beginning of May.'

'Can I see him?' asked Joe.

Ellen rose and he followed. The little man stood by Thomas's side, and said, 'Thomas Kane, I am your cousin, Joe Johnson from Melbourne, and the least you might do is say hallo, but if you don't – then I'll do the talking. How do you do?' He took Thomas's hand and shook it energetically. 'All the more room for me not to be interrupted, I hate being interrupted,' and like a performance, Joe Johnson began to talk.

He told them the story of his branch of the family. Convicted as felons for an attempted local conspiracy in 1797, two Kane brothers had been transported to Van Diemen's Land, now Tasmania, and even though their sentences ended within fourteen years, they were never allowed to return to Ireland. They settled and prospered, farmers first, then builders, then steel manufacturers, and now, two generations before Joe, the respectability of white collar work, owning one of Melbourne's largest insurance businesses, and getting interested in these new aeroplanes.

'They told me I'd find the house easily, you were the only ones around here with a car, typical Kane.'

378

He regaled them – wonderful stories of the bush, and the kangaroos, and then he said, 'I have a surprise for you.'

He moved the mahogany table behind Thomas a little to one side, then wheeled the bed-chair around: throughout, Thomas had neither flickered nor stirred. Placing two chairs side by side, as if for people awaiting a performance, he called Essie and directed her and Ellen to sit down. As they sat there, Joe went out to the hallway and they heard the clasps of his suitcase snap open. Returning, he said in a masterful way, 'Now, where's your phonograph?'

'You mean a gramophone?' said Ellen. 'We don't have one.'

'Oh?' Joe looked crestfallen. 'Bugger. Sorry, dear.'

He looked all around the room, then at the table.

'Mind if I move these?'

To clear a space on the table, he moved Ellen's empty crystal bowl and its lace doily to the top of the piano and dusted the table with his sleeve. All this time he had a mysterious flat package under his arm, which he now laid on the table, and unwrapped to reveal two packages. From the larger, square one he took out a gramophone record, with a dark red, gold-printed label, and he laid it flat on the table.

'You've seen one of these?'

'Well, we know what it is,' said Ellen, 'we're not complete goms.'

'"Goms". That's a good one,' chirped unabashed Joe, and arranged the record on the table with the same care as if it had been on a gramophone. He then turned his back, shielding the unwrapping of the second parcel from their view; he was assembling something, and also seemed to be affixing it to his arm.

'What are you doing, Joe?' called Ellen.

'The audience is getting very restless,' said Joe. 'All in good time.'

He spun around, and on the light grey stripes of his forearm sleeve, sat a wooden cut-out of a brightly coloured bird, neither parrot nor parakeet.

'Permit me to introduce you,' cried Joe, 'to the Australian native bird, the kookaburra, otherwise known as "The Laughing Jackass". And this,' he cried on, pointing to the record on the table, 'is a recording of how it sounds, but since we have nothing to play it on, I will just have to do it myself.' He cleared his throat, steadied himself like a concert singer, and held the arm with the wooden

379

kookaburra as stiff as a falconer's. His other arm started to flap like a wing, and from his mouth came an extraordinary sound, like a guttural merry shriek.

'Oooohahahahahahaha-haghhhagh-Oooohahahahahahaha-haghh-hagh-Oooohahahahahahaha-haghhhagh': he kept this up for at least a minute and a half, pausing only to take deep breaths, and stopping only when his face had become dangerously red, and then abruptly said, 'That's it.'

Essie and Ellen applauded. Joe bowed and bowed and said, 'I think that calls for an encore.'

This time, however, he did not flap the free arm as if to simulate the kookaburra's flight; instead he took a pencil from his pocket and, standing beside the gramophone record, kept describing a circular motion over it.

'Ordinarily,' he said, 'as I'm sure you know, the motion is the other way round, it's the record that goes around and around, not the needle.'

'Yes, we'd heard that,' said Ellen drily.

'Very well then,' said Joe, 'let the encore begin.'

He moved the arm with the wooden bird on it up and down, and kept the pencil going around in a circle and then began the screech again.

'Oooohaghhhagh-Oooohaghhhagh-Oooohaghhhagh.' This time, when he had ended his screeching, he made another noise as slowly his flapping bird arm came to a stop.

'Pidyp. Pidyp. Pidyp. Pidyp. Pid. Yilip.'

'What's that?' asked Ellen.

'You ignoramus,' said Joe (he pronounced it 'ignor-ih-mus'); 'that is the noise the bird makes as it settles back on the branch.'

'A good job you told us that,' said Ellen.

Joe Johnson left the house at nightfall. He hugged Ellen, and patted her cheek. 'You're a dear girl,' he said. 'G'bye, Tom, we'll meet again. G'bye, Essie.' Turning to Ellen, he said, 'My dear, y'know it is all going to be all right, don't you? 'Course it is.'

'Mr Johnson,' she said, 'you still don't understand. He wasn't injured in an accident. Thomas was shot.'

Joe looked at her. 'It still makes no odds,' he said, 'this is a house full of life, not of death.' With a new thought, he said, 'Do you know about the dolphins?'

Ellen shook her head.

'We have dolphins in Australia. Dolphins must keep moving in order to stay alive. If they stop they die. If a dolphin is too sick to move, the other dolphins get around it and keep nudging it through the water. That's all you need to have here, my dear – a bit of dolphin work.'

'Oh,' said Ellen, reflecting long after he had gone, 'wasn't that nice? Wasn't that nice? Essie, did you see how natural he was with the Master?' Then in a musing voice she murmured, 'A bit of dolphin work? A bit of dolphin work?'

25

'No. No. No.' Jack Hogan spoke firmly. 'This is a good job here, Miriam, and we're staying here. No. I don't want to move again. No, they are not all laughing at you, dear. No, they are not. Besides how could you know? You never go out and meet them.'

Miriam said, 'I'm sick of this dump, Jack, this hole of a place. All there is to do here is walk.'

'That's what you said when we were in Pallasgreen, Miriam, and you said the same when we were in Kilmacthomas. We have to settle somewhere.'

'I'm not a good wife to you, Jack, and if we were living somewhere else, I would be.'

'That's what you said before, Miriam, and you're not a bad wife.'

'Jack, stop telling lies, you're always telling lies. You pretend to people that I have your dinner ready on the table when you come home and I do no such thing. I never cook a meal for you, I'm not able.'

Jack denied that he ever said such a thing, but he coloured.

'I don't sleep in your bed alongside you, Jack, and I don't know where that's going to lead. As a matter of interest, Jack, do you care for me still?'

Standing at the cupboard, he suspended the breadknife and bread in his hands, and looked at her.

'You never asked me that before, Miriam. Not in twelve years.'

'That is because you seemed to agree with yourself about the way I was.'

'How d'you mean?'

'My mother told you I was – what?'

'"A bit of an oddity",' quoted Jack.

'So, you never tried to stop me being "a bit of an oddity"?'

'Is that what you wanted me to do, Miriam?'

'It would have meant that you didn't treat me like any old farmer's wife.'

'Miriam, I never know what new tack you're trying. If you're serious, Miriam?'

'I am serious, Jack. I hate these long walks I have to take all on my own. But I do a lot of counting, Jack.'

He looked up. 'What is it you count, Miriam?'

'I count the money you got out of marrying me, Jack.'

Mrs Greege said, 'Your friend was stocious last night by all accounts.'

'Who?'

'Who but himself? Jack. Taking the two sides of the road.'

'Dr Hogan? Drunk?'

'As a lord.'

'Are you sure?' said Ellen.

'Certain sure. Three sheets in the wind. Arthur Grant had to drive him home. Nor was it the first time, either. No wonder the wife is as odd as two left shoes.'

Father John Watson wrote a letter.

Thursday,
30th September 1926

My dear Ellen,

What can I say? I can only presume that you have been too distressed, and too frantically busy with everything: it is most unusual not to hear from you, as you are such a prompt correspondent.

I have just called again to Brunswick Square, and never have I seen a house so transformed from lightness to gloom. My heart and my prayers go out to you. In equal proportions, I have heard of your misfortune and your bravery, and all I can say at this moment is how deeply compassionate and sympathetic I feel. We are not privy to every part of His Divine Scheme.

I have deliberately not visited, even though in my

previous two letters I asked your permission. However,
if I may, I shall now come and visit you, and your
charming baby, and perhaps offer some spiritual aid.

>My deepest thoughts go to you.
>Yours faithfully in Jesus Christ,
>John Watson, S.J.

Those marks Ellen saw on the windscreen frame of the car in the garage, those small peppered dents in the edge of the metal frame and on one section of the glass, had the same appearance and consistency as the small black-and-blue marks, those thick, discoloured dots, now all but faded from the back of Thomas's right hand.

'Medium-heavy calibre,' wrote the Sergeant in the Amnesty Receipt Book, having accepted a shotgun.

The first cartridge had struck Thomas's right hand obliquely, bouncing some shot off the skin, then travelled across the car, scattering into the windscreen, some of it missing baby Helena's wrapped feet, one grain slightly nicking Ellen's left hand which was cradling the baby. Other shot from that cartridge exited through the open side of the car beyond Ellen's shoulder, and spent itself in the ditch on the far side.

'Choices. Choices. I have to make the effort,' Ellen thought aloud. 'I wonder if I wrote to Herbert would it help?'

She said to Essie, 'Essie, some night this week, I'm going to ask you if you would do both the Master and the baby, because I have to go down to the school to fill in forms and things, would that be all right? Oh, Essie, you're a trump,' she said, when the big woman beamed at the responsibility. 'That's what you are, a trump card. I'll be back about half-nine or so. I've a lot of things to do.'

'Ah, sure, yes, Ma'am.'

Miriam Hogan walked always in the same fashion: parallel to the road, for miles at a time, and when a cart or a bicycle approached, she sometimes crouched to the ground inside the ditch and watched carefully as, unseeing, they passed by. This morning she looked at Jack's untidy face at breakfast and decided. She would head west: climbing the hill past the church, and dropping down

the other side, she would make for the town, which she did not
intend to enter. The light rain did not bother her at all, fine. The
Dispensary front door does not slam, the wood had swollen last
winter and it must be forced to a gentle close. At ten o'clock, Jack
talked to a woman with a child in the surgery. Miriam walked for
five miles or so, always keeping close to the road, behind the
high hedges, enjoying trying to identify through the bushes the
occasional passer-by. Then, disturbingly, up ahead, she saw a man,
just as she climbed the last slope of that steep hill to the town, and
he walked as she did, in the fields, just inside the ditch. Head
down, peering, searching, he had just come through the bushes
from the road, and now he turned back and, as he did so, he saw
Miriam, started, and returned quickly to the road. She watched
his retreating shoulders as he cycled up the hill standing on the
pedals to get up speed. Miriam Hogan reached the place where
he had been staring, and she stood and stared too. Nothing to be
seen in the field; through a gap in the hedgerow, however, she
observed, as if they had been framed, the earthen weals along the
far roadside bank down which the Kanes' car had slewed on a sunny
morning in May. Miriam walked closer, then clambered out on the
narrow road. She found the marks on the road surface where the
car had first swerved: even though the heat of the summer had
melted some of the tar, the wheel gouges were there to be seen.
She paced it: eighteen yards, she reckoned, from the first swerve
to the last tipsy resting-place. An ash sapling had been wounded
in the car's lurching journey, its bark torn from the slim bole. Back
and forth, back and forth, Miriam walked, looking, looking. She
plucked at grass, at leaves, wiped her hands on the seat of her
camel-coloured skirt. Climbing back inside the ditch, Miriam
turned her face eastwards and home again, and at the last minute
kicked something in the grass.

She walked past the Dispensary and kept going. Behind her, she
heard the noise of Jack's car, the clattering rev he always gave it,
as he emerged on the road from their pathway. He honked and
drew up; Miriam flapped her hand at him in a sign he knew, and
he waved cheerily and drove on. Miriam called to the school and
saw Ellen supervising the children's play. She walked straight
over.

'Don't wait a minute longer,' she said in her abrupt manner, always unable to look in the eye of the person she addressed, always looking down and to one side. 'Get further opinion, my husband is too feckless to manage it for you. If you don't do it I will.'

'Why do you say that? Wait, wait,' called Ellen, but Miriam had turned back and begun to leave the village: to Ellen she looked fairly unstoppable.

'Try Dr Morgan,' Miriam shouted back. 'He's all right again.'

'That's what Nurse Cooper said,' shouted Ellen; 'come back a minute, will you.' Miriam strode off.

The second trigger had been pulled in a reflex action caused by the kick of the gun as it jerked up after the first shot. Half of the cartridge's load went wide, above and ahead of the car's occupants: the other half, a small hard cluster of grains, hit Thomas full on the right temple in a slightly downward trajectory.

'This is the angle, look,' the detective had said, getting the Sergeant to hold a string's end at about the height of the car roof, and he climbed on the ditch to show a descending path. 'So, the assailant was standing about there, or a little farther in? I see.'

Some of the pieces of shot had been recovered in the emergency procedures by Dr MacDonnell, who, even though he had no military experience, recognized the type of metal with which he was dealing: on the Tuesday, forty-eight hours later, with the arrival of some lucidity in Ellen, they all began to agree on what had happened, though without telling her.

'I wish,' said Ellen aloud to herself, 'I could get a slap of salt from the sea on my lips.'

'D'you want these, Ma'am?' Essie interrupted the reverie, and held out a pair of small green silk sachets Ellen had herself stuffed with lavender.

'Let me smell them. Oh, Essie, are you started on those drawers already? Oh, great!' Ellen sniffed them. 'Oh, they're nearly faded,' and Essie looked down at her with all the dear bovine, inarticulate sympathy she could muster.

'Arrah, Ma'am, Ma'am,' she said, when she saw the tears in Ellen's eyes, 'there'll be a day when it'll come right. There will, Ma'am, there will with the help of God.'

'The Master got that lavender in for me, Essie. Specially.'

On the day he planted it, Thomas said, out of the blue, to Ellen, 'Tell me. How much do you believe in God?'

'Thomas! That's nearly blasphemous.'

'No. Straight question. How much do you believe in God?'

'But I believe in Him a hundred per cent.'

'What I mean is. What is the feeling like?'

Ellen held out her fingers to count. 'First thing in the morning I say my prayers. You know that. Then I start the children off with a prayer, maybe a decade of the Rosary if it is a special feast-day, like Saint Monica, maybe, and you know I've great devotion too to Saint Joseph, Thomas. If I could only persuade you to say the Rosary with me in the evening. Then I have my night prayers. And I often say a prayer to myself during the day.'

Now, she crunched the little lavender packets in her hand and pressed them to her nose.

Tuesday, October 5th

My dearest Leah and Herbert,

I need to write this letter to you, even if I never post it. [She did.] I have so many things to consider, and even now I can't easily bring to mind the most difficult of them. I have come down to the school to write this, just like Thomas used to do when he wished to be alone. I've left him washed and clean and fed. Few signs of recovery, I'm afraid, and they give me a very big problem. Is now the time to put a big effort into finding him new medical care?

In fact, I have an awful number of problems, and since you, Herbert, asked me to try and work out my life, I thought the best thing to do was to open the whole thing up and get things fixed one way or another.

I was awfully young when I married Thomas, and when I discovered he was very violent, I got terribly upset. I even wondered whether I should (a) leave him, but there wasn't anywhere I could go. And (b) Helena was on the way and I wouldn't get a job anywhere and I certainly didn't want to go back to Brunswick Square; and even though I knew the two of you would take me in, I knew

too that you wouldn't have enough room for me to stay
for long.

When she addressed such topics, Ellen's stomach troubled her;
she broke off and, shielding the candle's flame in the mild air, went
to the girls' lavatory. Returning, she stood by the door, and looked
at the few lights of the village houses. Since Thomas's prostration
she had avoided passing the Quinn house too closely; the day she
visited the Canon she had walked each time on the far side of the
road, going through the village and coming back, eyes cast down.
Since school reopened, she did the same, yet had to pass the house
every day, the door always firmly closed. Only in the last week she
had begun to look at it directly – as she now did, at the single light
in the dim window.

Do you see the kind of mistakes I was making in my
thinking? Was it that I always paid too much attention
to my faith and not enough to my natural feelings? I look
at Helena now and think – how could such a dear little
dote ever be a murderer (or murderess, I think it is
called)? Then I look at Thomas and I think – I wish I had
not listened so closely to my religion and had brought
myself to be more of a good wife to him. The things that I
thought were sins were not sins at all – and the things I
thought were not sins might have been.

Dear Herbert, you said to me that there were facts it
was all right to be angry about. I feel myself getting very
angry now, but the writing of this letter is helping me
very much. What I think I'll do is – I'll try and go back
and list what you called my 'Choices', Herbert. Despite
all the awfulness of it all, and my day-to-day trying to
pretend Thomas's condition is some way normal (which,
of course, it has become), I feel there's something
building up, both in me and in the general state of all
this.

I suppose this letter makes no sense at all, but I'm
having to try every means I can think of to work things
out. In a queer sort of way, the full shock is only hitting
me now, not in any fashion that will knock me out, but
in a way that has suddenly wakened me up to the fact that

388

I have urgent things to do – and the first of these is to
get something medical done very fast.

You are dear friends to me, the two of you, and Rachel,
and Sarah. Tell them the cats were asking for them, and
my warmest love to you both, and from Helena too. (And,
I suppose, from Thomas.)

Your grateful friend,
Ellen

P.S. Essie is turning out to be a trump of the highest suit
of cards.

As she sealed the letter, Ellen had one last thought: on the back
of another envelope she made a list:

1. The doctors.
2. The school.
3. The car.
4. Father J.W.
5. The Bad.

Placing all the correspondence in her writing-case, she locked the
school and strode home.

'I'm back, Essie!'

'Is that you, Ma'am? Are you back?' replied Essie.

'Essie's always quick on the uptake, Thomas,' remarked Ellen
quietly as she took off her coat standing in front of him, and shook
out her hair. 'I'll just get my writing-pad and sit beside you.' She
had moved the best lamp in the house to the table nearest Thomas.

'"Dear Doctor Morgan," "Malaria", Thomas, I'm writing to him,
all right? "You have probably heard what has happened and I
understand you are back at work. Can you please come and see
us?" Thomas, is it "Yours sincerely", or "Yours faithfully"? I'll put
"Yours – faithfully", I think, I never know which.'

'"Dear Canon Williams,"' she read aloud as she wrote. '"Enough
is enough. Unless you make your mind up within seven days, I
will organize a petition among the parishioners to be sent to the
Archbishop, and a delegation to the Department in Dublin regarding the Principalship. It isn't good to have things the way they

are."' She lifted her head, put her tongue back in her mouth and said, 'Don't you agree with that, Thomas?' She read it again and said, 'So, "Please let me have your reply as soon as possible. Yours sincerely, Ellen Kane. Mrs." That'll soften his cough, as you'd say, Thomas. And Thomas, don't go mad, I'm going to ask Michael Condon to teach me how to drive.'

Ernestina Stephenson proved to have unusual physical durability. To her brother and all who worked for them, and the Harpers and her Uncle Henry, she manifested all summer only what Jack Hogan repeatedly called 'the symptoms of daily life'. After a few days confined to bed, she told him that bed is 'a place where people go to die', and she 'bloody' wasn't going to do that. Cyril's absorption elsewhere and the richness of the harvest for all her relatives meant that long stretches of Ernestina's day went unobserved. She could now slip into her bedroom for frequent rests unknown to anybody, and thus revitalize herself, maintaining the appearance of a normal daily round. The doctor called once a week and Ernestina told her brother, 'He's just friendly.' By the end of September, however, the spells of what she called 'tiredness' grew ever so slightly longer, as she told Dr Hogan, and came ever so slightly oftener.

'But no bleeding any more?'

'No. None.'

She covered her extending absences from the centre of the household with a tale of a project – she had embarked upon a large embroidered bedspread (indeed, she had even purchased all the essentials) and it was 'requiring all my concentration'. Her brother raised no queries, extremely pleased that his extra-mural adventures no longer seemed to whet Ernestina's harsh tongue. If she was friendly with Dr Hogan – what of it? That was her business. God knows, a farm this size caused enough problems: that damned engine: would he sell the yearling, hardly a yearling now, but coming up to prime form?

'I wish Ernestina,' he said one day, 'we could have a bit more meat. We've the roast on Sunday and we have it cold on Monday and Tuesday and Wednesday, and we have a roast again on Sunday, and we have only eggs on Thursday or something. Eh?'

Ernestina replied, 'It was good enough for us that way all our lives, what's wrong with it now?'

Next day, Cyril said, 'Ernestina, are you going to need all that space in the garden for your raspberries next year? You hardly picked any this year, and a great crop you had, and the hotel in Mantlehill will buy carrots from us. And I could put them in there. If you're not needing the space.'

'Shove your carrots in somewhere else.'

Sunday,
October 17th, 1926

Dear Mr Condon,

I am sorry it has taken so long to get you your money for fixing the car, but you know my circumstances and it is only now that I have been able to get the money out of the Bank where it was in my husband's name. Thank you for waiting for so long, and I notice you didn't call or send me a reminder or anything and I very much appreciate that. Also, I was very rude to you when you helped me so much, and I hope you will accept my apology, but you could see the state I was in.

I know it is a foolish question, but in a magazine my sister sent me, I saw a picture of a woman driving a car. Is it possible for a woman to drive my husband's car, and if it is, how would I go about finding out how to do so?

Thanking you again.

Yours faithfully,
Ellen Kane (Mrs)

On Tuesday morning, Dr Hogan's Austin Seven drew up outside the school, and he and a passenger hurried through the rain. Knocking sideways on the open door, he simultaneously caught Ellen's eye and she walked down the classroom, something of Thomas's magisterial-ness in her stride.

'Hallo, Ma'am.' He always had a sturdy greeting.

'The very man, when will we talk about getting some new doctors to come and see the Master?'

'We will, we will, Ma'am, I'm sorry to disturb you, but I brought this man to see you.'

'Oh, good! Are you a doctor? Where are you from?'

The stranger, raindrops on his spectacles, did not work on

391

the land, nor did his jacket and grey trousers suggest wealth or profession.

'Indeed nor I'm not, Ma'am.'

'And who are you then?'

Jack Hogan said, 'I don't even know if you know this, Ma'am, but the time of the polio, the Master and me discussed those letters you used to get.'

'Oh?' said Ellen. 'I thought –' addressing the other man '– that you might be a doctor or something.'

'No, Ma'am, I am not,' he said.

'But you're very sober altogether,' she said.

'This man is the Postal Superintendent in Thurles, and we came here first, we're going on to see the Sergeant in a minute. Or maybe into town to see the Superintendent.'

Ellen asked, 'What? Or – why, I mean . . . ?'

'Ma'am, this man here is after tracing the person who wrote them letters.'

'No?!' Ellen exploded in disbelief.

'I did, Ma'am, 'twas easy enough, that handwriting. We compared it a lot.'

'But how did you – find out?'

The man looked embarrassed.

'Hah,' cackled Dr Hogan, 'the Post Office kettle is for more than making the tea.'

'You mean you steamed them open?'

'I did, Ma'am, but I had the agreement of the Guards. 'Tis illegal except where the Postal Authorities feel there's something wrong, and one of them letters could be construed as a threat.'

'A bad threat,' endorsed Jack Hogan.

'But does the person know?' asked Ellen.

'She doesn't yet, Ma'am, but she'll know any day now, she'll be in the barracks soon, I'd say.'

'So it was a woman?'

'It was, Ma'am, and not any old go-the-road either,' said the Postal Superintendent.

'Well, well,' said Ellen wonderingly.

'You know her, too, Ma'am; at least she knows you.'

'I couldn't even begin to guess,' said Ellen.

'She was at the same Station Mass as you,' said Dr Hogan.

'Oh, my God!' Ellen opened her mouth. 'The long woman with

the bicycle; she has black hair going grey, parted in the middle,' she exclaimed.

'How d'you know that, Ma'am?' asked the Postal Superintendent.

They arranged that Dr Hogan would call for Ellen on whatever afternoon the Sergeant agreed, and take her to the police barracks to meet the woman, and decide charges.

'By the way.' Dr Hogan stuck his hand in his raincoat pocket. 'The wife gave me this for you.' He handed Ellen a lightweight packet – a brown bag folded over its own contents, tied very tight with white string and sealed with sealing wax.

'What's in it?' asked Ellen.

'Haven't a notion,' he said.

'Good-bye now, Ma'am,' said the other man, who seemed a little disappointed at Ellen's general lukewarmth for his discovery: he waited a moment as if for gratitude, then turned and followed Dr Hogan into the rain. Ellen opened the package at Thomas's desk. Around a spent cartridge Miriam Hogan had wrapped a page of blue notepaper. 'I found this inside the ditch at the place where you and your husband had your "accident". Just before I saw it in the grass, a man was searching near the same place, and when he saw me he ran away.' No signature, no identification.

Ellen shut her eyes in fear.

Val Vousden told the man from the *Echo* of his great new project.

'I see myself as a bridge. The music-hall is an urban entertainment, and now I want to bring the countryside into it, so I'm going to revive this Band, because they were the greatest musicians in Ireland, and I want to have them on the stage with me, it will, kind of, represent the new country. And besides which they've had a terrible tragedy in their village and this will rally them. So if you put in your article my request that if anyone knows anything about the Band or its uniforms or its instruments, I'd be most grateful. I have some information already, and that's what I based my famous monologue on. And now I have eleven men, and uniforms all made and repaired, and instruments being fixed up.'

'What was that eejit talking about?' asked the Editor when the man from the *Echo* got back to the office.

=

On Saturday afternoon, Essie had taken Helena for a walk down the road in the pram. Ellen, diverting herself briefly from counting whether she had all her bills paid, went back to the page in the ledger marked *My Choices*, and wrote:

1. I could send Thomas into a home.
2. I could keep him here – for ever.
3. I could neglect him and hasten his death.
4. I could take Helena and disappear.
5. I could –

She paused, went back and underlined the word 'death' three times. Staring at it, she wrote above it, in tiny writing, 'revenge' – and shivered. The ledger flapped shut and she restored it to its drawer, which she locked. She checked Thomas quickly, and for a moment looked at him coolly, then got her bicycle, went to the gate and saw Essie on her way back with Helena, cycled slowly towards her and said, 'I'm just going up to the church to say a few prayers. Will you be all right?'

Essie replied, 'Ngrand, Ma'am. No hurry.'

'Hallo, sweetheart!' And Helena grinned and grinned and waved her arms, her mouth forming an 'O' as she 'uh-uh'ed.

'Hallo again, sweetheart,' said Ellen, and she poked Helena in the tummy. 'I'll steal you, so I will.' Helena gurgled and laughed. Ellen tickled her again, and Helena beamed, and then giggled.

Earlier, Ellen and Essie stood over Helena who lay naked on the towel on the table.

'Look at the folds in that little stomach,' said Ellen smiling. 'You're a disgrace, so you are. A Dis. Grace.' And she bent down and blew air right on Helena's plump navel and the baby laughed. When Ellen did it again and again, Helena laughed uncontrollably. Then Essie laughed. Then Ellen laughed; all three females rendered themselves helpless.

'Ma'am, she's like she was butter-fed,' said Essie finally wiping the tears of laughter from her eyes.

'And then I promised Dr Hogan I'd go up and see that Stephenson girl.'

'Ngrand, Ma'am.'

'Bye, bye, baby, bye-bye, Helena. Peeps? Aaah!' Ellen, leaning across the handlebars, played 'Hidey' with Helena who chuckled, and Ellen cycled away.

—

Someone, the year before Ellen arrived, had painted the plinths of the Sacred Heart and Saint Patrick statues an eye-hurting puce. Built in 1860, at the height of the post-Emancipation zeal, the church's capacity amounted to three hundred people in a completely straight structure: a high, gently arched wooden roof of light oaken rafters, and six tall pointed stained-glass windows on either side, the names of the donors inserted on the glass of each one. On either wall stood two confessionals, the Canon's name above one, black letters on a piece of white card; the Curate's on the other: each confessional door had a piece of purple velvet curtain hanging from the top to waist height. Rows and rows of pews, all stained the colour of mahogany, a little cross inserted on the outside of each one, ranged back as far as the door almost, leaving an open, stone-floor space just inside the front door. In the middle of this space, stood what Thomas called 'The Corral', a new, whitewood enclosure intended for the choir, but the brand-new harmonium had as yet proven entirely unworkable: it had been shipped with part of the pedal mechanism missing; since she came to Deanstown, Ellen, to her regret, had only played the harmonium once – in Silverbridge church at the Confirmation.

Ellen, having donned the headscarf she had put in the bicycle's basket, genuflected and slipped into the place she normally occupied, traditionally the Teachers' pew in the body of the church. No sound could be heard anywhere within the building: in the distance faintly came the voices of some children playing. She changed her mind and went to a seat nearer the tall, rural-baroque white altar, like a spiky wedding-cake, with its gold-coloured sanctuary lamp and its engraved glass tabernacle door.

Identifying, as she always did now, the exact spot on which she had stood when marrying Thomas, Ellen took out her rosary beads and began:

'In the Name of the Father. And of the Son. And of the Holy Ghost. Amen.' She finished the Sign of the Cross, drew her hands together.

'I believe in God, the Father Almighty, Creator of Heaven and Earth, and in Jesus Christ, His only son Our Lord, born of the Virgin Mary, suffered under Pontius Pilate, was crucified, suffered death and was buried. He descended into Hell, the third day He rose again from the dead. He ascended into Heaven and is seated at the right hand of God, the Father Almighty. From thence He shall come to judge the living and the dead. I believe in the Holy Ghost, the Holy Catholic Church, the Communion of Saints, the Forgiveness of Sins, the Resurrection of the Body. And Life Everlasting –' Ellen stopped. She sat back in the pew, rigid, for several minutes.

Still lost in thought, she stood up, did not genuflect, walked slowly from the church, and stood outside the door. On a nearby tombstone she sat down, until the cold penetrated her skirt. She closed the church gate behind her, climbed on the bicycle, and then freewheeled down the hill. She inhaled something deeply through her nose: 'Woodsmoke' she acknowledged.

The Stephenson stud farm may be reached by another avenue which winds up along the crest of some high fields. From half a mile away Ernestina sees the figure on the bicycle approach and is thrown into a panic. Alone in the house, she knows she does not have the energy to make tea, nor does she wish anyone other than Dr Hogan to perceive the full extent of her illness, and how awful each day now feels – and if a stranger, especially someone with authority, and above all someone with a tragedy of her own, now appears, how can Ernestina not blurt?

Ernestina closes the window and half-returns to bed, pressing the pain place in her back. She counts the tablets in the little white drum-box, and subtracts them from the figure on her piece of paper.

'Ba-rang.' The bell was always too heavy for the house, and what in the hell was the point of having a huge ship's bell in a farmhouse, for God's sake? We aren't a bloody man o'war, this is a stud farm.

'Ba-rang.' It can be heard in the sheds. Bloody. Bloody, bloody. She saw this Kane woman at the garden party. People spoke well of her, said she was kind, if hot-headed. Ernestina watched how the Kane woman glinted with pride for having hooked that tall good-looking man. The bloody Sinn Feiners. They could be good-looking buggers when they wanted to be. That's what Mama said, too. Ernestina has taken off her glasses, without which only she knows how blind she is, and she puts them back on, and goes to the window, opens it and looks down.

'What are you doing?' she yells, unable to see the figure who by now has come in under the eaves to the front door.

Ellen reverses a few steps and looks up and along the top storey until she finds the open window, and then sees a part of Ernestina's head.

'Hallo. I'm ringing your bell.'

'For what?'

'Dr Hogan asked me to call': Ellen shades her eyes with her hand; 'to see Ernestina.'

'I'm Ernestina.'

'I know you are. We met at your garden party. Hallo there. Again.'

'We didn't meet. We saw each other. I'm terribly busy. I have another big party coming up.'

'That can't be true. Dr Hogan told me you were very unwell.'

'When did he say that?'

'Oh, ages ago. How are you now, Ernestina?'

'I'm very busy.'

Ellen steps back farther until she can get a better look at Ernestina – who jumps away from the window, not quite fully concealing herself behind the curtain.

'I'm Ellen Kane. We have something in common.'

'We haven't. You're a Catholic.'

Ellen looks stumped. Then she calls up, 'I'd like to talk to you.'

'No. No.'

'Dr Hogan said I should.'

'I don't care.' Ernestina moves back farther as Ellen roves about below trying to get an ever better glimpse. Ernestina catches sight of her own full-length profile in the mirror: has it been a mistake to wear this satin nightgown of her mother's? A honeymoon garment – 'everything I had was in peach or pink' – and it gapes terribly at the bosom, that rotting, knobkerried bosom. She gathers the ribbons and tries to tie them, but they are so old that one snaps. Her hand falls defeated. The outline of the thick bloomers may be seen easily underneath, and particularly against this light.

Down below, the visitor, Ellen Kane, calls again.

'Lovely flowers.'

'None of your business.'

'But they are lovely.'

'Go away.'

'All right.'

A sound of footsteps: Ernestina goes to the window. She watches as Ellen Kane picks up the bicycle where it leans against a black metal *jardinière*. Ellen Kane walks away and Ernestina, still tense, stops lurking and approaches the window again to watch her. Expensive skirt, good blouse: lovely legs. That smashing dress she wore to the party. Rich for a Catholic. And only a teacher.

'Go on. Go,' Ernestina calls, but the effort, even to speak, is becoming too much. One last shout left.

'Look at you. You have everything. Look at you.'

The visitor half-turns.

'What did you say?' she asks, not unmenacingly.

'I said. Look at you. With your smart clothes and your tall teacher. How many children are you going to have, ten, I bet?'

The visitor turns fully.

Ellen shouts. 'You bitch. You dirty bitch.' She throws the bicycle down on the ground. 'You bitch. Who cares about you? Blast you.' She looks for a stone, finds one and throws it at the window, misses, jerks her arm painfully in the unaccustomed movement, holds her elbow, in a squeal and bursts out sobbing.

Ernestina goes downstairs and opens the front door. Ellen, standing there, holding her elbow, looks up and sees her.

'I only came to talk to you.'

'Come over here, then.'

'Didn't anyone tell you?'

'About what?' Ernestina lies.

'About my "living dead" husband, that's what they call him?'

'They did.'

'Thomas was hurt. He's paralysed, and he can't talk and he doesn't open his eyes. He's lying there in the house. D'you want to come and see him? I don't know what to do.'

'About what?'

'About anything.'

'I can't make you any cup of tea, so don't ask me for one. I haven't the time.'

'Is there anything you need?' Ellen asks.

'You can't get it for me.' Ernestina steps out farther. 'It would be like asking someone to go to the lavatory on my behalf.'

Ellen smiles, even though this guttural girl is perfectly serious.

'What is it? I could try.'

'I'm too busy – to do something that I liked doing.' Ernestina paused, then her sludgy plainness surging with a rush of trust says, 'Do you know where the rivers meet?'

Ellen said, 'I know it well.'

'I used to go there and scream. Nobody can hear you there. And I used to take off my clothes and go in the water.'

'It's gone a bit cold now. If I – do that, will you, can I, call back some day soon and talk to you?'

Ernestina nods, and then she backs into the hall, and closes the door very gently.

Ellen set off down the other, more legitimate avenue, and cycled to the river where Thomas and she had sat, their first 'occasion of sin', as the priest in Confession had called it. Not a soul to be seen anywhere: she opened the field gate and ricketed down the bumpy path to the grove, and threw the bicycle down.

Standing on the bank of the river, by the corner of the seat, she opened her mouth.

'Ernestina. Ern. Est. Teen. Nah.'

A quiet shout. Not good enough.

'Ernestina. ERNESTINA.' She shook her head,

'ERN. EST. TEEN. NAH!'

Birds fluttered away, and Ellen walked to the edge of the dark water.

'ERN. EST. TEEN. NAH!' she shouted again, then again, and again, and again.

Her body reverberated. She began to shout all kinds of things. **'MEAT! FLOUR! SCHOOL! CURSE! ME!'** Then she let go her biggest shout. **'ELLEN!'** and then shouted out the seven sacraments.

'BAPTISM! CONFIRMATION! BLESSED EUCHARIST! PENANCE! EXTREME UNCTION! HOLY ORDERS! MATRIMONY!'

She moved to the water's edge, kicked a shoe off and touched the water with her toe.

'DEATH!' she shouted, and followed it with, **'LIFE!'**

She began to take off her clothes. **'I AM GOING MAD!'** she screamed. Only four garments: blouse first, then the light bodice: then skirt, then knickers. Her toes made marks in the little soft mud.

'FUCK OFF!' she shouted, not quite certain of the full implications of the word. 'I AM GOING MAD! PRIEST! LIFE!'

She walked into the slow green-and-black river which after the summer had not yet become again deep enough to swim in, and she stood there, water up to her hips, hands by her sides, as white as the statue of a goddess. 'ERNESTINA! YOU'RE DYING! THOMAS YOU'RE DYING! I'LL GO MAD IF I WANT TO!'

Ellen scratched at her abundant crush of pubic hair.

'DIE!' Pressing her hands to her face, her shouts began to subside; 'PRIDE. COVETOUSNESS. LUST. ANGER. GLUTTONY. ENVY. Sloth.'

She saw the face in the tall sedges, staring at her, and screamed at it. The startled boy jumped to his feet, Michael Quinn, and he ran as hard as he could.

'I DON'T CARE!' roared Ellen.

In a moment, she lowered her head and stood, both hands folded as if in duty over her groin. Then she turned and waded from the river, climbing up through the reeds and cresses. She sat on the wooden bench, her heavy buttocks leaving wet marks on the old plank.

'Thomas, my love,' she said aloud.

She could still see the boy running away across the fields towards the bridge.

'I'm all right now. I will be all right now. I'm going to be all right now. Thomas, my love, my dear love.'

In due course, Ellen dressed and rode her bicycle home, and did not get there until six o'clock. Essie met her in unusual agitation.

'Ma'am, nthere's a gngentleman here!'

'Where? Who? Is he a doctor?'

In excitement, Essie's speech defect intensified. 'Ma'am, I couldn't gnstop him. He's gnupstairs, Ma'am.'

'Oh, thank God': Ellen had a fear of anyone harming the unprotected and unprotectable Thomas. 'Who is he?'

'I gndon't know, Ma'am, gnhe says he's gcoming to stay, he gmight be a Protestant gminister, Ma'am, he's wearing a ngrey suit.'

'Oh, Father John!' Ellen lowered her voice. 'Oh, God! I wasn't expecting him so soon.'

He had heard Ellen arrive and he came downstairs, smacking his lips softly, a perennial habit. A handshake with both hands: a holding-out at arm's length to inspect: a look of deep compassion. As never before in his presence, Ellen felt embarrassed.

'Look. I'll show you. I have a letter half-written to you. You must think me terrible.'

'Look, I bring gifts, from your loving parents. From all the family. Have you forgotten?'

Her birthday. Yesterday. 'They clubbed together.' Not even with Ernestina did she recall her birthday.

'Isn't that a massive parcel?' Father John Watson S.J. smiled.

'Very like a fish,' Thomas said of him. 'A pike, those spiky teeth.'

'Open it. I am so glad to see you again, my dear Ellen, so glad we shall be able to talk.'

No time taken rolling the string.

'The bus conductor had to help me carry it in.'

'I hope he didn't come any farther . . .'

'No, no, this is a house of the sick. I told him so.'

No time to fold the paper. On top lay a silver piece of metal, with a black end to it.

'That's the handle.' A high-domed, wooden, lacquered box, with a lock. 'A gramophone, and there are records in my case.'

'But we have a gramophone record. A man brought it to us from Australia.' She rushed to Thomas's room, saying 'Hallo, Thomas,' not pausing, as she usually did, to be arrested by the sight, and rushed back again with the record.

'I'll do it,' he said, 'I'm used to it; we have one in the Provincial's House.'

Father John Watson wound the gramophone and put on the record. The kitchen filled with the sound of the kookaburra, a dreadful laughing, eerie and hacking sound, and not at all as pleasant and amusing and warm as Joe Johnson's version.

'What is this?' asked Father Watson, not a little taken aback, especially at the fact that Ellen laughed so loudly almost in tune with the record.

'It's a bird, Father John,' she told him, 'look, it says "From the Series of Thrilling Sounds: The Voice of True Nature." It's a bird.'

26

Long into the night, John Watson, intimate orator, addressed Ellen.

'Moments of endearment,' he murmured, retracing incidents from her childhood; 'And may I remind you of your great spiritual strength? Your natural solicitousness for Christ's will.' In his fat hand a glass of port the colour of black blood: he sipped gently: 'I advise you to recall such good times, when you were . . . when you were still, aah, ah'm? What is the word I was looking for? Still – untroubled. By this dreadful burden, yes, untroubled.' When Ellen first described him to Thomas, she said, 'His eyes. They're funny. His eyes are younger than he is, do you know what I mean, Thomas?'

John Watson now said, 'I feel it my bounden duty to warn you of one thing, dear Ellen. You must not give in to hatred now, hatred of Thomas. You must be so close to that, you must so wish to hate him. For him lying there, demanding so much of you, and proving such a burden.'

John Watson said, 'I was always a little, a little surprised – that you did marry. And indeed I often wonder whether Thomas had somehow persuaded you, against your . . . against your – it was all so rushed, wasn't it? Whereas I, who know you, dear Ellen, who know you so well, who know your soul as well, if not better, than you do, would have assumed, and I think rightly, that your prayers would have been enough for you? No?'

John Watson stretched his short legs. 'Isn't life funny? There is Thomas in the next room. Prostrate. You know, the ways of God. They're not our ways, Ellen. I was only thinking after Mass yesterday – poor Thomas. If he is lucid, is it crossing his mind – is it crossing his mind, that he himself must have rendered so many men insensible, I mean – eternally insensible? Even without a chance to make their peace before meeting their Maker? Although I do not subscribe to the vengeance theories, or the punishment theories, "live by the sword, die by the sword", sort of thing, no, 'no, no, this is not a vengeful God who watches over us, but at the same time . . .'

John Watson asked, 'And you, dear Ellen, how in the name of the dear Lord have you weathered it at all? I know, I know, don't tell me.' He raised a hand. 'Your prayers, your wonderful devotion to Our Blessed Lady. I know. At the same time, I sense you may have – perhaps – aged? There is a – there is a – what is the word, there is a – *glitter* about you I have not seen before.'

'Father John, do you remember the wedding here? Wasn't it a great day? Now, wasn't it?'

'Oh, Ellen, dear, the joy of that day, and the fun. So nice not to have had it at an hotel, wasn't it? Although –' He laughed and shook his head in amused ruefulness. '– I have to say, I must have eaten something that didn't agree with me. No, no.' He waved away her quick furrow of concern, 'I was fine in a few days, just the old tummy, I suppose.'

She surveyed him sitting in Thomas's armchair which the little priest had drawn out of the shuttered bow-window towards the range, and as Thomas did with a cup of tea, Father John balanced his glass of port on the edge of the kitchen table above his right elbow.

'About your age, Thomas,' Ellen had answered, 'although, wait – no, he's older, I counted, he must be, he must be . . . nearly fifty.'

'I suppose what I really want to say,' Father Watson summarized, 'is – you will probably survive better, dear Ellen, if you release yourself from memories so, so . . . I mean, if you dwell on, or . . . No. Let me start again. If you turn to new pastures of thought, rather than brood – and as we know, brooding is unhealthy – if you fill your mind with thoughts not so intimately associated with Thomas. If you move forward from memories of your marriage, which must now be so painful . . . and prayer, your own great advocate, prayer. Yes. Yes. That's it. Prayer.' He gazed into the fire.

'Where we find strength in our afflictions, Ellen, is not always within the affliction itself. My idea is that you should go back to – when you were yourself, as it were. My idea is that you should seek for succour outside those later days. Poor Thomas. So much pain and grief to you. Do you remember our long conversations, as we walked by the river, or out on the Ballysimon road on a

Sunday afternoon? And your dear, if I may say so, innocent enquiries into theology? And your earnest desire to find the right spiritual pathway?'

Ellen listened more – much more – than she talked.

Eventually, she said, 'Father John, will you say an earlier or later Mass than the Canon? Because I think it would be a good idea if you helped to give out Communion with him?'

Through the window Ellen could see the sharp cold smile of a quarter-moon reflected in her dressing-table mirrors. Around the landing, a creak and a puff: John Watson, at last in his bed in his room, blew out the candle. In her cot, Helena gave a tiny whistling cry, a baby dream. Ellen, alert, waited. Snoring began; Father John, yes, remember, he even drank nearly all that second glass of port wine.

Ellen put on the dressing-gown from Aunt Lil, and crept down. By the light of the embers in the range, she lit a new candle from the kitchen drawer, and melted the butt until the candle adhered upright to a saucer. The door to Thomas's room squeaked only when beyond halfway open: she sidled in: he lay swaddled in the dimness. Ellen placed the candle saucer on the floor, and standing at the back of the bed-chair, manipulated the two silent cranking levers raising Thomas to a shallow angle. Gathering the folds of her nightgown and dressing-gown safely away from the candle, she came around and squatted in front of him.

'Thomas,' she began. 'I am going to nail that man. Oh, Thomas, I shouldn't say that. Oh, God.' She gazed up into the insensate, open-mouthed, beloved face.

'No. I should say it. I should. I should. You would agree with me. You do agree with me. Don't you, Thomas?'

Through the blankets she fumbled until she had secured the shape of his foot, which she clasped.

'You do agree, don't you? You do. You do. I know you, Thomas. You do agree. You have never forgiven him for what he did to us. You were right. It was none of his business.'

Ellen tilted forward, from her hunkers to her knees, and clasped his foot with her other hand. 'Thomas Kane, I have changed. Oh, my dear love. This is the first day I can ever remember that I did not say my morning prayers. I said no prayers last night either. Thomas, I don't care. I do care, I do, I do, but when I say I don't care, that isn't what I mean. What I mean is. Oh, God, my head is full of wild thoughts, Thomas. What I mean is. You may be taken from me. But if you are, I won't care – provided – what is it you always said, Thomas? That your job was to keep your balance in life? Do you remember? You used to tease me – that was why we had to have six boys and six girls? Balance.'

She took her hands from Thomas's feet and pushed her hair back. 'Thomas, I have to whisper. Everyone's asleep. But I feel so wild. I'm like a fishwife telling her Confession. I haven't been good to you. I haven't nursed you well. How many things wrong? I don't know, Thomas, if you can hear me, but if you can, encourage me. Jesus Christ in Heaven, Thomas, encourage me.'

Her rhapsody gaining, Ellen went on, 'Bless me, Thomas, for I have sinned – in thought, word and deed, against YOU, my beloved husband. Through my own most grievous fault. I feared that you would breed murderers in me. I told that man, that awful man – remember you pointed him out to me, that very first foggy morning, his bicycle and his cap, I had my scarf on me still, and I had my hand on my hip, God, I remember it – I told him although I didn't mean to, that a revenge he might take against you would be understandable. "He who takes the sword" I said to him. And I knew that you knew about that McAuliffe woman's husband and where he was. And who killed him. I lied to you. About little things. About huge things. I shut you out of my bed, and I shut you out of my body. The body that I spent my days thinking about. How about that for mortifying the flesh, Thomas? Was I mad? I'm mad now, Thomas. I'm mad for you. Mad for you. And mad about you. And mad over you. Thomas. Jesus. I even contemplated suffocating you. With one of those pillows you're lying on. Or starving you, and pretending you had begun to reject food. Who would know? And d'you think Dr Hogan, that solid-gold eejit, as you'd say yourself, d'you think he wouldn't certify the cause of death? They'd all say what a mercy; what a relief! But Thomas, when I met you I knew nothing about love, and I knew nothing about what I'm like. And now I know one thing, that what I want out of life – is you.'

She laughed, hand over her mouth. 'Oh, Thomas – is that what you'd call "a turn-up for the books"? That I'm talking about the love of Man instead of spouting about the love of God?'

Ellen bowed her face until it touched his blanketed knees. The white long shape of Thomas seemed to extend and grow into her hair and shoulders. In the not over-warm room, she began to perspire.

'Thomas, I lost my way. I wasn't fair to you. I always had everything my own way. I always got what I wanted. But now, Thomas, I am going to get what I want, but I don't want it for myself, I want it for you.'

Ellen stood, her hips aching. 'Thomas, there are things I can't even speak to you about, about feelings in my body, when I'd stand in the school listening to the children recite their prayers, and I'd feel without touching what we had been doing at home, in our own privacy; this was before "Canon Law". Thomas, I asked you once – and blast you, I could never get you to talk about anything like that, you said it was "women's business" – I asked you once what we did in the night, what it made you feel, and you said to me, "Fierce", and even though I liked it, I didn't know what you meant. I know now. My dear, dear man. Fierce. Fierce!'

Ellen bent down and across Thomas, as she had to do when turning him with Essie. She moved the blankets sufficiently to expose his pyjama-ed shoulders and some of his chest, where the hair had turned quite white, and arranging her body, embraced him as fully as she could. For a long minute she half-stood, half-lay there across him. Beneath her, the breathing stroked through the body; the beating of his heart thumped on, described by the doctors as 'too strong'. Ellen lay her face on his, and whispered in his ear. 'Thomas, if I can – in any way whatsoever – I am going to bring you back to life. Back to life.'

Tenderly anchoring the blankets to keep him warm, she picked up the candle and climbed slowly to bed, not caring whether the stairs creaked.

She slept as deep as a drunkard until the cracking knock on her door in the morning: she had outslept the calling Essie and the crying Helena.

At eight o'clock, downstairs, dressed for Mass, Ellen put in place the first phase of her revenge.

'May I surprise you, Father John?' she asked. 'Can I go to Confession to you?'

At the dim end of the hallway under the stairs, she arranged a chair for him, a kneeling cushion for herself. The priest leaned forward on one knee, a Rodin Thinker in black with a purple stole, a hand over his eyes.

'. . . For I have sinned in the . . . the three weeks,' she lied, 'since my last Confession.'

'My child?'

'Father, I spoke badly of people.'

'My child?'

'Father, I might for a moment have lost my faith in God.'

'God tries us all, my child.'

'Father, He has tried me very hard. My husband is paralysed and insensible.'

'But – look. God has given you the strength of the Sacraments, my child? This is a Sacrament you are partaking of now.'

'Yes, Father, that's true.' In the distant kitchen, Essie's voice droned affectionately at Helena.

'Father, but I am a young and healthy married woman with no husband.'

'Yes, my child.' He paused. 'What, may I ask, are you leading to?'

Ellen blurted studiedly. 'I ask God to forgive me impure thoughts.'

'Many, my child?' asked the grave, oaken voice.

'Sometimes, Father. And – they confuse me.'

'Are they specific, my child?'

'How do you mean, Father?'

'Are they, ah'm, how shall I put it? Are they, how shall I say? Directed?'

'No, just impure thoughts about . . . Just impure thoughts, Father.'

'In the abstract, my child?'

'Yes, Father. No, Father. I mean, how do you mean?'

'Or in the concrete. I ask fearing scandal?'

'I don't get you, Father?'

'Impure thoughts about, well . . . Men whom you know, my child, men with – even – wives of their own. You may be committing Scandal, in your head, admittedly, but it is the gravest, "Woe to the Scandal-Giver", the gravest sin of all. The sin of Scandal?'

'Oh, Father, I never thought.'

'Grievous Matter. Perfect Knowledge. And Full Consent. In which case, therefore. Grievous Matter, my child, and, this is. But

407

no, this is not – mortal. Because no Perfect Knowledge. Is that right?'

'No, Father. Not scandal, not men with wives. He isn't married . . . I mean.' Ellen stopped. Paused. 'I haven't worked it out yet, Father, I need the grace of Absolution and Penance to help me.'

'My child, God will help you, and He will forgive you in your special circumstances. Feel sure of that. Now for your Penance say the Joyful Mysteries of the Rosary, and offer them up for this man of whom you think.'

'Thank you, Father.'

'Now, a Perfect Act of Contrition . . .'

He went back to the city on Monday afternoon. Ellen waved the bus good-bye, and returned to the house, thoughtful hand on chin. One letter; no time until now to open it.

> Dear Mrs Kane,
>   Yes, I did hear the bad news and I am very sorry
> indeed. Just as I regret that this old complaint of mine
> kept me from delivering your daughter, but I believe she's
> a fine infant in any case. ['The handwriting as bad as ever,'
> she smiled.]
>   Perhaps Providence inspired you [Ellen grinned at the
> irony: 'You old atheist'] but bearing in mind the description
> of your husband's condition (I read the salient details in
> the papers and I meant to write to you but I still had the
> shakes), you could not have asked a better man than
> myself for a second opinion. I think I know the exact
> surgeon to get in touch with, he's a man who knows about
> the silent areas of the brain; but I'd like to see your husband
> first and I'll come out this coming Thursday, if that's all
> the same to you. I bought myself a car and I'm going
> everywhere in it, I'm even calling on patients of mine who
> aren't sick at all.
>
>   Yours with best regards,
>   J. A. Morgan

Ellen jumped to her feet, and swung Helena above her head and danced around.

'Read that, Essie! Essie, read that!' she cried. 'Weeeeeeeeee!!'

Essie said, 'Ma'am, he must be hiring a spider to write his letters.'

'Read it! Read it! Weeeeeeeeeee!!' Helena, rich in gums, laughed.

'Right! Helena! Your best dress and matinee coat!'

She plonked Helena on Essie and ran along the kitchen, hitting her thigh hard as she rounded the table. 'Thomas! Thomas! Dr Morgan is going to do something!' At the parlour door Ellen clapped her hands in rhythm and danced to an imaginary jig. 'Thanks be to God, Essie! The first ray of hope! The first ray of hope! I knew it! I knew it!'

Ellen took Helena for a walk and played hiding games with her over the slim marbled-pearl handle of the pram. A woman in a cottage came out to admire the chuckling, arm-chugging baby: 'She's the spit-and-image of you, Ma'am.'

An unusual feather lay in the roadside grass: Ellen gathered it, tickled Helena's little nose. That night, all chores done, Ellen lit a lamp and took it into Thomas's room.

'Now, Thomas,' she said, settling in the chair as if for a long chat with a friend, 'isn't that wonderful about Dr Morgan? I can't wait. Look, I found this feather on the road, what do you think it is from, a seagull? I've lots of news for you. Jack Carty was asking for you yesterday at Mass. The Canon complained about the Dance last week, dancing too close again. They're all bound for Hell, he says, without even a stretch in Purgatory on the way. And he was ratty about a speech somebody made at a Gaelic League meeting in Shronell. Mrs Quilty had an extraordinary coat on her, I don't know where in the name of God she got it. The Relihans were asking for you, their daughter is going nursing after all. You'll be glad to know your bosom friend, Father John W., is gone back. Essie made the grandest meat loaf ever, although I think she put in too much onions, myself. Could Helena be getting a tooth? Look.' She lifted her skirt. 'I hit my thigh off the edge of the table and it's gone black-and-blue, and even a bit yellow. Look. It nearly tore the suspender off me.'

In the kitchen, folding clothes, Essie heard the drone of the voice coming from the Master's bedside and assumed the Mistress had begun the Rosary.

=

409

The barracks did not possess a cell decent enough, in the Sergeant's opinion, 'to put a sober woman into'. She was kept in a locked bedroom of the married quarters overhead. The three callers, Dr Hogan, the Postal Superintendent and Ellen, waited in the General Office while the Sergeant fetched her.

'I'll just lock the front door now for a while,' he said.

'Wait 'til you meet the Sergeant,' Thomas said to Ellen on her second day in Deanstown. 'He speaks as if he's saying his prayers. He's as monotonous as ditchwater.'

The Sergeant intoned, 'If anyone wants to get in they'll have to hammer hard. My wife can keep an eye on the door.'

Dr Hogan looked at Ellen: she did not laugh.

'I nearly passed out,' she said to Thomas that night, 'when he said he'd get the wife to keep an eye on the door. I could hear your voice, Thomas: "Which eye, the good one, or the one over to the west?" Jack Hogan was doing his best to get me to laugh.' Ellen's high spirits anticipated Dr Morgan's visit next day.

The woman did not return Ellen's stare.

'Her name, Ma'am, is Edel Crowe, a fine farm and respectable brothers.'

In her middle thirties, Edel Crowe wore the same black clothes Ellen had seen on her the morning of the Station Mass.

'She went to the Ursuline Convent, Ma'am, and only left school when she was eighteen. She did a Secretarial Course in Stephen's Green in Dublin.' No, the Sergeant's voice did not come from intoning prayers, it came from giving evidence. In each of his sentences many words began with capital letters.

Unworked hands, with the surprising pleasantness of freckles: Edel Crowe sat looking at nobody. In the drab green General Office with one official book and three chewed, unkempt pencils on the single table near the fire, each of the four people observed her differently.

The Sergeant saw the puzzlement of a woman from a well-off family attempting to commit a crime, with no history of any such thing in her people, and the nuisance of it was, he'd have to get the nurse in when they were taking her to the jail for the Remand. In the eyes of the Postal Superintendent as he leaned on the counter, she had good handwriting, and he would be cross-examined in a case that would get into all the papers. Jack Hogan, his hands deep in his raincoat pockets, saw a look of Miriam about her. Ellen considered something wistful and troubled in Edel Crowe: her own aggressive shows of unconcern often concealed defiance, or fright.

'Ma'am, I haven't drafted a Charge yet, but I'll need a Statement from you,' said the Sergeant.

'Can you do without it?' asked Ellen.

'I suppose,' said Dr Hogan, getting it wrong, 'it'd be very hard on the Mistress to have to stand up in court.'

'I have to Proceed via a Statement, Ma'am.'

Ellen said, 'Sergeant, can I speak to her on her own?'

'No, Ma'am, that'd be against Regulations, leaving the Prisoner alone with the Injured Party. Sure you'd never know what'd happen.'

The Sergeant had a private thing against Edel Crowe's brother – not the one gone to England, the one farming in the home place: he did not come up with the goods when the hint was dropped regarding a free sack of potatoes and no questions about the dog licence.

'No, Ma'am, against Regulations.'

Ellen moved over to stand near him and his silver belt buckle.

'Sergeant': she looked up at his bushy face: 'I would like very much to speak to Miss Crowe alone.'

Behind Ellen's back, Dr Hogan nodded affirmation with his head and brows: the Sergeant hesitated.

'Ma'am, we'd have to remain nearby, in the immediate Vicinity of the Prisoner . . .'

'Within shouting distance, maybe?' said Ellen, 'in case I need you.'

The three men walked through a door opened by the Sergeant which led to the rear of the barracks, and there, within view of Ellen but far away, they stood between the whitewashed walls of the corridor, talking, and trying not to look back at the dayroom.

Ellen sat on a chair two feet away from the woman and looked at her.

'Now, Edel Crowe,' she said, 'I'm the woman you wrote to, and I'm the wife of the man you wrote to. As you well know. And I have two things to say to you. The first is what the Sergeant would call a Statement. This is my Statement. You're a living, lighting bitch to do what you did. I never did a thing to you that I'm aware of. It wasn't my fault if you didn't manage to get my husband before

411

I even knew him. Nobody but a bitch would do what you did. And a right bitch at that. You frightened me.'

Ellen eased back. 'Now, I have that off my chest. Here's the second thing. Why did you do it, why did you write those letters? For all you know, I might be the sort of woman who could be a friend to you?'

Edel Crowe, for some strange reason, bore a curious resemblance to Thomas Kane. No more than a chance of life – they had no blood connection, ancient or recent, no breeding secrets, no consanguinous history. She did not answer.

Ellen softened her tone and said, 'Come on, tell me. By the way, I am not going to press charges, so there will be no court case and the whole thing will be quietened, I'll see to it. I promise, I give you my word of honour.'

The woman still did not reply.

Ellen tried one more time. 'It isn't a bargain, that, I'm not trading with you, or trying to. I'm not having charges anyway. I haven't had things easy. To look at me, you might have thought I had a lot of things that were great. Look at me now. Come on, tell me. Please. Why did you write them?'

The woman said, still not looking at Ellen, 'I meant every word I said in those letters. I had a flair for your husband.'

'Would you have it if you saw him now?' asked Ellen.

'I would. I know all about it. About what happened. I saw it in the papers. And every chance I get, I ask people about him. I hear how he is. I'd look after him.' Then she flashed, 'I'd get him proper doctors. More than you've done.' She had a voice as cultured as Ellen's own.

Ellen blushed but did not rise. 'I wish I'd known you properly,' said Ellen, 'without any of this thing happening. We might have got on very well. And if you were – sincere about the Master, why did you try and hurt him?'

'I felt hurt myself.'

'Thomas, I couldn't wait to tell you.' Ellen prattled on as she spooned the thick soup into Thomas's mouth that night. 'The thing is, she must have wanted to marry you desperately, and how can I complain? She was here before I met you. I know, I know, what you'll say, that she's a troublemaker.'

＝

412

'You felt hurt?' squeaked Ellen to Edel Crowe. 'But that's the same as taking the law into your own hands.' She turned impatiently, then faced back. 'Look. I said. I'm not going to have you charged with anything. Just don't ever do anything like that again. All right? I couldn't take that sort of thing now.'

She called the Sergeant, who blustered.

'If you insist,' she said, 'I'll go to court, Sergeant, but not to charge her. It is a witness for her I'll be, and anyway I'll say I didn't want charges brought, and my husband didn't either. So you'll have to face Justice Hipwell yourself.'

'Boys, oh boys,' said the Postal Superintendent.

When Edel Crowe received her coat and made to leave the barracks, Ellen asked Dr Hogan, 'You're not going to let that woman walk home on her own in the rain, are you, it's nearly dark. She'll get her death of cold. No, no,' she said, putting down his protest. 'You can call for me on the way back. Besides, I have something else to talk to the Sergeant about.'

The Sergeant rubbed his jaw hard, the gesture of a man contemplating shaving.

'Oh, God, Ma'am. That's fierce stuff you're saying there. Oh, God, Ma'am, and it was what, May, June, July, August, September, October, we're near November. Six months ago? Whewww!'

The Sergeant and his Superintendent had asked questions; not a shred of evidence existed – other than gossip.

'What use is another cartridge to me?' the Sergeant asked Ellen. 'Sure we have a cartridge already. Ma'am, I'm telling you. All kinds of people were questioned. The Super himself stopped people on the road. But sure what could people say to him if he started asking again now, only – "What are you asking me them kind of questions for? Are you going round asking everyone else what Mass were they at of a Sunday last May?" That's all we'd get from anybody, Ma'am.'

'So what could I do, Thomas? You couldn't move that Sergeant if you put a horse hauling him. D'you know, I nearly felt myself slipping back again to the worst times, if it wasn't for Dr Morgan tomorrow.'

Essie had gone down to the village to bring back the large

seven-pound bags of sugar for making the apple jelly. For hours on end, Ellen had continued to record even the tiniest change in Thomas. Eyes open, flutteringly or lazily a slight roll of the head; anything even approaching recognition in the demeanour. Her reports all said the same thing: 'Only minute changes. Nothing you could hang a hope on.'

She fought off the voice of despondency whenever it awakened in her. 'Am I glad, Thomas, I have all these notes for Dr Morgan tomorrow? Dr Hogan never looked at them, nor asked me. But John Morgan – he's very solid, isn't he? Here we go, Thomas, don't laugh, this is the song I'm teaching them in school.'

'O'er the fields she passes to and fro,
By the cornstalks standing row by row.
Poppies whisper as they see her go,
"Marionina, little friend,
Whither would your footsteps wend?
Come and teach us how to bend.
Marionina, Marionina –
Come, Oh come, and teach us how to bend."'

Ellen bowed and straightened up, laughing.

'Oh, Thomas, look!' She raised the skirt to mid-thigh. 'The bruise is an interesting shade of yellow, don't you think.'

She whisked the skirt from side to side like a can-can dancer.

'I think it is anyway,' she said, with a laugh-seeking flounce.

'And, Thomas, the other thing about that Edel Crowe woman. I forgot to tell you, she had lovely hands – and the most beautiful scarab ring I ever saw, in a glassy sort of green stone, I wonder was it a real emerald?'

People who knew him said, 'You have to hand it to Val. When he puts his mind to something, he gets it done.'

Again, Val proved them right. He had made 'marvellous progress altogether' with the Deanstown Band.

'Ma'am,' he said to Ellen in the school yard – Val leaned across the wall while the children milled back and forth behind him during the morning break – 'the original band, I'm finding out things all the time, had up to twenty-four men and the drum-major, not fourteen, and I think I'm going to be able to get nearly nineteen fellows altogether. Mrs Heffernan is a genius with a needle and thread and she has two more women sewing the extra tunics, she's cutting the patterns herself; the pants aren't that important, they were a kind of a dark blue colour, but really anything would do for the moment, the red stripe will unite them anyway, won't it, but the tunic was very important altogether, the blue and gold you know, and we're going to rehearse all the winter. The school won't be big enough for the morning practice, the Canon says we can have the hall.'

Ellen described him later to Essie: 'He looks like a kind of a cross between a bony old grandfather and a leprechaun and he has red cracked cheeks like a pippin apple. He's probably a very nice man, but I don't know what in the world to make of him. He talks like this –' and Ellen mimicked Val Vousden's up-and-down voice.

'Ma'am, how are things with you?' Val asked.

'Ah, sure not bad, I suppose, even though there's no sign of a change in the Master': another advance – she could now bring herself to discuss it openly with any who asked.

'What is it he has, Ma'am?' asked Val. 'Is it brain damage itself?'

'I suppose so, Mr Vousden.'

'And nothing to be done for it?'

'We're all the time making medical enquiries, Mr Vousden, but nothing yet, I'm afraid. In fact I have someone coming to give another opinion today after school.'

'Is it hard to look after him, Ma'am?'

'Oh, it is, Mr Vousden, it is. The great fear is if he catches a cold, that's the thing that worries me the most.'

Val told Mrs Heffernan that night how much he liked that Mrs Kane – 'She has a way of speaking that respects a person, a bit like yourself, Ma'am, in that respect.'

A moment later, 'Mrs Heffernan, do you think that Mrs Kane would consult a man who wasn't a real doctor? I mean, if the man didn't have the certificates, but he could cure people like?'

'A quack?'

'Well, I'd prefer to call him a healer?'

'If it was my husband, God be good to him, I'd try anything.'

Val Vousden, about to leave the Deanstown area for three or four weeks, said, 'I think I'll make a few inquiries. I've forgotten the person's name.' Mrs Heffernan broke off a piece of thread with her teeth.

'But I thought he'd nearly be here before I got home from school?' Ellen said anxiously to Essie. 'He'd never be out this late, would he, a man that age, and he's hardly used to the car yet, surely?'

Dr Morgan did not arrive on Thursday, nor on Friday, nor on Saturday – on which night Ellen had a dreadful time, a fit of weeping of a kind she had not had for weeks.

'Oh, Thomas, I'm sorry, "Weeping and gnashing of teeth" isn't that what they say we'll have to do in Hell? Ach, Thomas, I sometimes wonder which of the two of us is in "the exterior darkness"? Oh, I shouldn't be talking like this, he'll be here tomorrow or Monday; he probably had a baby to deliver, or an emergency thing or something.'

Dr Morgan did not come on Sunday; two of Thomas's brothers and his two sisters arrived in a hackney car, and stayed for their tea, distracting Ellen.

'If he comes on Monday, it will be very inconvenient,' said Ellen.

'I'm getting as fat as a fool, Essie,' said Ellen as they ate dinner, one of Essie's specials, porksteak stuffed with breadcrumbs, and peas and roast potatoes.

Around the corner of the house, they could hear the engine of the car being cranked up.

'Did you ask Michael Condon had he a mouth on him?'

Essie said, 'I did, Ma'am, but he said he's after his dinner.'

When Ellen returned an hour or so later from her first, swaying driving lesson – guided by a watchful and amused Michael Condon in a flat field, mercifully dry – she felt exhilarated.

'Essie,' she shouted, 'ESSIE! It was great. He said I was very good. No Dr Morgan, I suppose?'

'No, Ma'am.'

'I wonder what's wrong with him, maybe he's sick again, and then he couldn't write.'

'I've tea made, Ma'am.'

'Lovely! I'll have a quick read of the paper before I start the Master. Michael Condon has very bad teeth, Essie.'

Across the front page of the *Irish Independent* ran columns of

close type: BIRTHS: MARRIAGES: DEATHS: Ellen scanned them
expertly and turned to the general news on the next page, then
the next, at the bottom of which she shouted.

'Oh, no! Oh, God, no!'

**The death took place (suddenly) at his home on Thursday last
(as reported in our late editions on Saturday), of Dr John Alexis
Morgan, MD. He was aged 67. A native of Landerstown, Dr
Morgan was educated at Clongowes Wood, the Royal University, and Guy's Hospital in London. He served in two Colonial
campaigns, and was invalided out of the Far East, suffering
consequently from recurrent malaria. A widely respected and
popular figure, whose medical expertise was generously available to one and all, he will be deeply missed by his wife and
grown-up family, and by members of Athlunkard Boat Club
and Corbally Golf Club.**

WINTER 1926

27

Next day, the weather bowed Ellen's head, echoing and cloaking her dejection during the five-minute walk to school. Many children and Miss McGoldrick funked the extreme rain and wind. Ellen took all classes in Thomas's room; why light two fires? When she called, in Irish, for quietness, the habituated children stood up expecting prayers.

'No. Sit down again. Fold your arms.' This departure generated expectancy.

'Since you were all good enough to come to school, and not like the cissies who were afraid they'd melt away in the rain.' They sniggered. 'Or be blown away like thread, the ninnyhammers.' They laughed. 'We'll have something nice today.' She wrote a word on the blackboard. 'Now. A penny for the first person who tells me the meaning of this word.' Ellen smiled into their thickets of blankness. 'No? All right. A penny for anyone who can pronounce it. Come on. Try.'

Lips moved without sound: they hunched their shoulders, hands over covered mouths. 'John Ryan, come on, you big fosthoock.' He coloured and laughed and shifted his hobnailed feet. 'Sheila Carroll?' Sheila went, 'Surrr. Ik. Ullem.'

'Nearly there. Nearly there. Who's next? Miss Nobody? Or Mr Nobody? All right, all right.' With the long knitting-needle she had used as her pointer since Training College, Ellen took them through each part of the word.

'Now, there are four parts in this word, or four – what?' She nodded slowly several times as only the older ones struggled to spew out the word 'Syllable'.

'There are four. Syllables. And "syllable" itself has?' She held up three fingers on her left hand. 'Three. Syllables. Verrry Good. And the first syllable is? It isn't "Surr", like you call the Master. It is "K", the "c" is like the "c" in "Cat". So it's "Kurr". What is it?'

They sang a chorus of 'Kurr'.

'Now, the second part, or syllable, is very easy. What is it?'
Several said, 'Ik.'

'That's right, it may be spelt with a "c", as you can see, "i.c.".
But it is called "ik". So put the two together and what have we?
Kurr. Ik. Curric. Kurr. Ik. Now the third part or syllable is only
one letter and it spells –' she rounded on the most junior child in
the room, a tiny Viking-blonde girl in a fair-isle cardigan. Ellen
said, with a mock-fierce face and large smile, 'You!' The child
jumped back, and then blushed and giggled to her deskmate. Of
the room at large, Ellen asked, 'The third syllable is, simply, "u",
the letter "u", so we have what?'

They ventured, 'Kurrikyou.'

'Exactly. Exactly. And the fourth syllable or word-part is – Come
on. Yes, that's it.' She encouraged the tentative sounds. 'Yes.
"Lum". So we have Kurr. Ik. You. Lum. All together. One syllable
at a time.'

They chorused, 'Kurr. Ik. You. Lum.'

'Quickly.' She led them.

'Curriculum.'

'Good. What does it mean? The "Curriculum" –' she beat time
in the air – 'is the list of things you have to learn in school. Irish.
English. Arithmetic and all your sums. Catechism. History. Geography. Put all of those together and that is what the "Curriculum"
is. Now today we're not going to have the "Curriculum". We are
going to have something different. We are going to have some
Nature Notes. Just nice things about the countryside.'

She lifted the lid of the high desk, fumbled thoughtfully within,
fetched one of Thomas's books and from it took a tree leaf he
had pressed between two sheets of writing-paper. With a flick of
stamp-paper, she stuck it to the blackboard.

'Now what leaf is this? This is the leaf of the – Alder tree. Hands
up anyone who has seen it before?' Several hands shot up in the
air.

'Good. Good. It has red berries and sometimes it has flowers,
they're white or pink. Now.'

Ellen returned to the high desk and settled herself on her
cushions. One hand clasped on the other, she leaned forward,
relishing.

'Libate. Libate,' Miss Humphrys had cried in Teacher Training.
'Knowledge is a god, pour libations for it.'

Ellen flooded them with interesting knowledge; that it was also called 'dogwood' because hunters used to boil the leaves, and use that juice to wash the fleas and lice off their hunting-dogs: once a dog had been washed in the juice of the dogwood tree the lice did not come back for a year and a day; that before the Celts discovered how to make really hard weapons from their discovery of iron, they carved and seasoned dogwood branches into knives and daggers; that the Red Indians of North America used it as a mix to make the tobacco last longer, and they boiled it too, not to clean their dogs, but to tip into pools and lakes because the taste of it in the water made the fish drunk and made them easier to catch. At which the children laughed.

Energetically she took them through the shape of the leaf, stepping to the blackboard and running her fingers around its edges as tenderly as if tracing the boundaries of her own mouth. Together they wondered how it flew on the wind – did it flip over, did it float? She told them that several varieties had poisonous berries, that it was sometimes called 'Nightshade' and even more mistakenly 'Deadly Nightshade' which was a different plant altogether, but the berries of some alders were poisonous and the safest thing was to eat none of them. So the morning passed with Ellen teaching them to look even closer at the leaf, and the membranes, and the stem, and wondering how they might describe what the leaf was made of – skin, or leather, or hide, or what?

The postman came – late: soaked: cursing. His waterproof cape half-protected the letters: envelopes' edges caught the rain.

'Put it there on the mantelpiece so that it will dry,' said Ellen to the child who fetched the only letter.

She called a halt and bade them begin lunch: 'Tidily!' Returning the leaf to the book in the desk, she turned over the pieces of writing-paper between which it had been pressed. In Thomas's handwriting she read there a familiar quotation.

They told me, Heraclitus, they told me you were dead,
They brought me bitter news to hear and bitter tears to shed.
I wept as I remembered how often you and I
Had tired the sun with talking and sent him down the sky.

It bore a date: '22 August 1922'.

Feeling a shiver of more than guilt at the intrusion, she returned the quotation to the book, closed the pages and flipped through the rest of the volume, *A Child's Encyclopaedia of Nature*. At the back lay a folded newspaper page; she drew it out and unfolded it, still propping the lid of the desk up with her forearms: the *Irish Independent* of 23 August 1922 bearing the news of the previous day: General Michael Collins's assassination in the Civil War. Ellen returned to the quotation and read it again, concluded her business beneath the desk-lid and closed it.

'Essie, clear a big space. A big, big space, Essie. The Master is going to spend his days in here – in the kitchen – from now on.' Ellen closed the school early, taking advantage of a lull in the stormy rain.

They moved the sewing-machine even farther into the deepest recess of the bow-window, and shoved Thomas's armchair with it. Essie and Ellen hauled, with Helena propped on cushions smiling when either of them coo-ed at her. The bed-chair just fitted through the doors: 'Thomas, you'd have a fit if you saw that chip off the paint, wouldn't you, love?' He had been dressed in a warm check shirt, brown corduroy trousers and thick tweed-wool socks.

'Now, Essie, doesn't he look a lot homelier? Doesn't he?'

That night, when Essie had gone to bed, Ellen went upstairs, fetched her nightclothes, soap and towel. The shutters safely closed, she undressed directly in front of Thomas. All customary modesty abandoned, albeit in this total privacy, Ellen washed in front of him, and dressed for bed. When she had finished, she kissed him on the mouth, something they once did every night except during 'Canon Law'. Although dry and unresponsive, his lips felt warm. She took his dull hand and traced it across her breasts, then, kissing the hand, replaced it inside his blankets.

'You're not dead, Thomas Kane,' she spat, 'you're not dying on me.'

At that instant, her neckhairs chilled and nausea lurched across her stomach. Footsteps on the gravel. Are the doors locked? Did Essie lock the doors? Footsteps. The lamp. Too late. Did the shutters obscure every view into the room? The footsteps stopped, ranged a little either side the front door, paused again, receded a step or two, returned, and finally receded: she heard a tiny 'ching' as the gate closed, then a fading slow clip-clop of hooves on the road outside.

'Essie,' Ellen hissed up the stairs, 'Essie?'

Essie read novels of a kind Ellen wished Thomas could observe. Lurid, on cheap paper, they bore titles such as *Her Heart was a Liar*; Essie read them far into the night, had a trunk full of them, and did 'swaps' with friends. Ellen tried giving her George Eliot, but Essie said of George, 'He's very thick to get through, Ma'am.'

She appeared at her door, looking out over the edge of the banisters.

'Essie, there was somebody here!'

'Ma'am, there surely wasn't? Not at this hour of the night, sure 'tis nearly eleven o'clock.'

'Essie, there was, I heard the step.'

Essie, seeing the Mistress's distress, clumped softly down the stairs. She wears bedsocks! If Thomas only knew!

'Essie. There were steps on the gravel. And then when he went. A horse.'

'Oh, Ma'am.' Essie looked crestfallen, but not frightened. 'Oh, Ma'am, you'll have to go to the Sergeant.'

As she walked to school next morning, bleary from the lack of sleep, and dull with a menstrual ache, a catching-up voice called her from behind. The man tipped his cap.

'Mornin', Ma'am, how's the Master these days?'

He skidded his foot to stop the bicycle, and Ellen felt her lip skin and the muscles around her mouth go flat and tight: her palate dried as if chalk-dusted.

'He's just the same, thanks.' Ohhhnn! My Jesus, Mercy. Mary Help.

'And you're keeping well yourself, Ma'am? And the babby, sure she must be gettin' big now?'

'She is indeed, grand and big, thank God.' Walk! Keep walking!

'The lad said to tell you he was asking for you, you know he's gone off to Sacramento. You know, Michael.'

'Has he a job out there, that's good?'

Ellen reached the school.

'Ma'am, wait a minute, would you?' Ellen reached the door: not a soul in sight.

'Ma'am, I called last night, but ye were all gone to bed.'

'I go to bed very early now.' Cold words. Over her shoulder. Lock. Stiff.

She did not look at him. He tried a friendly gambit, a conversational tone, her interests at heart.

'I called, Ma'am, to say to you, you should have that Crowe woman charged.'

Fingers slipped on the big school key. The Sergeant told him. The Sergeant told him. The Sergeant told him. The Sergeant told him. The Sergeant told him. The Sergeant told him. The Sergeant told him.

'You should, Ma'am, 'twould be good enough for her.'

She slammed the door behind her. He heard her lock it. In a small moan she said, 'Oh, Jesus in Heaven.' In a louder tone he said to the unhearing closed door, 'Good day to you now, Ma'am.' He wheeled away.

Ellen had reached near-hysteria. She asked the Assistant, Miss McGoldrick, to send one of the children for Dr Hogan. The child came back three-quarters of an hour later to say there was nobody in.

Miriam Hogan watched the child, guessed it had come from the school, followed it, listened to Ellen, said, 'Two things, do you hear me? One – I'll go to my uncle, he's a Bishop; that will get some action out of the Superintendent, if not out of that clot of a Sergeant. Two – invite everyone you can think of to come and visit. Make sure a lot of people are seen all around the house all the time.'

The Superintendent, known to mix not at all in the community, said to Ellen, 'I assure you, Ma'am, we will keep a very close eye on you. I assure you.'

On a sudden journey to the Depot in Dublin, he asked for help in initiating a new investigation. Nothing went in his favour: the Deputy Commissioner, a friend, said that the month of May was now too far past for any fresh inquiry to have any chance of a good result.

'It isn't as if anybody was murdered,' he pointed out.

The Superintendent argued that the man 'might as well be dead', and the Deputy Commissioner suggested that a good course of action might be to start a quiet search of his own, and 'talk to everyone'.

Concerning this, the Superintendent said he had already been doing exactly that and was coming up against a 'wall of silence. Talk is one thing, witnesses or proof is another. A wall of silence.'

'Centuries of practice,' commented the Deputy Commissioner.

'Look, John,' he said, stopping in mid-stroll near the Zoological Gardens in Phoenix Park at lunchtime, 'see it two ways. See it first as a policing matter. Make sure that woman has some noticeable protection. If you have a young fellow in your division who's looking for lodgings, get him to stay in the village or very nearby. Make sure he's seen cycling past that house very often, or better still pushing his bike past it. Then just talk. Did anyone go over the ground?'

He shook his head when the Superintendent reminded him of the empty cartridge case (the Sergeant had not handed in the one Miriam Hogan found). 'Useless. Any shotgun would have it. You see – you haven't a thing to go on, only rumour. If we arrested everyone on the basis of what the neighbours say, the whole shaggin' country'd be behind bars.'

'You see the thing is,' said the Superintendent, 'supposing something happens to that woman? Where are we then?'

'Ma'am, there's no use in any more padlocks, sure look at the gaps in them hedges.' Essie seemed sanguine.

'What choice do I have, Essie? I have to make myself feel safe, at least.'

Ellen wrote twenty letters to all sorts of people, and asked them to come and see Thomas. When the Superintendent called, he endorsed the measure.

'That way, Ma'am, any intruder who knows the area will never know whether there's somebody here or not.'

He comforted her further by telling her that a young Guard had just moved into the village in new lodgings, 'a big strong fellow, a Mayo man, he's built like the side of a church.'

Something nagged Ellen on the Friday afternoon, just as she left the school and faced towards home. Wasn't there a letter? That wet day, the postman. Wasn't there a letter somewhere? On the mantelpiece or somewhere? Where was it?

=

'They are lovely, you know. I tried not to bruise them, although one or two have a little bump, if you give me a knife I'll straighten them. This is the first time I made them and I'm afraid I ate two of them before I came up.' Ellen slid the lemon tartlets, still on a tray, out of the paper bag.

Ernestina said, 'I don't eat pastry.'

'Will the men eat them? Or visitors? If I'd known that I'd have baked a nice fruitcake, a porter cake or something. Do you like caraway seeds?'

'I hate them.' Ernestina sat back on the pillows and sighed, 'I think I'll bake a Madeira cake tomorrow myself.'

Ellen silently placed the tartlets' tray on the table inside the door and came to the bed. Sitting on the counterpane, the bed so high Ellen's legs scarcely touched the floor, she took Ernestina's hand.

'Ernestina. Listen to me. I'm going to tell you something. My life is awful. I am frightened something is going to happen to me. I am in a round of chores that would test a hospital. I am tired all the time. I have a husband but I have no husband. He's in a living death, and I have to live alongside that, and I have to look at it every day, and worse still, in a kind of a way, I have to watch a new life growing alongside, and bring up a child that will have a father but won't have a father, and a father who'll never be able to talk to her.' Ellen nodded her head for emphasis as she brought out every point. 'But it'd be ten times worse if I tried to deny everything that was happening to me.'

Ernestina closed her eyes, and then held up a hand to stop Ellen speaking further. Ellen sat there, staring down at the white face, the closed, dark-pigmented eyelids, no spectacles today, the uselessly inappropriate and ancient nightdress, all ribbons and torn lace: once it might have looked like something somebody saw in the cinema; now it had no warmth in it, and little decency.

'She came in last night,' said Ernestina, her eyes opening and phasing.

'I know, I know,' said Ellen, thinking Ernestina was dreaming aloud.

'She was down in the kitchen, I heard them laughing.' Small beads of moisture gathered on Ernestina's white forehead.

'Yes,' soothed Ellen.

'You think I'm dreaming,' said Ernestina, and subsided again. 'I never slept last night.'

Ellen said, 'This is a lovely room, you know. Would you like me to freshen it up a little for you?' and stood.

'Wait.' Ernestina called, and Ellen sat again.

'I mean it. She was. In the kitchen.' Her breath halted. 'You'd think he'd have the decency – or she'd have the decency – not to come in until I'm better again.'

'Oh,' said Ellen, realizing. 'The Merrigan girl?'

Ernestina nodded without speaking, two deep nods.

'She's working in a butcher's now.' Again, she slipped back into her white-faced, stagnant-breath tranquillity.

Ellen looked around the large room. The square-cut windows, with small leaden panes, had been made deep enough to contain a three-sided window seat, covered with long chintz cushions. On the wall between the windows, partly obscured when the curtains hung wide open, was a large regimental photograph, with a printed caption of many names in little black tiers beneath it. Tall old dried flowers, long past their attractive days, stood on a table large enough to contain an unusually big white china ewer and basin. Behind the door hung several coats, and what seemed like a man's dressing-gown: tall boots on the floor failed to stand up straight. A walk-in cupboard door stood open, all the visible clothing in complete disarray, some on the floor, some garments hanging crazily off each other. Cardboard boxes stood piled: Ellen saw the edge of an old towel peeping from one box. In the far corner of the room, arranged to catch the light from the window, stood a round mahogany table, and a chair: on the table, still in their packets, lay scattered threads, and cloths, and a half-opened brown paper parcel of what looked like several yards of excellent white linen. The remains of uneaten meals were strewn amid three teapots and a coffeepot on the same table, and propped amid the debris stood a photograph of two laughing girls in the bonnets and parasols of a summer's day: Ellen recognized Ernestina as she must have been fifteen years ago or so. Beneath the table a nest of discarded towels lay on the floor, half-covered by a bundled sheet, with some papers and documents scattered nearby.

Ernestina started awake again.

'I always doze when I haven't slept very well.'

Ellen asked, 'When did Dr Hogan come to see you?'

Ernestina replied, 'He's useless, that fellow. But he's nice, he's harmless.'

'Who makes you a cup of tea?' asked Ellen. 'I'm going to open the windows and let in a breath of fresh air.'

'What do you mean "deny everything"? What do you mean by that?' Ernestina received a sudden small charge of vitality.

'Is that your father?' asked Ellen, pointing to the regimental photograph.

'No. Uncle Henry. When young. Do you mean, I should tell my brother to get his own meals until I recover?'

Ellen said, 'Oh, we met him, at your party here, your uncle, in the summer.'

'Wasn't that the most irritating afternoon in the history of the world?' Ernestina said, and continued half-aloud, 'But if I admit to anyone.'

She stopped, and Ellen, freeing the second window catch and pushing back the curtains even more, turned and said, 'I know what you need, you need a dose of Sheila Cooper.'

Ernestina's laugh sounded more like a gasp. 'I'm going to get up for a while. She's barred from this house. She had a terrible row with my mother. She called my mother "an old hawk".'

Ellen moved across the room quickly to help Ernestina stand upright. Ernestina said, 'Spectacles are the greatest nuisance. When you take them off, you can't see where they are in order to put them back on again.'

Ellen handed them to her from the floor, and, inspecting the standing girl, asked, 'Would you like me to get a fresh, clean nightdress for you?'

'I haven't one. Do you know what my cousin Emmerson's father is getting – a telephone, of all things. It is costing them hundreds of pounds, hundreds.'

'Where do you want to sit? Over here? Lovely fresh air,' and Ellen walked beside Ernestina to the table by the window.

'Isn't anybody coming to clear these?' Ellen asked.

'No. I put the run on her. She was carrying stories about me.'

'Old hawk or no old hawk, it's Nurse Cooper for you,' said Ellen, and Ernestina smiled again, brightened by the light of the sun.

'"My lady",' she mimicked.

'"My lady", indeed,' mimicked Ellen.

'That will be a laugh,' Ernestina said, 'I always liked her.'

Everybody replied to Ellen's letters inviting them all to call and see Thomas.

'But it is a great idea,' said Leah, when she, typically, was the first to arrive – on a Saturday bus, without the children or Herbert. 'This is Herbert's theory, isn't it? To bring life to Thomas, bring life to where he is?'

She brought with her a cutting from a catalogue advertising a new Valor oil heater.

'Herbert said, "Why not have the world come and see Thomas?" so – hallo, Thomas,' Leah greeted. 'You're lucky to be in here out of the cold and the damp. Herbert sends you his best regards.'

'Show him your new skirt,' said Ellen, and Leah did. Alongside Ellen, she stood before the bed-chair and talked to Thomas. Essie, in the scullery, looked up into the kitchen and saw the two women standing there, one tall and red-haired, the other very much smaller, talking animatedly to the Master as if all three of them were involved in an enthusiastic discussion. Essie's face betrayed not a second's surprise at the scene: she went on wiping the saucepans dry.

'Herbert said to tell you, Thomas, that if you were up and about he would be trying to persuade you to go into politics. You know how he doesn't like any of them, De Valera, Cosgrave, Mulcahy, "the whole tainted crew", he calls them. Well, he says the only thing that would make him change his mind would be if you went in there and straightened them out.'

As they sat to eat at half-past one, Leah turned the bed-chair around so that Thomas was made to face the table, and even though his position, owing to the height and design of the bed-chair, raised him above the level of the table, at first glance he looked like no more than an invalid included among the family, sitting there ordinarily, his eyes closed, skin marbling and a little waxen.

Ellen remarked upon this to Leah. 'For a second there,' she said, 'out of the corner of my eye, I thought he was all right.' She put her fork down and lowered her head.

'Hoi!' said Leah softly, 'not allowed any more. Come on. Chin up.'

On the other side of the table, learning to negotiate a high baby-chair, sat Helena, being spoon-fed by Essie, murmuring, 'One for the moo-cow?'

'But look,' said Ellen, in a gesture that included Thomas and Helena, 'can't you see what I mean?'

'It is still not allowed,' said Leah. 'What you are doing needs all your courage, so you have to keep your courage up.'

'Strict,' said Ellen.

'I mean it,' said Leah. 'You said – you're trying to bring him back to life. Now, come on.'

Leah had called to Brunswick Square in case the Morris family wanted to send anything to Ellen. Her mother gave Leah a leg of lamb to bring; Bob wrote a note to say he would come out for the day on the bus on Tuesday, and sit with Thomas while Ellen was at school. This fitted the first week of Ellen's jigsaw into place: now each of the next seven days would have visitors.

As she was leaving, Leah approached Ellen and spoke to her from behind. 'I wonder. I wonder, it would only be until next week or so, Ellen would you have . . . ? I mean, ten would do, or even five.'

Ellen went off to fetch her handbag, saying conversationally, 'Do you know what it is, that new hand-cream is very good . . .'

'And don't think,' continued Leah, 'that I have forgotten one penny. Or the length of time outstanding. Herbert, he doesn't know about any of this, and I really haven't enough . . .'

'My turn to shush you, now,' smiled Ellen, still permitting Leah not to look at her.

On Monday after school, Ellen marched the sixth class to the house. She pushed the bed-chair back a little to allow all eleven of them room to stand in a bunch inside the bow-window.

'Now, Master,' she addressed Thomas, who, on Ellen's instructions, had been dressed by Essie and Mrs Greege that morning in one of his good suits, 'I have to fill in the Progress Record for October, and I wanted you to hear how good they all are.'

Turning to the pupils she said, 'Now, first the poem, then the song. I'll start you off.'

Nodding her head, she spoke the opening line, and by the second line they had taken over in a full and good swing.

My eyes are filmed, my beard is grey;
I am bowed with the weight of years.
I would I were stretched in my bed of clay,

> *With my long-lost youth's compeers.*
> *For back to the Past, though the thought brings woe,*
> *My memory ever glides –*
> *To the old, old time, long, long ago,*
> *The time of the Barmecides.'*

The children gathered strength, and became unstoppable by the time they entered the second verse.

> *'Then youth was mine, and a fierce, wild will,*
> *And an iron arm in war,*
> *And a fleet foot high up on Ishkar's hill,*
> *When the watch-lights glimmered afar,*
> *And a barb as fiery as any I know,*
> *That Kurd or Bedouin rides,*
> *Ere my friends lay low – long, long ago,*
> *In the time of the Barmecides.'*

Ellen had chosen the poem on account of Thomas's love for it: he quoted it often: conveniently, it came within the Department's generous curricular brief. When they rolled on, to the verse which began

> *'I see rich Bagdad once again*
> *With its turrets of Moorish mould,'*

she did not even flinch at the lines

> *'I call up many a gorgeous show*
> *Which the Pall of Oblivion hides.*
> *All passed like snow, long, long ago,*
> *In the time of the Barmecides.*
> *All passed like snow, long, long ago,*
> *In the time of the Barmecides.'*

'Very good, very good.' She unclasped her hands, and from her bag took a tuning-fork. 'Now.' She banged the tuning-fork on the edge of the kitchen table and listened, then hummed, then maintained and increased the hum, checked it by hitting the tuning-fork again, then came down a key in the humming, and stopped.

433

'Ready? One, two, three, four.' They began.

'Proudly the note of the trumpet is sounding,
Loudly the war-cries arise on the gale;
Swiftly the steed by Lough Swilly is bounding,
To join the thick squadrons in Saimear's green vale.
On, every mountaineer!
Strangers to flight and fear!
Rush to the standards of dauntless Red Hugh!
Bonnaught and gallowglass,
Throng from each mountain pass,
On for old Erin,
O'Donnell Aboo.'

'One verse is fine,' Ellen said, and turning to Thomas, 'They know all the words, Master, the whole four verses, and they know the interpretation.'

She turned back to the class.

'Now, what kind of a song is that?' They all raised their hands.

'A marching-song, Ma'am.'

'That's right, a clan marching-song.'

'Which one of you knows what a "bonnaught" is?' Several hands shot up.

'A class of a soldier, Ma'am,' said a number of voices together.

'Good, good. And a gallowglass?'

In a more slender unison, three or four voices murmured, 'Another kind of soldier, Ma'am.'

'Yes, but what kind?'

'One with a heavy sword, Ma'am,' ventured one boy.

Ellen affirmed. 'Yes, a heavily-armed footsoldier,' she said.

'And who was Red Hugh?'

They all knew that. 'Red Hugh O'Donnell, Ma'am, one of the earls of Donegal.'

'And what does "Aboo" mean?'

'It means, Ma'am, "Up", it means a cheer.'

'Yes, a cheer,' she said. 'You're all very good, aren't they, Master?' and she dismissed them.

On Tuesday, Bob Morris arrived, climbing heavily off the bus outside the school wearing a new Homburg hat.

'But why didn't you stop at the house?' Ellen said, 'Now you'll have to walk back up the road on your poor leg.'

'I brought my stick,' he said, 'I wanted to see you first.'

'Did you bring your pipe?' Ellen asked.

'I did,' Bob answered in some surprise. 'Why?'

'I want you to have a good smoke and make sure you blow the smoke in Thomas's direction,' said Ellen. 'He used to love –' she corrected herself: '– he loves the smell of that tobacco of yours.'

On Wednesday, Michael Condon came to take Ellen for another driving lesson, and Ellen persuaded him to sit and talk with her in front of Thomas, and gradually she led him by example to include Thomas in the conversation, as she asked him all kinds of questions about cars, and the new developments, and how many cars there were in the whole county by now, and who owned them, and how many makes of cars there were altogether in the world, did he think, and was it true the Canon was thinking of getting one, or was it the Curate?

Thursday brought the results of Ellen's most successful letter. Eight people came to the house at five o'clock, followed shortly after by another three: she had written to the members of Thomas's Union committee. The Hon. Secretary wrote back, saying how clearly he had understood her letter, and what she was trying to do, found it admirable, and ended by suggesting they might hold the meeting with Thomas there, if she didn't think that was too big a crowd in the house.

'The marvellous thing, Essie,' said Ellen, 'is that it forces us to get the parlour back to rights.'

'Why was I so moved by it?' Ellen asked Nurse Cooper that night, when they had all gone. 'Was it because every single one of them behaved as if things were completely normal, and all through the meeting they referred to Thomas, telling him things that had happened since the last meeting? And they all picked up his hand and gave him a good genuine handshake when they came, and as they left. And you know, the women, they didn't bring cakes or anything, they just expected me to provide them. Which I loved.'

Sheila Cooper said, 'Now, on that account, you're entitled to shed a small tear – only one, mind you.' She then launched straight into an account of Ernestina Stephenson's condition.

'The poor girl. She isn't in a good way at all. I mean, she always had a good physique and it is standing to her, but all the same –'

On Friday, Val Vousden called by appointment.

'Ma'am, I won't be one bit taken aback, the things I've seen.'

Ellen had begun to discover that the more she spoke openly to people, the less abashed they found themselves.

Val bowed to Thomas, and said to him, 'Sir, I have very good news for you. The band, as you'll know *via* your Mrs, has started practising, the Canon is after lending us the school. And we're doing grand. Mrs Heffernan is a Trojan with the uniforms. Now, Sir,' he addressed Thomas grandly, 'a lot of that is down to you, and you haven't had a chance to hear my new monologue; 'tis famous already, 'tis called "The Deanstown Band", but I'm going to give it to you now, if you don't mind.'

Essie came to the kitchen door and leaned against the jamb of it, watching. Helena banged the table of her high baby-chair with a spoon. Val stepped up, bowed and launched into his recitation; Ellen had to stand behind him so that he would not see her trying to choke back the laughter, and when it had finished she and Essie applauded: Helena gooh-ed.

Over his cup of tea and slice of porter cake, Val said to Ellen, 'Ma'am, d'you recall a conversation I had with you outside the school a few weeks ago, and I asked you what was wrong with himself?'

'I do, Mr Vousden.'

'Call me Val, Ma'am, that's what all my public calls me. Well, I went away, thinking very hard, and I made some enquiries. And I was wondering – would you be at all interested in taking the Boss to see a man who wasn't an official doctor like, a man who specializes in curing people though, and he has a particular interest in things of the head. And the man I was thinking about is over near Doneraile, and, as I say, he's not an official doctor, like, but he has great success with the cures. I don't know for certain, but I think he might be a seventh son of a seventh son.'

Ellen wrote down the name and address.

Father Watson came on Saturday's bus, and stayed until Monday morning. Ellen asked for Confession again.

'Father, I have two grievous matters to confess.'

'Yes, my child.'

'Father, my impure thoughts will not go away.'

Ellen, with all her classmates, had marvelled when young at the inviolable secrecy of the Confessional. The holier nuns insisted that priests received Divine Grace to erase memory or identity; 'In other words, a priest could have a murder confessed to him and meet that man in the street and never know. There's Divine Grace for you.' Their more practical Sisters inclined towards a theory of mundanity and weight of numbers: priests simply forgot because they heard so much of the same from so many. In that whispered tumult, the sins of individual penitents melded, then faded. Ellen made different calculations regarding Father John's Confessional role: he did not customarily hear Confessions.

'When do these thoughts trouble you, my child?'

'In the morning early, Father, when I wake up, and at night when I lie down to sleep. Alone in bed.'

'Are they directed to any one person, my child?'

'Well, as I told you before Father, at my last Confession, there is one man in my mind.'

It was quite improper of Ellen to breach Confession's timelessness and anonymity like that, but John Watson did not rebuke her.

'Is he known to you, my child, or is he a stranger?'

'He's a very old friend, Father.'

'Have there been any impure actions between you, my child?'

Ellen in a shocked tone said, 'Oh, no, Father, he's a very good man. A very holy person.'

'You must put impure thoughts from your head, my child. God will help you. He will understand and make allowances for your very difficult position in life. That which you once so rightly and beautifully . . . so beautifully, what's the word – enjoyed, or perhaps I should say, experienced, has been taken from you cruelly. Nonetheless, you must pray diligently and assiduously to seek to avert temptation. Now, my child, you said there were two grievous matters.'

'Yes, Father. I have been thinking of murdering someone, and I want to know would God forgive me? Not my husband, Father, someone else.'

Father Watson smiled, and even laughed a little.

'No, my child. He would not forgive you, the gift of Life is His and His alone. We may feel murder in our hearts, my child, but a good person cannot bring themselves to do it.'

437

He absolved Ellen, and stayed a little while in prayer after she had returned to the kitchen from the hall.

Throughout the week-end, she showed him warmth, this cold, confident priest. One or two visitors dropped in briefly after last Mass in Mooreville; Father John hosted the parlour, leading from an armchair. As Ellen left for school on Monday morning, Father John came downstairs to enjoy a leisurely breakfast cooked by Essie. He and Ellen made arrangements that he should come and stay for Christmas.

Ellen found the missing letter: some exercise copies had also suffered dampness that day in children's schoolbags, and had been put out to dry near the fire: a child had gathered the letter up in error, and now returned it. Ellen glanced at Edel Crowe's handwriting and hurled the letter in her basket: 'Blast her, anyway.'

'Did Father John get away all right?' Ellen asked Essie after school.

'He did, Ma'am. Isn't it strange,' said Essie, 'how the priests are not good at talking to a baby at all?'

'They've no interest in them, Essie,' said Ellen.

Ellen spoke to Thomas at length every night. Sometimes she merely prattled on, sitting there as Essie did the last chores. Damping down the slack to keep the fire in; laying the table for the morning, the cups turned upside down to ward off the fire's floating smuts; preparing the oatmeal for the porridge; all tasks Thomas once did.

On most nights, Ellen waited until Essie had gone to bed. She undressed in the kitchen, standing in front of Thomas fully naked as she washed, then raising her arms high above her head to put on her nightdress. Ages ago, she had sent away to New York for a *de Bevoise Step-in Corselette* and it had arrived on Saturday: (she saw Father John take a good look at the long, narrow box which Ellen had opened and left on the hallstand shelf).

Now she tried it on, wriggling and jiggling. 'What d'you think, Thomas?' and raised her hands above her head like a Spanish dancer.

'Thomas?' The nightdress slipped down along her body, and she wriggled to help it fall to the ground, 'I feel vicious now. I feel

438

vicious. I made the mistakes, but you were the one who was right.
I was wrong. You can do nothing about it. But I can. And I'm
putting it all right. Thomas, you may live, or you may die, but
your debts will be paid.'

She kissed him on the mouth every night, sometimes more than
once. She kissed him now and talked on.

'I am not going to rest until I have paid back the people who
hurt you. I have been well and truly paid back. Now it is our turn,
Thomas, dear, and I am doing it. No wonder Father John says to
me that I've changed. He'll see. They'll all see. Remember the
ploughing, Thomas, "as if God had reached down with a knife and
cut a furrow along the ground". Wasn't that what you said good
ploughing was, Thomas? Well – that is what I'm going to do. Good
ploughing.'

Michael Condon, although short, had the strength of the farmers.
He also had a good suit, and he had put it on specially for the
outing Ellen had requested. Between the three of them, Essie,
Ellen and Michael Condon, they manoeuvred Thomas into his
heavy grey coat, out of the house and into the car, which Ellen
herself had polished for the occasion. With pillows and blankets
they stayed Thomas in an upright position, wedging his head gently
against the hood, closing the door to fix his shoulder. The mists
had cleared, promising a sunny morning: Essie would take care of
Helena, whose pudgy arm waved from the door.

'Will you drive a bit, yourself, Ma'am?' asked Michael Condon,
of whom Leah, when she first saw him, said, 'All these good-looking
men.'

'Not for a bit,' said Ellen, 'you get us started and get us away
first.'

'Fair enough, Ma'am.' He secured her in the dickey seat: she
pulled the wool bonnet down over her ears.

'I don't know if we're on a wild goose chase, Essie,' Ellen had
said last night.

'Ma'am, sure what of it?' said Essie. 'A person should try
everything.'

'The parish will know, I suppose,' brooded Ellen.

'Sure what harm, Ma'am, they'd do the same themselves.'

Ellen called as Michael opened his door, 'How far away is
Doneraile?'

'I don't rightly know, Ma'am. 'Tis a bit far.'

'Do you think the Master'll feel the cold, Michael?'

'Them hot-water bottles should do the trick, Ma'am.'

Beyond Mooreville, Ellen changed places with Michael.

'Hold on to yourself now, Thomas,' she said.

It proved the best drive she ever had.

'God, Ma'am, a few more of these drives, and you won't need me at all,' said Michael at their destination.

It took them three hours exactly: they found the healer's house easily, a cottage down a long but mercifully un-rutted lane. The man came to the door to see the car. He then went back indoors, saying, 'You'll have to wait, I have a client in here.'

'Have you any hot water?' Ellen shouted after him.

He didn't bother to answer, so she took the three hot-water bottles to a farmhouse they could see a field away, and returned very quickly.

'Here you are, Thomas,' she said. 'I'm after cleaning them out of house and home, all their hot water gone.'

She felt Thomas's hands and began to warm them.

'Of course,' she said to Michael, 'I have to watch that I don't burn him either.'

'His colour is a bit healthier, Ma'am, after the drive.'

The healer's previous 'client' turned out to be a greyhound, led away limping by its owner, after which the healer came to the car and looked in.

'I know that man,' he said.

'Do you?' said Ellen.

'Master Kane,' said Michael Condon.

'Kane. The very man. He was very well known around here, so he was. All north county Cork knew that man, Ma'am. He nearly stayed here one night. You know, in the old days, like.'

They half-carried, half-dragged Thomas into the cottage: a hen cluttered out as they entered.

'Prop him up there, now, Ma'am, on that high chair, so that the head is clear of the back of it, that's it, rest it on the spar – there.'

Then Ellen and Michael Condon were invited to sit down by the fire. When Ellen's eyes got accustomed to the gloom she found the cottage surprisingly neat, with postcards from America on the wall above the fireplace, between two orange and white china spaniels.

She gave the healer a brief history.

'They say 'tis brain damage, do they?' he ascertained.

'They do.'

The healer walked all around, peering at Thomas's head: how he could see in the dimness Ellen did not know.

'Ah, it was there it was, right.' He found the place on Thomas's temple, 'and 'tisn't long healed?'

Ellen watched with anxiety, then could stay sitting no longer, and rose to join him.

'Well, ointment is no good, that's for a fact.' The healer walked around again. 'Ma'am, he's as strong as a horse.'

'He's not as strong as he was, to tell you the truth,' said Ellen. 'I notice a bit of a failing in him lately.' She had not so far confided this worry to anyone.

'The winter does that, Ma'am. It does it to all of us.' The healer wore a stained brown leather finger protector on the index finger of the right hand. 'And the doctors say there's nothing doing?'

'Nothing.'

He bit his lip for a moment, and went out past the cottage window, returning a moment later with a heavy parcel wrapped in damp sacking.

'You'd think to look at him sometimes,' said Michael Condon, while the healer was out, 'that the Master was full alive.'

Ellen did not reply. The healer put the parcel on the kitchen table, and unwrapped from it a pair of flat wet stones, each one slightly larger than the size of a man's hand.

'What are they?' asked Ellen.

'They're the amulets,' he said. 'In my family over two hundred years. They're healing stones, Ma'am.'

'Why are they wet?' she asked.

'That's part of the whole thing, Ma'am. You could keep them stones there by the fire and they'd always be wet, winter and summer. We don't know why.'

Ellen, out of habit, felt Thomas's forehead.

The healer came forward. Standing behind Thomas's chair, he held the stones, one in each hand, and fixing his gaze on them, pressed them gently to the front and back of Thomas's head. He

441

spoke in a language Ellen did not understand, not a chant, not a prayer, just a series of statements, spoken rather flatly, except that each one ended on a slightly dramatic rising inflection. Staring hard at them once more, he then held the stones gently to each of Thomas's temples. Ellen winced as he pressed a stone to the location of the damage, but the healer was gentleness itself.

Again the strange dialect, and this time for longer: when it ended, and he took the stones away, the healer looked drained and disappointed. He returned the stones to their parcel.

'Well?' Ellen asked.

'No response, Ma'am. It might be that something will come out of it, but usually I feel a bit of a jolt if there's going to be a cure. Now I won't be charging you for that, Ma'am.' He had a wart at the corner of his lip.

At the car, Michael Condon whispered, 'Did you hear that tongue he was talking in, Ma'am?'

'I didn't understand a word of it, Michael. The odd word of Latin maybe. Did you know what he was saying?'

'No, Ma'am, but I'll tell you what it was. 'Twas Shelta, the tinker's language, Ma'am.'

That night, preparing for bed, Ellen, as she undressed before Thomas, said, 'I know, Thomas, you would mock me from here to Kingdom Come, for going to a quack doctor; I can hear you laughing now in my head. You'd say, "that bloody old wizard", wouldn't you, Thomas? And, yes, you'd be right. And you'd say, "That fellow is the opposite of anything", wouldn't you? But you wouldn't be able to answer me this. Why is it I'm so disappointed that he didn't cure you there and then? I know I'm too sensible to believe he could have done? And why at the same time did he give me hope for the first time that you might get better one day? Thomas, the old part of me, the part that was there before I met you, sometimes tells me I'm going mad. Out of my head. But I saw that old rabbit-catcher that day after the pond, and you so young and vigorous-looking when you were skating, that is what dead looks like, not what you look like.'

Two days after, on late Monday morning, Ellen saw Essie lumber frantically towards the school window. Ellen could hardly understand what she was saying.

442

'The Master, Ma'am. Oh, Ma'am. I'm after having a look at him, he's looking awful bad, Ma'am; he's feeling very hot.'

Ellen told the most senior boy in the school to put on his coat and follow her to the house. She raced up the road, Essie a long way behind. She ran through the door, skidding to a stop in the hall. Thomas's cheeks had never been so red.

'Oh, Jesus Christ, Oh, God.' His forehead felt scorched. 'Oh, Thomas.'

28

'You stupid woman! You stupid woman!' Miriam Hogan snapped at Ellen. 'Do you not know anything at all about medicine? A quack? You took him to a quack? Some fool in a dirty old cottage somewhere, and you thought he'd heal this man?'

'I thought . . .'

'Don't think. Act!'

'What? I mean, what will I do? Will we move him into the hospital?'

'For him to get worse? Do what I tell you!'

The schoolboy Ellen had sent to the Dispensary found Miriam alone. She led them now through a series of procedures: sealing the windows with brown paper; keeping the temperature even; instructions to bathe Thomas every four hours; never leaving his side. Hot water was to be made permanently available; wrap him in clean cool linen; the fire to be kept even with regular tiny supplies of coal. They took turns massaging Thomas's chest, bathing his forehead; Miriam showed them how to make poultices and apply them – almost too hot to bear, never to burn his skin. Miriam controlled the panic, delegated, ordered, cooled them.

Dr Hogan arrived. 'None of your airiness here, Jack. Use your brains, any you have left. Come on! How is he?'

''Tis the lad all right, the boy is on the way,' said Jack with the stethoscope, 'd'you see?'

'The lad?! The boy?! What are you talking about? Can't you speak the King's English, Jack.'

Jack, a little aggrieved, a little defensive, said, 'I'd say, Miriam, that man could develop pneumonia. That's what I think. Or d'you want a second opinion?'

Miriam said, 'No time for that. What we need is consistency. Tell us all the correct procedures. Now!' She turned to Ellen. 'Quick. Write these down. In handwriting that we can all read.'

Jack intoned, point after point. The morning quickened into dread.

=

'I have never seen,' said Nurse Cooper some days later, 'a human being change so much, and I have seen a lot of things. It's like she grew a new self.'

New and harsh. Ellen, the pious and virtuous woman, the girl Thomas often teased as 'a goody-good', the girl Canon Williams called 'Miss Prim', already disappearing, vanished completely: a woman with a different nature, cold and hot and frantic and aggressive, coped with this new pressure.

The Curate called, offering prayers, Rites. 'No time for that now, Father.' She closed the door.

All the details of duty, all the well-behaved vestiges, froze. Thomas slipped and slipped. Dr Hogan and Nurse Cooper conferred.

'Tell me plainly,' Ellen's words lunged at them. 'What are the hopes of getting him back?' Exposed to one emotional atrocity too many, a soldier under fire, Ellen's courtesy disappeared.

'A thin enough chance,' said Nurse Cooper.

'I do not care,' said Ellen, 'if I never teach another day. I do not care if I never say another prayer. I do not care if my life turns me so that I have to scrub floors, but I am going to do everything in my power. I want no mouldering rabbit-catchers in this house.'

All others around her – except Miriam – suffered exhaustion within that first sleepless seventy-two hours. As if hastened by demons, Ellen drove herself.

'I don't care if I collapse,' she snapped.

Miriam said, 'You're right. You're right! Go on! Go on!'

Ellen called every child in fifth and sixth class into action, and sent them out across the parish with short, urgent messages. From Dr Hogan and Nurse Cooper she demanded the clearest possible instructions on the best, and perhaps only possible, means of keeping Thomas alive, of keeping down his fever, of preventing pneumonia; she made the pair of them bring their medical books to the house, and checked everything they told her – she questioned and questioned and questioned: once, she even snapped at Essie. The house became a hushed cauldron.

When the neighbouring women whose favours she called in began to arrive at the house, she allotted each one a firm duty. They nursed Thomas, changing him all the time, out of

445

perspiration-soaked clothes, but keeping him warm while doing so, administering such medication as the doctor had found useful, feeding him with the greatest possible care, finding, for instance, the best meat to mince and break down almost to a *purée* in order to nourish him, and they talked and talked to him.

And when each woman left to go home, worn out, Ellen, still full of fire, thanked them, ticked them off on her roster, and asked them to tell their menfolk to call and sit with Thomas. And each woman said to the other how useless it was all going to prove, but it was as well to go along with it.

Ellen slept in two-hour breaks, three sleeps in every twenty-four hours. Apart from those short periods, she did not take her eyes off Thomas for more than a minute or two at a time.

'Miriam, will you keep an eye on the baby?' she asked.

'I will not, thanks,' said Miriam. 'I hate children.'

When Leah stepped from the bus, she found an Ellen no longer intent on speaking in the right tones, or adopting the 'good posture' she had always hoped for: she saw the brusque side in full flight. No small talk, no hint of self-pity, no mention of prayer or God, or the Church or the Sacraments, no holy epithets, no morbid interests.

'A kind of furious calm, Herbert. And she's aged, she's no longer a young one.'

'Why wouldn't she?' said Herbert. 'Wouldn't anyone?'

Dr Hogan suffered daily: Ellen tore into him. 'Think again, Dr Hogan, think again. Is there pneumonia there or isn't there? Is the man going to live? You've been in the war, you've seen crisis, is there a crisis, or isn't there?'

Dr Hogan rose to it. 'No, there isn't a crisis – yet.'

Miriam said, 'There has to be somebody with that man night and day. What would you call a crisis, Jack?'

Jack said, 'I mean, what they call a crisis in pneumonia, the moment when things go either way, d'you see?'

To Bob Morris, bewildered by his daughter's newfound force, Dr Jack Hogan said, 'What I want to know is where did she come from at all? I never saw a woman with that kind of fight in her, did you? Is it from yourself or from the mother she gets it?'

Ellen said to her mother, 'Mama, I haven't time to look at your new coat, I haven't time to pay you attention.'

The Canon arrived. Ellen directed, 'Pray over him and only that, Canon. No, you may not give the Last Rites, no, you may not give him Extreme Unction, that man is half a century away from the Last Rites.'

When the Canon began to protest, she said, 'Canon Williams, did you hear me?'

Late that night, telling Nurse Cooper about the Canon, she said, 'Can you find such a thing – anywhere in the world – as a man who isn't pig stupid?'

The Canon came back next morning.

'Ellen,' he said. She looked up at him in surprise, never having heard the word 'Ellen' from his lips. 'I'm just saying.' He faltered. 'Look. God bless you. Whatever happens, God bless you.' He turned away. The long, scratchy face of him.

'Well, thank you,' she called after him.

He turned around briefly. 'Oh, by the way, the job is all right. The Principal. Yourself.' He hurried off.

'Oh!' In spite of everything, the excellent news penetrated.

The men from the farms came each evening, slow footsteps on the gravel, and then the throat-clearing knock on the door. Self-consciously, they held Thomas's hand the way she showed them how, and within a short time found themselves relaxed and involved. Essie and Mrs Greege and Mrs Dalton and Mrs Relihan made rounds of sandwiches, and for over a week and a half Ellen Kane drew the entire community together in the effort to save her husband's life. Nobody queried the size of the effort to which they had begun to contribute: they all spoke of it in a paradoxical combination of natural acceptance and wonder.

Ellen never established – to her intense annoyance – whether Thomas had suffered pneumonia. At nine o'clock on the Thursday morning of the second week, Dr Hogan and Nurse Cooper conferred in the hallway, and calling Ellen, said they believed the worst had passed, 'definitely'. She ascertained some follow-through procedures, looked to the two women sitting with Thomas under Mrs Greege's supervision, and to their astonishment, put on her coat, collected her basket and went to school. Men came around that evening and other women, as arranged; however the word had begun to spread that the Master was out of that particular danger. On Friday, the Canon appeared at the school door just as the junior children were released at half-past two. Ellen walked to meet him: Jeremiah Williams was concealing something behind his long back. He stood in the doorway.

'You'll find these very tasty,' he said, offering a paper bag of apples. 'I have them in hay since August, it keeps them grand,' and he walked away.

Ellen tidied up the school paperwork – not much, but it had fallen behind, thanks to the useless Miss McGoldrick, still a Temporary Assistant – every applicant's letter for the job had, in Ellen's opinion, proven them unsuitable.

At four o'clock she walked home at a more rational pace than she had walked anywhere for days. Everything seemed in place: Nurse Cooper and Mrs Greege sat by the range chatting.

Ellen ate from a plate on her knee, then said to them, and to Essie, 'I'm going to sleep, see you all tomorrow,' at which they laughed. She kissed Thomas and Helena, climbed the stairs and slept for twenty-one hours.

Ellen made a pact with herself.

'No celebration of Christmas, no cards, nothing like that. Essie, there'll be you, and me, and Thomas, and the baby, and Father Watson.'

Then, a week or so after the Thomas crisis had died down, she sat alone one Saturday evening in the kitchen, listening to Essie move around in her room upstairs, as she seemed to do for hours every night before bed. Ellen had never dared to ask what exactly Essie did in that clumping time.

'Thomas.' She turned to him, laying a hand on the side of the bed. 'Tomorrow I am going to have a talk with Dr Hogan, and I have some hard questions to ask. Oh, Thomas.' She rested a hand on his cheek.

Jack Hogan called mid-afternoon and she sat him in the parlour: he seemed relaxed enough, notwithstanding the heated way Ellen had dealt with him during the intensive care of Thomas – for which she neither made, nor felt, apology.

'In your honest opinion?' she asked.

'Only my opinion,' he defended; 'others'll tell you different.'

'Go on. I can ask others for their opinions.'

'In my opinion –' he looked uncomfortable '– what will happen

448

is this. The sort of crisis he's just come through will happen again. And again. And again. D'you see, each one will leave him weaker than before. You realize, don't you, that what you have there lying on that bed inside in that kitchen is a medical miracle. I mean, if this wasn't a Catholic country, there'd be people'd say, well . . .' His voice trailed off.

'Catholic country or no Catholic country, what about life?'

'But, Ma'am, you're a great one for calling a spade a spade, you can't call that "life", d'you see. You said that yourself. I mean to say, how long can you go on keeping him alive? I mean, one day, Ma'am, you're going to have to face, well . . .'

He did not finish the sentence. Ellen twirled a finger in her hair.

'I don't know what to say to that,' she said.

'Ma'am, I'll say it again. The man is a miracle. It is miraculous. It nearly isn't natural. Since what, the ninth of May? Ninth of June, ninth of July, ninth of August –' he counted '– seven months to the day. D'you remember the day you took him out of the hospital? We all gave him six weeks to live from that day. D'you see, none of us knows how you did it? 'Tis against the grain of anything we ever heard of. That's the thing you have to realize.'

'No,' said Ellen, but to herself, not to Jack Hogan. 'A force beneath the force.'

'Ma'am, that is mad talk,' said Dr Hogan, 'that is what I call baloney. Dangerous. The medical fact is that your husband suffered damage to his brain, he's in what they call a coma, and he's shown no signs of recovering and no matter what way you look at it, you can't get away from that.'

'If I keep him alive,' said Ellen, fiercely, still ignoring the doctor, 'I am certain good will come of it.'

'Well, you asked me my opinion and I've given it to you. Look, why did I ask you to go and see that poor Ernestina Stephenson? Why?'

'So that she would have a woman to talk to, to visit her, I presume?'

'That's true. But, Ma'am, you've no experience of death or tragedy, and I also thought, d'you see, that seeing her the way she is, I mean that girl is finished.'

Ellen struck the side of her chair.

'Get me some more doctors.'

'Ma'am, I got you the best doctors you'll find. The men in Cork is the best there is.'

'Get them back here.'

'They won't come.'

'Ask them.'

'What would they come for? They were here already.'

Ellen leaned closer. 'What time of the day is it?'

'Four o'clock.'

'I know it is.'

'Then why did you ask me?'

'I didn't mean what time on your watch. I meant what time on your breath?' She sniffed and went 'Grrrrr! Don't ever come in here again with a smell of drink on you' – but Jack Hogan had an irrepressibly genial demeanour, and he left the house cheerfully. Ellen walked to close the gate after him. Across the road, in the field just inside the wall, Miriam Hogan suddenly stood up into view, like a ghost in the December twilight.

'Oh, you frightened me!' exclaimed Ellen.

'Don't you believe a word Jack says,' Miriam said.

Ellen replied, 'Well, that's not very loyal of you.'

'Oh, good,' said Miriam. 'If you ever want a companion to go anywhere with, on a walk, or out at night or anything, let me know.'

'Thank you, I will,' said Ellen. 'I won't ask you in, if you don't mind. I have an awful lot to do.'

'I wouldn't come, anyway,' she laughed, making Ellen laugh too.

'I asked Jack to get a second opinion.'

Miriam said, 'They don't like Jack very much. Where did he say they'd come from?'

'Cork again.'

Miriam laughed. 'They're very proud in Cork. If they can't fix it themselves they'll send him to London. They'd never admit to Dublin that they couldn't cure somebody.'

Two days before Christmas Eve, in the late morning, Ellen began to cry. The tears flowed silently at first, then noisily. Essie stood there, looking. Ellen stopped and blew her nose several times. The storm had lasted five minutes or so.

'Such a difference, Essie,' she sniffled, pointing to Thomas, 'between our first Christmas and our second Christmas together –

and will we have a third Christmas? Where will we all be this time next year?'

'Oh, Ma'am, sure the Master's still with us, and while there's life, there's hope, they say.'

Ellen, who hated proverbs nowadays, jumped to her feet, clapping her hands.

'Right, Essie, that settles it, I'm going to put up decorations and we're going to have a Christmas candle on Christmas Eve when Father John comes, that settles it.'

The postman arrived at four o'clock, in good and cheery fettle, having been thanked copiously in many houses for his year's work. Ellen shivered, then bristled when she saw the handwriting, and, opening the letter, quickly looked first to see whether Edel Crowe had signed it.

> Dear Mrs Kane,
>
> You never answered my first letter. I said in it that I wrote to my brother the surgeon in London, a long letter all about you. ['I hope you signed it,' Ellen muttered.] I told him everything that happened, and all about your own misfortune. He since wrote back to me and I enclose his letter; as you can see he wants you to write to him: he is not, unusually, coming home for Christmas, which I hoped he was, so that he might be able to see your husband. Let me know your answer.
>
> Yours sincerely,
> Edel Crowe

'Essie, d'you remember me talking about those Crowe people?' Ellen asked, as she shook out the contents of the envelope, dropping the second letter on the floor.

'Them anonymous letters, Ma'am, was it?' Essie called back from the scullery.

'Yes. What kind of a crowd are they at all, remind me?'

'Oh, Ma'am, you said they've plenty of money.'

Ellen skimmed the note, fastening on the sentence, 'Please tell your Mrs Kane to write to me here. I can't do anything unless her doctor or she herself requests it.'

She called out again, 'Jesus, Essie, do you know what? Edel Crowe's brother. He's a surgeon, over in London.'

'I knew that, Ma'am.'

On Christmas Eve, at the lighting of the Christmas candle by the youngest of each household, every family murmured, in Irish, the soft, secular prayer, 'That we may be all alive at this time next year.' In the morning, at the foot of the hill in Deanstown, Canon Jeremiah Williams, P.P., rose late, steamed noisily and long and yellow into the enamel chamber-pot, parted the lace curtains and looked at the grey day, then humped himself down backwards to his cold pillows.

'Girls are always lazy to start,' said Nurse Cooper to a first-time mother. 'Boys are savages.' The baby drowsed, and Nurse Cooper laid her down in the crib, and as the young woman then drowsed, from her stiff white uniform pocket, Nurse Cooper drew a tiny green bottle. 'Little dab of perfume,' she said, placing her finger behind each of the damp mother's ears, then on her wrist pulses, and then at the 'V' of her breasts. Nurse Cooper turned down the gaslight, leaving only a mild, flickering glow, and withdrew, leaving another new mother and baby to sleep. Outside the window, the town was dark and quiet.

In the small pool of light from the candle on the windowsill of the village, Timmy Quinn looked at the moth he had captured in a matchbox. His older sister surged forward to see it and the boy grunted, then screamed and fought her off; the sister put a kind arm around him and said she was only joking.

He had a spartan room along a bare, planked corridor within a sober brick building; therein, Father John Watson, S.J., put aside his breviary. Beneath his high window, the yellow street lamp softened in the swirl of a mist off the river. Inside the glass, Father John Watson opened a drawer and for some moments looked at an old church magazine photograph of the young Ellen Morris. He put it away again, and began to polish his shoes and pack his small travel bag.

=

Ernestina Stephenson slept, therefore long-legged Miriam Hogan received no reply to her knocking and ringing, and strode home again.

In her little notebook that she kept hidden from Herbert, Leah counted the row of figures and dates of borrowings with the letter 'E' opposite them.

Mrs Greege turned over and over in her lap the exquisite piece of silk fabric the Mistress had sent to her, delivered by one of the schoolchildren; no note, nothing, just this wide grey silk.

Through dark farmland Val Vousden dozed: the bus climbed hills of steep unseen pasture by Kilworth before the last long run down into Cork, woods on the right, the gleam of dark water on his left. Val Vousden disembarked at Glanmire, met his young friend Bernard for 'one drink and one drink only'. Bernard walked with him as far as Shandon, where they parted.

Val's sister said, 'You should take off that uniform. You look like the Chocolate Soldier in it.'

Father Watson, complaining of the hazards of bus travel, brought a small box of chocolates with him, which he flourished proudly. Essie, possessed of a glance with major potential for askance-ness, said of the chocolates: 'Sure, they weren't too heavy for him to carry anyway, Ma'am.'

'I checked with the Canon,' said Ellen to her Jesuit; 'he'd be delighted to have the extra Mass in the morning. In fact he announced it last Sunday, so I'm very glad to see you.' They smiled. 'Although I'll go to Midnight Mass, myself, if you don't mind too much, it'll help the house to get on.'

'My dear Ellen,' he held both her hands. 'You are a wonder. I heard all about the extraordinary nursing you did for Thomas's pneumonia, you rallied the whole county it seems.'

'So long as he rallied,' said Ellen. 'And it wasn't ever pneumonia.'

Ellen had placed the new Valor heater in the corner of the hallway.

'Oh, Lord, Ma'am, I won't, I couldn't go to somebody I know,' had been Essie's response to Ellen's offer that Father John could hear her Confession.

'No, Ma'am, sure I'm grand, sure I have no sins on my soul, sure where would I get the time to commit a sin?'

'Thomas,' Ellen had hissed last night. 'He's here again. Thomas, I know I am terrible to do this, but I don't care, he deserves all I'm going to do to him.'

The heater smoked faintly, but warmed the cluttered tiled hall.

'Father, since my last Confession, I find that I have become weaker.'

'Weaker? In what way, my child?' The hand fleshed the jowl, as John Watson gravely listened.

'Father, I can resist those impure thoughts less and less.' Ellen and Essie had paid Thomas greater attention today than for some days.

'He's entitled to Christmas too, Essie.'

Father Watson asked tentatively, 'Have you confined them to impure thoughts, my child?'

Ellen paused, timing like an actress. 'Yes . . . Father.'

'How often, my child?' She never took her unblinking eyes off the rotund profile.

'Twice . . . Father.'

'When, my child?'

'In . . . the last few days, Father.' No noise is heard when the deadliest traps close.

'Do you know why, especially then, my child?'

When considerate, John Watson's voice slid like satin.

'I knew I was going to see him . . . Father.' Dropped to a whisper.

'Does he know, my child, that you have deep feelings for him?'

'He knows, Father, that I regard him as my . . . deepest friend . . .'

As she walked to Midnight Mass, hat pinned tight, scarf wound firm, Ellen talked to herself half-aloud, both through agitation and the fear of the dark road. In the night sky she looked for the star that, as a child, she believed had been the guide to Bethlehem. Occasionally a quick step overtook her, then a cough, and a 'Good-night, Ma'am' reassured her.

'I'm always puzzled, Thomas,' she had said to him once on the way home from Evening Devotions. 'How do they know it is us?'

'Amn't I always telling you?' he replied, 'they know everything.'

The heels of her black court shoes rang on the road: a light frost gathered.

The church shuffled in all its hillside lights. She did not attend Communion: all right, people would put it down to not being able to organize the fasting since mid-day, on account of the Master and the baby. They came to the seat, tapped her shoulder, whispered, 'All the best for the Christmas, Ma'am. All the best now.' Ellen mouthed thanks.

In the light of the candles and the oil-lamps around the walls, her freckled face shone pale and vigorous; her 'boxer's nose' in shadow. She folded one hand over the other until it was time to pick up the Missal and find the red-printed flimsy pages with their Latin rubrics. The Canon, mercifully, took cognizance of the lateness of the hour, and his own need to rise early, and said a short Mass. In the porch afterwards, several people waited, again to wish her well. Their bicycles and murmurs swished past her on the night air as she set off down the hill; she strained her eyes in the direction of the Stephensons' house, but no glimmer of light could be detected at such a distance.

The road's darkness thickened into Hogan's Bend. Leafless, the trees and hedges stood silent, all conversation between them exhausted for the moment; their bare branches spread beseechingly. Ellen thought she heard something and halted her step, then walked on tiptoe. The snurry of a horse as it shook itself through its nostrils. And again. No sound of hooves on the metalled road, meaning the horse had stopped. She tiptoed on. Ahead, to her left-hand side, the shape loomed: a standing horse, a figure astride. The horse's head swung around and the horseman stirred. 'Hold! Hold hard!' the voice said unenthusiastically.

'Pewarrhhlupp!' rattled the horse's vast rubber-coral lips in the dark, its head giving a gentle plunge. Ellen's eyes and mouth widened simultaneously in a soundless wail. Jesus, I'm wetting myself! Not another soul on the road; no point in going back, everybody gone. No house between here and the church. On foot, no match for a horse. She tiptoed on, as far to the far side as possible, trying to slide through the dark. The horseman did not move: the horse enjoyed another jerking shudder, shifting its weight across all four legs like a ship on a wooden sea. The horseman said in a sleepy voice, 'Ah, would you hold, would you?'

Sidling, Ellen reached a soft hand to the crown of her hat and withdrew her Tara brooch long hatpin. On an October night on this road Thomas had shown her the Pleiades, and told her the sad story of Electra, the lost Pleiad. On a' night walking from the Evening Devotions in May they had stopped to marvel at the moon . . .

Ellen bustled silently and excitedly into Thomas's room. Essie had left a lamp for her; the red Christmas candle still burned brightly in the window; not a sound could be heard. Her cheeks glowed bright red, and she panted. She kissed Thomas passionately on the mouth and sat beside him, looking, looking. Some days he half-opened an eye; once he even showed a brief flicker of having heard something. Once, his smile half returned – but was it merely the muscles of his mouth in some grimace of effort?

Taking off her hat, and with concentrated attention, and rapid breathing, wiping over and over and over the large Tara brooch hatpin, and then sticking it into the lapel of her coat, she said, 'Thomas Kane. If a kiss could breathe life into a human being, if it could, if it could . . . D'you remember, that you often thought how you would like to have pumped life into the growing baby?' She clutched each side of her head, and half-frantically said, 'Thomas! Thomas! Oh, God!'

In bed, Ellen stretched herself rigid beneath the sheets, her fists clenched, arms outstretched like a cross.

'Oh, how nice?' she had exclaimed the day Thomas said, 'It comes from "*crux, crucis*" the Latin for cross. So a crux is the essence, or the real trial of something. The very heart of something vital.'

In the morning she woke dry and exhausted to a passing shudder of horror and indifference to everything. Then, the sweetest sound in all the world awakened her: Helena's crowing began later in winter. Ellen went to the mirror, perused her own face and expression with minute care. She lifted Helena out of the cot, felt her bottom through the lumpy layers.

'Dry? Still dry? Who's a pet? Who's a pet?' She jiggled the baby, and climbed back into bed, tucking Helena in beside her. The baby kicked and made eager shapes with her mouth. Ellen held a hand near Helena's face: the baby grabbed it and inspected every detail roughly. Leaning on an elbow, Ellen then lowered her face as near to Helena as she could, allowing the baby to tug her nose.

'This is a great game, isn't it? Isn't it, Hellie?' She blew on Helena's face making her little hair lift from the forehead. 'Wait 'til your Daddy sees you? Ow!' Helena had reached farther than the nose and pulled a strand of hair. Ellen detached the hand and returned it to her face, allowing it to roam. She found an ear and proffered it to Helena who took it like a lifebuoy.

'Don't grab, little thing. I don't know what I'm going to do if I have boys, if they're like you.' At which Ellen stopped smiling. 'Oh, Hellie.' She sighed. 'I have no one to talk to, only two babies. You and your daddy. Three counting Essie.' She tiptoed her fingers across the baby's fat stomach up to her chin. 'But. We have a great New Year coming, don't we?' She paused, sad. 'Dtth. Am I fooling myself, Hellie, am I? Oh, Hellie, will I ever tell you all these things, all these awful things that are going on . . . ?'

Christmas Day 1926, a damp day, in which the sun came out and went in again, passed quietly and with gentle introspection and stillness. Father John Watson, S.J., M.A., fell asleep proprietorially in front of the fire. Ellen Kane had to put ointment on the little half-moon cuts her fingernails had made in the palm of her left hand.

29

The first group of high-stepping Wren Boys called on the morning of Saint Stephen's Day.

'D'you give them money?' John Watson asked Ellen.

'The wren, the wren, the King of all Birds
Saint Stephen's Day he was caught in the furze.
Although he be little his family's great,
Rise up little laddies and give us a treat.'

'Ma'am, 'tis grand to see you so light in yourself,' commented Essie. Ellen laughed over-excitedly as she recognized most of the Wren Boys behind their painted faces and women's clothes.

'Where did you get the eye-fiddle?' Ellen teased one. 'You should wear it all the time.'

'Eye-fiddle? You mean a mask?' said Father Watson. 'How interesting? I wonder if Shakespeare used that word?'

Ellen gave them some coins and handed around a plate of cold meat slices, from which she told them 'not to snap the food like pigs'. After a quick moment of reflection, she invited them in to sing for Thomas: Helena screamed with fright at the high hats and the red ribbons fluttering from the holly boughs they carried over their shoulders, one of which nearly brought down a garland of the coloured paper decorations slung across the ceiling. Their energy reverberated in the kitchen: with mouth-organ and concertina, two danced a reel in front of Thomas's bed-chair. Five groups of Wren Boys called that day: each sang for Thomas.

As they watched the departure of what they hoped laughingly might prove the last band, Father Watson said, 'Do you think it really a good idea that they should invade poor Thomas's privacy so much?'

That night several of the Wren Boys told their parents, 'I'd say the Master won't last long.'

Essie lit the lamp as dusk began to fall: the fire in the parlour grate roared with high flames. Wren Boys excepted, they expected no other visitors.

Yet, 'Come in, come in,' they heard Ellen say; she seemed unsurprised.

Father Watson, in his self-appointed role as host, rose to greet the newcomers. The two men stooped a little through the doorway, more out of habit than necessity, as they entered the parlour: one in uniform, the other not.

"D'evening, Father.'

'Good evening, gentlemen.'

'Sorry to disturb the Festive Season, Father.'

'This is Father John Watson, an old friend of the family,' said Ellen. 'This is the Superintendent and, of course, the Sergeant.'

Father Watson said, 'May I offer you . . . ?' He indicated his own glass.

'Ooph, no thanks, Father.' The Superintendent rubbed his hands together vigorously, 'on duty, I'm afraid, all hours, Sunday and Monday, Christmas and all.'

'Oh, too bad for you,' Father Watson nodded understandingly.

'Ma'am, we want to have a word with yourself, if we could?' said the Superintendent.

'Sit down, sit down,' said Father Watson, and the men looked from Ellen to him.

'It'd have to be private, Father.'

'Oh, goodness, of course, of course . . . unless, my dear Ellen?'

'No, grand, thanks, Father John,' said Ellen.

'Well, I still have some of my Office left to say,' and the priest left the room.

An hour later, Essie said anxiously to Father John in the kitchen, 'D'you think I should take them in tea, Father?'

He pondered the advantages of inspecting the various faces should he have to open the door for the tray, and then decided against it. Another hour passed, and the noise of feet preparing to depart came from across the hallway. Ellen preceded the men and reached forward to close the kitchen door, thereby sealing off the hall. Some more conversation took place, and the men took their leave.

Father Watson said, 'Good Heavens! Did they interrogate you?'

'No,' Ellen said, brittle and aggressive. 'Essie!' she called. 'You-know-who. He was found last night on the road.'

'Oh, my God, Ma'am!' said Essie, making the Sign of the Cross.

'Heavy drink on him,' said Ellen lightly. 'The horse bolted under him, and threw him.'

'Is he hurted, Ma'am?'

'He's dead, Essie.'

They all heard the ticking of the alarm clock on the bookcase, the first wheezes of a boiling kettle.

Father Watson broke the surface of this brief pool of silence. 'My dear, I don't understand the significance of this at all . . . ?'

'A man with a big houseful of children here in the village,' said Ellen quickly. 'They used to come to school to me. Essie knows, don't you, Essie?' The women's faces gazing at each other excluded Father Watson and the universe.

'Oh, thanks be to God, Ma'am. Thanks be to God.'

Essie's fervent tone of voice bypassed her cleft palate.

Nurse Cooper visited next afternoon, and talked to Ellen.

'Look, my dear, there is one thing. He is not getting better.'

'Sheila, stop. I didn't close an eye last night.'

'You see. Even you're worried.'

'No, it wasn't that. You heard the news, I suppose?'

'I did.' Sheila Cooper held the pause, then resumed. 'Apart from that –' she gestured again to Thomas.

'Were you talking to Dr Hogan?' accused Ellen, returning from her reverie.

'No, as it happens, I haven't seen Jack Hogan for a fortnight.'

'Sheila, if Thomas dies, he dies. I have pledged myself to do everything I can to keep him alive.'

'Girl, you know there is no medical history anywhere of anyone surviving like this; if the man wasn't so strong . . .'

'I know, I know, he'd be dead long ago . . .'

'No, that isn't what I was going to say. What I was going to say was, if he wasn't so strong he wouldn't have been able to swallow so violently. He wouldn't be able to take in food.'

'If his throat muscles are working, then the rest of him could work again one day,' defied Ellen.

'No, you're not necessarily right. You fed him, like we showed you, by using the fact of involuntariness; we all swallow involuntarily, look how difficult it is not to swallow if a fly goes into your mouth, that's what has worked with him.'

'His lungs work. And his chest? And his windpipe?'

'Pure chance, nothing else does.'

'His bowels work. I know it full well,' said Ellen, 'and his bladder.'

'But – as he fails to be fully nourished all through, he has no exercise – he will slowly slip down and down. A day could come when even that great nursing effort will no longer work. And that day might come not too far away.'

'You haven't seen him for a week. Do you see a change in him?'

'I do,' said Sheila Cooper, 'I do.'

'Look, for all we know he could be listening to every word we say. Supposing – supposing he "wakes up" one day, won't we have fine fun when he tells us he was listening to every word?'

'Ellen, he isn't *The Sleeping Beauty*. It isn't a fairy story.'

'Sheila, don't say that kind of thing to me.' Ellen yelled. 'Now, don't! If you do, we'll fall out, you and I. I've had somebody trying to say that to me nearly every day since last summer. Supposing I'd listened and let go of Thomas – where would I be now?'

'Shhhh, dear. Shhhh.'

Ellen burst into tears and howled, then lay back in the chair, eyes closed.

'But, Ellen, it is a medical fact. You cannot bring him back to life.'

'Sheila, I won't give up trying until the day Thomas is buried. Now, look. I'm doing all I can. The surgeons are coming from Cork in a few days. I have written to that man Crowe in London. I can't hurry things any more than that.'

In the next twenty-four to thirty-six hours Ellen found space to reach for her new resilience and collect herself.

Father Watson stayed three further nights, until New Year's Eve, and thereafter visited Deanstown no more, nor did he ever see Ellen Kane again.

'Now!' Ellen clapped her hands. 'Forget your little sips of port, Father John. Whiskey tonight, it's the last night of your holiday. And wine, we have some somewhere. And Essie made something special for you.'

In the scullery earlier, Essie said, 'Ma'am, I can't make you out, you're leppin' around the place like a young one.'

461

'My mother used to call it "rampaging", Essie,' she whispered. 'I'm "rampaging", so I am.'

Ellen, taking out some as-yet-unwrapped wedding gift linen, cutlery and glasses, asked Essie to lay the parlour table. The priest watched the parcels come undone.

'Are we expecting company?'

'Yes, Father John. You.'

'Oh?!'

All day, Ellen, febrile still, had raced like a dervish.

'Ma'am, I never seen you get so much done,' said Essie. 'Never.'

At Thomas's final changing for the night, as Essie took the basin and soap out of the kitchen, Ellen kissed Thomas's neck so hard she left a brief red mark.

'Jesus, Thomas, Jesus.' She pushed her face into his hair.

Father John Watson came down the stairs at six o'clock with a scrubbed face, and he inspected the parlour table set a-sparkle in the firelight for two.

'I find this quite exciting,' he said.

Ellen, who had changed into the 'famous grey dress', as Thomas described it, poured him a drink and sat him down.

'No lamps yet,' she said. 'I love the look of a firelit room before the lamp comes on.'

'Like Dickens,' he said, 'just like Dickens; all we need is snow outside.'

Ellen bustled a little more, and on a quick final trip to the kitchen, she reached into the blankets and crossed a pair of Thomas's fingers, whispering, 'My lovely Thomas. Am I going mad, am I?'

She returned, and sat in the other armchair facing Father Watson in the flickering light.

'Would you like to know what we're going to feed you?' she asked him affectionately. 'Or would you like it to be a surprise?'

Essie, in a clean frock and apron, brought soup and fresh soda bread.

'There's even sherry in that soup, Father John,' said Ellen.

Dining began. Ching of spoon on plate. Breathy grunts of joy. She opened up his reminiscences.

'It must have been quite peculiar for you watching the little girl grow up, was it?'

'I think,' he said, soup on his chin again, 'I shall never forget the first day I realized you were a young woman. You were about seventeen, I suppose, and you had a blue dress with a white collar.'

'I remember it well! It was, it probably still is, one of the things I ever had that I was fondest of. As a matter of fact, I remember wearing it specially for you.'

'And you had lace gloves.'

'I did. I bought them at Cannocks. From Mrs Doran. Goodness, you remember everything.'

'And black shiny shoes.'

'Yes! Patent leather! They had black buttons like little eyes.'

Essie brought the next course.

'Oh, dear Heaven!' he said. He threw up his hands in a gesture of ecstasy at the meat on the dish.

'The best they had,' said Ellen.

'Oh, well, of course, as you can imagine we never get anything like that in the Provincial House.'

'We roasted it,' Ellen said. 'And basted it.' The long slob of fillet beef shone like a blooded champion.

'You'll carve, Father John?' and she poured a glass of wine each. They sat behind full plates, and set to work, she silently, he grunting little noises, tapping a foot.

'How come,' she asked, 'you never thought of marrying, Father John? I mean long ago, before you entered the priesthood, did you ever have a crush on anyone?'

'I think I was an idealist,' he said slowly. 'I think the theology, the laws of the Church attracted me. The idea that Man can make laws to govern what goes on in his soul – very attractive, very attractive.'

'The mind always?' Ellen nudged.

'Yes. Yes.' He paused. 'I think. I think.' He pulled a piece of gristle loose. 'Excuse me. I think – if, but you never know how life unveils itself. I think if the right opportunity –' he spoke so carefully '– if the right opportunity could have been seen, not just come along, but could have been seen. If that had happened. What I think I'm trying to say is – that if I knew then what I know now. But isn't that the case with us all? But, anyway, I never did marry. As you know.' He chuckled sweetly.

Ellen said, 'I remember one winter. You caught a bad cold. Mama said to me that I was more concerned about you than I would have been about one of our own family. She was cross about it. That must be what, about, five, six years ago, I wasn't twenty-one yet. I remember that so clearly.'

They ate on. Sooner or later one of them might have mentioned Thomas, but neither did.

'Hoh-ho! – look at that!' Father Watson applauded the sherry trifle; Essie, with a sharp knife, pared slivers from a chocolate bar all over the top. From the cupboard in the corner of the room, Ellen conjured.

'My father's trick with trifle. A glass of Madeira.'

'You are spoiling me! Spoiling me!'

John ate two large glass dishes of trifle, one after the other, and leaned forward, elbows on the snow-white cloth, twirling the almost-empty second glass of Madeira.

'I wonder whether this isn't sinfully good,' he said. 'Only joking, only joking. But that glorious food, and this, this Madeira, and the most intelligent woman in the county. And one who wasn't, if I may say so, hiding behind the door when it came to good looks being given out.'

Ellen smiled.

'Thomas,' she had said one night, 'I am going to commit great sins. On your behalf. On our behalf.'

'Father John, it is so lovely to talk to you,' she said. 'Inside or outside Confession.'

Thus lit, the flame travelled slowly along the fuse.

Essie came with a pot of coffee.

'No!' he said, 'I can't believe it!'

'True,' said Ellen, 'actual coffee. Mrs Winer sent it out.'

'But I haven't had coffee for – it must be four years!'

'We'll go and have it by the fire, and let Essie finish clearing. Essie, that was lovely, truly lovely,' said Ellen.

'Yes, my compliments to the cook,' said Father Watson.

'Oh, Father, I did the whole thing myself,' contradicted Essie.

By the fireside, Ellen Kane and John Watson looked at each other warmly, then back into the fire.

Ellen, in a pitched demureness, said, 'Do you know, Father

John. I had almost forgotten what it was like to have a conversation with a man. Do you know what I mean?' She laughed. 'That must sound so funny to you, because you have conversations with men all the time.' Her voice tinkled.

'Oh, I know well what you mean, my dearest Ellen,' he said.

An occasional sigh from the fire.

'Isn't that . . . weak of me?' she asked.

'I don't think so. You are a healthy young woman.' Ha! – the phrase she had used in Confession to him.

'Yes,' she said very thoughtfully, 'ye – esss.'

He gathered his shoulders.

'God forgives. You do know that?' he said. 'All our sins.'

She looked at length into his face and sadly smiled.

'Yes. Yesss.'

Behind him, Momentum tiptoed invisibly into the room.

'And which of us?' he continued, with just a little falter, 'Is not human?'

Ellen made a little haste to agree. 'And the Lord created us, Father John.'

'He did. And He knows us. And we are His children. And He forgives us.'

Thus, on 31 December 1926, at half-past nine in the evening, in the lamplit parlour of a remote country village, to whose cultivated schoolmaster he had once behaved so patronizingly – 'Fancy, my dear Ellen? The classics out in Deanstown?' – thus was Father John Watson destroyed.

'Yes, He forgives us. Indeed,' he continued. He looked down at the backs of his hands: 'Canon Law himself', Thomas called him in one particularly bitter moment with Ellen: 'when you mentioned to me your own difficulties with . . . your thoughts, and God forgives them too, my dear Ellen, and when you mentioned the "one, good man" of whom you spoke, to whom your, what's the word, your "difficult" thoughts were directed, for a brief moment, my dearest Ellen . . .'

He leaned forward, his small eyes shining, this man with a reputation for excellent, clinical Reason.

Ellen scarcely moved: an adjustment of the shoulders and jaw, no more than that.

'Father John?' Her broad, soft voice spoke the question with sad and lethal wonderment. 'But wasn't that in Confession? I mean, I thought . . .' A small bewildered pain crossed her face. 'Isn't the Seal of the Confessional . . . ?'

He put his hand to his throat, wrestling with the silk of the invisible noose there.

'Oh. My dear. Oh. Ellen. Of course, you're right, you're right. Oh. Hrumgh.' He coughed. He coughed again. Ellen fell silent.

That was all. No more took place between them. A word or two, an attempted but never completed, 'My dear Ellen, I am so sorry,' and a tentative reply, 'I suppose in the morning, Father . . . ?' – but the question was left unfinished. Both, from different perspectives, understood the precise extent of their devastating transaction. Archbishop Edward Ahern was known by all the priests in his Archdiocese to enquire into all the circumstances of the Reserved Sins he was asked to absolve, the time, the place, the number of people present, the reasons. One such confession had lasted up to two swingeingly interrogative hours.

Mutely next morning, Ellen accompanied him to the gate. She held out her hand: they shook hands. She did not wave, and he did not look back.

Indoors, Ellen bent over Thomas, and took his face in her two hands, whispering, 'You and me, Thomas. You and me. And Helena. And Essie. I promised you. I love you.'

On *The Princess* bus, a tear of condensation rolled down the windowpane beside poor Father Watson's outward gaze into the damp lands.

1927

30

'You're not as nice as you used to be,' said her mother.
'How nice do you think what I have to do is?' replied Ellen.

Leah saw the point and said, 'Fair's fair. We must, I suppose, change to meet you. But don't lose all the lovely things in you.'

'No,' said Ellen. 'I realize, though, that I never had a life of my own before. Strange, isn't it, that trying to give Thomas back his life, should bring me mine?'

'Herbert predicted it,' said Leah.

Sailing under her new colours, Ellen asked the two tall men from Cork: 'Are you competent to judge?'

Hearing their answers, she said, 'I won't forget your honesty. You don't know how decent and helpful that is. I just wish I had known it all a lot earlier.'

The taller of the two said, 'Of course, Dr Hogan is your doctor, and we can only get involved if we are called in by him.'

She told them of Maurice Crowe, and the background to his letter, and established with them his credentials. They talked on.

'We have two radiograph machines, and we have had them for some time, but we're not that happy with the results,' said the quieter man. 'What we'd like to do, if I can speak for Dermot –' he indicated his colleague '– is another physical examination now, and then write out our recommendations. And even if we're not involved ourselves, we'd like to get behind you and support you. I mean, this is a very interesting case for us altogether.'

They spent an hour with Thomas, while Ellen fretted elsewhere. When they sent their written report, they enclosed a copy of their letter to Maurice Crowe. Whereupon, Ellen wrote to her father for 'a good deal of money'. She calculated days, dates and times, and she sent for Nurse Cooper and Dr Hogan. She snuffed out Essie's excitement instantly.

'We have to stay very cool about this, Essie, very cool.' Calming herself further, she wrote a simple letter to the Canon, but withheld it until she had conferred with the doctor and the nurse.

'You have to admit it yourself,' Jack Hogan said, 'you have to admit there's a disimprovement in him.'

'I do,' said Ellen, 'but there's the letter. Look. There's what the surgeons in Cork said. The man's colleagues in London are interested. They might operate.'

'Yes, but I mean, what are they, experimenting or something?' Jack Hogan was sceptical. 'They have no real results, d'you see. Look, they even say that in the letter. "We make no promises." And how in the name of God are you going to get the man over to London?'

'This letter,' spat Ellen, 'is a lot bloody better than any medical help I've had in this county or country. All talk, that's all I get here.' She turned to Nurse Cooper. 'Sheila, if I can work out a way of getting him over, will you help me?'

Behind Ellen's angry energy, Sheila Cooper saw the fear, the last-chance terror.

'Of course I will.'

'Mad, the two of you are. He won't last as far as Holyhead,' said Jack Hogan.

Saturday, 8 January 1927.

Dear Canon,
    I have been given an opportunity to try and have my husband operated on in London. I have to ask your permission to be away from school for an indefinite period: it could be three weeks, it could be three months. What I think will happen is that we'll get him over there soon and he will be there for several weeks, and I should stay with him. Then when he comes back either he'll be in hospital in Cork or here at home, in which case I might be able to get back to school or not. I'm sorry I can't be more definite.

Yours sincerely,
Ellen Kane, (Mrs)

Essie brought back a reply.

470

Dear Mrs Kane,
    Thank you for your letter. Please accept the enclosed.

Yours faithfully,
Jeremiah Williams P.P.

The letter contained a twenty-pound note.

Maurice Crowe sent a telegram:

> Come any day from 2nd Feb. Given typical travel
> difficulties, we will hold situation open one week from
> that day. If coming no need reply. Will need patient here
> at least, repeat, at least, three to six weeks after.

Serene and forcible, and with everything in order, Ellen made all
her arrangements: a second Assistant Teacher to run the school –
my God, the value of that Inspector calling, no inspections for
four years! Michael Condon agreed to drive to Dublin, return to
Deanstown, and be ready to come back again to meet the Mail
Boat. The county had as yet no ambulance of its own: Ellen wrote
to Dublin to find an ambulance they could use for the return
journey. The unspoken question hung everywhere: 'But will there
be a return?' Thomas had faded – no doubt: the ruddy waxiness
grown grey, the hair a little coarser; paradoxically, he showed one
or two signs of rising nearer to the surface.

They decided to leave the question of Ellen's lodgings in London
open to chance: the hospital would know of a place she could stay.
Helena would be safe with Essie: Ellen's mother offered to come
and stay, so did Thomas's sisters and brothers, so did everyone,
especially Leah who brought a large, bulky envelope from Herbert.
'He says this will support you, and nourish you, but not to open it
until things get looking blue as they will; you know Herbert, how
cheerful he is.' They chuckled.

An overnight bed was arranged at Maryborough Hospital, halfway between Deanstown and Dublin, should they need to break
the journey either way.

The night before departure, Ellen turned to Essie who was feeding Helena in her high chair.

'Oh, Essie, tell me I'm not gone out of my mind.'

Essie, from a family of fourteen children, never caressed or cuddled in her life, and never likely to be, dumped into a convent as a lay sister, in other words a labouring drone, saw the Mistress sit down in a crumple, and putting down Helena's dish where the baby could not thump it, went across and drew the most awkward arm in the world around Ellen's shoulders.

'Ah, Ma'am, sure, look – all the things you done for the Master, he'd be dead long ago only for you, wouldn't he?'

Michael Condon arrived at a quarter to nine, as scrubbed as the morning itself: the car he hired, a Lancia, seemed as big as a bus. Nurse Cooper appeared with a packed bag.

'Where are you off to?' asked Ellen.

'Guess.'

'But.'

'Shut up, my lady.'

The Mail Boat left at a quarter to nine that evening: Essie's sandwiches proved invaluable. Three times at roadside houses, people heated Thomas's food, thinking it for a baby: Ellen's practised skills prevented them from coming out to see the deathly passenger. At the dockside as they wheeled Thomas up the gangplank in a bath-chair, Nurse Cooper holding his head straight, a familiar voice said 'Hallo' in Ellen's ear – Miriam Hogan.

'Where are you going?'

'With you.' Ellen did not have time or concentration to spare on resisting.

At Holyhead they were told, 'No trains to London. A strike.' Enquiries only yielded, 'No telling how long it'll last, no telling, could be a day, could be a month.'

Miriam Hogan said, 'A cab to Liverpool. A boat to London. I had to do that last year, big strike then.'

'In this fog?' said the shipping line official.

Liverpool had no fog. 'Good omen,' said Miriam Hogan, who startled Sheila Cooper and Ellen by her efficiency and merriment.

'I can't actually bear to be at home with Jack. I mean he's the greatest eejit, with his "d'you see", "d'you see". If a dog bit Jack he'd say, "D'you see" – "Juicy Jack", I call him to myself. And to his face.'

Later, she came into the cabin. 'You might as well know this,' she said. 'If there is fog in London, we won't get up the Thames until it lifts; they'll just wait in the fog. Maybe for days.'

Sheila Cooper and Ellen were feeding Thomas, and stopped in their tracks.

'But, butbutbut –'

Miriam stopped Ellen's anxious budding query: 'I got the Captain, men will do anything for you if you have a good pair of legs, to send a wire to Surgeon Maurice Crowe, and I told him,' she said, 'in your name, "Mrs Ellen Kane", exactly what we were doing and why, the name of the ship and if we were delayed, what the reason might well be. It cost four pounds of Jack's money.' She waved a hand and sang in a little song. 'Or, should I say, my money. Or, should I say, my dear departed Daddy's money.'

Maurice Crowe checked the shipping lists, and the weather, and sent an ambulance to Tilbury docks. Within two hours of his arrival, four days after leaving Deanstown, grey Thomas Kane was in a silent and antiseptic ward, under the most intensive professional care he had ever received. Ellen was given a bed; the other two slept sitting upright on benches in corridors; the universal sorority of nurses brought them tea and blankets and consideration.

'You're very like your sister,' Ellen said to Maurice Crowe, who flicked her a sidelong look.

In the morning, Ellen was interviewed at length by three distinguished-looking men, called 'Mr', not 'Doctor', in whose company Maurice Crowe seemed an equal. They noted down everything, returning again and again to 'the circumstances of the injury'.

They asked, 'Do you know how many of these "pellets" were removed?' They asked, 'Do you know whether his wound was aggravated by anything that happened in the collision? By which I mean – did his head hit any part of the car?' They asked, 'To what extent did he show any signs of consciousness; was there ever a moment when you thought he might come round? Did the doctors who attended after the event, did they say he regained even partial consciousness?'

Which had always been the most puzzling part, because that was exactly what Dr MacDonnell said; he said 'despite the bleeding he seems to have woken up a little, but he hasn't come the whole way.' At the end, one, an Indian gentleman in an immaculate grey suit, asked Ellen why, in her opinion, her husband had stayed alive against the medical experience of two or three similar cases. Ellen blushed, unable to answer.

As she walked down the corridor later to join Miriam, who waited, the Indian gentleman called her, and she stopped.

He said, 'I could see I embarrassed you. But it is a very important question.' He stressed the last syllable in 'important' – he said 'impor-*tant*'.

She said, 'I would have felt very foolish giving the only answer I knew. You're all so –'

'So what? We're only highly trained. I want to know your own answer.'

She said, 'I tried to give my husband life; I tried to bring life into him.'

'How?'

Ellen told him – the talking, the schoolchildren singing, the whispering, the 'normal' life going on around him, the meeting, even, of the Teachers' Union group in the kitchen, the buying him new shirts and holding them under his nose in case he could smell the fabric.

'Did you ever feel foolish doing all that?'

'No, not really. I feel a bit foolish telling you.'

'You shouldn't. If you lived where I came from, it would be the thing everybody thought was the most natural. The impor*tant* thing is – it was what kept him alive. In my opinion.'

'Mine too,' she said. 'What's going to happen next?'

He said, 'We have a suspicion that he has suffered some membrane damage. There are silent areas in the brain. They can suffer damage that does not damage life. Your husband would have been killed outright by a single, heavy-calibre bullet. Shotgun pellets don't often penetrate as deeply. We're going to radiograph him and see is there anything to look at. There may be something pressing on something else. If there is, we may operate.'

Ellen could not stop herself asking the one question she did not want to ask. 'What are the chances?'

The man blinked his brown eyes: 'Very difficult to say.'

=

Hospital Administration directed the three women to a bed-and-breakfast in Goswell Road, a ten-minute walk from the hospital. Immediately thereafter, Ellen spent five of her worst days ever. The men found something in the radiograph – they would not specify – and decided to operate. It would take two days or so, to judge whether they could operate immediately or whether his strength needed to be built up. They had to gamble, Maurice Crowe said, between Thomas's obviously deteriorating condition, and whether he still had enough strength to endure major surgery. The journey had sapped: a bronchial noise had been detected: they had to wait to ascertain its strength or possible departure before they could be sure.

Miriam Hogan provided compensation, in the form of an opulent flat rented for at least a week: she became adjutant and quartermaster all in one – and morale-raiser, irritating Nurse Cooper with her firm assurances that Thomas would recover.

'But you have no medical evidence,' hissed Sheila Cooper to her in the kitchen of the flat.

'My nose tells me,' said Miriam Hogan.

'Ah, you and your nose.'

Ellen's despondence told a different tale. She drifted here and there, taking in little, or briefly achieving animated interest, then lapsing into silence again. On the third evening she urged the women forth to enjoy themselves. When they had gone she took from her bag the bulky envelope Leah had given her. It contained a little card painted by the girls, a man in a hat with a big smile and a message, 'Get better, Uncle Thomas, with love from Rachel and Sarah'; a card from Leah: 'Dearest Ellen. We will be thinking of you night and day.'

The third item, in Herbert's handwriting, ran to several pages of foolscap, and had a note from him attached.

Dear Ellen,

I don't know if you ever read the *Song of Solomon* or the *Song of Songs*. It is my favourite piece of anything in the whole world, better than an ingot of raw silver, and although all the scholars say it was written by King Solomon himself, it feels to me as if it was written by a woman. It is about a husband and wife, or, to be precise, about a bridegroom and a bride, and all their friends and neighbours who observe them. It might be useful to you in the coming times.

Good luck,
Herbert

Ellen read the opening lines copied in Herbert's clear hand:

O, give me the kisses of your mouth,
For your love is more exquisite than wine . . .
Your perfume has a delicious fragrance –
Your name is to me as sweet as the finest perfume . . .

Too much, too much. She folded the pages away.

Nobody felt it a good idea that Ellen should hang around the hospital throughout the long, long surgery. Except Miriam Hogan. In the cab taking them there, Ellen said to her, 'You're a dark horse. Why are you never like this at home?'

She replied, 'If Jack can't pity me, he'll collapse altogether and drink his head off.'

'But,' asked Ellen, 'when you go back . . . ?'

'I might not go back. And then I might.'

Ellen had to fight to be allowed to Thomas's bedside: 'The fear of infection,' they said.

'Let her in,' said the Indian surgeon.

'He seems unchanged,' she said in a very small-voiced whisper, observing the acres of bandages.

'No, he is still sedated.'

'When or how will we know?'

'If he is still alive in the morning, that is a first step. Do you want to know what happened? We found some things pressing.'

'I thought so.'

'We have to tell the police.'

Ellen said, 'The police at home know.'

'We have to tell the police anyway.'

'Yes, good. People should know. How long before we have any idea of the long-term chances . . . ?'

'Two days, three days. If he is alive in the morning. There will be some change. If. But do not expect too much.'

All three women sat up all night in the flat, playing cards. When Ellen fell asleep they covered her in her armchair with a blanket and sat there with her.

Thomas was alive in the morning, and Ellen haunted the hospital, night and day. When, on the third afternoon, she saw Thomas move his mouth slightly in what looked to her like a non-involuntary way, she sat perfectly straight until she saw it again, a moment later, no mistake, infinitesimal, maybe, but he did it, by himself.

'I'm here, Thomas, if you can hear me.' She put on her best accent, the one he called 'posh' for best occasions. 'I'm here.'

Friday, 25 March: Michael Condon drove from Deanstown to Dublin and met the Mail Boat. With Sheila Cooper and Miriam Hogan in the car, he followed the ambulance bearing Thomas and Ellen to the Richmond Hospital, where Thomas was looked at briefly by the renowned Mr Adams McConnell, and Ellen was given an overnight bed in an adjoining room. Thomas did not speak; nor did he exhibit acknowledgment.

'He will be weak,' said Mr McConnell. 'You can expect that.'

'What else can I expect?' asked Ellen.

'Impossible to say,' said Adams McConnell kindlily.

They set out at half-past eleven on Saturday morning, driving as slowly as a funeral, Michael Condon ahead. Exhausted by the slowness of the journey, Ellen, despite herself, dozed in the back of the ambulance, and when she woke each time with a head-jerk, wished that Thomas did not still have to be sedated. They availed themselves of the hospital bed overnight in Maryborough. Miriam Hogan grew impatient and caught the Cork train; she reached Deanstown late on the Saturday afternoon.

The Canon announced at nine o'clock Mass on Sunday morning that Master Kane was 'coming home today after his major surgical operation over beyond in London; would everybody please offer up their prayers for his recovery. He was to be in Maryborough overnight; he'll be back among us around twelve or one o'clock, if it please God.'

March was going out like a lamb again, balmy and bright. After the Canon's announcement, most of the congregation never went home after Mass, they made straight for the village, and stood there waiting for Thomas: the children played with water splashed from the pump. Women in the ochre houses handed out mugs of tea. Mrs Hand asked the Sergeant did he mind if they 'gave out a few drinks'? He trapped her into untypical generosity by saying she wasn't breaking the law if the drink was free.

His friend Bernard said to Val Vousden much later, 'I s'pose, Val, 'twas as good as any opera house, was it?'

Val said, 'Bernard, 'twas, boy. 'Twas. I think, I think – 'twas my finest moment. Bernard, the sun was splitting the heavens.'

Just before half-past twelve, two of the boys raced up the hill.

'Coming! Coming!'

Through the trees beyond the Parochial House, they saw first the gleam of the Lancia car driven by Michael Condon at a slow pace, followed within a few seconds by the white ambulance. They surged forward from the village walls; Mrs Hand leaned out the upstairs window, her Sunday hat still on. The Sergeant began to count – what, sixty, seventy people? Canon Williams emerged from his avenue and began to hurry ahead: hatless he strode up the hill, his long coat flapping. The car and the ambulance slowed down to change gear for the steep incline.

Children jigged about: Bob Morris walked forward and stopped, leaning on his stick, stroking his moustache: Rina and Jim and May broke from their little group of three and began to walk nearer the pump. At the other end of the village, Dr Hogan's car drew up near the Master's house, and out got Miriam and Jack and walked forward quickly, like people hurrying to a fair. Mrs Greege sat in her trap, her sons either side of her, her severe face turned back towards the Dublin road. Between the trees on either side of Thomas's gate, Essie peeped out, then rushed in to put something warm on the baby.

A stranger might have imagined these people had gathered for a football game, or to observe a passing celebrity, as their forebears had for the Prince of Wales: men put out their cigarettes, broke off their conversations and lined the road from the pump to the pub: children climbed and sat on the demesne wall. The old, rival-rous joke came true: 'All to one side like the village of Deanstown'.

Then, everyone turned in astonishment from the approaching car and ambulance as, from behind them, clanged a blare of sound.

Up out of a lane from the houses at the rear of the blacksmith's forge, up through the muck, daintily high-treading the ankle-deep cowdung outside Hanafin's farmyard, came Val Vousden waving a baton; his gold-braided tunic sparkled in the noon light like the breastplate of a quirky Ruritanian god. Behind him, in their blue-and-gold tunics, all made by Mrs Heffernan, marched the new Deanstown Band, their trumpets and cornets and cymbals glinting and blazing and clanging. Val held his baton aloft and waved it as if he had suddenly found it to be a magic wand.

Not perhaps all playing at precisely the same tempo, they swung into the road and marked time there to the metallic whisper of the cymbals. Then, playing 'O'Donnell Abu' with a fabulous rush of energy, they moved aside to let Michael Condon pass in the Lancia with the white-walled tyres. Outside the school, the band formed up in front of the ambulance, causing it to slow down and stop briefly.

Led by Val and his baton, the Deanstown Band, the ambulance, and the people of the village in their Sunday suits diffidently paraded the one hundred and fifty yards from the village to the Master's house.

Inside the ambulance, Ellen, unable to keep back the tears, said to the inert, white Thomas, 'Thomas love, if you can hear. They have the new Deanstown Band; your friend Val, they're all put in the county colours of blue-and-gold, and they're marching ahead of you. They're playing you home.'

The villagers marched too – and the strangers: Bob Morris could not see because his eyes were full of tears, and if he blinked the tears would fall; and Leah Winer and the girls in their little white anklesocks, and Herbert.

Had anybody thought to look off to the right, up through the high fields in the sunlight, they would have seen, away in the distance, on the upper road, a small, dull procession. A hearse-horse with a single, rather tatty black plume strolled in front of one car and a handful of people. They walked down an avenue that connected with the upper road, and then to the main road along which Thomas's ambulance had just driven. Ernestina Stephenson was being buried in the family plot, beneath the rooks in their cypresses and elms, in the Protestant churchyard near the river at Silver-bridge. Uncle Henry, walking behind, observed Ernestina's last request. He read aloud from this dear, clumping, loveless girl's favourite text:

> 'Look, the winter is past
> And the rains are over and done with.
> Flowers have begun to appear on the earth;
> The time of the singing-birds has come
> And the voice of the turtle-dove
> Shall be heard in the land.'

31

On leaving the hospital, Ellen had been given two sets of instructions, one formal, the other informal. The first said that Thomas needed absolute quiet except for the domestic round – no callers, apart from those essentially closest to him, no intensive activity, no pressure of any kind. The second directive was delivered by the Indian surgeon, who said to her, 'Whatever you were doing before, redouble your efforts.'

He did not enquire what she meant when she murmured, 'Dolphin work.'

At Deanstown on that Sunday afternoon, she had to control the numbers of men who wanted to help with his stretcher. As those nearest saw his appearance, their minds recoiled. That night the fireside talk all flowed on the same current.

'There isn't any way a man looking like that is going to pull through.'

'Did you see the face on him? Like a ghost.'

Thomas safely indoors, Ellen came out again and said in general, 'I can't give you tea or anything, you'll understand.' In particular she said, 'Mr Vousden, how can I thank you?'

Then, she answered the only question in which anyone had any interest.

'I don't know any more than you do how he'll be. There wasn't any point in keeping him in London, or in hospital, even. The doctors had done all they could for him. It's all up to – up to what, I don't know now. But he has to get peace and quiet.'

'Is he awake, Ma'am?' one woman asked.

'No. He's asleep,' she said, an acute deflection, and thanking them again went indoors.

Leah, Herbert, the children and Bob had come in a hired car, and when their driver had been fetched from the pub, they left. Jack Hogan took out his stethoscope but Miriam forbade him to examine Thomas. 'He has to rest, Jack. For goodness' sake! He's not a toy of yours.'

Miriam, Sheila Cooper and Ellen herself undertook the routine of preparations laid down by the hospital: the observation charts; the

481

slow reduction of sedatives; the methods of judging whether they could begin to exercise Thomas's arms and legs; the minute inspection for any sign of consciousness; the counting of any hand or eye movements over specified periods. Sheila Cooper measured out the first allocations of medicines, the iron, the calcium. They bathed and changed Thomas, who seemed to Ellen far less pliant than before – 'Maybe it is because I haven't handled him for nearly seven weeks,' she fretted.

When he had been settled for the night, Ellen took time to renew acquaintance with Helena: 'You're so big, you've grown as big as a house!'

'Look, Ma'am,' said Essie, pulling back Helena's lips.

'Oh, oh – teeth, teeth, teeth!' squealed Ellen. 'You'd swear,' she whispered, when she joined the girls for a cup of tea at the parlour table, 'that Essie grew the teeth herself.'

As Miriam and Sheila left, Ellen shook their hands and said simply, 'Thanks, girls. Thanks.'

With a new household roster established after a week, Ellen returned to school. She sent out word-of-mouth to reinforce her message of that Sunday arrival – that for the moment the Master was allowed no visitors. This was taken as confirmation of their suspicions: Michael Condon was reported as saying that when he himself took the car to Dublin and climbed into the ambulance, he thought the Master, 'if anything, worse-looking'.

'Anyone who goes to hospital – sure they never come back,' said the pessimists, always in the majority.

'The Canon wants to say a special Mass for the Master,' reported Jack Hogan.

'No. No,' said Ellen. 'I have to put a stop to that,' and she wrote a note saying, 'Not for the moment. It gives me too much of a requiem feeling,' and Jeremiah abandoned the plan.

Back at school, Ellen gave another *Nature Notes* class, illustrated with drawings of 'the birds you see in the fields'. They identified the robin, the thrush, blackbird, sparrow, wagtail: 'What's different about the wagtail? This is what's different. All the others hop, but he runs. What does he do? He runs.'

Crow, pigeon, pheasant, yellowhammer, plover, swan, water-hen: they sang out all the names as Ellen revealed the pictures, and they baulked only at the different breeds of finch: 'This is the goldfinch. Some people have them in cages as songbirds. The goldfinch has one thing about it different to all the other birds. It has a very strong beak and can even crack open the stone of a cherry.' She gained their most concentrated attention from two birds they never saw: the owl and the cuckoo. 'The first thing about the owl is – the owl is a lot smaller than you'd think. And the owl has maybe the softest feathers of all the birds. Why? Because the owl hunts at night and the soft feathers on its wings make it easy for the owl to hunt at night.'

When it came to the cuckoo, Ellen said, 'Hands up anyone who has seen a cuckoo?'

Several of the older boys raised their hands.

She asked of each, 'And what colour was it?' One said red, another blue, a third red-and-blue, a fourth yellow with black spots.

Asked Ellen, 'And did any of you ever see a cuckoo with a little silk green waistcoat and a tall hat?' They all laughed.

'The thing about the cuckoo is – everybody thinks they've seen the cuckoo, but very few people ever see it, it is one of the shyest birds of all. The cuckoo is a brown bird, not red or yellow or blue or green.' They all laughed. 'And it is quite big, as big or bigger than a thrush, and it depends on not being seen, because it gets into other birds' nests while they're out, and lays its eggs there, and when the young cuckoo is hatched, it heaves all the other little birds out of the nest and keeps all the food for itself.'

All Ellen's routines changed.

'A funny thing,' she said to Sheila Cooper, 'everything about my system, you know, since the baby, d'you remember I told you how irregular everything was, it all seems to be getting back to normal again since Thomas's operation.'

'I wonder why that is, my lady?' said the raised eyebrow.

With the house organized into rotas, Ellen said to Essie, 'Would you take over the baby completely until we see how everything will turn out.'

=

The mornings alternated between Ellen and Sheila Cooper; Ellen and one of Sheila Cooper's young nurses; and Ellen and Mrs Greege. One of those women then stayed near Thomas while Ellen went to school. In the afternoons and evenings the roster reversed, with Miriam Hogan – who could never promise an early morning – joining in: Ellen reserved the evenings almost exclusively for herself.

Sheila Cooper found the demands unexceptional, and relished the care required of her. Mrs Greege remained contradictory: snide and forbidding to Ellen – yet capable of great tenderness towards Thomas. The young nurse had fallen for a young man not far away whose name she would not divulge, adding spice to their daily proceedings, as they tried to winkle his identity from her.

With the exception of her daily presence at school, Ellen vanished from local view. She did not appear at Mass; the gate to the Teacher's house remained firmly closed: the helping women had their lips sworn tight.

'Just give me this last one favour,' she asked them. 'While it is still touch-and-go – say nothing to no one.'

Mrs Greege said, 'You didn't take long to learn, did you?'

When Essie went shopping, people plied her with questions, but Essie had long ago learned the value of appearing stupid as a means of keeping out of trouble, and she drew on it now to the full.

Mrs Hand reported nightly to her customers on any visible activity near the Master's house.

'There was a big car there today, and two men got out of it, I thought they was there before, they had suits on them, but they weren't the same men at all, they had English accents and 'twas a Dublin car, not a Cork car . . .'

And, 'I seen Dr Jack go in there twice, but there isn't a word outa him, sure he doesn't even come in here now, only for the odd minute now and again, and all you'll get out of him is "All serene".'

And, 'The Mistress herself, she's looking like she's in a hard bind, I mean to say, she's looking like she's, oh, up against it altogether. And the house itself is gone like the grave, I mean they've the gate shut and the front door shut, and the clothes on the line, 'tis all sheets and towels, and there's smoke outa the chimney day and night; they must be spending a fortune on coal. She wouldn't let the Canon in the other day, nor the Curate either.'

And, 'I heard that friend of hers, that priest, the small, fat fellow, I heard he's gone off on the Foreign Missions somewhere, Africa, or something. I wonder what happened there, eh? . . .'

On Easter Sunday morning the Canon asked the congregation for a Decade of the Rosary there and then, 'for a full recovery to health by the Master,' adding tactlessly, 'in case the news isn't very good from that quarter.'

Ellen needed not to know the parish's speculations. Thomas's weight loss before, during and after London had been dramatic: she now began each day with porridge for him, milky, runny porridge into which she added the gold from the fresh honeycombs. After every feeding of Thomas, Ellen stood back and surveyed him.

'If looking at him could cure him,' said Mrs Greege, 'he'd be back to rights long ago.'

Leah arrived with a new mincer, and they minced bacon and beef and mutton.

'He's in a deep sleep at the moment,' said Ellen, 'and due to wake in about an hour or so, so we won't go in to see him yet.' When they did, Leah was only permitted a brief glance from the doorway.

Herbert rubbed his hands together that night very hard, very slowly.

'Ach!' he said, 'that does not sound good. No, that does not sound good.'

Leah described the Thomas she found: very drawn and with a pallor she had not seen before; the long jawbone accentuated by the plaster not yet removed from his temple; as yet no word, no sound, no recognition.

'What did Ellen say?'

'Very little. The nurse, that marvellous Cooper woman – she told me a lot. She said the London doctors told her privately that there was hardly as much as a half-and-half chance. What happened was that something hit a part of his head but didn't affect the brain directly, it pressed on something pressing on the brain. They got everything out, they think, but he was so damaged for so long. If only, they said, she'd brought him to them last August or September.'

Herbert said, 'Ah, she wasn't able for anything like that then.' Then he asked his wife, 'What do you think?'

Leah thought, then answered. 'I think. I think – that if by any miracle she gets him on his feet, or even smiling, she'll have a good chance. But I don't know . . .'

To the two surgeons who made the trip from London – not, alas, including the Indian consultant – Ellen reported, 'One day he's up, the next day he's down. The mouth is working a little, and the other day he moved his fingers – like this': she made a motion as if removing something stuck on the tips of her fingers; they asked her to repeat it: 'Right hand or left hand?' they asked.

'Left hand' – which excited them a little, though not nearly so much as it had excited her when it happened: she had just settled Thomas's pullover about him, and laid his hands on the arms of his bed-chair, when she saw the fingers move. With dread, the dread of hopes again dashed, she lifted his hand carefully, re-settled it – and the fingers moved again. She shouted to Essie, and the two of them stood there gazing at Thomas's whitened bony hands, sight-seers at a natural phenomenon. In school, Ellen taught that day with a giddy heart – and then had to endure a week when no further movement was detected.

She took the surgeons through the charts one by one: food intake; bowel movements; sleep patterns; eye movements. They stayed for three and a half hours, accepting only a cup of tea.

In the hall she asked, 'What do you think now?'

The one she did not like said, 'I'm encouraged. Although I have to say – even if there is a noticeable improvement, and we have to record what you have told us as improvement – you must remain aware that it could go either way. And that is, in my view, the only way to look at it. In fact, you could say – it has to go either way. In fact, there are four possibilities. If he does not regain full consciousness, he cannot live for ever like this. If he does regain full consciousness he may be impaired for life; in other words, he may never be the same vigorous man mentally or physically, although he will be able to look after himself. Or he could make a full recovery. The fourth possibility is – he could die very quickly and quietly, in his sleep, and quite soon. The body gives up, you know. My guess is, from all you've told me about him – if he gets at all active again, he will make a complete and total recovery. But it's a big "if". If he doesn't, well, no woman could have done more for any man . . .'

At the school, a sudden and heated row broke over Ellen's head. Mrs Hand knocked on the door, supported by Mrs Leamy.

'Ma'am, I'm going down this minute to report you to the Canon, so I am.'

'What?'

'I'm going down to the Canon this minute.'

'What's wrong?'

'Ma'am, the things you're putting in them children's heads. And you're not teaching them hardly any prayers.'

'I beg your pardon, Mrs Hand,' said Ellen with asperity. 'You're the very woman who came here to me, here at this door, two years ago and told me I was teaching the children too many prayers. And with all due respect to you, I'm the one paid to teach the children, not you. Indeed, if you spent a little more time cleaning up your children, they'd be a bit better served.'

As she began to close the door, Mrs Hand inserted a foot.

'You're not supposed to be teaching the children the things you were telling here yesterday. That's not what the Canon pays you for.'

Mrs Leamy said, 'Them things are none of your business.'

'The Canon doesn't pay me. The Department does. And that's none of your business. And if you don't mind, I want to go on doing what I'm paid for, so move your foot out of the way please.'

'I will not! I will not!' Mrs Hand pressed at the door: Ellen resisted: Mrs Leamy pressed, and the air was filled with grunts and rattles of the latch. The months of lifting Thomas had made Ellen muscular: she succeeded in closing the door and bolting it. Mrs Hand rapped the window so hard a pane cracked tinily. After some minutes the hefty women moved outside the wall of the yard and stayed there. In an hour, they went away.

On the previous afternoon, Ellen had begun: 'What is a Treaty?'

Faced with the usual vagueness, she answered her own question. 'A Treaty is a signed agreement by the two enemies in a war that they will stop fighting. The Irish and the English signed a Treaty in 1921 and that gave us the Twenty-Six Counties and gave England the Six Counties. Now what happened after the Treaty?' No hand rose.

'I'll tell you what happened, because this is part of the history of your own country. There was a Civil War. A what?' She made them repeat it. 'A Civil War,' they sang.

'Now what's the difference between a Civil War and any other kind of war? A Civil War is a war between people who are friends and neighbours, or who were friends and neighbours. Some people say that a Civil War is the worst kind of war. Now – there were some people in Ireland who didn't want the Treaty signed, and there were some who did. A lot of people around here, for example, did not want it signed; a lot of people in other places did. In some cases, one brother wanted it signed, another didn't. Or a father agreed with it, but a son didn't. So a Civil War broke out and it was very bad because people who were friends fell out with each other, and they even killed their friends and neighbours and relatives.'

Ellen told Mrs Greege about the altercation with Mrs Hand and Mrs Leamy.

Mrs Greege looked at her. 'You haven't learned everything yet. Keep your mouth shut about them things. Go back to the prayers.'

'I will not.'

'You should,' said Mrs Greege. 'People don't want to be reminded. Isn't that right, Master Kane?' she called to the bed-chair across the kitchen. To Ellen she said, 'If the Master was alive, he'd tell you the same thing.'

'Alive?' Ellen shrieked. 'He is alive!'

'Thomas,' she said that night, 'that's the first bit of embarrassment I ever knocked out of Mrs Greege, and d'you know what? I don't care. The children should know these things. What surprises me is the priests don't tell them. It should be part of their Catechism class.'

Obviously, they got at the Canon. A note from him said that in a fortnight's time he would conduct a short Catechism examination. Ellen said to Thomas, 'I suppose I'd better cave in a bit. But it won't change the way I feel.'

At the end of April, with all medical and nursing practices running smoothly, Ellen sat down late one night beside Thomas in the silent house.

'Thomas dear,' she began, 'I don't know if I have it in me, but I'm going to go flat out now. I don't know if this is going to be the last all-out effort I can make, but I don't know either what else I can do after this. Thomas, please, please, give me something. If you're in there and if you can hear me, show me. Show me. Give me something. I'll even tell you what I'm going to do,' and on her splayed fingers she ran through a list of her intentions. At the end she said, 'And after that I'm finished, Thomas, "bunched" as you'd say.'

She continued, 'Thomas dear, do you remember the first time we really and truly walked out together? You said to me, "Are you by any chance going home to Janesborough this week-end? Because if you weren't," you said, "there's a new hotel opened by a past pupil of mine who went off to England and made money." And you said you were going to go over there on Sunday.'

Ellen recounted and re-lived the outing.

They drove up along a high wooded avenue on the mountainside to a large house with tiny wooden eaves.

Ellen said, 'A lovely place.'

They looked out over the valley, with the river in the distance.

'Do you know those Encyclopaedias of Knowledge, Thomas, with the pictures of ancient Greece and all of that, ruined temples, or artists' impressions of what it must have been like?' Pointing out of the window, she had said, 'This view reminds me of that, the groves of childhood, that kind of thing, the trees in the distance, the river, and so on.'

Thomas had remarked, 'The owner – he won't take a penny. He won't let me put my hand in my pocket.'

'I heard him,' said Ellen, and smiled. Frost had made the air clear and sparkling, and Ellen wore her burgundy-coloured paisley dress and her maroon cardigan.

Thomas fumbled a little and poured a glass of milk from the jug on the table. A man stood at the door, saw them, came over and said 'Hallo, Sir,' to Thomas and shook his hand, and went out again.

'Mikie the Lady,' Thomas whispered, 'he's a bit girlish and that's what the boys around christened him. He's a spoiled priest, did six years, and cut before he was due to be ordained, but he's very holy.'

Mikie the Lady came back, contrived to get an introduction to Ellen, and told her, 'The Master taught me in the third, fourth, fifth and sixth book. I'd never have passed *Pons Asinorum* if it wasn't for him.'

When he left them, Ellen asked Thomas for a translation, 'being from the city,' she said, with an arch, teasing smile.

Thomas told her that 'book' meant 'class', that 'third book' meant 'third class'. Classes were formed by a philosopher called Duns Scotus. *Pons Asinorum* means "the bridge of asses": she interrupted tartly, 'Well I knew that' – and he continued, 'Euclid's fourth theorem: if you couldn't get across that, you remained an ass for the rest of your life.'

Ellen smiled. 'I never asked you how did you get into teaching?'

'I didn't want to be, although I wanted to do something for the country, I wanted to be in the law or something. But my father died when I was sixteen, nearly seventeen, and even though I had a King's Scholarship I couldn't take it up, because there was no money coming in. The youngest was only two, and all my mother had was my father's pension of two shillings a week, you couldn't feed a bird on that. So I had to forget about school and go and work for the farmers, and I worked for farmers during the day, thinning beet and hoeing drills, or in parts of the year lambing and calving, and then in the nights I worked in a pub, and I did that for eight years until enough of the family were working to bring other money in.'

Chops with gravy; jelly with custard; a cup of tea and biscuits: Ellen had never ceased smiling all through the meal. As they left, the owner made a fuss of her, too.

'This man is a genius,' he said, pointing to Thomas.

In the car Thomas said, 'And I couldn't get one ounce of information into his skull. 'Twas like trying to teach the wall.'

'Did you go to night school, so?' asked Ellen, trying to pick up the thread again.

'Oh, it is a long, long story,' said Thomas.

'Thomas,' she said now, 'you are entitled to your long story, and you should be free to live it again and to remember it. I came out here, to this village, thinking I was educated, and then I found myself having to fight like an animal for my life and yours. Thomas, I don't know any more what education is. But I didn't know what love was, not even when I married you. By God, I do now.'

=

490

May Morris wrote, in a letter in which Bob enclosed money, 'When Rina's holidays start, will I send her out to keep you company? She's very useful now.'

Ellen's brief note thanked her all the same but, no.

'You're a pagan, I'd reckon,' Ellen said to Miriam Hogan next day. 'What do pagans do?'

'Why? Do you think it is paganism will bring him back?'

Ellen looked at her but said nothing.

'Pagans take off their clothes and dance,' continued Miriam.

'I can't see Essie and Mrs Greege doing that,' said Ellen.

Miriam whooped with laughter.

'Get him flowers,' she said, 'and bring him young animals to see, and hold perfumes in front of his nose, and sing to him. That's what the Greeks would have done. That's what we'd do if we still lived in a tribe. Cast spells for him. Show him the moon when it comes out. Wash his face in cold rainwater that you catch yourself in a basin. Let the baby rub his face. Bring in a clump of grass with dew on it. Did you ever shave your legs? Well, then shave your legs in front of him. Let him smell your armpits. Rub your clothes to him. Put your skin near him. Read him love stories. Put the cats on his lap.'

Ellen interrupted, 'They climb up there anyway, Blackie is always there, we nearly have to pull her away, he's nice and warm for them.'

'Get him a dog. But above all, rub him, put your fingers to his mouth, rub your chest to his face, show him yourself.'

Ellen, for all her new feistiness, had a shocked expression on her face.

'Miriam! How do you know all this?'

'I daydream all the time, you know all those times I'm walking the fields? I think a lot. Jack forgets how well educated I am. He thinks I truly am what my mother told him, "an oddity". I think about things all the time and I link them to what I see out in the fields. Rain is a wonder, people don't realize that. And what do you think all that out there is for, the grass and the sky and the mountains and the clay? Look –' She held her arms above her head and twirled slowly. 'I often do this when I'm at home, when Jack is out. I take off all my clothes and I dance in front of the long mirror. Jack isn't intelligent enough to look at me or touch me the way I want to be seen and touched. When I saw how unintelligent he was about me, I nearly tore myself apart, I tried to mutilate my body so that he wouldn't want to come near me.'

'Miriam Hogan, do you know somethihg? I think you are gone a little mad.'

'A little soft in the head?'

'Not the full shilling.'

'A bit empty upstairs, maybe?' Miriam winked in slow motion.

'And Miriam, do you know something else? I think you're right to be that way. I'm beginning to think it is the only way to be.'

'For a woman, anyway,' said Miriam.

A horse-and-cart drew up outside the gate.

'It's all right, Essie, I'll go out,' said Ellen.

'Hold the rope, Ma'am, hold the rope,' said Dan Allen. 'Don't let him buck.'

'I'll have him back to you in a few minutes,' Ellen called over her shoulder.

To the toddling Helena's squeals of delight, her Mamma led a black-and-white calf right into the kitchen. Ellen held the calf's neck tight on the halter; the creature wobbled and buck-kicked a little: inside the house the calf looked large and highly amusing. Taking Thomas's hand, Ellen guided the calf to his fingers; the calf nosed around, then swinging its head gave a cry, then nosed again, then began to suck. It left a sweet milky scum on Thomas's hands, then licked Helena's hand who squealed in delight and fear.

'Oh, Ma'am,' said Essie, 'there'll be scutter all over the floor.'

Ellen took Thomas's palm and rubbed it on the calf's rough back, and back up to its ears and around its jaw, then led the calf back out.

'I haven't an iota why she wanted it,' said Dan Allen that night to Mrs Hand behind the bar. 'She only had it in there five minutes, and she led it out again, and thanked me and wanted to pay me.'

Next night, Ellen said to the departing Nurse Cooper, 'Don't. I'll lower him later.'

Although prepared for bed, Thomas continued to sit upright. Just before midnight, Ellen approached and said, 'Here, Thomas, here, look.' Slowly she took off her cardigan, then unbuttoned her blouse. 'Oh, Thomas, to think I wouldn't do this if you were in the whole of your health?' She lowered the straps of her slip and stood above him naked to the waistband of her skirt. 'Here?' She raised each arm and thrust each armpit into his nose. 'Smell me.' She then lowered her breasts and drew them across his face, slow, warm, pliant brushings across his eyes, nose, mouth, cheekbones, chin, down into the cradle of his neck.

On Saturday morning, she went into the garden with one of the large brown kitchen bowls used for eggs, or cake-batter. Essie and Sheila Cooper said to each other, 'What in the name of God is she doing now?' Ellen stooped and gathered handfuls of clay; from the gooseberry and blackcurrant bushes she broke little twigs; in the kitchen she held them close to Thomas's nose, crumbled the clay in her fingers as if it were snuff.

Rainwater, just a little basinful collected during a heavy shower, the smell of the honeycomb, the underclothes she was changing from, the newly ironed linen – all of these Ellen applied to Thomas's senses, usually held under his nostrils. Once, and once only, the desperation broke through. Late at night, with Essie upstairs on her clumpings, Helena asleep, Ellen undressed and began to shave her legs.

'Look, Thomas, you never saw me do this before, look.' Slowly she drew the razor down along her shins, holding the leg up to inspect it, and rubbing her hand along it, from the inside ankle to the outside thigh.

Not for days had there been any vestige of encouragement by way of a new flicker of life from him, not for days, and Ellen sat back in the chair, wrapped her arms tight around her naked bosom, moaned in frustration, held one foot yet in the basin of water, and could not summon the energy to shave the other leg.

'I think,' said Nurse Cooper that week, 'she's getting a little frantic. I'm worried.'

'Leave her alone,' said Miriam Hogan, 'leave her alone.'

'Come on,' said Ellen. 'Think of a song.'

'What about this one?' asked Miriam. 'Hey, big man, big man,' she said to Thomas. 'Do you know this one?'

'I have a song to sing-oh.'

Ellen joined in.

'Sing me your song-oh.

493

It was sung to the moon by a lovelorn loon
Who fled from the mocking throng-oh.
It's the song of a Merryman moping mum.
Whose soul was sad and whose glance was glum,
Who sipped no sup and who craved no crumb,
As he sighed for the love of a lady.
Hey-de, hey-de, Misery me, lacakaday dee.
He sipped no sup and he craved no crumb
As he sighed for the love of a lady.'

'Oh. "Sipped no sup, craved no crumb" – not entirely the best choice of words in all the circumstances,' said Miriam and they roared with laughter.

In the third week of May, with Easter well behind them, the people of Deanstown slowly became aware that the silence surrounding the Kane household had intensified even further. Those self-appointed watchers from behind the lace curtains of the village reported Mrs Greege's increased visits; Nurse Cooper's hurried arrivals, almost daily, then daily; Dr Hogan's extended stays; Mrs Hogan 'never left the place'; the Mistress's dark frowns as she raced to and from school; the children reported her as 'different, she don't laugh as much'. Ellen wrote brusque letters cancelling all who would call. The house had completely withdrawn into itself: the villagers, picking up the mood, talked and talked, paying gloomy compliments. 'Well, the one thing is, you can't say she didn't fight for him, that's for sure.' They shook their knowing heads. 'D'you know what it is. The Mistress wasn't at Mass this nearly five months.' Prayers continued for the Master.

'Any day now,' said Mrs Hand, 'you'll see Mrs Kirwan there': the local midwife who also laid out and washed corpses and acted as the undertaker's agent. Mrs Hand continued, 'Did you see his brothers were over? Two of them cycled over on Sunday and they were there no time, and they left with faces as long as a Tuesday on them. Mr Vousden, what do you think?'

'Well,' says Val, 'the Band is going to play there Sunday, outside the door, whatever? Sure 'tis the least we can do.'

'Thomas,' said Ellen. 'I have a good one to tell you. You know those Gannons, don't you, over there near Mullinahone? Miriam

Hogan was telling me: the Gannons have cousins in America who were home recently, and one of them was standing with that Gannon man, you know the man with the brown hat on him always, and the sun was going down. And the Yank, the American cousin, said, "That sure is a lovely sunset." And d'you know what the Gannon man said? He said, "I s'pose 'tisn't bad for a small place like Mullinahone." Isn't that a scream?' She laughed – and subsided.

She called, 'Essie, bring in that cake, is it fresh out of the oven?'

Ellen cut into the fruit cake. 'Blast you, Thomas Kane, you're going to eat this whether you like it or not, you used to love it. Will anything get you back to life, will anything?' and when she crammed the crumbs into his mouth, he gagged a little and jerked his head.

That night she took out Herbert's long handwritten piece of paper, and began to read, first to herself and then as she warmed to the text, aloud to Thomas, skipping forward as she found the most beautiful passages.

> 'Like an apple tree
> Among the trees of the forest
> Is my love among all other young men.
> I love to sit in the shade of him
> And the fruit of him is so sweet
> To the taste of my mouth.'

She looked up at Thomas's face and then down at Herbert's handwriting.

> 'He has led me into the banqueting hall
> With his banner of love waving over me.
> Feed me cakes with raisins in them.
> Refresh me with apples,
> For I am fainting with love.'

The light from the lamp shone half-across Thomas.

> 'Look, the winter is past
> And the rains are over and done with.
> Flowers have begun to appear on the earth;

The time of the singing-birds has come
And the voice of the turtle-dove
Shall be heard in the land.'

Ellen jumped to her feet and read with one arm held out dramatically.

'My beloved is mine and I am his.
He feedeth among the lilies.
Until dawn breaks and the shadows melt away,
Turn to me my love
And be like a swift gazelle
Or a young stag on the mountain of spices.'

Ellen slammed the paper down on the table, ran to the hall door and opened it. The May moon had risen long ago and now coasted high to the due south. She rushed back in and scrabbled at the locked shutters, breaking a fingernail, which she sucked.

'Thomas, look!' and sang, 'The young May moon is beaming, love. The glow-worm's lamp is gleaming, love.'

She doused the oil-lamp, whirled the bed-chair around, until the moon through the window shone in his face like a torch.

'Look,' said Ellen, 'you can see the cities there. Look. It is his face I can see. The man in the moon. When I was a little girl, when I saw the moon first, I asked my father to get it for me. Thomas, I want you to be able to show Helena the man in the moon. Thomas, you know the prayer I taught you, *Saint Patrick's Breastplate*, don't you? Whenever I think of that time, of you, out there in the fields on the run under the moon, with your gun in your bad, your evil, killing times – I know you won't ever talk to me about that, you never would, you must have been ashamed, or something – I used to think, what if *Saint Patrick's Breastplate* wasn't a prayer but a kind of suit of armour, and that my dear Thomas might have been able to wear it. The words of it, Thomas?' Ellen recited, 'Christ before me, Christ at my side . . . all that part?'

Ellen continued, urgency increasing, 'Well, there's another part, a part that's never said as often. One of the lines in it is, "The whiteness of the moon at evening". It is my favourite part. Thomas, make me a promise. Promise me you'll live, promise me you'll get

496

better, promise me that on the whiteness of the moon, will you?'

And so, night after night, week after week, her solitary impassioned colloquies continued, and she drew the household into an ever tighter and frenzied circle about her and her man, Thomas Kane. Only one person outside the circle ever saw that chalk-white, supine Thomas Kane again, as he lay in that now dreadful chair-bed, and that was Val Vousden. The band gave what Val called 'a recital' on the gravel in front of the house. Ellen permitted it, and opened the door and the windows.

'Can I see him itself, Ma'am?'

'On one condition,' she said, 'and this has to be a solemn promise.'

'Val is always as good as his word, Ma'am,' he said.

'You mustn't answer any of their questions about how he is.'

'Fair enough, Ma'am,' said Val, 'I won't even tell Mrs Heffernan,' and he never uttered a word.

The gate rattled early, just after eight o'clock. Ellen looked out of the window, and saw a curious figure, a man with a bicycle and what looked like a pedlar's tray across the handlebars. Propping the bicycle against the wall, he called through the bars of the gate. 'Anyone?! Anyone?!' She opened the bedroom window and put out her head.

'What do you want?'

'Is this the Kanes' house?'

'Yes.'

'I want to see Master Kane.'

'He's not here. Go away.'

She closed the window. The man shouted on. Ellen opened the window. 'I told you! He isn't here. Go off with you.'

The man tried to climb the gate, but could not negotiate the spikes.

Ellen opened the window a third time. Where the blazes was Sheila Cooper? She's usually here by now when it is her morning on.

'If you don't go away I'll call the Guards!' She lowered the sash again, and stepped behind the long lace curtains.

The man abandoned the gate and disappeared: then she saw him

497

climb the wall and crash through the high laurel hedge, Thomas's pride and joy.

'Jesus!' said Ellen. She opened the window yet again.

'Where are you going? Get out. Get out. I'll send for the police, I will.'

The man ran across between the apple trees, prancing high to avoid the wet grass, and hurled himself against the front door, rapping the knocker so hard the frame of the door jumped. Ellen raced downstairs and opened the parlour window a fraction beside the front door.

'Who do you think you are?' she shouted.

'Who are you?' he asked, the white teeth flashing in his dark skin.

'What do you want? I'm not buying anything.'

'I've something here for Thomas Kane. Master Thomas Kane.'

'What is it? I can take messages for him.'

He dug into a large pocket and pulled out a small brown paper packet.

'This. But I want a reward.'

'How much? And a reward for what?' He came to the window and handed it to her. 'Judge for yourself.'

Gingerly Ellen took the packet and felt it. Small, soft: so insubstantial there might be nothing in it. Sheila Cooper appeared at the gate, had a key to the padlock. Ellen closed down the window, stepped back into the parlour, but kept the curtains apart so that she could keep an eye on the man. She turned the packet over in her hand.

He rapped the glass hard. 'Open it, I haven't all day.'

She unfolded the packet as slowly as ever Thomas might have done. Inside sat a twist of newspaper which she also unfolded. Grubby, a little twisted and slightly green, lay her gold cross, the one ripped from her neck on her wedding morning. She disappeared from the man's view, and he heard her open the door.

'Where did you get this?' she demanded, un-harshly.

'Ask me no questions, and I'll tell you no lies.'

'But you're not the same man who took it?'

'No, but I know the scoundrel.'

'Wait 'til I get my bag.' Ellen returned with her handbag, took out her wallet and handed the man a five-pound note.

'I didn't mean that much,' he said.

'I do,' she replied.

He looked at the money then at Ellen. 'Is there anything else you lost that you'd like me to go looking for?' She shook her head.

Sheila Cooper said, 'What are you doing with yourself buying from a pedlar?'

Ellen showed her the cross, told her the story.

32

Ellen exhibited the missing treasure to sleeping Thomas, and to Essie: by now Ellen knew how to tell Essie a story: much detail, lurid where possible, adjectival, with mimicry: Essie gasped satisfyingly: 'A n-miracle, Ma'am.' Helena jig-stumbled about in red dungarees, crashing into doors, climbing on chairs, pursuing Soot who got away easily, if a little furred and miffed.

Notwithstanding the brightness of the morning and its startling event, Sheila Cooper wore a tight expression, as when about to raise a difficult matter.

'D'you remember when he was threatened with pneumonia? And you sent out for everybody from around the place to come in and help? Well, they're all anxious to know how he is, they're asking me every hand's turn I take, and I can't tell them a mortal thing – because that's the way you said you want it?'

'Sheila, the only reason I wanted a bit of privacy –'

'Secrecy, it is –'

'– All right, "secrecy", the only reason I wanted nobody to know anything was to give us a chance to get him right.'

'Why didn't you go to the other road? You saw the way it worked before?'

'What other road?'

'Get everybody in. Say, instead of us standing him up, propping him up to see if he can flutter a bit more into – into normal . . . the men could do that, couldn't they, a couple of big tall men like Michael Connors – or the Canon, come to that?'

Ellen reflected, forefinger between teeth.

'Yes. Yes.'

'Yow! Yow!' Helena squealed as Blackie pounced tail-high slowly across the doorway.

'No. This is why,' said Ellen, opting for authority. 'I know how . . . how particular – Thomas is. He's very, what? He's very, I don't know, not fastidious, that isn't the full thing I want to say. He'd be put out, he'd be . . . Look. Supposing I asked the same

500

thing again as we did at the pneumonia, and supposing Thomas, you know – "woke up" suddenly, and it was somebody holding him he maybe didn't even like very much. No.'

Ellen grew firmer. 'I see your argument, Sheila. But I'm after coming this far. And if there's any fraction of a chance – I want to be the one who's there. What I'll do if you like, is, I'll write to everyone and tell them, that's what I'll do.'

'All right,' surrendered an unsatisfied Sheila Cooper, 'but you'll be writing an awful lot of letters. You can start this morning with Mrs Stack, Mrs Hanafin, Mrs John Looby and Arthur Grant's wife. And that's only yesterday's crop.'

> Dear Mrs Stack,
>
> Nurse Cooper was telling me you were enquiring and I can't tell you what your interest and sympathy mean to us all. The Master is much the same, although lately we have been seeing, I think, and I hope I'm not imagining it, signs of improvement.
>
> The doctors told me in London what would happen is, we should pay him the greatest possible attention in the greatest possible calm. So we stand him up every day and we exercise his arms and his legs, that's all to get the circulation going, and we rub his cheeks, and we rub his head carefully, and his shoulders.
>
> They said I should be on the watch all the time, because as the brain heals itself, the last stages of healing can happen quite suddenly. It is, of course, all very tiring, but that is the way things are, and I hope I'll have more news for you soon.

She said to Sheila Cooper, 'Will that do?'

Sheila read carefully, and said with sympathy, 'Ah, well,' recognizing that Ellen had omitted the despair, the always-frustrated eagerness, and the crucial information that things might very easily slip the other way, that Thomas could likely die in his sleep or, as Sheila put it to Mrs Greege, 'sigh off to eternity in front of our two eyes'.

When she returned from school every afternoon Ellen asked Essie and anyone else who happened to be near, 'Any news?' in the same way her mother had used the phrase with pointed coyness in the months directly after Ellen's marriage: both questions had similar meaning: 'Any new life?'

Once, the young nurse told Ellen, 'I know one thing, Ma'am, the way he opened the eyes this morning wasn't the way they fall open, d'you know that old fish sort of a way; this was like his eyelids had their own muscles again' – but nothing further, nothing at all.

Ellen's private nocturnal colloquies continued throughout late May into the fluctuating weather of early June. One hot, thundery night, she unbuttoned Thomas's pyjama jacket and sponged him gently with a cool cloth, then towelled him with tenderness and allowed him to lie for some minutes open-chested.

'Oh, dear man – if only you'd snore or something, some sort of noise.'

33

The framework of the old village may still be traced very clearly and easily. Admittedly, prosperous bungalows have replaced all but two of the ochre, estate cottages, and smaller farms have been bought over and merged into greater acreages. The Castle has largely disintegrated: crusts of old stucco may be stumbled across, embedded in the earth. Only a corner of the brick kitchen garden wall lingers; the greengages have disappeared, and the Castle pond has dwindled to a tiny marshy fen. A headstone of bland marble in Silverbridge Protestant churchyard bears the legend,

Ernestina Stephenson
1894–1927
Erected by her loving brother, Cyril
AND THE VOICE OF THE TURTLE-DOVE SHALL BE
HEARD IN THE LAND

Stands of lime trees have grown in many fields; myxomatosis once eliminated the rabbits – they have returned to the blue-green grassy banks; and the mountains still look near when it rains. In the new school, glowing white on the edge of the village, summer holidays remain the same: closed in mid-July until the last week in August or, more usually, the first week in September.

On the Friday of the second week in June, 1927, Ellen decided she would revive Thomas's custom of having a sweet giving-out on the last day of the holidays, and she sat at the high dais writing a note to Newey's in Mooreville 'for delivery in plenty of time, a wide assortment of toffees, chocolate toffees, liquorice and fruit drops, six lbs in all'. In the bright sun of the morning, she had risen well, early, breezed down the stairs to Thomas, ahead, unusually, of Essie. She opened the shutters and approached that first dread moment – the daily test of checking Thomas's forehead and breathing to ascertain that he had lived through the night.

503

Next, Ellen opened wide the front door and the back door: because she was so early, she could make a start on Thomas and with Essie's help have him finished before she left for school – he too would have a lovely fresh beginning to the day.

Kettles on, in a moment she heard the rabbiting and chattering and thumping and little singing, meaning that Miss Helena was on her busy way down the stairs, bumping her bottom on each step, and then bursting with self-praise when she made it to the hall without misfortune. Helena put her head around the door, and grinned, and stood up. Ellen grinned back and laughed at little Miss Comical, steadier on her pins each day.

Essie's great noises began shortly after, step by thudding step. Did she have somehow to visit and re-establish each corner of the room before braving the day? Essie descended, and soon came her inevitable opening words.

Ellen whispered one night, 'Thomas, d'you know what it is? If Essie found me sitting on the chamber-pot, she'd say, "Sure I'll do that for you, Ma'am."'

This morning, Essie took the porridge saucepan handle from Ellen, and said, 'Sure I'll do that for you, Ma'am.'

Ellen had finally assembled her school basket.

'Ma'am, what'll I put on the baby?'

'Is it going to be sunny?' pondered Ellen. 'She'll be out again, I suppose? Are her red dungarees still clean enough?'

'And, Ma'am – will I bake a fresh cake of bread, say another white?'

'Yes, that'd be great, Essie.'

Thomas looked fine, clean: Essie and Helena walked to the gate to say goodbye to Ellen: much waving took place between mother and baby daughter. Eventually, by the time Ellen reached the village, Helena could just about be persuaded by Essie to return to the house: Helena always closed the gate with a resounding clang: Essie always tried to coax her in before one of the carts passed by on the way to the creamery, delaying matters a good five minutes more.

Essie had entered the convent straight after her unnoticed years in the primary school. No question ever of her taking Vows: in ways He knew and saw and appreciated, Lay Sisters supported the work of the convent, served God, His 'special flowers' in their plainer, coarser habit – the first clothes Essie ever had, she told Ellen once, 'that weren't somebody else's, Ma'am.' Cleaning proved her initial *forte*: windows, walls, the wood in the oratory: Reverend Mother told her she had achieved a reputation for floor polishing.

Helena went, 'Unh! Unh!' – a sign she wanted something: Essie handed her down the coloured tin they kept the dishmop in. Ellen worried recently to Leah whether the 'Unh!' sound was natural to a baby that age, or whether Helena had picked it up from Essie's cleft palate.

'You know, I suppose,' said Sheila Cooper, 'that the Boss here will probably have to learn how to speak again?'

'Oh, God, Sheila – and Essie with him all day,' retorted Ellen, and the women rolled about with kind laughter.

Essie could not find the cream-of-tartar, went to the pantry to open a new packet. Bending down, she backed her enormous rump into Helena, who whacked her.

'Nah, now, n-babby, are you n-beating Essie?'

Helena continued whacking, in thorough enjoyment.

Essie returned to the scullery, and with vast hands drew the flour in from the high rims of the bright tin basin. She took the brown jug and heaved forth a little of the thickening sour cream, watching the dribble of thin curd complete with the white clots.

'She is very cheerful, isn't she, very?' commented Mother Angela, 'always in good humour.'

'Do you want to do anything about the singing?' asked sister Mary Cecilia diplomatically.

Mother Angela smiled, her hands in the folds of her deep cuffs, shivering a little as they crossed the cold yard. 'Only not to let her into the choir, I suppose.'

Essie sang 'Slievenamon' as she baked, a sound that matched the scraping of the knife on the tin of the basin. Essie dabbed Helena's nose with a little flour: Essie then wiped the flour from her own hands on her elephantine hips. After a moment or two, when the baking had become uninteresting, Helena scrambled down off the chair Essie had placed adjacently, and wandered off. Essie, too concentrated on the basin by now, stopped singing and moved the chair out of the way.

'Yee-yee-yee. Yee-yee-yee!' Helena paused. She did her

emphatic jump, relishing the sound of her heels banging on the kitchen floor. Essie heard, paid no attention. Helena chuckled, a chuckle that rose at the end, signifying surprise and delight. Again she chuckled, with a sense of some enquiry: 'Yee-yee-yee? Yee-yee-YEE?' Then, 'Ahh-be. Be. Bu. BE?' This was a conversation: Essie turned her head, hands still deep in the cloggy mixture.

She could see Helena in the space between the kitchen table and the end of Thomas's bed-chair: something had caught the child's attention: and gold, dazzling sunlight drenched the kitchen.

Helena bounced again, and then crouched: she was playing a game, one which puzzled her, but did not threaten – but with what? Had the cat climbed up on the Master's bed?

Essie, holding her hands carefully akimbo, moved to one side, and when she took in the full view, suddenly reached for a cloth. Wiping her hands she moved forward along the scullery, up the step, past the open pantry door which she drew closed out of habit (leaving flour on the doorknob) and into the kitchen doorway. Helena again said, 'Be. Bu. BE?' and chuckled and smiled and poked Thomas's leg.

Essie stared. Helena looked at her, then back at her own father, and pointed and chuckled. Essie, her hands still in the dishcloth, backed carefully, back, back, to the scullery, dropped the cloth, slipped out of the back door and lumbered under full and rapid thick-legged sail around the side of the house to the gate. Three carts approached in their typical convoy, returning with the skim milk from the creamery, churns slopping water from the pump. She stopped the first one and asked him to turn around straight away and go down to the school and get the Mistress quick; she'd go herself only she couldn't leave the child in the house on her own.

'I will walk slowly,' Ellen told herself toughly. 'I will walk slowly, I mean my normal walk.'

The carter had only said, 'You're to come real quick, Ma'am, the servant-girl said.'

'Quietness, now,' she told her children. 'Delia, you're in charge,' and she then opened the door of the Juniors and said to her Assistant, 'I have to go up home for a minute.' The carter offered her a lift and she smiled her refusal.

'Ma'am, I hope you won't kill me for sending for you.' Essie waited just inside the gate under the evergreens. 'Oh, Ma'am.'

506

'Essie, what is it? You're never like this. Essie! What's up? Are you all right?!'

'Oh, n-Ma'am, the n-Master.'

'Essie! Come on. What is it?' Ellen's own face was turning red, and then patchy white. Essie could not say. Ellen ran along the gravel, crashed through the front door. Nothing.

Helena grinned, and ceased pushing a chair around, held up her arms to be lifted. Ellen ignored her, turned back to the hall to greet Essie.

'Essie, what in the name of God . . . ?'

Essie, who could see Thomas behind Ellen, pointed, growing even more agitated. Ellen turned and caught Thomas's faint smile. Essie leaned back, in shock, against the jamb of the door into the hallway . . .

Thereafter, Ellen scarcely slept; for the next two nights, she sat by his bed and held his hand. One day weeks later, Ellen sent Essie down to the Parochial House with a very private note – to ask Canon Williams whether he had a walking-stick or two she could borrow: he had, but told Essie he 'wouldn't lend them to Saint Peter himself'.

In summer, they never closed the outer doors of the church, only the wood-and-glass inner ones. On Sunday, 14 August 1927, the Canon arrived at a quarter to nine, and as usual, five minutes later, the bell rang. The altar-boys reported, 'They're all in, Canon'; the two oldest lads, deputed to light the tall candles, came back with their long-poled tapers, leaned them into the corner of the sacristy, and formed up with the others in soutanes and surplices in front of the Canon.

The sacristan said, 'How much wine will I put out, Canon?' He asked the same question every Sunday, and he always received the same answer.

'A good drop.' At which point the Canon always asked, 'Have we anything after?' – meaning a child for Baptism, or a woman for Churching, the ceremony of purification after birth, or a blessing of Holy Water.

'No, Canon, the fine weather drags them all away quick.'

Jeremiah Williams dipped his hand in the water-font at the sacristy inner door and added the Holy Water drops to the sweat-beads forming on his brow. He yanked at the right shoulder of the tall, homelily opulent chasuble.

The leading boy looked back: the little procession moved off. It rounded the rear of the altar swiftly and emerged swerving across the polished floor of the Sanctuary. The congregation rose, a muted shuffling sound, with the usual coughs, even in high summer. They sat down again as Jeremiah bowed to the Blessed Sacrament in the tabernacle. He climbed the steps, placed the covered ciborium with the gold-embroidered *I H S* in the middle of the altar-table, and turned to his right to find his spectacles and the card bearing the opening prayers.

As he descended the steps, all the acolytes genuflected with him and the entire congregation sank to their knees; standing, he spread his old hands and cleared his throat.

A large, alarming noise halted him, a hard, metallic clang from the yard, and a loud, revving engine noise. At the back, the men nearest the door, farm boys and labourers, down on one knee, their caps dangling from their hands to the stone flagged floor, started in suddenness, pulled mouth-ish faces of enquiry. Outside, the green Singer car, reversing, hit the wall of the church again, not as seriously as the first clang, and not at all dangerously.

'I'll tell you one thing,' they had been saying for several months, 'the Mistress, she's a wild woman in that motorcar. Do you know what it is? She have no aim.'

The first men to reach the door saw the Mistress pull the car forward a bit, then cut the engine.

'Her face,' they said afterwards, 'it was only fierce,' and they mimicked her jutting jaw. They saw her jump out, the brown cloche hat clipped firmly to her head, scurry round the car and look at the metalwork to see whether her appalling 'aim' had caused any damage. No: she opened the passenger door.

The hood was closed, so it took a moment or two to register that it was the Master she was helping out of the car. He stood upright, 'more or less of his own accord', as they later said, and put out a hand to steady himself on the car.

'He had his good body-coat on,' they reported. 'A big, heavy grey coat. And the day sweltering.' Ellen chose the right-hand door: a màn's rough hand from inside held it open for her.

She paused in the porch, reached up to adjust Thomas's lapel and collar. She removed his hat, placed a drop of water from the font on his forehead. Steering Thomas by the elbow first, then holding his hand, and then grasping him firmly by the arm, she walked slowly up along the aisle at his side. He looked straight ahead as he always did; he moved slowly, he moved stiffly: but the austere severity of his public face, the straight-edged mouth, had almost returned in full.

The Kanes reached the Teachers' pew a third of the way back from the altar. Thomas did not genuflect, although Ellen did, still reaching up to hold on to his arm. The Canon had watched their progress all the way.

Thomas encountered a little difficulty negotiating the entrance to the pew, a little stumble at the step; Ellen eased him down just inside, where he always sat, and she then stepped high over his feet and knelt by him. Thomas moved as if he would kneel but Ellen, looking at him, put out a restraining hand. He turned his head – 'A bit stiff, only,' they all said afterwards – and gave her a small, soft, slightly rueful smile.

Canon Jeremiah Williams surveyed Thomas, and Ellen, then Thomas again, and nodded. He turned back to the altar, and spreading his mottled hands once more, intoned, '*Introibo ad altare Dei.*' Those whose Missals included English in black print alongside the crimson lettering of the Latin, read, 'I will go in unto the altar of God.'

Ellen held the Missal over to her right for Thomas to share the page with her. The altar boys responded, '*Ad Deum qui laetificat juventutem meum,*' as the Master, the Mistress and the parish of Deanstown read in silent unison, 'Unto God who giveth joy to my youth.'

FRANK DELANEY

A STRANGER
IN THEIR MIDST

TO MICHAEL SHAW

*When he smiled the room grew warm. His brown eyes
welcomed all. In any business deal, nobody ever felt that
he alone had won, and they alone had lost, because,
in commerce's most humanitarian dictum, he 'left room
for the other man'. Within this company of ours, he
forged and devised and invented and strove. He made,
in the very fullest sense – he made the careers of many
of us.*

These words come from the funeral eulogy given in
1989 for Dennis Sykes by his successor. The Chairman
also said, 'None of you at this memorial service will take
offence when I say that we have never worked with – or
for – anyone as clever, anyone as *intelligent* as the man
for whose life we here give thanks today. He was our
leader, our inspiration, our dear friend.'

The eulogy rose and grew into a hailing piece of praise-
singing. Some jokes, the poignant recollection of a kind
deed, his prodigious memory for family enquiries and the
thoughtfulness shown towards everyone – typists, drivers,
cleaners. The eulogy contained no original words, perhaps, but no unnecessary lies. Apparently. The Chairman
delivered it beside a twinkling photograph of the
departed, who wore a silver tie.

Nobody mentioned, nobody knew, Dennis Sykes the
emotional criminal, the sexual psychopath. Who practised
seduction, manipulation, destruction of the heart. He

9

dreamed up, organized and executed, crimes against the spirit, against trust. Like a hired killer, a lone gun (he always referred to his penis as 'my Weapon') he reconnoitred, spied, assessed: he measured his booty in units of female vulnerability: he struck, and he vanished. With no regrets. All this he did with as much secrecy as possible. He understood secrecy, saw it as a kind of hidden energy source.

Dennis Sykes was one of the first of what came to be called a 'clear-desk executive'. In the interests of perceived efficiency, he had nothing in front of him except the file he was working on at that moment, and a large and beautiful blotting pad, with leather corners. This blotter remained perpetually snow-blank: no doodles. In 1984, at the age of seventy, he retired, wealthy and distinguished, from the chairmanship of Consolidated. His last company days show the warm-smiled, humane business leader, photographed bright and dapper in side-by-side handshakes, giving diligence awards to young graduate engineers in their first year with the company.

Nowhere do the photographs or the house magazines reveal a depressed man, his imagination full of revenge fantasies. Nor did anyone record that during seventeen years at Consolidated, Dennis Sykes never hired for his own office even one pretty secretary or female assistant. As part of his life-scheme, he kept his secret 'exercises' fanatically remote from his public activities, and therefore he chose to work with sober and restrained, untempting women.

Outside Consolidated, he golfed, and led the usual accompanying social life. People invited to his home for cocktails or less frequently dinner, teased him over not having a wife: how a woman would have loved that house:

10

how a wife would have untidied that fastidiousness and had rose petals falling on his shining mahogany.

In other circumstances – were he perhaps a less clever or educated man, but just as depressed – Dennis Sykes would probably have killed. He might simply have gone out and seduced women in a systematic pattern in order to take them somewhere safe, and then attack them. His wish to destroy women had all the hallmarks of a killer, and it was restrained by the white-collar society in which he moved. In Scotland and Ireland, he was also curtailed by the parochial size of the communities in which he lived and worked. Yet, in their secrecies he flourished, with his hidden life full of duplicitousness. And his destructiveness caused damage from which people never recovered.

1

Ellen Kane released the handbrake abruptly, and the green, glossy car jerked forward. Men of the parish standing in their gossipy line outside the gate doffed their caps and stared hard. In the passenger's seat, Thomas Kane sat upright, rigid and dignified, with bleak eyes. An unbarking dog chased the wheels, and skidded in the summer's dust. Slowly, with her chin raised so that she could peer over the steering-wheel, Ellen negotiated the sharp right-angled turn of the high churchyard wall. Straight as an arrow now, the car at last departed, and birds fled the trees at the noise.

On the steep descent to Hogan's Bend, neither spoke, and the sunlight disappeared when they entered the black nave of overhanging trees. When they emerged, Ellen indicated the plunging mare in the field on their left: her commentary began.

'Can you believe he paid three hundred guineas for her? Three hundred guineas!'

Outside one of the cottages, a young wet-lipped adult went 'Uuuhmmmnrh!' in delighted fright, and pranced awry as the car gleamed past.

'Poor creature,' murmured Ellen, 'but they say the new baby is normal. Thanks be to God.'

Up in the fields to the left, by that famous copse of the best hazelnut trees in the county, a horseman looked down at them against the sun, his hand shading his eyes.

13

Ellen with her amazingly good sight, said, 'Look, look! There's Cyril Stephenson, and they're saying he will, that he really will, marry her.'

Thomas Kane nodded.

'Thomas, are you able for a big breakfast?'

They drove past the dispensary. Ellen chattered on; 'The Hogans aren't up yet. I s'pose they'll go to last Mass in Mooreville.'

She had worked out a method of reminding him how the parish lived. With never a direct statement, she made oblique references only, and spoke of many things as if he automatically understood the references. 'I *knew* Mrs Greege paid too little for that paint on the haybarn last year. Look, the paint is all blistering.'

Up to their right, she pointed happily to the ruin of Deanstown Castle. The turrets and casements shone golden in the morning sun, a place fit for the streamers and flags of a jousting tournament.

'What are you thinking, Thomas?'

He shook his head, and folded his hands again.

They passed the Greege boy who stood at a field gate preparing to take cows across the road. He saluted. Thomas even tried to turn his head to look back at him.

'Easy, Thomas. You'll see him again.'

She yawned: Ellen had conceived three weeks ago.

This August Sunday morning was their first outing, his re-entry into their small community. Up to eight weeks ago, Thomas Kane had lived in a coma. For thirteen and a half months, he had lain stretched on a day-bed in his own home, with his wife living out a frantic, but powerfully-directed life aimed at his recovery. Mid-morning, Friday, 17 June 1927 – she later wrote the date in violet ink in her housekeeping book – a carter rapped at the school window and said, 'Essie says you're to go up home, Ma'am. Yes, Ma'am, *now*. She looks a bit urgent.'

Out of breath after her short run from the school, Ellen forced herself to stand still, to make no movement. She did not raise Thomas's heavy head, whatever the temptation; she did not take his pulse or his temperature. If anything, she pressed back a little, withdrawing the child. Right behind her, Essie, the big, mottled servant-girl, breathed as she always did when agitated: a little hissed moaning: 'Gu-nnnhhh-sss, gu-nnnhhh-sss.'

Helena, thirteen months and walking early for her age, sensed the stillness in the room and made whispering, conspiratorial noises. Ellen stood poised, suspended. No gambler ever eyed a dice closer: no sailor ever surveyed a threatening rock so watchfully. The death-faced, supine man closed his filamented eyes again.

Ellen said, quite sharply, 'Thomas?' in that tone of voice that has lost patience with someone feigning sleep. '*Thomas?*'

Nothing happened. She turned to Essie with an enquiring and disappointed shrug, but the servant-girl pointed again. He had reopened his eyes, and they blinked as lazily as a lizard's. Then he looked at her, but did not focus.

Day after day, week after week, Ellen had wondered – and she said it to several – 'What will his first words be?'

She never voiced the 'If . . . *if*'; she could not afford to; had invested everything in 'when', not 'if'; she kept two calendars side by side on the kitchen wall, last year's and this year's.

In the novels she read, an unconscious hero or swooned heroine always asked, 'Where am I?' Her husband Thomas Kane, his mind and spirit absent from her for over a year, said nothing at all.

15

As his eyelids found the strength to stay open, she stepped forward and took his hand. She turned the palm upwards, and rubbed his fingers as if attacking frostbite.

'If you can hear me, love, grip me, would you?'

His eyes focused on her and he coughed, releasing a little saliva; she wiped it with her finger.

'Thomas, do you know me? Do you know who I am?'

He blinked, once, then once more, then sighed, then closed his eyes again for a second or two, and when he reopened them, she said, 'Your eyes – they're a bit sharper now.'

She leaned towards his face, smiling as she did when picking Helena from the cot in the morning.

'Thomas, you're Thomas Kane. That is your name. I'm Ellen, your wife, Ellen. You've been hurt, you've been hurt for a long time.'

She straightened up and turned to Essie: 'I don't know what to do.'

'Bathe his forehead, Ma'am,' and the servant-girl hurried once more, this time to the back-kitchen to get a basin of water and flannel. As Ellen began to apply them, Thomas closed his eyes again. He put out his tongue, and licked the wet towelling of the facecloth. She looked down to see him make a flicking gesture with his fingers.

'I'll stop, will I?' she asked him, leaning back – and he spoke his first word in fifty-eight weeks.

'Do.'

In a wide circle, Ellen turned the car gingerly through the gate and saw its brass headlamps reflect golden sunlight on the bay-windows. At the front door stood Essie, holding up wriggling Helena.

With imperious hand, he did not permit Ellen to help him from the car; he even reached back inside, fetched his hat, and, holding it like a president, walked unaided to the house. She followed, removing the pin from her brown cloche and shaking her hair. Briefly she checked whether she had put a dinge in the car when she hit the church wall on the way in to Mass.

Sunday always meant a fresh tablecloth, but Essie had laid the white Belfast linen, the best. The servant-girl hung about waiting for a little praise, and Ellen smiled and nodded. Thomas smoothed the cloth as he sat; his clean, rounded fingernails traced the sheen of the damasked shamrocks.

'Couldn't Helena go down for her sleep now?' Ellen asked Essie. The child was held forth generally for kissing purposes.

Alone together, as they started breakfast, Ellen smiled at him. Both hands smoothed down her bosom in excitement.

'You see. You see! You did it! Your first outing! Oh, dear man, I'm proud of you.'

Thomas looked at her, then without a word turned to gaze out of the window.

Wildfire had carried the word of Thomas Kane's recovery. In an hour the news had spread. Mrs Hand in the public house said she knew something would happen because that morning, with not a puff anywhere, 'Lovely summer's day, a day like you'd write away for, we had a fairy wind here, didn't it run down through the village and rip a slate off the roof of the pub?'

Miriam Hogan found a fossil in the quarry the previous evening, and put it aside knowing Thomas Kane would have a view on it – when he could.

By six o'clock all knew everywhere in 'Deanstown and District', as officialdom called the place. By nine, after milking-time and supper, forum after forum opened up: the cross-roads; Hand's pub; the tree below the Canon's house where they played cards; Ryan's gate.

No two oracles bore the same tale. The Master was up and walking. He'd asked for potatoes, sick of that bread-and-milk, could you blame him? No, he was not up at all, not by any long chalk, he was only after opening his eyes and his speech wasn't working yet. Someone that someone spoke to heard from somebody else that someone saw him at the window. No. How could he be up at the window this quick?

As to his first words – what did they speculate? What did they actually insist that he said?

Easy to guess his first question: a hard man would want revenge, so he asked – 'Who did it?'

So they said.

By eleven o'clock on that balmy night of big summer stars, that was an established fact: 'Who did it?' – with variations such as, 'Who fired the shot?' and 'How many shots?'

Their comments had to remain speculative. Nobody got near the recovering man, and nobody would until this morning, his first reappearance at Mass. When Ellen Kane struck crisis, this soft and protected city girl abandoned her convent piety. She quarried ferociously for resources within herself, and discovered that privacy made her strong in that small, invasive community.

Therefore, for that crucial eight weeks after his awakening, from June to August, she kept them out. His dignity had to be guarded. To nobody could she, or would she, show his changing face, his staggering steps, his anger at his own debility. Even inside the house, she had to rush and hide from Essie his desperate, rock-hard erections each morning. This unanticipated embarrassment led to

18

her moving Thomas back into their own bed sooner than she had expected.

Besides, Ellen needed all her concentration: she had to make adjustment after rapid adjustment. He panted with anxiety as she left to go to school each morning. When she returned he would not let go of her hand. In that first week, he once tried to slap her face in anger as she said her afternoon 'Hallo'.

As each twilight fell, she closed and locked the gate, and when he developed sufficient mobility, took him into the warm dusk and walked him up and down the gravel path, into the garden, back again, around to the garage, back again. He staggered often; he stopped and started. A hidden onlooker would have reckoned this was someone trying to sober up a drunk.

'What will I do about all he has missed?' Ellen asked the doctors, who arrived some weeks after she had sent them her telegram: 'THOMAS KANE RECOVERED FROM COMA TODAY. THANK YOU. THANK YOU. ELLEN KANE.'

They considered, looking one to the other.

'Don't overload him.'

One said quickly, 'He may feel odd.'

'Odd?'

'People who have bad illnesses, and who recover from them, especially *accidents* –' how he chose the word – 'they sometimes feel they themselves are to blame.'

'But he wasn't.' She never lost that childhood quickness.

'Now, Mr Kane,' they asked him, 'how have you been?'

A letter gave notice of their arrival via Liverpool and Dublin. She dressed Thomas in the suit of his wedding. The couple stood by the door as the surgeons from

19

London, gleaming in this countryside like Martians in pressed grey suits, walked to meet him.

Thomas had the presence of a senile ambassador, as he slowly ushered these metal figures into the house.

They asked him ungushingly, 'Have you had any regressions?'

Thomas looked a little puzzled, and they amplified, 'Meaning, is all life normal? No blackouts or dizziness, no ailments associated with the head?'

Ellen again interposed. 'Not really, have you, Thomas? Not that I've noticed anyway.'

'Your trauma was acute,' they continued.

Thomas looked slowly from one sleek, relaxed man to the other. Ellen said, 'He wanted to know a few days ago, he asked me – which of you did the actual operating, the surgery?'

The answer came with a smile attached. 'There were five pellets, and a fragment of another. Three of those were close enough to the surface, two were farther in, one very much so. It became a question of, well, lightness of touch, really.'

Her lips sucked in, Ellen nodded.

Thomas began to speak: then stopped.

He stared straight ahead between the two men. Tears flowed unimpeded towards his mouth. He gazed at *The Monarch of the Glen* print in its gilded long frame, a wedding present. Nobody said a word, not even Ellen.

One man remarked, after a moment, 'Well, here we are. Here we are. You seem to me as if you're going to be right as rain.'

The other looked down into his empty cup. 'Yes, I will, please, Mrs Kane,' he said, when Ellen held the teapot aloft.

Thomas allowed his tears to dry, and sat motionless

during the rest of the visit. In due course the surgeons prepared to leave. Still, Thomas sat: eventually he stood to shake hands, and by the window watched them walk to the gate. He had red patches on his cheeks, bright as the dots of a clown. Ellen accompanied the Englishmen to their car and waiting driver.

'How would you say he is?' she asked.

'Astonishing. Complete recovery, I'd say.'

The other asked, 'How do you think he is emotionally?'

Ellen, from lack of comprehension, echoed, 'Emotionally?'

'Does he – does he get moody?'

'Yes, but – well, he was always a bit that way.'

Out of loyalty, she did not pursue: instead she asked, 'How much should I tell him – about, you know, about the time he was unconscious?'

'Tell him as much as he can take,' they concluded.

'He doesn't seem to like being told of things that happened while he was –' she halted.

'Tell him slowly. Spoon-feed it to him. You know how to spoon-feed by now, I should think.' A smile. 'No overloading. As I said. And be circumspect. I mean, like they used to do with the shell-shocked men, the soldiers. Remind rather than tell. Do you know what I mean?'

'Shell-shocked?' repeated Ellen. 'Yes. Yes.'

All smiled.

Up to then she had deflected Thomas's questions, promising answers when he had recovered further. That evening of the doctors, she began working carefully backwards. Of the actual shooting she spoke least, and finally told him in one terse, quiet burst.

'You called to take me and Helena home from the nursing-home. It was a lovely May morning last year.

21

You put the hood down on the car. Coming down Canty Hill, the accident happened. A man out shooting hit you on the side of the head. The car crashed and there we were. I was up and about within a week, Helena not a scratch. But poor you. The pellets put pressure on your brain.'

He stared. And stared.

She pressed on, looking him straight in the face, as she had done with her parents while lying in childhood. 'Dan Quinn. The poor fellow died the following Christmas. The family all left and went off to England.'

Neither glossed, nor glossed over, she told him no more, and never would. He never asked.

Day in, day out, he took her hand as she raised him from his bed, led him like Lazarus into the light. At night she lay with her cheek to his face and whispered, 'Welcome back, my dear, dear man. Welcome back.'

As she sat across from him, she splurged in her excitement.

'They all wanted to see you, didn't they? Did you see the crowd in the church, Thomas?'

Everybody perceived the appalling difference in him. They had waited weeks for this: they had prowled past the house for a glimpse. And would have climbed the trees by the windows had they not feared being seen. Now, how their eyes feasted. That night, by the lamplight in their kitchens, speaking with little puffs of wonder, they mimicked his gaunt walk into church – stiffened necks, their heads held rigid. His shoes with steel heel-tips used to ring firmly on the stone floor. Now, he clinked like a broken bell – one, two, three, pause: one, two, three.

They said afterwards, 'Wasn't it in a way like the opposite of a funeral? D'you know what I mean?' All

22

through the Mass, they scrutinized him. They took in his unprecedented hesitancy, his uncertainty, the half-vague expression on his face. Was this ever the same proud and aloof martinet, their great gunman-hero of the Troubles, who held himself as if banded with steel hoops?

They watched her as keenly: nobody had seen her for weeks. At his elbow they saw her display the pages of the Missal to him, and guide him through the prayers with a finger. She steered him upwards when he should stand: she sat him down again.

At the end of Mass nobody moved until they did – not even the slackest worshippers, who usually ran like hares before the *Last Gospel*. All stayed to watch.

The inner door had a glass panel: a frosty Crown of Thorns. Here, the couple stopped. As she stepped forward to negotiate the complicated door-handle, he stood waiting, not looking anywhere. A man helped, cap fisted to his breast – with a nod and a whispered 'Hallo, Missus'. Like damaged royalty, the pair stepped through the doorway, into the sunshine of the open church porch, and Thomas Kane blinked his long white face in the glare.

The congregation bulged out after them, but in the yard most people held back, content to walk far around him and stare. Children, agog, jostled for a better view. Senior men and women of the parish began to approach, and they spoke awkwardly to him, the men sweating in the August warmth.

Their thoughts showed. Should they shake his hand – or was it still lifeless? How could you welcome a person back when – when, well, he had been here all the time?

Eyeing the press of bodies, Ellen threw an invisible cordon around her confused husband. She clasped his arm with demonstrative responsibility: she glanced up at his face from time to time. Some of them said afterwards that she kept looking at him as if checking for something.

'Thomas. C'mon.' Ellen flicked a handkerchief from her sleeve and unfolded it. She reached up and dabbed a gem of sweat from his temple, where some blue flecks remained on the skin, and would never quite fade.

He looked over their heads, his eyes distant to the other hilltop, and took a deep breath, about to speak. Now they all pressed forward – but no. No word. They stepped back, disappointed: they had hoped he would wonder aloud who fired the shots. Among the few tall slabs *in memoriam* of dead canons and *monsignori* lying beneath the parade of beeches on this hilltop, the knot of people stood gazing at their local myth. Kindly they backed away from him, in the front yard of a country church whose walls today are painted a bright heliotrope. The tall man at their centre had returned from the dead, and his wife had brought him back, her plump lips in her worried face.

After eating, Thomas and Ellen sat by the bay-window. Dandelions gleamed like yellow stars in the long grass under the two apple-trees. At three o'clock, Canon Williams, coat open and flying, stalked through the gate. He flicked again his dark ageing eyes to Ellen's breasts as she arranged chairs outside the front door.

'I've new glasses, haven't I,' he said into Thomas's face, 'and I can't with them see as far as the end of my nose. I declare to God the collections got smaller since you weren't here, getting money out of this crowd is like getting blood out of a turnip.'

He sat. 'I'll pour myself out if 'tis all the same to everyone' – and he tipped the bottle of stout towards a glass, both vessels held at an angle to make a wide 'A' in his hairy hands.

He poured. 'I was thinking and I seeing you at Mass

24

this morning that you used to be a wonderful figure of a man;' sipped the cream froth on the black ale: 'A wonderful figure of a man.'

Canon Jeremiah Anthony Williams took another sip. 'We stormed Heaven for you, so we did, didn't we, Ma'am, we had every child from here to Timbuctoo in some clatter of a novena or another. We had so.' Yet he had refused to lend Ellen a walking-stick for Thomas's early upright days.

The Canon gazed ahead. 'I never liked Dan Quinn, I never did at all.' He shook his head. 'Nor did you, Missus, did you?'

Ellen, sharp as a tack, moved on him, asking in a hard voice, 'Canon, would you like something to eat?'

Soon, Helena, cheeks red and fresh from sleep, twinkled in and out through the door. Her pretty, plaid skirt flared like a tutu.

She said, 'Hallo there,' to the Canon, and showed him her skirt: he ignored her. His collar rose dignified to his chin, scoring a red weal above the Adam's apple. He snorted catarrh inwards, burbled, sipped stout again, then fell into one of his leaden reveries.

A village woman called Mamie arrived, and brought a gift to stave off her unwelcomeness – a finch in a small painted cage. Thomas rose from his chair, turned the cage this way and that.

Mamie preened at his admiration of the little bird, and ran her hands through her thin hair again, half-laughing. Thomas Kane flicked his fingernails on the tin of the cage.

The Canon said in a burst, 'Miners take songbirds down the mines to tell them of danger. If the bird dies, they know there's a dangerous gas around.'

'Good job there's no mines in this part of the country, so,' laughed Mamie.

Helena played 'hide-y' with Mamie, who winked at the child, and Helena stumbled off in a giggle.

'Fire-damp,' uttered the Canon. 'Yes, yes. That is what the mine gas is called.'

Thomas reached a long finger towards the caged finch who hopped back in dismay.

'Fire-damp. And. Talking of fire,' asked the Canon, 'is any of ye going to Dromcollogher for that memorial, that's next Sunday they're unveiling it.'

Thomas looked at him, puzzled.

The Canon comprehended. 'Last September. 'Twas while you were out cold. In your ould coma. The picture-house, and fifty they say now, or is it forty, I don't know. Dead, so to speak. There must be a lot you don't know, so.'

Thomas Kane glared at him, put the finch's cage on the window-sill, walked indoors and closed the front door. A moment later Ellen opened it, emerged and said, 'Essie made a sponge-cake. I think the Master's a bit tired.'

'Does he even know about Lindbergh?' asked the Canon.

The Canon munched. 'We should tell him everything he missed. Sure he probably knows nothing. Isn't that a queer one all the same, a teacher that knows nothing?'

'I think,' said Ellen primly, 'he will be all right. I'm making sure he knows all he needs to know.'

'Death is always looking for customers in new nations,' said the Canon, a man shaped by irrelevance.

Long after, when the visitors had gone, Thomas re-appeared on the stairs.

'Oh, you must be exhausted,' said Ellen.

He walked through the hallway into the kitchen and sat down in his own wide low armchair. Helena came barrelling through with a gurgle and began to climb on her father's knee. He plucked her firmly from his thigh and planked her untenderly on the floor. She tried another climb. He detached her again, and this time he skelped her hard; his hand bit into the thigh beneath the fluffed-out plaid skirt and its pretty lace edge. Helena squealed, gasped and wept in fright: for moments the child could not catch her breath. A blue and red weal bloomed on her skin.

Ellen did not voice her shock. She led Helena away, distracting her with the finch in the cage: 'Look, Helena – birdie, birdie!'

He dozed in the armchair. Sunday night filled in, always a time of stillness. The house quietened and they went to bed.

'Thomas,' she said, 'I have news for you.'

She turned to see his face. A waning moon and the night light of late summer kept the room semi-bright. 'You know me, I'm as regular as clockwork.'

His eyes flicked open.

'Dear man, if it's a boy we'll call him after you, no arguments.' He said nothing.

'If it's a girl, we'll call her – "Grace". What else could we call a child so conceived?'

He still said nothing, and closed his eyes fervently: impossible to tell whether in joy, or in dread.

They had days filled with gold in that first year of their marriage. Like all newly-weds of the time, they knew no familiarity with the bodies of others, and not much with their own. Once they discovered, though, how beloved is the skin of the beloved, they never stopped touching each other when alone. He – who could have believed it?

– deferred to her, asked her an opinion on every matter.

They had the codes of twins, or sweet conspirators, and the same dependence each upon the other. She could not get close enough to him: at night, when she crowded him in his chair, or got her arms around him in bed, she would try, it seemed, to climb inside his actual skin.

Her kisses landed everywhere. Only his ears were taboo: any touch there irritated him. Otherwise she kissed every fibre of his face and head and neck, his closed eyes, the corners of his mouth, the hollow above the bridge of his nose where his black eyebrows met – kisses, kisses, kisses, and the little 'pok' of her lip-sound that went with them.

No man could have been more different then from the taciturn and forbidding face he showed to the world. Night after night, and on dreamy gold dawns or frosty mornings, he talked to her in their deep bed. Murmurs. Whispers. Questions. Stories. Except during those difficult times, when he had to accommodate her piety while pregnant.

Now, she did the talking. She told him of Helena's first steps, of the child's first word – 'Dada! Dada!' Of the Teaching Union meetings she organized in the house so that his colleagues could pretend to include him. Of the children reciting their poems over his supine body so that his brain might hear, however faraway, the sounds of words that he loved. The food she placed on his tongue: rhubarb with ginger; coconut chocolate; the dust of grated orange peel. Of how she held fresh flowers and wet earth beneath his nose; of how she touched his face with silk or tweed, or new grass: 'There was only one sense I knew was not working, your dear eyes. So I tried all the other four. Sort of like the Last Rites, Thomas, only in reverse. You know how the priest anoints the Five Senses. I suppose that's what I was thinking of.' She counted in a remembering tone: 'Hearing. Smell. Taste. Touch. Yes.'

The night she conceived, in those nervous, gasping weeks after his awakening, she knelt beside and above him, and raised the nightdress to her waist. She pointed, tracing a finger along her abdomen.

'See. This line appeared on my stomach after Helena was born. They told me after the birth that it's known as "the life-line".'

In the gloom, she peered at his eyes, allowed her tongue a moment's rest on her lower lip. He beckoned and she lowered her face: he drew his forehead and eyes across her breasts. As she climbed across him, she bent and kissed his mouth. A small bruise like a mauve stain lurked for days afterwards on the edge of Ellen's lips, where he had kissed her too hard.

2

Dennis Emmett Sykes was born in St David's, south Wales, on 1 September 1914. Twenty-nine days later, his father died in mud and shrapnel, at Vitry-sur-Beche. Dennis's mother, with her tiny baby, had, initially, considerable difficulty: war pensions had not yet been properly put in place. Bernadette Murphy knew nobody in St David's: she came from Wexford, and a year earlier had met Patrick Sykes, while both on day excursions to Liverpool. As she had abandoned her Catholicism in order to marry the squat and pleasant Welshman, she had no good way of making friends by the usual local means of church, chapel or meeting-house. Her husband had few in family. A brother, estranged from him, lived in Swansea. Their dead mother descended from Irish labourers who had crossed to Wales for work on the railways.

However, Bernadette Sykes, *née* Murphy, from a family of ten children and swingeing poverty, had two assets. She was unusually pretty, with classy looks that made her seem like someone from a higher, wealthier stratum; and she had a combination of numerate intelligence and emotionless cunning. Her bereavement never fazed her. She had known within months that the marriage would eventually prove difficult: her bridegroom never had her speed of thought.

The day after the news came from France, she sat at her kitchen table in St David's to plan her survival.

Assessing all her possibilities, she figured that her marriage connections were useless – other than the house. Paddy Sykes had been an engineering foreman's mate at one of the medium-size collieries in south Wales. The company had just introduced a policy of housing some employees, but were not quite ready when Paddy Sykes had asked for permission to marry. They almost did not offer him the St David's cottage, sixteen miles from the colliery. Bernadette, though, having seen it, took it immediately – for its prettiness, and for the distinguished general air of the place: near the old monastery, within sight of the sea inlet.

When her husband seemed doubtful, she cajoled: 'We only have to be here until we get a place nearer your work.'

Thus she ended up with a house so attractive, even if small, that one of the mine-owner's wives complained what a pretty summer house it would have made. Later, the photographs of the house helped confirm the status and identity Bernadette was about to invent.

What an advantage that sixteen-mile distance from the mine proved. In mourning, she would have been expected to fraternize with her late husband's workmates and their wives. Once the dismal small service ended in the Methodist chapel near the colliery, she, baby Dennis in arms, accepted the condolences in the hallway – and the envelope from the General Manager's office. She returned to St David's that night, and very few of them ever saw her again.

Her first act, once that 'recovering' month of October had passed, took her to the village post office shop, where she purchased a notebook and borrowed a copy of the electoral register. At the kitchen table, she listed all the names in the St David's area, and along the coast, a resort and retirement area for wealthy folk, and all their addresses. With the mine condolence money, she bought a pram, and mobilized. Then on fine afternoons, walking miles, she systematically assessed the wider locality, noting down especially the large houses where, according to the register, the address showed a single resident.

One afternoon, she left the baby with a neighbour.

'The doctor. Trouble with the milk': she indicated her bosom (although she had long since stopped breast-feeding).

'Grief, I suppose,' murmured the neighbour.

An hour later, Bernadette knocked on the door of one of the larger houses in Pembrokeshire, which, according to the register, had as its owner an E. G. Hilton.

Bernadette said, 'I'm simply looking for work.'

The woman at the door, pleasant and rosy-aproned, asked, 'Can you typewrite?'

Bernadette shook her head.

The woman said, 'Pity, he'd take on someone who could. He has a lot of letters, see. Financial matters and that.'

After checking local newspapers, Bernadette went by train to Cardiff the following week. Typewriters, she discovered, cost a lot – more than she brought with her. And – 'to learn you must go to school,' they said. 'But there are correspondence courses.' She read their catalogue, at lunch, in a pub.

The watchful barman said, 'I think you're in the wrong place.'

'I'm only having a sandwich.'

'Girls work here. Working girls.'

She looked at him. 'I'm a working girl.' A full understanding arose. 'Or I would be if I got the chance.'

'You don't look it.'

'What's wrong with my looks?'

'Oh, no, I mean – you look too good for – work.' The barman leaned against the pillar by her chair.

'That's my stunt,' she replied. 'I don't look it.'

'Are you working this afternoon?' In the huge, three-quarters-empty pub, nobody could overhear.

'Depends.'

'On what?'

'How much?'

She turned three grimy tricks in a room nearby: three pounds. Bernadette bought a Royal typewriter. They arranged for her to have it delivered free when the van next went near St David's: scheduled for the following Thursday.

She went home, gave the neighbour some chocolates as a 'thank-you' gift, and took Dennis in her arms. For several weeks she checked her body for infection, and never prostituted herself again.

Tongue sticking out of the corner of her mouth: lamp drawn closer the better to read: baby asleep: for eight months the young widow Bernadette Sykes lived the life of a hermitess. Her neighbours understood that delayed shock sometimes produces grief and withdrawal.

The *Typewriting and Shorthand Correspondence Course* arrived with a handbook called *The Perfect Secretary*, and the package taught its purchasers how to get up to 'London Speeds', 120 words per minute short-hand and 60 words per minute typing. She returned to the Hilton household.

The same woman opened the door.

Bernadette said, 'I can typewrite now.'

The woman said, 'But he's dead.'

'When?'

'Nearly four months ago.'

Bernadette shook her head in disappointment, her auburn curls, specially ragged last night, flying out.

'Thanks, anyway.'

The woman scented something and as Bernadette turned the white ceramic gate-knob, called down the ivied path, 'But his widow's here.'

'Widow?' She turned.

'They were estranged, see, but never divorced. She might need help.'

At this moment, Bernadette pulled her greatest stroke. Waiting in the hallway, she noticed the family photographs, read the captions. The women all had boys' names (Protestants, of course, as Bernadette from Ireland recognized): 'Billie Hilton'; 'Charlie Gage'; 'Gussie Hilton'; 'Nicky Hilton'.

'Go in now,' said Mrs Rosy-Apron.

The woman at the desk, elbows in mounds of paper, had a small, fierce, well-bred face.

'What's your name?'

'My name,' said Bernadette Sykes, formerly Murphy, 'is Bryan Cooper.'

The woman registered and said to her, 'Can you clear all this? Intelligently?'

To which 'Bryan Cooper' replied, 'Without question'. She never said, 'Madam', or 'Mrs Hilton', or 'Ma'am'. And thus did Dennis Sykes's mother's survival begin.

Mrs Asia Hilton, who did not wish any part of her late husband's complex administration, left St David's a week later. In her absence, when 'Bryan Cooper' came across a piece of paper she did not understand, she simply wrote to the originator – broker, lawyer, bank, Government Stock Issue department – asking for help. At the end of one year, Bernadette had settled the entire affairs of the late E. G. Hilton and sent his will for probate. She worked five days a week, nine to five, for an excellent, agreed salary. Amid myriad and complex finances, she never stole.

Mrs Hilton did not even once have to return from her house in Northumberland, having been persuaded of the remarkable effectiveness of this young woman with a 'past' too painful to discuss – perhaps an outcast from a somewhat good family somewhere in Ireland, who cares?

The next move looked after itself. Asia Hilton recommended 'Bryan Cooper' to her young cousin Dorothy Bayer, who had just come through 'a foul divorce'. Dorothy came to Pembrokeshire for a rest, exhausted after proving that her twenty-five-year-old husband, his senses hammered numb by a shell in Ypres, was not fit to administer the funds. All the other Bayer-Hilton men died on the Somme and on Vimy.

'But I must be able to keep my house in St David's,' said 'Bryan Cooper', who had by now bought it from the mining company. (She attributed the 'unexpected capital' to 'a small legacy from Ireland', rather than a year's utter frugality plus Asia Hilton's generous wages and bonus.)

'Of course, of course,' said Dorothy Bayer, looking at the photograph of the house and saying, 'How pretty.'

'And you know, Mrs Bayer, that I have a small child?'

'I do,' said Dorothy Bayer. 'You can live in one of the two lodges. Ensure that they're warm. Northumberland gets cold.'

Bernadette Sykes leased the house in St David's to a couple from London – husband recovering from war wounds – and got herself to Alnwick.

Dorothy Bayer read magazines the way other women

of her day ate chocolates – in bed, with greed, and little thought to digestion. 'Bryan Cooper' gathered each finished magazine and devoured it likewise – but with a view to learning. In one, she read a short story, which described how a young man, bastard son of a cook-housekeeper, became the toy and plaything of the house's rich young women, and went on to marry wealth.

As her son Dennis neared the age of three, sweet child, his mother taught him little rhymes and songs to which he danced. One afternoon, when the time was right, he entranced Dorothy Bayer. She had no children, did not want children, but at twenty-five, whatever her riches and liberties, still had a biological clock.

So, Miss Bayer clapped her hands when Dennis Sykes, in his sailor suit in the summer of 1917, sang 'It's a Long Way to Tipperary' – Dorothy led the local war effort. Even more enchantingly, the child recited 'The Green Eye of the Yellow God':

He was known as Mad Carew by the subs at Katmandu
He was hotter than they ever cared to tell;
But for all his reckless pranks he was worshipped in the
*   ranks,*
And the Colonel's daughter smiled on him as well.

As Bernadette planned, Baby Dennis Sykes was taken up by Dorothy Bayer. She rode him on horseback in front of her: she drove him around the estate and into the village in the new car, standing him up in the passenger seat. He had to sing and recite for all her friends everywhere they went: he became her doll, lips by Botticelli. All the while his mother, watching, watching, chose his clothes for prettiness and dressed his hair in angel curls. She taught him new songs and poems, and hoped desperately that his looks would be hers, and not Sykes's from Port Talbot.

Above all, she manipulated young Mrs Bayer into taking Dennis to her heart and house. Dorothy kept him always around, the only child in the place. When her friends came to call, they brushed his curls. He spent hours in Dorothy's bedroom as they all tried on clothes, and they chatted and chittered and chattered. They bathed him, tried their new body oils on him first, even perfumed him, a plump and dimpled little rent-boy. Once, with shrieks, they taught him how to rouge their nipples and little Dennis pranked on, encouraged by their squeals. When the girls were not there, Dorothy, alone, prattled to him as mindlessly as if he were a spaniel, and he thus witnessed every aspect of her boudoir.

In Dorothy Bayer's bedroom – 'Dots' as she insisted he call her – he saw everything, including Dorothy's irritation at the fact that it took ages to depilate her hairy thighs.

'Dennis, do come over here and talk to me. I'm bored.'

So he grew, pampered by his mother's rich employers. Occasionally he played with another child, a steward's daughter who lived in the town of Alnwick, but usually he spent hours every day with Dorothy and friends. If not, he curled on his mother's office floor, a brown-eyed, golden-haired cherub, reading the advertisements in *Woman's Weekly*.

Membership of a ten-child family had early produced in Bernadette Sykes, *née* Murphy, a desperation for privacy. She turned that passion into 'Bryan Cooper's' discretion and reticence.

To explain away Dennis's surname to the Bayers and friends she murmured, 'A big mistake. But a boy should have his father's name' – and she would go no further.

Her Irish accent modified until it became 'charming': and with her efficiency such a legend, employment never failed her. The Bayers passed 'Bryan' around among their friends. Rich enough to take no interest in her, they never enquired into her life, sent nobody to St David's to check on this odd woman's background: enough that she saved them such headaches. She became a kind of county-society administrative secretary, who, huge advantage, had no men friends, and no lovers.

'Once bitten three hundred times shy,' she claimed, making them laugh – and feel safe. And added, 'I have my son to rear,' enabling them to enjoy a tinge of vicarious conscientiousness.

Her triumph lay in sinking herself so totally in her work that they did not notice her, and rarely had occasion to talk about her. If they did, they compounded her fiction that 'Bryan Cooper', genteel Irish, had eloped with some rake who then got himself killed on a bridge he was building in South America. Or something like that.

Thereby, she freed them so that she could use them discreetly. In the early years with them, working beneath their sight-lines, she created a life of comfort while maintaining an outward show of modesty. As her son grew, she exploited them in another way.

Dennis had inherited – and increased upon – his mother's intelligence. In the village school he shot so far ahead of his classroom peers that his teacher, Miss Campbell, felt liberated by him, could give him extra books, tuitions. In all the earliest little school tests, he scored full marks. Systematically, although it seemed random, his mother also kept him at home from school – 'illness'. The ploy worked: Miss Campbell came up to the house with books and homework. On those visits, her occasional accidental conversations with young Mrs Bayer clicked, and now, Dennis's mother could set out to fulfil another of the Bayer circle's fantasies – the cliché of the servant's brilliant son, which Bernadette understood from her magazine fiction.

One day, she mentioned to Dorothy a modest and small preparatory school near Manchester. Nothing too flashy: Bernadette knew where to draw the line. She did not want them pulling out of his financial assistance when they understood that a servant's child was going to 'too good' a school.

'They're strong in mathematics. His father wanted him to go there –' Pain flitted across her face briefly.

At the age of nine, sweetly uniformed and fully funded by the Bayer-Hiltons, Dennis went to boarding-school.

On his first Christmas holiday, Dennis came home by train and bus. After tea with his mother, he ran up to the house to see Dots.

'In the bedroom, as usual,' they told him in the kitchen, and in he charged: it was about six o'clock in the evening. She stood there, stark naked, drying herself with a towel. But where was the wonderful warm greeting for him, the hugs and kisses, the admiration?

'Haven't you grown?' she said coolly. Then out of the bathroom strolled another woman whom she introduced casually.

'This is Bobbie. Bobbie, this is Dennis, he's the secretary's son, he's at school. Where are you at school, I've forgotten the name of the place?'

Bobbie, a genuine redhead, shook hands with Dennis, and said, 'The secretary's son? I didn't know Bryan had children?'

Dots said to Dennis, 'Bobbie and I love each other. Aren't you thrilled?' The women touched noses gently.

Suddenly embarrassed, Dennis left the room and heard Dots call, 'Oh, you're not jealous, are you?'

Thereafter, he never again sought Dorothy in her bedroom, even though he had enough shrewdness to remain exceptionally affectionate whenever they met. Besides which, Dorothy had discovered travel, and rarely stayed long at Alnwick.

At boarding-school, Dennis Sykes studied intensively. He could draw well, had excellent mathematical capacities, fast brain, plus high verbal skills. Debating, stage-managing the school play, the library – he took on all the activities of boys too small for, or not good at, games. Although he never joined in any of the school fads – collars turned up, hair parted in the middle – he monitored all relationships with bonhomie. He knew everyone amiably, no one well.

Commerce occurred early. By whatever means, he seemed to persuade as much food as he wanted from the (female, naturally) kitchen staff, and by selling or giving it to chosen boys he purchased acceptance.

At the same time, in his paradoxical way, he developed a distancing air: in due course he came to recognize that this aloofness empowered him, because people mistrusted it. Some of this separateness got put down to study, a swot. In all his examinations he finished in the top three of the class, mostly at number one or two. Alongside, he read voraciously: novels, life stories, newspapers, the *Reader's Digest*.

In his last two years, he took off academically like a comet, uninterruptedly top of the school, always likely to win his university scholarship. Of this achievement, he remained openly proud all his life, and never forgot that August day, a week before his eighteenth birthday. When the letter arrived, he wandered in a dreamy glow all over the Bayer estate.

Late that afternoon he found himself in Dorothy Bayer's deserted bedroom. He stood in front of the cheval glass, where Dorothy habitually stood, on the spot where the carpet had been worn through to the boards by her feet. She had long gone to Ischia for the summer.

Dennis examined himself. With her ivory hairbrushes and combs he fussed with his hair, as those rich girls had done. He peered at his brown irises and long lashes; he picked up the perfumes and smelt them. Slowly, he took off his clothes, squatted, examined his genitals, turned, tried to inspect his anus. Next, strutting back and forth, prissing and preening like the mannequin they once made of him, he sang one of those little old lisping songs to the mirror:

Hallo Patsy Fagan, you hear the girls all cry,
Hallo Patsy Fagan, you're the apple of my eye;
You're a decent boy from Ireland, that no one can deny;
You're a harum-scarum, devil-may-care-'em –

Dennis stopped, turned from the mirror, looked the length of the room and walked to the adjoining bathroom. There, he opened every cupboard, examined every jar, every tin, every phial, bottle, packet and pill. Next, he went to the rows of wardrobes and rails in the dressing-room, pulled out with minimum disturbance, and sniffed, every garment. Finally, he invaded every drawer and inspected every item of clothing, looked at the labels, the stitching – smelling, smelling everything. As the shadows gathered, he sat on the edge of Dorothy's bed, burst into tears and did not dress or leave the room for another hour. All his life, when alone and in distress, he sat forever with

a finger on a wrist, taking his pulse as if ascertaining that
he still lived.

Dennis spent that summer reading, and cycling through
the countryside. He used the abundant pocket money
from his mother to watch women. Always women: in cafés
he observed them having tea, or working as waitresses.
In shops, he made meaningless inquiries just to gauge
how they reacted to him. As they stood on street corners
chatting, or walked ahead of him, he watched, following
a little, or walking by.

3

Helena obeyed, white-faced: she clasped each hemi-sphere of onion, like headphones, to her ears. Ellen bandaged them firmly into place with a long torn strip of old sheet. First she bound it widely under the child's chin, and eventually tied it on the top of the little girl's head in a big merry bow.

Ellen leaned back, hands folded like a renaissance madonna on the pregnant curve of her large stomach.

'Now, Helena,' she comforted. 'All we have to do is wait.'

From the doorway, Grace, motionless with fascination, watched her older sister. Neither said a word. Helena's blue eyes shone fearful, her legs not reaching the floor from the chair.

Hard footsteps on the yard: the little girls started. He loomed.

'They're just watching,' Ellen said pre-emptively. 'Helena's poor earache. We're just fixing it.'

Helena screamed, and her hands panicked towards her left ear.

'Ooh, that was quick, that was *quick*,' gasped Ellen, and rushed to take off the bandage. Helena's screams rose. She began to roll her head from side to side, getting out of control. Thomas looked on.

Ellen grabbed the child's head and began to undo the bandage.

43

'Helena, Helena! Easy – easy, love. Okay. Okay. Shhhhh. Shh. It's all right.'

Grace's eyes widened at her sister's sufferings.

'Easy now, eeeee-asy now.' Ellen soothed and soothed.

Thomas pleated his lips in approval of the old cure. After a moment he walked by, into the depths of the house somewhere.

The child was moving beyond reach of comfort. Ellen unlooped the bandage rapidly and took away the left hemisphere of onion: she peered at it, and Helena sagged and gasped in sudden relief.

'See! See!' Ellen held the flat, fleshy side out, a conjuror showing the audience the missing card, 'See! It worked!'

One russet earwig, tail waving like a man fallen into a barrel, had embedded itself head first in the onion.

'No more earache, Helena. See? And the other ear. Is it all right?'

The child nodded dumbly, and Ellen removed and inspected the other onion half.

'Now, the washing of the ears, there's a little bit of blood. Grace love, get me that clean towel will you.'

Grace moved to the table to pick up the earwig-containing piece of onion.

'No, Gracey, no,' Ellen commanded not unhumorously. 'Sweetheart, I bet Helena would like some bread with sugar on it.'

Ellen towelled the child's head and face, and hugged Helena: 'You're as brave as anything.'

Once her husband had made that first Sunday morning appearance, Ellen Kane regenerated quickly. The village knew she was making apple jelly again, because she sent for a windfall in late September. Betrothed girls once more began to visit for advice. Women bearing new recipes, other pregnant mothers – the parish streamed afresh to her door. She wondered at their frequency. Did they come because what she called 'normal business' had been resumed, or because they hoped to glimpse, even meet, Thomas? She knew they had called him 'the Living Dead', a morbid curio of the countryside.

But they took home no reports of him. He avoided all her visitors. Some observed distant sightings – but after that first ghostly Mass, nobody saw him regularly and normally for a full year: longer than most people expected. In time, he had resumed his Principalship of Deanstown School. By the early 1930s, he had returned to his stature as a main force in local matters, tall, grey-faced and austere, with a young wife and a growing family.

Nothing much ever changed in Deanstown, and the pace of the village allowed the Kanes to find their own tempo again. No hurry. His recovery, wrote Ellen in her ledger, could be 'like a flower opening, or a tree growing'.

As for her, whom they watched like a queen – she *seemed* back to her own, old self. A question for everyone; advice, food and old clothes to the desperate poor; on fine Sunday afternoons, she still met the Protestant Miss Harpers on the road for talk of flowers. When she trained the choir, she still beleaguered the unfortunate harmonium.

Yet – there was a fresh cautiousness, a watchfulness. Difficult, they said, to put a finger on it. If you hadn't known her well before 'the incident', you would never see this change in her. It fell across her demeanour like a faint shadow: they said she was always watching in case something went wrong.

From now on, the parish scrutinized her even more than they observed each other. If that were possible. These people survived by eyeing their neighbours. The underground currents of hatred and bile that drench those who know each other too well had flowed among them for generations. Few had gone untouched by violence. Most struggled for a living. Some had lately received a few envied fields from the Land Commission in the breaking-up of the gentry estates. In their passion for secrecy, all tried to know each other's business, and competitive envy kept them alive.

Ellen could have painted Deanstown as one great, long, humpy dragon, with each scale a neighbour's face. To any outsider, the people of the village and the parish constituted a single, and often troublesome beast, that had to be fed, and kept calm. When it prowled out each day, the dragon could be fought, as her husband did. He stabbed the lance of his tongue into its ignorance; he thumped his fists into its face. Or Deanstown could be appeased, spoken to friendlily but with great caution, given offerings – as Ellen chose to do.

From the moment she married Thomas Kane, she understood that the village was a vital part of her life, as clearly defined as any relationship she had ever known. She set out to win the villagers over – insofar as they ever could have welcomed someone so new. Her care for their children in her classroom impressed them: 'The young ones even – they don't even want to come home from the school these days.'

Then, as they watched her in difficulties, their natural doubt of an incomer halved: 'Oh, the way she looked after that man and he stretched.'

As Thomas recovered, Ellen's intelligence was released, and she could advance her place in the community with greater clarity: 'Oh, yeh, she's back to us again.'

Just like their lives, pregnancy followed pregnancy, and she began to balance adroitly the difference between privacy and shared experience. To show the way, she took Helena for the first government-ordered inoculations – but said nothing of the child's panic. She lent sheets and candlesticks for wakes, baked for funeral breakfasts. A rumour of typhoid had her visiting the cottages, explaining the leaflets, helping to boil the water: she never divulged Thomas's distaste in such things, for such people.

And, unlike him, she welcomed their favours returned. When Grace got croup, Ellen tried every cure they offered: poteen rubbed into the baby's chest; a teaspoon of whiskey every four hours; camphor balls boiled permanently near the child's cot.

Tacitly, by testing her boundaries, most of Deanstown learned her one golden rule. Ellen Kane never discussed her husband's temperament no matter what they observed, nor his health no matter what they rumoured. They granted her this licence ungrudgingly: they turned away their own chagrin at such secrecy by praising her, by hailing her 'innocence', her 'modesty', her 'devoutness'.

Within half an hour Helena grew frisky again, cotton-wool in each ear, bread-and-butter-and-sugar in her hand. Ellen bound Grace's hair in green ribbons. At eleven o'clock, the Kanes left the house and climbed the wall across the road into the Demesne. All around them, too distant yet to identify, other people walked in the same direction, their talk borne on the autumn air. Thomas Kane soon strode off in front.

In the second field, Miriam Hogan called out and ran up.

'Locusts. Wait until you see, we shall all turn into locusts today. Or vultures.' Miriam made talons of her two hands. 'Have you ever been to one of these fiascos? We will be fighting over spools of thread. Will there be a thousand people here, will there, will there? That's what I want to know?' said Miriam. Morning dew darkened the light leather of her boots.

The village never liked Miriam Hogan. She never behaved in a way they could address; she made smart, cutting remarks. Of which she boasted to Ellen: *How to Deal with Their Curiosity*: 'Smile blandly and ask about their drunken brother/father/husband – or better still mother/sister.' *How to Avert the Most Personal Questions*: 'Say to her – Was that the Vermin Man/the Health Inspector/the Debt Collector/the Cruelty Man I saw knocking at your door the other day?'

To fight back, the dragon's salacious tongue stained Miriam, and its breath blackened her feckless, drinking husband. They quoted her, mockingly: 'Maybe Jack met somebody' – meaning he could be found in his cups anywhere in the county, brought home at night on a cart by a farmhand.

Up the fields ahead of them, the auction banners, MOLUMBY & STAKELUM, hung out over the leaded windows of the Castle stableyard.

For years, Jack Hogan entreated.

'Miriam, it is perfectly ordinary for people to want to have children.'

She used a variety of obstructions.

Argument: 'If it is born deformed? Or mental?'

Silence: 'Ah, come on, Miriam, come on, talk to me.'

Distress: 'The smell. I hate the smell. The smell, Jack, of what comes out of your thing.'

As he jumped to defend himself and all male biology, or to say how could she know when they had never, not even once in eight years, done what married people do – she shouted like a pouting child.

'I do know the smell, I do know, I do! When you're drunk sometimes, you leak it onto the back of my night-dress when I'm asleep, and it smells like stale wet news-paper and I hate it.'

At least, thanked Jack, she no longer scratched, no more of that dreadful, scabbed tearing of her lovely, sable skin.

'No, Mrs Gardiner,' he told her mother, 'she's all right. Miriam's good, she's a grand girl and wife. She's all right.'

Miriam said, 'Jack has a dispensary all the morning over in Outrath and he'll come on after. Unless he meets some-one. Very smart, the auctioneer, to hold it on a Saturday. Where's Thomas?'

Ellen pointed to Thomas, ahead by half a field, Helena and Grace in his wake by several yards.

'How is he these days?' asked Miriam. 'I can hardly walk myself, I'm bleeding like a pig this morning, I knew yesterday and d'you know what, I'm sick of it, three weeks, five weeks, four weeks, six weeks, I defy all calendars.'

Ellen said, 'That's the thing about having babies. All that stops for a while. Miriam, what have you your eye on today? That's what I want to know' – a teasing mimicry of Miriam's catch-phrase. They fell into step beside each other, one woman tall and barren, one strikingly fecund.

'They say he shouts a lot at school these days,' said Miriam, eyeing the distant, straight-backed Thomas. 'Yes, a lot,' said Miriam. 'No patience, they say. A sideboard, maybe?'

Ellen wore her hair up today.

'Jack had a boy in the dispensary the other day with his hand hurt after Thomas's "discipline" in school. Did you

49

know that?' Miriam looked down at Ellen, whose face had reddened beyond pregnancy's blush.

She called out to her girls. 'Gracey, stay with Helena now, won't you?' Fixing her hair she said, 'Oh, Miriam, we're looking for a table, a good dining-room table. Of course there's nothing wrong with the one we have, but Thomas says, that if we're going to have such a big family we have to have a table that we can pull out. And add those extending leaves to.'

Miriam pressed. 'But blisters? As big as coins? On a young fellow's hand? Not fair. No. I mean the lad is only ten years of age.'

Ellen hastened. 'Oh, look, Miriam, there's Cyril Stephenson's aunt, they're taking over the Glebe, Captain Wallace's old house, they arrived yesterday, they say she's a scream.'

'Munch and Viva,' said Miriam cryptically.

'Munch and Viva?' asked Ellen puzzled.

'Ulverton. Her children. If you'd call them that. They're ancient items too.'

'Munch and Viva Ulverton?' Ellen laughed. 'Munch and Viva? Is that what they're called? Funny names.'

An auctioneer's lackey shook a powerful handbell, and it ba-ranged off the Castle walls. Ellen and Miriam quickened their steps.

Miriam, still forcing the issue, asked Ellen, 'Is there anything anyone can say to him – about toning down his "discipline", as he calls it, in school? I mean – men are saying there'll be trouble. There will.'

Ellen, when uncomfortable with a topic, had a way of holding herself stiff and unreachable; for a moment or two neither questioner nor topic existed. When she chose to emerge from this storage, all hope of resurrecting the subject died.

She murmured thoughtfully, 'A sideboard? A sideboard, Miriam, you're bidding for? Children!' she called. 'Stay where I can see you.'

Miriam re-directed her frustration to the *Notice of Sale*, her voice climbing.

'The cheek of it! Saturday-the-12th-of-September-1932-Monster-Auction-at-Deanstown-Castle-Sale-of-Furniture-and-Effects-by-Order-of –' and she yelled. 'Jesus! *Admission a shilling*. Don't say we have to pay in? For the love of God!'

She hooted at the man with his blue, numbered tickets, 'I'm not paying, I'm buying!' – and waltzed herself and Ellen past the assistant. He and his sagging jaw cared less. Hours ago he discovered that his writ would not run: nobody paid.

In the old grass courtyard, Ellen caught up with her two little girls and straightened their coats and their ribbons. Up the slopes from the Lake, by the Concubine Tower, the last distant stream of people pushed forward in a thick insect trail.

'Make sure! Make sure! Make sure!'

The Auctioneer stood by the entrance, as outrageous as some bald, cabaret ringmaster.

'Make sure you have your money in your fist! Come on now, girls, today's the day you *don't* keep your hand on your ha'penny.'

Miriam said to Ellen, 'I think that's supposed to be quite a rude thing to say.'

Ellen laughed back, 'You'd know, Miriam, I wouldn't.'

'Miss Goody-goody,' said Miriam.

—

51

With motley chairs from within the auction stock, Molumby & Stakelum had turned the old Servants' Hall into a saleroom.

'There y'are, girls, we'll be auctioning what you're sitting on today. Priceless, I'd say, only priceless.' The Auctioneer ignored Thomas's withering look. 'Ah yes, we'll be selling what you're sitting on.'

Miriam laughed: Ellen blushed. Thomas, by the wall, waiting to choose a suitable chair, continued to stare at him, unwilling to lose in this contest of dignity, and the Auctioneer said, 'You'd better sit down now, sir, or we might sell yourself into the bargain, there's all kinds of queer things in this catalogue today.'

He walked away, winking to a pal, and Thomas looked hard but unavailingly at the man's disrespectful back.

In this small community, the people's ears seemed unusually large and cupped – genetically formed for the catching of other people's business. They leaned forward for this Sale as they never did in church.

'Well, I declare to God, look at the lot of you,' said the Auctioneer. People laughed.

'Is Dinny Kavanagh here?' he asked. A man rose at the back.

'Dinny, the wife says you're not to go home without buying a commode,' and the Auctioneer, pleased at the joke with an old acquaintance, rubbed his hands.

A sparrow flew from one rafter to another. Two expensive women, strangers, came forward to the front-row seats they had claimed earlier with their folded coats.

'Dealers,' whispered Miriam to Ellen. 'Buzzards. They'd bid the coat off your back. None of us'll get anything half-good here today.'

==

52

Deanstown looked around and marvelled. Their servant ancestors had cleaned this furniture: ball-and-claw mahogany, leather ottomans, salon chairs with gilt legs and saffron brocade. By the Auctioneer's podium, rows of huge paintings leaned against each other, some almost three-quarter way up the high bare wall. Gossip believed the best pictures had been taken away to London and Paris, and even a few to Dublin. For any of those left today, not even the Canon had a wall large enough. Grass grew through the stone floors.

Most people had come out of curiosity, or at best for practical items – pots and pans, any bit of bedding which had never been affected with damp, bric-a-brac. One man, known at all such auctions, had come to buy brushes – shoe brushes, clothes brushes, sweeping brushes. All who knew him enjoyed the fact that he had a small brush of a moustache beneath his nose.

The sale began. Grace alerted Helena urgently. The Auctioneer's assistant held up a doll: the patter opened.

'Right, lads, there's not another doll in the parish like this one, whatever you might think of your missus.'

Everybody laughed, some cheered.

'Which of you is she going home with?' Hair-oil glistened on his forehead.

'God, that's a *Jumeau*,' whispered Miriam to Ellen.

'Is that good?'

'What'll we christen her? I'll tell you what. We'll call her Lucky, she's my luckpenny for the day. Now who's going to start the bidding on Lucky?'

Grace tugged Helena's hand desperately and pointed to their father. He had shown interest.

'I'll give you a tanner,' shouted a voice at the back.

'You will in your fillet.' The Auctioneer caught Thomas's eye, saw the fingers, and took the bid.

'Five shillings, now there we are. Five shillings starts me for Lucky the Doll. Who's going to go in against that, any advance on five shillings, any advance?'

A hand said six shillings and Grace hunched her little shoulders in excitement as Thomas went to seven.

The Auctioneer called, 'Come on now, warm me up, warm me up. Any advance on seven shillings, she's a doll in a million, buy Lucky and be lucky. Eight, I have eight, come on who'll make it ten bob, come on a half sovereign as it used to be when men were men and geese went barefoot. Am I hearing ten bob, am I? Ten bob, who's ten bob, ah, we have ten bob, thank you, madam. Ten bob here, sir, will you rise me, who'll rise me? Hold her up there, Eddie –'

The lackey held the doll like a lantern.

'Not as high as that, Eddie, there's decent people here,' said the Auctioneer. 'Eleven shillings, I have eleven.'

Thomas dropped out of the bidding at fourteen shillings: the doll went for three pounds: Helena, wistful, and Grace, irritated, subsided.

Canon Williams, standing stretched up against the wall, bought a walking-stick topped with a dog's head.

'If he has any more walking-sticks,' whispered Ellen to Miriam, 'he'll soon never need to use his legs again.'

Two pairs of candelabra went for more than they should have done: rivalrous wives. A long man draped S-shaped like a hook around the back of his chair and looking at everything sideways, bought a riding-crop, he who had never owned even a pony.

'He'll use it on the bicycle,' someone heckled.

The Auctioneer targeted Ellen and Miriam when he

saw them laughing. To buy off his banter, Miriam bid, and again and again and again, for a delicate parasol with black-and-cream-and-red *chinoiserie*.

'But six quid!' whistled Ellen.

Item by item the Castle's history came tumbling down, down, to the minor fripperies. The long-closed household had not functioned since 1914. At the onset of the Great War, black marketeers filched the lead from the roofs and sold it to munitions dealers. When bad weather came, good-spirited neighbours broke in and removed the best of everything to the security of the stableyard wing. The land agent later said that some items vanished in the neighbourliness.

A woman, beaming like a moon, paid two shillings for a half-bottle of lavender water and pressed it to her nose: 'The smelling salts of history,' she said grandly.

One little oval tin of sun cream showed a palm tree and bore the word 'Cannes'. The purchaser said this was the French word for 'tin' and passed it from woman to woman. Her sister worked for gentry in Buckinghamshire: 'That's what France smells like, I remember my sister describing that smell exactly. Her mistress goes to France every summer of her life, and she comes home smelling like that.' They goggled as she put the tip of her little finger into the cracked pink cream and applied it as daintily as a society filly to her goitred neck.

Lots 200–380, Domestic Utensils, brought the auction to its feet. Nurse Cooper from the nursing-home, her profession rendering her unembarrassed, bought all the chamberpots and two commodes.

'I'd say we'll have a dirty week-end,' released the Auctioneer.

55

Ellen bought a wide copper preserving pan.
'This winter's jam?' remarked Miriam.

Thomas Kane, alone as ever, viewed everything. Occasionally he took out a wad of old letters and wrote a tiny note on the empty back of an envelope. Those near him stared from time to time: five years on from his recovery, he was still a curiosity. If not too absorbed, he returned their inquisitive glances with a glare. His dress sense had returned, blues and greys of soft cloth; and his fingernails again the cleanest ever – as they said. The face and head never moved, only his chilly eyes.

Most of the remarkable furniture went to dealers, including two small cabinets that Miriam said were worth a mint: 'Olbrich. Austrian.'

The two expensive women sitting in the front row bought them. Several men, standing by the wall, one behind the other, leaned forward or back to make comment. None outbid another. When a significant piece of furniture, or a maker's name materialized, acknowledgement or recognition passed among them.

In turn, the Auctioneer played to them whenever he gave a brief auction pedigree.

'Now, the comrade [he pronounced it "cumm-a-raid"] of this very piece was sold up the country the month before last for record guineas.'

Thomas fastened on these dealers, and watched them closely. As each bid, he frowned at their smiles and collusions. They took no notice of this tight-mouthed man. Thus they never saw the moment of sadness in his eyes as *An Irish Versailles*, a painting of the Castle in the eighteenth century, entered the bidding at a hundred guineas, a price Thomas could not approach.

One of the smooth men bid and won. Brief contest, a mere finger-flick, his hand as close to his chest as a card sharp. At the Auctioneer's knock, one of the women turned back and raised the eyebrow she used for smiling with. The buyer inclined his head towards her.

By four o'clock, the Sale reached the farm items. Ellen, Miriam and most people prepared to leave. None of the heavy agricultural equipment could work again without grave attention. Men bought ancient harrows, rakes, ploughs and hay-turning machines for spare parts or for scrap.

Outside, Thomas saw the dealers laughing arm-in-arm, picking their steps in the mud from the castle down towards the Lake. As he walked briskly past them, one said, 'Excuse me, what's the quickest way of getting back to the main road?'

He stopped and faced them. About to speak, he changed his mind, shook his head in disdain and anger at them, turned and walked away. From the green crest of the ornamental lawns, Ellen stood and watched Thomas. He walked down the Bell Walk, towards the kitchen-garden wall, his shoulders stiff with disapproval.

Miriam ruffled Helena's hair and said to Ellen, 'Helena has your lips and Grace has your eyes. A fair division of the spoils.'

'Daddy walked away very quick,' said Helena, 'he's gone down the long way.'

'Very quickly,' corrected Ellen.

'Well, I'll see you so, Ellen, I think I'm going to go for a long walk, Jack won't be home until cockcrow if he wasn't here so far. You didn't spy him anywhere, I suppose?'

'No,' said Ellen.

'He must have met somebody.'

Miriam waved a resigned hand, and flapped away.

Ellen Kane herded her two children, and gave them the preserving pan to carry between them. She began her walk home down by the lime trees, towards the main road. If she timed it right, she would come tangentially to Thomas's shoulder. From the brow of the hill by the sunken fence, she could now see him again: he strode down these sloping beautiful fields between the beech hedges.

Helena and Grace, sure of the route, ran ahead and Ellen, hands deep in her coat pockets, contemplated their skipping. When they reached the place where their path joined their father's route – he was now out of sight once more behind the hazel woods – they raced each other back to Ellen. Grace banged on the preserving pan like a drum.

Soon, all three climbed the wall together in front of their house. Ellen looked back into the fields, saw Thomas coming and waved. He did not return the gesture; perhaps he could not have seen her.

Ever since his recovery seemed final and assured, she had tried many stratagems to raise difficult matters. Throughout the past five years, she worked out moments in which she could be alone with him, where he could neither leave their room, nor evade conversation. Yet, if she blurted, as she had twice, 'Why won't you talk about yourself?' he shunned her for three grim days.

At odd, strange daytime moments, he thawed. The smell of October woodsmoke did it once, and summer's new potatoes, like little white babies, his own crop brought to table. She made a raspberry cake one Sunday

– Leah and Herbert had taken the children on an outing to the Grey Valley. Thomas, never lifting his eyes, reached across the table and held her hand.

In bed, though, he had never changed. The first roughness after his recovery waned once his urgency calmed down: he became as tender as before. This bred Ellen's dilemma: how to adjust her spirit and her family to a man infinitely sweet when inside her body, bitter as acid in his discipline towards their children? After a day of cutting slaps across their legs, shattering them with hurt, or corrections spoken abusively – and to two children aged five and three – he still buried his face in Ellen's shoulder that night.

Not a soul could she tell, not even Leah. Thomas's passionate requirement of utter confidentiality had also become her creed. Nor could she have claimed uniqueness: just another local woman married to a man of uncontrolled temper.

As they entered their gateway, Ellen heard the loud call.

She turned in delight. 'Oh, Leah, but where were you? Where were you? I never saw you? And what in the name of God did you buy?'

Leah Winer, and her husband Herbert, walked to meet her: their two shy girls came too.

Ellen exclaimed again: 'Did you come on the bus? And what time are you going back? Are you getting a lift? Isn't it great I have a fresh chocolate cake baked?'

They stood aside from their greetings to let a crowded car rattle by on the narrow dusty road.

'Come in, come in, Thomas will be here any minute.'

Rhona Ulverton looked out of the Lagonda window and said, 'This place is like Bombay.'

'We're just as poor ourselves, Mamma,' said her daughter beside her in the back.

'This country is finished,' said Rhona. 'Bloody finished.'

'*We're* finished,' said Viva.

'This dreary place!' exhaled Rhona.

'We'll just pretend not to be finished,' said her son, in front beside his uncle Henry.

Viva Ulverton shook her head and smacked her wet violet lips. She drew a finger along the back of her brother's neck.

'A chicken. That – is – what – you – look – like.' She tapped his neck in time to her words. 'Munch – a chicken, you look like a chicken.' Viva tugged a knitted hat so hard down her forehead that it left a red circulation mark an inch below her hairline.

As they drove past Ellen Kane, Rhona turned. 'Jesus, she's pretty. Who's she? Now – she. Is. Pretty.'

'That's twice you said it,' observed Viva.

'Once would be too much where you're concerned,' interrupted Munch.

Rhona asked, 'Henry, who's that flower?'

'Mother, can't you ever call me "Munchin"? My full name. All I ask. You gave it to me. "Munch" sounds like an instruction.' Today, little or no saliva lapped his mouth; today he had done his best to clean himself.

'Or a description. No, an instruction, that's funnier,' said Viva. When Munch was like this they pressed normality upon him.

'She,' said Henry Wallace, 'is a Mrs Kane: she's the wife of that fellow, d'you remember the ex-Sinn Feiner who was in a coma for ages.'

Sometimes Viva went too far, or forgot. 'And you've been wetting the front of your trousers again, it's actually turning yellow, actually yellow.' Viva leaned forward and peered over his shoulder. 'Munch, you should never wear light grey trousers, your pee is a horrid yellow.'

Rhona looked back again. 'Well, she's too pretty for this place.'

'City girl,' said Henry Wallace, Rhona's brother, 'Janesborough. Litter of children by now. Husband's a sour pill.'

'Mother, you might as well have called me "Do". Or "Fetch". "Munch". It's a terrible name.'

Rhona sighed. 'We have had this conversation, my dear boy, a thousand times in forty years.'

He protested, 'I wouldn't mind but I like the full name. "Munchin". "Saint Munchin".'

'A saint?' shrieked Viva. 'You want to be called after a bloody Irish saint?'

Rhona said, 'A sour pill? Henry, can a man married to a woman like that afford to be a sour pill?'

'Of course he can, Mother,' said Viva, 'this is Ireland. Married people can do what they like to each other. *If* they're Roman Catholics.'

Rhona, still reflecting, concluded, 'If we had a half-decent civilization, a pearl like that woman would not be buried out here.'

'Mamma, that is ridiculous, what about those beautiful Indian women?'

'Exactly.'

Herbert Winer said, 'No, no, the kitchen table, don't disturb the parlour. And only a cup out of our hands, Ellen, we have to go back.'

'Now come on, what did you buy?' asked Ellen.

Leah, not usually hesitant or reticent, shook her bangles, a sign of embarrassment. 'Well –' she began. 'We didn't buy –'

Herbert took off his spectacles, peered into them from

a distance, replaced them and said justifyingly, 'I find those auctions confusing.'

Leah, who had clearly been expecting a different type of remark from Herbert, gathered courage and speed. 'Although we could have bought all round us because did you hear? Our good news?'

Ellen alerted.

Herbert said, 'Now, now. Don't burden people.'

'Good news a burden?' Leah queried.

'It often is. Ellen, where did you say Thomas was?'

'He'll be here any second, he should be here now. Grace, go and see can you see Daddy.'

Leah's words flew out. 'We came into money. A lot.'

'Wha-at?! Oh!' Ellen turned to her friend. 'Oh, Leah!'

Herbert winced. 'Leah, why don't you listen to me? People get upset by money.'

Grace bounced back into the kitchen. 'No, Mamma. Daddy's not.'

'Not what little chickie?' smiled Leah.

'Cluck-cluck,' mimicked Grace.

'But Herbert, that's wonderful news,' said Ellen.

Herbert sighed: Leah shrugged.

Up the long, gravelled avenue, the car listed a little to starboard. It stopped at the door. In the empty hallway, Viva asked, 'Is Cyril bringing his little Roman Catholic to meet us?'

'Ask him,' Munch Ulverton said from the window, and sang out like a ship's watch, 'he's ten yards away and bearing down fast.'

Cyril Stephenson said, 'Hallo, Uncle Henry, hallo, you must be Aunt Rhona, thanks for your letter, no, she's away.'

'Are you lovelorn then?' asked Viva. 'Do you miss her? I'm Viva, this is Munch.'

Rhona Ulverton said, with her gift of instant intimacy to a nephew she had not seen since he was two, 'Oh, Cyril, it isn't any of my business, but couldn't you think again? I'd rather you married a Nonconformist nearly, than a Roman Catholic. Christ, this house is cold. Are we sleeping in your house until the furniture comes? Have we enough furniture by the way, have you any spare? We need another bed?'

'The auction,' said Henry Wallace thoughtfully, a very long man. 'You should have bought.'

'With what?' asked Viva. 'Beads? Wampum?'

Cyril said, 'We still have the old beds.'

'Didn't people die in them? Oh-ho, no-oh, thanks, I'm not sleeping in them,' said Munch. 'Ghosts, ghosts.'

'Munch,' said Rhona, 'go for a walk, dear. Jesus! Look at this floor!'

The planking beneath Rhona Ulverton's feet needed attention, but she held herself as if already reigning over the household. Face-powder that she spread on her liver-spotted hands had flaked again, and dotted her black blouse-cuffs. Her nephew, Cyril, who blushed quickly, and who never wore anything but a check sports jacket – his wife-to-be once asked if he wore it in bed – looked out of the window at the rusting tractor derelict in the fields. It had never functioned. The factory blamed Cyril, said he tried to drag too heavy a load, refused to observe the guarantee: Cyril's life ran like that.

On account of the large windbreak to the west of the house, twilight came early to this room. Rhona paced.

'Cyril, this is an announcement. Now that we are back – I'm refusing to be bound by the whole politics of everything. We chose to return.'

63

Viva barked, 'Mamma, you are so manipulative! You'll get us into trouble!'

'Cyril,' Rhona pleaded, 'I didn't want to do what so many others did. I didn't want to go to Scotland. Or Belfast. Or whatever. If we went over to Devon or somewhere, Somerset, say – we'd still be Irish. Paddies. Yes, we'd be Paddies, we'd be the very same as the Catholics. That's no choice.'

Viva said vehemently, 'But Mamma, for Christ's sake. We have *no money*.'

'So, Cyril,' Rhona continued, 'be warned, I expect to be active in this locality. By which I mean political. We're surrounded by ignorant people. These bloody peasant gunmen, they can't run this country. I'm jiggered if I'm going to let all that we have evaporate. Christ!'

'Mamma! The guns are silent now.'

Behind Rhona's back, Henry Wallace caught Cyril's attention and shook his head slowly and reassuringly.

'God Save the King,' stated Munch to nobody.

'They're not silent. This country isn't fit to rule itself. Did you see that thing the other day where one of the members of parliament brought a pair of six-guns into the debating chamber with him?'

'Mamma! That wasn't yesterday, that was nine bloody years ago,' Viva phutted.

Thomas did not reappear and Herbert played with Helena, who read for him her new book, and Grace who explained to him every article of her doll's clothing.

Inevitably Leah said, 'I need your mirror, dear,' and followed Ellen upstairs.

They whispered dramatically: Leah told all: an ancient uncle, fifteen thousand pounds and a small-ish commercial property in Cork with an income of eight hundred pounds a year.

'And you know what he's like. He's been flinching ever since. Saying we'll be obliged to pay in some other way. That we'll fall ill, or one of the girls won't do well at school.'

'Poor Herbert,' murmured Ellen.

'And we argue about it.'

'But,' queried Ellen, 'you two never argue?'

'We do now. He won't buy anything and I want things.'

'Awwwh!' sympathized Ellen.

'Anyway,' said Leah with finality. 'And you, dear?' She patted Ellen's pregnant bump. 'You look in a bloom.'

Ellen smiled. 'It is still tiring, I'm amazed at how tired I get.'

'And Thomas? Is he – ? I mean, how is he?'

'Oh, fine. Oh, Leah, you may even be able to move to a new house.'

'By the way.' Leah fished into her handbag. 'Yours.'

'What's this?'

'Two hundred and sixty pounds. All told.'

Ellen pushed the envelope away. 'No, they weren't loans, I can't take that.'

'Yes, you can. Or I'll give it to the girls and then where will you be?'

'Oh, Leah, I was only helping you out.'

'Fifteen or sixteen times, some helping out, huh.'

Ellen turned over the envelope but never opened it. 'It was a pleasure to me. But Leah, is Herbert, is he going to be all right about the money?'

'Who knows? I don't. Maybe he doesn't. Who knows?'

Rhona looked through the door at the rhododendrons, the monkey puzzles and Cyril's red roof.

'I don't think I realized until today that these two houses were so close to each other. Just as well. I can't walk much any more. Viva, my stick, would you.'

Rhona leaned on Cyril's arm. She stopped by the huge mirror.

'What do you see, Cyril? The family nose, for one thing. You have it too.' Rhona pointed her stick into the mirror at Cyril's nose. 'You look much nicer in the mirror. Isn't that an odd thing?'

Rhona and Cyril walked past the dead plants and their stippled-brass pots in the vacant old house.

Outside, Cyril Stephenson said sheepishly, 'You'll like my fiancée, Auntie Rhona, she's very likeable.'

'She's a Roman Catholic,' sang Viva behind him, smelling the inside of the knitted hat, her shingled hair curling into her eye.

'Quiet, Viva. And Viva, I am sure your cousin Cyril doesn't want to know about you and your own little Catholic in Ranpore, does he?'

Viva reddened: Munch stilled.

'He slugged her and he left her,' Rhona said to Cyril. 'Black eyes he gave her. I used to see them from my bedroom, and Viva, well, Cyril, you know the phrase "bent over backwards for him".' To Viva – 'Didn't you, darling?' Rhona laughed.

As they walked under the trees, across the 'U' where the main avenue bifurcated to the separate houses, Viva lagged behind, pretending to fix her hat.

Rhona, who truly needed neither a walking-stick nor an arm to lean on, continued, 'Now come on, Cyril, continue. You're set on nuptials. Is that what you're saying?'

Cyril nodded dumbly.

'Well.' Rhona arched her neck. 'If you are going to marry, I'd better accept it. We shall have to celebrate.

When can we celebrate? When can we *meet* her? A glass of madeira one afternoon, maybe?'

Cyril mumbled an unclear something.

'I hate weddings,' said Rhona. 'I hate them.'

Munch said, 'I don't think we'll be going to this one, Mother?'

'Of course we will. Of course we will.'

Munch insisted. 'Oh, no, we won't, and do you know why? There won't be a wedding in public, the girl will be excommunicated, that's why.'

'Not a good year to marry a Roman Catholic, Cyril,' said Rhona, 'this Eucharistic Congress thing, cardinals from kingdom come. The whole Irish'll be in a fever.'

'Nineteen-Thirty-Two – the Year of Fervour. That's what the papers say,' declared Munch. 'A fever of fervour.'

'I didn't say I was marrying this year, Aunt Rhona.'

Herbert said, 'I missed Thomas. Do you think he knew we were there?'

'Ellen said he was fine. And she looked fine.'

'Even if I'd seen him at the auction,' said Herbert, peering through the window of the bus.

'Of course, you know Ellen, she will never say anything.'

'He's a man who knows what to do about things,' said Herbert with approval.

Leah glanced at him, but did not challenge. Herbert continued.

'I often feel for him. All that time out of his life. He must think we all know things he doesn't, things that he missed.'

'He has a good wife.' The late sun through the bus windows caught Leah's great frizz of red hair.

'I mean. His face when I asked him, d'you remember,

what he thought about Lindbergh? Why does that haunt me?'

'Things haunt you, Herbert. That's why.'

The Ulvertons dined on corned beef and cabbage with Cyril Stephenson that night.

'Small helpings again,' scoffed Viva, 'nothing new in this house.'

'I hated that auction,' said Rhona before she went to bed. 'More of the old order gone.' She walked like an ageing heron, but when alone and unseen, moved more spryly: she was only fifty-eight and wished to appear more venerable.

'Mamma,' said Viva, 'Deanstown Castle never belonged to our side, it was owned by French Catholics.'

'Yes, but French Catholics aren't like Irish Catholics, they have a bit of style about them, they're not bloody slaves and prudes.'

Miriam stood in the hallway, wincing.

'But you are, you definitely are, and you said you wouldn't get drunk again. You said.'

'Ah, Miriam. Who was there anyway?' he coaxed. 'Look, smell.' He hawed on her.

'Yu-htsss!' She recoiled, twisting her mouth away.

'Seriously, Miriam.'

She sat on the stairs. 'I asked her. I asked Ellen – d'you know? About the boy's hand that was swollen?'

'Did you make your tea itself, Miriam?'

Miriam shivered in the dim hall, drew her feet up from the brown tiles. 'And she said nothing. As usual.'

Jack clicked his teeth, scratched the palm of one hand. 'Whuh-huh. Did your man come with the new ointment, d'you know?'

'Although – she looked great. Great. She won't say a word against him, though.'

Jack said, 'Miriam, I'll tell you one thing, I'm never again putting that new petrol in the car, it gave the engine the hoose, like a calf or something.'

Miriam shook her head. 'And he was there, too, moving around as if he walked inside a glass case. He put up a bid for a doll. The girls are getting to be lovely little things. That's what he's like, like a glass case, no, not like the glass itself, like one of those figures in, oh, like, Jesus, I'm too tired to think, those tall domed glass cases you see in museums, you know, old uniforms.'

'Thomas?'

They stood in the bedroom. Every night he washed beneath his arms with a cold face-flannel.

'The boys in school. When you have to discipline them.' He stood at the ewer in pyjama trousers; she walked over and pressed her big pregnant stomach to his back; she laid her head between his bare shoulder-blades.

'If their hands hurt afterwards, you know – when they get an answer wrong, or something. Maybe you don't know your own strength.'

She felt his spine stiffen and she clung. He stood in rigid silence and Ellen Kane knew he could stand there all night, unmoved and unmoving.

4

At one point in the 1920s, Bernadette Sykes calculated that Dorothy Bayer's income from all sources amounted to six thousand pounds a day. The Bayer-Hilton old money lay in property and other possessions; new cash arrived daily from investments. Two centuries of marriage alliances in Europe, South America and South Africa, had increased the core fortune. Among recent generations, infertility, war and homosexuality whittled the family down to a few outer cousins. Only the widowed Asia Hilton remained at the heart of the fortunes, and, childless too, Dorothy Bayer.

When Dorothy returned to Alnwick from Tunisia in September 1932, Ramsay MacDonald's tax laws had begun to reap. Dorothy may have oozed languor, but she lived by shrewdness: despite some unusual chemical indulgences learned in north Africa, she retained a clear view of her wealth.

'We have to make some decisions, Bryan Cooper,' she said. 'Tax paid is wealth lost.'

Without (as usual) showing too much knowledge, 'Bryan' pointed out that Trusts had advantages; Dorothy concurred and began to liquidate several income-generating assets.

'Yes, I'll form Trusts for all the people I love;' 'Gerry' – Geraldine, who, many years since, had replaced 'Bobbie' (and others in between) – became the first beneficiary.

'But,' sighed Dorothy, 'what about my Dennis? What will he do?'

Years earlier, Dennis's mother learned the value of timely silence – and after such a long moment Dorothy decided.

'Oh, well, let's give Dennis a Trust too,' she said. 'But not a very large one. A man must earn his own living, we don't want him turning into a little tart, do we?'

By now, Bernadette had secretly rearranged her own future. In the years of administering the properties and estates, she discovered that insurance companies and other financial institutions paid commission on new business. Gradually, she carefully restructured all the appropriate policies – and thus guaranteed herself a life of security.

In personal terms, her accent, demeanour, appearance and presence had also reached levels of consistency. Firm within herself, she never unlocked the greed and breeding that she once feared would let her down. Dennis was at university, financed by his scholarship and, soon, by this new Trust of Dorothy's: the estates were running smoothly: at forty-two, she had space to re-think. Her new solitude, and her financial safety, told her that she had achieved her goals: time to move on. This mood ripened one day in Newcastle-upon-Tyne.

Over and over she had congratulated herself on never having let a man through her defences: her secrets remained intact. Of late, however, she seemed to notice that not a few had begun to observe her with interest. One, the accountant for the solicitors with whom she most often dealt, asked her to lunch. Bernadette accepted, and discovered two facts that alarmed her.

He said to her, 'I hope you don't mind this remark. But

your careful twin-set doesn't altogether conceal something exciting about you.'

Although she answered, 'Mr Cathcart, long ago I lost my heart and never got it back,' his overture registered a great deal lower than her head and shook her composure. Awake that night, she concluded that if her body now seemed ready to betray her, then her guard was dropping, meaning her long task was over.

More worryingly, the accountant, malicious at being rejected, had remarked as they parted, 'I love the way you've taken the Bayers.'

'*Taken*?' she queried.

He winked, and waved good-bye.

Some months later, the first instalment of Dennis's Trust Fund arrived at Alnwick. Bernadette opened the envelope, verified the cheque, and sent it with the letter she had already written.

> Dear Dennis,
> This is the first payment from a Trust that will give you an income for the rest of your life. I have therefore seen to it that you will always have at least some financial means. The money will increase because interest rates will go up.
> As I have also benefited from Miss Bayer's money, I am now going to give up working for these people whose sort I have always hated. But I had to do it for you, to get you a start in life.
> I will go back to St David's, only for a few days, and then I will do some travelling, as I have always wanted to. It is my turn to have a decent existence, and maybe I will meet someone suitable. When I find somewhere in which I think I will settle, I will get in touch with you.

But I have set you on course. With the brains you
inherited from me, you have guaranteed yourself free
education with your scholarship and bursaries. Miss
Bayer says you can use the lodge for holidays for as
long as you are at University.

Until we meet again,
best wishes for your studies.

Yours,

Mother.

Dennis ran to the Dean's office in such distress that
they let him use the precious telephone.

Dorothy herself answered.

'No, my Dennis, she's gone. Went yesterday. Didn't
you know? Oh, yes, she told me a month ago, I thought
you knew. No, she didn't go to St David's after all. In fact
she's left the keys of St David's here for you.' Dorothy
paused, then said, 'Hallo, hallo, are you there, Dennis?
Dennis, darling, are you all right? Do come here for the
week-end if you're feeling peaky. Although I shall be in
Edinburgh, I fear.'

Like a mad fiend he walked through that day of dismay.
It rained when night fell; anguished and breathless, he
stood under a shop arcade; the rain stopped and he walked
on. In a doorway on Lantern Street, he found a prosti-
tute, and for a ten-shilling note, she plucked deftly and
agitated rhythmically until he ejaculated into her hand.

He rested against the brick, making meaningless conversation to her in the archway. A raindrop inside his
collar chilled his neck. For a further ten shillings she
lifted her skirt and let him look, and he tooth-combed his
fingernails softly and edgily through the lank hair at her
crotch. In their third transaction, she hauled at him softly
once more, the coldness of her hand an exciting detail.

When semen whitened her black skirt, Dennis drifted away and hailed a taxi to the University.

At the mirror in his room he scanned every lobe, aperture and follicle of his head and face. He inspected his underwear and genitals, sniffed his hands, then washed them with fierceness and sadness. High on a cocktail of triumph and self-repugnance, he climbed into bed and fell deep asleep.

Several dreadful weeks followed. In the early, early mornings Dennis sat up against his pillows and, finger to his pulse, stared at the thin line of red which brought the dawn to Manchester. Once, he went to the doctor and complained of breathlessness, but never gave away any possible emotional causes. Over and over, he patted his face as tenderly as if he were his own child. He ate nothing, drank goblets of tea; he washed his hands again and again and again. Then, like some god gone wrong, on the seventh day he rested from his distress.

To recover, he began to formulate what would become his story and his attitude. His peers already knew little about him, this gregarious but never forthcoming, slightly pretty swot. So he felt free to replicate – if unwittingly – his mother's example. In other words, he reinvented his own life.

To begin with, he returned to Lantern Street. One of the other tarts identified the whore he described – 'Betty'. Later that night, Betty duly reappeared. Thereafter Dennis saw her once or twice a week, and on Betty he tried out his new identity – to test credulity, to gauge reaction. He always chose the same type of meeting: a door, alley or archway; no intercourse, vaginal or oral; one-sided verbal exchanges – he had no wish to learn of

Betty's life, or full name, even when she offered. After each ejaculation, he told her yet another tale from his great new fiction, and she listened – with attention, so it seemed.

She did not respond in depth, was not required to – but he was pleased to retain one comment she made: 'Any man with as much spunk as comes out of you is going to be rich.'

When he had sufficiently invented the fiction of where he had come from, he next wished to decide where he was going. To do this, he needed to map-make. Clinically, he charted the pattern of his visits to Lantern Street. Any reverse in study, some slight, some hurt or depression in his general life, a feeling of unease – all such contentions sent him to her. The need turned into a scream on two occasions. A loving letter from Dorothy Bayer, with a cheque for Christmas, gave Betty more cash than usual – and a complaint about an aching wrist. She also observed a development: Dennis had never uttered a swear-word in her presence up to then: when he did, Betty said, 'That's more of a man!'

His harshest demands came after a chance meeting with the aggressive Alison Kettley, the Alnwick steward's daughter. Dennis bought the girl coffee, he had to; she asked. At the marble-topped table, amid the spilt sugar of the Saturday afternoon crowds, Alison pried into his student life, fingered his scarf, asked about his adventures – she 'would bet' he had girls in love with him.

To his dismay, she began to talk about his mother.

'She must have loved your father hugely, to have carried a broken heart all those years?' Bernadette's fictions endured.

Dennis nodded.

'Such a looker, too. Did you know that? Did you know

75

that she was, I mean, she is, such a pretty woman? Boys often don't know that about their mothers. She must be so proud of you, is she? If you were a few years older she'd have you marrying Miss Bayer. We used all think that's what she was up to, getting you a rich wife out of that family. I bet now that she's left Alnwick, your mum comes to see you really often does she? And all that money she was left by your father? You'll inherit that, Dennis. Where's she living?'

Talk, talk, talk – but he practised his warm-eyed look. Later, Dennis manoeuvred her through the streets with such svelte force that they had reached the railway station before she knew where they were headed. Alison gasped that she had forgotten two chores, but Dennis's smile so rewarded her that she entered the train thrilled and philosophical. As he waved from the platform, he congratulated himself on having kept her from meeting other students.

That night, Betty of Lantern Street said, 'Go easy, go easy, you'll hurt yourself. Oi! Oi! Stop, you're pinching my arm, stoppit.' Two streets away, two hours later, Dennis bought Carla, black, strong and impatient at his delay, for which she charged him extra.

When Dennis moved to Birmingham for postgraduate work, he began the long and safe journey into the myth of his past. To make the legend consistent, he gave it very few major component parts. That way he could never forget, never make an error.

To the widowed mother in Glasgow, he added a wealthily married sister called Dorothy in Witwatersrand. By now, his father had been a sportsman, an engineer and a gambler, cast out by a good family. One grandfather, a clergyman, had married money. Dennis just missed his

University blue owing to injury. As an undergraduate, he had been almost engaged to an unnamed blue-blood – but, probably for class reasons, the girl left him for another; he remained heartbroken. The legend rolled on.

His academic brilliance needed no invention. Although never visibly boastful, it somehow happened that all who met him knew of his distinctions within minutes.

Only once did he return to Alnwick, having checked that Dorothy was abroad. Others had just come to live in the lodge; he told the cabbie to drive by. Dennis never entered the house proper, simply collected the keys to St David's, where he walked and walked the lovely coast. As before, his treks always ended up in towns; he haunted the summer cafés and teashops of Tenby.

On that riviera south coast of Wales, how the girls and the women jawed! Dennis watched and overheard everywhere. Always with enough money in his pocket to afford a room in a hotel – never, never a bed-and-breakfast – he eavesdropped, while pretending to read his serious-looking books. Clothes. Men. Relatives. Men. Children. Family. Mothers. Money. Relationships.

He heard. Yet, he avoided contact.

'Not yet ready,' he told himself. 'Wait, Dennis, wait.'

To grant himself a more withdrawn air, he even bought a pair of horn-rimmed spectacles with clear lenses.

'For a play,' he told the optician. 'I'm up at Cambridge, *Bitter Sweet* – you know, the Noël Coward. Yes, you're absolutely right, it *is* lovely. Marvellous fun.'

Girls did approach him: why not? Very good-looking: obviously well-to-do: blazer and knife-pressed flannels, and clean, so clean: he smiled them away. Not yet, Dennis, not yet.

Next year, he discovered that people had come to live in the St David's house. His mother had sold it by remote control. All her goods, packed by a neighbour, had been sent to a furniture store in Bristol. Where, they told him, they had sent it to a shipping office, who took it to a boat bound for the south of the world. Dennis walked from the shipping office to the water's edge and sat for an hour, completely still.

'Bryan Cooper' vanished – with many thousand legitimate pounds. When she first left Alnwick, she did not go far: her cunning told her no need: she rented an excellent apartment in Torquay just as the summer season ended. Two trips to London fitted her out in the amber and grey colours of that autumn's fashions, plus a black coat and three black dresses. She called herself 'Madeleine Ring', a widow. Twice a week she dined alone in the Imperial Hotel, choosing the absolute best of the menu, and being shrewd with the half-bottle wine-list. By the third week, with the discreet collusion of the pompous, gossipy maître d'hôtel, she had sized up a divorced man from South America – who proposed.

Bernadette never had one ounce of mothering in her; she felt only duty. Whether she missed Dennis, how can we ever tell? When Patrick Sykes made her pregnant, a logical consequence of all marriage, she accepted the burden of a baby's dependence by looking ahead to his earliest possible maturity, and with it her own freedom.

Had Dennis been unintelligent she would have shipped him off somewhere, a children's home, a working farm, into service. If she had not pulled off her various coups with the Hilton-Bayer set, if she had failed to get out of south Wales, she would have sent her son down the mines at the age of fourteen like all the other boys in and around St David's. In recent years, when she ever contemplated his possible life ahead, with the typical prospect of a daughter-in-law and grandchildren, she shuddered again.

Accordingly, her cool decision to vanish had nothing to do with his feelings – only hers. Her care of him had also been a manipulation of him – towards money, preference, and above all unto her own eventual liberty. Once that had been put in place, and once he had proven his intellectual ability to build his own life, she felt no more ties.

Her coolness of spirit and her simple greed had kept her life on straight lines, led her to play a long game. Through the Asia Hilton experience in Pembrokeshire, she first carved out an understanding of herself that connected to money and possessions. At Alnwick, she found how powerfully she could manage the rich, and their ways and means. Her greatest vulnerability – a fear of others' poor opinion of her – came under control after she discovered the advantages of false identity.

It never occurred to Dennis to register his mother as a missing person. Such a course of action simply did not fit her. It took a long time, though, before he could stop himself in public staring at every remotely similar woman. In the years following her disappearance, Dennis believed he saw Bernadette twice: once from a train window at King's Cross, once in Paris, on the Boulevard Haussmann. On both occasions he was wrong. He never knew what became of her, and when they came to clear out his effects, no trace of her, nor of any family existed anywhere, no 'departed mother in Glasgow', of whom he told such dotty and loving anecdotes, no 'wealthily-married sister in Witwatersrand'. Nothing.

All the big engineering corporations kept in close touch with university faculties. Dennis was offered one, two, three, four jobs during his postgraduate studies. He opted for a surveying firm in Liverpool. Was it because his father had met his mother there? We do not know. Some wish to give himself a family past? He never said.

It was in Liverpool that he established his permanent general pattern. Get in. Settle down. Good digs, first, then a flat. On his own. Always. At work, get well-liked and admired for performance. Pleasant to everybody, 'especially secretaries and clerks, because they talk, they have to, their work is so boring.' Outside, check the population at large. Inside, check the society of the workplace. In both, assess the means of creating 'friends'. Next, measure those circles against each other. Figure out where to circulate for good commercial practice – plus: in what milieu to move with social safety? And, finally – where to live the secret life?

Public. Private. Secret. Three lives. 'Public' meant 'warm'. 'Private' meant 'genial, if gently aloof'. 'Secret' – he prowled. That is how Dennis Sykes lived the three lives. Committed in work. Shy but loyal with such companions as he made, always office-derived in those early days. In secret, he learned soon the charms of devastation.

His first 'field experiment' resulted in a most satisfying piece of emotional savagery. Two Liverpool foundries had merged; the parent company closed one plant and wished to enlarge the other. Dennis's employers liaised with the Council in discussions to widen roads, to increase the capacity of a railway bridge. He did the first surveying, and reported an extraneous difficulty. One house would suffer. Increased loads, noise and dust would spoil the enjoyment of its long, lovely garden.

'I think we should confront it,' he said in his quiet way. 'Meet them. Go and see their faces.'

He rapped the lion's-head doorknocker. 'Them' was an

American woman alone; husband worked weekdays in London. She and Dennis sat facing each other, armchair to sofa, drinking coffee.

'No, I will take the decision,' the American woman told Dennis. 'I have to. He's away Monday to Friday.'

'That can't be easy?' He pursed a sympathetic lip.

'You said it!'

She, a stranger in Liverpool, had made no friends yet. Dennis sensed her irritableness, primed her: 'Does – does your husband, does he, ah'm – *have* to work in London?' – and then listened.

She spoke, he reckoned later, five minutes non-stop: then came the embarrassment, then the gratitude. Dennis listened. Dennis listened on.

Audrey Gee said, 'You know, I've never had a chance to say it all before, I've never said it. Not even to him. I mean not fully. I'm sorry to pressure your ear like that.'

'No, no. Shush.' He waved a hand.

When he returned to the office he said he felt certain they might 'crack this nut', but it would take a few weeks.

He wrote – his fine handwriting on the firm's letterhead.

> Dear Mrs Gee,
> Thank you for the coffee. If you need further
> advice, please get in touch. I will keep you informed
> as to progress.
> Yours faithfully,

Dennis prepared himself for Audrey as a priest for a rite. He remembered some creamy languorous girl, drawing on new stockings, and recounting an *amour* to Dorothy.

'Then, he put his hand –' How she stood, and posed, both for the cheval-glass and Dorothy.

81

'Just here.' Leaning like a fashion model, one hand on one bare hip, she asked the rhetorical question.

'Now, why is that so – oooh!?'

The girls laughed deliciously.

Second and third visits to Audrey began to yield a gentle familiarity over the drawings unrolled on the dining-room table. Dennis picked up clues, and on his fourth visit brought the week-end *Sketch* which had a special photo supplement on Wimbledon.

'Oh boy! What a memory you have!' Two weeks ago, Audrey told Dennis that her sister back home had played a schools championship against Helen Wills Moody.

She stood in the hallway glancing at the newspaper. Dennis closed the front door behind him. Audrey had a mirror on the closet door at the end of the hall. She stopped momentarily to fix her hair. Before she could walk on, Dennis, right behind her, stood and put one hand on her hip.

Quietly he said, 'Don't move. Just – just – don't move.'

He spoke very softly.

They stood there. One hand only, on one hip. Then she turned and, slightly taller than him, put her head down on his shoulder.

All afternoon he stayed tenderly near. Sitting beside her, he lodged a hand on the edge of her lap. When she stood, he rose and touched her hair, lifted it a little, let it fall. As she gazed into the long garden, he stood behind her, his shoulder just touching hers. In the hallway again, before he said good-bye, he put his fingers in her mouth.

Next morning she had a note pushed through the door: it only read, 'Thank you. *Thank* you.' No signature.

=

Four days later, he came by. Each afternoon she had taken care to dress with edge, just in case, just in case . . .

Dennis stepped inside, stood with his back to the closed front door. He covered her face with his hand and spread his palm like butter all across her features.

They halted on the stairs twice, scrabbling, kissing, falling to their knees on the landing. He calculated every move, every breath. She kissed with her eyes closed, he with his eyes open, as he would forever.

Standing above her as she lay on the bed, he hesitated.

'What?'

He lowered his eyes. 'I believe – I believe I may need instruction.'

'Oh, Jesus! Oh dear, sweet Dennis.'

The widening of the bridge went ahead.

'I must say,' said Dennis's office admiringly, 'I don't know how you did it. If it were my house, I'd never agree.'

Audrey overruled all her absent husband's objections because she had a secret. She knew she would not have to live in the house much longer. Dennis had struck – but only when he knew for certain that he was being moved to London.

'Darling Audrey.' Every Monday over the four months, he had found her frantic after her wifely week-end. A Wednesday, consequently, more leisurely in mood, seemed suitable for the *coup de grâce*.

'You know there's going to be a war.'

She said, 'I can think of nothing else. Can't you avoid it?'

He had checked and re-checked the shipping time-tables.

'When I was a boy,' he said wistfully, 'there was a post-card my father had sent from Santiago. That is where

83

his first office was. It had a blue sign. On a terracotta wall.'

She lifted a breast, and with it touched his face and eyes.

'Audrey, would you – if I asked . . . ?'

'Come with you?'

'She had green eyes, my first girlfriend,' he reminisced fondly forty years later. 'And sort of off-black hair. She was, she was – great *fun*.'

Audrey embraced his head. 'Where? When? I'll be there.'

He made the elaborate arrangements. She left a note for her husband. Half an hour before Stanley Gee was due to arrive from London for the week-end, Audrey departed for the docks, panting like a bride.

Afternoon after afternoon, evening after evening, 'Your tongue,' she said, over and over, 'your tongue. Oh, Jesus, Dennis, honey. Oh, Jesus Chriii-iiiii-issst!'

'No,' he said each time he lifted his sweating curly head, 'I'm the one who knows where the honey is.'

Lying back he asked, 'What did you daydream about? About men, I mean? Before I came into your life? Did you used to think about men – and that?'

He licked the back of her ear, moistened the edge of her hair.

'Yeah, but I never thought –' and that habit he had of never letting her finish what she was saying, of stopping her words by laying his cheek to her lips. Four and a half months of immersion.

On the days before he arrived at the house, Audrey would hug herself and say out loud, 'How I love him! How I love him! I wonder if I'm good enough for him?'

Each day she had a new greeting for him. 'Who do you

look like today, Dennis? Let me see, I think you look like –'

After they had seen *Bringing up Baby*, Audrey changed her mind and said, 'No, honey, I was wrong, George Raft has too sharp a face, you're like Cary Grant. Yes, you're Cary Grant.'

Not once did he say, 'There's no need to apologize.'

Not once did he say, 'You're too self-effacing.'

Not once did he say, 'Yes, of course, you *are* good enough for me. Don't be silly.'

Every little service, every cup of tea, every sandwich she brought to the bed – he accepted them like a firm little sultan. Yet, each afternoon before he arrived she still asked herself out loud, 'I hope I'll be good enough for him today. How can anyone love someone so much?'

Audrey looked in the mirror and hoped for a big moon at sea, so that they could lean on the rail and gaze at the stars and the ocean.

She embarked as Dennis instructed, on a dockside full of exotic cranes, with barges in the river. In the cabin she drew from her new suitcase a new slip, a new négligé. He had done all the planning; she had done all the booking.

They had before them a nine-week voyage, an 'advance honeymoon, and think, honey – no war, I won't have to fear you'll get killed overseas.'

'Qualms?'

'Nope. Oh, no! Because I guess, I guess – I'm leaving an all-right marriage for a thrilling one.'

He had warned that he would not come below until under way, had smiled in that crinkle that made her body fizz: 'I'm bringing you a gift.'

As the boat cleared the harbour, a train passed overhead, en route through Crewe to London. In the first-class compartments sat Dennis Sykes, wearing a suit of chalk-striped navy-blue, with a white, foaming pocket-handkerchief. He shook out his *Times* and settled to read. Out to his right, the lights of a ship slipped away and Dennis blew a mental kiss to all who sailed in her, and to all in Santiago.

In his pocket he carried a letter, from his old to his new office, which began, 'You are getting, if I may say so, a bit of a treasure this time. DS is a remarkably clever and able chap – and terribly popular.'

Dennis Sykes had a habit of rubbing the edges of his fingernails against each other. He had no self-abusive gestures, such as picking at skin, and he virtually raged if he cut a finger or bruised or scratched himself. Dorothy Bayer took a photograph of him once – a three-year-old boy with long curls and the lips of a decadent angel. He wears a button-through little tunic with an over-elaborate white collar, and he has cocked his head archly – a cherubic show-off. Over twenty years later, in the London office-group photograph, the lips have merely grown to manhood, and dark wavy hair hides the forehead; the eyes mistrust the camera.

Public. Private. Secret. After Liverpool, Dennis added very few geographical moves to his *curriculum vitae*. Between 1938 and 1949, he worked for the same company, a fact of which he was proud: he believed it demonstrated stability in him. He meant to grow into a sharp and ambitious executive, ready for each significant moment that came along. Every movement in his career took him upward. Alongside, he built his private income astutely by spending carefully; setting out to earn as much from investment as from employment, he more or less succeeded.

The way in which he approached work typified the life-method he had worked out. A seeming lightness of touch, with quips and accommodating-ness, concealed a ferocity of commitment. He worked harder, longer, swifter than any colleague his age. No extra work fazed him; no new complication irritated. With unnoticed control, he used his superior capacity to become a rescue service for over-worked colleagues: 'If you're busy, I'll finish that.'

While doing so, he watched how the company functioned. Preferment, he observed, came to those who got nearest the senior managers. Dennis chose the Deputy Managing Director and made him the recipient of all his design and client problems; by doing so he gave the man an opportunity to develop a protégé. They discussed, experimented, exchanged ideas; they drank together – Dennis never touched alcohol, but encouraged the other man to relax. Together they kept up with the literature of their profession, and discreetly considered personnel difficulties in the firm.

The senior man trained him. *At meetings never contribute until asked. Service the primary requirement. Innovative but solid drawing-board and site work. Elegantly presented and conducted. Put the client first, then the project. Listen. Listen.*

Within a year, by dint of drawing and listening, and by means of ideas, courtesy and evident responsibility, 'DS' had made himself into as perfect a young managing engineer as the firm could have wanted, or ever had. Promotion jumped him two grades, unheard-of for a man in his twenties.

Method. Perception. Control. It had begun to work – especially control. Therefore – private life next. He had long perceived that he needed extensive social experience. All in good time. The time is now. At Dorothy Bayer's he had taken in the rudiments by osmosis. But now – how to move easily in company; how to become liked by women; yet how to avoid involvement. At the same time, he wanted to know every wild and absorbing carnal trick. Could he get both?

The conundrum absorbed him. Although conducted entirely in secret, the affair with Audrey, with its element of sexual instruction, had boosted his self-confidence in dealing with women. Intimacy. Sweat. Tight curls of hair like little serpents. Such a drug. And to think it could lead to power. To stay always in command, though, he needed ever more experience.

One path to follow: enjoyment without commitment. He wanted this combination for two reasons. Popularity with important wives and daughters would enhance his office reputation. Plus – he needed 'bodies' for his secret life. All things bright, Dennis, he told himself, everything on course. Young, evidently comfortably off, clothes-style already admired, and he had never known women liked men's hair so much.

'I wear rags of silk in it every night,' he teased the women in the office, 'silk from China. In little rolls, red and yellow.'

He began by swimming in the nearest pool. Maturer, but still young, women colleagues, of senior responsibilities, took to him. He accepted one in every four of their invitations – to a party, or a supper, or a lunch. Dennis listened and smiled, listened and smiled.

He primed their instincts, filled them with images of Dennis the caring son: 'My mother – anyone know how to ease the pains of rheumatism? Her knee –' and he would tap his leg. And Dennis the emotionally interested. He would look pensive and they would ask why: 'Oh, a

88

friend of mine,' Dennis would sigh. 'His marriage is going wrong. I have to go round and see them tonight – but I never know what to say – in these situations.'

Soon, these slightly older women colleagues told him everything. Past loves, passions, unrequitements – he heard amazing things: of abortions in backstreets, of ruinous obsessions; incest. Upon which the confessor would say, 'It's like talking to a girlfriend talking to you, Dennis.'

Dennis would smile but make no move.

Which led them to ask among themselves, 'Is he a bit – pink? You know – no girlfriend in evidence?'

He heard – and kissed one of them. Once. On her doorstep late at night, without coming in 'for coffee'. Then he apologized, and when she told all the others of the kiss in all its splendour, they concluded, 'No – definitely not pink.'

After that one tongue-and-lips kiss, he increased his attractiveness by holding them all warmly at bay. By which means, he also kept his doorstep unfouled.

Without knowing it, the women leaked him information: who was being moved off which contract; what manager was now favouring whom among Dennis's contemporaries; who was having problems with what client. He even knew the content of his own Annual Report before his Annual Interview. With such intelligence at his command, Dennis moved like a panther into all corners of favour.

All also told him about sex, even though they called it love. He learned how they dreamed, how they hoped. Knowing they included him in their wishes, he played gently along. At the point when he had four girls in the same office hovering and crazed, each never telling another of their love for him, he received his second promotion. Unusually high he rose – therefore, time to escape gracefully into darker suits and stiffer collars, to move up the company hills, in among the management wives. He heated up the ailing-mother-in-Scotland story – 'wasting disease, you should see the medical bills.'

Or – 'She desperately wants me to marry, but do you know what she said? So that she would have a daughter-in-law who could nurse her.'

They loved him even more. As they smiled in disappointment, they understood why he could not yet wed.

While the public and private lives were being set up and managed, the secret life raged on beneath. When he 'played', as he called it, Dennis followed an undulating pattern. First came a period of extraordinary promiscuity, typically lasting a period of some weeks, for which he always paid in cash. After, for some months, he would, as he put it to himself, 'lie fallow'. Then, out again, and into the fresh carnal burst he hurled all the pent-up insults and reverses since the last period.

He did not like it. Even if the self-disgust had a power source within it, even if the sheer release made him walk tall with the force of its secrecy, he wished for more control over it. He knew control must be available; he knew he could tame these outbursts and convert them – to another pattern of behaviour. They could be different, methodical, useful. Sexual activity could have a purpose, like an energy harnessed. He could use seduction for professional advancement, and it could still satisfy that curious, unexplained but utterly driven sense of revenge. But – so difficult to learn. Whom could he tell – or on whom could he practise without having to say why? Then one Saturday morning in 1940, he found his tutor.

==

On the corner of Lisson Grove stood a mansion block of flats needing repair. Attractive prices, therefore, and if you had money for renovations, you got rapid access to a high standard of London living. Furthermore, if your repairs seemed comprehensive and exciting, people in the block talked about you, speculated, invited you for drinks. These buildings had their own social micro-climate.

Dennis Sykes stood inside the open door of his new apartment. The decorator swiped different colours in wide soft swathes across the walls as a test. A bony woman walked by.

'I like that russet terracotta,' she said. 'Are you one of the boys?' Then she said, 'Forget it, you're not,' when she saw Dennis's puzzled face. 'Thank God, darling.'

Her name was Binnie Maxwell. 'I'm on the floor above. 34B, same as my bust.' The decorator laughed and arched an eyebrow at Dennis.

Binnie glared. 'When Michelangelo here is gone, why don't you come and have some coffee?'

She had a leather sofa.

'Dennis? And how old are you, Dennis?'

'Twenty-six.'

'If Herr Hitler really starts chucking the ordure – Dennzy, you'll be cannon fodder.'

'No. We've talked about it. The company says I'm to be Reserved Occupations.'

'Another cigarette, please?'

'What do you do for a living, Binnie?' He lit it for her, and the sofa-leather creaked.

'Reserved Occupation, too, darling, but whisper it please, I'm also a lady. I'm a *fille de joie*.'

Binnie, mid-thirties looking fifty, racked with coughs and mascara, formed the core of a like-minded and like-bodied bunch. Obliquely well-bred, most were the daughters of financially-stressed divorcées whom the titled and rich had cast aside for younger flesh.

'*Les Louches*', Binnie called them, and they lived on their wits. Some had unsteady inheritances, or allowances. Several had addictions. All needed money, usually in desperation. They got it in tough ways: tarting on a closed and abusing circuit; servicing elderly wealth; hitting the resorts after wives had gone home.

Binnie had a frail side, too. For all her wild living she longed for some kind of protection, some kind of undemanding stability that would yet not deny her the raciness of it all – 'I have to box on the ropes too often, darling.'

She and Dennis clanged together like a pair of magnets. Binnie, smelling Dennis's rapaciousness, offered the deal. He, a near neighbour, would frequently be so nice to come home to: she, a woman of the world, had a lot of knowledge to impart.

They shook hands: she kissed him with her thin, carmine lips, then broke away to the high bar stool by the peeling kitchen counter.

'Phase One: the practicals,' and she wheezed with saloon laughter.

On their first full afternoon together she told him, 'Of course we start with an advantage, darling.'

'What's that?'

'For a little chap, you're hung like a Zulu. Not at all dinky in that bureau.'

Soon, she made other expressions of agreeable surprise, and he made her laugh like a whisky drain. The tuition began.

'Darling, look in our eyes all the time. Lead us gently but firmly and always, always push us down to a soft landing place.'

'Darling, here. Put your tongue just inside our lips, and run it around. Lick the inside of our lower lip. Lick it like your tongue was a little busy snake. Aaaahhh!'

'Darling, the most wonderful stunt of them all. Say to her, "I was dreaming about you last night." And then quick as a flash, say, "No, tell you later. A lot later." Nothing more flattering, darling, than being told by a man that you've been on his mind while the bugger's been *asleep*, for Christ's sake.'

Binnie sighed, 'Now – slip him back out, darling, and lie back. Thaaa-at's it. A little rest, shall we? A little nicotine relief for Binns and Denns? And then we begin all over again.'

She taught him how to use his fingernails lightly up and down her spine, how to run his tongue from ankle to thigh – 'Always, always on the inside, darling. On the outside you might as well be tongueing the table-leg. No-no-no-no-no-no, darling, that is not *at all* what Binnie means by ball-and-claw.'

For several consecutive week-ends, they spent afternoons and early evenings in bed, with Binnie hailing Dennis's fortitude, and correcting his ploys: 'Think of it as training the animal, darling, think of me as an animal-trainer.'

In return, Dennis, glad of the sweats and aches, bought her cigarettes, drink, and food. Early at night, before the hard people came out to play, he took her to meals in the solid, well-fed restaurants where she would never ever see the folk from what she called 'the bright side' of her life. Afterwards they went back to Binnie's where they clanked and tussled some more.

Yet, even if he stayed until three in the morning, Dennis never slept overnight, always closed the door of 34B behind him and like a jaded musketeer slipped quietly down the dark green stairwell, his empty scrotum aching.

In Phase Two, Binnie taught him about targets.

'Watch wives, darling. Watch the corners of their mouths. In fact, watch the corners of all women's mouths. Mine don't droop, darling, do they? Say what you like about me, call me a fast and lanky jade if you will, but the corners of my mouth do not *droop*! And I am proud of that!'

She dragged on the cigarette with horse's lungs.

'Watch this. You go to a party. You find a woman, a wife. She's – heavy-ish. But not too heavy. Or bony – not as bony as me, nobody is. But too bony for her own good, and evidently wed to a wealthy animal. He will have sleek fur. So will she – but the gloss will be a little dull. Bit artificial, paid-for rather than natural. Listen to her for half an hour, keep refilling her glass. Don't, for Christ's sake, *talk* to her. Listen. *Listen* to her. You know about listening. Next afternoon, you'll be round there for tea and buns and handkerchief-pandkerchief. Binnie knows, darling. How does she know? Because while you're round there, Binnie's actually hogtieing the article's animal? That's why the corners of the wife's mouth are drooping, darling, poor wet hen that she is. But – for Christ's sake darling, tell them you're married. Otherwise, they'll be round here with their pointy teeth – going after you like pike in a fucking trout stream. Another of your ciggos, please, darling.'

Binnie paced towards the long window and looked down at the traffic; shadows of the afternoon darkened her high, thin, nude haunches.

She turned, thin long breasts a-swing.

'Why am I telling you this?' He lit it for her; the lighter

94

flame gilded her face. 'Yes, they are tears in my eyes, you little shit – no! Don't ask! No! Shut up! None of your fucking business.' Binnie tightened her act again and slipped back into character.

'And another thing, darling, if you're into social bull-fighting, you can have the most wonderful anarchy, the greatest fun stirring it between husband and wife. In a way a woman in the same position never can. Heed Binnie, darling, and you'll be the social equivalent of one of those guided rockets Herr Hitler is supposed to be building. Yes, ye-es, go to it, Dennzy.'

She turned and, cigarette askew in her lips, began to hammer the bed fiercely with her fists.

'And be delicate when reporting back. Binns is not made of fucking tin after all. Am I?! Am I?!'

Dennis launched himself: Phase Two: The Social Life – Intimacy without Commitment. With ease, he built a separate existence away from the office and, above all, away from clients. New circuits: he purchased a car, joined a motor club; he bought clubs and played golf. New women: alphabetically, and in code, he kept count in his notebook: Clarrie, Diana, Elizabeth, Faith, Hazel, Iris, Joan, Lorna – one a fortnight. Or so.

All feared losing their comfortable homes: all knew disappointed marriages. Most had for years gone along with the ordinary pretence of marriage in exchange for the patterns of house, car, clothes, by which they now felt comforted.

Dennis brought relief. At least they could tell him what hurt at home.

Marjorie remarked, 'I've never had the courage to tell him how his hogging the newspaper at breakfast annoys me.'

Nicola said, 'And he didn't even know that to give some-body a gift of gloves is a bad omen, it means breaking a friendship. Not that we were best friends, we've been just – well – married, I suppose. I'd love my husband to be my best friend.'

Olive complained, 'And I go to the most careful lengths, I choose the writing-paper carefully, I've always been extra-careful about the way our address is printed on it, about the lettering, and then suddenly I find that half of it is missing, and that he hasn't even said how nice it is.'

Petra said, 'I'm married to a man I don't love.'

Dennis clucked and shook his sympathetic head.

He soon understood that he had guessed the paradox right: sex and business could mix if kept apart. 'The Binnie System', as he called it, brought him a dividend even beyond the sex-without-emotion, a career bonus by way of by-product. While warming briefly these sad-faced, hurt and cautiously angry women in Kensington, Burgess Hill, Wimbledon and Harrow, while 'apologizing' to them for his 'marriage', they also told him all their husbands' business strategies. As he studied their bodies, Dennis also learned of their friends and associates. Each night in his flat, he wrote down all the names they had mentioned: husbands, companies and connections. As well as storing for future reference, the information enabled him to appear knowledgeable of industry and finance, to drop names as delicately as a Chinese diplomat.

Rarely did he see Queenie, Roberta, Sheila, Thomasina twice. How sweetly and wistfully they parted, she still in a robe, secretive and kissy behind the closed front door. But Dennis reassured them on the telephone two days later – that it was a once-only time for him too, and now, oh, how guilt would haunt him! He felt 'funny' seeing his 'wife' that evening, he explained ruefully.

Dennis had only three breaks in this routine, when three times he contracted Non-Specific Urethritis from Binnie. Red-edged and oozing, he showed Binnie.

'Me, darling, I fear,' she said. 'I'm a carrier. Apologies all round. But my friend Edmund will look after little Dennis's every need. He has a clinic for these things. He's a hickory-dickory-dock. So to speak. A dick doc.'

5

As her family increased, Ellen Kane found that she stood in the hurtful middle between her children and her husband. The cold and jagged outer ire he showed in the earliest days of his recovery never abated; it often intensified. Those cyclical undulations of mood, common to many men of his age and time and experience, began in him at a higher level up the roller-coaster. His household angers were more vicious; in his calms, bitterness lurked a bare inch below the lid. And yet, and yet – once the bedroom door closed behind them, he had such tenderness for her: lips pressed to her hair, hand held in both of his.

It took her several years to regulate the confusion caused by this split in him. She watched him closely, looking for perhaps one clue, a key that would release him. What, for instance, could she make of his sudden disappearance sometimes, after he had been particularly harsh to a child? Once or twice she found him sitting on the chair in their bedroom, his head erect, eyes closed, like a man keeping pain at bay.

In front of the children, she had to brave him with tact, diffuse his powerful, general force. Never smile, she learned, when a crisis of what he called 'discipline' blew up as suddenly as a bomb. Be grave, she discovered: take his side somewhat, to appease him: but never quite join in his harshness.

Afterwards, she had the next difficulty – of how to calm

an afflicted child while not betraying her husband's authority. She hugged; she kissed; she praised the weeping daughter or son for other things, and for hours afterwards never failed to smile with warmth when they caught her eye. If she prayed after such incidents, it did not mean that all her old piety had returned, but that she meant to give example to the children. With all these warmths and diligences, Ellen believed that by and large she had reduced or explained to the family their own bewilderment. Some of her loving worked: the children did not grow resentfully, nor – on the face of things – uncontrollably distressed.

Helena seemed to have the greatest difficulties, to such a degree that from above, her mother, and from beneath Grace – and even the younger ones – often rushed to buoy her up. Ellen spent particular time in developing Helena's reading habit. By the time she was ten, the child, as pretty as porcelain, could immerse herself in a book. When she had finished the latest Laura Ingalls Wilder, sent by cousins in America, or a new Eleanor Farjeon from the school library boxes, Helena could sit and dream, untouchable. By these means she occasionally escaped any gale of violent 'correction' that suddenly swept across the kitchen from where her father sat. She never raised her voice, and in following her mother's lead of creating family exchange, she taught Grace and the younger ones impossibly long passages from vivid poems.

Then saw they how there hove a dusky barge,
Dark as a funeral scarf from stem to stern,
Beneath them; and descending they were ware
That all the decks were dense with stately forms,
Black-stoled, black-hooded, like a dream – by these
Three Queens with crowns of gold – and from them rose
A cry that shiver'd to the tingling stars

– and the young ones would shiver in delight and repeat the words, with Helena nodding as if keeping time to music. Her mother encouraged and encouraged – and fed her warm milk to try and cure Helena's recurring diarrhoea.

One April Saturday night in 1937, Ellen conceived again. A few days after Grace's ninth birthday, a red-faced man appeared at the gate, embarrassed not exerted, and asked for help.

'What kind of help?' asked Ellen: it was late morning.

'Urgent help, Ma'am. The car's broke.'

Ellen no-nonsensed him. 'It's "broken" not "broke" – and since when did a broken car become urgent?'

The man replied, 'Since John McCormack got into it, Ma'am.'

Ellen dropped her hands into the dough. 'Jesus, Mary and Joseph!'

'That's the form, Ma'am.'

She clarified. 'You mean to say that John McCormack is out there in the car? On the road?'

'I do, Ma'am, that's the form. His wife is along with him there, and the son.'

Ellen, flustered at first, began to organize.

'Bring him in, bring them in, we'll at least give them a cup of tea. My husband knows about cars.' The man went.

'Helena!' Ellen called, and sent her to fetch Thomas from the garden.

'Grace!' – who was sent to find other children, so that faces could be wiped.

Essie lumbered in and was sent for a clean apron and a clean tablecloth. Thomas appeared.

'Wash your hands,' Ellen urged, 'John McCormack is coming through the door at any minute, his car broke down.'

'What?'

'Go. ON!'

Thomas hared upstairs, Ellen ran after him, and they changed like lightning, in time to see from their window the small party step through the gate. Lily McCormack wore a small velvet hat and pearls and, on the gravel, walked carefully in suede shoes.

Thomas, peering, said to Ellen, 'He's bigger than I thought,' and they raced downstairs again to stand at the door as a couple, just in time to shake hands and introduce themselves.

The embarrassed driver spoke to Thomas, who sent him to Hand's pub, where a mechanic from Dublin, in charge of the steamroller on the New Road, had been staying. Ellen led their visitors to the parlour.

Thomas spoke first. 'I was saying to my wife – you're bigger than I thought.'

McCormack smiled; 'A big noise comes out of a big drum.'

Scuffles in the gravel outside: the children wrestled to peer in at the window.

General talk began – of the difficulties with cars, new roads, weather. Tea appeared: John McCormack began to praise the scones.

'Well, you're lucky,' said Ellen, 'I put them into the oven just as your man came through the gate.'

Lily said, 'I wish I could bake like that' – to which her husband replied, 'Just as well, or I'd be even bigger.'

It became a Kane household joke for years: 'Mama – can we have some of John McCormack's scones?'

All the time, Thomas had not stopped smiling or half-smiling – in a rictus of shyness; or in genuine pleasure at having one of the world's great singers in his parlour; perhaps from a feeling that he knew he had the capacity

101

to belong in such company. He commanded the room, steering the conversation from one adult to another and if necessary extending the courtesy of an explanation to the McCormack boy, who sat as meekly as all boys in their best clothes. Thomas had a habit of looking at the back of his outstretched hand when making a point, and of then turning the hand palm upwards, flat, to conclude the statement. He sat upright, forward on the edge of his chair, courteous, forthright and confident.

So, it was Thomas who accepted when John McCormack turned to Ellen and, tapping the dark piano said, 'Mrs Kane, since you're after giving us the fruits of your talents with your lovely baking, I hope you'll let me repay the compliment.'

Thomas beamed. 'You're going to sing for us? Well, well, that's just tremendous.'

'Have you any music of your own here, Mrs Kane?' McCormack asked. 'Because we have some in the car.'

Ellen said, 'I have, but surely you know them by heart?' and she smiled.

'Of course I do, but I want you to accompany me.'

'Oh,' was the only little sound she could make. 'Oh.'

Thomas helped. '"Panis Angelicus", maybe?'

'Yes, yes, we have that.' Ellen foraged within the piano stool.

Thomas rose, went quickly to the window and pulled back the lace curtains, alarming the lurking children – startling them even more by the fact that he was smiling at them.

'No,' he said, 'no, stay where you are,' and he lifted the window open. Then he whispered to Helena, 'Get Essie to come out here and listen.'

Inside the room, Ellen had at last arrayed the sheet music. McCormack, in his dark suit and yellow tie, bulky as a grizzly bear, stood on her right as formally as if on a concert platform. She settled, and with all the composure she had absorbed from Sister Agatha at Teacher Training, played the opening bars. Then, when she nodded gently, McCormack began.

Panis Angelicus.
Fit panis hominum.

The great voice, with the power of gold, they said, could be heard, they said, at the weir four miles away, they said. And, listening, Thomas Kane sat with fingers splayed across his own lips in astonished pleasure. The children outside the window stood still. Essie, out of sight, froze her big body at this molten sound that seemed to hang in the air above the house and the garden. A man on the road with a pony stood like a statue of stone.

Ellen played the piano calmly, and now played on, in simple accompaniment to every note that was sung. Thomas Kane took his fingers away from his thin mouth, and he joined his hands in his lap as if in prayer. Lily McCormack, who had heard it all before, still sat transfixed. The last note lasted as long as a long kiss.

When it was over, McCormack bowed to his blushing accompanist: 'Mrs Kane, I can assure you, if ever you need a job as my pianist –'

The mundane man who drove the car arrived in time to say that the engine had been fixed and was now making a grand noise once again.

All evening, Thomas murmured in wonder, 'John McCormack? John McCormack in our house?' Twice he told Ellen the story of McCormack meeting Caruso.

'And he says to him, "And how is the world's greatest tenor today?" And do you know what Caruso said?

He said, "And since when did McCormack become a baritone?" Well, well. John McCormack? Singing in this house!' He laughed. 'We should be putting up a plaque.'

As they lay in bed, he stroked Ellen's shoulders over and over, down to her hips and back to her shoulders again, then stroked her spine with hands as soft as kindness.

'The excitement of it!' he said over and over. 'The honour. You played the piano for John McCormack. My wife!'

'You must tell the children how you feel,' she said.

'No. Oh, no! This is for you and me,' he replied in the darkness.

This, however, is how the Kane household heaved with pain and confusion. The following afternoon, even though still agog with stardust, Thomas addressed Helena ominously.

'But what was the name of the hymn he sang?' A Sunday visit had been paid to a distant farm.

Suddenly, all the others in the car fell silent. He asked again.

'I don't – remember, Daddy.' Helena's breath caught.

'What are you, a little fool? With your mouth hanging open? I'll ask you once more. What was – the name – of the hymn – Mr McCormack sang?'

Helena's lips contracted: she squeezed her fingers, and said tentatively, 'Was it "O Salutaris" – Daddy?'

'I'll give you "O Salutaris" when I get you home. You'll have your legs bared for me when we get out of this car tonight, Miss. Now – I'll ask you again? What was it?'

Helena shook her head wordlessly.

Thomas said to the windscreen, 'Are we rearing a complete fool? A clown? What are we wasting food on? Why are we feeding her?' He hissed on his teeth.

Grace nudged her mother's shoulder from behind, but Ellen did not intervene. Helena's face had turned completely white and not another word was spoken.

In the kitchen, the others sat at the table silent. Soon, Helena walked through them blindly. Her long white stockings were down: red marks faded from the backs of her legs. Even the small ones were silent as they heard her climbing the stairs.

Grace whispered fiercely, 'Mama, Mama, you should have stopped him doing it, he's always doing it, you should have stopped him.' No answer.

The Kanes once more ate a silent evening meal. Thomas did not appear in the kitchen for some time. When Ellen searched, she saw the light of his old carbide lamp in the garage: not a sound came forth: she peered through the crack and saw him merely sitting on an old chair.

Upstairs later, Ellen went to see Helena, who lay quietly in bed.

'Dear girl, aren't you undressing at all?' Helena had climbed under the blankets fully clothed, coat included. Ellen took her hand, and Helena tightened her grip so hard that Ellen had to ease it. She stroked her daughter's blonde hair over and over.

'Here. I've been keeping this for you.' She handed Helena *The Story of the Amulet* by E. Nesbit. 'This was my very own copy.'

Helena took it and put it under her pillow.

'Aren't you going to read it, love?'

'No, it'll only tell me what I'm missing in this house.'

Ellen stroked and stroked, saying, 'Shhh, now, shhhh, love, shhh. The hymn, by the way, was "Panis Angelicus". *Panis. Angelicus.* Will you remember that?'

'He told me while he was slapping my legs. He told me three times. Six words. Six slaps. *Panis. Angelicus.*' At last she began to weep. Ellen gathered her and sat with her in the dark until the girl fell asleep.

To change her own mood, Ellen went downstairs and washed socks, even though Essie tried to stop her. Then, finally, preparing for bed, she eyed Thomas.

'I never asked you, Thomas. Did you sleep well last night?'

He half-smiled. 'Last night? Like a log.'

'I bet,' she said, and chuckled to get his attention, 'I bet that there will be news soon from that department –' and waited until he turned.

'You can't tell that quickly, can you?' He reached forward and loosened her hair from the fixings at the back.

'What will we call it? I know I'm right. I've known with each of them.' She put her head on his chest. He grabbed her hand and held it.

'If it's a boy we'll call him – "McCormack",' he smiled.

She eased his hand away. 'Oooh, Thomas,' and rubbed her fingers. 'Don't you know your own strength?'

'Did I bruise you?' He looked down solicitously. Ellen shook her fingers loosely.

'You have such huge hands.'

He hugged her again. They lay.

'Thomas?'

'Nn-mm?'

'I know you are so anxious that the children use their intelligence, and that they know things. No!' she said panickily, 'Don't stiffen your body.'

He raised his head. 'Are you about to criticize me? I hope not.'

'Oh, Thomas! That dead voice you use, it's like steel.'

He rose quickly, put a cardigan over his pyjama jacket and clumped his way downstairs. Ellen still lay awake when he came to bed two hours later.

In the decade since Thomas's full recovery, the children's pattern had been established. At three o'clock, they had a meal after school; an hour's play afterwards, and then, until tea at half-past six, lessons with Thomas at which Ellen hovered.

'They must be ready for secondary school when the time comes,' he said frequently.

Age difference brought no concessions. Helena, aged eleven, was asked the same addition and subtraction as Grace aged nine, and down the line to all except the very youngest. Then came the learning by rote, in the manner of the period's education. Like Evensong, the Kane children could be heard at home, long after classes had ended, chanting tables and spellings. Thus they grew up sharing a high, if curiously uniform, standard of intelligence. Grace, alone, went beyond the mere recite-to-memorize, and showed the least fear of using her imagination. By and large, however, she, too, had to conform to the 'learn-it-off-by-heart' dogma drummed in by her father, and supported, apparently, by her mother.

No visitors were comfortably received in the house during the evenings of the school week. Afterwards, Thomas, and only Thomas, read the papers in front of the family; Ellen did the crossword when the children had gone to bed at night. As an extension of the education, Thomas read out news items he considered appropriate to their lives. In March, they all gasped at the fire in Texas which killed five hundred schoolchildren. In May, the *Hindenburg* exploded, and Thomas gave them the history of airships. From mid-June to the General Election in early July, he taught them the political process.

Grace asked, 'Who are you going to vote for, Daddy, is it Mr de Valera?'

Thomas looked hard at Ellen across the table. 'Tell her.'

Ellen said, 'Gracey, it is very bad manners to ask anyone whom they vote for.'

Occasionally the outside world arrived with the postman. In September, Father Peter Nolan in Wolverhampton, a friend of the Morris family – of Ellen's mother, in particular – sent Ellen one of the new English threepenny pieces. It sat propped up in a glass for all to admire, high above the tallest child's reach.

Apart from such bright bolts, outside matters came in so rarely and then under such control that anything worldly seemed magical. A film came to the school, dental care instruction: animated molars fought off black, pitchforked invaders called 'Bacteria'. In another ten minutes of flickering black-and-white, gap-toothed exotic children smiled up at Irish priests and nuns on Foreign Missions. For whose upkeep the girls delivered magazines such as *The Far East*, and travelled the parish to collect the subscriptions from the parishioners.

On one such journey, both girls saw a cow about to be serviced by a bull. The farmer had a rope around the bull's neck; the big wrinkled beast slipped and slid on the stone-flagged yard and the farmer winked at the girls, saying the bull needed 'a dose of coaxy-orum'. When they relayed their puzzled story at home, Helena and Grace had never seen their mother so angry; she forbade them to go near that farm again.

Next day, Ellen reconsidered her rage, using different justifications. She suggested to Thomas that, with Helena now eleven, perhaps it was time the two older girls began to meet more people.

'Why?'

'They need social development, too.'

'Why?'

She played one of her few good cards. 'Thomas, love, we can't have them looking backward. Helena'll be going to the convent in September. She'll have to get a chance of being accustomed to people outside the house.'

He looked up from the parlour table where he had been writing.

'They're never to talk about life in this house. Do they understand that? All those people would love to know our business.'

'Oh, they know that, Thomas, they're good girls. And anyway,' she added, 'I suppose they can't say anything if they have nothing to say.'

He looked at her sharply but made no comment.

'I'll start them cautiously,' she concluded. 'I'll watch carefully which houses they visit. They can run errands for me.'

In this way, Helena and Grace met Mrs Ulverton. Ellen sent them on a visit to an old brother-and-sister farm, where Rhona also called.

'Oh, by the way.' Rhona had an unconscious rhymer lying within her who sprang to life now and then. 'I brought you a bird, though Munch says I'm absurd.'

As Helena and Grace watched, amazed, this exotic, strangely-spoken woman, whom their mother knew, began to undo her blouse. Beneath lay a peach satin slip and some white, enormous arrangements. In the no man's land beneath her bosom and above her waist rested a large parcel wrapped in newspaper.

Feeling it, Rhona remarked, 'And it's still warm. You see, newspaper is so good to us all. If you want to keep cream cool wrap the jug in newspaper. If you want to keep a goose hot, ditto. That means the same, ditto means "the same", child,' she explained to Helena. Rhona had just killed a neighbour's gosling, but did not know whether such a young bird could be cooked.

'Here, help me,' and Helena, standing up, took the gosling from above Rhona's waist with all the ceremonial care of a doctor handing over a new-born baby.

'I use my greaseproof paper more than once, there's a good tip for you, child, the greasier it gets the more it insulates, and after all, it's all only food. Now, child, what is your name, pretty things you two, whose love-children are you?'

'Helena Kane, Ma'am.'

'And yours?'

'Grace Kane, Ma'am.'

'Ooh, good manners. Helena of Troy, and Grace and Favour, and how old are you both? Or should I say each?'

'I am eleven since last month.'

'I'm nine since April.'

'And so precise. Pretty children. That's *my* daughter – over there in mauve.' She indicated Viva, who waggled long fingers at them.

'Now,' Rhona sat and addressed the large cold farmhouse kitchen. 'I want to hear all your views on this bloody excommunication. Is there anything we can do about it, I mean can we stop it? It is barbaric.' Neighbours shuffled.

At which moment, the woman of the house, thick spectacles gleaming in the lamplight, ushered the girls out of the house and sent them home with eggs for their mother.

Unfortunately for Ellen's new scheme to widen the girls' horizons, Thomas met them at the door.

'What new words did you learn?'

Grace, still as excited at Mrs Ulverton as if she had seen a parrot, blurted, 'We heard "bloody excommunication". And we heard "barbaric". That's all, we knew all the other words. Oh, and we were asked whose "love-children" we were?'

'Fetch your mother,' said Thomas.

He asked the girls to repeat the words to Ellen. She contrived to have the girls expand the context.

'I won't have it,' exploded Thomas. 'That woman will fill their heads with Protestant ideas.'

Ellen traded again, and won. 'As long as they know we're right,' she said. 'The wrong views of others will only reinforce their faith.'

Then she lost, by not thinking ahead.

'In that case,' said grim Thomas, 'they had better all come to the excommunication.'

'Oh, Thomas!' She bit her lip.

'Yes?' he asked unbrookingly.

'It – it used to be a very harshly worded business.'

'All the better. Remember – "the fear and love of God", the fear is important too.'

'Even the little ones.'

'Oh, yes, oh, yes. No question. They'll remember it all their lives.'

Ceremonies cemented the church's power. To practical effect. The children's First Holy Communion every year boosted retail trade: new dresses and veils, new suits and shoes. Confirmation every three years brought a state visit from the Archbishop, with local catering. Occasionally the Church received a golden opportunity to demonstrate its darker authority.

=

Archbishop Edward Ahern, and his Administrator, Monsignor Tom Kelly, sat like cassocked impresarios.

'The bigger the church the wider the message, your Grace?'

'Yes, Thomas.'

'Therefore, Mooreville. And – early in the Mass, middle or late, your Grace? Canon Law leaves it open.'

Edward Ahern said, 'The latter, I think.'

Monsignor Kelly, who was a pedant, replied, 'By that, your Grace, do you mean the last-named of the three? "The latter" can only be one of two, it is a construction very like "the alternative". Do you see what I mean?'

'Yes, Thomas. I mean, as late as possible. After the last Gospel, even.'

'Yes, your Grace, yes.' He approved. 'Yes. Yes. But they won't be away until nearly one o'clock? And after half-eleven Mass, isn't that a bit long?'

'No longer than on Easter Sunday, Thomas. Or a Confirmation,' replied Edward Ahern.

Powerful psychology: the Monsignor beckoned an altarboy to remove all flowers. Edward Ahern watched from a throne to one side. The small Monsignor began to excommunicate Joan Merrigan whom Cyril Stephenson had at last married.

'A child of this Archdiocese has placed herself outside the fold.'

The candles on the altar had been doused; the crucifix draped.

'Her name is Josephine Brigid Merrigan, known as Joan Merrigan. She abandoned Mother Church for selfish reasons, namely to marry a non-Catholic.'

All sacred vessels had been ostentatiously removed from the altar.

112

'Thereby she allied herself to a man who can never see the face of God. And now Mother Church, after many efforts to have the child reconciled, will abandon her, and reject her.'

The clappers on the sanctuary handbell were bound in black crepe cloth.

'She will be consigned to the exterior darkness. On her deathbed she will not receive the consolation of the Blessed Sacraments, nor the valedictory comfort of Extreme Unction.'

No sunlight activated the colours on the stained-glass windows.

'She will not pray with her family, nor will there be a place of welcome for her children within these walls, they will not exist in the sight of God. As she has chosen to put herself distant from God, so He now chooses to forget her.'

The little Administrator paused, wiped his brow. Congregants in the front pews looked only at their hands or at the floor. The altar-boys in their scarlet and white sat still.

'If she calls for God He will not hear her. Though she writhe with agony on her deathbed, or in all the days of her life, He will not ease her pain. Though she kneel and plead with Him, He will not heed her. For her there will be no Communion of Saints. For her there will be no glimpse of the sight of God. That is what the word of Holy Mother Church, the term "Excommunication" means. The word of God.'

Not for years had so many people packed this church. Nobody coughed. Archbishop Edward Ahern held his crozier at a powerful slant.

'Let me repeat her name: Josephine Brigid Merrigan, known as Joan. She is no longer a member of this Church or Catholic community. She is shunned by God, by His Blessed Mother, by Saint Joseph and all the Saints. Her prayers no longer have efficacy; they no longer go up to Heaven. A murderer, provided he show contrition and do penance, will have a greater chance of passing through the gate of Heaven than Joan Merrigan will henceforth.'

A tear rolled down Ellen's face; Helena caught her breath; Grace looked across at her father on the outside of the pew.

'And it is His wish that her former community, embracing her family, her parents, brothers, sisters, nieces and nephews. And her new neighbours in that part of the archdiocese to which she has now removed herself. It is God's wish that they become aware that she has been decreed by God unfit for our society. That is also what "Excommunication" means.'

Grace and Helena shifted. The younger Kanes snuggled under Ellen's sleeve. Thomas sat upright, his eyes never leaving the face of the Administrator, his head a gleam of austerity.

'Josephine Brigid Merrigan, known as Joan, is hereby excommunicated. And to you, my dear brethren, gathered here this morning in the love of God, I say this. Even though it is not technically a sin, if you find yourself consorting with an excommunicated person, it would be as well to seek your confessor's advice. As the proverb has it, you cannot touch tar and not be blackened. Let us kneel and pray for her poor, unfortunate soul.'

In the Kane car, mother and children spoke not at all.

Thomas said, 'Well. There you are. She would not listen to anyone. She thought she was right. She would not take heed. And that is what happens to people who do not take heed. Are you listening?' He addressed his remarks over

114

his shoulder to the children in the back of the car. Nobody replied.

'I said. Are you listening?'

Grace ventured, 'Yes, Daddy. We are.'

'And what did I say?'

'You said, "That is what happens to people who do not take heed."'

'Good girl. And what is it that happens to people who do not take heed? They get excommunicated. What happens?'

Grace replied, 'They get excommunicated.'

'Are you the only one back there with a tongue in your head, Miss?'

Helena, alerted, murmured, 'No, Daddy.'

At two o'clock, the Winers came, Leah still gesturing in argument with Herbert on the unfairness of his never learning to drive.

'And I, Ellen, I! I. Look. My hands! I have to drive all the time. I have to turn the starting-handle.'

She subsided with the mood she found.

'The children have had a shock,' whispered Ellen to Leah. 'We had this excommunication today. It was very grisly and upsetting.'

'But why did you take them?'

Ellen evaded.

Leah took the hint and declared, 'An outing.' She called. 'Girls. Girls. Best feet forward, we're going for a drive.'

The Grey Valley represented some kind of collective memory for the locality, a wild place, of strangeness and ancestry. At its deepest it had sheer sides of limestone, haunted in summer by strangers on bicycles with sketch-

pads, or small hammers and satchels. They captured the
gentians and whins in their purples and yellows; they
hacked serene fossils from the ripples of shale that shelved
like an ebbed beach down to the gorse.

Shaped like an upturned, three-quarters-open fist, the
valley cradled thirty or so houses. Those dwellings from
which children had done well in America had been able to
continue thatching their roofs. Others yielded to cheaper
measures – mainly corrugated, galvanized iron. All maintained their colour codes of ages past: russet-washed walls,
or *belle-époque* red, or whitewash, or deep green, or
mauve, or bluewash.

Leah, Ellen and the girls climbed from the car and
stretched. Grace ran ahead, then turned back and said,
'Oh, Mama, why didn't I bring my paints. Look!'

Helena, a book omnipresent under her arm, trotted
after Grace into the wooded interior, and the two women
strolled the path behind them.

No invader, not even Cromwell, had violated the Grey
Valley, and Deanstown people rarely told outsiders that
it existed. Those bicycling summer strangers, in their
khaki shorts or billowing flowered dresses, had read of it
botanically or geologically, in specialist publications. The
Natural History Museum in Dublin still displayed the
great honey-coloured ammonite found there in 1907. An
English botanist claimed that the Grey Valley had a micro-
climate.

'The thing is. If you look at Herbert. We never used
to differ.' Leah clenched her fists. 'But he has changed,
Ellen: he's changed.'

'My father always says that men aren't generally well-
known at all, that they're very different inside themselves.'

Houses in the valley contained priceless handmade

116

furniture that had been built-in over two to three hundred years. Kitchen dressers still had chickens in the open-drawered compartment beneath, straw peeping out between the slats. One wall-bed, which folded out by night, had been made in 1598, and the maker's adze-marks still ridged through the generations of pink lead paint.

'And did you ever think,' asked Leah rhetorically, 'that you would hear me say what I'm going to say now? I'm going to say that we'd have been happier while we were still poor.'

'Of course,' said Ellen, 'men want to earn, don't they, they want to earn the things they have.'

In the deep, foggy wood, Helena and Grace called to each other.

Grace chanted, 'Bliss-bliss-bliss-bliss. Bliss-bliss-bliss-bliss.'

Helena chased Grace, then hid, then frightened her from behind and they chased again. Then Helena dropped her book, reached up and began to swing from a bare old elm branch.

On the valley's floor, beneath the greenery, rock formations had created areas like ice floes. Leaves piled in a bronze mulch. As the girls ran on, the women walked the dark pathways to the interior, and eventually lapsed into silence, savouring the peace of this foggy oasis.

6

In his three chosen lives, Dennis Sykes matured quickly. The partnership had huge and essential contracts from the War Office and assigned him, as promised, to Reserved Occupations: he designed airfields and hangars; he engineered the secret bunkers to which the politicians would retreat if Hitler got across the Channel. On his private circuit, his value increased as husbands vanished into the maw of the burgeoning war. Indeed, on one significant day, he was the only man under fifty when Royal Wimbledon hosted Moor Park in their annual fourball.

And for the secret life, Binnie remained a sufficient receptacle. He had met her just before his twenty-sixth birthday, and, infections excepted, their heavings had continued apace. As she had asked, he kept his suburban pathfinding hidden from her, unless he wished to taunt her. His barbs always took comparative form: he would look at her body thoughtfully and say, 'I sometimes wonder . . .'

'What, Dennis?'

'Nothing.'

'C'mon.'

'Nothing.'

'Come ON!'

'Well – whether I like the more, the more, well, the fuller bodies I meet?'

'You are such a little shit!' – but it drew tears.

—

Prostitutes rarely figured again: he had adjusted his revenges and found how to satisfy them in his London and Home Counties 'social' life. Then, in mid-September 1942, Dennis began to discover the pleasures of broader horizons. The war swung between the RAF bombing Dusseldorf and Bremen, and Hitler laying siege to Stalingrad. With pride the firm appointed DS to their most secret project.

'Possible necessary relocation of ultra secure building,' said his mentor, now the Managing Director. 'Deep under Stirlingshire or Ayrshire, perhaps the eastern Borders. Should the Americans fail Europe, Herr Hitler's jackboots could grow seven-league status. Scotland's farther away.'

Binnie fidgeted. 'Well, darling, mission accomplished around these parts, eh? The chaps say, according to your reports, that you're "A man's man", and the gels say, "He really likes women". Talk about having it both ways, but not fully. Dennzy, dear, don't ever go sweet, will you? Never go pink?'

'No fear,' said Dennis, 'no fear.'

'Are you sure? You're for ladies, darling, not for men.'

'Sure.'

'Sure as eggs is *ova*, darling? Speaking of which.'

Binnie had three abortions during her intensive two years with Dennis. Each time he wrote what she called 'a respectable cheque'.

Before they left the restaurant, Binnie said, 'Top of the tree, now, little Dennis, darling.'

He asked what she meant.

'Well it's one thing, darling, to pierce the hearts of all these creatures in the Home Counties. But Scots ladies are different, purer. And the Scottish gentlemen, they watch their wives as closely as they watch their money.

They see them as their chattels, Dennzy, darling. So –
big challenges for a little boy.'

Binnie bag-of-bones, with her smoker's cough, rinsed out
by abortions, alcohol her dominant body fluid, outlived
Dennis. A rasping, pink-flannelette, Bette Davis look-
alike, she slumps today in one of those Home Counties
homes called The Cedars or The Pines. When Dennis's
obituary appeared in *The Times*, she held it up to a friend.
  'I used to know him. Unhappy little fella. Never
pretended it, though.'

After six months' research in Edinburgh, with secret
briefings back in London, Dennis, under orders, moved
into the countryside. In the Cheviot Hills, at Mervinslaw
near Hawick, he found Iain and Mona Nicolson. They had
no children and a calm household. The Agriculture and
Fisheries Department, Dennis's 'cover', preferred its
'operatives' to stay with 'approved' local people. Given
the powerful nature of his work, the hosts had to know
what secrecy meant, or ideally have 'official' experience.
  Ten years earlier, Iain Nicolson had come home from
'Government security' in Africa. While he supervised the
finances on the Mervinslaw estate, he met and married
Mona, a secretarial factotum for the Countess of
Mervinslaw. Her mistress was a lady-in-waiting to the
King and Queen when in Scotland: Balmoral for the summer holiday, functions at Holyrood House. These required
that Mona stayed once a year in Edinburgh; otherwise, she
and Iain had not spent a night apart in their clockwork and
rigorous marriage. They were fifty and thirty-eight when
they met Dennis Sykes, who, within weeks, had begun to
divide the couple as never before.

—

Husband and wife both liked him; to each other they spoke of him enthusiastically. Iain Nicolson's resentful nature eased because Dennis was the same small height; Iain had also found a male talking companion for his 'six-o'clock dram'. Mona saw in Dennis, rare object, a man interested in clothes and furniture, in flowers, even, and society gossip. And he knew so many people, discussed names she had only read in magazines.

On his third week (Dennis never rushed things, no need) in their large, stone, dormer-windowed house, Dennis said to Mona (out of Iain's earshot), 'If you don't think it impertinent of me, that colour suits you.'

Mona looked down at her blouse, plucked it out a little to inspect. 'H'm? Some people say green's unlucky.'

'Works with your hair,' he said, 'that tinge there,' as he pointed vaguely to the brushed wings of grey.

Mona, after that pause in which the hesitator is lost, said, 'Iain never notices things.'

Dennis practised his look of surprise. 'Not even – you?'

Mona might have blushed, but took it in her stride. 'Maybe if we lived in the city?' she said. 'Iain's not a city man.'

'Full many a flower is born to blush unseen,' murmured Dennis. He then allowed Mona to see him stare at her breasts. Next day, she dressed less austerely.

Dennis had learned well. He initiated with Mona conversations which dwelt on the senses. When he brought up the subject of touch, he said, 'Let me see your hands.'

Mona showed, and Dennis was careful to look, not touch.

He murmured, 'I have a doctor friend who believes that the hands [Dennis held out his own] can cure anything.' (He had no such friend, and apart from Binnie's

Edmund, did not even know a doctor, had not met one since breathlessness at university.)

Whenever he thanked Mona – for food, or a fresh towel – he spoke quietly, so that the softness of his voice obliged her to draw a little closer. When alone with her in the house, indeed when addressing her, he looked first at Mona's mouth, and then straight into her eyes.

Above all, he made her laugh: 'I heard that Lady Milly Haig has a wooden leg and that she has her maid polish it with furniture wax.'

Mona changed a little, confusing Iain. She had her hair altered and Iain did not like the new hairstyle; he licked disapprovingly upwards at his moustache.

Dennis said brightly next evening, 'I met a man today, don't know his name, he was *very* complimentary about your wife when he heard where I was staying.'

Iain Nicolson blinked. 'Oh aye?'

That night, he snapped at Mona – in front of Dennis.

Next morning, Iain long since gone to work, Dennis said, 'None of my business, but is Iain, is he a bit, well – ?'

She said, 'Moody? Yes, snappy. Wee men are a bit like that, aren't they?'

'Me too?' he asked with a grin. She shook her head; he saw that she did not find the subject amusing.

'Like Napoleon?' wondered Dennis. In the kitchen he sniffed the wind near her. 'What's that perfume? What's it called?'

For the following week, he paid Mona no attention, allowed himself to be utterly absorbed in his work, smiled vaguely at meals, deep in papers. In due course, he apologized for his preoccupations.

Mona came to breakfast one morning in – for her – a completely unprecedented white sweater.

Iain looked at the sweater, at her. 'Can you work in

that?' She did not answer. Dennis's eyes licked the sweater – then he turned to Iain earnestly for 'advice' on the size of a local laird he was about to meet.

Iain drank twice as much as usual that evening, called Mona 'foolish' in a discussion about the war, and went brusquely to bed. Dennis raised a sympathetic eyebrow.

Within two more days, Dennis was touching Mona's elbow as he poured her evening drink, before 'sharing' some of his work questions with Iain. Two weeks afterwards, Dennis stayed in bed untypically late. Shortly after he heard Iain leave for work, Mona rapped gently at Dennis's door; 'Would you like a cup of tea?'

He made room for her to sit on the bed, and they talked. A week later, Iain went to Stirling for the day, leaving in the very early morning. Dennis again received tea.

On the day Dennis left Mervinslaw three weeks later, Iain took his leave of him and wished him well. At the front door an hour later, Dennis said to Mona, 'Do you, ah, do you ever – have occasion to be in – I mean, what I'm asking is, do you know Glasgow?'

She looked away and said, 'Ah'm, I have a friend there, whom I haven't seen for a while –'

Dennis asked, while also looking into the distance, 'What's – what's the best, I mean, the best way of, you know – of, well, getting in touch with you? Do you still answer the Countess's phone?'

'In the mornings, yes.'

He took both her hands, and with tenderness kissed her twice, just each side of her mouth. 'I will, as you know, be writing a note, but, I mean – to both of you.'

She nodded in understanding; he released her hands and walked to his car.

He telephoned: Mona failed to find Dennis at the rendezvous he gave. This was not surprising. On that promised evening, he had gone back to Mervinslaw, where, over a drink, he asked Iain Nicolson whether he could have seen Mona in Glasgow, no, he must be mistaken? Dennis had had his own studio photograph taken, and in the next breath he presented a copy to Iain, who put it on the sideboard with warmth.

Dennis contacted Mona at the Glasgow rendezvous, apologized most tenderly, blamed 'matters hush-hush', laid another false trail, kept her from home a second consecutive night, never met her. She came back flustered, and with badly-delivered excuses. Small Iain became a suspicious man, especially when Mona received a postcard from Glasgow with just a '!' on the back. It took the Nicolsons some time to repair their marriage.

7

The parish held pagan oddities. For generations, the Shea family owned a healing stone that never dried, dripped eternal moisture. Over in Corrbridge, a yellow light swooped across the sky when a Clinton died anywhere in the world. Bede Regan had a potion to cure ringworm in animals and children; he got it from his friend, Chief Burning Cloud, in Wyoming where they had worked on the railways. Look at that Carney woman. One fight with Peter Gleeson, and Peter Gleeson lost his whole herd of calves. Those animals died like flies the day after the Carney woman was seen running through them at dawn scattering ashes.

Oddly, this spirit of otherness, of superstition, preserved the two Stephenson mansions. In the years after the Civil War, many such great houses fell in flames all over the country. Pub talk, and old rebel songs, aroused clandestine arsonists who, on their way home at night, reduced much of the Ascendancy to embers.

Not in Deanstown. A respect, born of eerie wariness, prevailed towards that family up there on the ridge. In the Wallaces and the Stephensons something strange had always run. The hallway of the dower house (now Rhona Ulverton's) was once filled with long, striped masks, and drums, and spears with tufts. Someone had seen an angry little human head on a mantelpiece. There was a leg-bone lying in a glass case.

Even that farmland felt queer: two fairy forts; an old cemetery; and how come they had more mushrooms in their bottom field than the rest of the parish? Walk through the Ulvertons' woods to this day and you will see trees with two different growths sprouting like Siamese twins from the same bole. Nobody had sufficient lore of flora to understand that Rhona's ancestor, the great amateur botanist Captain Wallace, had merely grafted and budded in fits of spring fever. An oak still bloomed there last year with camellia-like flowers; and a lilac with the red tight buds of japonica.

Consequently, such a rite as excommunication fitted them. 'Look at that Mrs Ulverton,' clucked the village. 'Was she related to them other Protestants, the Maudes,' they wondered, 'where the devil stuck every deathbed to the wall?'

See her hooked-ish nose, the purple lipstick, her scarab ring? That devil's-head walking-stick contained poison in the prongs of the horns.

Rhona, unwittingly, contributed to this view of the family's bent towards quasi-sorcery.

'I can fly,' she told homegoing schoolchildren. They believed her. 'But I am not in the mood this minute, I'm not wearing the right-coloured clothes. Watch out, though, when I'm wearing vermilion.' She pulled a string of yellow chiffon from her open mouth, made a coin disappear completely and then found it in her shoe, blew cigarette smoke from her ears.

'In India,' she told them, 'I grew up watching the fakirs. Did you notice how I pronounced the word?' Only one grinned.

'Smart boy wanted, eh?' said Rhona to him sideways.

She resumed. 'Those fakirs – they knew how to climb

126

a rope and disappear. Stop here tomorrow,' she instructed, 'and I'll show you.'

As they walked along the road towards her next day, she waved a pull-out set of six dangly postcards. Between the first and the final picture, the fakir climbed the rope and vanished.

'I can do that,' she said, pointing to the rope-trick, 'my nickname at school in India used to be "Magic", I was known as "Magic Wallace". But I need jodhpurs to climb a rope. Otherwise everybody would be, wouldn't they, looking up under my skirt and seeing my knickers.'

The children dissolved into giggles.

When Mrs Ulverton became friendly with Mrs Kane, Deanstown whistled in surprise. Until Mrs Hand recalled that well – didn't Mrs Kane always after all sprinkle the crops with Easter water on John's Eve, cause being she found eggshells in the potato ridges one year, someone trying to steal the crop? And she had, after all, taken her comatose husband to a healer with stone amulets in north Cork. The stones failed. But a cure is like fork-lightning, they said – you never know if it will hit.

The excommunication predisposed Ellen towards the Ulvertons and Stephensons. In this, justice, kindness, humanity, diluted her usual religious loyalties. Her feelings intensified after a conversation which produced a surprise from Thomas.

On their return from the Grey Valley that evening, the girls scattered. Herbert and Leah, with Thomas sitting by, listened carefully to Ellen's account of the morning's terrible rite. Ellen quoted: 'It is God's wish that they become aware that she has been decreed by God as unfit for our society. That is also what "Excommunication" means.'

Herbert, considerably shocked, summarized. 'To be an outcast. Terrible.'

Thomas looked at him carefully.

'Think of it,' said Herbert slowly, fixing his skull-cap yet again. 'Think, Thomas. If you could not face that village tomorrow in case you loved someone. That girl might love that man she married. What does it matter so long as he's a decent human being? I mean to say, I mean to say. Look at what's happening to us. I mean to say, under Adolf Hitler.'

'Why give such a man his full name?' whispered Leah.

Thomas respected, and may even have feared, Herbert's calm wisdom.

Ellen asked, 'Should we do something?'

Herbert replied, 'Such an ordeal. Do you know them?'

Ellen shook her head. 'They don't mix at all. You know. Protestants. But – they're not from here, they're from India.'

'Ordeal?' echoed Thomas. 'That's an interesting way of looking at it.'

In bed, Ellen murmured, 'What could we do? About the Stephensons, I mean.'

Thomas surprised her. 'Well,' he said slowly, 'that elderly woman, Mrs Ulverton. Talk to her.'

Ellen swivelled her head. 'But – but I thought you didn't like her?'

'Herbert knows what he's talking about.'

'He does, doesn't he?' admired Ellen. 'He's not a bit vague.'

Ellen, characteristically, spoke up.

'Strange that we've never met. But we never see you or your family out anywhere?'

'No.' Rhona wore an old black riding-coat, and a long ivory skirt.

The women connected immediately. A week after that conversation with Herbert, Leah and Thomas, Ellen set out for the Ulverton house, heavily noticeable in her 'John McCormack' pregnancy.

In a shower of rain, she stood under a tree. Suddenly, like a figure from a dream, Munch Ulverton loped across the fields. He bowed while striding, and carried on past her. Ellen next heard the woman's voice calling 'Munch! Munchin!' and on the brow of the hill Rhona appeared, trying to shake life into a crazy umbrella. She came down the hill more spryly than Ellen would have imagined. Near the tree she stopped, and looked askance.

'My son.' She indicated the fleeing figure. 'He will catch cold. He's used to a hotter climate. I can't chase him, I'm sixty-three.'

'Step in here and shelter,' said Ellen, making way. 'You'll catch cold yourself.'

Rhona lowered the umbrella and walked so directly to Ellen, and with such hard intent, that for a split second Ellen feared the tall woman would strike her. Instead Rhona held out her hand in greeting.

'So – your manners are as sweet as your looks. That is the first word of kindness anyone has spoken to us in the last three months.'

'No?' said Ellen in disbelief, and then corrected herself, 'Oh, of course, the excommunication.'

Rhona looked down at her. 'The forbidden word? You dare use it?'

'It was all – unfair,' said Ellen. 'Uncharitable.'

'But aren't you Queen Catholic around here?' said Rhona.

'I'm not.' Ellen blushed. 'I only pretend to be, but you

129

mustn't ever tell anybody. I have to be like that for the children's sake. I found the excommunication – I found it so unkind. Unkind. And indecent.'

'You're very open.'

'I amn't always.'

'Only my grandmother ever said "amn't". If you're going to be open with your secrets – well, you can completely trust me.'

'I guessed that,' said Ellen.

'Here's my secret. Or one of them. We have no money,' said Rhona, 'and we're often hungry, and now we have no credit. Since the "excomm." as we call it. That's why we never met, that's why we never see anyone. We have no means of returning hospitality. I used to entertain all the time in India. D'you imagine how I feel now? Here? Penniless? I was reared for entertaining, for being a hostess – it was what I was. Now I can't even sit by myself at my own table.'

'Why can't you?' The shower passed by. Lemon sunlight broke through.

'I've had nothing to eat for three days.'

Ellen said, 'What?! My God in Heaven!'

'I mean it. Last week too we didn't eat for three days.'

'Can't your daughter get a job? Or you?'

'No one hires Protestants like us. You know that. You look embarrassed, you shouldn't be. Everyone has secrets, even you have.'

Ellen took the big decision: she spoke her besetting concern. 'I know. I can't get my husband to be calmer.' Then she bit her lip, stuck it out as a preliminary to tears.

'It's all right, oh, it's all right.' Rhona laid a hand on the younger woman's arm. 'What am I to call you? I'm not going to call you Mrs Kane, are you Eleanor?'

'Ellen.'

'Perhaps your husband is a lonely man? Does anything work?'

Ellen swallowed the tears and replied, 'And I want to bring my children up, I mean, I want to rear them well. I want them innocent for as long as I can, I want them merry. And nice to people. Yes, innocent.'

'My grandmother,' said Rhona, 'believed that love and affection were better than a warm bath.'

'Now, today for example, my husband, he's in better humour because he got a gift in the post of something he's never had before, a box of cigars.'

'Oh! Oh!' Rhona exclaimed. 'Bless you, bless you! Oh!' She halted in recollection. 'Of course today is the eleventh of the eleventh, I knew something would go right when the numbers lined up.'

Ellen asked with a half-laugh, 'What is it, I mean, what's the –?'

'Will you meet me here next week?' asked Rhona, moving away.

'I will.'

'Same place, same time?'

'Yes.' Ellen still looked puzzled.

'Cigars! Cigars! Have you magic powers, or what?'

Ellen laughed. 'Lord, if only I had. Cigars, though?'

Rhona stalked off, still speaking. 'By the way – that brown coat doesn't suit you. And the next time we meet don't give the impression you're trying to please me, you don't have to, I like you.'

Ellen said, 'Now I don't know where to look.'

Rhona, from a few feet away, the grass wet at her feet, spun around and said, 'Do you really want something to think about?'

Ellen cocked her head to one side like a puzzled bird.

'Think about my son,' said Rhona, 'my dear beloved

131

son, Munch. I think he's mad. I mean – insane. If he is,
I shall be so hurt.'

Their five and a half years in Deanstown had brought the
Ulvertons no influence. Nothing had happened in their
lives. So much for Rhona's brave political words. Her greatest fear – that they would dwindle into friendlessness – had
been coming true. The excommunication hastened it.

Lack of money controlled everything. Henry Wallace,
tighter than wire, helped not at all. Instead, he and his wife
hovered five miles away, watching, poised to buy any
remaining heirloom: the famous silver humidor, say, or the
Meissen tea-service. So far, Rhona defied her brother and
avaricious sister-in-law, with some desperate scraping. A
small batch of Tate & Lyle shares came via Trinidad, a
remote great-aunt's bequest. Residual colonial pension
payments on her long-dead husband arrived out of the blue
as a result of a clerical error made in London.

Once or twice, in hunger, her stomach plunged almost
down to danger point, to inanition. She awoke one morning dizzy, her hands not gripping. Natural foods were out
of season; mushrooms and fruits long over. All credit in
Mooreville had vanished; the shopkeepers there, ultimate
insult, had even stopped asking for repayment once they
knew of the intended excommunication.

Somehow, some desperate how, Rhona conjured food.
She found a box of apples in hay; she stole a winter hoard
of nuts from a tree. 'Bugger the squirrels,' she told Viva,
'our need is greater.'

Late that week, a straying heifer fell in an adjoining
ditch and died; the farmer could not be bothered to
recover it; Rhona bartered with the butcher – he could
have a quarter of the beast in return for his work. Did
she lure or chase the animal to its death? Nobody could

prove anything – yet, on neighbouring farms they strengthened their fences.

As to cigars – she rushed up the terraced lawn calling to Viva.

'Dress! Pack! Quick!' That evening, Rhona sold her mother's Georgian hairbrushes to Henry and his wife. On pawn principles – to be redeemed or not, and she fought off their protests. By way of revenge, Munch was billeted on Henry for three days.

Rhona and Viva took the train from Goolds Cross. En route, she explained to Viva.

'Your grandfather had a remarkable taste in cigars. He had a box at Hound's. I had forgotten.'

Mr Lusk at Hound's fetched a ledger. The record had been maintained intact. When David Wallace died in 1910, Hound's had held exactly a hundred and eleven pounds' worth of cigars in his box.

'Good omen,' said Viva, who also liked these things. 'One, one, one – again.'

Mr Lusk had the jelly eyes of the inquisitive. He spread the papers on the glorious wood of the counter.

'Now, the position is this now. When the late Mr Wallace died without having given us instructions as to what should become of his cigars, we waited a decent interval and we sold them now. A decent interval. Are ye married yeerselves, girls?'

'You sold them?' boomed Rhona.

'If we kept them, Ma'am, they'd have gone like all humanity, dust to dust now. But hold on, hold on.' Mr Lusk had the patience of men in old purveying trades. 'We didn't know the first thing about what to do. We wrote to the widow, and we even sent a letter around by hand – d'you see?'

Mr Lusk pointed to brown-ink entries made in the ledger. 'But, out of grief or what now, we'll never know, the poor woman never replied.'

Rhona knew why: alcoholic haze.

'So the money sat here now, so it did, accumulating at the rate of somewhere between a fluctuating three-quarters to one and a quarter per-cent-per-annum.'

'Where is the cigar money now and whose is it?' asked Rhona.

Mr Lusk beamed; a good-natured man, Mr Lusk, with a cyst on his forehead.

'Oh, 'tis here, Ma'am, and now – 'tisn't ours so 'tisn't. 'Twill be in the Ledger. We do it every half-year.' He hauled again at the huge marbled book and hummed a 'yah-de-dah-de-dah-de-dah' under his breath. 'We do always round up or down to the nearest pound. To this very day. And now you'd be surprised how it comes out even in the long run. We'd be half a guinea up on one year and the next year we'd be half a guinea down, now we do always say 'tis the same half-guinea.'

Rhona, tiring, said, 'I daresay it is. But – is there money? Now?'

'If you're the heir. The heiress, I suppose, although these days you can't be too careful.' He stubbed a big finger and read, 'Wallace, David Warrington Jasper, San Giovanni, Sandycove: accumulated to end of financial year, 1937, that is to say, April 4th; six hundred and eighty-six pounds.'

And from Mr Lusk, as to be expected, 'And you'll notice now – no shillings nor no pence.'

'The money doesn't work,' said Viva, 'at between three-quarters and one-and-a-quarter per cent interest, even if you compound it. On a hundred and eleven pounds it

134

wouldn't be that much.' Today her hair looked like a schoolmarm's.

'Ah, Miss.' Another thing about Mr Lusk: he had letters after his name in finger-wagging. 'The cigars now – they were worth a hundred and eleven pounds the way the original gentleman, the original Mr Wallace, paid for them. But the year he died wasn't there some sort of a row in the international trade markets and you couldn't get Cuban cigars for all the tea in China, that's a joke we have here, Ma'am,' he explained to Rhona. 'And now a gentleman in the Vice-Regal Lodge, he said he'd pay what we asked that we thought fair, and he paid four hundred and forty pounds for the whole box. A good investment. So the interest is on that, not the hundred and eleven. D'you get me, like?'

'We get you. Like.' Rhona proved her identity, an ancient passport, in her maiden name. Mr Lusk said, 'We'll draw up a cheque, Ma'am, and we'll send it round to the hotel. I s'pose you're in the Hibernian.'

On the street, Rhona said, 'I'm exhausted.'

Simultaneously, each said tenderly to the other, 'Don't cry.'

They clasped hands. 'The worst thing has been not being able to tell anyone,' said Viva.

'No, the worst thing has been not being able to feed my two dear children,' said Rhona. 'Now, I need to buy some powder, have you enough scent, dear Viva?'

Deep in some kind of gratitude, they stood quietly, self-effacingly, on the street for a moment, the two tallest women in Dublin that day.

Rhona came home to Deanstown, and clawed back the Georgian hairbrushes from her brother Henry: 'Never you mind where I got the money!'

She kept her appointment with Ellen. For an afternoon hour the women strolled back and forth in the same patch of field, near the same tree. Behind them, the dower house with its colonial portico smiled through the woods. Rhona told her cigar story; Ellen exclaimed. Then Rhona stooped to listen. Out in the open fields, with no apparent context, the two women absorbed each other. One, tall and aristocratic, and vividly dressed, carried a silver-topped cane; the other, small, bulged almost outlandishly in her pregnancy.

'How is your husband? Is he – well?'

Ellen said, 'The main problem is – I'm no more than a kind of a go-between.'

'Explain, my dear.'

None of the children asked Thomas directly for anything they needed. Few of them spoke openly or straight to him: none easily.

Cash for schoolbooks: 'Mama, tell Daddy I need –'

Pocket-money for an outing: 'Mama, the school is going to Dublin for the Spring Show, and we've to bring five shillings for the bus and the whole day –'

'Aha,' said Rhona. 'It's like the king who will listen to one courtier only – and only in private.'

'That's a good way of putting it,' agreed Ellen, 'but they all assume that the court chancellor, that's me, will get all their favours granted.'

'I don't like men when they won't be friendly,' said Rhona. 'Dear girl – you need a *modus vivendi*, you do.'

'A way of living?' Ellen the teacher could not stop herself translating. 'Do I?'

'You need a means of surviving your poor husband's lack of rationale. May I think? Look! I knew that goose was laying!' In the grass she found a small cache of big eggs and stowed them in her skirt pockets.

Ellen said, 'I am taking a terrible risk. He hates anyone talking about him, in any way whatsoever.'

Rhona pointed to herself dramatically. 'I have been called a marble mausoleum. My secrets die with me.'

'I live,' said Ellen, 'in the fear that something awful is about to happen.'

'Anxiety. My husband suffered from it. How many children have you? I've lost count, I mean how many beyond those two lovely girls?'

'Before you go,' said Ellen. She led Rhona to the hedge-row, where a napkin-wrapped parcel lay among the nettles like Moses in his basket. 'Three others, and this one invoiced': Ellen patted her stomach.

'What's this?' asked Rhona.

'I'm a lovely baker they tell me,' said Ellen, without immodesty. 'These two are my best. There's a meat pie and a gooseberry tart.'

'I will eat them with pleasure. Thank you.'

They had parted when Rhona called out, 'Don't forget one thing. You have a rare natural gift – of affection. It'll carry you through anything.'

Inventively, the two women found many means of seeing each other. Thomas was appeased by references to the excommunication: 'I suppose it's a good thing to show people we're not all savages.'

To Ellen the relationship became vital, because it repeated a pattern: it re-ran the Mrs Greege experience. In the doldrums of those awful early days and weeks after Thomas's shooting, the house plummeted into near-squalor. Hidden behind her locked gate, nobody witnessed Ellen's weeks of unwashed hair, the same clothes day after day, a baby infrequently bathed and changed.

Then, Herbert Winer visited intuitively. The tender provocativeness of his enquiries first led Ellen to recognize the frailty of her situation. He directed her to find resources within herself, rather than within piety.

Herbert spoke gently but at length. Herbert pointed out her isolation. Herbert urged her to seek help from a senior woman. Herbert ruled her mother out; May Morris's need for attention would have diverted the concentration from where it was needed.

Ellen wrote in her housekeeping ledger after Herbert's visit, 'I have the following choices as to what to do with my life and this predicament.' After deep thought, after contemplation that was at first plaintive and then energetic, she recognized that only one woman she knew in this place of strangers had the inner fire to help her.

When Ellen first came to Deanstown she lodged with Mrs Greege, who tried to regard her as a kitchenmaid, and insisted she scrub the floor; then she unapologetically opened all Ellen's letters and parcels. An unlikely saviouress this woman may have been; harsh and cutting the words she addressed to Ellen; antagonistic their joint history. But – she came when asked. Ellen now believed that Mrs Greege's intervention saved Thomas Kane's life, the bathing, the powerful nursing, the instinct. Likewise, now, Rhona Ulverton – only infinitely kinder, and in need herself. This time, Ellen had chosen an emotional rather than a practical ally.

For the 'John McCormack' baby, a boy, Rhona came to the nursing-home, with a small posy of the earliest possible snowdrops.

'I regret they're not celandines. They're supposed to grant a new baby the gift of keen sight.' She smiled. 'And I brought no dance music with me, we should all dance when a baby is born.'

Ellen asked in a discreet *sotto voce*, 'Did Essie, did she come to see you?'

Rhona nodded. 'Delicious, too. You were right, you are a great baker.' Rhona leaned forward. 'Ellen, my dear, will you help me with something?'

'Of course, of course.'

'How can I keep my son out of the asylum?'

'Oh, the poor boy! Is he violent?'

'Oh, you *are* a good girl. Most people are afraid to ask. No, he's violent like a lamb is, or a mouse. But he is so difficult. People in the village. They want him put away. He frightens the animals. Apparently.'

'I'll think hard,' said Ellen. 'Of course I will.'

A month later, her own depression began. Through the glass partition between the classrooms, she saw her husband humiliate his own son in front of the entire room. As the boy stumbled over an answer and blushed, Thomas called him out, made him hold forth his hand and gave him four slaps of the ash stick. Ellen, hardly knowing what she did, dismissed her classes and left the school an hour early. Thomas watched, never intervened.

Later, at home, he asked, 'Did your clock go wrong or something?'

'No.'

'Did you know you let the children go home an hour early?'

'Yes.'

'Why?'

'No why.'

In her heavy tweed coat Ellen left the house and walked.

The black moods continued for two and a half months. Her depression worried them all, and scared Thomas. She

139

had never been silent at mealtimes; now she could not even respond to a ripe story about a neighbour, or a report of some strange event in the farms. In brief respites, Ellen knew enough to wait, that a remedy would appear the way birds returned in the spring.

Rhona saw her that first week, said a knowing 'Aha!' and simply walked by her side, in silence.

During the next week, 'No, do not try and cheer up,' insisted Rhona. 'I won't have it. No, never mind about Munch. When you're ready. When you're ready. Not before.'

Finally, weeks later, Ellen told Rhona what triggered it.

'The child was humiliated. Humiliated.'

'You made an error,' Rhona observed. 'Of judgement. You should have said to him immediately, "Please don't do that to our son again." You should have said it up into his face.'

'Oh, you don't know my husband!'

'Try it!' said Rhona. But Ellen never raised the subject with Thomas.

Throughout 1938, Rhona's moral support gradually reduced Ellen's anguish at Thomas's parental harshness. Nor did she feel as fearfully isolated by his paranoid fear of neighbours' inquisitiveness. The knife's edge of his humours, along which she had so long teetered, had become a slightly softer, broader place to walk.

Rhona employed contrast in their discussions.

'I mean, your husband, he's not like Hitler, Ellen, is he?'

'No, Rhona, oh no.'

'So – in your own words, what is it you loathe?'

Ellen explained how she hated Thomas's failure to apply

140

the same intelligence to his feelings as he did to his working life.

Rhona said, 'Easy. He is a man of parts. Some parts have spikes. Some have hurts. Some have warmth. Blunt the spikes. Put balm on the hurt – if you can find it. Heat yourself on the warmth.'

'Easier said than done,' said Ellen indignantly.

'When we have no choice,' said Rhona, 'we have to use our energy to put up with our lot. Not be passive, not lie and moan. Say, "Well, that's tough, he's like that." But don't let him get away with it.'

In return for such support and sympathy, Ellen virtually fed the Ulvertons. Essie belted to and fro with full and empty bowls and jars and great pans. Tact became paramount. For Rhona's latest conjuring trick – learning how to poach salmon at night – Ellen provided the accompanying vegetables. Or, saying, 'The children hate the taste,' she would share home-made butter from Thomas's sister-in-law in Bishopswood. Or ask for an opinion on a new soda-bread recipe, or potato cakes.

In September 1939, war broke out. Munch Ulverton lay in the roadside ditches and fired imaginary artillery at passing strangers.

'Poor Munch,' Rhona said to Ellen, 'and I love him so. My heart is broken. I loved his father, and I had so hoped that when Munch grew up I would have new conversations with an adult male. I love Viva too, but I can never bring myself to tell her so. I'm often horrible to her.'

'I'll tell her,' said Ellen.

'Would you? Please?' asked Rhona.

'Of course, I will.'

To Rhona's delight, Munch would do anything for Ellen. She called him from the ditches, wiped his briar-torn face

141

as if he were Christ and she Veronica. To Rhona's greater delight, Ellen gave Viva tea one Sunday, and said, 'There is no shame in having mental illness in the family.'

'Lunacy, we call it lunacy,' said Viva, who picked skin from her hands all the time.

'Call it what you like,' said Ellen smartly, 'there's still no shame in it.'

'Mamma is useless.'

'Oh, no she's not,' said Ellen. 'And I've never met a mother who likes her daughter so much.'

Viva turned a bright red, but did not look displeased and for the first time managed enough tenderness to walk Munch home from the stream where he said there were U-boats in the water-cress.

By 1940, the Kane household's emotional structure was forever fixed. As Rhona summarized it, the home ran in three concentric circles of relationship. The outer circle comprised all the children, in their groups and cliques, revolving around each other. They posted watchmen for their father's irruption into their wary ring. The next, inner circle contained Ellen's relationship with the children – bouncy, loving, teasing, warm, strict. Finally, in the innermost circle, Ellen conducted her secret marriage to Thomas.

Years earlier, she gave up hope of ever seeing again in daylight the man who used to round the corner of the house, or walk in from the garden, with a smile. In bed, however, he still seemed to find his old love for her. Like a swimmer coming up from the deeps with a treasure in his hand, he would approach her with gentleness, then lie exhausted on her shore. Downstairs next morning, something would annoy him, and the knives of their lives would again be unsheathed.

Even if he never discussed his harshness to the children, he knew Ellen loathed it. He had ways in which he tried to circumvent, or apologize for, his cold, bullying attitudes. In May 1941, he discovered a source of liquorice ropes, her favourites; he brought home a dozen on the day of a library meeting. He bought lemons, too, if ever in stock either at Mooreville or Janesborough. If a war report seemed particularly important, or bizarre, he scissored the piece from the newspaper and folded it carefully to keep for her: they talked for an hour about Pearl Harbor.

About the house and school, though, his unrelentingness did not thaw, and no matter how she told herself that she could see a red heart beneath the pack ice, she never knew what mood each day would produce. On his bad days, the awful times of his supine silence long ago had a kind of echoing innocence.

All the circumstances of the society ensured that she could not leave him: no divorce, no separation, no laws of marriage other than union. Therefore she compensated, as did all women of that time and similar circumstance, by investing in her children. Apart from never shielding them from Thomas's excesses – certainly never sufficiently for Grace's demands – she found riches with them. She mothered them abundantly, never sentimentally. Although she would not discuss their father, she never otherwise played them false, and she behaved in general as an amused and amusing, loving parent. Just once, on a grievous occasion, she fought him on their behalf, but without their knowledge.

On Christmas Day 1941, Helena gave Thomas a green tie, and Grace gave Thomas a spotted handkerchief; both girls had saved birthday money; they had hand-painted

143

the wrapping paper and woven the string from coloured raffia. He opened the packages carefully.

To Helena he said, 'I'd never wear a green tie, did you ever see me wearing a green tie?' – and handed it back to her. Grace watched apprehensively, as he then opened the wrapping around the blue handkerchief. He unfolded it, inspected it – and walked away.

This happened in the hallway; Grace and Helena looked at each other with horror. Typically, Helena's tears began.

Grace tightened her mouth: 'I'm going to talk to Mama about this.'

'About what?' asked Ellen, coming downstairs, baby in arms.

'About Daddy,' said Grace, in a voice just below a scream. 'Do you know what he's after doing. He's after throwing Helena's Christmas present to him back in her face.'

Ellen dealt with it too slowly, did not shush Grace in time.

'In our faces. He threw them back. He's a Bastard!'

'GRACE!' Ellen, hampered by the baby, moved forward, but too late.

Grace opened the kitchen door, and shouted, 'That's what you are, a bastard, a bastard, a bastard, a bloody bastard, a bastard.' She hurled the balled wrapping paper at him, and in her new dress ran from the house.

Thomas rose calmly, took his hat from the hallstand, put on his scarf, chose his second-best coat, collected his walking-stick and set off.

In the fields, Grace sometimes glanced over her shoulder. Thomas, in no hurry, strode three hundred yards behind her, swishing at the grass, a man out for a walk. She ran and ran. Both eventually disappeared from view, over the slopes.

Almost two hours later, the white dot of Grace reappeared in the distance. He had caught her just before she made it to the safety of the Grey Valley, and Thomas now walked directly behind her, policing. Every few yards he reached out and stung her legs with the tip of his stick, or flicked it sarcastically to her buttocks through the thin white party dress. From her bedroom Ellen watched alone.

When they neared the house, the children heard Grace's squeals. Ellen stood at the hall door, the kitchen closed behind her. Grace rushed to her, but Ellen fended her off and said, 'Go upstairs, Grace, and begin to wash.'

Ellen quickly steered Thomas into the empty parlour and closed the door. Nobody heard what transpired between them. Helena applied mercurochrome to the series of stinging cuts on the backs of Grace's legs.

Behind the parlour door, Ellen swallowed hard and said quietly, 'I felt every blow you gave Grace. Don't move, Thomas, don't move,' as he made to leave the room. 'Sit still. Say nothing, nothing. Just think on what I said.'

'You did brilliantly well,' said Rhona. 'And you say he blushed? Yes, yes! Embarrassment is a wonderful weapon. How was he afterwards?'

'Odd,' said Ellen; 'he was very affectionate.'

Until the schools opened on the seventh of January, all those Kane children remained quieter than usual in a house into which a stronger chill had drifted.

They said that Miriam Hogan had a miscarriage in March 1942, but few women in Deanstown believed it.

'Must be another immaculate conception,' they cackled.

Over four to five months Miriam did appear to change shape, and she moved from customary peakiness to apparent bloom. Nobody asked about her 'condition'.

145

Aged twenty when Jack married her, and now even wealthier since Mrs Gardiner died, Miriam was forty in 1942, a year older than Ellen.

Rhona Ulverton saw through the 'pregnancy', and caused the 'miscarriage'. Too alike, the two women never became friendly. The Ulvertons, uncomfortable in their poverty, hated the way Miriam dropped in. Ellen Kane had become accustomed over the years to Miriam's disconcerting way of appearing: in a doorway, over a wall, popping up from behind a hedge. Thomas, in a rare moment of light-heartedness, said, 'She'd have made a marvellous guerrilla.'

On St Patrick's Day, as Miriam walked along the Stephensons' and Ulvertons' shared avenue, Rhona appeared in a heavy coat and a man's hat. Miriam, again true to form, wore no coat, only what appeared to be a light summer dress, making her bulge unmistakable.

'Oh – oh, my dear girl,' said Rhona and she claimed later she said it artlessly, with no malice aforethought. 'I was going to say come up to the house and I'll lend you a coat on this bitter day, but with all that padding around your stomach you won't need it.'

Miriam fled. Someone saw her climbing into the doctor's little green car, 'thin as a rake as usual'. She did not return for two months.

Rhona said defensively to Ellen, 'She's a silly little bitch anyway.'

In April, Helena began to menstruate. Grace followed immediately: two years apart in age, two weeks in maturity. Thereafter, as some euphemism would forever be required, they would call it 'the aeroplane'.

On the last Saturday morning of the month, the house was filled with a harsh and huge noise. Ellen later paraphrased when telling the story, 'You know, like in the Bible, "And there came a noise as of a mighty rushing wind," only it wasn't the Holy Ghost.'

All rushed to doors and windows, excited and shouting. Low over the roof of the house, against the sunlight, the wide black shadow dipped and waggled. It rose again, struggled up above the trees and limped through the air towards the Castle.

Thomas gathered a notebook and pencil. All followed him. Up ahead, through the old gate, they could see the tip of the tailplane, a black and grey upward fin.

At the top of the slope a figure appeared in the gateway, his hands to his face. Thomas turned to his own oncoming family and shouted, 'Stop! Wait here!' But the stranger held both hands in the air like a supplicant facing a gun-man. His face streamed with blood. As they watched, the young man took off his flying helmet, laid it on the ground, then spread his arms wide and dropped – a kneeling cruciform.

Thomas called to Ellen, 'A German! A German plane.'

All drew level with the kneeling airman.

Ellen said, 'He's cut. Is he badly hurt, do you think?' She stepped forward a pace. Her bosom rose with the exertion of the rapid walk. 'Are you hurt?'

The man looked at her and said, with a nervous smile, *'Ich spreche kein Englisch.'*

'I beg your pardon?' asked Ellen, her smile for strangers in place.

'Ich spreche kein Englisch. Ich bin Deutscher.'

Said Thomas, 'Maybe he doesn't understand you. Try something else.'

Ellen raised her voice to more or less a shout and asked him, pointing to his wound. 'Is that cut deep?'

'Blood. Red.' The German boy looked confused – then

147

with his sleeve began to wipe his own bowed forehead.

'Awhhh, goodness me,' said Ellen. She stepped over and shook the aviator's hand, then helped him to his feet. He staggered.

Thomas looked on, did not offer to help.

'Girls!' commanded Ellen. Helena and Grace walked over, and Ellen handed Helena her handkerchief. 'Wipe his face. Over there.'

Helena, so tall for her age, only had to reach up a little. Gently, gently she dabbed the cut on the German's forehead. Grace, responding to another instruction from her mother, began to undo the leather cuff buttons where blood also appeared. The boy made himself completely available to them, and stood still. Thomas began to write in his notebook – the day and date, the time, the description of the young flying officer, the number of persons present.

With a shout – 'Master Kane, are all you safe?' – men arrived; one brandished a four-pronged fork in hand; all had been working in the fields.

Thomas spoke. 'It seems to be a German war aeroplane that has got into difficulties, and the pilot seems to have hurt himself, I'm just taking a record of the details for the authorities.'

Four-pronged-Fork strode forward and began to threaten the airman's face.

'Have you bombs with you, have you?'

The boy recoiled and Ellen, placing herself between the flier and the farmer, turned and snapped.

'What do you think you're doing?'

'Ma'am, but he's a German!'

'Do you not know your politics? This country is innocent in this war. Ireland is *neutral*!'

—

They took the young pilot home, down through the fields. The farmers, under Thomas's direction, stayed to 'guard the aeroplane'. Michael Ryan went to fetch a rope so that they could tie it to the old gate 'in case your man escaped and took off again.'

At the house, they sat him at the kitchen table. With slow, unthreatening movements, they eased off his flying jacket and the heavy vest-shirt underneath, until he sat naked to the waist.

Ellen sent for Doctor Hogan: 'In case there are any broken bones or that.'

Grace took up a vantage point at the table, and watched as Helena sponged the boy's blond forehead. Ellen checked his shoulders, back and chest for bruises. Essie stood by, refilling the basin where blood ran like a thin red oil, drifting in the water. Grace placed a dreamy hand under her own watching chin.

Thomas arrived with the Sergeant, who peered at the stranger through the bay-window, then entered the kitchen cautiously. The boy stood, clicked his heels and saluted: '*Heil Hitler!*' – to which the Sergeant said, 'Hallo yourself.' The boy sat again, and Ellen began to help him dress. The inevitable news arrived that Doctor Hogan could not be found: 'We'd never want to have the plague come,' said Ellen.

'The military'll be here shortly, Ma'am,' said the Sergeant. 'We sent a wire to Southern Command in Clonmel, that's what Procedures says we're to do in the event.'

'There'll be no Procedures until he gets something to eat,' she replied. She and Essie fed the boy, now dressed in a shirt of Thomas's. Bacon and eggs, sausages and black pudding, tea and soda bread with her own apple jelly: all watched him eat. When he had finished, he stood, bowed and burst into tears.

The Sergeant turned to Thomas and said, 'He's not what you'd call much of a soldier. Hitler'll never beat Churchill at this rate of going. If all he has in his army is crybabies.'

'Sergeant!' rapped Ellen, and he subsided with an embarrassed shrug.

They bade the airman good-bye when the lorry arrived. Sixteen soldiers disembarked with guns; they lined the gravel from gate to house. Some, such excitement, crouched under the evergreens. The young man first bowed very formally and deeply to Ellen.

She shook his hand and said loudly at him, 'Now, I hope you're going to be all RIGHT! And that you get back eventually to your mother and your family in GERMANY! These people won't harm you, we're very friendly in THIS COUNTRY!'

He clicked his heels again, bent over her hand, but did not kiss it. Then he shook hands with Thomas, who had to put aside his notebook and pencil in a hurry. The flier saluted the Sergeant, and when he came to Helena, took her hand and kissed it carefully, and said, 'Danke. Danke.'

Then he twisted a button from its metal clip on his jacket and handed it to her, clicked his heels and bowed.

'What did it mean, what he said? "Donk", or "dunk", what was it?' hissed Grace to Helena in bed that night. 'I think it meant "beautiful". I think it's the German for "beautiful". It is, it is, I bet you. He said you were beautiful.'

Next morning, even through the rain, Grace at the window could see the tail fin and part of the fuselage peeping over the distant side of the castle wall.

'Helena, if the rain stops, we'll go up and look all over it. Because the soldiers are coming with a tractor the next few days to take it, the Sergeant told Daddy. Oh, Helena, what's up, why're you crying. Oh, lookit, you're all bloody, you cut your bottom or something!'

Helena said, 'Get Mama, quick, but don't tell anyone.'

Grace returned minutes later. 'I whispered. She looked real hard at me and said she'll be up in a minute.'

Ellen arrived.

'What is it?' Ellen had a small parcel under her arm.

'I don't know. I think I'm sick. Look.' She pulled back the bedclothes. 'Will it wash out?'

At secondary school in Mooreville convent, the Kane girls were known not to mix well. Each time they mentioned any other girl's name at home, Thomas made a disparaging remark about the family. Thus, the Kane daughters made no friends, and on the cycling journey to and fro, sought only each other's company. Consequently, they were denied the usual, colloquial channel of puberty information.

Ellen unwrapped the parcel. 'I've been expecting this.'

'I have a pain.'

'Where?' asked Grace.

'Will Daddy be angry?' queried Helena.

'No, love, he won't know.'

'But he will be cross,' she insisted. 'He'll see the sheets?'

'I'll hide them,' said Grace.

'Shush,' said Ellen, 'and Gracey, you'd better listen too.'

Ellen spread open the contents of the parcel and covering the bloodstained sheets for the moment, sat on the edge of the bed. She began.

'Now. God gave women the blessed right to have children and to bring them up in His image and likeness. It is a great honour.' Ellen had been rehearsing this since the day Helena was born. 'This is how it happens. In

151

foreign countries, because of the heat – or the cold – they all have to marry very much younger than we do. So they marry when they have a lot of energy. At sixteen or so.'

Grace chimed in, 'That's you, Hellie, that's you.'

'Quiet, Gracey,' said Ellen. 'Now. In order to have babies, women have to carry around food in their tummies. A little of what you eat every day is stored up in a tiny room inside you and that's called your womb.'

Grace, tossing her long hair, said, 'And blessed is the fruit of thy womb, Jesus.'

'Exactly. Now. Because you couldn't go on storing up food forever God cleans it out every month. Every twenty-eight days – and it comes out as blood.'

'Out of everyone?' asked Grace. Helena said nothing; she stared at her mother's face and listened.

'Everyone.'

'Even Essie?' asked Grace, and Ellen, with secret knowledge of Essie ('I'm flooded again, Ma'am'), smiled.

'Indeed even Essie.'

'And Mrs Doctor Hogan?'

'And Mrs Doctor Hogan.'

'Forever and ever?' pressed Grace who had never heard anything so interesting.

'No, Gracey. First it stops when you're having a baby. And the second time it stops and forever is when God knows a lady is too old to have babies any more that it wouldn't be good for her or the baby. At about fifty or so, although John the Baptist's mother, Saint Elizabeth, she was over sixty when he was born but that was a special message from God. So what this means, Helena,' and Ellen smiled at her oldest child, 'is that God has now told you, He's sent you a special message, that you're going to be able to have babies when you marry.'

'But,' asked Grace, 'how does getting married affect it? Can she have babies or can't she?'

'She can and she can't,' said Ellen, funking it. 'God doesn't *mean* her to have babies until she's married.'

'But how does it work? If she knows now she could have a baby, then she could have one, couldn't she?'

'Only if she's married, Grace.'

When Ellen dropped the 'y' from her usual affectionate 'Gracey', her second daughter knew to steer clear.

Ellen said, 'Pay attention the two of you. There are rules about this. First of all, you're never, ever to tell anyone, especially not a boy or a man. It is none of their business. You can tell each other, or you can tell me, or if you're not feeling well in school, you can tell a teacher. Preferably not one of the nuns. One of the lay teachers. Because sometimes, like you have now, Helena, you get a pain with it.'

Grace butted in, 'Funny message from God, so.'

'God's ways aren't our ways, amn't I always telling you that? Now, when it comes, this monthly message from God –'

Grace butted in again. 'Is that what we're to call it?'

'No. You're to call it something that will hide it. Your Auntie Rina calls it her cousin, she says, "My cousin is after getting off the bus." Or Leah says, "Her nuisance of a relative." I only say, "My friend has arrived," because it's a message from God, therefore it must be my friend.'

'I know,' said Grace, bouncing on the bed. 'We'll call it the aeroplane,' and in spite of herself Ellen laughed. Helena joined in.

'This little belt goes around your waist, love,' said Ellen to Helena, 'and these loops, look. And these are like little face-towels, or flannels. I got you the very best towelling.'

Two weeks later, Grace cycled home from school, for

once not racing Helena. As she freewheeled into the back yard and Ellen greeted her, Grace sang, 'God's been in touch. I'll need one of your parcels.'

Her mother laughed.

Where Helena had stayed in bed for a day and a half, Grace pranced – and organized a picnic for both girls next morning to the Grey Valley. Ellen encouraged such excursions, protected the girls' privacy, their right to such times. The Grey Valley was their counterpoise to the Castle, where their father roamed incessantly. He never came to the valley, was disliked there. The girls, consequently, looked forward to their rambles with leaping hearts, and always returned refreshed, peaceful, animated. Grace said the valley had warmth even when everywhere else was cold.

By half-past ten on sunny Saturday mornings, their chores finished, the girls climbed on their bicycles, sandwiches packed; they purchased lemonade in Silverbridge en route. In the valley, they climbed the stone sides, scrabbling and halting and looking. They discovered beetles, and the trails of foxes, the sett of a badger which they treated as reverently as a shrine. Hidden in clearings among the deep grasses and heavy-hung groves, they lay and turned their faces to the sun.

Helena liked the high white cliffs of limestone at the far end. Grace loved the nestled houses, and ran her hands over the large settles that sat outside fixed to walls, where people sat in the evening and chatted, the men smoking, the women darning.

Occasionally, Ellen joined her daughters, and the three enjoyed days of which they talked again and again. Helena found a pointed stone – Ellen said that it must be a flint arrowhead. And she sat peacefully beside Grace for two

hours and more, and watched her draw. On rare afternoons, she even lowered the shoulders of her own blouse
and lay with the girls to catch the sun on her shoulders.
Helena gathered the alpine gentians and the moss and
the powerful little orchids that botanists said grew
nowhere else in the country: Grace drew them in pencil,
then coloured them at home.

Always when leaving, they stood on the eastern rim
and looked back, watching the chimney smoke climb the
evening sky, waiting until, at the far end, a light or two
appeared in the windows. As dusk fell, the valley disappeared into a velvet pocket.

In these pursuits, and in other small, careful ways, the
Kane girls grew, in a centrifuge of innocence, in a naïvety
controlled and imposed by their mother. No boyfriends:
Ellen's prayers for purity had the force of Thomas's insistence on discipline. They moved up the grades of secondary school unsullied. In their late teens, Ellen, still in
control of their lives, dressed them staidly, in shoes and
socks, coats and suits: a lace collar seemed risqué.

Their father joined in this eternal purification. He
excised from newspapers and magazines any articles with
even the faintest carnal tinge. Once, from the *Reader's
Digest*, Thomas cut 'How to Have Fun in Bed' by Cornelia
Otis Skinner, but forgot to erase the title from the
Contents page. Grace showed it to Helena on a week-end
home from college, and they puzzled upon everything
from pillow-fights to breakfast.

Ellen, taking a cue from Thomas, removed all magazine
advertisements showing underwear or foundation garments. She sacked a dressmaker for describing too
graphically with her hands how 'Empire Line' meant a
fall of cloth from directly beneath the bust.

Grace, more than Helena, sensed the naturally erotic

denied them by their parental conservatism. When she challenged once or twice – she had heard of a shop in Cork where you could buy a black under-bodice – all Ellen had to say was, 'Ask yourself what Our Lady would do. Could you see her wearing foundation garments the colour of sin?'

Grace muttered, 'They didn't wear those kind of clothes in Galilee, it was too hot, and anyway she's always wearing white or blue. And black would show through that.'

Ellen would have no argument.

Academically, the children set a local record – no other family in the history of the parish had ever received second- and third-level education. Helena gained first-class honours as a Domestic Economy teacher; Grace came first in Teacher Training in Janesborough, Ellen's old college.

As the girls became women, containment of their father proved a little more possible. In one good example, Ellen persuaded him to light the candles at Helena's twenty-first birthday party.

'I never had birthday parties,' snapped Thomas.

'I did,' retorted Ellen, but with a smile: one of Rhona's ploys. She further manipulated him into good grace by inviting people in front of whom he could not misbehave – her own parents, plus Leah and Herbert, and a selection of neighbours she knew he found impressive. Not the Ulvertons: Ellen always kept Rhona for herself.

People who left the party together spoke of the two oldest Kane children: 'Beauties – and as tied as twins.'

Helena had Thomas's build, tall and rangy, and her aunt Rina's blonde hair. Grace looked so like her mother, small, voluptuous, that she teased people with photographs of Ellen taken nearly thirty years ago.

8

Dennis Sykes returned to London in late 1945, and received official plaudits at a secret dinner for three hundred people, whom Churchill praised as 'the unseen'. On his thirty-first birthday, the firm made DS a partner, and he throve in the myriad post-Blitz rebuilding contracts. Binnie and he struck up again, though never as powerfully – more friendly than raw. She had had, as she said, 'a good war'. An elderly American munitions industrialist found her warm streak, and rewarded it with money that did not run out for several years.

In London, Dennis found a new breed – the officer widows. At one stage, he ran seven concurrent relationships. By 1948, even his voracious palate had tired, and in his longest 'fallow period' – almost twelve months – he never even 'hunted'.

In 1949 Dennis landed in Dublin, Managing Partner of the firm's new Overseas Division. With recruitment among local engineers and graduates, he set up a forceful office.

This prowling urban animal noticed an outstanding fact: when you got close, everybody in Dublin seemed so *rural*. Finding them easy to approach, he began to ask people at work, or the barber, the waiter: 'Where are you from?'

Very few said, 'Dublin.'

All had either come direct from the country, or descended from people who had. He soon heard the joke, 'A Dubliner is somebody who doesn't go home for the holidays.'

From the evening newspapers, Dennis noticed that it all stratified consciously. County Associations sponsored weekly dances: the Mayo Men's Association, the Kerry Men's, the Galway Men's. Dressed to the nines, he went to one of these dances one night, the Monaghan Men's Association in the National Ballroom. The night failed him. They seemed so raw and ill-paid, and he had over-dressed. Nor could he understand what they were saying in their thick, involved country accents; and they danced like brown bears.

At breakfast next morning, he told his landlady where he had been, and how different he found it.

'They're all very innocent,' she said, eyeing him carefully. 'Very innocent,' she repeated. 'This is a very innocent country.'

A land of virgins: his appetite roared into heat. Dennis Sykes cased the city, like a robber seeking plunder. He checked restaurants carefully: impressive but not flashy. Three of the cinemas had dining-rooms, the Carlton, the Metropole and the Capitol, white table-cloths, white linen napkins; the waitresses wore white starched caps. Girls whose banter, he observed, con-tained no sexual knowingness: he could ask them the most double-meaning questions, and receive innocent replies. Women never dined alone: only with aunts, or husbands, or in families. Therefore, he drank soft drinks in lounge bars, where he got two jousts. Both ended in disaster.

'You dirty thing,' said one.

'I'd only let a husband do that,' said the other.

Research, Dennis, research. He drank on – and listened.

'Mothers and priests. That's how Irishwomen grow up. Mothers and priests. They know nothing about men.'

'Nationwide?'

'A nation once again,' said a bank clerk. 'Virginity is a national institution. I had a girl once and she used to arrange, if we were going to the pictures or that, that we'd meet on the steps of the church. And go in to say a prayer for purity.' The bank clerk laughed. 'I think she had a contract to supply purity to the south of Ireland.'

Such a challenge.

Dennis laughed. 'The mothers I can understand,' he asked. 'But the priests?'

'Hah, you never heard a fire-and-brimstone merchant. That's another great national resource, fire and brimstone. Listen. There was a scheme on here not long ago. Now, you know they wear pins in their lapels to show if they don't drink. Pioneer pins, they're called, it has the Sacred Heart on it. They have a pin too that you wear if you speak Irish, you'll see it, a little silver ring. Or if you're an expert, a native speaker, a gold one. And a while ago, someone came up with the idea of a chastity pin. They did,' he insisted to Dennis's incredulous face. 'Oh, aye. A genius called Father Goode. "The Goode with the Bad" they call him; he's always giving out to women about their morals.'

Dennis realized that 'morals' meant what he had in mind.

He heard Father Goode late one Sunday morning.

'Don't tell me you might be interested in taking instruction?' asked the landlady in delight.

Dennis smiled noncommittally.

Father Goode, astride the pulpit like a horseman of the

Apocalypse, attacked courtship. One by one he listed its evils:

Touching: – 'It will lead,' he cried, 'to inflammation.' Dennis did not quite know what he meant.

Kissing: – 'Two mouths sliming together like slugs, God alone knows what they were eating or drinking beforehand.'

Immodesty: – 'Women wearing tight clothes, they stick out in them, my dear brethren.' Delivered with, Dennis observed, a flair for alliteration: 'Lewd. Libidinous. Licentious.' Whether the predominantly female congregation understood the language, it listened tensely.

Dennis made notes when he came home. A catechism, purchased at the church door (and left lying around in his room sufficiently 'hidden' for the landlady to find), showed him that the Catholic Ten Commandments differed slightly in sequence from the ones he had learned at Sunday school in Alnwick. Next evening, a large, playful smile on his face, Dennis wrote his own Ten Commandments.

Thereafter he took his time, bought a small sweet house in Heytesbury Street, moved in the renovators. When his appetite temporarily outgrew masturbation, he visited Binnie in London.

Renewed after Binnie's body, and invigorated by her comments – 'A land of opportunity, Dennzy darling' – he returned and dived back into his researches.

He saw her eventually. Age – forty-one or so: height – 5' 3"; large-faced, quiet-eyed, buxom – in the Oriental Café, South Great Georges Street, early on a Saturday afternoon, among the coffee things, the spoons, the napkins, the saucers. He followed her that afternoon – on the 16 bus to a pretty little house in Terenure: no other residents. Then, he tracked her for weeks.

To the laundry in Camden Street where she worked.

To Mass on Sunday, where she sang in the Pro-Cathedral choir.

To the cinema, almost every Sunday night, one in three with a girlfriend.

She walked in Bushy Park. Alone. No man in evidence. A lot of time spent alone, he noted. For tracking purposes, Dennis had an assortment of hats, caps and coats.

Two week-ends away in three months: from the quays she took the bus marked 'Roscommon'.

Above all, she sat with her shopping bags in the Oriental Café for an hour from two o'clock every Saturday afternoon of her life: a beaker of coffee, a large currant scone with butter and a soft slam of raspberry jam, the *Evening Mail*, and then the eager first pages of a library novel.

Where to strike? How?

Dead easy in the event: he knew her table, sat at the next one. She arrived, struggled with a tray: he helped, then, after her pleasant thanks, lapsed into his book, the title held so that she could see it: *Dubliners* by James Joyce, what else?

Next week, when she smiled and said, 'Hallo again', he allowed his face to recall her.

'Ah. Yes. Hallo.'

'You're a slow reader,' she smiled.

Again, a moment to recollect; then a compliment, 'Oh, how observant of you.' Then a dash of homely naïvety. He looked at the book jacket and said, 'Relish, really. I'm reluctant to finish it.'

'Oh, isn't it lovely,' said she, 'when a book does that to you?'

'Yes. Yes.' Dennis pleasantly returned to his reading.

Week Three, he helped with her tray again.

'You're housetrained,' she said. 'You're not Irish?'

He smiled with his brown eyes. 'How did you know?'

Rose laughed. 'A woman could be hiking coalbags and an Irishman wouldn't help her.'

'I'm half-Irish,' he said. 'Irish mother.'

Said she merrily, 'I knew there was something good about you. And the other half?'

'Father? Oh, dead, a long time ago, killed in the First World War.'

Next week he didn't show. Tactics.

The following week, she said, 'Oh, there you are.'

'Hallo. Nice to see you again,' said he.

'Were you away?' said she.

'Yes. My mother's very elderly. Well – I mean, she's been hanging on by a thread for years. I go to see her as often as I can.'

'Where is she?'

'Scotland. Just outside Glasgow, place called Helensburgh.'

'That's a nice name of a place,' said she, drawing her crumbs to the centre of her plate.

'Yes, the man who built the town named it after his wife.'

She lit her cigarette, then thought of offering him the packet; he waved a refusal with the second and third fingers.

'You're not married yourself?'

'No.' He shook his wavy head.

She laughed her little silver laugh. 'Man your age, should be ashamed of yourself, you're like the Irish fellas.' Not quite a coarse voice, a little deep, but there had been some local attempt at refinement.

He smiled his famous rueful smile. 'Yes, you're right.' She was perfect meat, perfect, just the right degree of forwardness. 'But. Well.'

'Now, no excuses.' She genuinely had no guile.
'No, no excuses.'

First: I am the Lord thy God. She must be rendered completely devoted.

Her name was Rose Glacken. Today, not her usual shopping clothes: Rose wore a bottle-green twin-set, plus those nice beads Nuala gave her a few Christmases ago. And a good skirt, that small herringbone pattern, a Gor-Ray, she bought it in Kelletts. Nylons were a bit more plentiful now thanks to somebody out in Loughlinstown who had imported a huge amount from America. Her brown court shoes, newly soled and heeled: she collected them the day before yesterday from that little cobbler in Harold's Cross: a bit of a detour getting on and off buses, but worth it.

They talked of other things. Of the war: yes, Dublin had had bombs, more of an accident really. Over on the North Strand. No, he was in what they called a Reserved Occupation, lucky, yet he felt bad about it.

Of his house. 'Heytesbury Street.'

'Oh, very nice,' said Rose.

Rose asked him, 'But what do you do with your time? I mean when you're not working? You read, what else do you do?'

'I think,' he said. 'I think.'

'It has to be said,' agreed her friend, Eily, 'a man who thinks in this day and age is a rare article.'

Thereafter, Dennis Sykes systematically ruined Rose Glacken and her ordered life. As surely and intuitively as if divining for water, he found her lethal streak of duty. All the women he had enslaved and then walked away from, had that pressure point in common – responsibility:

163

conscientiousness, some passivity. Better if they were tarnished with a little greed: his evident financial well-to-do-ness hurried them if they proved slow.

Second: Thou shalt not take the name of the Lord Thy God in Vain. As a tactic, all previous boyfriends must call from me expressions of the vilest jealousy.

'And if I can ask you the same question,' he said the following Saturday. 'Why aren't you married?'

She smiled: 'Past history' – and he allowed her to see his brow darken just a smidgen.

'I had a friend who broke off his engagement,' Dennis said later, 'because his fiancée couldn't stop talking about her past boyfriends.'

Binnie taught, 'Always discuss relationships. They are meat and drink to women, little Dennis. Viandes et Vin.'

'Oh, I can well understand that,' said Rose. 'I have a friend who's as jealous as anything of her fellow's girl that he had before her. In my case, there was only a couple of times we went out. It came to nothing, he wasn't going to get the farm until he was pushing sixty, 'cause his father was as healthy as a fish, he's still alive, and his mother wasn't going to let another woman in.'

'Was he good-looking?' asked Dennis quietly.

'He had curly hair,' Rose said. Dennis smoothed his own locks.

One more week should do it, Dennis believed. Correct.

Seven days later, she said to him, 'If you're not doing anything Sunday, a few friends of mine are dropping in.'

Against Dennis's rules. In his secret life, he would not be 'vetted' by friends. Absolutely not.

'Oh, no! Oh, no! I can't.' He sucked a piece of regret. 'How very civil of you. But I have to go and see this ancient creature out in, I think it's called Palmerstown,

164

an old friend of my mother. And I don't know what time
I'll get back.'

A lie, a complete lie: he was golfing: 'But will you ask
me again?'

'Oh, I will, of course?' Rose fell down, down. 'What
about the following Sunday?'

'Yes, please. Thank you. You'd better give me the
address now.'

He wrote down the address carefully in his beautiful
leather notebook, checked it meticulously with her and
said, 'I'll be there.'

Last sip of Grand Oriental coffee. Quick tentative
question: 'Do you ever hear from that old boyfriend
now?'

Hasty reassurance. 'Not for years.'

Third: Remember that thou keep holy the Sabbath day.
In a pious society, women are likeliest to be most bored
and therefore most susceptible on Sundays.

He stepped like a dancer up her little Terenure pathway, with its diagonal red and yellow tiles. A fire in the
grate; and the table set for tea for two in the neat parlour;
Rose looked both rounded and suitably pointed – she'd
bought a new bra the previous afternoon in Arnotts. Today
Rose was wearing a pink Kayser slip and matching
knickers: that stiff roll-on still pinched, one of the sus-
penders dragged to the side.

Rose Glacken, like so many women of her age, took
love where she found it: nieces, nephews, ageing relatives, firm friends. She would, say, have willingly nursed
aged parents; would have sacrificed all aspects of her life
to take, say, her sister and her sister's husband through
lifelong illness, had such occurred. No effort of nurture
could be too great. To pass the long time, Rose, stable,

rarely took a drink, unlike Nuala. Nor did she yet rely on prayer, although she had long ago begun the spinster's pattern of repeated socializing with the same friends. Of such fine heart, she told herself that she could love a man, a good man, truly love him – even in the way he wanted to be loved.

Sundays, though, were tough days, down days. Passable in summer: walks, cycles to the mountains, bus trips to the shore. Dreadful in winter, although Rose luckily had the element of a real, coal fire in her grate; Nuala could only afford electric or gas heaters, those narrow blue flickering bars of thin comfort.

Oh, to have a man to talk to on a Sunday: that came straight from daydreams. A well-mannered man, too. Who brought an armful of the Sunday papers in case she had not seen them. Who wiped his feet on the mat. Who admired the colour scheme immediately. Immediately.

Who – and he not even a Catholic – was able to discuss Father Goode's sermons. And once Dennis uncovered that Rose went to hear Father Goode frequently, he knew, if any doubt lingered, that he had found marvellous quarry.

'He's very powerful, isn't he? I mean, he's a very powerful speaker.'

Rose, in her parlour, agreed.

'When has he been at his most powerful?' asked Dennis.

'I heard him one Easter,' she said, 'the Easter before last, and he tore into women about the way we dress in front of men going to dances and that we can expect men to want to – to want to not respect us.'

'Is he very specific when he's like that?'

Rose said, 'Yes, and he's a fright to go to Confession to, he asks very direct questions.' Dennis allowed her to fall silent and muse.

'Darling, don't give me that guff about the heat of the fire,' hooted Binnie.

Because Rose's nipples had risen under her new blouse as she recalled Father Goode and his prurience.

Fourth: Honour thy father and thy mother. Never choose a woman with a family who can interfere.

'Are there many in your family, Rose?'

When he discovered the sad answer, Dennis made his first move.

'I'm terrified of *my* mother dying,' he said, then stepped from his chair by her fire and kissed her tenderly on the top of the head. Nonchalant. Confident. Brotherly. But in doing so he put his hand for a second on her neck, and then sat down, and for the rest of the evening behaved like a gentleman, and a little aloof.

Yes, good: both parents dead; the proceeds from their farm in Roscommon helped buy the house in Terenure. Pristine and aromatic with floor polish and, in season, flowers: it simply waited for a husband. Inside sat Rose at her loom. Did she have moral guardians? A lone sister eighty miles away in Roscommon, married to a man thirty years older, and both a little unwell, with no children, therefore, no troublesome visitors for week-ends.

'Happy birthday, dear Rose!' – a Cusson's Gift Set of soap, talcum powder and lavender water: mauve box, mauve ribbon.

After the reams of bashful gratitude, Rose said, 'I'll tell you one thing, you'd never get an Irishman walking into a shop and buying that for a girl. Or if he did he'd get his sister to do it.'

'I buy all my mother's clothes,' said Dennis, 'and in fact when I'm buying her a present it's always clothes

I buy her. But of course I've known her taste a long time.'

Rose made tea. Dennis stoked up the fire and they sat in their opposite easychairs.

'Come over here,' and he indicated where she should kneel down. She squatted by his knees, her back to him, and they both watched the fire in silence.

'It's your birthday, Rose.'

He placed a hand on the back of her neck, then bent down, turned her face up to him and kissed her – softly and not long – several times, then ran his hands through her hair. She caught the hand, held it, then let it free again and it roamed and roamed through her hair, and they kissed and kissed. Very soft kisses, never prolonged, no tongues.

As he left, he said to her, 'You'll have to buy a sofa for this room,' and grinned.

Red-faced from the fire in the grate and the kisses on her face, she touched his moustache.

'What's Father Goode going to say to me?' she asked.

'I'll wait for you outside the church,' he joked.

Binnie always said, 'Women are addicted to kissing. If men only understood that they'd conquer the world.'

'I thought we did already?' asked Dennis.

'Darling, there are only two things around which the world revolves. That –' she made a 'gimme-cash' gesture with her fingers, 'and this –' she pumped a strong forearm. 'Moola and muff, darling. Pence, darling, and puss. But – kiss. Kiss. Kiss us. Just, kiss, us.'

After every meeting now, he kissed Rose. Especially on Sundays, after, perhaps, a walk, or even an uxorious silence digesting the Sunday papers he had brought. He kissed her and kissed her. And left her lips waiting for kisses like fields waiting for rain.

'When I wake up of a Monday morning –'

He corrected with a smile: 'Ah – *on* a Monday morning.'

'Of or on, my lips are full of your kisses.'

Rose in love.

Fifth: Thou shalt not kill. Of course not. Nevertheless, use just a little agreeable violence. And call it Passion.

He declared Heytesbury Street finished in May: it had been completed and furnished long before that. The cork popped.

'Never? Not until now? Well, well. I hope you like the taste. Do you know how champagne was invented, though? Oh, *you'll* love this, Rose. Wine fermented too long in a monastery in France and when the monks came to pour it they found it full of bubbles, and then when they tasted it they said, "Look, we are drinking the stars."'

He raised his glass. She tasted and swooshed, 'Oh, it's gone up my nose.'

He laughed kindly.

They walked indoors from his little garden, and he cooked her lunch. She marvelled at his skill, his kitchen command. That evening, by his fire, as they both knelt on the floor, he removed her blouse and her bra. Just what he hoped for, exactly the right amount of hanging weight he loved! And he thanked her for the privilege, and still he kissed her and kissed her and kissed her. He stilled her flinchings by his gasps of admiration and his devotion, then assisted her in her modesty by hugging her so tight he could not see her. Never once touching her nipples, he circled them and then helped her to dress, apologizing.

'Passion. I got carried away.'

169

'We're only human,' she helped.

Within a month she was helping him undo the blouse buttons, and he was making jokes.

> *There was once a young couple of taste,*
> *Who were beautiful down to the waist.*
> *So they limited love*
> *To the regions above*
> *And thus remained perfectly chaste.*

A verse of Binnie's, who never said anything a mere once.

'Oh, Dennis you know everything,' Rose praised.

Sunday after Sunday, they knelt by his fireside or hers, naked to the waist, adoring.

Heavier kisses, wild pawing at Rose's hair, drawing it through his fingers over and over. He sucked her breasts as if to milk them.

Lying back with a subsiding gasp, he said, in the dreamy version of his voice, 'The Milky Way was formed because Heracles drank too fiercely from his mother's breast, and as she tore it away to stop the god-baby hurting her, her milk squirted out across the sky. That's the Milky Way.'

Rose thought Dennis a genius.

Impossible nowadays to imagine the depth of innocence in those country girls. Rose Glacken, and younger by a generation, the Kane daughters, and all their friends, older and younger – all the women growing up in country parishes had minimal carnal information. A few *double entendres* shouted in banter as they cycled through a village; or a chance viewing of animals' copulations. If unfortunate, they had been pawed, or worse, by relatives or neighbours. Pregnancies without the girl knowing the reason for her swellings were not unusual. Families lived in terror of the stigma of illegitimacy – it caused havoc

170

to land inheritance rights. Ignorance was deemed the best defence.

Dennis Sykes seduced Rose Glacken by two means: one, by assuring her she was now old enough to enjoy all the fruits of life, and after all what was Confession for? She didn't always have to go to Father Goode – she should find someone sympathetic to the idea of Love? And, two, by the use of his Sixth Commandment.

Sixth: Thou Shalt Not Commit Adultery. Tell them there's never been anyone else. If they're single, always tell them it's your first time.

'But – how do you know,' asked Rose, 'how to kiss?'

'Same way as you do. You're a wonderful kisser.'

'I'm not.'

Dennis said, 'You mean I do it all on my own? No, Rose. Wonderful. Maybe it's just the natural force of loving inside you. And of course we both read a lot.'

Rose nodded, happy to agree.

He smiled shyly. 'Do you feel like a child, Rose? I do.'

By now he customarily put his tongue in her mouth. He took it out and asked, 'Makes a nonsense of sin, doesn't it? As if God would keep a girl like you out of Heaven on account of me?'

Rose replied, 'I found a priest in Clarendon Street who's real nice.'

'"Really nice",' corrected Dennis.

'Yes, he's very nice.'

'Besides which,' said Dennis. 'We're like children playing.'

Seventh: Thou shalt not steal. Her intimacy must be appropriated openly; I must know everything about her, especially the three 'Ms' – her mates, her money, her monthlies.

Friends – three very close: Nuala, oft-quoted by Rose; Eily, clever and bookish, and Mary Pat, a keen dancer; all of the same age, and (could be tricky, so watch it) all *desperately* interested in romance.

'You must meet them.'

'When we're ready.' Good touch, the 'we': hint of promise.

He asked, 'What are their boyfriends like?'

'They don't have any. That's why I tell them so little about us. You know. People get jealous.'

Not the full truth from Rose; her friends were expressing some alarm, and she knew it, at her long evenings with Dennis the Mystery Man. But she had begun to relax more and more, and at his encouragement, did a lot of the kissing. Of late she did not always wear her roll-on, or her stockings, when he called. Once, she even had to throw the key down when he arrived early and caught her in the bath. Ever the gentleman, he sat and read while she assembled.

'Here.' He thrust at her one Saturday afternoon an enormous bunch of flowers.

'God! Dennis! This is like *Social & Personal*.'

'An investment came through rather well. I can't wait to tell Mother.' All untrue. Well, technically Dennis had a point. 'Bryan Cooper' had invested so shrewdly that Dorothy Bayer's Trust took a sudden lurch upwards: one squad of dividends came from a company contracted in the rebuilding of Dresden.

'Don't forget. If you ever need help,' said Dennis.

Rose said, 'I have a thousand I could let loose.' On money, the great point of peasant confidentiality, Rose told Dennis everything.

'Give me three weeks with it.' Dennis smiled his cat's smile.

He returned with the money doubled.

She gasped and offered: 'I've another three thousand.'

Did she lick her lips? It seemed so.

Dennis shook his head. 'It doesn't always work. I'll tell you when the next good time comes.' And she reminded him almost every fortnight.

Yes. Worth five hundred of his own money, Dennis reckoned.

One week-end, picking up the acid on her breath, he asked, 'Are you all right, Rose?'

She blushed.

He put an arm around her. 'I watch you very closely,' he said. 'I keep an eye to see you're all right.'

'Some months are worse than others,' said Rose. 'And I mean, I'm not as bad as Eily. She has to go to bed for two days.'

Dennis clucked sympathetically. A thoughtful half-hour later, he announced, 'We'll go out for our tea,' and on the doorstep that night kissed her chastely, did not come in.

Unexpectedly, he dropped by next night. She was ironing. He looked.

She remarked, but unblushingly, 'Stop looking at my undies.'

He smiled.

Eighth: Thou shalt not bear false witness. Wrong! Thou shalt always bear false witness.

All going according to plan.

Including his success at keeping her from ever meeting his colleagues; 'We have a very difficult project; we are so – so touchy with each other, that we all agreed to avoid each other socially for the moment.'

Including his success at avoiding her friends: 'Put it this

way, Rose. Before long, there may be a very, shall we say, a very appropriate occasion to meet them, I mean – an excellent reason for a party. And we'll get your sister and brother-in-law to come for the night. Besides which – I'd rather spend the precious time with you.'

Once or twice, when Rose pressed harder for social exercise, he frowned. She hated to see Dennis frown. When displeasure appeared, she let him 'play' longer next time, and for his next visit baked a cake. Once, when she asked how much he earned, he told her. She took it like a lady – but with glittering eyes when telling Eily. To whom she explained the burden of the aged mother in Helensburgh.

He also used his displeasure to invade her, and to make rules. A little after a 'mood', he would say a little edgily, 'How is Father Clarendon Street these days?'

'Great, he never asks too many questions. Not like Father Goode.' Rose mimicked. '"Did he touch under your clothes, my child? Where did he touch you?" Nuala used to say we should all agree to answer, "In Palmerston Park, Father."'

'Speaking of which, Rose,' Dennis replied, and reaching a hand up, snapped the elastic in her knickers. 'Let in some air one of these days, it's a hot summer.'

Week by week he undermined her modesty.

Some evenings, out of the frustration of waiting for the ripe time, Dennis on his way home handed some of his folded banknotes to the whores with their big lips and their shiny skirts on the banks of the Grand Canal.

Ninth: Thou shalt not covet thy neighbour's wife. If she ever shows the slightest interest in another man, drop her until she comes crawling back.

He arrived late one Saturday afternoon to the Oriental

Café and saw Rose in animated conversation. Dennis allowed her to see him leave in a hurry. Within an hour she rang the bell at Heytesbury Street. Surlily, he opened the door; he turned his back and walked ahead of her, into the house; he stood looking into the empty fireplace. A light breeze blew through the open French doors.

'What's up?' she asked, behind him.

'Who was he?'

'Oh, Dennis! Is that it? The man in the Oriental? That's Billy Nicholl, they own the laundry, I've known him since he was sixteen. It was his father made me manageress.'

'You never said.' His jaws bit into the words. For an hour he froze, an hour of mood, an hour of her cajoling, an hour after which she wept at last. Then he allowed her to thaw him. By six o'clock, the late sun heating the carpet, she lay naked. Dennis's tongue started the long-postponed work: Rose had her first orgasm in association with his displeasure at her.

Thereafter, Confession and Absolution came into their own: Rose never hung back again. If she had become addicted to his kisses, she began to die for his tongue. Rose asked for more dates: she got them. One Saturday, in the strange heat of an Indian Summer September, he kept her up all night, taking her to the edge of her own control and back again.

'Fair's fair,' he then said, unbuttoning.

'Statues look different, don't they,' whispered Rose.

Tenth: Thou shalt not covet thy neighbour's goods. Thou Shalt Physically and Rampagingly Possess Them, Lock, Stock and, yea, even unto Barrel!

At work they noticed the change in Rose. Nancy Hanley a presser; Nancy who had eight children despite her husband's working the Liverpool boat – 'I wish to God he'd a-been doing Africa' – noticed it first.

'Some fella's polishing Rose's shilling,' she said to Maureen Phelan, both women blueing the shirts, perhaps even Dennis's.

'Well, whoever he is, there's a tune in her fiddle right enough,' replied Maureen. 'I hope she'll be all right but.'

Rose had always been so fair to them; good about time off for sick children, strong in her compliments when she spot-checked the work going out; bonus at Christmas; holiday money.

'The thing to watch for,' said Nancy, 'is if she stops going to Mass.'

'No,' contradicted Maureen, older. 'Them country girls always goes to Mass. The thing to watch for is if she stops going up to the altar rails at Communion.'

Which Rose did. He had blasted his sermon into her.

'The inside of you,' gasped Dennis in wonder – and was that a tear in his eye? 'The inside of you is like silk, Rose.'

For the next three and a half months, Rose learned Dennis's rhythms and preferences, fourteen weeks which took her from shyness, to abandon, to a private sense of shame about which she could do nothing. At the end of which time he had her reactions as trained as a pet monkey's.

Hallowe'en, 1951. Rose rang Dennis's doorbell. No answer.

Feeling certain his mother had been taken ill, perhaps died, Rose returned to Terenure and baked his favourite dark fruit cake. A week later, certain that his mother's funeral had just about happened by now, she put a note through the letter-box. The week after that she did the forbidden, the unthinkable: she rang his office.

A voice said, 'Who's calling?'

'Oh. A friend of his.'

Impressive transfer to another voice, who asked, 'Who's calling him, please?'

'I'm a friend of his.'

Impersonally, the voice said, 'No, Mr Sykes isn't in today.'

She thought of asking the police; she even scanned the newspapers; essentially, she fought off her instincts.

Saturday morning, five days later, she said, 'Who are you?' to the woman who answered the Heytesbury Street doorbell.

'Ackland. We've just moved in.'

'But – I thought Mr Sykes lived here.'

'He did. But he's left Dublin. Oh, do you know where there's a good laundry around here?' asked the fresh-faced woman, whose husband worked at the British Embassy.

When Rose went into Holles Street Maternity Hospital after the first complication, she wore Eily's mother's wedding ring and she was able to give her own address, Mrs R. Glacken, 15 Mayhill Terrace, Terenure.

'Wasn't that lucky,' said Eily, 'having an address of your own like that?'

She miscarried; by chance it happened in a check-up visit to the maternity hospital, and ended as a wide, soft red squelch in a bathroom, with much sympathy from the nurses.

'And you there? Actually in the hospital at the time?' said Eily in wonder. 'God, Rose, you're always lucky.'

=

Rose sat in her quiet little sitting-room for two months, and then went gently back to work.

'Hanging's too good for a shagger like that,' said Nancy Hanley to Maureen Phelan, because eventually in Dublin everything gets out.

'He's a fool to himself,' said Maureen; 'he'll never meet a nicer girl.'

In Dublin next spring, Rose Glacken accepted finally that Dennis was not coming back, and she invited Eily around for 'a bonfire'. They sat by the fire in Rose's parlour, and Eily watched in amazement as Rose put letter after card after photograph after letter, on the coals. She read one especial letter lastly, but not aloud, before she consigned it.

> Darling Rose,
> You asked me last night what it was I felt that you give me. I tried saying the sun, moon and stars, but you wouldn't have it, and then I promised you that I would go away and think about it. Now I know.
> You give me myself. I was nothing until you came along, a small figure in the landscape, over-devoted to his mother, solitary, accustomed only to sitting quietly in my lodgings, reading or thinking.
> Before you I had only had desultory relationships with girls and never for very long. And now there is even the chance that we might march onwards side by side. What more can a man ask – to have a girl such as you?
> My love always, forever,
> Dennis.

She folded it, and put it back in the green, deckle-edged envelope, and said to Eily, 'It was the day after that letter, that was the day he went.'

Eily said, her glasses winking in the firelight, 'Well, he's going now, isn't he? Watch him burn, the bastard.' She pointed to the flame-licked letter. 'He'll burn hereafter, too.'

'No,' said Rose, 'that's where you're wrong. That's what I learned. His likes get away with it all the time. What we have to do is not let them make us get sick.'

'Will we kneel down and say a Rosary?' said Eily helpfully.

9

Electricity came late to Deanstown. Rural Electrification had been planned for several years, but the mountains supervened. In addition, farmers and smallholders refused to allow cables across their fields. Cattle would die from rubbing off the pylons. Storms would bring down wires, burn grass.

Lurid folklore added extra hazards. Firesides heard what exactly happens to a human body when electrocuted – what shade of blue it turns; how far out of their sockets bulge the eyeballs; when the fingernails crack open; why the penis ('the lad himself') springs erect.

Many, on visits to cities, had met electricity and disliked it. Bill Clements, who married late and then to a woman of only forty acres, took her on honeymoon to Janesborough, all of thirty miles away. ('Exotic,' commented Ellen.) The new Mrs Clements returned telling how Bill 'sat up in bed, and he blew and blew at the light, and it wouldn't go out, and he had to call the girl downstairs up.' Other stories told of people going blind in the new glare.

They might have been a tribe fearing some bizarre, silver force that would sear their innards, confound their reason. Wasn't electricity used to try and make mad people less dangerous? Didn't it change the patterns of the inside of the head? The old gunmen said, 'Any power that's hard to control is a dangerous thing.'

It might alter Life beyond their future. To many, electricity meant lightning sheets, cracking against the high summer skies, or the blue zig-zags, whose rainy voltage split rocks. Everyone knew of someone cleft from poll of skull to sole of boot while sheltering under a tree. Everybody had heard of lightning running like a mad chrome ghost along the galvanized iron roof of some barn, tearing at the rivets with its wizard's talons.

Electricity belonged with miracles when safe, with death when untrammelled. Electricity danced along water. Electricity struck the metal eyelets of boots; it tore harness-pieces from horses' foreheads; it flew like a bright fast metal comet along the ground, hitting horseshoes, turning riders and carts upside down.

'Think,' they said. What might it do on the loose inside a house with, as John Shea pointed out, 'every man woman and child in the parish sleeping in an iron-framed bed?' In the middle of the night would their mattresses and palliasses be upturned and would they find themselves pitched rafter-high? Think of the speed of electricity – upon you, like violence or gunfire, before you knew it had seen you. There were men they heard of – in the next county – who watched it turn corners seeking the metal food it desperately needed. With a loud blue-red-turquoise-flash, it rendered that metal to powder.

Electricity was the gelignite of the gods. Small wonder that entire countries in Africa and Scandinavia and the Far East would have nothing to do with it.

So the stories ran. So the regressed part of Deanstown viewed this new force, that threatened to hurtle across their land and shake the mountains when it danced.

—

After college and their first teaching posts, Ellen made one stipulation to Helena and Grace – to come home every second Sunday by one o'clock for a family meal. They could bring some washing with them for Essie to do, and they had to make a small financial contribution 'to the education of the younger ones'.

She always made an exception of the New Year's first Sunday, given how much they had been at home for the festive season. Thus, neither girl heard the exciting news of the Rural Electrification Scheme until halfway through January.

Ellen showed them the Notice. 'The boys say the very first thing they want is toast with scrambled eggs on the new cooker.'

Helena asked, 'Are we definitely getting it?'

'We have to,' said Grace. 'This place is like the dark ages.'

'Oh, Miss, oh, Puss,' mocked her mother sweetly, 'is it awful for you altogether?'

'At least,' said Grace, 'we'll be able to see our faces in the mirror for a change.'

'And would that be such a good idea?' asked Ellen. All laughed.

'Is everyone applying?' asked Helena.

Ellen laughed again and said, 'Your father is on the committee collecting the names and listing geographical difficulties. You know – getting the poles across fields and that. And you'd be amazed at some of the objections. There's an old woman up in Banter and she says "Yerra, it'll never catch on." And there's another old fellow over in Cairncrow says he doesn't want that "oul' lightnin' sparkin' and fizzin' at him outa the wall"' – Ellen did one of her mimicries.

She had grown up with electricity, and her immediate

comment had to do with how dirty the house would prove when all its corners were lit up.

The Application Forms came to Thomas at the school, great boxes of them, and the senior schoolchildren distributed them on allotted days off, one form to every household. Some returned, requesting more forms. For instance, the Canavans in Horganstown asked for three – one for the brother, and one for each of the sisters. The siblings in that house had not spoken to each other since the parents died twenty years ago.

In the village, notices appeared. 'Evening Meetings will be held at Deanstown National School on Monday, Tuesday and Wednesday, the 14th, 15th and 16th of January, 1952. Admission Free. Questions Welcomed.'

Fog came down on the Monday night, and swirled like an old friend through the high and mysterious trees. By the lights of his oil-lamps and his stoked school fire, Thomas Kane introduced men in spectacles who carried blueprints and survey maps. The people sat crowded, cramped and smiling among the desks of their childhood. Feet shuffled; neighbours muttered and buzzed.

The first man, courteous and warm, stood before them as strange in his strong blue suit as the school inspectors used to seem. 'National Supply' was explained. They learned the history of Poulaphouca reservoir supplying Dublin, and of the Ardnacrusha scheme which harnessed the Shannon. In the film that whirred against the white, thick wall, a double-decker bus drove through one of the great turbine pipes. New, holy words floated through the flickering room – 'Head Race', 'Tail Race', 'magneto'.

When the film ended, the man and his colleague unpacked a number of flat cartons. They heaved and wrestled the heavy contents across two conjoined trestle tables at the top of the room. Thomas moved a lamp closer, and the men stood back to unveil their trump – a map of the village and district in relief.

Look: there flowed the river, made of a silver ribbon. Ridges of wrinkled, earth-brown plasticine made the mountains. Tiny balsawood boxes, painted bright, created the farms and the village – 'There's the master's house, there's the Canon's,' they whispered. The green metal trees came from doll's farms. .

One by one, the gentlemen plotted little pylons into slots. By the light of the school lamp, their minute tines squared like shoulders as they marched through the undulating map, toys on a child's counterpane. From these pylons, the tiny, tiny serried rows of poles, made of creosoted half-matchsticks, radiated off to right and left. On 'cables' of metal thread, thin as gossamer, the 'power' floated to the eaves of the little houses. The junior gentleman moved Thomas's lamp away; the senior man clicked a hidden switch cabled to the film-projector battery beneath the table, and a street light illuminated a building with the minutest of lettering over the door: M. J. HAND: LICENSED TO SELL WINES & SPIRITS. Gasps.

Then, one by one, the little houses on the relief map, both in the village and along the outlying roads, lit up, until eventually, as a *tour de force*, a hidden 'moon', on a rigid wire so thin it could hardly be detected, glowed last of all with the words *Deanstown & District*.

The electricity gentlemen called for questions. Viva Ulverton had eaten apples throughout the meeting. She peeled each one elaborately in a spiral, taking as many risks as she could, but never breaking the skin. Eventually, she had a continuous narrow whorl of apple peel

184

which she wound around her finger and then ate. She champed the cores like a hyena and asked, 'How much will it cost?'

They offered her national figures, provincial averages.

She shook her head, asked again. 'How much will it cost?'

They smiled at her, with the county breakdown, the typical household: Viva said, 'No. How much will it cost *me*?'

Nobody gave her an answer she liked. She rose and left, throwing her huge shawl over her shoulder.

That first Electricity evening did much to counter the old superstitions. Deanstown welcomed conjurors. Since the German warplane, nothing so diverting had come by, and that was ten years past. The travelling shows never played the school any more, not since Thomas threw them out. Canon Williams had grown quiet in his ancient old age, and he made no more lightning visits: how he used to throw houses into frenzies of respectability! Nor did he lambast them from the altar.

True, they joined in impersonal successes, from outside the parish. The county team had won three All-Irelands in a row: 1949, 1950, 1951. Word had it that Vincent O'Brien owned a horse that might win the Grand National. At last, though, they had something of their own to talk about.

Just as well. The war rationing – which should never have reached this far into a neutral country, should it? – would end soon, and no longer provide conversation. Those Ulvertons proved useless as a spectacle, now that the mad son was in and out of 'the Hospital' (as everyone called the asylum). Through her father's friends in Janes-borough, Ellen had found a place for Munch in the quieter wing, and he came home when doctors observed he had entered a 'good phase'. From time to time in there, he met Cyril's excommunicated wife, who often disappeared 'for a rest'.

Mrs Greege died. Ellen laid her out, with the best linen and her own good candlesticks. Her sons approached Thomas for financial advice. In two biscuit tins and a suitcase under her bed they discovered twenty-four thousand pounds in banknotes. More poignantly, they found intact the wedding gift Thomas had returned to her in May 1925 in revenge for her disrespect of Ellen. To post it, he had cruelly reversed the same wrapping paper in which Mrs Greege had sent it. The boys handed it to him, thinking their mother had somehow mislain it.

The Home Economics of Rural Electrification: How to Light a House for a Penny a Week; How to Cook for a Farm Family for a Week for Half-a-Crown. Everyone who had attended the first meeting, plus fifty per cent more, came to the second. Could the school fit them all?

A woman with a pleasant face and a small enamel badge bearing a lightning flash, held up a grill-pan; then some baking tins; then many brochures of electric cookers. She explained.

'And from now on, ladies, dirt is gone from your cooking forever – and as for your men. Well, I have bad news for them. A week's supply of hot water is only going to cost fourpence.' All laughed.

'Look, ladies,' she said, with Ellen near the front nodding in the agreement of a woman who had seen it all before. 'These are pictures of the way a cake of bread will rise in an electric oven. Now I know some of you get great results already, and that's because you're great bakers. But when you have an electric oven, even your husbands will be doing the baking' – at which, of course, they laughed and laughed.

The woman turned on an oil-fuelled generator. On the table sat a small electric cooker. She greased a pan, she cracked eggs.

'Watch the speed,' she said, 'it does an omelette with.'

Not everyone knew what an omelette was, but they watched. She impressed them with her wristy one-handed cracking of eggs on the rim of the bowl. Onion and butter smells filled the room.

'See – no flames, but all the heat you want. And it is *concentrated* heat.'

This placid conjuror, her buttocks square beneath her large skirt, heeled the pan back and forth on the round, metal cooker-plate. Little rivers of egg ran fugitive from side to side, seeking the heat at the edge of the pan that would cook them too. One last circular glide of her wooden spoon around the rim and – 'There y'are ladies!': the omelette lay folded in surrender on a plate.

With a fork she offered morsels. A wag suggested, 'Taste it yourself first, Ma'am,' and she, who came from similar stock, said, 'You'll get none.'

She played her heckler. All through the morsels that she visited up and down the benches and children's desks, she told him, 'You're getting none.' Finally, with a flourish, she pounced upon the wisecracker with the last fluent piece.

'Come on – open your mouth, we'll see will this shut you up,' to the delight of all.

He blushed and took it. As she walked away, she asked, her back turned to him, 'Well, did you like it?'

'Not bad, not bad,' he said with a merry grudge.

'Well,' she said, facing him, 'you're going to be a busy fella – for I put number Nine [a well-known cattle purgative] in that bit you ate.' Her victory was complete.

From a box beneath the table she drew, with the care of a jeweller showing samples, cakes she had prepared in advance.

'See the height of that sponge,' and they admired the little domed mountain sprinkled with powdered sugar.

'Slice into this,' she said with the fruitcake. 'Now, ladies! Doesn't that beat all the arguments you hear that electricity makes our fruitcakes sink. It does no such of a thing.'

The sleight-of-hand escalated. 'If you have someone special coming home from England, what about a Battenberg cake?' They ooh-ed and aah-ed at its marzipan beauty. Tapping the desk in rhythm with her words, she said, 'You can't. Go wrong. When you control. Your own heat.'

Finally she drew forth the staple diet of the countryside, a cake of risen soda bread. She did not cut it, she broke it, and it came away in her hand. They peered, tapped, prodded and sniffed.

'How long?' she asked them. She could have sold the Elixir of Life from a Medicine Show in Tombstone. 'How long did that take?'

Nobody answered.

'I'll ask you a question you all know the answer to? How long would that take in your own bastable oven on top of the fire with *spris* [the ember piled on the iron lid of the pot] – you all know that?'

The room said, 'An hour and a half to two hours.'

'In this – thirty-five minutes! And at the same time you're cooking the dinner here on top. And you've no smoke, and you've no ashes to clear out, you've no mess, or bother, or old filth.'

=

As the evening disbanded, women asked Ellen, 'What about makes of cooker, Ma'am?'

'Well, the make I'm getting is the big Belling,' she declared. 'It has a good big oven, it'll take a fifteen-pound turkey or a sixteen-pound goose, and it has a drawer underneath for keeping the plates hot, and it has a grill. And there's three plates on top, one is rectangular, and then there's a big round plate and then a small round one.'

'What about for the cleaning, Ma'am?'

'I think we'll buy the Electrolux. Because the long tube and the different-shaped nozzles means you can get into corners, and God, girls, we're going to need it. When that light switches on, 'tis then we'll see the dirt.'

One woman, who once gave Ellen an excellent recipe for lemon tartlets, and who, a naturally embarrassed woman, shifted her shoulders up and down when speaking, said, 'We have the Sacred Heart lamp ordered already and that's the only thing.'

'Oh, so have we,' said Ellen, 'there's a great run on them.'

True: the most common item they would order in the preparation for electricity was the little lamp to shine in front of a picture of the Sacred Heart of Jesus. A red glass dome encased a three-dimensional blue cross that flickered and glowed permanently. In front of this the families would now kneel when saying their rosary. At present, they had small fat oil-lamps, with red glass globes and wide, blue-striped wicks.

'Think of it, girls, no more paraffin oil, no more smells, isn't it great?'

Ellen rubbed her hands, enjoying her self-given role of leading the women into general acceptance. The myths of electricity had been made by the men.

'Ma'am, tell me now.' John Relihan's wife from Kiltynan turned every utterance she made into a matter of importance. 'Do you yourself, like, do you think 'tis safe?'

'Oh, of course I do,' chirruped Ellen. 'I grew up with it, it is a Godsend, that's the only word I can think of for it, a Godsend. God sent it to us.'

When Ellen got home (Thomas always stayed to lock the school and leave it tidy for the morning), Helena, surprise, waited. She had been visiting nearby.

'And don't you look nice?' said her mother.

'Mama, did you hear?' Helena blushed in excitement. 'Did you hear what they're paying the new cookery demonstrators? Nearly twice teachers.'

'Do you know what, we must have been thinking of each other? I was just saying to myself coming up the road, because we had a cookery demonstration tonight – wouldn't that be a lovely job for Helena?'

'I'm going to apply. Will Daddy be cross if I do?'

'Apply anyway,' said Ellen, and winked.

The third meeting, called for Wednesday night, was, as the expected bombshell meeting, the most crowded of all.

Two senior men, of gravity and authority – 'They look more like surgeons,' Mrs Hand said – waited in a car until all the foggy stragglers seemed to have at last entered the school. The men shook hands with Thomas, and he introduced them to the audience: Mr Michael Quinlan and Mr Andy MacCarthy. A third man, unannounced and unintroduced, came in late, nodded to the two officials, and took up a place in the shadows, standing by.

Mr Quinlan, smiling, hesitant, opened the meeting's topic – 'Where Deanstown and District is Going to

190

Get its Electricity From.' He outlined their geography.

'Ireland is a saucer-shaped country, with high mountains all around its edges and a lot of liquid in the middle, all the lakes.'

Most of the people in the room had heard almost identical words from Thomas Kane, and they all smiled with memories of schooldays. So far so good. The official next addressed the particular difficulties of their large area.

'Deanstown is not necessarily the obvious choice for a focus of all our planning, but it is the most centrally located problem we have,' he said, 'and therefore it acquires a new importance.'

They nodded quietly.

'Especially as it is going to be a place in which we have to exert the sort of new skill the whole world is interested in. What we do here will have an influence on projects in Africa, in India, in South America. Deanstown will lead the way.'

For weeks, he and his colleagues, smarting from previous bad experience, had been working on a form of words. In the car on the way from Dublin, Mr MacCarthy and their passenger had 'heard' Mr Quinlan's words, like an actor rehearsing lines.

'Here in Deanstown, we cannot get you the kind of supply much of the country has.'

How quickly he had elided into the communal spirit, how swiftly he had become one of them.

'So much derives from the Shannon and similar sources, as with the great scheme at Ardnacrusha. But here, the mountains are in the way.' He paused. 'Now I know that faith can move mountains –' he allowed them their chuckle – 'but we are only humble engineers.'

Was he a Corkman? He might have been; there was a

trace of Cork in that accent, but he'd probably been in Dublin a long time.

'We've looked at this problem in every way. We've even flown over the entire area in an aeroplane, and you'll be glad to know that most of your roofs are in very good repair.' A smile again. 'And we have considered every way of getting the electricity in here, and we have rejected all but one, because, ladies and gentlemen – Deanstown and District is a special case.' Buzz-buzz – and again he permitted it.

'So, instead of bringing you electricity from the Lee scheme in Cork, or from Ardnacrusha, we are going to *build*. We're going to construct. A special. Local. Scheme. You will have your very own electricity, and it will be generated and provided locally.'

Each listener turned to his or her neighbour.

Mr Quinlan pressed on. 'Now. You'll know from the talks you've had here during the week, that electricity is generated, for Ireland's purposes anyway, by two methods. By the turf- or peat-burning stations in Clonsast and the Midlands. Or by harnessing the water, like the Shannon at Ardnacrusha. And as you know, there is another way of harnessing water. At Ardnacrusha we took the widest part of the Shannon, where we had the biggest supply of water and we redirected it into channels at such speed that it was able to turn the huge turbines. In other words, we have to give water strength and force – if it hasn't enough already. There is another way of doing that, and for that' – he held up the big photograph they had already seen on Monday night – 'we're going to use here a smaller version of what happened at Poulaphouca. We're going to build a dam. A hydro-electric dam.'

'The Ulverton one,' everyone said afterwards, 'she started it.'

192

Some hazelnuts Viva ate tonight, which she had previously cracked, and whose kernels she dipped into salt from a twist of paper.

'Oi?' cried Viva, and Mr Quinlan turned. 'Don't any of you know what happened at Poulaphouca?' She pronounced it 'Poolapooka' and Thomas, from his high desk, corrected her: 'Powel-ah-Fooka.'

'Powel-a-whatever-you're-having-yourself,' Viva replied in the lamplight; and her cheek to Master Kane sent an approving hum around the room. 'When they built that dam,' she said, 'two thousand people lost their homes.'

'No. That's not quite correct,' said Mr Quinlan urbanely.

'Right,' said Viva, who had the full, and suddenly tense, attention of the room. 'Give us the correct version.'

'Some displacement of domicile is inevitable in projects of such magnitude,' said Mr Quinlan.

'What's that in English?' someone said.

'In Poulaphouca, because Dublin is such a huge supply zone, we had to take a lot of land into consideration.'

'I notice,' Viva said, 'you're very careful not to tell us where you're building this dam here.'

Mr Quinlan said, 'I was coming to that.'

'I bet you were. Could you hurry up?'

Whatever his experience, his status, his general demeanour and presence, nothing in Mr Quinlan's upbringing had prepared him for Viva Ulverton. Viva, when swimming naked in the river where others had gathered on summer afternoons, did not even deign to cover her breasts when towelling. Nor was there any point in Canon, Curate or Minister having a word with her: Viva had let it be known after the excommunication that if she saw a clergyman on their land she would shoot, and claim bounty.

Mr Quinlan turned to the blackboard and took down the large and glamorous photograph of Poulaphouca Dam, then gestured to Mr MacCarthy, who with his smooth and pleasant smile took over.

'Ladies and gentlemen, good evening, my name as you heard is Andy MacCarthy.'

Viva crunched her last few hazelnuts. 'Get to the point.'

'I am, I am.'

'You're taking your time about it,' she said.

He rubbed his hands and began. 'The thing about a dam is that it must be sited in a place where you can get a lot of depth. So that the water gathered there is deep enough to put very considerable pressure on the dam wall. And the strength of the water pressure that comes through the dam – that is permitted to get through the dam – comes from releasing some of that force. Like a big hard tap. Or a hose nozzle. Have you all here seen a hose or a tap?'

'How could they?' said Viva. 'There's no running water around here.'

Andy MacCarthy smiled and said, 'Nevertheless I hope you get the idea.'

'They do,' said Viva. 'We're not fools here, and if you're not going to tell them, I am.'

Mr MacCarthy produced a series of charts: many had illustrations of taps releasing water.

'This is the force you need,' he pointed to the first tap, a dim, dull trickle, 'to light a bulb of twenty-five watts.'

'You can always tell a man,' said Viva, 'who's afraid of coming to the point if he knows he's going to cut his finger on that point.'

Mr MacCarthy smiled bravely. 'And this,' he said, 'is the sort of force you need if you're going to light a hundred-watt bulb. You'd need two of them for this room, for instance,' he said helpfully.

Viva addressed the packed room. 'You none of you know what he's up to, do you?' she asked caustically. Her Anglo-Irish accent and forbidding bearing quelled any likely hecklers.

Mr MacCarthy's next chart showed a much healthier tap, in brighter flow. With an amateur attempt at drama he reached for a last chart.

'And this,' he said, 'is the kind of water-power you need to bring the electricity to Deanstown.'

Waves beat on a blue shore: a seagull wheeled, caught forever in Mr MacCarthy's big coloured picture. 'You need oceans of power,' he said. 'Oceans of it.'

Viva snorted. 'You're afraid to say, aren't you?' – and she stood. 'Who's here tonight from the Grey Valley?' she asked.

Several hands rose. Viva fluttered her fingers like a fan-dancer.

'Your houses are going to be filled to the eaves with water soon,' she sang. 'Because that's where the dam's going to be. They're going to empty the Grey Valley of people and they're going to fill it with water.' She waved her skirt in a frou-frou and sat down again.

Andy MacCarthy turned to her. 'How did you know that?'

Viva smiled at him, a big, gay smile.

Mr Quinlan came forward, smiling like a nervous deacon.

'If I may reinforce what Andy, what Mr MacCarthy, said? You are pioneers in a technological development that will be copied all over the world.'

He raised a hand to quell the buzz.

'We also have a huge financial consideration. If we don't

bring in this hydro-electric scheme, you will never get electricity, nor will a very large section of the county.'

Viva said, 'Around here, they don't care about anyone else.'

Mr MacCarthy re-entered the conversation, and glid smoothly over her.

'We chose the Grey Valley,' he said, 'because it is geographically ideal, and because there are no large farms. There's quite a bit of scrubland in it, you have to admit.'

He began to explain the valley's aptitude for the dam project.

'It is the only natural high-sided valley anywhere within reach, capable of containing enough water to house a hydro-electric dam. Not only that, you have the River Carry and the River Lene.' He pointed to his map.

'They're close enough to the mouth of the valley to be easily diverted, and powerful enough to fill the valley. You see – we have to ensure that the water levels never drop.'

They expected opposition: they had planned for it. In their meetings and conferences in Dublin, they had dealt entirely in anticipation. In the end, it all fused into one substance: money. Thus, Mr MacCarthy and Mr Quinlan decided in advance when to play their ace. The budget allowed for it; they would play it only when people seemed extra-restive. Mr MacCarthy nodded to Mr Quinlan: the moment had come.

'And of course,' said Mr Quinlan, 'we didn't get around to talking about *compensation* yet.'

Compensation. Instantly the room quietened. They understood compensation as salmon understand a waterfall. In effect, money for nothing. Mr Quinlan became the good parent.

'Compensation will be paid for every person, for every man woman and child in the Grey Valley. Compensation that will not only be adequate. Compensation that will be generous. This project has international funds behind it. Because several countries are interested in how a project of this compact size will be able to generate such huge power. This dam is something special.'

He knew he had them, and he warmed.

'Now – normally compensation for the kind of disruption the Grey Valley residents will have to go through would take two forms. They would either be rehoused in something comparable elsewhere, usually better. Or they would be given the cash to do so. On this occasion we will be doing a bit of both. In fact –' when he smiled, his nose changed shape '– in fact, a lot of both.' He never, ever, throughout the entire project uttered the phrase, 'People will have to leave their homes.'

The room was his. No question. He knew it; Mr Quinlan knew it. Finally, with authority that increased at every word, Mr MacCarthy said, 'I want to introduce to you – and he will speak to you at another meeting next week – the man who is in charge of the project. He is a very distinguished engineer, even though he doesn't look old enough to be long out of short trousers. And you will be seeing a lot of him. He will be living here.' He beckoned to the man in the shadows.

'Ladies and gentlemen, this man will be with you for the next year so get used to looking at him. As you'll hear in due course he is an Englishman, but he has a bit of good in him, his mother is Irish. His name is Mr Dennis Sykes. He's the man who will build the Deanstown dam.'

Dennis came forward and they looked carefully at him as he smiled. The light in the room dimmed a little as, simultaneously, the oil in both lamps, always filled at the beginning of the evening by Thomas, burned below the halfway mark. Then both wicks recovered, and went on to draw on their second half of fuel supply. The room brightened again.

Mr Quinlan said, 'Well, that's all, now, ladies and gentlemen. Oh, there is one more thing. Mr Kane here, whom you all know and respect.' He indicated Thomas, a sentry in the flickering shadows by the fireguard.

'He will be your representative to us. He will be the man who will take all your complaints to us, and I think you must agree that your interests could not be in better hands. So when we get this project going, Mr Kane will be keeping an eye on everything on your behalf. He'll note down your queries about poles going across fields, about wiring houses, about where your meters will be put. And so on and so forth.'

Dennis's brown eyes roamed the dim schoolroom, with its Mercator's Projection Map of the World, with its partition. Through the many panes of glass, from waist height to the ceiling, Thomas Kane with his unblinking eyes and his raven hair in those days, and his forceful physical presence and his strong demeanour, wooed Ellen Morris when she first stepped off the bus to teach in his country school.

'Well,' said Ellen. 'What did you make of all that?'

'I knew all along,' said Thomas.

Ellen whirled. 'And you never said.'

'They asked me not to.'

Ellen faced him. 'Thomas, the girls are going to be very upset.'

Thomas looked surprised. 'Why?'

'Well, the place is special to them. Extra special. Since they were small.'

Thomas Kane never told anyone that he had no welcome in the Grey Valley. He had accused the place of failing to harbour a wounded colleague during the War of Independence. It had also and ever been his contention that the children from the Grey Valley were among the most stupid he had ever taught.

'Interbred,' he said. 'They're pig-stupid. And unsteady.' As with all things he disliked, but to which within all manner of reason he could not object, he had always ignored coldly the girls' Grey Valley expeditions.

Now, he made a face with his mouth.

'Oh, well,' he said, putting sugar in his tea and picking up the newspaper. 'Can't be helped. I've seen all the maps. It's the only place they can put the dam.' He shook the newspaper. 'You can't hold up progress.'

10

Next week, all the Grey Valley people arrived for what
had become known as 'the Compensation Meeting'. Even
the oldest tribespeople rumbled out, some of whom had
been too infirm, they claimed, to go to Mass. The women
wore grey or black fringed shawls, the men had huge
boots. They sat around the schoolroom walls, on benches,
in respectful and shy silence. Since the news reached
them, the word 'compensation' had echoed off the high
limestone cliffs above their houses in the valley, had whispered through the dense thickets. In conversation, many
had already spent the compensation money before they
got it – or even knew how much it would amount to; and
they looked forward to new houses, with no damp, with
sound windows.

Mr Quinlan was back: he welcomed them all. On the
blackboard easel behind him stood a large and glowing
'Artist's Impression' of the valley. He told them the picture would be raffled in a free draw when the dam was
built. Miriam Hogan and Jack stood at the back of the
room in their tall expensive clothes; Jack sent his hand
over and over his sandy hair.

Mr Quinlan said, 'Now those of you who were here last
week will remember that I introduced you to the man in
charge of all this excitement. Still there's nothing lost by
introducing a good man twice. Here's our Chief Engineer,
Mr Dennis Sykes.'

Dennis began. As he spoke, the room stared. Predictably, the men did not like the look of him – too well-dressed, too sure of himself, little bantam-cock. The women took in the gleaming cuffs, the razor-pressed trousers, the white stiff collar on the blue-striped shirt; the brown eyes, the abundant, unoiled hair, the smile. Viva Ulverton stood to her full height (she claimed her stoop came from bending down to hear what people were saying to her). Miriam Hogan crossed her legs without knowing she did. Ellen, equally involuntarily, closed her coat across her bosom despite the fact that she sat near enough to the fire.

'Ladies and gentlemen.' Dennis used his hands when he talked, not quite like a Frenchman, but not with a countryman's reticence either. 'What is different about this project is the size. If this works – and I mean to see that it works – we will have built a system where in a third of the usual volume we will generate three times the amount of electricity. It is nothing short of revolutionary. This will be one of the smallest dams ever built and a great deal more powerful than many which are much, much larger. Where we have an advantage here –' he turned to the artist's impression – 'is this: there is an unusual sudden depth. At this end.' He pointed.

The painting on the easel showed the Grey Valley as a rocky deep cavity, whose floor was a cushion of bushy greenery. Commissioned and directed by Dennis, the artist had conveyed nothing of the valley's privacy. This air of secrecy began outside, where woods almost camouflaged the only entrance. Unless a stranger understood where to view the valley from – and only habitués, like Helena and Grace Kane, knew the exact spot on the ridge – he would never guess how many houses had been hidden among the groves and stands of thick woods and copses. A clue could be had in the late afternoons, when the light shifted around, highlighting the rising plumes of chimney smoke. Deliberately, the artist had now portrayed the valley as it had been before dwellings were built in it.

'Up here,' Dennis pointed to the last rising canyon at the sealed end, 'as you know, the two rivers flow from opposite directions. Here. And here. The River Carry and the River Lene. They're fairly wide, but – and this is most important – at this, their nearest point to each other, and to the Valley, they're very deep. And they're fast. They pelt down the side of Knockmore, which you don't need reminding is the second highest mountain in Ireland. It's only when they flow separately away through the country that they become placid, and turn into ordinary meadow-rivers. Now as you know, these rivers are rarely empty. Our plan is to divert them and bring them together for a stretch – here. Then lead them through here – by blasting a channel in this end –' He waved the pointer Thomas used for singing lessons.

Dennis created a dramatic pause, then said in urgent, controlled excitement, 'Now here's the beauty of it all.' He clenched an upturned fist like an orator. 'After they have made our electricity, the rivers will again join their own beds where they now flow. And in fact – listen to this, ladies and gentlemen. No grazing land anywhere will lose water. That stretch, where we take the rivers away from their original courses, is all scrub and moorland.' The room sighed in wonder.

'So – the water will pour down here and fill to this height.' Dennis removed the artist's impression and replaced it with another. This second picture had obliterated all physical aspects of the valley interior – the bushes, the foliage – and presented the place as a huge, ovoid skeletal bowl surrounded by high cliffs. 'It will in fact fill to here.' He pointed to a blue line near the top of the valley. 'How simple! Water comes in one end. It creates a deep and powerful enough lake – which is contained by the wall of the dam, and some of it is allowed, in a controlled fashion, to pour through the turbines.'

'Jesus God,' said Miriam Hogan later, 'did you hear the way he said "rather"?'

'In due course,' Dennis purred on, 'in fact if the valley growth patterns are anything to go by, in no time at all, we will have a *rather* beautiful, new tree-fringed amenity – here, on the edge of these meadows. The only thing will be – anyone going swimming will have to remember it will be about half a mile deep.'

He produced a third and final artist's impression called, in glorious lettering, THE DEANSTOWN & DISTRICT HYDRO-ELECTRIC DAM: OPENED 1 FEBRUARY 1953.

Dennis interpreted the gasps of the room as he pleased, and said, in a confirmatory tone, 'St Brigid's Day, an ancient feast-day. Yes, we will build it that fast. Little over a year from commissioning to completion. It will be a world record.'

The artist had painted a smooth and brilliant curved dam, like a picture from a futuristic comic. Through the dam, the water pumped like streams of foam; tiny men in white coats stood on important platforms looking up at the dam wall in awe. Of the Grey Valley no more could be seen.

'And just a word about that timescale,' said Dennis. 'In the end it will all happen very quickly, and it will be very exciting. I hope you'll all be there.'

Mr Quinlan eased forward. 'Now. Who's going to ask the first question?'

=

Nobody, least of all Dennis Sykes, foresaw how he would lose control of that meeting. The first twenty minutes or so raised no difficulty. How will the compensation be decided: will it have to do with the size of the smallholding, or the square footage of the house being vacated? Had any relocations been talked about yet? Where were they looking at? Would those new county-council houses being built in Mooreville be part of it? Will there truly be cash as well as rehousing? How much? Would local men get jobs on the scheme?

Mr Quinlan's nose curved more and more, as his smiles suggested that they could hardly believe their luck. No opposition. No attacks.

How far would the power reach beyond Deanstown, would it supply the North Riding? There was a rumour that if it did, Deanstown would get its electricity cheaper.

Miriam Hogan, still focusing on Dennis, returned from her reverie when the pensive old woman sitting just in front of where Miriam stood, turned round and said urgently, 'Give me a hand up.'

Her name was Mollie Stokes. Helena and Grace knew her well. She smoked a pipe, still spoke much Irish and often asked the girls to read to her, saying her eyes were fading. They had never been fooled. Anyone who could crochet in that half-light would have no difficulty with print or handwriting. Last year, Grace told Helena she would one day find a way of teaching Mollie to read 'without Mollie knowing what was happening'.

Helena laughed at Grace's idealism. 'You won't catch her. She can hear the grass growing.'

Mollie Stokes gathered her shawl and held up a hand like a child at school asking a question: 'Sir?'

'Yes-ss,' said Dennis, crisp and benign.

Miriam Hogan gushed afterwards, 'What I want to know is, where did he get such good manners?'

Mollie Stokes said, 'Sir, I listened to all you said, and I looked to your pictures.'

People whispered her identity to each other: Ellen wondered whether she was the woman the girls had talked about so affectionately. Mollie began a calm account of her day.

Morning sun in her eyes, winter and summer. Woodcocks. Pheasants. Apples, and even cherries red as a child's cheek. She was born in her bed, as was her mother and grandmother, and the whole line of Stokeses back to before the curse of Cromwell. Ninety next Whit, she wanted to die in that bed, be shrouded and waked in it.

Mollie Stokes had reached her understandings of life in and through the Grey Valley. It explained to her thunder, and colour, and solitude, and the taste of food that she grew herself. She got from the valley her sense of Time, of health, of calm; it had taught her growth, and the seasons of the year, and logic. Death threatened with less fear; life's burdens could be anticipated because, as she said to little brown-eyed Dennis Sykes, 'That valley is my system, Sir.'

She, and the others who lived there, had ancestry and descent, had means and nature, had sequence and recurrence. If spiritual advantage comes to those who have unbroken blood continuity in one place, if they have accumulations of simple understanding by which they can live fulfilled lives, the people of the Grey Valley had more than most. Without having the means to articulate it, they none the less understood, as did Mollie Stokes, what they would now lose. Compensation might appeal and even appease, but their spirits would none the less be charred by the loss of their old place.

Dennis Sykes, accustomed to women, recognized immediately the force of Mollie Stokes. He stepped back a little, let Mr Quinlan take charge – who gestured it back to Dennis. For a moment or two, any forthcoming response seemed to bobble between the two men, wordless ping-pong. Dennis finally accepted the challenge and spoke with good grace and thoughtfulness to the standing old woman.

'I know exactly what you mean. I recognize what you are saying, that you know already what you are going to lose. And I think you are also saying that there are no values in money that can compensate for what you must leave behind you.'

Mollie Stokes nodded: she looked like the old woman with the samovar in a Russian play. Dennis drew a deep breath.

'And,' he said, 'I'm very sorry. Very. Sorry.'

'Is there nothing to be done?' she asked, then stood immobile and unblinking.

Dennis repeated, 'I really am. Very – sorry.'

He turned again to Mr Quinlan, who raised helpless shoulders. Nobody said anything for some eternal seconds. Someone's foot scraped on the wooden floor.

Mollie Stokes broke the silence. 'In that case, Sir,' she said, 'I may as well do my mourning now.'

Only Thomas anticipated what she meant. He was probably the one person in the room who could have stopped her. But he had heard her long ago, and, perhaps overwhelmed by the memory of her force, and by the emotions her voice would call up, he failed to move. Mollie Stokes opened her mouth and began to keen.

Victorian and Edwardian travellers through Ireland described the keening women. The term came from *caoine*, the old word for 'lament'. In her *A Lady's Tour of the South-West and West of Ireland,* Mrs Florence Handscombe wrote, 'Three women arrived with the coffin on its farm-cart. They were dressed in poor black, their hair blown by the sea wind, and their eyes blackened around the edges as if with sticks of charcoal. From the moment the funeral entered the overgrown cemetery, they began to "keen". To "keen" is to make a wild, high noise. It disturbs the hearer with its intensity, and its griefstricken shrill cadences rend the heart.'

Vita Sackville-West compared the keening women of the west of Ireland 'to the worst that German legend can yield, or Furies and Harpies can render. For many months afterwards, I woke at night, harsh voices in my ears, their tragic blackened eye-sockets staring at me from diverse points in the dark room.'

General Arthur Crabbe believed that 'not even the Indian dervishes at their most fearful can reproduce the wild effects of these simple but terrifying creatures.'

Mollie Stokes had serviced many funerals, keening in a voice that the opera stage would have acclaimed for its range. On the long notes she remained without vibrato. The short notes built to peal after peal of bereavement and misery. All who heard it chilled at the sound: Dennis Sykes smiled at first in embarrassment, then turned a little white and looked away.

Miriam Hogan looked at Jack who shrugged his eyebrows. Nobody left the schoolroom.

At funerals, when keening for their own beloved, such women usually lapsed into a kind of desperate sobbing, punctuated by sudden high returns to the keening, as if somehow their voices were still tearing through the fabric of their normal behaviour. More composed relatives then led them away, and – perhaps even more harrowing in some ways – the sound floated back to the graveside, even from a long distance.

Miriam Hogan reached out a long, thin red-freckled arm and coaxed Mollie Stokes from the room. Those people bunched inside the door made way. Mr Quinlan, Dennis Sykes and their sentry Thomas Kane, watched the small old woman protected by the tall younger one, hesitate in the school door and then walk out into the night.

Lost to eyesight, but not to earshot; her high-pitched sobbing, which borrowed notes from seagulls and eagles, lasted several minutes more.

Finally Mr Quinlan broke the silence in a voice he dare not raise.

'Ladies and gentlemen, I think that's all. Mr Sykes will be coming to live nearby. Mr Kane will channel all enquiries. Thank you. Thank you.'

He withdrew, a shattered glass. The people dispersed.

Dennis Sykes reintroduced himself to Thomas Kane.

'Mr Kane, that was, I suppose I may use the word "extraordinary". I certainly can't think of another word.'

Thomas nodded. 'Yes. It's a very old tradition, it's called "keening", it was an old mourning custom.'

He told Dennis some of the history. The smaller man listened, nodding as if in fascination.

Next, Thomas called across Ellen, and said to Dennis Sykes, 'Oh, this is my wife.'

Dennis Sykes took Ellen Kane's hand. Dennis had a dry hand, yet Ellen recoiled. He fell short of wrapping his grasp round the full breadth of her smaller hand: instead, his fingers invaded her palm, and loitered. Too long. Her hand tried to improve the encounter by shoving forward, into the handshake a little, but his grip, though

light, had no intention of changing. Twice she registered
– the fingers: the duration. A part of her brain thought
that this man shook hands like a thief – even though she
had never shaken hands with a thief.

With people moving around the room, and shadows
heaving across the light, the schoolroom lamps denied
Dennis an adequate view of Ellen's face. He craned
quickly, still could not measure. She seemed to him quite
an item – not as countrified as the other women; unusual;
almost Italianate; full-mouthed.

'How do you do, Mr Sykes?' Not a local voice: no burr;
a clear tone. He allowed the handshake to come to an
end, then put his hands like royalty behind his back.

'I'm bound to say I'm having an interesting time,' he
replied. She half-smiled.

He continued, 'My friends have wondered whether I
will find it slow here in the countryside. But you have
your moments it seems.'

'You're very welcome,' said Ellen, bowing her head a
little in her manners – but why did the words stick in her
throat, she wondered; why could she not say them as
easily and fluently as she had always done?

Thomas and Mr Quinlan conferred a little longer, then
Mr Quinlan fetched Dennis.

To whom Thomas murmured, 'Mr Sykes, this isn't the
time or the place to make arrangements, but sure we'll
see you again.'

And all left. To face unpredictedly intense complications.

Helena and Grace, in an exchange of letters, agreed to
meet in Mooreville, prior to catching the bus out home for
the week-end. Grace had heard, and now told wide-eyed
Helena, of Mollie Stokes's keening.

'Hellie, they're going to drown our valley, it's going to disappear.'

'I know. I know.'

'Hellie, our lovely place! Our valley! They're going to make it a lake!'

'I know.'

'All our foxes! And the badgers! And the wild apples! God, it's awful. Awful!'

'Awful,' agreed Helena.

'I've never been so hurt about anything,' said Grace. 'And you know about Daddy?'

'About him helping them? Yes, Mama wrote. She said in the letter, here it is, that he couldn't do much else. Apparently all teachers, all over the country, have been doing the same in all the electrification schemes. The school is where it is more or less organized through.'

'Yes,' said Grace, twisting her mouth, 'but you know him. Look at the relish he'll be doing it with.'

'Easy, Grace, easy.' Helena had many of her mother's intonations.

'No, Hellie, I won't go easy. This is only part of it. Look. Last week-end, I went and stayed at Ruth Clohessy's house, I told Mama and Daddy I was doing a week-end course in case they called to see me, I didn't tell them I was staying with anyone, you know what he's like about us mixing with people at all. And Hellie, I think I know now why he never wanted us going into other people's houses.'

Helena, leaning away, looked troubled.

'He doesn't want us to see that other fathers are nice to their children. Ruth's father talks to her, he says "hallo" to her when he comes in. God, he even ruffled her hair when he walked past her chair. He teased her, I mean, nicely. And he's the same to all the other children.'

Helena stirred her tea, and sighed. 'Yes, I've noticed the same, but I didn't want to say anything.'

'Well, I've noticed it for ages and ages, for years now, but I didn't want to say anything either,' emphasized Grace. 'And you know what Mama will only say, she'll say he's had a hard life or something. But Hellie, I'm sick of it.'

'Oh, Gracey, don't cause trouble.'

'Well, you tell me this,' said Grace. 'Why were we always ill? Why were you always getting diarrhoea? Until you left home? It's because we were all the time frightened, that's why. Look. Since I started teaching, the one thing I know is we're not allowed to frighten children in school. Or say hurtful things. Look at our father. Look what he always did. And still does to the younger ones.'

'Don't, Gracey, don't.'

Helena spoke in vain. Conflict began from the moment the girls entered the house.

Thomas said to Helena, 'Where in the name of God did you get that blouse? Was the circus in town or something?'

Slowly, over the past two years, the girls had been allowed by Ellen to buy their own clothes: Grace had argued and argued for their independence.

Helena winced – but Grace blew. She blew so high and so hard that Ellen, for the first time ever, scattered the other children out of the kitchen. They listened, anyway, at doors and windows. Thomas and Grace faced each other down in a shoot-out.

'What did you say to my sister?' snapped Grace. 'Apologize! Go on, apologize! No Hellie, I won't shut up, he has to say he's sorry.'

Thomas stepped towards her. 'Mind your mouth, Miss, you are forgetting yourself.'

211

'I suppose you're going to hit me. If you do, I will tell everyone in this parish. Go on. Hit.'

Ellen did not need to intervene: Thomas, amazingly, stepped back.

'Is this what all your "independence" is doing for you? Fine teacher you'll make,' he sneered. 'If this is what you think constitutes respect.'

'You're the one with no respect,' spat Grace. 'Look at the way you have just completely disrespected Helena.'

'I said – watch your tongue, Missy.'

Men would have stepped back from Thomas when they saw him like that. Not Grace.

'Go on. Bully me. Like you bullied every single one of us all our lives so far.' She had his eyes, and they blazed.

Thomas Kane had made himself legendary by knowing how to move through hedgerows and dark fields by night with a gun in each hand. He had stalked patrols of soldiers, taken out their rearguard silently and escaped through the trees; he had blown apart army posts from the inside. All these heroisms, between 1916 and 1920, when, inexplicably, he walked away from the violence in the middle of it all, had made him a hero. Otherwise, the other hard men of the parish, whose children he 'disciplined' at school, would have faced him long ago. Yet Thomas Kane had curiously weak antennae for general life. His wife picked up the slack, dealt it to him, guided him along the ropes of each day. After the keening incident, she had anticipated an outburst from Grace, even if not of this strength. Sure enough, Grace switched the issue.

'Look at you! You won't even lift a finger to help that old woman Mrs Stokes.'

'Grace, that isn't true, your father has a great sympathy with Mrs Stokes.' Ellen, when agitated, spoke with her hands pressed to her jaws.

'When will we see it? When she's in the County Home with all her possessions rotting at the bottom of this dam?' asked Grace.

'Gracey,' said Helena, 'Gracey. Easy.'

'You don't know what you're talking about,' said Thomas, but his rigidity now slapped no curb on his fiery daughter.

'This is what I'm talking about,' said Grace, and she held out her fingers to make point after point exactly like her father always did, but perhaps the mimicry was unconscious or inherited.

'I'm talking about the destruction of an old place of great value. I'm talking about the removal of our history from in front of our eyes. I'm talking about the disappearance of something we will never have again, those rare plants, the rocks with their fossils. I'm talking about buying people off so that engineers can have their way. How do you know that this is the only scheme that will work? We've only their word for it. I'm talking about the way they're going to appeal to people's greed, by giving them cash. And you, you of all people who have always complained that people are too conscious of money, you're going along with it, you're even working for them.'

Faced with her force, Thomas gave up his righteous position by deciding to answer her last point. 'I am working for the Government. It is my duty.'

'Duty! Duty! You made duty your god! Look at you! You haven't one friend in the world. Name one man you talk to. And I know why you've never had a friend. It's because you're afraid someone else could ever make you change your mind.'

Ellen shouted, 'Grace!'

All stopped. Helena caught Grace's arm. Thomas turned and walked away.

'Grace, you've gone too far.' Ellen did not know where to look.

Grace spoke with the brusqueness of finality. 'Mama, I haven't. And you know it.'

Grace took Helena's arm and said, 'Come on, Hellie, I'm going for a walk. Are you coming?'

Thomas went to bed at eight o'clock, and appeared to be asleep by the time Ellen joined him, an hour later. The girls had not returned.

Next morning, nobody spoke. While the family in general went by car, Helena and Grace walked to Mass together. When all returned, Thomas received his breakfast alone in the parlour. The other children sat quietly, except the youngest, Hugh, who asked, 'Why is everybody saying nothing?'

Grace smiled and said, 'We're trying to teach you the virtue of silence.'

Mid-morning, Helena and Grace left the house together, with a basket containing food. Ellen did not ask where they were going.

Thus ended the first altercation in the Kane family which challenged the autocracy of the parental knowledge. Nobody had ever before dared. Complete control over the children's opinions had held sway. Every item of information, or thought, or learning that they brought to the house had been altered parentally in some way. Mainly by their father: he put their world through his filter; he changed, challenged and reordered, until all things they ever knew or considered had been rinsed through his mind.

Ellen had continued to serve his utter writ, living separate lives, wife and mother: that according to her lights, seemed best, in the fitness of things. She had never contemplated that it had, eventually, to crack: too extreme. Now his wife did not know how Thomas Kane would react to this revolution under his roof.

At six o'clock that evening he gave his response, when he opened the parlour door and summoned Ellen.

'She.' He paused. '*She* – is not to come into this house again. Nor will I speak to her – until I have a letter from her setting out her apology in the form I have drafted here.'

He handed Ellen a sealed envelope. As she spoke, he held up a hand. 'No. I've said it.'

He closed the parlour door in her face. Ellen stood in the hall, looking at the envelope.

Helena and Grace returned.

'We went to the Grey Valley,' said Grace matter-of-factly. 'We saw Mrs Stokes.'

'Grace. Helena, love, you'd better hear this too. Grace, your father says he wants an apology from you. He has written out a letter to help you.' She handed it to Grace, who, leaning on the handlebars of her bicycle, took the envelope and, without opening it, tore it in half, then dropped it to the gravel.

'Oh, Grace!' said Ellen, in dismay, not anger. 'He says you can't come in unless you apologize.'

Helena picked up the torn letter and held it out to Grace.

She shook it away. 'Simple. Then I won't come in. Hellie, get me my travel bag, will you, and I'll go.'

'Grace! Grace!' said Ellen.

Helena went indoors and packed Grace's bag, while mother and daughter stood beside each other. Ellen talked; she wheedled, she attacked, she cajoled, she wept. Grace did not move. Helena came out, handed Grace her bag; the girl fixed it to the carrier clip at the back of her bicycle and rode away, saying, 'I'll drop you a note, Hellie, 'bye, Mother.'

Helena said to Ellen, 'This is awful.'

Late that night, Helena read Thomas's draft apology.

> Dear Daddy,
> I am heartily sorry for having offended you, and for having shown you such disrespect. I undertake and give you my word that I will never do so again, and that I will support all your actions on the Grey Valley.
> Your obedient daughter,
> Grace Kane.

Nor was it lost on Helena that the Act of Perfect Contrition, which they had been taught by Ellen to say every night of their lives in case God called during their sleep for their immortal souls, began with the words, 'Oh my God, I am heartily sorry for having offended Thee.'

Next evening, as Thomas and Ellen took a late walk, she remarked as if thinking aloud, 'I have to say – that was very moving what Mrs Stokes did in the school. I haven't been able to get it out of my head.'

Thomas cleared his throat. 'She keened like that at my father's funeral.'

Ellen looked up at him in amazement. 'You never told me.'

'She did.' He stopped himself speaking, as he always did when anything of feeling came near the surface.

'People get attached to land, don't they?' asked Ellen later. 'I mean, if it is only a haggard garden?'

'They do,' said Thomas, still thinking, 'they do.'

Ellen tried to clinch it, moved too soon.

'I suppose you feel a sympathy for her so?' she asked in a tone of hope.

He withdrew at a typical speed. 'No, I have a job to do.' And as he so often did, he vacillated, leaving her unsatisfied either way, 'But I understand her distress.'

'So –' she chose carefully. 'So – if a few people take Mollie Stokes's side, what way, I mean, in what manner do you think they should be spoken to?'

'Depends on who they are.'

Local debate had begun. As no compensation figures had yet been struck, hostile mutterings had started, initiated mainly by those outside the valley who did not qualify for cash or rehousing. Five other families in the valley had come out and said they would not leave, that the waters could close over their heads.

Ellen said, 'Well, the Griffins, the Careys, the Ryan Jacks, the Hallorans and the Healys. As well as Mrs Stokes.'

He followed her list. 'The Griffins are scroungers. The Careys no better. The Ryan Jacks don't belong there anyway, they're incomers, they only went there at the turn of the century. The Hallorans will smell money like a cat smells fish and they'll go where that is. The Healys aren't worth talking about.'

Ellen waited, then said, 'And old Mrs Stokes?'

'She'll be dead by then.'

'But if she's not.' Ellen stopped.

'H'm.' Thomas stood and thought.

11

One remark of Grace's cut into her father – her observation regarding his lack of close friends. It attacked his view of himself as a man who had command over his world. He knew from old days the value of comradeship, knew how a friend warned of a possible bullet in the head, or mopped a wound with a handkerchief or scarf. Although capable of relaxing with people in exalted positions, he had no confidants.

Now he began, not necessarily aware, to change this – difficult in a system where he required himself to remain above the people, in order to retain his authority over them. Not that a good confidant proved easy to come by.

Jack Hogan: too drunk too often, with a talkative wife.

The Canon: would use a confidence as a weapon in an argument, and now too old.

Herbert Winer: the husband of Ellen's friend, and anyway had to have everything explained to him twice.

On the day during which he most reflected upon Grace's remark, a confidant appeared, to whom Thomas would open his heart. Completely. The appointment had been made the previous week. Dennis Sykes asked Thomas in a letter if he and his wife would care to come to the Royal Hotel in Mooreville for a drink.

Ellen did not go, said she had arranged to talk to a girl – coincidentally from the Grey Valley – getting married the following week. Thomas arrived in the hotel on the dot of five o'clock. Dennis looked at his watch.

'Punctuality. The mark of the gentleman,' he said. 'How do you do, Mr Kane, how nice to meet you again,' and held out his hand. 'Mrs Kane not with you?'

Thomas explained. Dennis ushered him to the far end of the bar: 'I've asked the barman to keep this little corner free so that we can talk in private.'

'How are you getting on in general?' asked Thomas.

'Settling in, settling in. I have a house now, and I am getting a telephone, believe it or not.'

'A telephone? Yes, I suppose you would need one,' said Thomas.

'I'm being driven everywhere at the moment,' said Dennis, 'and – ah, yes, now you'd know. I have to buy a car, or at least the company is getting me one. What's a good make of car?'

Dennis Sykes had made careful enquiries. They told him Thomas Kane saw himself as an important person, liked to be viewed as a figure of authority. Kane, they said, acted as if in charge of everything, had no idea that many people hated him.

'A cold man,' they said, 'very big in himself.'

'A bad bastard,' said others in Dublin; 'he's vicious and he thinks he's above everyone. But – he's a man you have to keep in with, he knows people. Since the old days.'

Even if these remarks ran along a scale from half-mockery to sneering, Dennis sensed that people feared the teacher. Therefore – woo him.

Dennis believed in his own luck – provided he assisted it. On the very day he had chosen as the date on which to leave Rose, the Government approached with the

Deanstown project. An afternoon of discussions persuaded him. At a party two nights later, he met the people who would rent his house: everything up and running within three days.

'Amazing, Binnie, wasn't it?'

'No, little Dennis, there are only two kinds of people in the world, those who make their own luck and those who have none. In other words, darling – you and me.'

'Only drawback, Binnie, I'm going to be soon sick of these peasants.'

'Have you left her with one, Dennis? The Dublin lass? Bun in the proverbial?'

He reflected: they were sitting in the small bar at the Mayflower Hotel off Park Lane.

'Don't know. Still – not my problem.'

'Dennis darling, somewhere inside me – but I can't find the place – I hate you.'

'Come on, Binnie, I'm your star pupil!'

'But Dennis, darling, I'm a woman. Sister-feelings.'

He shifted. 'Oh, yeah? Well. She was nice. All right. But you know. Time to move on. God, she was boring, though. Bo. Ring. Still, I weaned her off religion, I did that for her.'

'And,' asked Binnie, 'you think that's a favour?'

Thomas Kane replied, 'I think the Wolseley is a lovely car.'

Dennis replied, 'Then a Wolseley it will be' – but Dennis had ordered a Wolseley long before Thomas Kane mentioned it.

'Yes,' he reflected. 'All that nice leather. And wood.'

'Exactly,' said Thomas Kane, his hat carefully on the seat beside him.

'I can't tell you how excited I am about this great

project,' said Dennis. 'This is my big opportunity. And I have to say I'm quite nervous. Now – a man like you, you must have had some challenges in your life. Tell me something – if you don't mind my asking you, if I'm not imposing on you.'

Thomas said to Ellen that night, 'He's an extraordinarily sincere individual.'

'No,' he said to Dennis, 'you're not imposing on me, not at all.'

'How do you overcome fear? I mean – I wake up at night sweating with fear in case I get this project wrong. In case the day we press the button to let the water into the dam catchment, nothing will happen.'

Thomas smiled – the smile he used for the Archbishop, the smile he used for John and Lily McCormack.

'Yes, yes,' he said thoughtfully, rubbing his chin. 'Are you a religious man at all?'

Thomas said to Ellen, 'And do you know something else, something really surprising? He's taking Instruction, he was attending a priest in Dublin. Father Goode in Merchant's Quay.'

'Oh, isn't that ideal,' said Ellen with a dry edge, but said little else.

'Oh, by the bye,' said Dennis to Thomas (a phrase Thomas soon began to use), 'I hadn't realized about Cardinal Newman's great connection with Dublin?'

'Oh, yes, oh, yes. Very much,' said Thomas. Who then returned to the subject. 'The thing about fear.'

Dennis leaned forward flatteringly to hang on every word.

'The thing about fear is. Fear is one of two things. Fear of that which you don't yet know anything about. Or that which you know from experience, and therefore you know you have good reason to fear.'

Dennis sat back and looked thoughtfully into the middle distance. He paraphrased Thomas's words.

'Mmmm. "That which you don't yet know anything about. Or that which you know from experience is worth being afraid of." Is that what you're saying? Gosh, that's an intelligent remark.'

Said Thomas to Ellen, 'He's very stimulating to talk to. He grasps things immediately.'

Dennis continued, 'So what you're saying is. I have to ask myself. Which am I afraid of? Something I already know. Say – if I had done something like this hydro-electric scheme, and it didn't work. Which isn't the case. Therefore what I must be afraid of is – that this project won't work?'

He stood to order another drink, absolutely refusing Thomas's intervention and protest.

'And they say,' said Thomas to Ellen, 'that the English aren't hospitable. I could hardly buy the man a round of drinks.'

From the bar, Dennis called to Thomas, 'Now I notice you like your water in a separate glass. Like the Americans.' He returned and mused and quoted. 'Mmmm. "Two kinds of fear." I can see now what Mr Quinlan meant.'

'Mr Quinlan? You mean the man with you?'

'Yes,' said Dennis. 'He's one of the head men. He said one of the reasons Deanstown was chosen, it wasn't entirely a geographical decision. Although it has turned out that way. One of the reasons was that the support on the ground – meaning you – would be as intelligent and sensitive to all our needs, he said, as we'd find in Ireland. I hadn't realized you were so well known.'

'Ah!' Thomas jerked his head in a modest demurral.

Mr Quinlan had said no such thing. He had remarked

that an old gunman he knew told him Kane was once known as an 'icy savage'.

'Have you lived here long?' asked Dennis. 'It's quite a lovely place. Did all that sense of – of – ' Nobody struggled for a word more impressively than Dennis Sykes. 'Civilization. Did all that civilization – did it come from that gorgeous-looking Castle? I'm looking forward to exploring it.'

He had also heard of Thomas's love of the Castle.

'It looks so like some of the châteaux I've stayed in in France,' said Dennis, who had never been to France.

'He's a much-travelled man, too,' said Thomas to Ellen.

'Jesus, Binnie, don't joke, this really is the back of beyond. I mean this is so remote the birds can't get there!'

'You'll be able to go native, darling, you can shag all those thoroughbred cattle.'

'There are no such creatures as thoroughbred cattle, Binnie.'

'Oh yes, there are, Angelica's new man-friend's got them.'

'Binnie, I have no indoor plumbing in my house, for God's sake.'

'What no bidets, no douches for the ladies? Dennis darling, what *will* you do?'

'Did you know that Dean Swift stayed there?' Thomas eagerly sought new listeners to the history of the Castle.

Dennis swivelled. 'Don't tell me he wrote my favourite book there?'

'And he seems very well-read,' said Thomas to Ellen. 'I mean he quoted from *Gulliver's Travels*, and not from the part we all know, not from Lilliput, but from Brobdingnag.'

'Goodness,' said Ellen, washing under her arms.

'No,' said Thomas to Dennis. 'He had that written before he came here.'

Dennis allowed his crest to fall.

'What a pity the place seems to be falling in ruins,' he said.

'Ach!' said Thomas. 'Don't talk to me. I fought and fought to save that place. I think it should be preserved, I mean it has a great history.'

'So important,' said Dennis, 'so important, a sense of history.' He insisted on Thomas joining him for supper – 'unless your wife might be discommoded?'

'And such a great vocabulary,' said Thomas, watching Ellen pull the nightdress over her head. 'Lovely to hear someone speaking good English. "Discommoded". "By the bye".'

'And you should see this guy they all defer to, Binnie, this headmaster. He's like – he's like a hillbilly in a suit, no, he's posher than that. He's like, he's like – a bad sheriff in a Roy Rogers film. He has these eyes as blue as the worst kind of glacier, he's twice my height –'

'Well, darling, in all conscience – *would* that be difficult?'

'Shut up, Binnie. He wears these homburg hats, he's really frightening. Ask him a question and he takes up to five, ten seconds before beginning to reply and he – he –'

Dennis stopped.

'He keeps putting his hands together like this.' Dennis made a gesture of prayer-folding. 'But he does it as if he has to control them otherwise the hands might of their own accord reach out and strangle you.' He twinkled at Binnie. 'Wife's a peach, though. Absolutely right for me. Little partridge. Face like a renaissance madonna.'

'So you're going to divide and rule, darling D?'

'Don't know, Binns, don't know. Doubt if she's ever had a production number.'

Binnie punched him. 'Christ, you're a vulgar little punk.'

Ellen, seeking the advantage of Thomas's mellow mood, straightened a pillow and murmured, 'I had a note from Grace. I think she might be home for an hour or two tomorrow night.'

'No.' Clear as a handclap.

'She's only passing –'

'No.'

'Thomas, she's –'

'No.'

'But –'

'Look. I spent the evening with a civilized and decent young man who understands the function of respect. She is not coming into this house until she writes that letter of apology.'

The conversation ended. Thomas slept and, as always after some whiskey, snored. Ellen heard the mantel clock in the parlour strike three before she began to doze.

Munch had come home for Easter, much spryer again, as he always seemed after one of his 'holidays' in the 'hospital'. He lurked in the woods when Dennis Sykes arrived; then, like an Indian brave, long-legged Munch raced the new Wolseley as it glid through the shrubs that lined the avenue. A last dash via the walled garden and thence to the kitchen where Viva sat glueing a mug handle and – 'He's here at last,' gasped Munch.

'Who? The dandy Jim?' Viva rushed to the window. 'He is, by Jove, he is. Mother! Quick, up the stairs. Fast.'

Rhona left the hall and lurked at the top of the landing.

Dennis tugged the bell-pull, and stood admiring the view through the windbreak straight across to the Castle.

'Mother,' Viva called dulcetly, 'a gentleman to see you,' and bowed to Dennis.

Rhona then made her entrance, descending the staircase like a dowager in an opera.

'Good afternoon.'

'Mrs Ulverton, I believe?' asked Dennis.

'Credulous of you – but entirely accurate. And you? Do you have a card?'

'No. My name is –'

'I know who you are, I'll tell Mother,' said Viva. 'This is the dam builder.'

'Viva!'

'Mother,' said Viva patiently, 'the man who is building the dam, not the damn builder.'

'Hooh!' trilled Rhona. Every moment of this had been rehearsed – with Munch playing Dennis.

'Mr Sykes,' said Viva. 'Isn't it?'

'You must be having the Dickens of a time,' said Munch from near the bamboo.

'Oh, forgive him.' Rhona smiled.

Said Dennis, 'Charming house.' He gazed around.

'Yes but do you get the joke?' insisted Munch. 'Sykes, Dickens. *Oliver Twist.*'

Dennis smiled.

'Not very flattering, is it?' said Rhona.

'No, that's all right, Ma'am,' said Dennis.

'No, I mean your name, Bill Sykes. Do come in here. We use the morning-room in the afternoons, that's the way we are. *Bill* Sykes. Shall I call you "Bill"?'

'My name's Dennis, Ma'am. Call me Dennis.'

'No. Sit down. You're too late for tea, I'm afraid, and too early for drinks.'

Viva sat across the table and, chin on her hands and elbows on the table, looked steadily at Dennis.

'I just called,' he said, 'because I'm making it my business to meet everyone affected by the electricity's arrival.'

'Thoughtful.'

Viva said abruptly, 'I know something about you.'

'Oh?' said Dennis, turning pleasantly.

'You are – a little fucker.'

Dennis shook his head as if to clear it. 'I beg your pardon.'

'By which I mean, you're pint-sized and you fuck women.'

'What my daughter means in her inelegant way, she's known too many military men' – one smile in Rhona's repertoire fluttered like a lace handkerchief – 'is that she believes you are a seducer, Mr Sykes.'

Dennis's mouth fell open.

'You do, don't you. Yes, you do fuck, admit it?' Viva pressed with glee.

'Don't worry, Mr Sykes, don't worry, in this house we like men who like women. It's all right. "As you were, troops." Were I younger, I'd take you myself. Please don't answer because you're likely to come out with some asinine compliment and I couldn't bear it.'

'I bet you never did it in a haybarn,' said Viva, 'because you'd have thistle spines up your B-o-t-Tom. Everyone thinks haybarns are great, but that's what happens.'

'Yes, Viva, we needed the depth and width of your experience, thank you,' said Rhona. 'Now, Mr Seducer Sykes, I suppose you have persuaded everyone to take your electricity?'

227

'Apparently not,' smiled Dennis a little recovered, but edgy.

'Ohhhhh? And why not?'

'Superstition in some cases. Fear in others.'

'Who says?' asked Rhona.

'Mr Kane has been canvassing.'

'He hasn't called here,' said Rhona, 'and we haven't decided.'

Dennis reached in his briefcase. 'Well, he has spoken to me about you, and that is in part why I am here. I have some forms here that will help.'

'*Forms* that will *help*? A contradiction in terms,' said Rhona.

'Mr Kane's idea,' said Dennis, his energy returning. 'You see, we have schemes whereby people can join, but if there's financial hardship, they can abate the payments –'

He got no further. Rhona rapped the table. 'What did you say?' She stood. Dennis looked up in alarm. Viva came and stood behind him, as tall as her mother.

'Out! Go, seducer. Leave!' Rhona glared.

He said helplessly, 'What have I said?'

'Little fucker in more ways than one,' said Viva.

Rhona snapped, 'My grandfather was at Sind. My great-grandfather co-owned the yard that built Cook's ship. Abate!'

Rhona swept from the room. Viva followed. Dennis sat alone, then rose, gathered his forms and found the front door. As he closed it behind him, he saw Munch behind the bamboo in the hall inside, waving, making a hand like a child saying, 'Bye, bye.' Rhona and Viva watched from the landing.

Dennis drove his Wolseley slowly down the drive. Inside him, in the woods, Munch ran fleet as a deer through the short-cut in the trees and, to Dennis's amazement, stood at the head of the avenue and waved good-bye again.

'Twins? No, no twins. Why do you ask?' said Thomas Kane when he and Dennis met the following night. 'A daughter and a son, that's all. No twins.'

'Well,' said Dennis, 'that is most confusing. You see, the son was standing in the hall when I left, and then a man looking exactly like him was at the gateway at the far end of the avenue when I drove out.'

Thomas smiled. 'Oh, that avenue loops quite a lot, so he simply raced through the wood in a short-cut.'

At Dennis's aggrieved look, Thomas remarked, 'Those people, they're quite – quite strange.'

As if to make up for the failed performance at the Ulvertons' – and Dennis had rarely had a failed performance – he turned it on for Thomas Kane. They had met, by arrangement, at the school. Dennis showed Thomas the Wolseley, let him drive it on a short spin.

'I approve. I approve,' said the teacher solemnly.

On their return, Dennis unloaded neat rolls of paper in drums. He uncoiled the first one on Thomas's high desk.

'Since you're so involved in this – it seemed only right to get your advice on one or two of the plans.'

Thomas, stiff with importance, took out his spectacle case.

'Now, this is what?' He looked at the drawings.

'This is the actual point of force, this is a cross-section.'

In one chamber of Dennis Sykes dwelt an uncontrived man, who planned, drew and executed engineering projects, who tested weight, mass, flow and energy, who led teams of other men excitedly and excitingly. From this, his only spontaneity, he made a reputation that would raise him up and up. He could not resist the challenge of imposing Man's will upon landscape, of making machinery subdue Nature. Now, still in the early reaches of his career, he pored over drawings with a country schoolteacher as enthusiastically as if he had been a student examining the works of Leonardo da Vinci. It proved to the good of his scheming that this, less calculated side of him assisted his campaign to capture utterly the support of Thomas Kane.

Before he arrived, however, he had invented a 'problem' on which he could consult the white-haired authoritarian. He wanted to flatter the man further – into thinking he had a contribution to make in matters completely beyond him.

'The difficulty,' said Dennis thoughtfully, 'is whether the fall of ground here, where the two diverted rivers will eventually meet, whether the fall of ground – at this point – will be enough to get the water through at a pace that will fill the dammed valley fast enough to meet our deadline. Because if you look here –' he produced another section. 'This is based on a geological survey of that far end.'

Thomas scrutinized.

'Now – we know we're going to blast this end,' continued Dennis, 'but there is a theory that we can only blast so far without damaging the underneath, core material. We can blast a channel, certainly, and it will be wide enough to accommodate the flow of water, but it might still be too high.'

Thomas's stern face always seemed grimmer behind the spectacle rims. He asked, 'In other words, because you can't blast as deep as you want – the water might have to climb a hill? If that's not putting it too simply?'

'Mmmm, quick grasp you have,' murmured Dennis, but did not labour it.

Thomas asked, 'And you're certain you can't blast down that far?'

'Not yet. We think so. There's one more survey. You may have seen the men, taking up cores.'

'Aha, is that what they were doing?' said Thomas.

'You must come on to the site more often,' said Dennis. 'Local knowledge is hard to come by. Of this calibre.' He almost lost the last words.

Thomas said suddenly, 'Have you thought about pumping?'

'Pumping?' Dennis lifted his head from the drawings. He looked at Thomas sideways. 'Pumping?'

Thomas showed him. 'A pumping station – just there, on that ridge. Would that be too expensive?'

'Show me?' Dennis animated.

'You know that at Shannon they pumped the water to create force. Into the Head Race,' said Thomas. 'The river is too placid otherwise.'

'Oh, my goodness, so they did,' said Dennis. 'So they did.'

The entire discussion was a set-up and a fallacy. At the far end of the Grey Valley, the limestone had proven soft enough to permit blasting safely down to any level they wished. Core sampling, a routine procedure, would go on until they ascertained that no serious flaws lay beneath the rock. This routine took place in all such projects to check for geological faults. Undiscovered underground channels could suck the two new rivers away, if the rock were blasted right through. A pumping station, therefore, had always seemed essential – but to control, rather than assist, the waters.

Yet Dennis Sykes allowed Thomas Kane to gain the

impression that he had made an important contribution – to a project that had long passed this stage of planning, even before Sykes joined the team.

'Pumping,' said Dennis. 'Pumping?' He straightened and sounded wistful. 'You should have been an engineer, Mr Kane. My late father was an engineer. And a very brilliant one, by all accounts.'

The school door clanged, and Ellen asked through the shadows, 'Thomas, is that you?'

'Come in.'

'Working without a lamp. You'll go blind, love.'

She started when she saw Dennis Sykes, who stood respectfully. Thomas introduced them again, and, more pleased than she had seen him for ages, said, 'We've just been looking over the plans for the construction, very complicated.'

'Your husband has been making some very valuable contributions,' said Dennis.

'Oh, I hope you are not straining your eyesight,' said Ellen to Thomas.

'I'm just going to take this man and give him a drink,' he replied.

'I'll run over and tell Mrs Hand,' said Ellen, moving away.

'No need, no need,' said Thomas. 'She'll know when she sees us.'

A postural stalemate began between the three people. Thomas stood and thought; she fiddled with the lapels of her coat; Dennis, hands behind his back, waited for Ellen to say something, judging the distance between him and her very carefully. He did not move his feet; he leaned a little in her direction. From Dennis, Ellen caught a faint aroma of soap, unusual on a man in Deanstown.

She opened her coat to tug down the hem of her woollen

jumper, patted it into place on her hips, closed the coat again, and settled it with both hands down the front of her body: she might have been buttoning armour.

'Yes,' said Dennis eventually, 'there isn't enough light left, is there?'

'What time do you think you'll be home, Thomas?' said Ellen.

Nor did she take any notice of his saying there was no need to tell Mrs Hand. Thomas Kane did not drink in either the public bar or the saloon of any pub in this part of the world. Mrs Hand and everyone knew that. Therefore, just before he and Dennis Sykes arrived, the parlour was cleared on Ellen's instruction, and the fire stoked.

Like eighteenth-century gentlemen, they sat facing each other.

'Everywhere I go,' said Dennis, 'people know who you are. That couldn't happen in England.'

'Really? Is that the case?'

Dennis nodded. 'People say you were a great – hero.' He halted respectfully over the word.

'Ah!' Thomas looked into the fire. He had taken off his coat.

'I know I'm the opposite side, so to speak,' Dennis began, 'but in England we know nothing of what happened here, it was never taught to us in school.'

'What?!' said Thomas, incredulity ablaze.

'Nope. Never.' Dennis shook his head.

'But – but that's extraordinary.'

'Not a word. All we know is that twenty-six counties of Ireland became independent in 1922.'

'And the other six still shackled.' Thomas shook his head.

Dennis asked, 'If I may, the thing I'd like to ask is – what was it like for a young man like you, obviously with great potential, what was it like suddenly to take up a gun and become a guerrilla?'

From that moment, Thomas Kane finally decided to make Dennis Sykes his close friend. He began, 'I'd have to tell you the full story. I'd have to go back a little before that, my own family background, and that sort of thing.'

'Please do. Please do.' The younger man spread his hands in kind invitation. Such were the gifts that made Dennis Sykes a successful chooser and leader. He had the capacity to make a figure like Thomas Kane trust him and, in Mrs Hand's parlour, Dennis heard a view of the man's life never before spoken, unknown to Ellen or the Kane children.

Thomas began. 'I was the oldest child of a family of eleven children, and I believe my mother had three other infant losses. My father's father lived with us, and both he and my own father were men of great intelligence. But that was no good. There was no system whereby we could rise much above menial livings. My grandfather was a quiet and lovely man, said little. He had the worst of things happen to him – he was predeceased by one of his own children. Which was my father.'

Thomas paused, sipped. 'I was eleven and very tall for my age. And one day my father sent for me from the fields where he was working. We were cottiers, a big family, small cottage, usual story. My father worked as an agricultural labourer. When I got there, it was a pleasant spring day, much sunshine and the big cloud formations we get around here. My poor father was standing under a tree, all alone. He was leaning against the bark, against the trunk, his head back. Like this.' Thomas in his chair indicated with his own high head.

'He saw me coming and he smiled and beckoned me. I, for some reason, began to run. Now, my father was the nicest man who ever lived. He had a smile in his eyes for everybody. He talked to me all the time, since I was – since I can recall. Going for water to the pump, he'd take my hand. If he found an unusual shape of vegetable he'd give it to me first. He'd watch the birds nesting, so's he could show me.'

Thomas stopped to reflect.

'Jesus! Talk about maudlin,' said Dennis to Binnie. 'He told me this long rambling sob-story about his miserable family. I had to sit there and listen like a confessor.'

'Father Dennis,' she coughed, 'that would get you the girlies' secrets. Father Dennis Sykes.'

Thomas continued. 'Suddenly I found I was having to support my father's weight. He said to me, "I have to go home." And we began to walk. I don't know how I knew, but I knew it was serious.'

The drama became so inherent in Thomas's voice that Dennis leaned forward without ploy.

'We walked home, and he said to me as he sat by the fire – my mother had gone to the village, the younger children were playing around somewhere – he said to me, "Find your grandfather." He liked his father the way I liked mine.'

Suddenly Thomas broke off and looked at Dennis, 'Isn't this a bit insensitive of me? I mean, knowing that, well, your own poor father – ?'

Dennis waved a hand. 'No, I've always wanted to know about other people's fathers.'

He nodded, and Thomas carried on. 'So. My grandfather came in. He looked at my father and said to him,

"Where are you complaining?" and my father said, "Here," pointing to his cheek and throat. To cut a long story short, I went for the doctor, who said he couldn't come. He told me to bring my father to him. We put him on a neighbour's cart and when we got to the doctor's surgery, we had to wait while the landlord's dog was having a splint put on its hind leg because the landlord's wife, "the Lady", as she was known, would not go to a vet, only Dr Williams would do.'

Thomas Kane paused, passed a hand over his eyes.

'Dr Williams looked at my father, said very abruptly "What's wrong with you?" My father said, "Pains, doctor," and began to show him. "I suppose you drink too much," said the doctor. "No, I don't," said my father. To cut a long story short, he said after a while, "You have cancer, it will be busiest in your jaw, you will live about four months." That's all he said.'

The teacher grew agitated. 'I helped my father out to the cart where my grandfather waited. There was no bed in the hospital, my father never even got a nurse. The doctor came to see him only once more. And I used to see that doctor driving in the gates of the house to the landlord and his wife, oh, once a fortnight. While my father rotted in front of my eyes. I never got over it. It made me silent. My children find me silent. That I know. My neighbours find me silent. And I *am* – well – silent.'

In an attitude of attentive sympathy, Dennis Sykes listened. Nobody came to the door: enough drink, as was the custom for Thomas Kane and his guests, had been provided to obviate the need for any disturbance: he had seen to that years ago, knowing the size and eaves-dropping range of Mrs Hand's ears.

Thomas Kane said nothing for a long time. Then he spoke again.

'And it is that experience that more than anything else helped to make me the way I am. I should have been a – a professor. A mathematician –'

'Well, yes, I can see that –' chimed Dennis enthusiastically.

'Or, a lawyer. Not buried in this place, not teaching the three Rs to this, this –' Thomas struggled for a word. 'This hole-in-the-wall.'

12

In the ordinary scheme of things, Dennis would have used Thomas Kane as his local touchstone, as his local protection, his eyes, ears and advantage: Dennis worked that way.

That following week-end he said, 'Binnie – you can only call me heroic. I mean, I listened. I actually listened. With some attention, I may say. To his boring, boring, droning story.'

'Little Dennis, darling, I've been thinking about you. You're all ulterior and no interior.'

'No, Binnie. I need the fellow. I have to stomach him.'

What Dennis did not yet know was the degree to which he would suddenly, urgently require Kane. He had not necessarily chosen the most effective local representative: Dennis, being an outsider, should have selected someone closer to the people, someone who heard things – not a man from whom the locals shied away. And there would be things to hear – as Dennis only discovered on his return from his seasick-making 'relief' week-end in London.

He drove back to Deanstown in foul weather, on the bad roads. Early on Monday morning he visited the site, to find that the men had stopped work on the main infra-structural artery: 'Aah, too wet, Sir, sure you couldn't get a duck to work in weather like this.' From under the trees they gazed happily to the dark-grey skies and leaned on their shovels.

Sensibly, he realized he would have to raise their wages: fortunately, the international funds were about to flow. He telephoned Dublin – but heard something else.

Dennis spoke to Dublin three times a day: from the Post Office in Mooreville: his own telephone had not yet been 'rushed in'.

'I don't quite get what you're saying. You'll have to interpret the signs for me,' called Dennis down the crackling line. 'Serious or not?'

'Not unserious,' said Mr Quinlan.

'Is there a balance that can be tipped?' yelled Dennis.

Mr Quinlan, who somehow seemed not to have to shout, replied, 'Well, as you know, I'm not an alarmist.'

Cried Dennis, 'What will they do?'

'There will be a letter in tomorrow's papers, apparently,' said Mr Quinlan. 'We'll confer again. Once you've seen it.'

'Do you know what the letter says?' called Dennis, mindful of listeners outside the call-booth.

'I can give you a whiff of gist.'

Dennis listened, and sucked a vicious 'Dtthh.'

'Can you get those telephone people moving?' called the irritated Dennis.

'Strategy: to commandeer irrevocably TK's support.' Dennis looked sideways at the quick note he wrote. 'Does TK know?' he scribbled – does he know that his own blasted daughter Grace Kane had left her teaching position to organize a Grey Valley Campaign?

'A fast mover too,' said Mr Quinlan in his whiff of gist.

He told Dennis's ear that so far she had enrolled the help of a historian from University College, Dublin, two from University College, Cork (one of whom had been born in the Grey Valley), a couple of scientists from

239

Trinity College, and the Deputy Director of the Natural History Museum.

'Yes, I'd say they're what you'd call medium important,' considered crackling Mr Quinlan; he pronounced it 'meejum'.

Grace guessed she needed a year. 'NN-mmm,' she nodded. 'A year's leave of absence. It will take a year. Or so. N-m.' She smiled like an attacker.

'What are you going to live on?'

Grace said, 'Um.'

'Your father's not going to help, surely?'

'Dlok,' clicked Grace with her tongue. 'Probably not,' she said.

'I can see your passion for it, though, and I'm a great believer in letting passion have a run for its money. Let me think. We'll talk tomorrow.'

Next lunch-time, Grace went to see her headmistress again.

'Well?' she pounced.

The Principal never ate the crusts on her sandwiches; she piled them like little planks all over the place. 'If you're fighting for these people – I'm assuming they want you to fight for them?'

'Oh, they do, they do,' said Grace.

'Grace, are you extending the truth?'

'No! Look –' Grace began to justify.

Miss MacNamara put up two restraining yet submitting hands.

'All right, Grace, all right, all right. I can tell that the hordes of Hy-Brasil wouldn't stop you. Goodness, you're like your mother.' Grace grinned.

'Practicalities?' asked the Principal. 'The food in your mouth, the roof over your head?'

'Oh!' Grace animated. 'I hadn't thought of that.' And she solved it swiftly. 'I could stay with that woman I was telling you about, Mrs Stokes, she has no one.'

'And she wouldn't be too hard on you in terms of what she'd charge you?'

Grace said, 'Oh, no. She'd now be very glad of the company.'

The Principal, tearing off a soft perforation of bread, said, 'I can't, you know of course, give you full pay for a year off. Matter of fact, I can't give you any pay for a year off. The Department wouldn't have it.'

Grace waited. Miss Mac's chewing would stop one day. It did.

'But if you'll agree, I'll mix things a little. And this is what I'll do. If you continue to take the adult classes four times a week. And you can do two on one night, if that suits, I'll be able to manage to put you on three-quarters pay.'

Grace clapped her hands.

'Ah. Ah. Provided. Provided.'

Grace had already complied in her own mind with whatever the Principal would demand.

'Provided – when all this is over, you guarantee to teach here for at least two years. And. And. In that two years, you do the adult classes free until you make up the three-quarters pay I'm giving you. It may even be up to three years, I haven't worked it out.'

Grace said, 'Oh, ye-ssss, Miss MacNamara, I will, I will. I promise.'

The Principal said, 'Well – I know you will.'

Grace left the room – and was called back.

'Grace, do you know where you're going to get the money for this campaign of yours.'

'Money?' said Grace.

'Yes, posters and train fares – you'll have to go to

meetings. You'll have to see people. They'll have to come and see you. All of that.'

'Oh.' Grace stopped.

'It's okay, it's okay. There is a fund in this school,' said Miss MacNamara, 'not very large, but never called on and entirely at my discretion. You know the photograph in the hall?'

'John Francis Clancy?' asked Grace.

'He left money for what he called "Civic Projects". He left it for the education of the children who wanted to find out how their country worked. Very loose rules, really. It's a bursary. I administer it.'

Grace ooh-ed.

Miss MacNamara said, 'I'll start you off with fifty pounds.'

'That's a fortune, Miss Mac.'

'You have to keep an account of every penny, receipts, everything.'

'I'm not going to have enough thanks in me,' said Grace.

Said the Principal, 'If you're seriously doing drawings of your precious Valley, I'd love a drawing of one of those fiddle-fronted dressers.'

'Oh, I'll do you a water-colour!' cried Grace.

'One last question. Your parents. What do they think?'

Grace said without a blush, 'Oh, you know what they're like.'

The letter had beneath it, 'We would welcome correspondence on this subject. Ed.'

Dear Sir,
We the undersigned wish to draw attention to a scheme being undertaken by the National Electricity Board, who propose to drown the renowned Grey

242

Valley of Deanstown for the purpose of building a hydro-electric dam. The Grey Valley is an area of outstanding natural beauty, with major fossil resources, unusual botanical life and a considerable depth of natural, built-in homecraft. It contains, for example, the last fiddle-fronted dressers and settles handmade onsite in this country: some of them are over three hundred years old and have been in constant use since before Cromwell.

Many of the residents do not wish to leave their ancestral homes, and their lives have become very distressed since the unilateral announcement – with minimum consultation – of this project. No alternative possibility seems to have been considered.

The undersigned seek the support of the nation in the preservation of the Grey Valley and we would ask all interested parties to convene outside Hand's public house in Deanstown on Sunday, 19 April for a march to the Grey Valley. At a rally, several of the undersigned and other dignitaries will speak. Funds to support this campaign will be gratefully welcomed.

signed:

Grace Kane, Campaign Co-Ordinator.

co-signed:

Thos. Considine, dept Botany, University College, Dublin.

Edward Cassells, dept Geology, Trinity College, Dublin.

Michael Edwards, Natural History Museum.

Elizabeth Miller, dept History & Folklore, University College, Dublin.

Anthony MacNamee, dept History, University College, Cork.

Michael Phelan, Folklore Commission.

=

Helena waved her arms and said with a feeble face, 'She has been given some leave of absence, Daddy. I don't know how much.'

Thomas shouted, 'What is she trying to do, embarrass us? Make us all look like fools in public?'

Ellen said, 'Let us get some more knowledge. Helena, can you ask Gracey –'

'The girl's name is Grace!' said Thomas. 'What more knowledge do we need? There she is in black-and-white.' He rapped the paper ferociously with the backs of his fingers. 'Where is she now? Where is she? "We the undersigned. Campaign Co-Ordinator." I'll give her Campaign Co-Ordinator.'

He caught Helena's arm: Ellen intervened, persuaded away his grip.

'Thomas, Helena doesn't know. I'll go and find Grace.'

The talk spumed, high as a hot geyser. In Hand's, the newspaper floated along the counter from drinker to drinker, accompanied by words such as 'comeuppance' and 'his high horse'.

Thirty miles away in Janesborough, the Winers read it at breakfast: Herbert always read the letters column first.

'Can there be another Grace Kane?' Leah derisively echoed Herbert's enquiry. 'Of course that's Grace. But I feel for Ellen. Caught in the middle again.'

'You don't understand that man,' said her husband mildly. 'He suffers. He suffers inside.'

'I understand that he makes everyone around him suffer,' snapped Leah.

Everyone who knew the Kanes had an opinion, took a position.

'No, Miriam,' said Jack Hogan. 'No, we won't march in that.'

'You're forgetting, Jack, that I was there. I was the one who got that man to London for his surgical operation. Has he ever as much as said a single word of thanks?'

'Miriam, where did you put the eggs?'

'And as for your trying to say the man may not even know I was in London, be that as it may, Jack, and it will be if life is true to form, it doesn't put a stopper in the fact that he thinks he's above everyone.'

'Ah, Miriam, these eggs are gone bad, look, their yolks are gone black. But sure – what matter?' said Jack with ease.

Last night in bed, for some strange and unspoken reason, Miriam had turned and taken his hand and placed it on her neck and kissed him on the mouth, a kiss fifteen years late but no less welcome for that: 'No less welcome, Miriam.'

Off the Janesborough bus, Grace cycled the last miles from Mooreville to the Grey Valley. By the southern road she went, avoiding Deanstown and her father's eagle eye through the school windows.

As she reached the climb, she learned how fast things moved on big projects. On the high far end, where the rivers would flood in, great lorries moved slowly up on the ridge like saurians. Their engine sounds, revving and slipping, rasped down towards her on the breeze. She turned the last bend to the Valley entrance, and in the other direction saw only the ring fence: no sign of the first excavations for the foundations of the dam wall.

So far, Dennis had initiated these works with a delicate air. He stayed away from the interior. No engine snarled on the Valley floor; only the wind agitated the trees. Although he had prowled the Valley from stem to stern, usually in the white light of dawn, he already knew that limit where molestation would begin. Oh – if he could build the entire thing as cleanly as possible. If he could just slide the dam wall across the mouth, and softly open the channel at the far end. And in the course of it all, let the Grey Valley continue to sit silent.

Problems: problems. He strategized through the nights like a boffin. Would the compensation plus the re-housing remove the objections by the actual residents of the Valley? If so, since they were his biggest threat, one potentially huge problem would evaporate. Before this campaign was mooted, he had figured on buying off the objecting Valley dwellers with a nudge up the compensatory scale, a nudge he would 'sell' to them. After which, the botanists, the historians, the geologists could be invited, openly and with small grants, to pay their last respects. Museum staff could take what they wished from the houses. Acknowledge the people's old furniture: emboss their names on the little museum plaques: all to be done quietly and constantly over a year: everything damped down, with Thomas Kane co-ordinating.

Then – flood the Valley and make the flooding dramatic, make it poetic. Invite the community to stand on the rim of the Valley and watch it filling in. They would drive, he said slickly to Mr Quinlan, from their new houses in the new cars their compensation had bought. He reasoned further that the natural shape of the landscape, the big lips of the valley behind the deep woods, helped him to conceal work-in-progress. He was right.

'Girl, I can't understand it,' said Mollie Stokes to Grace. 'There isn't a sound here, the place is as silent as the grave except for them few lorries at the far end.' She called them 'lurries'.

'Listen, Mrs Stokes, can I stay with you?' said Grace. 'Is that all right?'

'The company'll be lovely for me. I'm not right in myself since.'

'Did anyone come to see you?' asked Grace.

'No, girl, only that strange creature and she walking like a heron, you know her, that Protestant woman from over near your house, and her daughter with her.'

Grace took off her scarf, shook her hair. 'Oh – the Ulvertons. What did they say?'

Mrs Stokes said, 'They said I should fight to keep what was mine, that nothing in the world can buy the past.'

'And what did you say?'

'I agreed with them. But sure why wouldn't I?'

'And,' asked Grace, 'nobody from the electricity company?'

'No, girl, not soul nor sinner.'

'And,' asked Grace, 'you say there's no work hardly to be seen going on? At least nothing as much as you'd expect?'

'Child,' replied Mrs Stokes, 'there's nearly nothing.'

Grace said, 'Yippee! Maybe we've stopped them. I knew it, I knew it! I knew we could do it! Well, they didn't have much fight in them! Oh, Mrs Stokes, I think I'll run out and have a good look.'

Mrs Stokes's house stood near the Valley's entrance. Grace took the route she and Helena knew best, cutting up the lower slopes, through the early brush, until she came out on the first slides of shale that led to this part of the rim. On top grew thick hazel, arbutus, some aspens. Here they first saw the vixen and her cubs, even saw the dog-fox bring home a slain baby rabbit.

Thomas had said, 'Tell the farmers about those foxes. Chickens are getting killed.' The girls did not.

Grace stepped slowly down through the heavy groves. Cycling jolted her bladder, and she squatted in the ferns, inspecting carefully for nettles: this always made Helena laugh.

As a small child Grace always believed that the under-earth teemed with people – cities, schools, farms. Not on the same human scale, ten sizes down, she said to Ellen, who never discouraged. To please her mother, Grace added, 'And churches, Mama, and cathedrals. You can see the crowds going into Mass.'

As she crouched now, she saw through a gap in the ferns something which glinted. For a split moment she returned to that pleasing childhood belief. Far below – this was the highest point in the valley – a huge construction site had indeed begun to take form: some toy huts, several toy trucks, toy men moving. Grace yanked up her knickers, and rushed to the edge of the ferns. From here, you could see for miles; when the light was right you could even catch the weir. Beyond the woods, a tranche of the old commonage had been thickened with works: high wafers of planking; bins; a fence; a tall gate. It seemed, from where Grace stood, as if the people who dwelt beneath the ground had come to the surface at last, and had begun to conduct some concealed and sinister undertaking.

Mrs Stokes asked, 'But tears isn't going to improve all that, girl?'

Grace said, 'But I thought that letter might have stopped them. And that was why you weren't hearing any real work. I thought the lorries we saw were only for show.' She dried her eyes, and held up the letter in the *Irish Independent*.

'Read it to me, my eyes aren't that good the day.'

Grace read.

'A power of names,' said Mrs Stokes. 'A power of names.'

Grace regained her self-control and began to settle in. Mrs Stokes said, 'The room to the west' of the thick-walled house. From a deep woodlined alcove hidden by heavy curtains they pulled down the wall-bed.

'No draught of air in there, girl,' said Mrs Stokes, 'you'll be warmer than at a fire.'

Grace took off her shoes, lay on the bed, looking at the little carved embossed stars on the 'roof' of the bed. The bed-hangings, all handmade, had rich soft embroidery in yellows and blues.

'The county colours,' said Mrs Stokes. 'Blue and gold. And d'you see that patchwork? Four generations of women worked that. 'Tis blankets as well as a quilt.'

She folded it back to show Grace how the work had been built in cosy tiers. Under the dressy cover, each layer could unbutton from the next for seasonal adjustment.

'Your mother now'd love that,' Mrs Stokes said to Grace.

Acrid, pleasing smoke crept in, from the wood on the kitchen fire next door.

Ellen, in affection, reserved Grace's name from Thomas. But she did generate a quiet discussion with Helena. Was there more to this campaign than Grace's usual gift for drama? For example, was there someone 'putting her up to all this'?

Honesty compensated for Helena's timidity. She answered Ellen's myriad questions comfortably. About Grace's art classes; about the books Grace read; about Grace's view of Thomas. All questions came up quietly, not to judge or blame Grace, but to gauge her sincerity, her commitment. Ellen nodded as Helena explained patiently.

'I mean, Mama, don't think I'm getting at anyone, but there were times when the Valley was the only peaceful place on earth.'

Ellen made sympathetic noises and faces. 'I think, Helena love, I'll go and talk to her.'

Even the disliked people of the parish liked Ellen Kane – the Hands, the Burnses, the Brownes, the Cronins, sloppy people, leeches. They said she had 'even hands, she was fair'. Their children experienced no differentiation in the school. Ellen addressed her teaching duties as she did her marriage: richer or poorer, sickness and health. Oh, yes, get on her wrong side and you felt the blisters. If unfair she apologized; compare that, they said, to her husband whose lips had no shape for the word 'sorry'. With that woman you were the same as everyone else, no grudges, until you merited otherwise.

This row between her daughter and her husband disturbed Ellen, jarred the locus of her home. She had explained away or ascribed all other crises variously: blame, for instance, that past 'difficulty' in Thomas's life – followed, when he recovered, by the economic tensions of a big family, exacerbated by the uncertainty of harsh economic and political facts under a bad leader, the headstrong and devious de Valera.

So she spoke to herself, so she reasoned; and through all of this, and through the grim recurring daytime silences of her husband, Ellen Kane ran a good life, and in general outpaced the constrictions upon her. Rhona Ulverton, her confidante, had been such a help; how they talked; how they concluded with, always, a decision taken upon action for the best.

Now, sitting quietly with her housekeeping ledger, she kept doodling mad, interlocking, repeating, question marks.

When Helena came home for the week-end, she sent her with a pot of soup in the handlebar basket of the bicycle to see Mrs Ulverton.

'Tell her I want to see her. Any word of Grace?' whispered Ellen in the back-kitchen, shooing away Hugh who listened to everything.

'No. I thought you were going over to see her?'

'I'm trying to work a way of doing it without your father knowing.'

Helena whispered, 'Is he still –?'

'More than ever.' As she heard footsteps, Ellen raised her voice to normal mode, 'And be sure to tell her there's no need to send the saucepan back immediately, we're not in any hurry with it.' But it was one of the boys, whose footsteps sounded so much like Thomas's.

All news of Grace and her activities reached the Kanes as if by homing pigeons.

Always obliquely. Nobody ever said, 'Oh, I hear your daughter is going round putting up posters in all the pubs.'

They said, 'God, Mrs Hand is a fierce woman. She won't put up that poster. Sure, what's wrong with a poster, don't she put up posters for the circus, or for the thistle, ragwort and dock? I s'pose she's afraid of losing all that business from the workmen.'

Another woman remarked to Ellen, 'I think 'tis a shame them workmen going round tearing down them posters, I mean we all have our right to object to something.'

Thomas knew Grace had been in Mooreville, knocking on people's doors; had bought an advertisement in the *Nationalist* for the meeting; had booked seven people into

251

the Royal Hotel; was even expecting two people from London, a reporter and a photographer.

'Does she mean to make a total disgrace of us to the whole world?' fumed Thomas.

In face of this anger, Ellen did not go, but wrote,

My dearest Gracey,

I know you're busy – because we hear about you!

All I'm worried about is your health, that you're getting enough food and rest, and that you aren't making enemies.

I know you don't want to come home because of you and Daddy (who is well, thank God, as are all the others, Hugh getting as fat as a fool from eating as usual, but he's at that age). But I would love to meet you if you like.

Remembering you in my prayers always,

Your loving,

Mama.

When Helena reached the top of the Ulvertons' avenue, she saw Grace's bicycle against the pillars of the colonnade. They met in the hallway, and each said sweetly, 'Hallo, what are you doing here?' No touching, no handshakes even: the Kanes rarely made physical contact of affection.

'Mama sent me with soup.'

Grace laughed, and peered into the saucepan. 'I'll never guess – chicken and red lentils. Auntie Leah's recipe.'

Helena smiled. 'No, you'd never guess. But c'mon now, what are you doing here?'

'Enlisting supporters. How's home?'

'Mama's fine. She bought a lovely skirt in Hassett's Sale, sort of black herringbone pattern. Dad's like a –' Helena stopped.

'A fiend, a demon, a raging devil, a dervish, a bear with a sore head, a bull in a china shop –' Grace was enumerating on her fingers when Rhona called.

'Don't stand whispering in the hall like a pair of excited nuns, come in here!'

She lay on a chaise-longue, in the morning-room, her back to the light, clad in yellow and burgundy and gold.

'Helena, dear. Here to help your sister, I hope? We have all kinds of schemes, don't we, dear?' – to Grace. 'India or China tea?'

Both, uncertainly, said they would prefer China tea.

'Milk and sugar?' – and they both nodded: Rhona said, 'One doesn't have milk and sugar in China tea.'

Helena sat beneath a bamboo plant that had now somehow taken root within the wall. Grace took the other side of Rhona, and Munch drifted up and down the room, talking half to himself and half to his mother. Viva did not appear for several minutes, and when she did, her face wore a thick creamy covering, some kind of beauty treatment. She sat without comment.

Rhona hummed various tunes without finishing any bar of them; she also answered Munch's cross-talk. The table wore a wild cloth, red and blue spangles, painted elephants, tasselled, sequinned howdahs; the cups, large and shallow, seemed made of chintzed ivory.

Munch fumbled again and again in his crotch, sometimes with both hands at the front, and each time he did, Rhona gave a loud cough, then clicked her rings in a ching of embarrassment, and beamed at the girls.

Viva, lips immobilized with beauty cream, tapped Grace urgently on the elbow, making her start. When Grace looked up at her, Viva took Grace's hand and laid it on the sugarbowl, then indicated herself by prodding her own bosom. Grace divined Viva's intent and handed her the sugar. Viva took a cube, and, head back, popped it in her open mouth.

Rhona raised a hidden corner of the tablecloth, found a name-tag embroidered on it and held it aloft silently to Helena and Grace. She underlined the name – Rhona Mercury Wallace – with her long fingernail, whose varnish matched the hint of rouge on her cheekbones. Moments later she took her walking-cane, silently compared its elephant-head with the elephants on the tablecloth, and smiled at each girl in turn.

At that moment Munch made a dive for the door and Viva rose so quickly to stop him, that she dragged some of the cloth and spilled a little of all their teas. Munch subsided into an armchair. When Viva returned to the table, Rhona remarked, her eyes dark with concern, 'We have, as you will note, been having our little problems.'

'Mamma!'

'Are they blind, Viva?' and she continued tenderly, 'Viva, darling, you caused this. I told you that you must not tease him, and you must never appear again in front of him undressed. Not ever.'

'He is certifiable, Mamma. Why is he out?' pleaded Viva, trying to speak through the smothers of face-gunk.

'He's a dear boy [Munch was forty-seven]. Now, girls.'

Rhona sat back and drew her walking-cane to her, held the elephant's head between her knees.

'Did you find me diffident today? In certain parts of India tea loses its spiritual efficacy unless taken in some silence. Am I right in thinking you are almost exactly two years apart in age?'

Grace smiled, always the first to speak. 'Nm.'

'And you know about Love? Viva, darling, where are you going?'

254

'Mother, I've heard you on Love before.'

'You can hear it again. Stay.'

Viva stayed.

'Have men come sniffing yet?' asked Rhona.

The Kane girls looked at each other and smiled. Never kissed nor kissing; never read romances in magazines; the grip of the household had closeted them even from popular songs. When they left home, they were further sheltered. In Helena's Domestic Economy College, socializing with men was forbidden, and in Grace's Teacher Training, the girls took baths in their swimsuits.

Rhona said, 'Stand up each of you. Yes. They will be sniffing like hounds around you two. You, Helena, have the looks a certain sort of man likes, the type who likes a thin girl with a big bust. I, too, was most fortunate. Turn round.'

Helena stood with her back to Rhona.

'I see. And you, my dear,' she said to Grace. 'Turn round too. Yes, I thought so. Lovely creatures. You two will have so many men to choose from. So many. And all must be for love, none of this "good values" stuff, or any of that.'

In the armchair Munch held his hands in the air like wings and began to weep.

'Dear boy! Are you all right?' asked Rhona compassionately; coping with her disconcertment, she turned to the girls again, and tried to shut out the scene across the room.

'I know what I am saying must be heresy, heresy compared to what you have been told at home, at school and at college, but what is life without heresy? And here is another bit of heresy, because now you must go. I think, I really do believe, that no Irishman you will meet will be sophisticated enough to appreciate either of you girls.

Viva, do something about that would you? The poor boy's like an animal.'

Munch had sprawled disgracefully wide on the arm-chair, scratching vigorously.

'So look to the world,' declaimed Rhona, smiling at them, 'look to the wider world for your soulmates and you will be less disappointed, and the wider world will receive a bonus. Those teeth and those beautiful limbs you both have! And your eyes, and your colouring, blue with blond hair, and brown with black hair? Ohhh!'

She held out her hands, one to each. 'So lovely of you to come and see me. I shall be watching for whatever swain you produce, and I will approve or otherwise.'

She released Grace, gripped Helena tighter.

'One last thing, my dear. Are you living in mortal, daily terror of everything – your father, the Roman Catholic Church, the forces of darkness, the Man in the Moon, your own shadow? Ah!'

Grace began an intervention on Helena's behalf: Rhona held up a hand to interrupt.

'Listen to me, Helena, child. You are named after one of the greatest women the world has ever known. Helen of Troy. But not yet Helen of Deanstown are you? You're a sweet girl. And you can be brave. Your mother loves you, loves you both. I know. She tells me. But do you know what's at stake here? Do you know what heroics your sister is performing?'

Helena stood abashed.

Rhona continued. 'If this country is to have any future, people must object. Object.'

Grace said nothing, looked at Helena anxiously – who said nothing either.

'What's the matter with you, Helena? Speak, speak to me.'

'I don't know what to say,' replied Helena.

'Well,' said Rhona kindly, 'you could make a comment. On the validity of what I've just said. Or you could say, "I admire hugely what my sister is doing and it's time I got stuck into it too. And helped her." You now have an Easter holiday, your sister has this rally to organize, and she's trying to do it on her own. Go on, go and live with her in that old woman's house in the Valley, and try to keep some standards in this blasted land. Stop letting your father destroy your life.'

'Helena,' said Grace, hands out, expiating, 'I said nothing.'

'Didn't need to,' said Rhona, 'a clown could see it, Munch could see it – the talk of the bloody place, that man's arrogance. He's worse than a bloody bishop – an RC bishop, I mean. I adore your mother, give her my love. Give her my fondest love.'

Walking down the avenue, Helena said to Grace, 'Did you understand one word of that?'

'No!' and they laughed and laughed.

'What's a swain?' asked Helena.

'A posh version of pig?' suggested Grace. 'Swine. Swain.'

They laughed again.

Grace said, 'What are you going to do?'

'I think. I think –' Helena grimaced. 'I'll come with you.'

'Wheeeeee!' Grace danced.

So far as Ellen consciously knew, Helena departed that night for her own habitual accommodation. Yet, as she waved her daughter good-bye, something troubled Ellen. An untypical furtiveness in Helena? Why did she

257

suddenly take those heavy knitteds with her, so bulky in a bicycle's basket? Also, she had said so little about her meeting with Grace, brought minimal news of Rhona. Helena usually told everything: so, why did she seem evasive, uneasy? The queries rolled over and back inside Ellen's brain, over and back.

On the Wednesday afternoon of that week, Ellen lied to Thomas, said she was going to call on Mrs Martin Burke. Instead, she cycled to the Grey Valley. She told herself that she hoped to meet Grace: she suspected more, but knew not what.

Dennis Sykes, working with two surveyors on top of a crest, saw her. He stared into his binoculars until she disappeared into the woods, then anticipated that she would reappear on the upper line, a mile from the Valley's entrance. The two surveyors had not seen Ellen Kane – but Dennis, excusing himself, set off in pursuit; he crashed through the trees, down the incline.

She had her head down, exerting, pushing her bicycle up the steep slope when he walked through the high ferns, apparently lost in thought.

'Oh!' Both started: he transmitted extensive surprise and stopped. 'Hallo!'

'Oh, hallo – Mr Sykes.' They halted, and stood each other off on the ridge. Dennis pointed down – to the growing construction plant far below.

'Have you come to have a look? You should have come round to the site. What do you think? Great, isn't it?' He held his hand out as if promising her all the land she could see.

Ellen gazed, did not speak.

Dennis insisted: 'It is pretty marvellous, isn't it?'

'I'd no idea it was so –'

'Massive. And yet it is a small project.' He turned to her, hoping to dazzle. 'It's Ellen, isn't it?' He nodded. 'At least I think it is, your husband keeps referring to you as "my wife". But I seem to remember it's Ellen. Is this your first time up here?'

'Oh, no, Mr Sykes, we used to come here all the time, I mean, I didn't come that often. The girls did.'

'Ah, yes. The girls. How old are they?'

'Oh, I don't know why I still call them girls, they're young women now. Helena is almost twenty-six and Grace is twenty-four.' Ellen spoke as if to herself, tried not to look too much at him.

'I'm told,' said Dennis Sykes, 'that they're as pretty as their mother.'

Ellen had never heard herself called 'pretty'. Obliquer terminology prevailed in the countryside: 'an eyeful'; or, 'easy on the eye'. More usually, compliments came by comparison: 'I'll say this much for you, Ma'am, you're not a bit like Nellie Cunningham' – who had extensive whiskers, and a goitre the size of a myth.

To Dennis Sykes's compliment, 'I don't know about that,' said Ellen diffidently. Then she warmed. 'But they're nice girls. Well-behaved. And they're well-liked.'

'And I suppose Mother's cycling over to see that they're both settled in well?' Just a pleasant sense of enquiry.

Ellen, fast as lightning, said, 'Both? No, Grace is over here, only.'

Dennis put on his quizzical look. 'Oh? Forgive me, Ellen, I've a'hm –'

Ellen's face became a question, which he answered.

'Is your oldest daughter, is she the one with the lovely long hair, blonde? I know the other girl has your colouring?'

259

Ellen faced him. 'You mean Helena's here?'

'If that's her name. She came two nights ago, no, Saturday. I know it seems like we're spying. But we have to find out everything that's going on.'

'My husband doesn't know Helena's here, I mean –'

'You mean you did not know until this minute? Until I told you? Oh, no! I'm sorry. Sorry.'

Dennis stood beside Ellen. Ellen looked distressed, and he said, 'Look, this is none of my business, and yet it is my business. And I feel I can help in some way –'

No reply: he let a pause grow: he continued, 'I've come to admire your husband hugely, he is a remarkable man – he has told me so much about himself. His experiences and that. His family. He's even going to take me back to where he grew up.'

How often had the children complained that they knew so little about their father's family; how often had they been bitter that they met their father's likeable brothers so rarely. Ellen, who had seen the siblings together before Thomas 'changed', as she described it to herself, wondered whether he avoided his brothers because with them Thomas dropped his guard. She suppressed her sad rancour on the matter, looked at Dennis Sykes quizzically, and said nothing.

'And I really would do anything I can to help.' He gauged her all the time, looked at her forehead, her ears, her neck.

'Now there's this meeting coming up, this big rally, that your daughter Grace is organizing. I should imagine it is a matter of great pain to her father.'

She tried insisting. 'But my husband says very little about himself, Mr Sykes.'

'No. Oh, no. You're wrong, if I may say so. He says it

to me. And he does talk all the time about how all of this is upsetting him –'

Ellen looked at him hard and doubtingly.

Dennis remarked, 'You may not know this, but – men, you know. Well – they often tell each other things that they don't tell their wives.'

Seeing his lack of impact, sensing that a retreat might prove strategic, he modified. 'All good men like confidentiality. And great men need more than most.'

Ellen opened her mouth to say something, then closed it again.

'What were you going to say?' he asked quickly.

'Nothing.' She looked at him and changed her mind. 'When are you meeting my husband again?'

'This evening, as it happens,' and then Dennis Sykes trapped her into collusion. 'I won't say a word to him about meeting you like this. Okay? I mean on account of Helena. On account of this – this difficult new development.'

He smiled and held out his hand. Ellen shook it: again the fingers lurking in her palm; again, he held on for too long.

'Very nice meeting you alone, and in such a lovely place,' he said crisply, much too skilled ever to stray into smarm.

Despite herself she blushed.

Dennis remained on the heights, gazing down. First, he watched the swing of her buttocks as she walked to the path. He whipped his binoculars to his eyes as she hiked her thigh to the bicycle saddle on the roadway below. Why did she not go to Mollie Stokes's house? Anticipate, Dennis, anticipate: reflect upon this new development – he knew that Kane would call it his daughter's 'defection'.

What next, Dennis, what next? Can this family be turned upon itself to stop this idiotic protest? Wife doesn't seem susceptible: she must be made so. By whatever means.

Later that night, Dennis enquired, elbow to elbow with his principal road ganger, a man of great ears.

'That, ah'm, Mrs Kane?' The foreman listened and rubbed a lobe.

Dennis wondered aloud, 'Is she – she younger or older? Than she looks, I mean?'

'Ah, older, yeh.' The foreman wore a jacket over dungarees.

'Fresh, so?'

'Ah, yeh. She'd be rising fifty nearly. Else!' He called the woman. 'Else, your man Kane's missus, how long now is she here?'

Else Campion, with one tooth bucked, scratched her apron's strap. 'I know. For Joe had that dog, d'you 'member that good dog, we had, Saffron Stranger, d'you 'member, Liam?'

'An' didn't I make money outa him itself,' said Liam the foreman. 'Saffron Stranger, the very lad,' and turned explanatorily to Dennis. 'He was a coursing dog, like. And light, don't you know, for his size. And in wet going, oh, a pure bullet, wasn't he, Else?'

'He was so.'

Else never grew after the age of ten. On quiet evenings she stood on a crate behind the bar of Keaney's in the village of Silverbridge, conversing over her elbows on the counter; when she stepped down, she vanished and strangers became disconcerted.

'And that'd make her, that Mrs Kane, that'd make her have come here in 'twenty-four, no, I tell a lie, that'd be 'twenty-five, that's right, you can count it yourself sure.'

She yelled, 'I'm comin' Jimmy!' She lowered the voice, 'And they said at the time there was twenty-two years between them, I don't know for a fact, like, but the Canon over there, he had the birth certs, sure he'd have to for the wedding. And Kane was over double her age at the time, and if he was forty-four – so she'd be fifty. I'd say forty-nine for my own satisfaction, say.'

Liam gathered a huge ear in a hand and folded it. 'Aw, the fuck, hoh?' He murmured in wonder. 'Forty-fuckin'-nine? The wonders of the world.' The pliable ear comforted his hand.

'Fresh! Fresh!' said an amazed Dennis.

'Grand arse with it,' said Liam, who had divined, if never witnessed, his Chief Engineer's principal leisure. 'An arse you'd take home with you.' He spoke as slowly as a grave and lewd druid. 'Not that anybody'd ever, like. Drop the hand with her. And them dugs on her. She always had them, though, ever before the children.'

Dennis probed. 'Of course, Irish girls . . . ?'

'Ah, no, ah, no.' Liam rushed to defend whatever pliability he had found in the womenfolk he had met. 'Some are great sport. I knew a Roche woman. Where I was working the job-before-last. Two or three mediums of stout and she was the one'd be hauling you into the long grass on the way home. But there's other women and they thinks they pisses holy water.'

'Like, ah'm, Mrs Kane?'

'She keeps her hand on her ha'penny and the other on her beads. Don't she, Else?' he called, but tiny Else Campion had not returned to earshot. 'Oh, listen, sure Kane, he was to retire. And he wouldn't. He's going on an extension, don't you know? Else!?'

Else returned.

'Wadn't Kane for retirement?' Liam asked.

'He wor so, you're right dere.' Else made an 'O' in wonder. 'He wor to retire and he sixty-five, and they gev him an extension 'til sixty-eight, and the Canon said he wor to have another extension 'til seventy-one. That must be nearly up.'

Dennis pulled a mouth. 'He's a very fresh man for his age.'

'He is so,' said Else, 'sure the temper he have, 'tis that do keep him alive.'

Suddenly, Helena stiffened.

'What?' asked Grace, and rushed to the window thinking Helena had seen or heard something. The taller girl shook her head.

'No. Sorry. I mean.' Sometimes, her smile never developed fully. 'No, nobody there. Just, a shiver. A shiver of a feeling.'

Grace let the lace curtain fall from the cottage window.

'Someone walked over your grave?' she asked.

'Yes. Yes.' Helena held both hands to her mouth, a praying gesture.

'Hellie, look at this, I mean – only look!'

Like a builder, Grace ran her hands along the shelving of the deep window-sill and traced it into the shuttering, her water-clear fingernail following the natural grain of the wood. 'Look! I'm on the trail!'

'Trail?'

'Yes! Yes! I'm on the trail of the ghost! The ghost of the carpenter who made this! Look, Hellie! Did you ever see such a kind pair of hands?'

Grace opened out the old shutters, as Mollie Stokes came in.

'Oh, Mrs Stokes, did you ever see such lovely

work, and look if you open this here –' she pointed to a weakening section of the frame. 'Nobody else has touched this wood since he made it?'

Mrs Stokes nodded. 'He was famous at it, a man called Michael Banim. Not from here, a Wexford man, but he made for everyone around the place.'

'What year was that?' asked quick Grace.

'Others were that few years earlier, but this house. It'd be what? About the year fifteen-fifteen they say. Or sixteen.'

'What?!'

Even Helena said it, if milder. 'What? As long ago as that?'

Grace calculated. 'Two from six is four. Nine from eleven is two. Subtract fourteen-ninety-two from fifteen-sixteen, that's what I'm doing, Hellie, that'd say that this house was built only twenty-four years after Christopher Columbus discovered America – dear God!'

Mrs Stokes smiled. 'Are you all right here now, girls, the two of you? Are you warm enough?'

Helena nodded, as Grace continued wondering aloud and fondling the wood of the shutters – 'Fifteen-sixteen? Fifteen-sixteen.'

When Mrs Stokes withdrew with her good-night-and-God-bless, Helena turned her back and began to undress, then climbed into the large bed and moved inwards. Grace bounced around the room undressing, and, naked, searched for her nightdress. Briefly, she checked her body profile in the wall-mirror before letting the nightdress fall from her shoulders to her knees. She wiggled her bottom, in delight: 'Fifteen-sixteen. AD!'

Then climbing into the bed, she challenged her sister's angst. 'Hellie, you're sighing again?' she accused. 'Daddy, isn't it?'

'He doesn't know I'm here yet, and he mightn't know until . . .'

'Until when? I'm going to open the window.' Grace jumped out of bed.

'He sees me. Until he sees me at the meeting, the march. I dread Sunday week.'

'Will that breeze blow the candle out, no, it won't,' and Grace turned to check. 'No, don't dread it, 'tis going to be a great day. And if he does, what of it?'

'What will he say to me? What will he say?' Helena drew her lips back in a small worried rictus.

'Let him say what he likes and he won't anyway because we'll all be in public. Sssssttt? D'you hear that?'

Helena rose on an elbow. Grace stood by the window and whispered, 'Probably a badger. Or I wouldn't be surprised if it was a deer.'

No further sound. As Grace returned to the big bed that heaped and plumped like white clouds, Dennis Sykes walked on soft feet away from the cottage window.

13

One week later:

'I brought you this from London.' Dennis Sykes held out the package. 'I felt you'd like it.'

Thomas Kane opened the wrapping, folded the outer paper, then opened with careful fingers the inner layer of tissue paper. The book gazed up gravely: *Moncrieux's History of Guerrilla Warfare: 57 BC to the Guinea Campaign*.

'It's a translation, of course,' said Dennis. 'I thought you'd be interested.' He made a drinking motion. 'The same?'

'No, no, man, let me get this.'

'Sit, sit,' soothed Dennis, 'you can buy the next round. Water in a separate glass?'

Binnie said, 'Thanks muchly, my darling,' ever grateful as she folded the banknotes.

'Binnie,' said Dennis. 'I am in severe, extremely severe difficulty.'

'Explain.'

'I need to split the Kanes. Totally. If that girl's protests begin to succeed, she will at least delay us. And you know what happens if there's a delay. Everyone rushes to pro-long a delay. And then what happens? Sooner or later someone's going to put the idea of a public enquiry into

..ad.' He hammered the pillow. 'Fuck!

Thomas Kane looked at the book's index, fingered the pages, found one uncut, reached in his pocket for his penknife. Dennis Sykes placed the drinks on the small table.

'I would have thought –' began Thomas, indicating the book, and Dennis finished it for him.

'That an Englishman like me would resent you having been at war with us, with my country?'

'You say "at war", I notice,' said Thomas.

'And why not?'

'Well,' said the schoolteacher, fingering the newly-cut page, 'they called us "gangsters" –'

'We,' interrupted Dennis, pointing to his breast, '*we*, not "they". *We* called you "gangsters". And "hoodlums". To say the least.'

'How do you know?' Kane wondered.

'I've been reading my history. I have a friend in London, a university man, a professor, saw him at the week-end. He says Ireland was the most shameful period in English history.'

No: Dennis had spent the week-end with Binnie: she complained of his roughness. He pleaded frustration.

Thomas shook his head, pleased, bemused. 'You're a remarkable man. So – so, understanding. There's no doubt about it. And this book –'

Dennis said expansively, 'Well – you should know the history of your own soldiery,' he said. 'Just because you didn't wear a conventional uniform doesn't mean you weren't a soldier. And by all accounts we could have done with you on our side.'

=

Binnie soothed. By now he had almost calmed down.

'But they're like the Venetians, the Irish. So do weasel, Dennis. I beg you. Yes. Weasel.'

Dennis fumbled his spaghetti.

'Yes, you're right, Dennis darling. Split them. Split them totally.'

Leah came to stay. She made a good observer at a good moment, loving Ellen, part of her history. Awaiting Ellen and baby Helena's return from the nursing-home, Leah had been there 'that dreadful morning'. For the next weeks, she had seen Ellen upright again, walked by her side as Ellen came back into life, supported her: Thomas seemed without hope, without possibility in an unhygienic hospital.

A quarter-century on, gaudy and warm as ever, she walked from the late bus to the front door. Leah ignored any sombreness of atmosphere she ever found inside the Kanes' house, pretended the children's wariness of Thomas never existed. Always, however, she watched Ellen closely, and never so closely as when Ellen gave little away.

After greetings, and the dispensing of the small confectionery, Leah made Ellen find quiet time. This moonlit evening, they walked. Leah reported 'trouble in Ellen' to Herbert two days later.

Dennis brought more drinks and when Thomas went to the lavatory (a set of galvanized iron partitions in the Hands' back yard), Dennis tipped some more whiskey into Thomas's glass. Mrs Hand brought cheese sandwiches.

Dennis sat again beside Thomas.

'I'm worried about something.'

Thomas looked into his glass and listened.

'I met your wife, did she tell you that?'

'No,' said Thomas, 'she did not.'

'This march on Sunday next. I think she's going to march. And if I lose your support –'

Drink never suited Thomas Kane. It took him through animatedness, into bonhomie, and then into self-righteous, self-pitying anger. Dennis watched and timed.

'On the march? My wife?' Thomas Kane shook his head. 'She will not.' He repeated it. 'She will not.'

'Are you sure?'

'My wife does what I say.'

'But – she's a mother. And your daughters – ?'

Dennis left the sentence unfinished.

'Daught*er*.' Thomas emphasized the singular.

'No. Daught*ers*. The – the older girl is on now.'

'Helena?' He frowned.

Dennis nodded sadly. 'Moved into the Grey Valley ten days ago. That's where I met your wife.'

Leah's report fell into two parts – of the walking and talking, with Ellen meeting her problems squarely and, unusually in recent years, discussing them openly; and of the late evening, when Thomas returned, and the anger and division.

'Now, tell me about you?' began Ellen, and laughed. 'Do you know, I now think of you as my *wealthy* friend.'

'Oh,' Leah alerted, mistakenly. 'Is everything all right for money?'

'Oh, yes, of course. You know Thomas. The Great Provider Himself. What I really meant was, Herbert must be well used to it by now.'

'He still moans. Says we were better off when we were poorer. But, you won't believe it. I have my own cheque-book.'

Ellen laughed. 'What do I say? Congratulations? I'd be afraid I'd go mad if I had a cheque-book.'

Leah changed the subject – to Ellen. And reported when she went home, 'She has not lost any spirit, Herbert dear, she has gained it. Not that she was standing up to him as such, but she was managing him, not letting him get away. God, he's a problem.'

'He's a fine man,' murmured Herbert. 'He has qualities.'

Ellen Kane had a walk full of energy. Even though she picked her steps carefully, she thrust forward, bosom out. Leah's recurring comment about her beloved friend had to do with inspiration.

'She'll do everything she can in her power for those children. And for him, though in a different way. Do you know what she told me? She told me that she bakes twice when she's baking. She bakes for the children, same as anyone, and then she bakes specially for him. Not that it's any different, it's just that she lets him know.'

As Ellen ended her long résumé of Helena, Grace and their father, Leah looked down at her dark-eyed friend. She saw not Ellen Kane, a country schoolteacher in a small, backward and ignorant village, but a woman who had fought adversity from within herself, who had gone back almost to animal instincts to keep her husband alive.

'So,' concluded Ellen's long tale, 'I have to keep faith with the girls until this thing fizzles out. Because I think it will fizzle out. And I had better be there to help them with their disappointment. At the same time, I have to show him I support his official role.'

She never mentioned Dennis Sykes, who now preyed on her mind like a sin.

—

The women returned, sat at tea in the parlour, all children banished. Except Hugh, who hung around at the door.

'Cake later,' said Ellen firmly. 'Where's Daddy, do you know?'

'He's with the Engineer' – the name now given universally in Deanstown to Dennis Sykes.

'All this time?' asked Ellen. 'Does he know Auntie Leah's here?'

'Will I get him?'

'No-no. No-no,' she hurried. 'Off you go.'

Darkness fell slowly. Late birds, crows from the Castle, returned to their ivy, and one by one fell silent. The two women, figures in a painting, could be seen through the parlour window as the lace curtains billowed apart. Heads inclined towards each other, by the yellow light of the lamp-globe, they talked across the table, and listened. Leah's red lipstick shone: her nose cast a shadow: the red hair stuck out behind her, as ever.

Ellen explained. 'And I know, I know, I should do more. The girls say, well – Grace says – that I should have protected them from Thomas, I mean protected them more. But Leah, I did, though. For instance, every time he cut one of those thin ash sticks he used to punish them with – well, when it got too much for me, I used to go and find the stick and take it away. Secretly in the beginning. And then when I realized he thought it might be one of the children stole it, I did it openly. I never said a word, just removed it. Then he stopped using them.'

Leah nodded, in slow, deep nods.

'But now Grace says to me that he ruined things for everyone.' Ellen's soft voice rose in a hushed inflection of concern.

Leah murmured, 'And what do *you* think?'

272

'Oh, Leah, he's my husband, and you know me, I do things by thinking what I'm supposed to think.'

Amber tea in Leah's cup: she looked down at it: then she looked up at Ellen. 'Is there something now radically wrong? More than you're saying?'

'Yes. Yes.' Ellen, when cornered, stared hard into the eyes of her cornerer.

'What, dear? What?' Leah opened her palms. 'What's wrong? It isn't money, you said that?'

'No. No. I don't even know. I have a bad feeling. I never told you this, or anybody. But the night before. You know – the night before Thomas's – accident. I couldn't sleep. I was afraid of something, but I couldn't put a name to it. I have that feeling back now, and I have it worse than then.'

Leah asked, 'Is it about Thomas?'

'No,' said Ellen. 'And. Yes, and. It's about the girls, too.' She started. 'Oh, my God!'

Both women simultaneously heard the footsteps strike the gravel, urgent steps, faster than Thomas's usual walk.

'Oh, God. Look –' Leah stood. 'I'll say hallo first.'

She had no such opportunity. He opened the door, did not acknowledge Leah.

'Ellen! Come here please!' Without waiting for an answer Thomas said it again. 'At once, please!'

In the hallway he raged, 'What is the meaning of this, this business with your other daughter? You haven't told me.'

'I was going to,' said Ellen.

'Going to? *Going to?* When? At the end of the century?'

Quietly she said, 'Leah's here.'

'I don't care who's here.' His voice rose. 'What else's going on in this house behind my back and I not knowing?'

'Thomas. Two things. One – Leah's here: I said. And

273

two, you don't normally drink much, so what were you doing? You were with that Sykes fellow, weren't you?'

'He's not a "fellow", and don't call him that, he's a gentleman. What I want to know is – what kind of little bitches are you rearing, that they're doing this to me in public, and you not telling me?'

Ellen said, so that Leah behind the door could hear, 'Under no circumstances call the girls that. Under no circumstances speak to me like that. Ever.'

Leah reported to Herbert, 'And then, dear, she came back into the room and locked the door. He pounded on the door; he then went to the window; she closed the shutters calmly; then the curtains. She sat down facing me and said, "Leah, I'm very sorry. Now – why don't we continue our talk?" Thomas raved on outside and after a while we heard him going to bed. But yet – she slept in the same bed as him that night, and in the morning he was gone before I got up. I didn't see him again.'

Herbert wondered, 'Should I talk to him?'

'Not possible, dear, I'd say.'

Of the two sisters, Helena would not have known – but Grace should have sensed something. Frantic within her own activities, she never looked around to take the temperature of the village.

'Lukewarm,' they said to each other upon enquiry; and 'I don't think there'll be that many.'

'Poor organization,' smiled Dennis Sykes to himself. Only two people felt the thunder of the occasion, Thomas and Grace. Both issued instructions.

'Nobody from this house will even be at a window when that march goes past. Do you hear?' The other children nodded.

'And when the buses come,' said Grace, her hands full

of posters and glue and envelopes, 'we'll begin the march as soon as possible.'

Helena made only one observation. 'I think we should have obtained a clearer picture of how many?'

Grace went through the list: 'Each signatory to our letter promised at least twenty people. At least. It will be more. Dr Considine said he'll have thirty. Hellie, look. We've booked five buses. And this is only the beginning. Five busfuls at forty-five people per bus. Two hundred and twenty-five. Plus the locals. We could easily have five hundred people.'

'What's happening about the band?'

'I can't get him to answer my note,' said Grace. 'I even called again and he wasn't there.'

On Thursday morning, Dennis Sykes disappeared. Nobody saw him go; he left no significant message – merely a remark to the second-in-command: 'Urgent. I have to go. Hold the fort.'

He hoped to be back 'sooner rather than later', and at the morning site meeting had praised all progress.

The dam workers talked about him all the time. His nearest equals hailed his acumen, confessed themselves 'staggered' at his scope and grasp. Dennis had located his head drawing office at Rosegreen, eight miles away, in an old Georgian manor full of comfort and eccentricity. There, without any fixed point of his own, he directed the diagrammatic operations, moving from desk to drawing-board to wall-chart like some powerful butterfly, alighting on new ideas, sipping their nectar, and promulgating them to test their stamina.

He had appointed two senior assistants whom he met first and last every day: each brought him full reports of their half of the project. One took responsibility for the 'soft' work – the drawings, the purchasing, the contracts, the payments. The other handled the 'hard' end – men, machinery and operations, the construction drive.

Dennis controlled the impetus. From the beginning, he had pinned his soul to this project like a bright flag. He knew that every engineer in the English-speaking world would know of his success, that he had within his power the setting of an international benchmark. Using hour after hour, day after day, of more solitude than he had ever granted himself, he planned every detail: how he would delegate, where he would aim for breakthrough, and the management of time.

With the smoothness he knew his brain possessed, he fitted all the phases together in his mind so frequently that he could dismantle and assemble them like the parts of a gun. He oversaw every detail, down to the nuances of where to hire the greatest number of men – which parishes and even which townlands of which parishes? Hence his wooing of Kane: he recognized the potential of local difficulty, and perceived Kane to have a natural figurehead position.

Budgets, time targets, logistics: no wonder, he smiled from time to time, no wonder his libido had taken a holiday. No wonder, too, that no immature, virgin idealist could be allowed to halt this seething momentum. She had to be stopped: those things had a festering contagiousness. Which is why he left without warning, told nobody where he was going – and threatened Mrs Hand into secrecy by saying he could take away this new, fabulous drinking trade the dam had brought.

Sunday brought great warmth from the sun, the beginning of a premature heatwave. At half-past twelve, dressed in bright colours, Grace and Helena appeared in front of

Mrs Hand's public house. Grace wore a straw hat and carried leaflets; Helena appeared nervous. Rhona, Munch and Viva Ulverton arrived.

Viva said in her blurting way, 'How many? How many?'

Grace grinned and said, 'None yet. Two and a half hours to go. Why are we all here so early?'

'Excitement, my dear. And rightly so.' Rhona tapped her stick on the road. 'I hope they're coming from Dublin?'

'And from Janesborough,' said Grace, 'and Cork, and Thurles. And Clare. And Galway.'

'And you're here, I see. Good,' said Rhona to Helena. 'What are you staring at, child?'

She joined Helena's line of sight – Ellen, sturdily walking towards them.

'Don't say,' said Viva, 'don't say she's going to march.'

'Hallo,' said Ellen to all, 'hallo, girls' to her daughters, and after a general exchange, drew them to one side.

She had promised herself to behave normally, not to ask them why they had not answered her letters; she had promised herself not to engage with them in the controversy. Otherwise, she would have to tell them of the fury with which their father had behaved for the past four days – the swearing and door-slamming, the accusations.

'Are the two of you all right? *Will* you be all right? Are there many coming?' Ellen looked solicitously at each girl. 'Dear Gracey! You've been busy, your posters are all over Mooreville, everyone's talking about it.'

'About five hundred we think. About ten buses. Are you marching, Mother?' asked Grace.

Ellen shook her head – 'And you, Helena love, are you all right?'

Helena enquired, 'How's Daddy?'

Ellen nodded in a way that precluded further enquiry,

277

'He's fine. I just wanted to say hallo to the two of you. Now. Have you – have you everything you need?'

Both nodded.

'Mama, is he cross with us?' asked Helena.

'Sweetheart, this isn't the best time of all for us to talk about this. Daddy has a lot on his mind.'

'Mother, you're still doing it, you're still protecting him!' Grace turned away in disgust.

A bus approached. Behind came another, then another, then another, then two cars, then another bus, then another. Grace cheered. 'But they're so early!'

As the coaches stopped, wheels crushing the grassy verges, Grace ran towards them. 'You're all very early, but you're all very welcome,' she called, waving a rolled poster. 'Hellie, quick, look how many are here, look!'

With a smile at the Ulvertons, Ellen slipped away from the scene. At her gate, a hundred yards away, she turned, surveyed the gathering, waved to Helena, and disappeared into the folds of the trees in front of the house.

Rhona knew before Grace did, and murmured to Viva, 'Dizz. Ah. Stir.'

'What, Mamma?'

'Disaster. Look.'

Viva stared. A man descended from the first bus, walked to the roadside and began to urinate fatly. Behind him, others lurched out.

'Oh, my Christ!' said Viva. 'They stopped on the way.'

'Many times by the looks of it,' said Rhona: her purple chiffon stole waved in the breeze like Isadora Duncan. 'And those girls don't know what to do.'

'Help them, Mamma,' said Viva. 'Go on.'

'No. I won't. They have to learn.' She nudged Viva. 'Look! *They're* not teachers or students.'

278

Slowly, all vehicles emptied. Their passengers, men aged from twenty to forty, many unshaven, headed for Mrs Hand's pub. The sun grew hotter. A youth, cheap jacket over his arm, lurched over to Viva and said, 'Where's the fuckin' dam anyway?'

'Where did you come from?' Viva asked.

Grace walked over, baffled. 'Are you here for the rally?' she asked politely.

'Cork. They're from Janesborough, we all met in Mooreville.' He smiled foolishly.

'All of you? You all met in Mooreville?' Viva asked.

'What rally?' He eyed Grace.

Rhona butted in. 'When did you all meet in Mooreville?'

'Yes. Where's the buses we're supposed to be stopping?' He had a bottle in his hand concealed beneath the folded jacket. 'Half-past ten.'

'Half-past ten? Why?'

'Is the fella here?'

'What fella? What d'you mean?' Viva asked.

'Several rounds. He bought me on my own four rounds.'

Rhona asked, 'What kind of "fella"?'

'Friday night. Decent as anything. Couldn't buy a round for him, he bought everything.' The young man licked his mouth. 'Never let it be said the English aren't decent.'

Rhona asked keenly, 'Did he have a lot of black hair and was he small?'

'"A mystery tour", that's what he said, "give's a day of your time and you can have all the drink you can drink." Yeh, a'course he'd black hair. And a fiver each.' The young man walked away.

Rhona turned to Viva. 'No doubt you've guessed.'

'I'm getting there.'

'Master Sykes. A set-up.'

Viva said, 'Little fucker. But there are still the others?'

'Watch, Viva, dear. By the end of it, there will be fighting. Or else you will not see an organized protest here today.'

In all this time, the two cars accompanying the coaches had parked quietly, and their occupants had not emerged. Now they appeared, men in uniform. A senior, braided one asked Viva, 'Are you Miss Kane?'

Villagers came to their doors, but not to take part.

Viva pointed and beckoned. Grace returned. Red of face. Angered and embarrassed. Chagrined.

'I can't work this out.'

'I'm sorry, my dear,' Rhona said to her. 'I fear they're rabble material.'

The Superintendent asked, 'Are you the organizer?'

Grace affirmed.

'May I meet your stewards, please?'

'Stewards?'

He said, 'Over two hundred people, strangers, have come into your village to drink. They're all in that pub by now. You are expecting many more that you have rallied here. Right?'

'To begin at three o'clock,' said Grace.

'How do you propose to keep order? There are several known troublemakers in the village at this moment.'

'Help,' said Grace helplessly to Rhona.

By sundown, Grace's despair had subsided into, 'But why? Why?'

Rhona walked her up and down the avenue, up and down, a firm hand on Grace's arm.

'My dear girl. Cruel to say, but you've been outwitted.

The police simply had no choice. They had to close the village. They had to turn the marchers back.'

'But my people had no drink taken,' protested Grace.

'Worse again, dear.' Rhona paused. 'Do you not recognize what has happened?'

Helena, walking with them, murmured, *Agents provocateurs?*'

'I fear so.'

Helena and Mrs Stokes went indoors to prepare some food. Grace sat outside and watched the night fall to the Valley floor.

Forever after, Helena chided herself for not having sat with Grace. She wrote over and over again in her notebook, 'Why didn't I stay? By going indoors, I gave Grace the time to think.'

Rightly or wrongly, Helena attributed the beginning of the end, the essence, to that moment. Grace, deep in the depressive aftermath of the march-that-never-was, intensified in her determination.

'I can hear him gloat, that's the worst part. He'll be saying to Mother, "I told her but she wouldn't listen." He'll be saying to the others, "Children of every age should always listen to their parents." Can't you hear him, Hellie . . .'

Next morning, because they had written in advance, and slipped the letters by hand under the old doorways, Grace and Helena set off on their round of the cottages in the Valley. In this search for signatures to their petition, they had anticipated a victory tour, had expected that the rally would have given them stronger cards to play.

'I've two things to say to you, Miss Kane,' said the first woman they called to see. 'Mind your own business for a start. And the second is, 'tis all fine for you with your father and your stuck-up mother. But you never went without money or food or a pair of shoes to your feet, and now I have a fine house coming to me over in Mooreville near my daughter, and you trying to stop me getting it. G'off now, g'wan, and leave uz alone.'

Grace tried to fight. 'But the house and its age, and that furniture you have, the value of these?'

'An' lumbago to go with it, and arteritis, yeh? I'd sooner a good sofa from John O'Dea's shop any day. G'wan, g'off wit' yourself.'

Grace dipped into her next resource of bravery, and walked on. According to her notes, the Connaughtons owned a rare Carbery Settle, a highbacked seat fixed to the kitchen wall. From it unfolded a one-legged table, so that the sitters on either side could turn, face each other and dine.

'Take it away with you, girl, if you're that fond of it,' said Bernard Connaughton, with his cap to one side. 'Look at this.'

He showed Grace and Helena a letter from the County Manager confirming the offer of 'a bungalow with three bedrooms' in Mooreville, and 'a resettlement compensation of between £750 and £1500.'

Bernard Connaughton cocked an eye at the girls and asked, 'Will you match that? Or your father, 'ill he give me that much for staying?'

Grace said, prim and edgy, 'My father isn't involved in this. We're doing this on our own because we think the Grey Valley should be preserved.'

'Preserved for what, hauh?' The cottier moved off, stranding the girls outside his home.

Of the five houses visited that morning, Eddie Martin alone gave the girls some consolation.

'I was born here, and I never wanted to go outa here but in a box. My heart'll break the night they flood it.'

Grace said, 'They *won't* flood it, Mr Martin, they will not, that's what we're fighting. What I want from you is your signature, and I want a statement from you about the oldness of the furniture you have, and how old your house is.'

He sighed. 'The house is the same age as the rest of them, and there's no furniture here worth the asking.'

Helena enquired, 'Have you a settle-bed or anything like that?'

'I haven't. My daughter over in England furnished the house from top to bottom two years ago and she got rid of all that stuff, we burned a lot of it that winter following.'

Helena asked, 'Have you any pictures of it?'

'No.'

Grace said, 'But look at that thatch? Beautiful.'

He said, 'Well, 'atiz and 'atizn't. There's flax in it and I knew the day they put flax in 'twould be unlucky. Flax never brings luck in thatch.'

Thomas Kane became obsessed with Dennis Sykes. He sought Sykes's approval, his companionship, his praise. Like a man grasping at an urgent opportunity, he careened off at this new, comradely tangent. When the school closed in the heat of mid-July, Kane was to be seen striding in the dam area, observing, measuring, taking notes. He offered comments to Sykes, who accepted them as if they were nuggets of engineering pioneerwork.

Dennis assessed every turn of this relationship in terms of advantage. Notwithstanding his success at obliterating the rally (which Kane never discussed with him – hah! pressure at home), he still feared a call for a public enquiry. Indeed he puzzled as to why none had been mooted. One evening on the crest of the Grey Valley, not far from the point where Sykes had met Ellen, he remarked to Thomas, 'It seems as if you've become part of this family of mine' – and he waved his hand towards the workers, the trucks, the great ants crawling over the site far below them. 'This busy family.'

The massive foundations had now been finished, and the concreting had begun deep beneath the ground. On either lip of the long curved pit stood lines of cement-mixers like tiny watch-towers; each mixer had its own team and they raced each other to fill the pit up to ground-level.

'Yes,' mused Dennis. 'I *have* run them like a family. In a sense they're the only family I know.'

By now he knew the length of Kane's reactions. A planted thought, usually triggered by Dennis in a key word, took time to root: Kane had a proud reputation for pondering. Dennis had observed that the schoolmaster usually renewed such a subject four to five days later.

In their enclave north of Deanstown, the Stephensons and the Ulvertons met frequently. Their two large dwellings had come through a cold winter. Plaster fell away, leaving sores on the pink wash walls of the dower house. Rhona Ulverton repeatedly asked Viva to procure – knit, if necessary – woollen gloves: Rhona had spent many days beneath the heavy blankets and feared her limbs seizing.

A chimney collapsed on the manor one night and terrified Cyril Stephenson's excommunicated wife. Joan had slowly recovered from the worst of her depressions, and she now lay silent in their bed at night, a sullen woman, often tearful. She sighed for hours before sleep reached her, and next morning complained daily of the cold.

Rhona's tentative meetings with Cyril and the wife had

produced no financial solution to the problems of heating these houses.

The Stephensons and the Ulvertons none the less loved the place, especially in summer. Old plants grew around the doors. The gardens beamed. Morning glory and japonica flourished like bright bandits in unexpected nooks. Inside, the high ceilings and cornices downstairs remained in an excellent state of repair; the leaks had never penetrated. Feared subsidence had not materialized. Not a flake had fallen from the stuccoed ceilings.

Sunday morning: bumblebees in the blossoms on the high old brick wall. Cyril shrugged; Rhona, wearing a green eyeshade like an antique tennis player, stretched in her deck-chair.

'By when, Aunt Rhona?'

'They seemed unhurried. By September, October I suspect. Viva, no!'

Viva had appeared wearing shorts and a chiffon top through which her tiny breasts and plinking nipples could be seen as clearly as a relief map.

'Heatwave, Mother!'

Rhona rapped her stick on the paving beneath the garden bench. 'No! Look at Cyril's wife! She's sensible' – who, sitting on the grass nearby, wore a green woollen long-sleeved dress.

'Yes, and she's baking. Anyway, she's a Roman Catholic and they don't show their bodies, do you, Joan?'

Cyril's wife never answered.

'Go, Viva and change!' – but Viva escaped, ran down the green slope of the banked lawn, and reached her clearing in the woods.

'And Uncle Henry won't help?' asked Cyril.

The families had become a main topic of electricity

speculation. This remained unknown to them – although Cyril's wife, of the people, had suspected. Their enclave, beautiful and sleek when first built, now proved inconveniently sited. This group of houses, above even the glossy woods, had once struck fear into tenants' hearts. The supply engineers, not of Dennis Sykes's team, had finally – after months of dithering – told the houses of the extra work needed. To bring electricity through Wallace's Wood would cost two thousand: they could share it.

'Henry says he has problems finding the money for his own electricity poles.' Rhona sniffed. 'But I doubt it. I believe he's lying.' Rhona worried. 'Cyril dear, I think this is all deliberate. Are you telling me that if a Roman Catholic farm is in a remote place they will have to pay the same as us? And Christ we're not that remote!'

Cyril stood, made his hand into an eyeshade and gazed off at nothing; he looked briefly like some unambitious *conquistador*.

He sat again. 'What are you going to do, Aunt Rhona?' 'I think I'm going to fight – on other grounds – so that if I may make myself enough of a nuisance I can do a deal. I have an idea. God, Cyril, your father and your mother must be turning in their graves! I feel like a non-person in this country.'

Cyril nodded, afraid lest his wife would overhear: but she had fallen asleep in the sun on the grass, and beads of sweat stood on her pale face beside her open mouth.

'Yes,' he said softly, 'the RCs really show us now, don't they. We have no say.'

Behind him to the left, his own house basked. The sun lit the blond stone he could not afford to repair. Down the fields, the yellow, ragged-leaf ragwort rampaged through pastures he could not afford to meadow. He had one horse, and two tweed jackets, and a dark suit that had been his father's. If any of the twenty cows that sustained the house sickened, Cyril could only get a vet of the same religious persuasion who would understand. The man had to come from forty miles away, reachable only by letter.

In Rhona's house, some tiles had come loose on the red roof on an equinoctial night. She hoped that the tarred roofing canvas beneath would survive, would not melt.

'Yes,' finalized Rhona. 'That is what I will do. I will be devious.'

'How? The Kane girls? Their campaign will come to something?'

'No,' said Rhona. 'They're not doing well. That march fiasco. All that fighting and vomiting.'

Cyril said, 'Aunt Rhona, everyone's laughing at them.'

'I need tea. Viva! Viva!'

No reply came. Viva lay in a deep sleep, legs apart in the sun. That night she wept with the pain of the sunburn on her long-shanked inner thighs.

14

Ellen accepted briskly, without question, their truce.

'The Engineer's coming for his tea,' she told Essie.

Preparations matched those for the Canon or an Inspector. Ellen baked her best cake. Four egg yolks; four ounces of dark melted chocolate; four ounces of caster sugar: two large tablespoons of flour: at the end, fold in the beaten-stiff egg whites meticulously.

He parked on the road, and bore a gift wrapped in damp brown paper.

'Where,' asked Thomas, 'did you get it?'

Dennis smiled. 'A friend of a friend who's a good fisherman, and he was out early this morning. For your breakfast tomorrow.'

Thomas showed Ellen the great trout, and she smiled formally.

The girls had been invited – Thomas's truce concession to Ellen. Grace resisted, close to rage when she read the note: Helena complied.

As they sat to table, she cycled through the gate. Dennis saw her arrive, and attempted to give Ellen a conspiratorial look: she focused on Helena. Who came uncertainly in. All watched Thomas. He moved to make room for her.

'Have you met our oldest, Dennis?' he asked. 'Helena. Born in 1926.'

Dennis, eyes like a falcon, said, 'Uh-huh, you mustn't

reveal a lady's age. How do you do?' and he rose to shake Helena's hand.

Helena wore the lemon yellow dress, and her blonde hair curved under her chin. She moved nervously to sit by her father. Ellen watched Dennis's glances on Helena's thighs and waist. Thomas Kane's eyes watched nobody.

'Did you cycle?' asked Dennis Sykes of Helena.

'Yes.' She nodded.

'Strong wind today,' he said pleasantly. 'In that hot sun. Like France.'

'Does that ever interfere with your construction, Dennis?' asked Thomas. 'I mean, high wind?'

'It may later. When the men are working up on the dam wall.' Dennis Sykes turned to Helena. 'As a matter of interest, does it get hot where you are? I mean, deep within the valley?'

Helena said, 'Yes, I mean, no.'

She overcame her surprise at such open speech in so difficult a matter.

'No. Well, it does, yes. The sun comes at an angle, and it gets hotter for some reason.'

Once, at this very table, Leah and Ellen sat and observed Helena, then aged nineteen. She walked through the gate, head slightly tilted, unaware of the watching women.

'Do you see what I mean, Leah?'

Leah smiled with such affection. 'Yes, yes.'

'That innocence. I worry about her. Will she meet a nice man? Otherwise, how will she manage?'

'All that vul, vul – what's the word, she's very vul, oh drat it, I can't think of it.' Leah's bracelets clanged.

'But everybody likes her, that's the good thing. My heart hurts when I watch her.'

'Nerable!' Leah shot.

'Oh, *vulnerable*? Yes, that's a good word. Yes. The first-born.'

'The first-born,' echoed Leah. 'Yes, they're often vulnerable.'

Dennis Sykes praised things. He praised the strength of the tea, the pips in the jam, the dark moist sponginess at the heart of the cake.

'It's good and tense,' he said. 'A good chocolate cake should be tense.'

'Tense?' smiled Helena.

'You never married?' asked Ellen, determined to be polite, as Thomas had specifically requested.

'Nearly, once' – a master of the hint of eastern disappointment. In later life, he got his way at board meetings by knowing how never to overdo.

Against her wishes and her better judgement, Ellen's curiosity fizzed. 'Nearly? Once?'

'These things happen,' said Dennis. 'How many children have you, Mrs Kane?'

'I think you could call her Ellen,' smiled Thomas.

'Eight,' said Helena.

'Gosh! How lovely!' said Dennis the enthusiast, Dennis the wistful, Dennis the would-be family man, his brown eyes poignant.

Ellen asked, 'But do the English like large families? I thought they didn't.'

He smiled. 'A family of any kind would be welcome in my department.'

Thomas gave his rare, pleased nod. 'In my department,' he echoed, relishing.

And yet, the talk had some stiffness in it. Dennis, sensing this, visibly set out to warm the table. He told a long

290

tale of an ancient hoard found in a Scottish site where he once surveyed. Ellen watched everyone listening to him. Believing him. Especially Helena: who, still a little wary of her father's looming bulk beside her, looked many times at Dennis's expressive hands. At the end of the tale Dennis rewarded himself.

'Is it rude to ask for more cake?'

Even Ellen dived to help.

'Did you like the things they found?' asked Helena, her first direct question.

Dennis held their attention yet further by not speaking with his mouth full. He brushed the crumbs away.

'I thought.' He used both his ring-fingers to scrabble crumbs from his lip-corners. 'That I had never.' Quick swallow. 'Seen anything so – so lustrous.'

Thomas echoed again. 'Lustrous.' He looked at Dennis with firm approval. 'Lustrous.'

'You could almost see,' said Dennis, 'the fingermarks of the goldsmiths on the wide bracelets.'

At this same table twenty-five years earlier, Ellen Kane, *née* Morris, had fought for her own composure. Three feet away, her husband, 'the Living Dead', lay stretched on his bed-chair. At every meal she argued silently with him, or talked to him as if he heard. Each night, with Helena in her cot, and Essie lumbering like an Indian cow on the floor above, Ellen had ranted at life and at her comatose man. Fists clenched, she cajoled and imprecated. She hustled her husband, turned his face to the full moon silvering through the windows. Undressed before him. Painted his body from mouth to groin with her breasts. Called his name aloud, or whispered it. Drove at him with passionate confidences. Urged him back into his own life. Hauled him from his pallor and his oblivion. Cursed him. Now, at the same table, she sat with feet coiled around her chair-legs in tension. As she watched, the seeds of, to her, a worse tragedy were being planted – and beyond her reach.

Dennis Sykes's skill dominated the end of the night.

He turned to Helena and said, 'It is as good as dark now, why don't I give you a lift back to the Grey Valley, you can put the bike on the back of the car.' Precluding comment, he said to Thomas, 'That was a memorable thing for you to do. Bringing me into your family like this.'

Finally he turned to Ellen, whose hand he took. 'Mrs Kane, I can understand your suspicion of a man like me, coming in to a place he's bound to disrupt. The dam will change lives. I know that.'

Ellen, discomfited but courteous, said, but mainly to Helena, 'Mr Sykes it was very nice to have you for your tea. Helena, love, will you be cold without a coat? Take my light one.'

Helena peered forward into the night. She sniffed.

'Leather,' said Dennis Sykes. 'And wood. That's walnut, actually,' pointing to the trim in front of Helena's knees, 'the whole dashboard is walnut with leather.'

She drew a hand along it.

He remarked, 'I can see you understand these things.'

'Lovely smell.'

'How old are you exactly?' he asked.

'Just recently twenty-six.'

'Twenty-six. God! Talking about blushing unseen.'

'I don't blush!'

He said, 'No. I wasn't saying that. Don't you know the line?'

'What line?'

Dennis recited, 'Full many a gem of purest ray serene, The dark unfathom'd caves of ocean bear.'

Helena said, 'Oh? *That* line.'

'Finish it,' commanded Dennis.

Helena did so, without faltering. 'Full many a flower is born to blush unseen.'

Together they ended the quotation: 'And waste its sweetness on the desert air.'

One of Dennis's more reliable stock lines: he used it on Rose; he used it on Mona Nicolson; he used it on myriad others.

They had arrived at the Valley: trees hung over them in the dark. Dennis took Helena's hand as she stood by the car. He held her long fingers and said, 'I hope we meet again.'

She replied, 'We are certain to.'

'Certain to?'

'I mean – you and my father, and that.'

He asked, 'Can I meet you one night? I mean, as a secret?'

Helena could not see his face in the night.

He pressed on. 'Unless you have some boy or young man who wants to marry you?'

Helena said in amazement. 'Oh no, oh, no!'

'Whyever not?'

The girl shifted her feet on the earthen valley road. 'It – things – I mean, it doesn't go like that in our family. Or around here.'

He chuckled. 'You mean people don't marry?'

'No. They do. Oh, I mean – well, in my own life, I've sort of –' she paused, not having anything else to say.

Dennis remarked, 'I have the impression that your father likes me. Is that right, do you think?'

'Oh, yes, he does, I could tell.'

Dennis paused, allowing his implication to take root. Then he said, 'I must go now. And I am reluctant to. But – will you meet me again? I mean – as a secret to begin with? Given all the complications?'

Helena replied, 'But – my sister . . .'

'As a complete secret? Promise? Promise?'

'I promise.'

'Here? On this very spot? Next Wednesday evening? Late?'

'Yes. I will.'

'What excuse will you give your sister? You could say you were visiting your parents?'

Helena said, 'Yes, I suppose so.'

'In fact,' said Dennis, 'I have a better idea. Why don't you visit them anyway, and I'll call. By coincidence, as it were – and pick you up there.'

'By coincidence as it were,' echoed Helena. She so lacked self-esteem that her listeners frequently had to guess whether her inflection signified question or comment.

Mrs Stokes had gone to bed: Grace had not come in: when she did return from her night wanderings, Helena pretended sleep.

From early August, electricity fever had been rampaging. Perhaps the village had waited for any protests to die down; perhaps it took until then to subdue its wariness of that fierce blue flashing power. Slowly, it began to swing round. In due course, sceptics or recusants became figures of fun.

This new enthusiasm took two forms. Well-to-do neighbours conferred, pencilling remarks on brochures, gauging each other's finances according to the intended number of appliances. Even people with no carpets ordered vacuum cleaners. Housewives scoured their rooms, painted woodwork. Electricians came by, curly-haired men in blue overalls with urgent red flashes on their breasts. In thoughtful inspections they marked with great triangular pencils the places for power points on skirting-boards. Fire hazards became a topic: what to do with thatch? How far from the inside of a straw roof, now tinder-dry with age and the residue of smoke, might a light bulb be installed?

In the wiring enquiries, in the fumbling around under the roof, men found unknown things of their ancestry – old guns; pieces of ancient bacon; prayer-books hidden from the Penal Laws; money stored in the thatch. John Barron found a box full of three-pound notes. The bank told him they were called 'pig' notes, because 'one note could buy a pig back in 1880'. A new shop opened in Mooreville selling only 'Electrical Goods'. The ancient incumbent of the town, Joseph Comerford & Sons Hardware, had to hasten, and spoke indignantly of the upstart.

Many people began to pay visits to the dam site, as to a holy well. Dennis Sykes had wondered to Thomas if the Canon should come and bless the work. On the appointed day, Dennis provided more than one bottle of Jameson – and the Canon's beloved onion sandwiches. Nobody believed Jeremiah Williams would ever again make such a public appearance: they said he had had a stroke: why else would the Curate be saying both Masses at each end of the parish, Deanstown and Silverbridge, every Sunday?

Thomas drove Canon Williams, loading him into the car. The men, caps off, welcomed him at the site, steered him along the wooden walkway over the mud of recent rain. A senile Cortez on Darien, the Canon stood looking along the completed dam foundations, and the first rise of the wall. His lip had sagged a little: his left arm – did he hold it a little stiffly? That night the talkers could not agree.

He puffed as ever through his nostrils.

'Boys, boys. If I never saw the Hanging Gardens of Babylon, I'll see this. How many men?'

Thomas Kane, in all his authority, acted as aide-de-camp and said, 'All told there'll have been one thousand one hundred here for the completion of this bit, and then for the rest another one thousand two hundred and fifty will come in.'

Dennis Sykes, silent and respectful, nodded.

'All from the county?' said the Canon.

'Bar a few special workers,' agreed Thomas.

The Canon raised his right hand; a workman materialized with a glass bowl of Holy Water. 'In the name of the Father. And of the Son. And of the Holy Ghost.'

Thomas made Ellen laugh later.

'D'you know what he said? Dennis had this reception prepared for him, very well done really. Jeremiah took his usual two quick drinks, and settled down – and out he came with it, "D'you know what it is, boys? I'm as good a blesser as ever I was." You'd imagine there was some kind of championship for blessings.'

Grace watched the event from her vantage point. Hour after hour, she hid in these ferns and trees, observing.

'I feel like God. Or Gulliver,' she told Helena.

Her father's car had been arriving at the site every day. And every day she turned her head away briefly when it came – then forced herself to watch. For hours at a time she followed Dennis Sykes's movements far below, as he walked, walked. When Canon Williams emerged, the sunshine lit the rain pools on the brown clay. Grace stood in anger.

Her mother used to say, 'Grace, you are too wilful. Too wilful.'

'I never quite understand the word, do you?' Grace asked Helena.

'It means following your own will without regard for the consequences,' said Helena.

'What else have we to follow?' asked Grace.

'Mama means your prayers and that.'

The aborted, drunken march, and the abuse of so many cottiers had sent Grace into temporary retreat. Worse than that, one or two of the valley families had begun to prepare for evacuation.

Treading water, she began to draw, and set out to note down every plant she could identify in the Grey Valley. She persuaded Helena to smuggle from home one of their favourite books, *The Wild Flora of the British Isles*. Day after day, Grace made an appointment with herself at four o'clock to match what growths she could find with the illustrations in the book.

Sometimes Helena disappeared, wandered off by herself. When Grace asked, she merely gave a diffident excuse: 'Thinking' – or, 'I needed to think.'

Watched by Mrs Stokes, Grace also sketched every view of the cottage interior. She noted down the colours within, each piece of fixed work, such as shutters, the wall-bed, the details of the iron crane from which the pots hung over the fire. The patterns in Mrs Stokes's lace bedspreads and curtains took ages; Grace counted the patches in the patchwork quilt. In morning light, she sat at the open door and named and sketched the trees she could see.

'What are you up to, girl?' the puzzled woman asked.

Grace, grinning, replied, 'I am a recording angel, Mrs

297

Stokes, a recording angel, that's me. Here, Hellie, hold this' – and she fetched yet another pencil from her satchel.

Daily, Grace roamed the woods alone, looking, sketching – and always fetching up on the ridge, staring down at the works of the project. She rose near dawn and followed fixed habits, such as smelling the roasted apples of the briar by the door, and turning to watch the steam from her own morning urine rising in the thick, summer grass. The Grey Valley drew her deep into its grasp, and gave her ferocious purpose. By August she had begun to record every sound and mood of the place, the leaf, the branch, the fruit.

Each part of the day received colours from her. The morning began 'dove-grey', as she stood at the gable of the house and watched the other cottages materialize in the mist. Then it became 'mauve', as the sun tried to break through the high trees. On the many sunny days, she called mid-morning 'cinnamon'. She ordered Helena to find some cinnamon on a day-trip to Janesborough, so that Mrs Stokes could see what Grace meant by the colour. Mrs Stokes peered unknowingly at the cinnamon sticks in the long jar. Grace, impatient, took her to the front door and pointed.

'See,' said Grace, demanding as a child, 'that's cinnamon, that's cinnamon-coloured.' She held a stick of the spice to the light. 'Look! They say that's what Italy is like. Rome or Siena.'

Smiling, the old woman went along with it. By the Connaughtons' windows, the light had fallen on an old cart, making the derelict beautiful.

When Helena walked through the door, blinking and yawning into the early morning light, she found Grace on the wooden settle, paints open. Head on one side, Grace added grey weight to the wing-feathers of a wood-pigeon. She smiled at Helena.

'The sun shines straight through that nightdress, Hellie.'

Helena looked down, yawned again. 'Look at you fully dressed.' She leaned over Grace's shoulder. 'Oh, Gracey, that's lovely.'

Grace said, 'I wish I had all my things. I'm missing several crayons.'

Helena sat beside her. 'I can go home and get them for you.'

'Would you?'

Helena nodded – and deceived. 'I'll go, say, Wednesday.'

The girls sat easily side by side. Helena twirled her hair in one finger. They looked into the waxy shimmer of the morning's haze.

'Did you make Mrs Stokes any breakfast?' asked Helena.

Grace nodded. 'She said she didn't sleep. I think she's gone back to bed.'

Helena stretched her legs and looked down at them. 'Did you see that advertisement in the papers – for an ointment or a cream to take the hair off your legs?'

Grace laughed. 'Do men use it for shaving?'

Helena, in the middle of a yawn, laughed again.

'How was home last night?' Grace erased a line and blew the dust off the notebook page.

'All right. Mama was wearing that lovely cream silk blouse.'

'I told her,' grinned Grace, 'she's to leave it to me in her will.' Sobering, she asked, 'How was HE?'

'Oh – you know.' Helena said. 'Guests there.'

'So he was the perfect gentleman. Did he ask about me?' Grace busied herself.

'He couldn't have done, with all that was going on. What are you going to do today?'

Grace said, 'I don't know, yet. I thought of starting to count all the rare plants here, will you help me?'

Next afternoon, Thomas Kane arrived at the dam site. Dennis greeted him at the office door.

'Just in time.' To the office-girl he said, 'Tea, Mary? A cup and saucer for Mr Kane, I'll have my mug.'

They stood by the window. Dennis showed Thomas the latest workings; he verified for the teacher the next developments on the far end of the escarpment.

'Look at the birds,' he pointed. Overhead, they wheeled and drifted on the thermals above the valley. Some gulls had arrived, forty miles from the sea. 'We must be turning up a lot of worms.'

The tea arrived. Dennis said as they sat, 'I have to say – if it's not forward of me. Your daughter. Goodness, she's lovely.'

Thomas gave a small, embarrassed laugh.

'Does she have – is there a – a young man?'

'No, no.' Thomas shook his head. 'There really – there really aren't any – suitable. Any suitable *people* – around here. She'll probably have to go to a city if she wants to marry.'

Dennis smiled. 'Like her father did?'

Thomas laughed in surprise. 'Yes, yes. I never thought of that aspect.'

'Oh, by the way,' said Dennis, 'I want to drop in two new drawings to you. Will you be there on Wednesday evening?'

'Come for your tea,' said Thomas.

'I don't think I can. It'll be about nine before I get to you.'

Ellen cycled to see Rhona Ulverton. Munch, on his avenue patrol, saw her coming and ran alongside the bicycle, chattering like a guide. Ellen, untypically, answered in monosyllables. She handed him the bicycle carelessly; he grabbed it and began to cycle round and round in front of the house. Ellen pulled the brass handbell.

Rhona appeared, antennae waving.

'Come in immediately. What's the matter?'

Ellen asked, 'How did you know?'

'I watched you come up the avenue. You are agitated.'

'Yes, I am. I don't know what to do.'

The women faced each other in the hall.

'I think,' said Ellen, 'I think that fellow, that engineer, is after Helena. Rhona, am I wrong to be upset by that?'

'Tea. Immediately.'

'I brought some scones,' and Ellen handed over the parcel.

'How could you be wrong? Shall we kill him? I'm only half-joking.' Rhona took Ellen's hand. 'Calm down. Take off your coat. We have to plan. Tell me all.'

Ellen shook her head in worry, and draped her coat on a large cane chair. She followed Rhona into the kitchen, where she sat at the table and rubbed her face deeply. Rhona made tea.

'We have no butter, but here is some of your gooseberry jam.'

'He was in our house the other night for the first time. And then he gave Helena a lift back to the Grey Valley, put her bicycle on the car. I haven't seen her since. Although we had a note this morning to say she's coming

301

for her supper tomorrow night. And now my husband tells me Sykes is dropping in as well. Rhona, am I imagining things?'

'No. An absolute no. No mother easily imagines something so fundamental as her daughter's danger.'

'Rhona, Helena's so impressionable.'

'I'm glad the girls are home again.'

'Grace isn't, only Helena.'

'Is she a virgin?' asked Rhona.

Ellen looked shocked. 'Of course she is!'

'Relax, my dear, relax, just measuring.'

Rhona poured the tea, put jam on her own scone and sat down.

'Now. Read it for me.'

'How do you mean?' asked Ellen.

'Spell out for me what you see as the problem.'

Ellen spoke with emphatic hands.

A She never trusted Sykes from the moment she saw him.

B He had her husband around his little finger.

C It would suit Sykes fine to pursue Helena and then he would surely drop her when the project was over.

D If, God forbid, he didn't, she could not imagine a more unsuitable husband.

'Because,' summarized Rhona, 'he is clearly an amoral little shit. I've seen dozens of them. He's a user. He will use Helena. He will do what he likes with her.'

'Rhona, I saw him looking at her in the most, the most – *immodest* way. Helena never noticed – but she wouldn't know what I was talking about.'

'I understand,' said Rhona, in her wild chiffon.

'I mean – you may think I'm old-fashioned –'

Rhona interjected again, 'But I understand your

conventions. And how safe you find them. Yes, you are right, and we must fight. We shall have to see him off.'

'But how?'

As Ellen walked around the kitchen, she muttered.

Essie asked, 'What was that, Ma'am?'

'No, nothing, Essie, I was talking to myself again.'

'Couldn't be in better company, Ma'am.'

The day dragged. Ellen did chores she had put off for months: sorted, to repair or discard, blankets that the children had chewed when small; counted the available preserving jars; wrote into her ledger two recipes from wives. During each task she paused at length, reflecting and muttering.

'First things first,' Rhona said. 'Alert Helena. Warn her of such men.'

But the plan came adrift early. Thomas had accidentally met Helena in the village as she cycled towards the house. Ellen saw them arrive, saw, to her astonishment, Thomas smiling at his daughter.

Matters worsened. Thomas said as they walked to the door together, 'I've just been telling Helena that she has an admirer.' The daughter blushed.

Ellen forced a smile. 'And who is the lucky man?'

'A distinguished man, no less,' said Thomas, smiling again. 'Look, she's still blushing.'

'How are you? Don't you look lovely?' said Ellen to her daughter.

The next occurrence completed the undoing of Ellen's and Rhona's scheme. All three Kanes perked at a car engine in the still, late afternoon.

Thomas took his watch from his top pocket. 'He's very early. He said he would not be able to call until nine o'clock or thereabouts.'

The car drew up.

'I'm sorry to intrude,' said the spry man, 'but I didn't expect to be passing.'

'Come in, come in, you're welcome anyway.' Thomas held the door.

Dennis in his perfect manners acknowledged Ellen first, then Helena.

'Now you will stay for your tea, won't you?' Thomas led the way.

Ellen rubbed her forearms vigorously when disturbed; nobody noticed.

'Isn't this a lovely room, I've been remembering it since the other night. I love parlours,' said Dennis Sykes. 'So that's the very same piano you played for John Mc-Cormack, Mrs Kane, well, well!'

How did he control it so easily? How did he command the whole evening so that Ellen never had an opportunity to speak to Helena alone? In the days to come she analysed and analysed.

'He simply made the assumption,' said Rhona, 'that the evening would run like that. Assumptions are very powerful medicine.'

Ellen did fire one salvo. Long after supper, as they prepared to depart, Helena said to Dennis Sykes, 'Oh, I've forgotten something,' and ran into the house to fetch the drawing materials Grace had requested. Thomas moved away from the group for a moment, to fix Helena's bicycle to the car. Ellen and Dennis stood alone. She peered into his face.

'Mr Sykes, what are you up to in my house?'

He stepped back. 'Up to? What does that mean?'

'Mr Sykes, you are up to something. I know it. Please leave my daughter alone!' Ellen had not meant to hiss. 'And you needn't bother giving me your pained look either.' (A warning of Rhona's, who had pulled the face to illustrate: 'He'll look pained, his sort always do.')

Thomas returned: Dennis won.

'Your wife,' he said it with such a smile, 'is attacking me.'

Ellen became confused and embarrassed.

Thomas asked, 'What is it?'

Helena returned before anything could develop. Thomas waved the car and the occupants away and stormed in. 'What was that all about?'

Essie left the kitchen too.

'Come on!' he snapped. 'What was that?!'

'I told him I didn't want him near Helena.'

'You what?!' Even Ellen had difficulty in not recoiling from Thomas in this anger. 'God in Heaven above, what are you doing? Are you gone blank-stupid, or something?'

'You've never spoken to me like this,' she said.

'That man!' said Thomas, pointing a crooked finger like a scythe in the direction of the departed car. 'That, that, that *excellent* man – he may want to marry Helena! He's already told me how much he likes her.'

'I don't trust him,' said Ellen quietly, hoping that by lowering her voice Thomas would follow suit.

'Well, I do! And I've taken the trouble to get to know him!' He thumped the table; the lamp jumped, and flickered violently. 'He is an educated and considerate man, and very successful. Where else will she get a husband like that? I mean – she's not the greatest catch in the ocean, is she?'

Ellen, stung, replied, 'Oh, Thomas, you're wrong. She's sweet-looking, and she has the loveliest nature, she's a very nice daughter to have.'

He snorted. 'She doesn't know her mind from one minute to the next.'

Ellen retorted, 'And look at what you do with a daughter who *has* firm opinions, you throw her out of the house.'

Thomas said, with as much force as Ellen had ever heard him use, 'If that man wants to marry one of my daughters I would feel privileged to have such a son-in-law. At least he's respectful towards *me*.'

At first, Helena Kane puzzled Dennis Sykes. She talked about the weather as if it lived and breathed, she discussed clouds and rain as if they had human life. Dennis's training as a listener paid off handsomely.

He asked only one question. 'Who is your closest friend?'

'Grace. My sister. I tell her everything. These are her drawing books, and things.' Helena indicated the pile in her lap.

A rabbit ran into the headlights: Dennis stopped the car, waited until the animal freed itself from the dazzle.

Helena said, 'That was kind.'

'God's creatures,' said Dennis matter-of-factly.

For the second time in that week, they reached the part beyond which no road existed, the entrance to the valley.

'I'll walk with you a little of the way,' said Dennis. As he carefully manhandled Helena's bicycle from the car his elbow touched her breast.

The night had not sufficient darkness to cloak them completely.

'Listen.'

Helena stood by her bicycle.

He whispered, 'Not a sound. I love silence.'

'Not even a dog barking,' she said.

'When do your summer holidays end?' he asked in a moment.

'Two weeks.'

'Look. I'd love to talk to you for ages and ages. If I meet you somewhere, can we spend an evening together? We could drive into Janesborough and have our supper in a hotel.'

'I don't know. What to say.' Helena fiddled with the handlebars of the bicycle.

'Say "yes", say it now,' he urged.

'The secret part, that worries me,' said Helena.

'What worries you about it?'

'I'd be lying to my sister.'

'But your parents wouldn't mind, would they?' asked Dennis. 'And – does she, your sister, does she know we arranged to meet this evening? Which we did. Remember? We arranged to meet without anyone knowing we had made an arrangement.'

'No. I didn't tell her, I was going to, later. I don't know, I mean – Grace and I, we've never –'

Dennis clinched it. 'Okay. I'll ask your father. All right?'

'Yes, yes.'

'And just for the moment, don't say anything to your sister, I mean if she's not at home – she won't know. So it will be all right.'

He held out his hand and Helena took it.

'Thank you,' she said.

'Oh, no, thank *you*.'

Rhona broke a twig from one of the trees and swished it.

'That whole swathe of behaviour suggests to me that he is really very practised. Very practised.'

'Explain that,' asked Ellen.

'He knows how to divide opinion. Divide and rule. If you have two people who obviously have had much to agree on – like a couple who have been married a long

307

time. Then if you can split them – you have a power in you. He caused a row between you and your husband.'

'He did.' Ellen leaned against a tree, her skirt blowing in the warm late August wind. 'The worst ever. My husband never spoke to me like that before, even when times were really bad with him and the children.'

'Try this,' said Rhona. 'Try meeting Sykes on your own. Try having a conversation with him of a reasonable kind. Although I believe that he's a despicable and treacherous little shagabout, *you* must also satisfy yourself on the point. And at the same time you can get a better look at him. And you're a very good judge of character. Plus – you will disarm him.'

To begin with, Ellen had to disarm Thomas. When he said gruffly that 'Dennis' had asked permission to take Helena out, Ellen agreed.

'Of course. When?'

'Next Saturday evening. They will go to Janesborough. He will take her to supper.'

'Good,' said Ellen. 'Helena needs social experience.'

Thomas never even reflected surprise. She merely arranged further that Dennis should pick Helena up at Deanstown rather than the Grey Valley: a letter would be sent telling Helena.

Ellen sat in the chair facing Dennis Sykes. Thomas had gone upstairs to change from the garden; Helena had not yet arrived.

'Now, Mr Sykes. I believe I may owe you an apology.'

Dennis shook his head. He wore a navy polka-dot tie, small dots.

'No, Mrs Kane.' One of his hands lay mildly on the other, as if waiting to applaud.

She insisted. 'I was hasty with you, and I am sorry if I gave you offence. My girls are my pride and joy. I feel very protective of them.'

Dennis said, 'I understand. Mr Kane and I spoke about it.'

'Did you?' Ellen's eyes widened – and she regretted immediately having given away a position.

Dennis seized on it. 'Did he not say?'

Ellen, discommoded, began, 'He – we, sort of missed time spent –'

'Oh, yes, we had a long talk. I asked him for permission to take Helena out this evening. On reflection, and here I must apologize to you – I should also perhaps have asked you. So the apology due is mine, Mrs Kane.'

She recovered a little. 'We, I – know so little, we – we never met you, you're a stranger.'

Dennis replied, 'I've told your husband my life story.'

Ellen coped better. 'That is not what I mean. What I mean is – we run on very straight lines here, we –'

She stopped, then began again.

'Our lives are modest, Mr Sykes –'

'Call me "Dennis", please!' He laughed. 'I'm too young to be Mistered.'

This she would not yield.

'Our lives, Mr Sykes, are small. Our girls have their interests; they are careful girls; we brought them up carefully.'

'And beautifully, if I may say so.'

Ellen ignored the compliment. 'I brought them up to believe in their continuing life as it is here. As they know it. They are innocent girls. You will notice that neither of them has moved too far away from home.'

He decided to engage with her. 'But, Mrs Kane, if I may say so. They are in their mid-twenties. I mean –

many friends of mine that age have three children by now.'

Ellen fought back. 'I don't mean to give the impression that I don't want my daughters to marry.' Her voice ascended to a prissy note, usually a sign that she was confused.

'Well then?' Dennis sat back.

Ellen had no tact. 'I just don't want them to marry men I don't –' This time she did stop before the crucial, damning words – but too late anyway.

He pounced. 'Do you mean you don't want them to marry men you don't like?' In his concluding remark, he encircled her and took her prisoner. 'My dear Mrs Kane, if you don't know me – which is true, because I am a stranger here – how can you therefore know enough about me to dislike me?'

Ellen looked away, her cheeks reddening.

Dennis rose to go to the window, and broke the conversation. 'I think I see your daughter, do I, in the distance?' He looked at his watch. 'Punctual. Like her father.'

Thomas entered. Dennis repeated, 'Punctual, I was saying. Your daughter. Punctual like her father.'

Thomas laughed, and asked, 'Do you have a destination in mind?'

'Yes, Cruise's Hotel. I believe it is very good.'

'Oh, yes. And very famous.'

Ellen remained seated. The men left the room and met Helena on the driveway. Thomas took her bicycle, and Dennis held open the car door.

Thomas waved them good-bye and came to the door.

Ellen said, 'I'm going up to see Mrs Ulverton. I have some recipes she's tasting for me.'

In all the years Thomas never challenged the euphemism.

=

Rhona, alerted by Munch, walked to meet her. Ellen was cycling too fast, but responded to Rhona's police-raised hand.

'I can't, I can't!' Ellen flapped. 'Rhona, I can't have it! I'm worried. I'm so worried.'

'You're not worried, you're panicked. Now – stop!'

Rhona picked up the bicycle from where Ellen had pitched it. 'Come on,' said she. 'Talk.'

The words flurried out of Ellen's mouth.

'I did it. I did what you said. I sat him down and I looked at him. I looked into his eyes. I talked to him.'

'And?'

'And – I don't know what to say, I don't know what to SAY!'

'Come on, come on.' Rhona took Ellen's arm while trying with her other hand to steady the bicycle. She eventually let it fall again. 'Tell me. In your own words tell me. What is your impression of him?'

Ellen stood; Rhona held her arm.

Ellen gasped. 'He is worse than I thought. I hope I'm not exaggerating. Do you know what it is like when you think something or someone is really worrying, but I had this before, and I didn't act in time.'

'And?'

'And my husband got shot, that's what happened.'

'No, that's not what I meant. You looked in his eyes and what did you see?'

'I feel a fool even saying it.'

'Say it, Ellen.'

'Well, he's – filthy!'

'You can't mean unwashed.'

'No, he has a filthy soul. That's what I mean. He has a filthy spirit. He is unclean.'

311

Rhona said, 'If you genuinely feel that, then you must do all in your power to stop him.'

Ellen stamped her foot in frustration. 'I can't. That's what's wrong! Who will listen to me?'

'I'm listening to you,' said Rhona, and did something Ellen never knew before or expected: she reached down and embraced Ellen tight.

Ellen burst into tears.

'At last. At long last,' said Rhona. 'The number of times I've wished you would cry and let some of all that stuff in you out.'

When the embrace came to the end of its natural life, Ellen sniffed.

'He has everybody fooled, though. Rhona, nobody can see through him – and he's out with my beloved daughter tonight. What can I do?'

Rhona considered, then answered. 'My late husband had a saying. "To make good decisions you need good information." Therefore – we had better get some information.'

Dennis Sykes explained the etiquette.

'It feels ill-mannered, doesn't it? But think of it as coming downstairs. The gentleman always goes down first, so that the lady will have something to fall on.' He smiled. 'Likewise, when walking to a table in a restaurant, the man leads the way so that he can pull the chair out for the lady. I like these details, don't you? Now – are you comfortable? You're not in a draught or anything?'

'No. Not at all.' Helena looked around.

He asked, 'Been here before?'

'Oh, no, no.'

'Like it?'

'Oh, yes. It is very – grand.'

'Oh, do you think so?' Dennis smiled. 'You should see the Ritz in London. They have gold statues. And a ceiling painted like the sky.'

She smiled. 'I read about it,' and Helena looked at Dennis's hands.

He said, 'Of course you read a great deal. Your father told me. By the way – are you nervous?'

'Yes. How did you know?'

'Because I am.'

'You are?' Her voice lifted in surprise.

'Yes. Why wouldn't I be? This is like my first ever date.'

'Date?' She seemed puzzled.

'Yes.' Dennis realized she did not know what the word meant. 'A "date" is what the Americans call, well this is, you know, an assignation.' It still did not get through. 'When a man and a girl go out for an evening to try and get to know each other. Or when they are what used to be called "courting". That's a date.'

Helena smiled. 'Around home they call it "coorting", they say a pair are "coorting". It's meant to be very –' She coloured a little.

Dennis waited.

'You know – very – private.'

He said, 'You'll hear the word "date" in songs. Don't you listen to the wireless?'

'Only the programmes my father and mother say we can hear. And there's no wireless in my lodgings.'

'I see.'

He changed the subject as the menu came. 'Does your sister know we're here?'

'No. You asked me not to tell her.'

'What's your sister like?' he asked. 'And as a main course? Something quite balanced after soup, don't you think?'

Helena worried.

He said, 'Why don't you have the chicken with bread-crumbs and I'll have the same?' Much relief on Helena's face.

'Now,' said Dennis, 'it is my intention to get to know all about you. What you want out of life, what you dream of, when you're happiest.'

'She's very – lively,' said Helena, 'she's a lot livelier than me.'

'Who's your favourite writer?'

Helena thought; always, she answered slowly. 'Oh, I don't know. That's like being asked your favourite food, or the nicest flower. Lewis Carroll intrigues me. And there are days when I think a lot of Charlotte Brontë. Mama, my mother, is reading *Adam Bede* at the moment, I finished it last year.'

'George Eliot.' Dennis merely placed the name in the air between them.

Helena looked at him in enthusiasm. 'Oh, you've read her.'

'You forget. I was educated in England.' He saw Helena looking into her soup. 'They're called croutons. French. Made of toast.'

She returned to the earlier subject. 'And Grace draws very well. That's what she likes, I think I told you that.'

At which point, Helena fetched from her handbag a newly-taken photograph.

15

The 'Ulverton Picture' (as Ellen now calls it) was taken by Viva in that summer of 1952. It shows how the two Kane daughters differed.

Both smile easily enough at the camera. As they stand next to each other, their affinity is plain. Beside the elaborate if decaying garden furniture, both look not a little international: aristocratic Italian, perhaps; Finzi-Continis. The old-fashionedness of their simple summer dresses, seen against the brick of the walled garden, suggests an earlier period, almost Edwardian. Notwithstanding the anachronism, both look well-kempt, blooming in health. The photograph is waist-high, and close on their faces: Helena is tentative; Grace's eyes are bolder without being forward; hers is the passionate mouth.

This is the photograph that, when shown to him by Helena that night at dinner in Cruise's Hotel, told Dennis how to pursue Grace Kane. No lines from Tennyson; no sweet reminiscences of Hans Christian Andersen; no cultural enquiries.

'Fears?' he echoed to Mr Quinlan's question. 'Should I have?'

'We got a whisper up here of two dirty words, just a hint we got. That Kane girl.'

'Grace Kane? Dirty words?'

'No,' Mr Quinlan chuckled at the misapprehension.

'The dirty words are "Public Enquiry". Someone's put her wise.'

'Could it happen?' Christ, Quinlan was maddeningly slow!

'We-ell, if she got influential people. Legal folks, especially. They stand to gain.'

Dennis asked, 'How long do Public Enquiries take in this country?'

'The last one lasted eighteen months.'

'Jesus!' swore Dennis, as he stepped from the phone booth.

Grace bustled.

'You'll have to move your feet, Mrs Stokes,' she chanted. 'Or I'll be washing them like Jesus washed the apostles' feet.'

Mrs Stokes laughed and lifted both ancient legs. Grace scrubbed furiously and quickly, then wiped the patch dry.

'Back now to *terra firma*!'

'What's that when it's at home?'

'You can put your legs back on the floor!' Grace looked up and smiled, then sat back on her hunkers and frowned.

'Tell me,' she said, 'have you noticed anything different about my sister? I mean – lately?'

Dennis Sykes and Helena had 'walked out' on four occasions in three weeks. Anything more frequent, reasoned Dennis, would be seen as 'fast'; any fewer – uninterested.

'She's out more, and she's quieter,' said Mrs Stokes. 'That can only mean one thing.'

'What?' asked Grace.

'A fella. A boy. A young man walking her out.'

'No! She'd have told me! Mama would have told me.'

Grace spoke more readily to men than Helena, had an

easier welcome for them. Once or twice she came close to accepting invitations; each time she judged according to her liking for the man, rather than the idea of having an admirer. So far, nobody she had met proved attractive enough.

'You know when some of them shake hands, and you feel their hands and they're as hard as boards. I don't want that.'

She paused. 'Hellie, do you ever get the notion that we don't know a lot of things we should know?'

Helena answered with a vague, 'Yes.'

Grace warmed to the topic; they were sitting alone on the settle outside Mrs Stokes's.

'There was a girl in Teacher Training who was always in trouble. She was nearly denied a place in her finals when she told Mother Agatha our last Easter holiday that she used to go to dances. She showed me how to put on lipstick if I ever need to, and she wore slacks, I met her once in them.'

Helena laughed and said, 'Don't tell Mama you know someone who wears slacks.'

'Can't you see her face?' Grace mimicked. 'And hear her, "I bet Our Lady never wore slacks." And the lips pursed. We ought to tease her about it.'

The girls enjoyed the joke: Grace continued.

'Anyway this girl, one night she began telling us about a boy she was walking out with. She showed us how he kissed her.' Grace stuck her tongue out, and Helena went, 'Yeeacchh!'

Grace laughed. 'Stoppit, Hellie. She said it was really exciting. She loved it. The French do it all the time.'

The sisters frequently discussed which of them would marry first. By and large they agreed on Grace.

Helena said, 'I'm not certain about the lying in bed

together, smell of sweat,' and she shuddered, making Grace laugh.

'I'd just make sure I was just as sweaty,' she said. 'I'd work like a Trojan just before going to bed, and I'd give as good as I got.'

At which Helena laughed. 'No. I want to go to bed with perfume on.'

'And have him play a mandolin under your window,' said Grace, 'and send you flowers every seventh day. In case you forgot his name.'

Grace, a bitter tinge in her voice, said to Mrs Stokes, 'But we had an agreement. Hellie and I always agreed that whenever we met someone we'd tell each other immediately.'

Mrs Stokes replied, 'The only thing to do then, girl, is ask her.'

'I will,' said Grace. 'I will.' Her momentary dip had passed: her empowering cheerfulness returned.

Miss MacNamara said, 'You will do best campaigning against what most annoys you. Now – let's go through it. Point by point. One – you are not against the place getting electricity?'

Grace said, 'No.'

'Two – what you are against is the Grey Valley being flooded?'

Grace said, 'Yes.'

'Three – but you are not against the people there being re-housed and receiving compensation, and many of them would prefer that to living forever in the Grey Valley?'

'True,' said Grace.

'Four – so what is it that utterly sticks in your craw? Because that is the point on which you will have to fight. Truthfully now, Grace?'

'I can't bear the loss of my lovely place.'

Miss MacNamara said, 'No good. Although I sympathize with you, that won't help you. Try again.'

'How do you mean?'

'Grace, nobody is going to support a campaign because some exotic place that you like to browse in, is going to be destroyed. You have to give it public value.'

'Public value. Such as?' Grace frowned.

'How valuable is everything?'

Grace said, 'I went through that before. That's what the march was supposed to be for.'

'Forget the march,' said Miss MacNamara. 'Have you established what is the most valuable thing about the Valley?'

'The botany.'

'Not strong enough.'

'Well –' Grace reflected. 'Dr Elizabeth Miller from the Museum said that the built-in furniture in the Grey Valley was unique and that nowhere did such a perfect capsule of a European country's domestic past exist in the vernacular.'

Both paused and considered.

Miss MacNamara asked, 'How busy is the work-site these days?'

'Like an ant-hill.'

'Like they're in a hurry?'

'A big hurry.' Grace tapped a pencil against her teeth. 'Don't do that, child, it's irritating,' and Grace stopped.

The teacher continued, 'So – they're in a hurry. I see.'

She thought again, then asked, 'Grace, do you really believe you can stop the dam outright? I mean – truly?'

'I'd like to.'

'I know you'd like to – but do you truly believe you can? Answer me carefully.'

Grace pondered. She exhaled. 'I think. I think – that as long as he's going full tilt, it will go ahead.'

'But,' cut in the teacher, 'if you interrupt someone's momentum it's as good as stopping them forever. Did you know that?'

Grace said, 'Yes. Maybe.'

Said Miss MacNamara, 'Have you found out what the people themselves think of their furniture?'

'They're not pushed.'

'But it has value?'

'To the museum people, yes.'

Miss MacNamara said suddenly, 'Go for a Public Enquiry.'

'A what?'

'Get the historians behind you again, widen your net, do it with style. If you get a Public Enquiry, you'll make them consider an alternative scheme. On the grounds of the vernacular value.'

Grace began anew. Following the system Miss Mac-Namara outlined, she interviewed, without attempting to influence them, every person in the Valley who would speak to her. All their comments and observations, their feelings, their knowledge of the history of the furniture – all went into her notebook; and she made drawings of the pieces of furniture under discussion. Day and night she worked, and then, when she had a large collection, she began to compile a short document.

A printer in Janesborough went through it with her and Grace emerged with a five-page newsletter. Each page was headed with a drawing of a different piece of furniture: Mrs Stokes's Wall-Bed; the Carrolls' Paired Canopy Bed; John McCarthy's Fiddle-Fronted Dresser; the Hickeys'

Sledge-Foot Dresser with Clevy for Hanging Utensils; Mrs Ryan's Carbery Settle.

Underneath Grace gave the quotations she had collected from the families who owned the furniture – statements of their esteem, affection and family history, simply expressed. All the vernacular pieces, she emphasized, had been created as part of each house: built into the walls, or fixed to stone floors – and therefore immovable. And therefore certain to be drowned.

She sent the first printer's pull to Dr Elizabeth Miller, and asked her for an observation she could use to complete her newsletter. Dr Miller wrote back: 'The Grey Valley has the single greatest concentration of Irish Vernacular Furniture in existence. It belongs in its own environment, and will lose much even if saved and housed in a museum. To place a cultural value on it, I would suggest that by virtue of its concentration in one locality, it has as much a place in the culture of the nation as a latter-day Book of Kells, or St Patrick's Bell.'

Grace whooped. She went back to Miss MacNamara, and showed her Dr Miller's letter.

'Now you have your campaign,' said the teacher. 'Now – this is what you do. You finish printing your newsletter with this as the front page, plus your own account of the Grey Valley. No emotion, Grace, just beautiful facts. Then, when it is all printed, you send it off to every political figure, every distinguished academic, everybody you can think of, and you ask them to write back to you. Most important, find a list of leading solicitors and barristers: you can get that from the Incorporated Law Society. Send the newsletter to each one. When you have all their letters, plus the signatures of the people in the Valley, then you give the editor of the *Nationalist* first crack at telling the world. At that point, you ask for a Public Enquiry. You can even talk about a National Park.'

In the car coming home from Cruise's Hotel, Dennis discussed at greater length the implications.

'I mean – I'm her greatest enemy, I'm the man drowning the Valley.'

Helena thought, and replied, 'But – I never had a secret from her.'

Grace sat up in bed drawing. When she heard the latch lifting and Helena's footsteps on the stone floor of Mrs Stokes's kitchen, she called out, 'Come in if you're good-looking.'

Helena smiled around the candlelit door. 'Hallo, artist.'

Grace said, 'Come here to me, have you a fella?'

'What?!' – but Grace misread Helena's alarmed reaction for a hint of outrage.

'I knew it, Mrs Stokes said you must have. I said she was wrong. How're they all at home?' asked Grace.

'Great. Mama sent this.' Helena, grateful for the diversion, handed over a small warm rug, and a bag of oatmeal scones. 'She says to tell you the autumn is coming on, so be careful to wrap.'

'Did she say anything about my not going back to work?'

'Not a word.'

'Great,' said Grace, 'because I have big plans' – which she conveyed in detail.

Helena's betrayal of Grace deepened. As she put her dilemma to her mother, her father listened.

'I don't know what to tell her if he asks me to go somewhere with him again. Or if Gracey asks me again if I have a – friend.'

Thomas butted in aggressively, 'He's a more decent

322

man than you'll find around here. And you should be grateful that such a remarkable and successful figure takes an interest in you. Such a polished individual.'

Ellen opened her mouth to speak, but Thomas glared.

'Don't tell her yet,' butted in Thomas. 'And that's an order. Your sister is a troublemaker.'

Ellen soothed. 'I'll tell Grace,' she said, 'when the time is right,' and snapped the sewing thread with her teeth.

'By then,' said Thomas, 'her "campaign", that nonsense, that will all be a thing of the past.'

'I don't know,'said Helena, 'she now has very powerful material, and she's sending it to everybody.'

Ellen, gladdened, but not able to show it, asked, 'What do you mean?'

Helena pulled the newsletter from her bag and showed it to her mother.

'Grace is writing to nearly five hundred people asking for their support. When she gets their letters back, Mama, she feels she will have something valuable, and she's going to call for a Public Enquiry.'

'At this stage?' snapped Thomas.

'She'll then give all the letters to the *Nationalist*.'

Thomas fumed and ran from the room.

'Helena, love, keep out of it,' pleaded Ellen. 'And as for Mr Sykes –'

Thomas stormed back, in hat and coat.

'Helena, you are not to tell Grace you told us all this.'

Next week, having ascertained that Helena had still said nothing to Grace, Dennis praised her. 'There's such a thing as tact.'

The following week – 'And if she discovers that you and I have been walking out – as I hope we are?'

Helena, honest as ever, replied, 'I don't know what to say.'

'At least,' replied Dennis, 'you understand that Grace

323

will be hurt. She will see you as having taken up with the enemy. That's why I always suggested that you say nothing to her. Time enough when all this is over.'

The work on the Deanstown hydro-electric project became a wider attraction. On Sundays, people from everywhere gathered on the high ridges to look down and marvel. They saw a deep scar in the ground, and, now, the gum of concrete rising well above the top. The curve fascinated the watchers – a perfect lateral arc, of grey, with an edge like a scimitar.

As his first line of defence against the new Grace Kane initiative, Dennis put in counterweights. Through an agency in Dublin, he engaged artists and writers to create a large storyboard. This was taken out of the construction huts every Sunday morning and erected in a prominent position. With Thomas, he arranged a school tour for the Deanstown children, at which he gave them an illustrated lecture on how such a project was undertaken. Thomas invited other schools, and led other parties of pupils.

Dennis Sykes understood the potential in the power of Grace's argument. Sure, he already had the overwhelming support of the community. Certainly, they looked forward eagerly to having electricity in their houses. Equally, they basked in the 'worldfamousness' of the project. Yet, he had enough intelligence to understand that people from outside could be pressed into service emotionally – and financially.

He assessed his position. The Kanes, father and mother, were divided over his 'interest' in Helena. Thomas Kane made that clear.

'I think your wife doesn't like me.'

Thomas looked up from Dennis's project notes. 'Don't worry about that, my wife changes her mind about things.'

'So, about Helena.' Dennis held the pause. 'If my intentions ever became serious – ?' He left the question unfinished.

Thomas actually blushed a little. He shook his head. 'Leave all that to me.'

Pressure. Pressure. Keep up the pressure. The phrase Helena had unwittingly reported haunted him: 'The Grey Valley – as important a national treasure as the Book of Kells': that could sink him.

'I was thinking,' said Dennis, 'of changing the work schedules. I was thinking of creating three teams, A, B, and C, and giving prizes for getting sections of work done quickest. You know these men. Would they like that?'

Once again he had rubbed Thomas's ego.

Thomas preened. 'Yes, yes. I believe they would.'

Thomas's next remark gave Dennis a brainwave. 'In fact,' said Thomas, 'they were saying in the Post Office this morning that the men said – they could work harder if they had to.'

'In the Post Office?' asked Dennis.

At which point he decided his next two moves.

The first depended upon his influence over Helena Kane. He began to make notes of every conversation he had with her. On the nights he returned from a meeting with her, he wrote down the key words of the evening: 'soft'; 'kind'; 'easy'; 'nervous'; 'gentle'; 'frightened'; 'afraid'; 'children'; 'mild'. He noted that she did not use these words as meanings in themselves, but as the paint in her ordinary language. Extrapolating, he wrote a short character sketch:

Virginal: frightened: not unintelligent – but too meek to use her brain well. Obviously terrorized by her father, and in awe of her mother. Possible to speak to her unusually directly about sensitive matters; yet needs to be handled with kid gloves. If dealt with abruptly or hastily, she will fly away. Wants romance and tenderness and promises of a future which will have no hardship in it. Not much would push her into a nervous breakdown. For instance, she may only be kissed in the most chaste fashion. A devout girl, she will lie if asked to, so long as she can tell it in Confession. There will be nothing intimate of any kind in her life before marriage, and even within marriage only with difficulty.

He planned his strategy towards Helena accordingly.

Dennis the prude: 'I absolutely oppose any, you know – intimacy. Until people marry.'

Dennis the lover: 'I'm a romantic at heart – I like, well, poems.'

Dennis the companion: 'Isn't delicacy between people such an attractive, such a winsome thing?'

All the while he enquired subtly – usually by asking for comparisons – as to what her sister was like.

The sister sounds less patient, more passionate. This stands to reason, as the good quality of the relationship between H and G suggests that G is likely to be in contrast, and to have more of the mother's natural passion. Whereas H has the father's tendency to aloofness but without his innate violence.

He began to draw up an urgent timetable.

Rhona and Ellen met on the avenue. Ellen's anxiety had reached fever pitch.

'Any news?'

'Yes. Good news. I have had a letter,' said Rhona, and fished it out. 'Read it.'

326

Dear Rhona,

Odd that you should ask, not my usual line of country. But I did enquire, and I think I have come up with something.

Neville's brother in MacReady Armitage Bailey has a typist, a gossipy girl called Eileen or Eily. She has a friend who was 'wronged' by a well-off 'incomer', an engineer. Whether he left her in the family way, or whether she merely thought he was going to marry her and didn't, I cannot be clear, but if you like we can enquire who the girl was.

Apparently she was a laundress. Does that sound right? And what in the N. of G. are you up to?

Yours bemusedly,

Harriet.

Rhona asked, 'What do you think?'

Ellen said, 'Explain all that.'

Rhona took her time. 'My friend Harriet Armitage makes it her business to know as many people as she can. She's like that. If I ever want anyone found, you know, for mundane things, such as, well, polishing old ivory, that sort of thing – Harriet will know. She always knows someone. Who knows someone. Dublin is a small place. So – what do you think?'

'Enquire,' replied Ellen glumly. 'That's all we can do.'

'We can do more,' said Rhona, 'at least you can. If our enquiries work, you can go to Dublin. Gather evidence.'

'Oh, hardly!' said Ellen.

Rhona raised an eyebrow. 'My dear Ellen, it *is* your daughter. That little shagabout will be wanting to marry her next. I would go if I were you. Can I persuade you?'

Ellen said, 'Yes, but you'll have to come with me.'

16

Dennis set it out like this.

1 By October 7: begin 'approach' to GK.
2 By October 7: tighten up 'commitment' to HK.
3 By October 14: block all responses to GK's
   newsletter.
4 By October 14: Secure all TK's loyalties forever –
   at least until February 1.
5 By October 14: Compromise EK beyond recall.

He found her easily enough. From the site headquarters,
his binoculars scanned the ridges each morning. Soon he
divined that she had a pattern. At about ten o'clock, Grace
climbed the eastern end of the ridge. From the top of the
escarpment, with the sun behind her, she surveyed the
progress of the site work. Sometimes she sketched into a
large pad, then tucked it under her arm and descended
into the trees and bushes, the fur of the Valley floor.

Three mornings in a row he watched, until he had verified her paths. When he climbed the ridge, he could see
the cottage clearly: ironically, he had chosen that vantage
point as the one from which the switches would be thrown
to fill the Valley, and then light the village, on 1 February.

Rain delayed him for two days. On a morning of bright
sunshine, he moved. As Grace scrabbled the last yards to
the top of the escarpment, Dennis left the site and slipped
down into the Valley. He had chosen a position that would

directly place him in her returning path. The precise spot would enable her to see him first, and choose, should she wish, to avoid him. He would judge his next move from whether she acknowledged his presence – from which he would know immediately whether his hunches about her were right. In a conversation about the French, Helena had told him Grace's kissing story: what matter if she had begun it in great embarrassment: as she had stopped and started, Dennis 'helped' her along with it.

He arrived at his chosen place, and stood, legs apart. The upwind breeze helped, bringing in advance the tune Grace hummed, and the noise of her brushing against the shrubs.

Timing, Dennis, timing.

About ten seconds from the moment when she could first see him, he faced in her oncoming direction, opened his trousers, took out his penis and began to urinate. He did so in an exaggerated fashion, hand on hip, stream flowing and steaming. He could be seen in detail – a flash of white underwear, a glimpse, even, of pubic hair.

If she fled, Dennis would have to re-think. If not –

He heard her stop: had positioned his head so that he could peer from under the lid of his hard-hat – without her seeing his eyes. The impression he gave was of a man completely unaware of any other creature. He finished and began to button his trousers, then she crashed forward and stopped. Yes! Yes! She *had* hidden. *And* stared!

He looked up and started. 'Oh, I'm – sorry.'

'For what?' Grace clearly intended pretence.

He changed tack. 'I mean – did I frighten you?'

She scorned, 'It would take more than you to frighten me.'

'I'm sure that's true, but what I mean is – you gave me a start.'

'A start? A start in what?'

'Aha!' Dennis laughed. 'A language barrier. I see. A "start" is what we call a fright. I mean – I didn't expect to meet anyone, and I thought perhaps you didn't either.'

Grace said, 'It's a free country.'

Like an admiring little satyr, Dennis looked at the trees, and the skies, and the ambience, and threw out his arms and said, 'Yes, and the old saying is true, the best things in life are free.'

'But you're trying to destroy them,' accused Grace.

'I'm only doing my job.'

She pounced as he meant her to. 'Ah, so you admit it, your job is to destroy this place?'

'Heavens, you are spirited,' he laughed. 'No, and you know perfectly well what I mean.' He stared at her breasts in her green blouse. 'Anyway, I couldn't see you coming, you were wearing camouflage.'

Grace looked down.

He indicated. 'Lincoln green?'

'What?'

'Lincoln green. The colour. The colour of your blouse.'

'*Lincoln* green?'

'Yes. After Lincoln Forest, where Robin Hood was. He wore a suit of Lincoln green. Did you ever read about Robin Hood?'

'Yes. I did.'

'Oho!' He laughed.

Grace asked, 'What's so funny?'

'A girl reading boys' books. You must have been a tomboy.'

They stood facing each other. Neither moved. In a moment Grace gave way – she stepped back and fiddled with the branch of a tree.

'By the same token, how does a man know about colours? That's a woman's subject.'

'I studied painting.' Which he had not.

Grace hid most of her interest. 'What kind of painting – house-painting?'

Dennis smiled. 'No, but I'd probably make more money.' Now he relaxed. 'I studied all kinds of painting. Still life, you know, bowls of fruit. Life studies. Nude studies. Some landscapes. Animals.' He watched her closely.

Grace asked, still not entirely conversational, 'Animals seems a bit like your subject.'

He pretended not to see the irony. 'Yes, in fact. Shrewd of you. The anatomy is difficult to draw. That's why humans are interesting too.'

He looked at Grace and generated a silence. Then he turned and walked away.

Early in adult life, Dennis Sykes discovered what he called 'compartmentalization'. If he divided his mind and his activities into compartments, he could give his full attention to one issue at a time, and bring a burning focus to bear upon each. By fixing on it with all his concentration, like a magnifying glass held in the sun's rays, he could burn into that compartment, could achieve from it, or put upon it, exactly what he wanted and needed. This power gave him whatever firmness he had salvaged from his unstable, unfathered childhood.

He made Grace Kane a 'compartment'. After he turned away from her and appeared to head back to the dam project, Dennis looped in his tracks. Within about three minutes was abreast of her, up a slight slope – able to monitor her, but able to conceal himself if she suddenly turned to her right and saw him. She walked along briskly, head down, large sketch-pad clutched to her bosom. Like her mother, she talked to herself all the time; Dennis could see her lips moving and would have given his fortune to know what she said.

She stopped once, and stared into the distance ahead of her: he watched from behind a high and heavy briar-rose, saw her mouth move, her knuckles clench on the sketch-pad. As if having determined something, she shook her head and walked on. Dennis watched her out of sight, heard her call a greeting to the old woman.

Already as he walked back to the dam, he recognized his dilemma: how fast, how hard to move? Play her slowly? Should he dive in? Was there a middle course?

Thomas Kane said, 'You're going to have a visitor later today.'

'Who?'

'The new Minister.'

Beautiful. Beautiful. Another objective could be achieved at once.

'Are we neat and tidy?' Dennis asked Thomas. 'Is my face clean?'

Thomas, boyish only in the presence of Dennis Sykes, said, 'I'll have to inspect your fingernails.'

'Now,' said Dennis, 'you arranged this, didn't you?'

Thomas inclined his head. 'Well I did write to him to congratulate him on his appointment.'

'And,' said Dennis, taking up the story, 'you just simply suggested that he come and see the most advanced hydro-electric project in the world.' He gave an exasperated and puzzled exhalation. 'My goodness – your nous, that's the word for it, such nous!'

Thomas Kane did not appear displeased.

=

Rhona said, 'There are times, Ellen my dear, when a little judicious deception has a purpose, a greater purpose. This may be one of those times.'

'I hate telling lies.'

Rhona replied, 'Nobody likes them. That is to say, I don't like them either. There is a cause here, though. We have found our woman. And she will see us. And Sykes was the man in the case. The ruinous man. Your instincts were right.'

'How will we do it?'

Rhona thought. 'Tell your husband that you are coming to see the doctor with me in Dublin. If you do not elaborate, he will think it is a woman's complaint, and not ask questions, men do that.'

'I know.'

Rhona asked, 'Do you know where Terenure is?'

'I can afford a car to get us there from the station. Will you write to Miss Glacken, or will I?'

The Minister walked carefully, hands deep in the pocket of a raincoat. A man whose eyes moved all the time as if he had a kind of dancing myopia, he shook hands with everyone he saw. Thomas Kane and Dennis Sykes stood on the wooden walkway steps to greet him. The Minister snorted, put his head down, increased his pace and ran up the walkway.

'The man himself! And how are you?'

He held out his hand, and Thomas took it.

'This man,' said the Minister of Transport and Power to Dennis Sykes, 'without him I wouldn't be here.'

Dennis chimed in, 'Nor, Minister, would any of us on this site, I believe.'

'How are you? How are you?' insisted the Minister again.

'I'm well, Dan, and so are you, I think.'

'This man,' the Minister rapped Thomas's lapel softly with his knuckles, 'is one of this buckin' country's great heroes.' He turned to Thomas once again. 'But what are you doing here at all? Why aren't you in the school? A'course, 'tis Saturday, what am I saying?'

'Dan, this is Mr Sykes, the young genius who is in charge here.'

'And the wife, how is she herself, I heard you've lovely daughters. Hallo, Mr Siki, Dan Cantrell, Minister for Transport and Power.'

'Sykes, Minister, how do you do?'

'Sykes, Dan,' Thomas Kane corrected gently, 'Dennis Sykes.'

'Sykes, ah, Sykes, a'course there used to be a boxer called Battling Siki, d'you remember him? Now where's this damn dam? Hallo girls, Dan Cantrell, Minister for Transport and Power. How are ye?'

The Minister walked forward and shook hands with the typists.

'But you didn't say? I know 'tis Saturday, but I'm still asking how did Thomas Kane, the man I know to be a schoolteacher and the best in the whole buckin' province too, how did he get to be a dam engineer?'

Dennis smiled. 'Minister, he's a kind of unpaid, unofficial adviser. Without whom we would not have managed. I assure you.'

'They say you're ahead of yourself?'

A civil servant behind the Minister nodded at Dennis.

'Just about, Minister. If it had not been for this man's help and understanding, we would not have advanced nearly as far.'

'My God,' said Dan Cantrell, Minister for Transport and Power, 'but I could tell you stories about this man, so

334

I could. I remember one night, not two hundred thousand buckin' miles from here and lying with this man in a wet ditch –'

Thomas steadied himself. 'Now Dan, come on, the past is past.'

'See that!' cried Dan Cantrell, Minister for Transport and Power, 'this is not a man to boast. But I'll tell you one thing, there was never harder. What about them two Black and Tan officers? D'you remember staring them into the eyeballs –'

The civil servant intervened. 'Minister, the foreman here – he's a constituent of yours.'

The foreman came forward.

'Dan Cantrell, Minister for Transport and Power. What's your name now?'

'Paddy Prescott.'

'What Prescotts are you?'

'Ballingarry.'

'Ah sure listen, don't I know every chick and child in your whole family, hadn't you an uncle died of TB two years ago up above in Peamount Sanatorium. I was at that funeral.'

Dan Cantrell, Minister for Transport and Power, had a pulse in his throat like a frog. It fascinated many.

'But come back here to me a minute,' he said to Dennis Sykes. 'How come this man here is acting unpaid?'

At this moment Dennis Sykes clinched his second objective.

'Minister,' he said, 'I have asked Mr Kane over and over to accept some kind of fee, some kind of consultancy payment, some sort of honorarium or stipend. He has refused, he says it is no more than his duty. A matter of honour. Now, I believe – and I can prove it to you, Minister, and to your advisers [Dennis had learned many years

335

ago that civil servants liked being called 'advisers'] that without this man's help and advice we could not, as I indicated, we could not as quickly have progressed as far as we have done.'

The civil servant peered around the edge of the Minister.

'Minister, there is a precedent, for having local advisers on certain projects.'

'Right so.' Dan Cantrell took Thomas Kane's arm and addressed Dennis Sykes. 'He'll be an adviser to the Minister. And that's all there is to it. And why wouldn't he be?'

Like a thin gale, Dan Cantrell swept out of the office to inspect the dam earthworks and concrete, and in his wake Dennis Sykes lifted a pleased eye at Thomas Kane.

'Credit where credit is due,' Dennis said.

'This man,' mouthed Thomas silently, a mimicking echo of the Minister's oft-repeated phrase.

'I am being made an official adviser,' said Thomas to Ellen.

She stared and smiled. 'To the Minister?'

'Yes. For this. And he said "Who knows what else?" That's what he said.'

'Oh.' She clapped her hands. 'Well done. Well done. You can buy me a fur coat.'

He laughed. Then he said soberly, 'I should remark – it was at the recommendation of the Mr Sykes you don't like.'

Ellen recovered well. 'The important thing is that the Minister knows how seriously you take life around here.'

'Yes. Yes.' Thomas nodded gravely.

After some contemplation, Ellen said, 'Thomas. Next Saturday. This day week?'

'Yes?'

'Rhona Ulverton wants to go to Dublin. She asked me to go with her.'

'Why?' he asked, though not unamiably.

Ellen made a wavy gesture. 'A doctor. You know.'

'I see. Will you want a lift to the station?'

'Apparently Cyril has said he'll drive us. We'll go from the Junction.'

'Cyril?' Thomas laughed. 'You'll never get to the train, let alone Dublin.'

Next afternoon, Dennis said over and over, 'Third-Remember-that-thou-keep-Holy-the-Sabbath-Day.' He swished his way through the woods with a hazel stick he had cut, a long wand with a fork at the tip. Helena had arranged to meet him that night at her parents' after Evening Devotions.

Dennis took a chance on the afternoon; but first, he stood on the ridge and checked Mrs Stokes's house with his binoculars. No sign of young life; the old lady came out once, threw a basin of white water away into the long late grasses and went back indoors.

Where was she? From the ridge he searched and searched: no sign of her. No bird life seemed disturbed. Other than occasional smoke from other, hidden chimneys, the Grey Valley was as still as the next world. All of autumn had come down to the valley floor, and he smelt it as clearly as he smelt women.

The ridge shelved a little under his feet, the under-carpet of shale yielding a possible fall. He stopped, picked up a curious stone, flung it away, then continued. The renowned valley blackberries had gone unpicked; a few remained as fat and black as sin. He plucked several, avoiding the long briars that reached for his sleeve. A sloe stung his tongue so bitterly that he spat it out. Two rabbits raced ahead, their scuts bobbing into the deep low hanging growth. He found a path, and stayed on it, with branches so low even he had to duck. Aloud he murmured the line of an old poem, 'I saw old Autumn in the misty morn, stand shadowless like Silence.' He stopped and listened – like a hunter. Which is what he meant to be.

In his notes last night he wrote:

> Grace Kane: small and hot: legs like a Roman goddess: fat lips and strong eyes: would lead a husband a hard dance were she raised in a non-Catholic society: knows she has a body: is capable of telling lies quite easily: she saw me, I know she saw me. Don't wait. MOVE!

Now he went forward, on tiptoe, ear cocked. The humming – just ahead: a humming noise: a tune, but not recognizable. He saw her – she stood looking at a parasite on a tree, a growth of berries sprouting a red leprosy from the bark; she reached in and touched it, then returned to the sketch-pad, made some marks, then looked back. He stood. Unwatched, she groped back and pinched her grey skirt to ease underwear from a cleft somewhere.

Dennis strode forward.

'We meet again,' he called, his voice hard.

She spun. 'What are you doing here?'

'As we agreed. It's a free country.'

He stood right in front of her, 'Let me see.'

Grace made no effort to stop him, as he took the sketch-pad and stared. Only when he began to flick the pages did she attempt to prevent him.

He rapped, 'No!' and leaned back out of arm's reach.

Some pages earlier he found a rough sketch – of him, standing as he had been when he urinated while she looked. The sketch, full-length, had loose, fuzzy definition at the crotch.

Grace blushed bright-red as he handed it back.

'So – you saw? I thought you did.'

Her eyes defied his stare – but she was the first to look away.

He said, 'I dreamed about you last night.'

'A nightmare was it?'

He said, 'Maybe for you – but not for me.'

'Oh. Were you drowning me?'

He said, 'No. I was taking off your clothes. So that I could see you as you saw me.'

She turned back to look at him. He reached out, drew a hand softly along her face, from height of cheekbone down to mouth and down, down, quickly through her cleavage, down to her crotch, so quickly she hardly knew he did it. Then he turned and vanished into the trees.

Helena waited by the gate.

'My parents have visitors. Where are we going?'

'That hotel, that lovely old place I stayed in once.'

'Grabstown Manor.'

They drove. Helena said, 'Did you smell the autumn today?'

Dennis smiled and reached across for her hand. 'Isn't this the life,' he said. 'I may never leave this place. I think I've fallen in love with it.'

Over their drinks, both orange squash, they simply talked. He told her his invented life; she answered his questions about her family without seeing his motives.

That night, she had arranged to stay in Deanstown. In the darkness, he pressed his face to her cheek.

'Good-night, dear Helena. Can we meet next Saturday?'

'I don't know. I have to be here. Mama is going to Dublin.'

'Shopping?' asked Dennis. 'Why don't you go with her?'

'No. It – it is something odd. She said not to ask. Which is not like her at all. She and Mrs Ulverton have been writing to someone there.'

Dennis's antennae twanged.

In the car, as if writing in his notebook, Dennis assessed his orchestration so far. Thomas Kane flattered into abject loyalty. Time to ask for Helena's hand: but – next Saturday? Why was Kane's wife and that tall snotty bitch Ulverton, why were they going to Dublin? To dig up something? Bloody small country. Everyone knows someone who knows someone. Vital that the second Kane daughter fall utterly out with everybody – so that no one knows of my relationship with both. And those fucking letters? Had she now sent off all her Newsletters?

Move, Dennis, move! Now! Christ's sake! He braked, turned, changed direction.

Heavy, knee-high fog. He parked the car on the snout of the earthen path. One light showed; the old woman slept early, Helena had said. Only one other bedroom.

He walked straight to it. Curtains wide open: inside Grace sat up in bed; by her side on the floor a pile of letters, clearly ready for the postbox. She licked another and sealed it; she wore a cardigan over her white nightdress.

Dennis tapped on the window softly, softly enough to make her wonder if she had imagined it. He paused. She stopped and listened. In a moment he tapped again.

'Is that you, Hellie?' Grace had a rasping whisper, it came of her husky voice like her mother's.

Dennis tapped once more.

'Hellie, if that's you the door is open.'

Tap. Tap. Then a little scrape.

Grace climbed out: Dennis appreciated the thigh he saw. She came to the window, leaned across the wide sill, tried to peer out, hands either side of her eyes. Dennis stretched a hand in and tapped again. Grace wrestled the sash up.

Dennis spoke. 'It's me.'

'What?' Why did she not sound surprised?

'I have news for you.'

'What are you doing here?'

'Your father.' He knew all the most powerful introductory words.

'What's wrong with him?'

'Can I come in?'

Grace thought, then yielded. 'Be careful. Be quiet. I'll go to the door.' She took the candle. Dennis tiptoed in her wake through the dark kitchen to the room.

Grace never said, 'This is improper.'

Grace never said, 'I don't want to see you.'

Grace never said, 'Go away.'

Second draft of timetable: by Christmas all nuisance will have to be removed. G must be disarmed completely by then and – ideally – have gone from the area.

He sat uninvited on the bed, did not look around, behaved as a messenger.

'I'll come to the point. Did you know that your father has been made a special adviser to the Minister for Transport and Power?'

'When did this happen?' Grace looked at him.

Dennis looked her up and down, in her white lawn nightdress.

'It has been in preparation some time. Confirmation has just come through yesterday. Nothing to do with me.'

She sat on the rope-seat chair beside the bed. The candle flickered: Dennis took it from her, put it on the shelf. He said nothing, simply looked at her.

'Why did you come and tell me?'

He shrugged. 'Two reasons. One – fair's fair. There are now considerable powers ranged against you. Two – I wanted to see you again.'

'Why?'

'I like rebels. I'm one. You may not think so.'

In the silence that followed they heard Mrs Stokes snuffle-moaning in her sleep in the room across the kitchen.

'They never told me,' said Grace. 'Mama never told me. Why didn't she write?'

Dennis had figured accurately. In these circumstances Helena would have wept. With luck Grace would rage. She did.

Shaking her head, she clenched teeth and fists. 'All that talk about honour.' She said it over, and over, and over.

'I must go,' said Dennis. No reaction. After a moment or two, he said it again.

'I must go.'

If Grace had tears in her eyes, they shone with fury. She stood as he did. By the door he whispered, 'At least I got to seeing you again.'

He made to leave, then turned back. The psychological trick he had pulled on Rose Glacken was about to pay off again – associating intimacy with distress, affection with disappointment and fear. He took Grace's forearms and held her hands by her sides, then kissed her on the mouth. No movement on her lips, inexperience rather than lack of interest – so he moved her lips with his tongue. He stood back, and took both her hands: he spread them around her breasts. Like a child she looked down at her hands in his grasp; he dropped one hand and scraped his own fingernail lightly in her pubic hair as Betty had taught him in Lantern Street. Dennis scraped a second time; he reached in a little, pressed hard briefly – and left.

Next morning he saw Grace cycle from the Valley; on her pannier the bulk of several postal packets.

That night he called again. As she sat on the bed he tipped her very, very gently on her back and by way of a joke remarked, 'Never ask me again if I have a civil tongue in my head . . .'

He buried his face on hers. As he left, hours later, he remarked, 'Did you know that your sister's staying at home . . . ?'

17

On the train, Ellen leaned over to Rhona and said, 'Now the next problem is how to get Grace back into the fold.'

'Has your husband eased any since he got that compliment from the Minister?'

'Not towards Grace.'

The women had dressed exquisitely. Ellen carried what Leah called 'her inevitable brown-paper parcel'.

'If Miss Glacken is a single girl living on her own, she may need some fresh baking, and a fruitcake lasts a while.' Sometimes Ellen had a self-satisfied air.

At the dam site later, Dennis Sykes said to Thomas, 'How does the postal system around here work?'

Thomas said drily, 'Slowly.'

'If, say, your daughter's campaign was to bring in a lot of letters – how long would it be before she got them?'

Thomas reflected and said, 'If there were a lot, the postmistress'd prefer she collected them.'

'Are they stringent?'

'Stringent?'

Dennis clarified. 'Are they stringent in that only the addressee can collect? I mean – can one collect letters for a member of one's family?'

Thomas replied matter-of-factly, 'We open all the children's letters, not that there are many. My wife and I feel things are safer that way, there used to be a tradition around here of anonymous letters. We've always thought the children, especially the girls, should be protected from that sort of thing.'

The pathway's tiles gleamed as ever. Bright shone the brasses on the little hall-door.

'Which of you is which?' asked the large-faced girl gently.

'I'm Mrs Ulverton and this is Mrs Kane. Are you Miss Coleman or Miss Glacken?'

'I'm Rose.' She smiled tentatively, and led them in. Waiting by the little stairway stood Eily Coleman who introduced herself.

Rose said, 'Eily has to go, but she came around just to see that you'd arrived safely.'

Eily bobbed a little around the women and prepared to go. Ever since Man stood upright, no woman ever left a house as reluctantly as Eily Coleman left Rose Glacken's house that Saturday morning. Indeed, she even turned back, having forgotten her gloves. She admitted to Rhona's beady eye in the hallway that it was 'a bit early for gloves wasn't it' but she 'always had bad circulation'.

She called, 'Rose, d'you need tea made or anything?'

'We can probably manage,' said Rhona with a grin.

'A brighter set of colours on you would cheer you up,' said Rhona to Rose. 'But it is very good of you to see us.'

'I like maroon,' said Rose, 'but I thought this was a bit lighter when I bought it, until I put it on.'

'That can happen,' said Ellen.

They sat. Rose had prepared tea, sandwiches and cake. Ellen handed over the baking she had brought and Rose thanked her fulsomely. 'You shouldn't.'

Rhona led off immediately. 'Mrs Kane,' she said, 'will come to the point.'

'I gather,' said Ellen, still wearing her hat, 'that you know a Mr Dennis Sykes.'

Rose nodded.

'How well did you know him?'

Before Rose could speak, Ellen interrupted her with a blurt. 'You see, Miss Glacken, I'm worried sick. He's after my daughter and I don't think he's a sincere man.'

Rose gazed at the willow pattern on the teapot as if it were a crystal ball. The women waited for her answer.

'Sincere?' She said it softly. 'No. He isn't sincere. Does he still wear a watch with a light brown strap, a kind of tan colour?'

Ellen nodded.

'Well.' Rose continued her scrutiny of the teapot. 'He used to look at that watch behind my back when we were – if we were, if he was –' She struggled. 'You know – when he gave me a kiss or that.'

Rhona and Ellen had to lean forward to hear her. Rose drew her fingernail over and over across a little nep on the tablecloth. She had a small brown mole on her neck.

'Why should that be the thing I remember now?'

'Am I right to be worried?' insisted Ellen.

'There's a sweatstain on the watchstrap and that used to annoy him, and one evening here I asked him to take off the watch to see could the stain be polished away, and playing, like, I said to him, "Now you're not getting that watch back until you're leaving the house tonight." And d'you know what it is, I thought he was going to hit me. He snapped at me so hard that I gave it back to him in a fright.'

Rose looked up at the two women. 'What do you make of that?'

'He had to have control of everything,' said Rhona.

Ellen asked, 'How do you feel about him now?'

Rose's gaze returned to the teapot. She mumbled something.

Ellen said, 'Pardon?'

Rose said, 'Smeared. I feel smeared.' She made a dismissive gesture, as if washing herself down. 'I feel he dirtied me.'

Rhona and Ellen exchanged looks. Rose continued, 'I feel as if – as if, I don't know what. I didn't feel it for a while after he went, and then I began to feel as if, as if.' She paused. 'As if he came in here to, to – use me, like I was an old animal, a cow or something.'

She raised her face to look first at Rhona and then at Ellen, and then Rose's large placid and pleasing features collapsed. Her mouth arced downwards and her lower lip sank. No tears.

The three women sat there. A painter would have captured a woman as tall as a cossack's wife, her hand leaning on an ivory-handled cane; a small vivacious woman twisting her wedding ring; and Rose – a small hand fiddling with the nep of fabric on the tablecloth. Under the square rug, the lino on the floor had been waxed to local grandeur.

The visitors waited for Rose's words. She kept them waiting.

Rhona knew the uses of briskness.

'May I ask – where did you meet him?'

Rose began, 'He used to come and have coffee in the Oriental Café in South Great Georges Street.'

She told her story: of Dennis's slow build-up, of his attention, of his respect.

'How could I mind,' she asked rhetorically, 'even if I felt it was all a bit too perfect? All I ever had to say to

347

myself was the truth – that I'd love to have a husband. He seemed nice to me.'

The gifts; the attentions; the Sunday papers; the 'taking of instruction'; the waiting for her outside Confession – all later came to dust when he vanished without explanation.

'I still don't know why he went.' Her monologue faltered. 'Maybe he guessed.'

Ellen pounced – but softly. 'Guessed what?'

'Well. I discovered I was expecting.'

Now Rhona pounced – on Ellen. Leaning out of Rose's range of vision she wagged a powerful finger when she saw the beginnings of disapproval on Ellen's face. She had to wag again before Ellen released the purse-strings of her mouth.

In a voice as kind as a grandmother's, Rhona asked, 'Was the baby – adopted?'

'No. I lost it. At four and a half months I felt a pain and I went into Holles Street by myself, and when I got there I asked the receptionist to take me to a bathroom, and the nurses just got to me. They were kindness personified.'

Rhona asked the question nobody else would have asked, and that Rose needed most to answer. 'Despite all, do you miss the baby?'

Rose nodded, as dumb as grief. 'I didn't care if it was a boy or a girl even. And now, even though 'twas probably too late for me anyway, even now, if I met somebody or even' – she hesitated – 'even if he came back, I can't have any children. They told me.'

On the homegoing train, the first chance they got to talk without being overheard, both women homed in on the same point and simultaneously quoted Rose: 'Even if he came back?!'

—

Rose talked and talked. Every detail materialized. She had forgotten nothing. They marvelled at her recall. She described specific occasions, told them where she and Dennis had gone, even what they ate. His clothes, her clothes, his views, her cooking for him. Then came the questions she had never allowed herself to ask. Why she had never met his colleagues? The fact that he never wanted to meet her friends? How come he ran everything and she simply fell into his line of things?

Ellen and Rhona sat with Rose, as they had each sat with widows after a funeral. Each woman fed Rose from her own store of compassion – brusque, tender, turn and turn about. At the end, a silence.

Ellen broke it. 'Rose, I'm going to call you "Rose". My heart goes out to you. I've hardly ever met a nicer girl.'

Rose nodded.

Rhona said, 'Is there anything practical we can do – to stop this little, this little seducer ruining Helena's life?'

All considered.

'If he has any shame,' suggested Rose, 'the mention of my name, maybe. It might – it might tell him people know about him.'

'I can pretend,' said Rhona, 'that you're a friend of mine.'

As they left, Ellen shook Rose's hand warmly. 'I'll write to you,' she said.

Even as the women on the train planned, Dennis Sykes had moved ahead of them. He ticked off his objectives.

1 TK secured.
2 The *coup de grâce* about to be delivered on HK.
3 GK in hand (so to speak).
4 GK's effort about to be pre-empted on two fronts.

First, he approached the editor-owner of the *Nationalist* and bought the biggest advertising spread that newspaper had ever seen: 'To continue until April, all right?'

Said the editor, 'We support progress.'

Secondly, he had to make a small adjustment to Thomas's effort.

'But if you intercept *all* the letters,' said Dennis reasonably, 'then, if it were me – I would suspect. Shouldn't a few get through?'

Dennis looked forward to 'soothing' Grace's disappointment.

A problem remained, potentially – the Kane wife's trip to Dublin with that older of the two Ulverton bitches. For some unknown reason he felt persuaded that it concerned the girl, what was her name, in that funny little house with the cold lino floors?

Viva Ulverton moved his position from persuaded to convinced. Lately, she often unnerved Dennis by popping up: on the roadside; peering at him through the site fence; sitting on his car outside Hand's pub. She never said anything – just waved, or smiled, or skipped a little as if about to dance for him. On Monday morning, she sat on the saddle of a bicycle just by the site entrance.

He greeted her, pleasant as usual, his policy: 'Morning, Miss Ulverton.'

She pointed at him. 'Spoke in your wheel. Fly in your ointment.'

'What are you talking about?'

'Pebbles in your shoe, little man.'

Dennis grew cold: no effect.

'Wait and see, Dapper Dan.'

'Wait and see what? And who, may I ask, is Dapper Dan?'

Viva chortled. 'You are. Little fucker.' She wandered off.

Grace waited on the pathway down from the shale.

'You look nice.'

She shrugged. 'Easy words.'

'No.'

'Yes. You have a lot of words. They come easy to you.'

'Here.' He held out his hand. 'Give me your hand.'

Reluctantly, she agreed.

'Come for a walk.'

'I don't want to.'

He stopped and looked her in the eyes. 'Now what's wrong?'

She said, 'You made me sin. You made me commit a mortal sin.'

'How?'

'You touched me. Immorally.'

'I'm not a Catholic,' said hard and defiant Dennis.

'But you know about sin?'

'I don't see how a gesture of affection between two people can be a sin?'

She said, a little savagely, 'Affection? You don't know the meaning of the word.'

Dennis replied, equally aggressively, 'How do you know? You've hardly met me.'

'I know by your eyes.' She quoted him sarcastically. '*Gesture of affection.*'

'All right,' he said. 'Desire. Is that better?'

'A bit more honest, anyway.'

'So – you're so fucking perfect!' He watched carefully to gauge the effect of the expletive. She did not react. He took back the hand she had earlier snatched away.

'I've got the measure of you.'

'What do you mean?' she asked.

'One, you saw me on the pathway. I was pissing and you watched. You pretended you didn't. Two – you, with your Catholic sin and all that, you never batted an eyelid when I swore just now. Three, I felt your tongue move against mine.'

Grace repeated, 'You made me sin. I should not have let you – do. Do what you did.'

'What did I do?'

She replied, 'You know perfectly well.'

'Stand.' As she stopped he walked behind her, stood right against her back. 'And did you object?' he whispered in her ear. Grace did not answer. Dennis put a hand on her hip: shades of Audrey.

'And did you object?' he asked again: this time he spat the words.

No answer. With his other hand, Dennis reached around and smoothed a breast, then ran his fingernails in a circle until he found the nipple.

Grace said uncertainly, 'This isn't fair.'

Dennis dropped both hands to his sides. 'What isn't fair?'

'I have no one on my side.'

Dennis said, 'You have now. Let's walk on.'

She seemed near tears and he put an arm around her shoulder.

'Come on. I'm better than you think.'

They found a log and sat.

'Can't you make it up with your father?' asked Dennis.

'No. You don't know him,' objected Grace.

'He's very stern. Was he always like that?'

Grace, still avoiding Dennis's look, said, 'Mama said he wasn't. Until the accident.'

'Accident?'

'You must have heard.'

Dennis said, 'Only vaguely.'

'He was in a coma. Helena and I, when we were at school – people used to say to us that my father was shot, and that my mother afterwards –'

'Who shot him?'

'I don't know.'

'Your mother afterwards? What was it you were going to say?'

'I don't want to talk about it.'

'The man who shot him – was he caught?'

'He died.' Grace rose. 'I said! I don't want to talk about it.'

'All right, all right, keep your shirt on – or, rather, don't.'

Dennis's joke failed.

Grace said again, 'You made me sin.'

'Oh, for Jesus Christ's sake change the fucking tune, the band is getting tired!'

Dennis tossed an angry little head. He pinned her arm, put a hand roughly under her skirt and flicked. Grace tightened her legs; they struggled; she parted her thighs briefly, soft flesh above stocking-tops. He pressed two fingers right in, withdrew his hand, rose and walked away, leaving Grace looking after him.

Ten yards off he turned and called, 'I'll see you later.'

In that village community, there are still no such things as secrets. Nor do you ever hear what they say about you. But they know. The unconsummated Hogan marriage. That John Shea and his sister shared a bed. The small legacies. Or big debts. The death of Dan Quinn.

When Thomas Kane recovered fully, there was one civic duty he never again undertook: his wife successfully objected to it. In the past he had been a Character Witness when the court circuit came by. During the Hilary term of 1925, he testified on behalf of Michael Quinn, a boy accused of stealing. But the court convicted the boy, and asked Thomas to carry out the birching. Afterwards, the boy's father spoke vengefully to the righteous schoolmaster, to his wife.

During the investigation of Thomas Kane's shooting, nobody made allegations – and everybody knew. The police questioned only one man, the bulky and dismissive Daniel Quinn. No proof.

In the succeeding months, Ellen Kane heard the flint of heavy boots on the road near the house and on the gravel. Quinn came into her garden once, and helped himself to a bucket of potatoes. In fright, but with presence of mind, she immediately invited the Canon to do likewise – very publicly. Quinn did not do so again.

On Christmas morning 1926, Daniel Quinn's body was found on the roadside, near the church. His horse grazed the winter verge nearby. Quinn died of head injuries, had drink taken, the heavy spirit of Christmas Eve. The vet's examination, to ascertain whether the horse might also have kicked the man, revealed a small but powerful, irrelevant wound on the horse's shank. When the Superintendent called upon Mrs Kane, he took away for examination a Tara brooch hatpin; it was returned two days later.

The inquest jury returned a verdict of 'death by misadventure': thrown by his horse. Deanstown still agreed on the natural justice of the outcome.

'We all said he had it coming to him.'

Dennis asked, 'The horse, Mrs Hand? Was it put down?'

Breege Hand said, 'No, no, the horse was harmless.'

'But it threw the man?'

Mrs Hand practised jovial malice. 'Ah, now sir! We do all get frantic if we're jabbed.'

'Jabbed?'

'Jabbed.'

'Jabbed with what?'

Mrs Hand laughed. 'Men knows nothing. There's many a man round here since wouldn't let his own wife own a hatpin.'

'Who had the hatpin, Mrs Hand?'

'Ah, now look, wasn't justice done? Didn't the hand of the Lord help?'

'But the hand of the Lord didn't push the hatpin, Mrs Hand?'

Mrs Hand eased herself out of the conversation. 'No, nor it didn't.'

Dennis Sykes had enough bait to go fishing.

Almost ready for bed, Ellen heard the Sykes car. It stopped outside; moments later the door slammed; the car drove away; she heard Helena's footsteps on the gravel, then around the house, then the girl came through the back door. Ellen went downstairs.

'Hello, Mama.'

'Hello, love, you look very nice. Did you have a pleasant outing?'

'He's very nice to me.'

Ellen smiled carefully at her daughter. 'Do you like him?'

'Well, I do. What I mean is. I know you don't like him, but Daddy does and since he, I mean Dennis, since he started to be interested in me, Daddy is very nice to me.'

'But is he the kind of man you would marry?'

Helena said, 'If he's going to be that nice to me – I

355

mean, if, if –' She sighed. She considered. She began again. 'If he talks to me and tells me things, and if he doesn't bark at me. Tonight, for instance, he told me how much he likes children, he told me how much money he earns, he told me how much money he has saved. He said I was intelligent.'

Ellen protested, 'But you are intelligent, you are!'

Helena replied, 'He says that I say interesting things. He says that I know what I'm talking about. I don't feel afraid.' She took off her gloves. 'And tonight before Dennis called, Daddy actually showed me something to read from the paper and discussed it with me.'

Ellen said nothing, just nodded, then after a moment or two, asked, 'When are you seeing him again?'

Helena replied, 'He's taking me to the pictures in Mooreville on Tuesday night.'

'To the pictures?'

'Yes.'

'What's on? Is it suitable?'

'Yes, Mama, *Soldiers Three*. Stewart Granger is in it.'

'Oh, pity –' then Ellen bit her tongue.

'Pity about what?' asked Helena.

'Gracey loves Stewart Granger.' Ellen regrouped. 'Helena love – we have to *do* something. It is terrible that Gracey isn't speaking to us.'

'But Mama, it isn't my fault. And it isn't your fault.'

Ellen let the thought continue, then asked, 'And it isn't, I suppose, Gracey's fault?'

'No.'

'Then –' thinking aloud, 'whose fault is it?'

Helena said, 'It might be nobody's fault.'

Ellen rose. 'We have to think of something to do. I miss her terribly. I've written to her now three times and she won't write back to me, there's no reply.' At the kitchen door Ellen asked, 'Are you going to first or second Mass?'

Helena said, 'I'll go to first.'

'Goodnight, love.'

After Helena, he drove straight to the mouth of the Grey Valley. This time Grace heard him coming; the window stood raised. He whistled like a small animal or night bird. Grace pulled back the lace curtain.

'You?'

'Me.'

'What do you want?' All in whispers.

'You.'

'Stop it. Go away and leave me alone.' But she did not move the curtain.

'Why?'

'I have to get up for Mass. Tomorrow's Sunday. You upset me.'

'I did *not!*'

'Shhhh!'

'I did *not* upset you.'

She whispered, 'You did.'

'I didn't mean to. Can I come in?'

Grace defended briefly. 'The door is closed.'

Dennis indicated. 'The window is open.'

She made no attempt to prevent him hauling himself over the wide sill. He dusted down the flakes of whitewash from his black trousers. Grace stood there; the candle in her hand guttered a little in the breeze.

'A windy night was blowing on Rome,' Dennis quoted softly.

'What?'

'Nothing.'

He did not penetrate Grace that night. Nor did he take

357

off his clothes and climb beneath the heavy blankets with her. He did kiss her repeatedly, stroked her, touched her bare skin, smoothed down her nightdress again; laid his face on her shoulderblades, kissed her neck under the hair, traced her lips with his fingers, then his tongue. He talked to her, or rather he listened, mostly about her father. She described the Christmas Day she called her father 'a bastard' and how her father had whipped her home like a small dog. When she grew distressed during a whispered memory, Dennis found an erotic means of distracting her, of making her halt the story for a moment or two.

Dawn raked the sky. As he slipped away, he whispered back through the window, 'Was all that sin?'

Grace shook her head, full of sadness and premonition.

The rabbits raced ahead; a distracted small bird whirred softly by Dennis's head. He walked, half-loped through the thick shrubbery of the valley floor. Stopping by one house, he heard the sleeping moan of an old person, the re-settling grunt; then silence. A cat ran home. No chimney smoke, no bark of a dog. In a clearing, Dennis checked the sky, and saw the sun coming up, its light unimpeded by the tails of long red-tinged cloud. He changed his mind, cut off to the east.

On the far ridge, he turned to face the Valley below. It looked like Africa. Man might have been born here, sixty-five million years ago. Dennis could see no houses, only the wavy, milky haze that softly clogged the upper strata of the greenery.

He spoke aloud. 'Grace is right! She's right to fight!'

His words had no echo – not in the valley, not across the empty space of that morning, nor in his heart. With his next breath he turned to view his beloved project.

The dam had now risen truly above the ground. That grey thick curve of wall had the sinister force of those submarines he saw in wartime newsreels. So compact! So – so *powerful*! Along the top, a column of twelve men could march abreast. Dennis's specifications to the builder resulted in a neat site, the work-in-progress always ordered and under control.

It all had a majesty; the wide young walls seemed an organic part of the planet itself. A week tomorrow, the workforce was about to double and in six weeks these walls would then reach their final height. When it began to curve in, the full beauty would appear. Nature did not have all the tricks, did She? A man could take Her on and tame Her to make something beautiful. In a little over two months, a new landscape would exist here, a shimmering lake of grey and silver satin held firm at one end by exquisite engineering. What a day was to come! The sluice at the far end, the last of the works that would be completed, would blast open and in would plough the rivers, spuming and ferocious. This valley bowl would fill in, what, six hours? At which point, the dam would begin its eternal work. Time it backwards: February the first: dusk falls at four o'clock: therefore, hold a ceremony to loose the waters at nine in the morning; then return for the switching-on of the lights at, say three? Return? Nobody would leave: the party would grow and grow as people came to watch the flooding of the valley.

To do all this: to change people's lives! To transform the face of the Earth itself! Not only that – this is the smallest, yet the most powerful piece of engineering work of its kind in the world, almost a toy, no bigger in its curved length across than a large battleship, no, perhaps an aircraft carrier. Small, like me! Powerful, like me!

Elegant, like me! Came out of nothing, like me! No fear, no more. Fuck them!

Developments on Monday finally guaranteed Dennis Sykes absolute command. All had to do with the Kane family. They occurred between half-past two and half-past four.

The first took place on the hundred-yard stretch of road between Deanstown School and the Kane household. Ellen's day ended half an hour before Thomas closed the school at the statutory three o'clock. By twenty minutes to three, she had gathered her basket, donned her hat, smiled at Thomas through the partition and left. Autumn surrounded her, mild, warm and full of smoky thoughts. Carrie Egan filled a bucket from the green helmet of the old pump and waved a greeting. A hen stalked tediously in the thin-legged privet of Caseys' hedge. Ellen saw the black gleam before she heard the engine; inevitably he stopped.

'Hallo, there.' Until he died he would retain the habit of stroking his moustache as he greeted someone, a nervous reflex.

'Hallo, Mr Sykes.'

'Oh, look!' he sounded half-irritated, half-amused. 'You'll have to start calling me Dennis.'

He hauled on the ratcheting screech of the handbrake and got out. 'I knew there was something I've been meaning to say to you for weeks – that chocolate sponge cake.'

He made a circle with thumb and forefinger and punctuated the air between them.

'First-class.'

Then he looked Ellen's body up and down.

She attacked. 'Mr Sykes. I will not call you "Dennis". I will never call you by your first name. I will not have

360

anything to do with you. You are ruining my family. And I know all about you.'

He recoiled but kept his head. '*All* about me?'

'I know enough to make people suspicious of you, indeed to change their foolish view of you.'

'Now, Ellen.'

'I am "Mrs Kane" to you, Mr Sykes. Nor will I ever be more familiar. And if I have my way, you will be out of here as quick as your legs can carry you.'

'I believe you're mistaken, Ellen. I have a job to finish.'

'Believe what you like. Not that you believe in anything. No – I'm wrong. You do believe in something. You believe in wrecking people's lives.'

'Oh, come on! That's not on!'

Ellen played her card. 'Rose Glacken? 15 Mayhill Terrace, Terenure?' She puffed with triumph. Not for long.

He grinned. 'Oh, who's a snooper!' Dennis rubbed his hands with glee. 'Playing that game, are we? Nothing I like more. So – may I ask. Did you, in your snoopings, find out whether Miss Rose Glacken uses a hatpin? Or rides a horse?'

Ellen's mouth fell. He leaned back against the car, could afford to wait, no need to press. She began to come back at him, but – no words. He moved the matter forward, and not in the way she expected.

'Yes?' he said, in a jovial 'I'm waiting' tone.

Nothing. He had won.

Long pause. Reality. No pretence now, cold business: 'Here. We have to get on, you and me.'

'You and I.' Still she could not stop correcting people.

'All right. You and I. You're full of that sort of shit. But we have to get on.'

She tried once more, nothing if not courageous. 'You ruined that poor girl.'

'Love's labour's lost – *Mrs* Kane.'

'But you ruined her, she is – destroyed.'

Dennis smiled; he put on what Binnie used to call his 'glitter'. And stroked his moustache again. 'But she's alive.'

Ellen's shoulders conceded defeat.

Dennis said softly, 'Don't you know your Cicero. Very apposite in all this – *Mrs* Kane. "While the sick man has life there is hope." Must have been a time when that would have been a useful tag in your existence.'

Dennis opened the car door. He said over his shoulder, 'So in fact, we may now turn around and put to good use your earlier remark, what was it you said to me? "I know all about you." Yes, I believe that is what you said.'

He drove away, and was pleased to see that she stood watching him – probably, he hoped, in consternation – as he turned into the school playground fifty yards on.

Thomas Kane saw him arrive, released the school five minutes early. Dennis watched the motley children storm out.

'I must say,' he observed, 'it gives me deep satisfaction to think of the improvement electricity is going to make in their lives.'

Thomas smiled, 'Come in. Come in.'

'I won't stay. I just have two things I want to say. First of all, and most important. I met your wife on the road just now. Now – how can I put this to you?'

Thomas looked puzzled.

Dennis paused.

Thomas fixed the fireguard for the night, put a tall carboy of ink back in the cupboard.

Dennis began again. 'Your wife. Well – the conversation she and I had.' He pretended unease, then appeared to gather courage. 'Look, I don't know how to say this, I've never had to say this to a man before.'

Thomas now gave Dennis his full attention. The small man said, 'This is what I have to say. I would very much like, now that I've had a good look at both parents – I would very much like to marry your daughter, Helena.'

Thomas Kane laughed and rubbed his hands. 'Well, well, well. This is very good news. Very good news altogether.'

Dennis put out a hand: Thomas took it and shook it. 'It will be like having another son,' he said shyly.

'And it will be like having a father after all. We got on well, didn't we, from the moment we met?'

'We did indeed. We did indeed.'

Dennis said, 'I have such plans. If this entire project works out, I may even start my own engineering company, and to have your wisdom and advice. That would be just great.' He added anxiously, 'I hope your wife will be pleased.'

Thomas nodded, 'She will of course. She will of course. Every mother wants to see her daughters marry well.' He returned to his small, day-closing chores. 'Oh, this is excellent. Excellent.'

'Now, I have to go,' said Dennis.

'Indeed. Indeed.' The two men reflected for a moment.

Then Thomas said, 'You said there were two things?'

'Oh, yes. The postman told me this morning, there were what he called "several hundred" letters for your daughter – Grace.'

Thomas frowned. 'Leave that to me.'

Dennis contemplated. 'We have so much at stake now. Oh, by the way.' Dennis turned on his highly-polished shoe. 'Not a word to Helena yet. Please. I obviously want to –'

'Of course. Of course.' Thomas smiled again. 'And by the same token, I think I'll wait for a while to tell her mother.'

Dennis approved.

Effectively Grace Kane's protest ended that evening. She needed replies *en masse* by the middle of that last week in October. Had she received three hundred letters, she and Miss MacNamara gauged, a national newspaper would have taken up her cause. At the very least she would have persuaded some journalist to use the words, 'Public Enquiry'.

In her fantasy, all would have happened while the dam wall was still low enough to be covered in.

'What does the place look like?' asked Miss Mac-Namara.

'Well.' Grace hesitated. 'I have to say it doesn't look as bad as I thought. The thing is – the whole project is much more compact and neat.'

'How many letters?' asked Miss MacNamara.

Grace blushed. 'Eleven.'

'How many did you send out?'

'Over six hundred.'

Miss MacNamara gazed out of the high window. Behind her desk hung a picture of Eugenio Pacelli, Pope Pius XII, thin nose, thinner spectacles.

'Eleven out of six hundred. That's what? One in sixty?' She sniffed her fingers. 'Of the eleven – anyone significant?'

Grace said, 'No. One museum-keeper, who wrote from home. The point is – there's no typewriting – all the letters I got are in handwriting, so –'

'So there's no *official* response?' asked Miss MacNamara finishing the thought.

'No.'

'That's funny. Oh, well. Perhaps they all felt – that it was too late or something, or often people in positions of authority, they often feel they can't, they can't – well, go against something so official. Does this mean you have no time left?'

Grace nodded.

Miss MacNamara said, 'That's a pity. A pity. And you fought so valiantly.' After a pause she asked, 'What do you want to do now?'

'I want to go on noting down and drawing everything,' said Grace. 'There are only three months left.'

'And when,' asked Miss MacNamara tenderly, 'do you want to come back to work?'

'The first of February.'

'Your job will be waiting. You will be very welcome. Have you enough money?'

Grace nodded. The Headmistress changed briskly, 'Now something else, Grace. You're not looking well. Are you all right?'

'I'm not sleeping.'

'Of course you're not.'

Grace said, 'I – I.' She stopped.

'Is there anything you want to talk about?'

When her staff smiled about Miss MacNamara and her beard, and her walk like a very fast bird, they also referred to her warmth. Yet, not even her heart could bring Grace to ask for help in the dilemma over Dennis Sykes, and the raids he made, and her awful compliance, and the guilt he caused her . . .

Last night he called again, very late. Last night he talked to her a little – and he listened, and listened, and listened. Last night he kissed the insides of her lips and she felt the skin stretch as her nipples rose. Last night he

365

made her hot, and when he left in the small hours of the morning, slipping away through the rain, not even the breeze through the opened window could cool her cheeks.

Last night, when Mrs Stokes went to bed, long before Dennis the prince of darkness arrived, she sat by the fire and wept, now that she had failed and had nobody with whom she could share her failure. She wept because she missed Helena, who had not yet replied to the letters she sent – even though Grace wrote to Helena at her lodgings. She missed the jokes with her mother. And she wept because she had no words yet by which she could tell Mrs Stokes that she had failed, and that the Valley would be drowned after all.

'You're keeping me alive, girl,' the old woman said to her every morning. When it finally appeared as if no other letters would arrive, Grace feigned illness, left her room only to empty bladder and bowels.

Then, on the third morning, Mrs Stokes came into the room and said, softly, 'Child, I have a little bit of bad news. The big builders is in, they're in in force, there's hundreds and hundreds of them.'

The dam had reached the point where nobody could stop it now. All Grace had managed to do was raise a notional point-of-no-return, and that had passed and she had been virtually ineffectual. She and Mrs Stokes sat in silence.

18

Rhona Ulverton waited – for news of the *coup de grâce*.

As she left the train, she said to Ellen, 'Go for him. Go straight for his jugular vein. It runs along here –' and she made a throat-cutting gesture with the flat edge of her hand.

No news – except from a surprised Viva, who said, 'Sykesy-Ikesy is livelier than ever. I thought you two were going to spike his guns?'

Rhona handed bread-bearing Essie a note.

> My dearest E,
> What happened? Did you beard the maggot in his den? I yearn to know.
> With affection,
> R.U.

Ellen replied,

> Dear Rhona,
> I'm afraid we have to let the hare sit a while. Things are complicated: I'll explain later.
> Hope the bread is fine.
> With affection,
> Ellen.

Rhona's inner questions tormented her. Three times in the next four days she walked in ways and places where she had been accustomed to meeting Ellen. No joy. Munch had not seen her. Viva had not seen her.

Essie arrived, laden again.

'How is the Mistress?' asked Rhona.

'Grand, Ma'am.'

'Is she very busy?'

'She is, Ma'am.'

'Can you ask her – very quietly, mind – to meet me tomorrow afternoon in the Bottom Field?'

'I know she can't do that, Ma'am, she've inspectors in the school like, and she've to be there, for their tea.'

'The day after?'

Life quickened as never before. Deanstown and Silverbridge became Klondike villages; Mooreville a Yukon town. The shops carried notices of delivery dates for appliances. Comerford's Hardware Stores ordered a hundred electric kettles: people flocked to see them, on the prime shelves, fat as copper duchesses; each had a pleased-with-itself spout, and a thick projecting stub of round plughole at the back. Customers lifted the lid, looked at the grey worm of element inside, asked about Brasso as the ideal cleaner. Lily Campion even came out from behind the counter and showed them by means of a measuring jug that each kettle held six pints.

In plain brown cardboard boxes the irons came, and each had a long coiling tail of thick speckled flex cord, ending in open wires awaiting a plug. Women hefted the weight and marvelled at the glass-smooth plate underneath.

The village of Silverbridge stole a march on the town of Mooreville. Hogan's Stores took delivery of six Belling cookers a full week early, on the second Thursday in November. Word went out, as if a travelling show or a fortune-teller had come. Wife after wife hurried over the humpy bridge; they tapped every plate, twisted every knob.

Ellen wrote to her daughter.

My dearest, lovely Gracey,
It seems as if the Grey Valley will turn into a lake
after all. But maybe birds will nest on its banks, and
maybe swans will come.
Are you well?
Will you come home? Please? Or, if you want to
do things a different way, or if you want to talk first
and can't face us all at once, could we meet?
I miss you, we all miss you. Hugh keeps asking for
you, he says he has new jokes for you. We can achieve
almost anything by talking and your lovely friendly
joy and intelligence are sorely missed by this house.
Please reply.
Your loving,
Mama.

In the stillness of the night, Dennis listened.

Grace enumerated. 'They even say a silver fox used to
come into this valley, all the way down from the Arctic
Circle. There are gentians here we will never see again.
And all the fossils. They will all disappear. That's the
extent of the damage you're doing.'

He nodded. 'I know. I know.'

'These people. Mrs Stokes, she's heartbroken.'

He nodded.

'Compensation is only money,' Grace whispered.

Dennis whispered back, 'I have something to tell you.'

Grace listened now. Morning after morning she had
met Dennis in the Valley floor, where they kissed on the
edge of hostility. Before which she had climbed to the
ridge in rain and hail and wind to see him leave the site
and walk to meet her. When they parted, she grew
anxious – and rushed up the shale again, to track him the

whole way back to the construction hut. And day in day out, the grey wall of the dam rose and rose.

'Your newsletter.' Dennis watched her closely. He wore shiny, black riding-boots, his trousers tucked into them.

She looked askance and embarrassed.

'Two and a half weeks ago,' he said. 'Replies came.'

Grace said, 'I know. I got them. Eleven out of six hundred.'

Dennis shook his head. Grace leaned back against her pillows, as with a malady; Dennis, a hand on the patchwork counterpane, sat on the bedside.

'No.'

'What do you mean – "no"?'

Dennis traced a nipple idly through her nightdress. Grace wriggled away and asked, 'What are you saying?'

'I'm saying. There were several hundred.'

She frowned. 'No, I *sent* several hundred.'

'And – you got several hundred back.'

'I didn't.'

'You did. But you don't know it. Your father intercepted the letters. He collected them at the Post Office in Silverbridge, told the postmistress he would give them to you. I only found out yesterday.'

Dennis clamped a hand across Grace's lips. 'Shhhh! The old woman. Don't wake her.'

He held – until he felt her mouth ease; he took his hand away.

Grace swallowed and asked, 'How many letters?'

'He said, your father. He said. Well, he counted them.'

Grace hissed with ferocity. '*How many?*'

Dennis held up one hand, then the other. 'In hundreds.'

'Five hundred?'

'More. Five hundred and thirteen.'

'But? I got some?'

'Your father made a decision. He believed that if some replies reached you, you would not get suspicious.'

'Ooohhhnnnnhhhh!' It came out as a long whispered moan, true helplessness. Grace, since a child, when moved beyond endurance, put the heels of both her hands into her eyes. Perhaps in so doing she pressed ducts: in any event, tears never flowed until she pressed hard. She inhaled deeply and held her head back on the high pillows. From under her closed eyes, tears began to seep.

Two weeks ago, he said to Helena, 'I would never want you to weep. I want to give you so much protection.' When Helena smiled, he whispered, 'Ohhh! Your lovely face.'

Dennis began to inch forward. Grace, drawn by his hands, allowed herself to fall towards him: he stroked the black abundant hair, buried his face in it. As each draught of weeping hit her, he drew her closer.

A week ago, 'Dearest, sweet Helena,' he told her in the car, 'I can't bear the thought of you ever needing anything. My role will be to provide for you, to let you sit, and be. To give you time and love. To make your dreams come true.'

With his toes and heels he eased off the black shiny boots, and slid up along the bed. And stroked, stroked. Soon, of her own volition, Grace pressed her face into his shoulder. Dennis slid her down from the pillows, until he and she lay parallel.

==

371

On Sunday, he offered Helena the mysterious package.

'This is for you. A gift. For no reason other than for your being you.'

'You call it "gift" – we call it "present". What is it?'

He played with her. 'I'm not going to tell you. You must open it.'

Helena said, 'Oh. Oh.'

He tapped the leather bindings. *The Collected Works of Tennyson*. "On either side the river lie. Long fields of barley and of rye." Like it?'

He forced the bedding away until her legs lay exposed.

'Hallo,' he kept saying. 'Hallo.'

He slipped farther down, raised her knees and angled his pelvis under her. Much stroking, much, much stroking. Soon, and without ceremony or protest, he had gained careful entry. Patient, soft, holding her, not letting her raise her face; he stroked her hip; he stroked her hair with his other hand; he waited and waited. She never opened her eyes.

Last night, he said, 'Helena, darling – I want a special date with you one evening soon.'

'Why?'

'Nosey parker.' He tapped her nose.

With each half-thrust he whispered, 'Ease up, ease. Relax.'

He never hurt her, she never cried out; very little blood spilled. When he left, Grace had fallen asleep. She did not awaken until very late; an overcast morning had kept the sun hidden. For several moments she lay there, then she turned on one side, placed her head

deep in her arm and began to sob without a sound or
a tear.

Rhona and Ellen met in the Bottom Field.

'What happened? What happened?'

Ellen lied. 'I changed my mind.'

'You whaa-aat?'

'I changed my mind.' Set of lip, jut of jaw.

'But we said?'

'I know.'

'He will get away with murder if we don't stop him.'

Ellen said, 'We have to think of another way.' White
of face; staring straight ahead.

Rhona turned, stopped in front of Ellen, causing her to
halt.

'Ellen. Look at me! I'm an old fox. I know things. Something's gone wrong. What is it?'

Ellen stood, but not looking.

'Ellen, what *is* it?!'

'We have to think of something else.' Stubborn; head
angled away.

'I know. Helena, isn't it?'

'Who told you?' Ellen seized the excuse.

'Viva said they were seen at the pictures. And at
Cruise's Hotel in Janesborough. And over in Thurles.'

Ellen Kane could not have survived Thomas Kane's
righteous depredations for so long without some inscru-
tability. His morality had been forged by the use of the
gun. As he failed to grow, his morality never developed.
Accordingly, she had to devise her own labyrinth and
steer her family through it. An occasion such as this with
Rhona Ulverton, however knowledgeable and worldly
her opponent, posed few problems. By her silence she
led Rhona. When assumptions tumbled from the older

373

woman, Ellen chose the most suitable. Rhona reached it quite quickly.

'Your husband is encouraging Dennis Sykes to woo your daughter?'

Ellen nodded.

'In that case,' Rhona declared, 'I can easily use our new knowledge to discommode him.'

'I think we should wait. In any case, he will be gone in a few months.'

'But –'

'Look, Rhona. My best chance is to do nothing. Maybe it won't come to anything – him and Helena. Maybe he is only pretending to like her. In order to smooth his path while here.'

'That,' said Rhona, 'is almost certain.'

'In which case, let it blow over.'

Rhona said, 'It sticks in my gullet to have to do that.'

'Please. For Helena's sake.'

Rhona looked at her. 'If you wish. Nevertheless.' She raised a finger. 'I am going to say one last word. In all the years I have known you, I have never seen you so ashen. If you need me, you know I'm here.'

The final meeting of the electricity project for Deanstown & District took place in the schoolhouse on 20 November. In exceptionally mild weather, mist closed in early. Excitement ran high. Ellen did not appear.

Dennis addressed the meeting. 'Is everyone here from the Valley?' and a voice said, 'Only Mrs Stokes is missing.'

'Aah!' said Dennis sympathetically. 'Now – while Master Kane is doing his last calculations, I'll tell you exactly where we stand. Oh, by the way – the Department have informed me that all re-housing has now been agreed. Is that right?'

They nodded.

'Is there anyone here who feels worse off – I mean in terms of the house you've been given?'

No answer.

'All I hope,' said Dennis, 'is that the next community I work in, be it in Ireland or Iceland, will be as pleasant. I could not have done any of this without the help and co-operation you've all given me. The wall of the dam, as many of you have seen, is up to a great height. We are ahead of schedule. Thanks mainly to the quality of the workmen from around here. I have never worked with men who worked harder.'

Dennis clapped his hands, a one-man round of applause.

'Now. Let me tell you what will happen.'

He led them through each stage. On 1 January – 'what better day to start a new life?' – they would begin to evacuate. All transport and furniture removals would be provided. 'I know there has been some debate about the furniture you have, so if there's anything you want to bring – even if it is built-in to the wall, we will provide help.'

One voice said, 'Be glad to see the end of it.' Many cackled with the speaker.

'You can each have up to three trips to empty your house,' said Dennis. 'We want this to be as painless as possible.' They murmured their appreciation.

'By the last day of the month, all the work will be finished at both ends. Then the Great Day itself. We have photographers and reporters coming from abroad. As you know, the Archbishop is saying a special Mass at the site that morning at half-past seven. I know that's very early, but this is why. It will take only six hours, we calculate, for enough water to pour in. To activate the turbines. Those pumps are like atomic power.'

'Over Christmas, the last work at the far end will be done. On the morning itself, after he celebrates Mass, the Archbishop will bless the dam and then he will press the button that will blow the gelignite and unleash the rivers into the pumping mechanisms. And then into the Valley. No danger – but a lot of noise. Then you will see the greatest torrent you have ever seen in your life. Any questions so far?'

No, no questions.

'We will all go away and have breakfast. Or we can stay and watch; bring picnics if you like. To my sorrow we won't have enough to feed you all – unless the Archbishop brings enough loaves and fishes with him.' They laughed.

'Then.' Dennis got their attention again. 'At half-past three we will reconvene and observe the progress of the water. According to our estimates it should be three-quarter way up the wall of the dam; certainly it will have covered the tops of the trees by then, and a beautiful lake will have begun to form. I hope everyone'll be there. Because, all things being equal, we will turn on the electricity some time between four and five o'clock. As you know, if you choose the best spot up on the ridge, you will be able both to look into the Valley, and see down into the village. And you will see the lights of Deanstown being switched on.'

They applauded.

The schoolhouse door opened. Both lamps flickered. Dennis recognized her at once. Men standing at the back parted to let her walk through. Thomas Kane stood by the yellow lamplight and stared.

Grace, halfway up the classroom, turned to the people who had craned sideways towards her, and said with great calm, 'There is now one fewer house in the Grey Valley to be emptied. Mrs Stokes died this evening.'

'Go away!' Grace called from inside the locked house.

Ellen rapped on the door again and said, 'But Grace, Mrs Stokes has to be laid out.'

'We did all that last night. Mrs Allen helped. Now go away.'

'Oh, Grace, my love.' Ellen went to the window.

From behind the curtain, Grace said with perfect calm, 'I am not your love. I will not be your love again until you leave that man you are living with. Now go away and don't speak to me again.'

'But Grace, I'm married to him. He's my husband. Marriages can't break. He's your father.'

Grace said, 'He is not my father any more, not to me anyway. When all this is over, I am going to change my name legally. I do not want his name. He has betrayed me in every way.'

'Betrayed you? How?'

'Ask him. Now go away, Mother.'

Which gave Ellen no choice.

Dennis said, 'I wish there was a way in which I could help.'

Helena shook her head. 'If Mama can't talk her round, nobody can. Mama and Grace are very close.'

Dennis said, 'Are they very alike?'

'Yes.'

'Are you upset, Helena?'

'I miss her. And I feel guilty. Because I've been avoiding Grace.'

'On account of me?' Dennis chewed on his steak, turned his eyes on Helena.

She nodded. He laid a hand on her forearm. 'But, Helena – it will all blow over. In time. Yes,' said Dennis in his wise voice. 'Yes, it will.'

After dinner, they drove back by way of the dam. Dennis turned on the generator, trained the hand-spotlight on the far side of the curved dam wall. They stood in silence, Helena huddled in her coat.

'You know that I consider this beautiful, don't you, Helena?'

'I suppose so.'

He moved the spotlight again. 'Look at that curve. Look at the way the fog makes it seem like a kind of magic!'

Helena looked. Into the night, like a ghostly path to the future, stretched the high curve of the dam wall. The near levels had already been finished.

'We'll be able to walk along it next week,' said Dennis. 'Incidentally, will you give your mother a message from me?'

'What's that?' Helena's teeth began to chatter and she pulled the coat tighter.

'Tell her I met that Mrs Ulverton and I was able to do something about their getting a supply of electricity.'

'What?'

'Yes. I'm quite – pleased, really. Tell her Mrs Ulverton and I were able to work something out.'

'Oh,' said Helena, 'she'll be delighted.'

'She may be delighted too if you can answer the next question,' said Dennis.

Helena said in her mild way, 'Oh, yes?'

'This is the question. It is a very simple one. Will you marry me?'

'Oh!'

'I've asked your father.'

'What did he say?'

'He smiled like an angel. He is very fond of you.'

'Oh!'

'I thought we would announce our engagement at Christmas. Then we can take our time in deciding when to marry.'

Mrs Stokes had died in the afternoon. Word reached Ellen as to the manner of her death, and of Grace's involvement. Mrs Allen told Jack Hogan who told Miriam.

Grace came back from the Hanlons where she had been making drawings of their wall-bed. When the cat, hunched under the settle outside the cottage, ignored her friendship, Grace was alerted. The door was open; the fire almost out. She called. No reply. She called again. Odd. Mrs Stokes never went far.

Grace went to the old woman's bedroom door and listened. Silence. She pushed through, saw the dark shape, half-kneeling, half-sprawling, as if she had tried to climb on the bed. Grace put down her sketch-pad and rushed over. The old woman said something Grace could not hear. With great strength she manipulated Mrs Stokes up and on to the bed, on her side, then rolled her over. Saliva came from her mouth corners.

Grace said, 'Are you all right, are you all right?'

Grace lit the candle, and rushed it to the bedside. She felt the woman's pulse, no sign.

'Are you all right, Mrs Stokes?'

Mrs Stokes tried to speak. The mouth gaped too much and as Grace bent to hear what she was saying, the eyes began to glaze.

Doubt never arises that someone has died. A force withers; new space becomes available in the air nearby.

379

Grace sat on the chair beside the bed and gazed at the dead body. She never even knew she should close the eyes.

Grace's rejection sealed Ellen's feelings of despair, of isolation. Dennis Sykes had initiated the process by uncovering, and illuminating, the only foulness in her secret life. No good that she guessed he would never mention the feared and forbidden 'thing' again – in return, she presumed, for her own quiescence. No use, either, that she avoided him. Sykes even seemed to assist matters by calling to see Thomas at the school, but only in the afternoons, when Ellen had left. Nor did she see him much with Helena, whom he now met away from the home, collected her from her lodgings.

None of these facts contained any solace. All her resources seemed to be ebbing unstoppably down some dreadful tidal shelf. Such an impasse is often best dealt with by a degree of impassiveness. Ellen knew this from the year of Thomas's coma.

Which enabled her to judge carefully her response to Helena's agitated news: 'Oh, are you very excited?'

'Mama, I don't know what to say.'

'People in your position usually say either yes or no.' Ellen smiled.

'Daddy is nearly more excited than I am. Oh, Mama, do you think he'd be pleased? I mean do you think he'd like me more if – if I said, if I accepted?'

Ellen jumped in surprise. 'When did you tell him?'

'I didn't. Dennis asked him weeks ago. For my hand, I suppose.' Helena giggled in embarrassment.

'We must all talk it through,' Ellen stonewalled. 'We must talk through every detail. Did he give you, did the two of you, did you make any plans?'

'Just to get engaged at Christmas. And then he said,'
Helena smiled – 'we could take our time, and decide
slowly when to get married.'

'Have you said anything yet? I mean yes or no?' Both
women laughed.

'No, Mama.'

Gravity never left Helena alone for long. Her face
lengthened. 'I was thinking.'

'I know.' Her mother joined in. 'Grace.'

'Yes.' They paused.

On Monday morning, she watched Thomas teaching the
senior classes. He had pinned three elm leaves to a piece
of paper draped over the blackboard.

'The Elm,' he intoned, 'is one of the highest and most
dignified trees in the wood. Its principle is to grow smaller
leaves, but many of them. The Elm provides Man with
spiritual and temporal sustenance. It is one of the first to
flower in the Spring, and to many the fresh greenness of
its foliage is the sign that Spring is only a few minutes
away. Secondly, its wood, though not of a superior quality,
proves equal to many fundamental situations. The inner
bark of the Elm has been known to be capable of use in
the brewing of beer. Thirdly, because it can endure moist
circumstances, the timber of the Elm is used to make
carts, mill-wheels and coffins.'

At morning break, she strolled into his classroom.

'Do they know yet,' she asked, 'of the holiday dates?
The small ones were asking me.'

Thomas turned the calendar. 'The nineteenth to the
twenty-sixth, that's one week, the twenty-sixth to the
third, that's two weeks. If we say two weeks and two days,
that brings them back on the fifth of January. That's good,
that means the evacuation will be almost clear.'

Ellen said, 'By the way, I'm going up to see Mrs Ulverton this afternoon. And tomorrow, what are we going to do about Mrs Stokes's funeral?'

Thomas said, 'She's being buried during school hours, though. So there isn't much we can do.'

Ellen replied, 'I'll go.'

He replied, 'But it's at twelve o'clock.'

Ellen said quietly, 'I'll go anyway.'

'But what about – ?'

Ellen interrupted, again speaking low, 'Grace will need some moral support, so I'll go. Now –' she rubbed her hands together; 'what would you like for your supper?'

He shook his head in irritation but made no comment.

In the Valley, Dennis shook the rain from his sou'wester hat.

'Don't you mind being alone in the house at night with a corpse?'

Grace shook her head. She pressed herself to the tree. 'Feel,' she said, patting the bole. 'The wood is warm, almost.'

Dennis wiped the rain from his face. 'You know the reason I didn't call is that it didn't seem right.'

'I know,' said Grace. She put her arms around his neck and kissed him.

Ellen said, 'I owe you an apology.'

'My dear, for what?'

'Well. I dragged you all the way to Dublin, we went to see that girl. I gave you to believe that I would then confront Mr Sykes with it. And I did nothing.'

'So is it true,' Rhona asked, 'that he wants to marry your daughter?'

Ellen nodded.

'Then you had good reason for doing nothing. But you can't be happy about it?'

'I'm not. But I have to think of Helena.'

'Is she happy?'

'Rhona, I don't know. This is her first experience of a man being nice to her. All I can do is watch.'

'You mean, Ellen dear, that is what you have decided to do.'

Ellen smiled. 'Yes.'

Rhona said, 'Let's go back into the house, I'm getting cold. By the way, I have a confession, too. Sykes and me. I never confronted him, either. Do you know why?'

'I think I can guess, I got a message. You did a deal with him.'

'I'm afraid so. I'm ashamed.'

'Because he offered to find a way of getting you the electricity without it costing you the earth.'

'Was I very wrong? It was Cyril's idea.'

'Oh, Rhona, no. You have to keep warm.'

'Yes, and anyway – we both have his measure. With two such women as ourselves we should be able to keep him under control.'

Ellen smiled thinly. Then she warmed and said, 'If you want me to talk to Joseph Comerford and Sons about appliances –'

Rhona said, 'I couldn't sleep last night, and I thought of something else. Your daughter Grace.'

'Yes?'

'Have you catered for her reaction if her sister marries that little man?'

Ellen said, 'I hope to see her tomorrow.'

Fewer than fifty people attended. Mud fouled the priest's white surplice. Intoning the prayers in raised voices above the wind, the daughter never looked in the mother's direction. Whereas the mother never took her eyes off the daughter.

In such a short time – what, ten, eleven months? – these women's existence had been polluted, faeces thrown in a crystal bowl. Up to then, in common with many families in their comfortable milieu, it was possible to think of life as a series of bridges to be crossed: or a wide-ish road, relatively clear up ahead; at worst, perhaps, a woodland path, full of easily moveable debris – Thomas Kane, father and husband, being the briar-thorns.

Such separation as had taken place between this girl, Grace Kane, and her family, cannot easily be bridged. The rift grows more troubled when parent and child feel so alike, seem so full of resemblance as these two women. Wind flayed the graveyard, driving the sleety rain before it, hammering it like small icy nails into people's clothes and bodies and cheeks.

Who else could have held Grace's pain safely, could have poured balm on it? She still had no language to encompass her father's abuse. The stolen letters became an emblem to her, a symbol of pillage, a tarring and feathering of her honourable efforts. In the many mad hurts of nocturnal fantasy, she assumed that Helena no longer wrote to her because of Thomas's intimidations. One person, and only one, had the capacity to ease Grace's soul: one person could even have listened and understood the rapine perpetrated by her night visitor.

That person stood a few yards away, unlooked-at, perhaps, by her daughter, but felt. Grace, so closely like her mother in body and mind, never had to raise her head to know it was Ellen who had entered a room. If not feeling guilty about her children of a day, if ever able on a random morning to acknowledge a difficult truth, Ellen would say to herself, unstoppably, 'I love Helena – but I adore Grace.'

When Grace turned away at the end of the graveside prayers, Ellen at last saw her daughter's eyes, puffy and red. The graveyard is a small one, rising to a hillock in the centre, where silvered railings mark the commemoration place for republican dead. Ellen halted beside a green-mottled headstone.

There are few descriptions which accurately capture the savage, shifting, lifelong jabs of parental anguish. There may be none which describe the primal desolation that a child – of any age – feels when it knows it has lost parents who go on living. Grace delayed and delayed, sheltering, talking to strangers.

Some years ago, the great hurricane blew down the giant macrocarpa trees at the western wall, and today the prevailing westerlies blow through here even more fiercely than they did on the morning Mrs Stokes was buried.

When Grace finally braved the pathway, she did not greet her mother. Ellen stepped out beside her.

'Gracey, can we talk?'

No answer.

'Grace!' Ellen tried authority.

No.

'Grace! Please!' Ellen took her daughter's arm. Grace glanced down coldly at the hand, then, standing motionless, looked into the distance, through the rain.

'Grace, it's Christmas the week after next. We want you home. That cottage is empty now, poor Mrs Stokes. I know how you liked her, God rest her dear bones. And soon the Valley won't exist at all. You have to come home, love. Please!'

So much rain had spilled on Grace's face that tears could

not be measured. Dye from her scarf ran on her cheek, making a blue map. She dropped her purse and it fell open, spilled; Ellen bent to help; the women gathered coins from the mud, wiped them on their gloves. One by one, taking turns, they placed them in the purse, which Ellen snapped secure and handed back. Grace said, 'Thank you', bowed her head, raised her eyes again. She met her mother's gaze – and at that moment started the long journey back across their blood-bridge.

'Look, Mother.' Hesitant. Maybe tearful. 'This was all awful.' She chewed her lip, exactly like Ellen does.

'Oh, Gracey, the others miss you. I miss you, my dear, wilful daughter.'

'Wilful – ?'

'No, I mean it as a joke. No, please.' Ellen took Grace's gloved hand and smiled a smile from long ago.

We do not always know the exact moment when we are making life-destroying errors: we only know the moment after we have made them.

'Do, love. Do come back. I give you my word. And I need you especially now. I need your life and soul for the party.'

Ellen smiled again, hoping her joke would land. She rattled on.

'Even though we're keeping it very quiet. Helena wants it that way. Although *he* – he would be happy, I think, with a pipe band playing.'

Grace turned, eyes like black-flamed lamps. 'Party?'

'Yes.' Ellen smiled in encouragement. 'Your father is very pleased with her. Imagine.' She half-giggled.

The punch of dread. Fear. The end of life.

Grace lost breath. She instantly knew everything, immediately recalled in vivid flashes the hard texture of his small-man's body, the shard of his fingernail, how it caught her askew, and she had to twist her hip to avoid the sting inside her.

'Hellie's getting engaged?' Desperate exhalation.

'There's no wedding date yet.'

'Aaaaa, hallo, ladies, there, I've to lock, like.' A man with keys called them from the entrance to the graveyard. 'Aaaaa, the gates, like. Aaaa, sorry to disturb you.'

Grace did not ask the next question: Ellen answered it. But what can one do except speak on.

'Maybe late summer, we think. Depends on his, you know, Dennis's, his next position. Once the dam is completely finished.'

And nowhere to look, but up – to the sky and the rain. And nowhere to go, but away – forever and ever. One betrayal may break the heart; the second dismembers the soul.

19

Grace Kane disappeared. From the churchyard, Ellen, in distress, watched her daughter's retreating back: no point in even calling out. Steadily, the girl walked: not hurried, nor dogged.

At home, distressed to hysteria almost, Ellen wrote a letter. Or tried to.

'My dearest Grace.' Four times she began it. Four times she abandoned it. Splodges. Tears on the inky paper.

Helena arrived, and asked whether Grace had appeared at the funeral. Ellen replied ambiguously that it had not been possible to talk to her.

'Mama! What's wrong? Oh, Mama!'

Grace walked into Miss MacNamara's office at five o'clock that evening and asked for shelter. The headmistress looked at her and said, 'I will be finished here in half an hour. You can come home with me.'

Neither woman said a word on the cycle through Janesborough's suburbs to Miss MacNamara's neat and large brick house. Inside, she pointed Grace in the direction of bedroom and bathroom, and said, 'I will be down in the kitchen when you are ready.'

Grace did not appear that evening, nor the next. On the third morning, Miss MacNamara wrote to Ellen to tell her that Grace was safe and sound, if a little unwell; she advised no contact for the moment.

That night Miss MacNamara said to Grace, 'I don't know what has happened to you, and I only want to know if you want to tell me. This I do know. You are to call and see Dr MacMahon tomorrow at half-past eleven. I have made an appointment for you. I will accept no argument to the contrary. You will come back here and cook supper for me, which I will come home to eat at six o'clock. Thereafter, you will stay here until the first of February when you will resume work as one of my teachers, part of our bargain, if you remember. I do not require you to speak to me until you are ready, and I have told Dr MacMahon – who is also my doctor – that you may wish to maintain your silence. He, too, understands.'

Grace lowered her head.

At Dr MacMahon's, she undressed piecemeal as he asked.

'Please nod your head if the answer is "yes", and shake it if the answer is "no". Have you been raped?'

Grace shook her head.

'Have you lost your virginity?'

Grace nodded.

'Have you had sexual intercourse more than five times?'

Grace nodded.

'More than ten times?'

Grace shook her head.

'Is your monthly period late do you think?'

Grace shook her head.

He looked in her eyes, and in her ears; he took her pulse and her blood pressure; he examined her hair and her nails.

'Dress, please.' She stood casually and put on her clothes.

As she sat in front of him he asked, 'Have you had a

389

severe physical shock? Almost a bad accident, or anything like that?'

Grace shook her head.

'Have you had a bad experience, I mean a bad love affair.'

Grace stared straight ahead.

Dr MacMahon said, 'You know I must speak to Miss MacNamara, don't you?'

Grace nodded.

To Miss MacNamara that evening, as she called on her way home, he said, 'I have seen patients after the last war, and that was called "Shell-shock". You know what that's like. This seems not dissimilar.'

'What is your best guess, Doctor?'

'They also call it "catatonic". This is a mild version. Or it may be from choice. How and ever – something horrible has happened to her, some, I don't know – family trouble, something like that. Betrayal often produces it.'

Miss MacNamara asked, 'Will she come out of it?'

'Don't know. Don't honestly know. She should do, very fit. Very fit.'

'Anything I ought do – ?'

'Kindness and privacy. Nothing else.'

Grace missed the evacuation. Perhaps it was as well. It began at the farthest end, the point nearest the new pumping station, and how her heart would have caved in when the tractors came through with their trailers, crushing her beloved paths. Over the rise they came, like beasts stampeding methodically into the mouth of the Valley; they rolled regardless down the long line of hedgerow past Mrs Stokes's cottage. (No relatives had come forward to claim anything; the evacuators saw the heavy padlocks, made enquiries, shrugged: 'Their loss.')

Difficult right-angled turn: low, hard foliage brushed the smoke-stacks of the engines. One driver pointed out that those branches would have to be trimmed if any trailer came back piled high. Grace could have gone there, and sketched the trees before and after, howled at the barbarism of the sawmen.

They ravaged her earth, too: by the end of the day they were spreading gravel on that corner to try and ensure purchase – even for the bigger rubber wheels. The rain kept off.

In each house, the tractor driver and his helper asked, as they had been instructed by Dennis, 'Do you want to take anything built-in with you?' and they pointed to dressers, settles and wall-beds. Not one resident wished any of the vernacular furniture to be detached. All said something to the effect, 'Not at all, glad to be rid of it.' Grace could not have borne it; by then she was sleeping a dreamless broken sleep in her quiet city room.

For delicacy, it had been agreed to move one house at a time: two-hour intervals.

'They won't like their neighbours seeing everything they have,' advised Thomas. He and Dennis arranged to be at the entrance to the valley as each tractor emerged.

'Curious how little they actually have,' commented Dennis quietly, as the first load toiled past them. Thomas agreed.

'What's that?' Dennis pointed to a large wooden baulk on the second trailer.

Thomas peered. 'Good God!'

'What is it?'

'I'll tell you in a moment.' The cottier, his wife and their ageing, mentally infirm daughter walked past them behind the piled trailer: they acknowledged Dennis, ignored Thomas.

'What was it?' insisted Dennis.

'It was the roof-tree of the house,' said Thomas.

'What does that mean?'

'That's an old story. When people emigrated to America in the last century, they took the roof-tree with them, so that they would have some material with which to start building a new house.'

'But they're being rehoused,' said Dennis.

'It's in the blood,' said Thomas.

Grace could have recorded that incident: she could have made them stop for a moment, done one of her lightning sketches, thinking, 'Charcoal for the charred parts.'

Misty rain drifted in. The two men sat in Dennis Sykes's car. Another tractor noise drew them out again. This trailer had been piled high, high.

'Well-to-do?' asked Dennis.

Thomas nodded. 'All the children emigrated.' He called to the tractor driver, 'Is that everything out of that house?'

The man shouted back, 'Ah, 'tis, sir.'

'Where are they?'

'They've something hid they're waiting to get and they wouldn't look for it 'til I was gone,' said the driver, who crested the rise and reached the tarmacadam road in safety, then roared away down the hill-road towards Mooreville.

'What was that about?' asked Dennis.

Thomas smiled and said, 'We'll probably find out any minute now.'

He peered in the direction of the Valley mouth. Soon, two elderly men appeared. A small justice for Grace was at hand, a little crackle of retribution.

'Yes,' said Thomas grimly, 'I bet I know what this is.'

The men walked slowly towards him, one heavy on a walking-stick.

'Should we offer to drive them?' asked Dennis.

'No fear. Watch.'

Abreast, the men stopped. The one with the stick reached deep into the pocket of his greatcoat and drew out a large and obviously rusty Colt revolver. He pointed it at Thomas Kane. The trigger, he knew, would not pull.

'There you are, Kane. If this gun worked, I'd give you the contents. I'd empty it into your grey fuckin' oul' head, so I would. You fucker.'

His venom shook Dennis Sykes.

Thomas called back, 'A gun that wouldn't fire. Typical. You were a coward then, you're a coward now.'

The man threw the gun at Thomas; it landed several feet short.

'Pick it up, Kane. Put it to your head and pretend 'tis me. Fuck off to hell.'

'Big vocabulary as ever,' called Thomas Kane, and the men moved off.

'Whoooph!' said Dennis. 'Charming.'

Thomas stepped forward and picked up the handgun. He wiped the clay from it with a clump of grass.

'Now will you tell me?' demanded Dennis.

'Civil war,' said Thomas. 'We were on opposite sides.'

'But that was ages ago!'

'Thirty years precisely. But did you never hear the saying, "The English never remember and the Irish never forget." Look at this.' He displayed the gun to Dennis. 'No firing pin.'

Dennis took the gun. 'Whoo! Heavy!' He inspected it. 'Were you a good shot?' he asked. Thomas nodded.

Changing the subject he asked, 'Do you want to go and see those houses?'

Dennis said, 'No, I'll wait until they're all empty.'

Four more houses that day; four more tractors emerged from beneath the misty trees like creatures. On their trailers sat tables, chairs, bedding, cardboard boxes, tea-chests. These merry one-family processions looked like evacuees from some benign war, en route to the land they had been promised. One of the Valley's few children, a pal of Grace's, wore a saucepan on his head, and waved like a victor.

Tales had already begun leaking back to Deanstown of the Grey Valley people's ecstasy when they saw their new homes. Thomas Kane preened.

As the rain cleared, Dennis pointed. The curved wall of the dam could be seen through the glim. Some men walked along the top, seeing to things here and there.

'I am pleased,' said Dennis Sykes, 'at how compact it is.'

'And powerful,' chimed in Thomas Kane, 'like yourself, if you don't mind my saying so – compact and powerful.'

That night, Dennis Sykes went back into the Grey Valley to find Grace Kane. Christmas had been quiet and sombre. Helena said she wished to wear no ring just yet, not until Grace came home. Ellen Kane remained quiet, withdrawn even, but civil.

He shone his torch through the windows. In Grace's room, a white nightdress lay over the back of the chair. Her books remained stacked on their shelf. The cottage's back door had a heavier padlock than the one at the front: he drifted away.

The evacuated houses swung ajar. He wandered in and shone his torch all around. A settle had been opened down from the wall and left as if in use. He sat on it, caressing the timber with his hand. Grace had shown him her drawing of this piece. From his torchlight upon the chimney breast, he could see the cup-hooks on the rim of the high mantel, where they had not even taken away the oilcloth from the mantelshelf.

'Yes,' he said aloud, 'it could be Africa. Just as bloody primitive.' At the door something startled him. He flashed the torch at it: goddam barbarians – they had left without taking their cat!

Next morning, before Thomas Kane arrived at the observation point, Dennis stopped the first of that day's four tractors.

'Have you left any domestic animals behind?'

'Howja mean, like?'

'A cat or a dog?'

They shook their heads. The sun came out and the possessions on the trailers glowed in the watery light. One woman came over and shook Dennis's hand.

'God bless you, sir, I hated that oul' house, so I did, and I asking the council to get me a new house with years now.'

By the middle of the following week, just before Thomas Kane reopened Deanstown School, the Grey Valley had been totally evacuated. The last tractor left at three in the afternoon.

'While there's still some light left?' suggested Dennis to Thomas. They walked in.

'I'd forgotten how small it is,' said Thomas. 'It's like a pocket, isn't it?'

'That's what makes it perfect for our purposes,' said Dennis. 'It will fill perfectly and at great speed, and then it will hold the force of that water forever. Wonderful idea, isn't it?'

He watched the elderly man carefully as they passed Mrs Stokes's house. Thomas looked neither to the right nor to the left. They visited seven of the empty houses.

'No interest, I see, in preserving "vernacular furniture", that's for sure,' said Thomas in a jeering tone.

As they returned, he again ignored the Stokes cottage.

'So – all set?' he said to Dennis, as they reached their separate cars.

'Went smoothly, didn't it?'

Thomas nodded.

'Thanks to you,' said Dennis. 'Look how you handled all that, all the persuasion, all the commonsense.'

In her note to Miss MacNamara, Grace said she had decided upon a short holiday, probably in Galway, a lot of walking, and she would be in touch. But Grace took the bus to Cork. On the same morning, Miss MacNamara took the bus to Deanstown, and conferred with Ellen.

'I am not an alarmist, am I?'

'No,' agreed Ellen. 'You are not an alarmist.'

'But she has not spoken a word. Not one word. In the afternoons she went for long walks and returned absolutely silently. We ate together; she never spoke a word. Nothing but silence.'

Ellen said, 'And she my most talkative child.'

'Yes.' The women sat in thought.

'Ellen, are you worried?'

'I am. Dreadfully.'

'That's the way I am.'

Ellen said, 'Should we put out an enquiry, I mean through official channels, a police notice on the wireless?'

Miss MacNamara said, 'I would.'

This did not happen. Thomas Kane said, 'Under no

circumstances. This is just another means she has dreamt up of spoiling things. Of getting attention. How dare she?'

Ellen went for help. 'Rhona, Rhona, please! I know, I know, I feel it in my bones. I know.'

'I agree with you. Dear Ellen, I agree with you. Put the notice in yourself.'

'I can't – it has to go through the Sergeant and he won't do it without Thomas's signature, I can tell you that now.'

'Who do we know in Galway?' asked Rhona.

Ellen said, 'I don't know anyone.'

Rhona said, 'Nor do I.'

Ellen remembered. 'Miriam Hogan. Her brother's a Gardiner man, he's a doctor outside Galway. We'll ask her.'

But Miriam told Jack, and Jack told Thomas Kane.

On the twenty-ninth of January, Grace Kane came back to the Grey Valley. Via a roundabout, devious route, that began when she went to Cork, and deposited her from the bus almost twenty miles from the Valley. It rained heavily; Grace got to Mrs Stokes's house at one o'clock in the morning. In Cork she had bought a can of paraffin for the primus stove, several yards of strong thin rope and some sheets of thick oilcloth. The workmen had now closed the entrance to the valley, and she had to hike her bicycle over rocks and felled trees. The builders had begun the final sealing-off of that last remaining gap in the entrance.

She assembled a space like a bureau for herself at the table and wrote: to her mother, to the youngest Kane, Hugh, and, longest letter of all, to Helena. On the third morning she climbed the ridge at dawn and looked all around. Everything was in place. Nobody to be seen.

The dam waited, patient and firm. Smaller finally than

Grace had expected; and she had to admit that the curve made it an object of great beauty. She ducked beneath the briars: far beyond her, Dennis Sykes appeared, walking like a game-cock on the wall of the dam, leaning over the railings, checking their strength.

'If I had a gun,' spat Grace aloud.

Her words made a bird fly screeching from the tree nearby, and Dennis looked up sharply. When nothing developed he continued his cocky stroll, the early sun shining on his yellow hard-hat. Under cover of the foliage all the way, Grace eventually went back to the cottage, and when she got there had again to hide. High above, and in full view, workmen had begun erecting the great opening-day platform.

For the next two days, Grace lived like a small animal. Mrs Stokes's stores of smoked bacon would satisfy her minimal food requirements; the stream had drinking water; the old primus stove would make tea – no smoke could she show until after dark. Heavy blankets sealed the windows: no firelight could shed a flickering message into the night.

Heavy in its frame, she bore Mrs Stokes's old mirror from the bedroom to the kitchen. By tilting the angle, Grace had a face to whom she could speak – her own. Only once did her resolve waver when, in an unguarded glance, she saw a face so like her mother's: she returned the mirror to the bedroom.

The house welcomed her; all its night-time noises crackled and sighed, and she recognized every voice. Pictures in the fire, again: flicks of blue flame, with orange; and the pillowy bed had no memory of the bad nights and the shames.

In the morning when she woke, she rose immediately, did not lie long abed. She washed carefully and all over:

water taken in the previous night from the rain-barrels. No more prayers: they had stopped weeks ago.

All the time, she wrote her journal, pages and pages. When she heard the workmen leaving the sites, and their distant laughing gibes and farewell calls, and the lorries revving away in the distance, Grace slipped from the cottage and like a ghost toured the empty houses of the Valley. From them, she gathered bric-a-brac: a pothook, a broken cup, a discarded fishing-rod.

On the evening of the thirtieth of January, she took down all Mrs Stokes's crockery and prepared to fill every vessel she could find with woodland decoration. Next morning early, she gathered a last few gentians, and broke branches from trees and shrubs. The stone-flagged old kitchen began to look like a cottage-garden. Later that day, Grace manhandled the wooden settle from the fire-nook into the middle of the floor, and surrounded it with lamps and candles.

One last flit. She knew the Valley floor so well. The foxes on the edge of the shale: they might have cubs. Grace slipped and slid upwards, a pale half-moon helping, the flashlamp to be used only when utterly needed.

Her heart thumped: a light came bobbling towards her. She stepped aside, ducked low, trying to be silent on a crop of loose, large stones. A long torch approached, in whose light the black boots glimmered. Grace's hand closed around a stone, and she hefted it into her hand. Feet from her, Dennis walked on, a last traverse of the heights before his triumph.

In darkness and strong wind, under floodlights, Mass began at half-past seven. From the canopied viewing platform, the Curate and the Archbishop could see the people's lights struggling up the ridge. Needless to remark, Thomas and Ellen Kane and their family had reached the site long before anyone else from the village.

'Wish me luck,' said Dennis.

'You don't need it,' whispered Thomas, and Helena pressed Dennis's hand secretly. Beneath them, the valley lay in hard, cold darkness. To their right, great lights played on the wall of the dam. One long searching lamp picked out the rock which at nine o'clock would be blasted to let the twin rivers merge and become glittering torrents.

The morning light began to spread. Mass ended with the Archbishop's blessing and a singing of 'Hail Glorious Saint Patrick'. A breakfast in the temporary hut rang with laughter and congratulations. The American news cameraman enthralled Hugh Kane with his stories of war and bullets.

'Do you smoke Camel cigarettes?' asked Hugh.

Ellen asked the cameraman to ensure that Hugh did not make a nuisance of himself. Other photographers snapped Dennis and Thomas and the Archbishop. The evacuated residents, Guests of Honour, told everyone of their fine new homes.

At three minutes to nine, Dennis led the Archbishop out into the open air again. On a podium, wires racing away from it, sat a large red button. The Archbishop, Edward Ahern, stood theatrically still. Beside him waited the Minister for Transport and Power, Dan Cantrell, and Dennis Sykes – behind whom towered Thomas Kane.

All along the edge of the ridge, the villagers stood in lines. They leaned over, looking down; despite the raw February cold, they chattered and called as if at a garden party.

Ellen Kane remained impassive. Had Leah been there

she would have felt alarm at the way Ellen's mouth worked in tiny, ceaseless movements.

'Thirty seconds to go, your Grace,' said Dennis Sykes. 'I checked my watch with the wireless last night.'

'I get my time from the BBC,' said the Archbishop, and smiled his pastor's buttered smile. 'They have the best time.' He folded his soft hands again.

'Get ready, your Grace.'

Archbishop Edward Ahern stepped forward.

'Now,' said Dennis Sykes.

Archbishop Edward Ahern plunged the button and at the far end of the valley there resounded a great crak-crak, then a boom. In the cottage below, Grace heard it, but did not see. Some said the flash was blue, some green; all saw the smoke and the flying rocks. Then the waters began to tumble – slower than they had expected.

Above the hubbub Dennis explained to the Archbishop, 'They have to move slowly at first. If the stream flowed too rapidly the pumping station would be overwhelmed. But when they hit the pumping station – watch, your Grace, look!' he cried. 'Now they'll begin to roll.'

Before all their eyes, the waters surged forward and as if kicked from behind rolled down into the early slopes of shale that led to the deeper valley. At first no wider than a mountain stream, the waters became a spate, then a torrent, then a wide cascade, sparkling and bounding down.

'How long, say, before these places down here will be covered?' asked the Archbishop.

'We calculate by about half-past two,' said Dennis. 'That is why we have timed the switching-on at three o'clock or just after it.'

'A work of genius,' said the Archbishop. 'Where do I switch on?'

'Same button, your Grace. The wonders of science,' smiled Dennis.

They clapped Dennis on the back; they photographed him again and again, and even the Archbishop agreed that a drink at this hour on a cold morning was acceptable in such remarkable circumstances.

The water found its way into the valley floor in directions nobody expected. As the sun appeared fitfully, the watchers on the ridge (none of whom had left) shouted, 'Over there', or 'Look, down here'. Soon that part of the valley floor directly beneath the platform resembled a field after several days of rain, a field with a tendency towards getting waterlogged, a field where curlews alight. Those who bought foreign-missions magazines were reminded of rice-paddies.

People who had not brought picnics mooched in the general direction of the large festivities tent, and were not disappointed. At eleven o'clock, Bill Prendergast and his sons arrived and set up a stall selling ice-cream and sausages.

'Ice-cream! On this day of the year, your Grace,' marvelled Thomas Kane to the Archbishop with whom he got on so well. 'And then,' he continued, telling the old tale, 'McCormack just opened his mouth –'

Edward Ahern, a fine, straight man for his eighty-five years of age, said when Thomas had finished, 'I love that story, Mr Kane.'

Ellen Kane smiled with her mouth but not with her eyes.

At one o'clock they began their wagers. At what time would it begin to go in under the nearest house door? Any minute now? Wasn't that where the old Stokes woman died? Yes, it was racing now, the water, out across the valley floor and rising. By twenty past one, it was lapping the foot of the dam wall, covering the last high winter grass over there.

As they had been told it would, the gap had opened wide by the pumping station, where the water was now hurtling down like a real big river in spate, spuming, bucking; powering down. Dennis appeared on the podium, peered down. They saw him and cheered him, and he acknowledged the cheers like a little *Duce*. And still the crowds gathered, streaming up the hill, hurried on by the cheers from up on the ridge.

Inside the tent, Dennis Sykes heard it first, heard the changed note. He held up a hand to halt the conversation he was having.

'Listen.' That was not a cheer. 'Shh, listen.'

A gabble. A moan. The door burst open and a man's face gasped, 'There's a woman down in the valley!'

Ellen screamed.

From the podium they all saw her. Grace came to the door of Mrs Stokes's house in her white nightdress. The silver water, now flowing flat, wide and fast as a tide, plucked and lapped at her calves. By opening the door she had let the water course into the house. She looked up, shading her eyes against the winter sun. People screamed, and the crowd released a moan of wonder and horror.

Ellen pushed forward. Every hand on the platform held her back. Thomas Kane crowded behind her. 'Who is it? Who is it?' he asked, and nobody told him – until he saw his wife's eyes on him. He covered his face with his hands.

Grace looked slowly along the ridge, scanning the long

crowd standing on the lip behind the ropes. With no gesture, no acknowledgement, she walked back into the cottage and, with difficulty against the rushing waters, closed the door. With his binoculars Dennis saw light after light go on in the cottage.

People beleaguered him. The Archbishop commanded him.

'No, your Grace.' Dennis's voice rose in fright as he answered, explained. 'It takes nearly twenty minutes to get down. No, the pumping house cannot be switched off, there's nobody over there on account of the danger of the blasting. It would be – too late.'

The sun had begun to sink, and western light, Grace's favourite, flooded the kitchen. The candles and lamps now lit, she folded her last writings in the thick oilskin cloths, and bound them to her body. She had tied the settle to the iron fixings at the fireplace, and now she lay on the settle and tied herself to it. With her hair splayed out behind her, a dark Ophelia, she waited in peace for the waters to reach her.

The waters rose higher and higher; the watchers on the ridge saw the lights in the cottage flicker and go out, one by one.

Ellen never left the podium, never took her eyes off the cottage windows, never blinked, never wept. Helena, her mouth frozen open, hugging herself in unspeakable dismay, had been led away by the Hogans. Thomas Kane could be seen alone in the catering tent, sitting upright on a chair, eyes closed. Of Dennis Sykes, no trace. In silence at half-past three, as the waters slapped the dam wall, the Archbishop pressed the great red button, and the lights of Deanstown in the distance were switched on, fireflies far away.